A PROMISED SUNSET

M.T. JADED

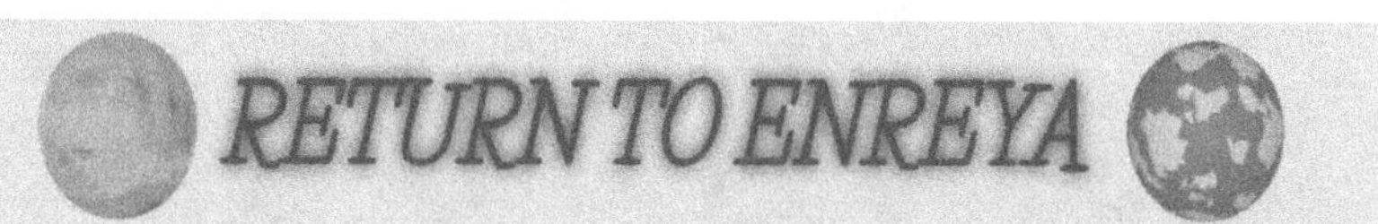

Copyright

You Should Know

- Certain words are capitalized to show respect from the character's POV.
- Alleged Kidnapping
- Possible Drugging
- Foul Language
- Intimate Encounters
- Violence
- On Page Death
- Mental Health
- Bullying
- Harassment
- Extortion
- Threats of Sexual Assault
- Recount of Sexual Assault
- Implied Child Abuse and Assault
- Body Weight Concerns
- Mentions of Suicide
- Alcohol Use

Contents

PROLOGUE
XAVIER/SUPPADE/DRUM

Xavier didn't understand why his Momma was crying or his Daddy's Energy was so angry. He handled everything, so he stood his ground and refused his parents' request.

"Why do we need to leave?" six-year-old Xavier defiantly asked. "We didn't do anything! We can stay and fight!"

"Xavier, I'm not about to argue with you!" his Daddy Caleb yelled, his deep voice shaking their townhouse and the ones around it.

Tears welled up in the corners of his eyes. His Daddy never yelled at him before, but he still didn't want to leave his home. He was born here. He was confused why his parents wanted to suddenly leave in the middle of the night.

"They won't find anything!" he said. "I made sure to get rid of the bodies." His tears now freely falling from his face.

His Momma's Energy changed as the memory of what happened finally came back to her. "Caleb! They attacked us. So many of them came rushing into our home and I fought back but I think I was knocked out from behind?" his Momma Kannika[1] tried to explain.

His Daddy turned to look at him. "I'm gonna ask you, what happened here?"

He looked down, wondering what he should say. The Golden Healing Angel next to him hadn't said a word since his parents and older brother arrived. He decided to be as honest as he could be with his family since it seemed like the Angel was right, only he could see the Angel, and even then, it was just the beautiful, sparkling, golden Energy the Angel held.

"I was at the park with Alex when I heard Momma scream. I came running back and saw a limo parked across the street, watching. I took out the human in the backseat and his driver with my Energy, but the man's daughter got away.

"I came to help Momma, who was on the ground. As I was checking on her, I was stabbed in the back through my Core." He paused and after a quick glance at The Golden Healing Angel, he continued, "My friend," he gestured to the Golden Angel standing next to him, "healed Momma and helped stop my Core from exploding," he ended.

"Did you use any Abilities around the kids at the park?" his Daddy asked, with an eyebrow raised. "And what friend? Alex? Cause Hayla is human!" His Daddy spread his

---

[1] *Pronounced- Can-knee-ka.*

arms, turning around to look at everything but could only see a clean and tidy home with no signs of so much as a trip and fall while they stood around.

"I used my Ground-step[2] Ability to run to our home, and I used my Flare Ability on the two in the limo. I didn't follow the man's daughter because Momma was attacked from behind and I came in through the bay window." He pointed at the unbroken window.

"Momma killed ninety-two of them and I killed the rest. Then I went to check on her and the twins when I was stabbed from behind...by Alex." He stopped speaking, knowing the questions were about to be randomly shouted out.

"Why would Alex stab you!? He's your best friend?!" his Momma asked.

"What do you mean you killed the rest? How?" his Daddy inquired.

"Why isn't the window broken or our home a mess? Where's the blood and guts?" his older brother Justin jokingly asked.

"What friend are you talking about Zay? There's no one else here besides the four of us?" More questions flew out of his Momma's mouth.

"What the hell happened to your Core[3]?!" his Daddy asked, and he knew his Daddy was using Enhanced Vision[4] to look inside him to see his Energy[5] and Core.

The rest of his family collectively stopped, and all turned to speak to him at the same time. "Where's the twins?!"

He stood tall and took a deep breath. Letting it out, he first explained to his Momma. "Alex was a part of the attack on us and stopped being my best friend when he stabbed me." He turned to his Daddy. "I realized Momma and the twins could get caught up if I just used my Flare, so I took the remaining fifty-five out using Ground-step and Up-jump[6] combined with the basic defense skills you tried to teach me."

He looked at Justin. "After the knife was pulled from my Core, my Energy exploded, but the Golden Angel kept my Energy confined to our home. That's when all the bodies, except Momma, the twins, the Angel, and me burned away to nothing. Afterwards, I used my Energy to clean and repair our home."

He looked back at his Momma. "There's a Golden Healing Angel standing beside me whom only I can see. The Angel saved our lives." He turned back to his Daddy. "I don't

---

[2] *See Universal Abilities #5*

[3] *An orb-shaped mass made of and containing the Lifeforce of Entities inside a human body.*

[4] *See Universal Abilities #12.*

[5] *The Lifeforce of Entities.*

[6] *See Universal Abilities #6A*

know what happened to my Core, but I feel different, like there's more to my Energy than before."

After looking at all his family's Energies, he finished his explanation. "The twins are safe. The Angel asked me to send them to MawMaw and PopPop for now."

"Then we should—" His Momma was cut off by NanaPoo and Abuelo rushing through a Portal.

"YOU'RE STILL HERE!" NanaPoo shouted, her Energy in a state of disarray. "I got a call from a Being officer in the precinct. They overheard about a raid on your home!" NanaPoo grabbed his Daddy. "You need to leave before the raid happens!" NanaPoo pleaded.

"The raid already happened," his Daddy calmly explained. "We were also ambushed on a fake fucking mission. They took out a lot of our people." His Daddy's deep sigh was felt in everyone.

Abuelo finally spoke, his voice breaking and he could see Abuelo's Energy in a perpetual state of sadness. "Doc...his family...gas leak...all of them." Abuelo sat down on the couch. "Bryston's family...bad brakes...mountainside curve...can't find Bryston's body." Abuelo's hands slid down his face.

"The plane...Eva...her family...vacation...exploded...engine malfunction. Robin...sick...never made it. Alivia...her kids...with us, but...her husband...our home...by cab...hit by a semi...sleeping driver. Doctors...don't know...him or the cab driver...gonna make it," Abuelo informed all of them.

Everyone paused and let what Abuelo said sink in and how. Abuelo never spoke so brokenly. He could see and understand Abuelo's Energy and as he stood there listening to what happened to his family, rage boiled up inside him. Now, more than anything, he wanted revenge. He wanted to kill every person who so much as thought about harming his family.

The Golden Angel placed a hand on his shoulder and from inside himself, he felt the words, *"Be patient and I shall give you all you need and desire,"* without hearing anything.

He ignored the words since they didn't feel like the Angel was saying them to him and started plotting how he could find the information he needed, but he felt more words.

"Why fight Fate when you can just trust me to give you what you desire?" the words asked him.

"Why should I wait to kill these horrible people?" he asked inside himself, hoping the words would respond.

"If you rush now, you will kill the only hope you have of achieving your Dream. Fate will guide you down the Path I am laying out for you," were the words he felt.

"If I'm patient and you go silent, I will forget about finding any information on them to find and destroy you myself," he angrily thought.

"Because of what happened to your Core, your words of destruction ring true. Those who are not your family will no longer be able to touch you. It is my way of protecting you."

He felt the words but didn't care about being protected, he wanted vengeance, sweet vengeance. Not the sour kind which only ended in a quick death, he wanted whoever planned and participated in this to feel utter agony before he ended their life. He wanted to wring every bit of despair from those involved.

"I am already laying down a Path for you. Those Marked are your sign," the words relayed to him and the tiniest smile pulled at the corners of his lips. Whoever or whatever was sending him these words could hear what he was thinking and could feel his emotions.

He was starting to listen to the words and calming himself down, with the help of the Angel's hand on his shoulder. He glanced at the Angel, but the Angel was more concerned about the conversation being had between the rest of his family. As he stared at the Angel, he wanted the Angel to stay by his side forever. Not because he wanted the Angel to save his family whenever, but because the Angel was comforting.

"Thrice you will meet the one you call The Golden Healing Angel, who will assist you, but the Angel also has a Fated Path. The third time you both meet, you and the Angel will be able to make that decision yourselves," the words informed him, making him release a breath of calmness.

"If I'm patient, one day I may be able to have my Angel friend by my side and get my vengeance," he thought, turning to give himself over to the conversation.

"So, the fake mission and the attacks all on the same night were a collectively planned hit on our family?!" his Daddy asked and Abuelo nodded.

"So, it's not about them finding anything," Justin said. "Over twenty human police officers just up and disappeared after conducting a "raid" on our home? Even if there were mafia members mixed in, they won't care enough to listen to anything we say. We HAVE to leave!"

"There were Beings as well," he said, pouting.

"The twins? Where are they! Are they even alive!?" NanaPoo cried out.

He looked away. "They are."

"They won't be if they know ya'll still alive," Abuelo said, standing to move closer to him. "What the hell happened here Xavier?" Abuelo asked, looking around the clean house.

He gave a small smile at Abuelo's renewed Energy. Eight of their family members were gone, but some of them survived. Abuelo would celebrate the memories of those who lost their lives while continuing to live and protect those still breathing.

"It doesn't look like anything happened here!" NanaPoo said, hanging onto his Daddy. "Please! You all need to leave before the Federals come and break down your door!" NanaPoo begged.

"I don't wanna leave!" he said, instead of answering Abuelo.

"You all will be safe in Sunset Country with MawMaw and PopPop," NanaPoo said through her tears. "Zay, open a Portal baby."

Abuelo handed him coordinates but he crossed his arms, refusing to even look at the paper. His Daddy came to squat down and pulled his face to look into his eyes.

"I know you have Enhanced Hearing, so you heard what my Momma told you to do. Ignore her again and face me," his Daddy's deep voice told him.

Out of respect for Abuelo and to continue hiding his Ability Level, he took a quick look at the paper in Abuelo's hand and closing his eyes, he began pulling enough of his Energy to his hands as he pinpointed the exact coordinates. He released his Energy, connecting the two sides and opening a royal-blue PPR[7].

"I can stay here with Abuelo and NanaPoo," he argued, and he looked at his Angel for help, but his Angel said nothing, only watched. He was afraid if they left, he would have to wait to see his Angel again.

His Daddy took a deep breath and exhaling it, he stood, gesturing to Justin. His Momma was already through the Portal after hugging NanaPoo and waving bye to Abuelo. His Daddy hugged his parents and with an "I love you", his Daddy walked through, followed by Justin dragging him, screaming, and unwilling through his Portal.

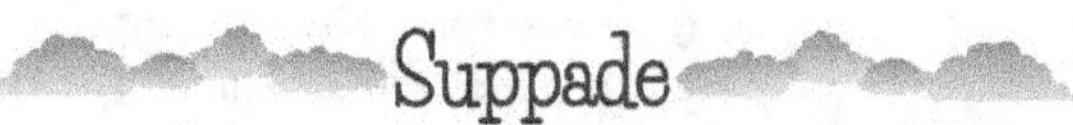

Suppade

He was now living in the small town of Sunset, halfway around the planet from his hometown of Little Atlanta. He hated it here. He understood that after his Daddy, he was the second strongest Being in town but still the most powerful on the planet. After clearing up what happened in Little Atlanta, his parents sat him down and explained.

"We can't go back right now Zay," his Momma told him. "We have no way to explain to humans how that many bodies just disappeared."

---

[7](Party Portal Rare) See Universal Abilities #4

"We gone stay in Sunset Town with MawMaw and PopPop 'til this mess calms down over there," his Daddy said, rubbing his forehead.

"We're going to change you and Justin's names so you can attend school," his Momma said, planning their new lives.

After listening to his parents say all the things he didn't want to hear, that night, he left Sunset Town and struck out on his own. Finding a small island in the middle of the Optic Ocean where no one wanted to travel through, be it by water or air, because of all the weird, unexplainable events, he set up a raging wall of constantly swirling water on three sides.

The walls of this Water Barrier[8] reached three hundred and forty-one point two miles high, pass the Breathable Ozone layer; the Tropicalsphere and right where the Nexusphere starts, to ensure no low-flying plane could pass over.

He found other small, uninhabited islands and set them up to look like a dragon from an aerial view locked inside a triangular Water Barrier. He used one island to plant his crops, another to grow rare flowers he found around the planet, one for his livestock and another for his experiments into Purifying.

He happened to come across an island which looked as though it was once inhabited and added it, so he could research the history of the now extinct people who once lived there.

He was only able to be happy for two weeks before Justin showed up. Not physically setting foot on his crop island, Justin sent his Conscience[9] in Energy Form to him as he was tilling the land.

Wiping a sweat from his brow, he stopped and leaned against his plow to ask, "What do you want?" He decided he could listen and plow, so he kept moving after his question. Lifting the wooden walking plow, he continued to trudge as Justin spoke.

"Mom and Pops are freaking out right now. They have the whole town searching the forest around our home for you," Justin informed him.

He kept plowing. "Well, you can tell them to stop. That's not my home. I'm making this my new home. If I go back, Dad's gonna force me to follow him."

Justin crossed his arms and tilted his head. "So, you're gonna live here all by yourself? What about the rest of us? Are you gonna leave us to fend for ourselves? Without you,

---

[8] *When a Being wants to protect, their Energy is used with this singular purpose, creating a dome around the Being or whatever/whomever the Being wants to protect. See Universal Abilities #3*
[9] *Also known as a Being's Mind*

our family is broken. They'll take everything Abuelo and Pops have built only to use it against our own people."

Justin straightened up to stare hard at him. "You want our family name to be the reason why T-PEC can now control the Being Community with no oversight, no one to tell them what they're doing to their own people isn't right?" Justin questioned him, but he kept plowing, uninterested.

Justin stuck his hands in his pocket and relaxed. "I don't know about you, but I'm pretty sure your invisible Golden Angel only knew you would be in Sunset. Think your Angel can find you here?"

Justin's words made him freeze, but he refused to look at Justin.

"How about..." Justin started, "you make Sunset Town somewhere your Angel would want to live, want to stay. That way, you can have your Guardian Angel beside you." Justin took his hands out of his pockets to lift them in a shrug. "None of us in Sunset Town will be able to see your Angel or tell your Angel where you are," Justin ended and he felt a knowing smile from his older brother.

He dropped the plow and turned to look at his older brother's Dual Energies of orange and red. "What about you? Aren't you pissed you're not next in line?"

Justin laughed. "I'm ecstatic! The only Path of Pop's I wanna take is the business route."

He didn't smell a Lie from Justin, whose Dual Energies remained calm, so his eyes found the ground as he thought about what he could do to make the town better. He looked up at Justin. "Dad won't be onboard."

Justin's hands found his pockets again as he looked around impressed at how much was plowed in two weeks. "How about you and I figure things out here first and then I will go back with our proposal to Pops, get him to understand," Justin offered.

"If he doesn't agree, I'm not going back," he said, his face turned up into a pout. He crossed his arms and set his feet determinedly on the ground.

"Right now, we both have to be willing to compromise to get what we want. Being demanding will only put people off. Show you're a man of your word and people will begin to believe your actions. Once that happens, whatever you say will hold the most weight in any conversation," Justin advised and he was willing to listen.

"Okay, as long as Dad is willing to hear us out, I'll go back," he compromised.

Once back, his Daddy held out his arms to him, and he ran into the open hug.

"Zay, Promise[10] me you won't leave Sunset Town until I okay it?" his Daddy asked. "If anything, they wanna get their hands on you, and I'll be damned if I allow them to attack my family again."

He heard the anger in his Daddy's voice and looked down at the ground, nodding. "I Promise," he replied, feeling the tiny Promise form in his damaged Core.

"You're Special Zay," his Daddy said, hugging him again. "I know you don't want to follow me, but this decision was already made for you from birth. It's the Path you choose which will define you as a Leader."

He exhaled a deep breath. He pulled himself out of his Daddy's arms and looked him in the face. "Justin and I have come to an agreement. I only ask for your support in ridding Sunset of humans. I don't want to live around them anymore. I want to be able to freely use my Energy when I want to."

His Daddy nodded. "You have become very reasonable after disappearing for two weeks."

"Justin showed me things from a different viewpoint," he said, leaving out exactly what he and Justin agreed to and did.

"We might as well put some of our wealth into this town. The only popular places are around our resort," his Daddy said, thinking.

He knew his parents met when his Daddy came to Sunset to scout locations for a new luxurious resort chain his Daddy owned. His Daddy was the only man out of all her suitors, to win over his Momma, the most sought-after young woman living in Sunset.

The town of Sunset was mostly poor, with fishing being the highest paid occupation. He held suspicion that his Daddy only built his resort here to spend more time with his Momma. It did bring tourists to visit but most stayed close to the oceanfront resort.

"Zay and I have some ideas to implement as you're building up the town," Justin said.

Within a few weeks of living in Sunset and now known by his Being-given name, Suppade[11] erected a shimmering, white Barrier over Sunset Town. This Barrier Purified[12] the air, water and land, making Beings and humans living under his Barrier notice the difference.

Humans had no choice but to move out as everything became toxic to them. The only safe places for humans were at the resort, which was still a popular destination point for cruise ships and the newly built airport, neither of which was under his Barrier.

---

[10] *When a small part of a Being's Energy forms a lock inside the Being's Core.*

[11] *Pronounced Sue-paw-day.*

[12] *Decontaminated.*

This caused Sunset and the surrounding areas to become flooded with Beings wanting to live under a Barrier which could replenish the Energy inside their bodies just by breathing. He never told anyone it was his Barrier, and he knew the Beings living there assumed it was his Daddy's.

His parents held true to their words. While his Daddy was investing in upgrading current businesses and starting new ones, his Momma was busy building new schools and setting up education programs. The small town started growing and expanding as his parents improved the quality of life in Sunset.

But while their parents were benefiting from his parents upgrading the town, the children didn't care and were cruel. He understood the children were enjoying a better life than before and it showed in their attitudes.

Students on this part of the planet started first grade after their seventh birthday and turned eight during the school year. He was six years old in the first grade, which was unheard of unless the child was smart, like the legacy his Momma left.

He already finished early education and was enrolled in first grade when he left The States[13] at six. Because of his aptitude for learning and being incredibly bright, the school board allowed him to continue in the first grade. While other students were eight, he turned seven at the end of their school year.

Every day at school, the children would make fun of him. The teasing was only made worse by the fact he was smaller than the other students and soon, things turned physical, with them throwing things, ruining his stuff, and learning slur words in his native language of English.

Suppade didn't care enough to make friends. He spoke to no one and kept his distance from everyone not his family. He understood that with the influx of Beings from around the planet now moving into and around Sunset Town, the children heard and regurgitated rumors from the other side of the planet about his family.

But he focused on honing his Abilities, ignoring the children and now teachers, who didn't condone what the children were doing to him but didn't stop it either. Only one Being in

---

[13] *The second largest land mass on the planet, known as The States, similar to America on Earth. There is a large border wall separating the closed, barrierless North from the mixed Beings and free humans South.*

the whole E-Level school would say anything or try to help him, while keeping the recommended distance.

Until one day, an E-Level Five student found him sitting by himself on the playground. The boy was apparently mad at him for something he did, but he didn't care. A crowd grew, but he sat through the insults until the end of recess. When he stood up, the E-Level Five student punched him in the face, and he blacked out.

When he snapped back to his senses, he was sitting in the principal's office with his parents. He listened as his parents explained they would cover the medical expenses and compensate the family. They would also move him to a different school. When he heard, he would have to move again, he pulled his legs up and hugged them.

"I don't want to leave again," he mumbled, wondering if his Angel would ever be able to find him if he wasn't in Sunset.

The principal was stating the child currently in the hospital with severe burns along with multiple broken bones and fractures, shouldn't have touched him in the first place.

"The school prides itself on teaching manners and respect, so there's no reason for him to switch," the principal said. "We will make an announcement that all students are to keep their hands out of others' personal space unless invited."

The principal's desperation started to show since losing him as a student would also mean losing an open wallet policy from his wealthy parents. The staff and students all knew he hated being touched; it was the one thing his parents stressed before enrolling him in school.

His Momma came to comfort him, leaning down to look at him. "Do you want to stay here Drum?" she asked, using his nickname.

He peeked at his Momma and nodded. "I have to stay here so my Angel can find me again," he meekly stated. He knew his family all considered his Angel his Imaginary Friend and he thought it was easier to not correct them.

She stood, turning to the principal. "Okay then. Any further incidents ignited by touching Drum will result in charges being filed for assault and Drum acting in self-defense." His Momma's matter of fact voice was comforting to him.

His Daddy's deep, booming voice sounded out, shaking the room and the principal's Energy. "We need to go see this kid's parents," his Daddy said, holding the door open.

His Momma gathered him out of the chair and helped him stand. When she was eye level with him, he felt her smile as she straightened his jacket and zipped it.

"Hopefully this will not go on Drum's *permanent* education records?" his Momma asked, her Energy giving off a threat underneath her words to the principal.

"Of course not!" the principal said, her Energy shaking.

"We will deal with the police at the hospital, so send them there," his Daddy told the Energy-scared principal.

He took his Daddy's hand and the comfort he felt from his parents gave him the courage to walk out of the office and the school with his head held high.

The next week, he returned to school. Everyone gave him extra wide berth not to accidentally bump into him. They also stopped the bullying. By lunchtime, he was feeling like he could finally breathe a little.

As he sat at his table alone, a young boy he knew was registered as Eastern[14], and in his class, pulled up a chair from another table and joined him. The boy's Energies was gangly and graceless, with his clothes being too big on him. He stared at the sagging uniform on the intruder.

The boy giggled. "I think my sister's hand-me downs look cute on me. What do you think, Young Master?"

He rolled his eyes and went back to eating.

"If you're free, we can hang out where I do odd jobs! I'm saving to buy a sewing machine so I can alter my uniforms." The boy turned to look at him. After receiving no response, the boy continued, "You know my nickname is Dot, but my name is Panya."

He turned to look at Dot. "You can call me Drum, and I think the nickname Queen fits you better than Dot."

Dot's Energies lit up. "I like the nickname better too!" Queen kicked his legs while they finished lunch in silence.

Without looking, he asked Queen, "Hey Panya, can you keep a secret?"

Queen's interest was piqued, and he nodded enthusiastically.

"Yes Suppade! I can keep a secret," Queen whispered, remembering not to get too close.

"Good," he said, flashing a smile.

But Queen didn't know how to react to being given the most adorable smile, and he held in his laughter at Queen's Energies coming to a standstill, unsure of what to do. So, Queen sat there and stared at him until he left to throw away his trash. Only then did Panya, formally known as Dot, now known as Queen, snap out of the trance.

---

[14] *Eastern is the name those of Earth's Asian descent called themselves as they mixed to form new languages.*

INTRODUCTION: MEET THE FOUR
SUNSET TOWN: SUNDAY (THIRTEEN-ISH YEARS LATER)

As nineteen-year-old Drum and his best friends were walking down the street headed to Queen's favorite fabric store, he didn't pay any attention to the tourists. It just so happens this street was popular for its open bar atmosphere and was regularly crowded with human tourists who have snuck in, looking to make a quick connection with a local before having to leave.

"Is it me or does Queen enjoy the attention?" Sport asked, as he walked alongside Drum's right.

Queen, who was on Drum's left quipped back, "If you looked near as good as me, you would want to show it off as well."

Sport looked up and down at Queen, taking in Queen's bright, olive skin, straight, black hair and chestnut brown eyes, giving Queen the look of a mysterious, handsome doctor, who just brought you back from the dead. Queen's Grace made it easy for people to gravitate to him, even telling him their darkest secrets.

Queen was also known throughout their town as "Knowledge", as he was able to know things before anyone else. He knew more about their schoolmates and those in town than they themselves did. Even adults would come to Queen to verify a rumor, or give personal information about themselves, in return for a possible Favor from Queen.

At first, everyone thought Drum would know since Queen knew, but they very quickly learned Drum never treated anyone differently after Queen learned their secrets.

There were only two rules when it came to dealing with secrets in town; never spread a rumor, and if it's not your business, don't tell. These two rules made Queen the most trusted person in town.

There was only one family Queen didn't know everything about. He felt he only knew exactly what they wanted him to know. It was driving him crazy for years and he set his resolve to finally be invited into Drum's home this school year.

Drum fought back a smile as he listened to his best friends argue. Every time they walked down the street; this was the common conversation between Sport and Queen.

Sport enjoyed the attention just as much as Queen. At six-foot six and a half, twenty-one-year-old Sport was the tallest of them. His family line was unknown, so even though he was registered as an Easterner, no one knew for certain. His light brown eyes and tan, olive skin would make some people stop and question his heritage as his deep brown hair was naturally highlighted with light brown streaks.

Sport was built like a professional running back, while being naturally gifted in any sport he played. Sport would often practice with Drum and his Dad, Mr. Caleb, Justin, and Major. This is what Sport believed helped him become a starting player on the High School's varsity teams in his first year and by his second year, he was made captain.

Sport was the only student in their Higher Education[15] school's history who held both positions his first year, starting player and team captain. Queen taught him the aesthetics of being naturally charming despite his build. This allowed him to "mingle" with single tourist ladies, despite his campus uniform. So much so, Sport was the most experienced out of all of them.

Drum didn't seem to care Sport was with much older tourists and never commented on it because he understood his best friend's frustrated Energy. There was someone Sport was head over heels for but was unable to confess to.

No one in daytime courses on their campus, openly dated. Everyone was waiting on Drum to ask someone. Anyone who wanted to be or seem "pure" for well-known, complete abstinence Drum, never openly accepted anything from anyone who liked them. No one wanted the embarrassment of being unavailable if they were the one Drum liked.

Since Drum seemed to have no issues flashing his smile, most everyone stayed "single" in hopes of finally catching his eye. Of course, it didn't stop the students from secretly hooking up.

Almost everyone on campus wanted to date Drum. He managed to naturally charm most of his schoolmates with guidance from Queen, Sport and the little one hiding behind his back to avoid being stared at by tourists.

Win was what Queen was in elementary school. Although Queen grew out of his awkwardness into a slim, graceful, handsome young man, Win was not so lucky. Skinny, gangly, and tall with a baby face, his shyness made everyone want to feed him and pat his head.

But Win hated when strangers would touch his curly, deep brown hair, making his mahogany brown eyes flash with anger, while his tan skin would redden. He was considered the most adorable Islander[16].

---

[15] *Is the term used by Beings to signal the University was for Beings only. No human is ever accepted since all Higher Ed schools are under Barriers.*
[16] *Islanders are the Spanish speaking population from Earth. Over generations, the Spanish language and people merged to become one.*

Drum would share his home-cooked food with Win, and since other students gave way to Drum, Win was less bothered and stressed. To everyone's surprise, Win's personality as cute and bubbly shone through.

Drum and Queen's friendship started after the incident in elementary school. And when Queen threw a fit because his Adopted parents wanted him to go to a different middle school than Drum, they became friends with Sport and Win. It was Drum who approached them both and asked them to be friends.

Sport watched sports religiously, so Drum found someone he could talk to about his favorite teams. With Win, Drum joked, saying it hurt him to see people waste food on a kid with a picky appetite, fast metabolism, and a small stomach.

Their first year in Higher Education started with Drum seeking revenge for a classmate who was assaulted by seniors from a different campus. This became known as The Surf and Turf War.

Outside of fighting to protect his schoolmates, Drum's personality was aloof, but charming if approached. He never raised his voice and was willing to help anyone from their campus with any problem they had. Which is what they were doing today. Helping a classmate.

They finally passed the bars and reached the street they needed. It was down a quieter back street, which only locals shopped on. As they walked along you could hear them laughing and joking about how many women it would take to milk Sport dry.

Win chimed in with the number three hundred and twenty-one, and they all stopped to stare at Win before Drum and Queen fell out laughing.

Sport blushed and was offended. "Why...what...that many...how could you think...?"

Win gave Sport a goofy smile. "Well, I figured by number three hundred and twenty, your big ball sack would have shrunk into a tiny almond. The last one would be the nail in the coffin."

Sport tried to grab Win, but his thin frame and use of his Elemental Ability[17] to use air, made it easy for him to leap back from Sport's reach. Drum was trying to hold himself up against a brick wall while laughing and Queen was on his knees grabbing his stomach.

"What?" Win asked, as he used air to glide behind Queen. "I know how large your member[18] and balls are. You're constantly showing—" Win stopped mid-sentence and ran as Sport did a small Up-jump over Queen, trying to grab him again.

---

[17] *Most Beings' Energies are only compatible with one element.*
[18] *Only Beings living under a Barrier use this word for male genitals.*

Sport's face was filled with embarrassment as Win ran behind Drum. Sport stopped short in front of a laughing Drum as Win used him as a shield.

"Me how "blessed" you are every chance you get." Win licked his tongue out as Sport went to grab him again.

At that moment, Drum stood, and Sport's arm quickly moved so they wouldn't touch.

"Words first," was all Drum said, as he smiled at Sport.

Sport became flushed with embarrassment, and he looked down to mumble, *"I just wanted him to see that one day even he…could achieve great lengths."*

Drum fell against the wall laughing again, this time at Win's expense. Win's red face was unable to retort back which caused Queen to fall out laughing again. Sport and Win both looked at each other, only to laugh as well. Those walking past the street smiled as they heard Drum and his best friends' laughter.

It was a rare occurrence for Drum to be in town. Ever since first grade, Drum spent every weekend out of town and school breaks were no different, but he would come home early when Sport had a game. So, he only spent time with his best friends during the school week. Even Queen didn't know EXACTLY what he did on the weekends and never pressed for information.

Drum never invited his best friends to his home and turned down any invitation to visit theirs. He mostly went straight home after classes unless Queen could coax him into a side trip or Sport wanted to practice. Drum would only participate in Favors he knew his best friends couldn't handle themselves and Queen was very selective when it came to accepting Favors which included him.

They finally made it to the store Queen wanted to visit and once inside, the others lazily walked and looked around while Queen placed his order. They left after Drum paid and continued walking down the street, following it to a small, restricted beach cove, just outside his Barrier.

They took off their shoes and started running in the sand. Sport took a rounded ball out of his bag, and he and Drum started playing football, sometimes ending up in the water, splashing Queen and Win, who were collecting shells. They were interrupted by a middle-aged human man coming out of the cave behind them.

"Shut the fuck up you fucking brats!" The human spat at them as he spoke. One would think the human was dressed in swim trunks, but they could see he was only wearing boxers.

Drum's face immediately changed and with an even tone, he spoke. "What's sooooo important that us brats can't have fun here?" Drum was offended a human was cussing *at him* in a vicious way.

"I'm... just...trying...to enjoy...umm"—the human cleared his throat—"the day. Leave you fucking brats." But the human's voice no longer held the anger from earlier.

Drum made no indication he was about to leave and asked, "Or what? Will you call the police on us?"

At the mention of police, the human paled; quickly changed his tune and held his hands up in front of him. "Just be respectful that there are more than just you here, and pipe down." The human started to go back into the cave but as he stepped back, Drum stepped forward.

"Win!" was all Drum said.

Before the human could block slender Win, he was in the cave. Seconds later Win's hurt voice sounded out. "QUEEN! HELP!"

The human panicked and looking for a way out, ran off towards the noise of a crowded area, but the sand seemed to slow him down.

"Sport!" Drum said.

The human didn't make it far before being tackled by Sport. Drum walked up but kept his distance as Sport held the human on the ground with an arm twisted behind his back.

Drum looked down, watching the human sweat from the excessive amount of Heat he was giving off. "What? Don't you want to have some time alone with *me* in the cave? Am I too *old* or too much like *you* right now? Would you enjoy it more if I change into my Form?"

The human tried to stutter out an excuse, but sand kept getting in the man's mouth, since Sport would push his head down every time he tried to speak. After picking the human up, Sport walked the stumbling man back to the cave with Drum following close behind.

They waited until Queen and Win exited the cave with a bundle wrapped in Queen's arms. He and Win moved towards the water keeping distance between them and the human. Queen looked at Drum and shook his head while Win was trying not to cry. Queen and Win kept the bundle close by the water, protecting it with their bodies.

Once Drum nodded, Sport roughly shoved the human back into the cave and turned to guard the entrance while Drum went inside. The bundle was being calmed and reassured by Queen that the human would never again touch them as a blood-curling scream escaped the cave.

Drum left the cave minutes later and Sport tossed him a towel. After cleaning his hands in the water, Drum used his Energy to quickly burn the towel. He and Sport left after making sure Queen and Win would be okay.

When the police arrived, Queen and Win explained they came here, only to find a human in the cave along with the bundle and called the police. The human was placed in handcuffs, but a second ambulance was also needed. The police were shaking their heads in disgust and disbelief at the scene in the cave.

They looked at Queen and Win, then back at the human on the gurney, completely sure the two young Beings in front of them weren't responsible for what happened to the human. Locals secretly knew alone time with Drum never ended well for the person unlucky enough to catch his attention.

"Is Young Master around?" a police detective asked Win.

"No. If he was, you would see him, wouldn't you?" Queen answered instead.

"I was speaking to the young man, what's your name again?"

Win choked through the tears. "Tawin sir."

"So, Tawin,"—the detective leaned down closer to Win—"is Young Master around?"

Win shook his head. "I just wanted to collect ocean shells!" Win burst out crying.

Queen held Win as he shot looks of anger at the detective.

Lifting his hands as if Queen were holding him at gunpoint, the detective backed down. "Fine, fine, just make sure I get your statements on my desk by tomorrow so I can put this fucker away for the rest of his short human life with some Beings who would be upset to know what he did today." The detective turned to walk away but stopped midway. "Tell him we said thanks for doing what we wanted…even though we didn't know about it." He walked off to the ambulance.

Win, with his forehead still on Queen's chest asked, "Is he gone yet?"

Queen sighed and patted Win on the back. They gathered their things and left the scene, quietly sneaking around the spectators and news teams to head back under Drum's Barrier, before using a Portal Key[19] to Queen's home.

Later that night as Queen was watching the news report of a trafficking bust, he received a text message. 'Thank you!' was all it said.

---

[19] *A pale violet key used to open a Party Portal to a set location.*

PANTU: A NEW TOWN, A NEW PLAN
WEEK ONE: MONDAY

He had to do it. Going from online studies to physical attendance on a campus at the end of the year was not ideal for a Higher Education Senior. He needed to complete his education if he wanted access to his trust fund money. That's what his parents said, but his only interest was where his parents hid the information.

Since his education was tied to his fund, his parents were able to contract a private tutoring company to test him in place of what people called high school grades, so a Higher Education campus would accept him. He tested in the range of highly gifted but never thought he would have any time to care about school.

His education was different from the other students'. His parents submitted his completed assignments online for him. They communicated with his Professors on his behalf and made sure he did his finals every semester. He was enrolled at the school since his first year. He was, unknowingly to the majority, the only online learner the campus ever admitted.

He also needed to take his medicine and be a "good little one" if he did not want his parents to lock him away again. Once, his whole life was planned out, but in an instant, it was shattered.

Stepping out of the car, he looked up at his new house for the next couple of months. The two-story, light blue and white house was kind of cute, but he would never admit it. The house was a downgrade from their previous luxurious home they shared with Indria, but an upgrade from the many places they lived since leaving his hometown.

He took a deep breath, and his lungs were filled with clean sea air. He looked around to see how close they were to the sea and noticed a young male, about his age, watching from across the street. Once their eyes connected, the young male turned and walked down the street.

His eyes followed and thought the young male was quite good-looking, but not more so than him. If this was his competition, he would have no problem tricking his parents into thinking he was doing better. People his age tend to flock to the best-looking to be friends with. Besides, the male looked like he could use a meal.

After remembering he was looking for the sea, he was surprised to know they were not at all close to it but being able to smell the sea from the house was nice. He smiled but quickly sighed, hoping his parents did not see it.

He was giving his parents the vocal silent treatment, only speaking with his Ma through text messages. He thought even that was too generous as they allowed Coin to stay behind with his Grandparents and continue living in The City, the country on the planet Torven[20] where he and his parents are from.

After travelling so far from his hometown, he was surprised to find nothing was known about the place or the citizens, since it is closed off from the rest of Torven. Once in a library, he looked at a map of Torven and saw his birthplace is called something different by those outside The City.

His parents made things worse by moving him to the edge of the continent, to some weird town which was prideful of their knack for being busy year-round. He made himself hate it long before they crossed over the town line.

But he would go back, once this school year was over, he would return and claim everything that was his. Compared to the years they spent away from The City; four months was not a long wait.

Patience was all he needed. His main plan was to leave without his parents once he finished Senior year and received his fund information. He never wanted to see them again.

It was the first week back on campus after a four-week break, so he decided to stay at the house and help his Ma unpack what little they had. Although he never said a word or looked at her, his Ma rambled on about their new town.

He was surprised when his Ma told him there was no need for gasoline, since their vehicles ran on what people here called Neutral Energy[21]. She would use her Light[22] to start the car as the owner or authorized driver and then the Neutral Energy in the air would power the vehicle.

He needed a new phone since the one he brought with him stopped working once they crossed the county line. He learned all their electronics and the utilities in their house ran on Neutral Energy from the air to power everything they needed.

He also figured students would be too excited about what they did during break to care about a new student. He needed to be in the spotlight if he were to trick his parents.

It was easier to find weak-willed people who floated along the edge of the crowd to be his fake friends and even better, fake Woman. He needed people who were as desperate as him in order to make it through the rest of the school year, so when Monday came, he had a plan.

---

[20] *Torven is twenty times the size of Earth and what humans named the planet.*
[21] *Energy which can be processed by any Being.*
[22] *What those from The City call Energy.*

It is time for you to wake up!

Opening his eyes Monday morning, everything looked foreign to him but felt familiar. He quickly adjusted when his Ma knocked on his bedroom door and called out for something named breakfast.

But the adjustment wasn't understanding. As information quickly poured into his head, he realized he was not in The City anymore and it had been a week since they moved to this town. As he glanced around the almost empty room, his eyes landed on the closet.

"Uniform," popped into his head and he climbed out of bed to get ready for the day.

Although he said nothing, as he finished getting dressed or while eating breakfast with his Ma in the kitchen, banging around pots and pans while trying to figure out the multiple uses for them, he paid attention to everything, with information about this new house occasionally popping into his head.

On the drive to his new campus, he stared out the window at the stunning scenery passing by him. Everywhere his eyes landed, the unobstructed starlight made the colors of everything radiant. He needed to close his eyes a few times to adjust to the brightness around him.

When he climbed out of his Ma's car and looked up at his new campus, he was shocked a school on this part of the continent was as beautiful as it was. It was clean and well taken care of. As he looked around, admiring the landscape, the smell of the sea made him crack a smile. He had smelled this scent before, had he not?

He looked down at his phone to hide his face and text his Ma that he would be fine, she could leave. He would figure out the campus himself. Apparently, the Dean wanted to have a conference with him and his parents before he started, to take them on a tour, but he was against it.

He did not want to be seen on campus before his first day as it would ruin his plans, but after realizing the size of the campus, he sighed, wishing he would have taken the tour.

Looking up, he started to walk up the steps of the Admissions Building with a smile on his face. But his eyes did not stop at the entrance, instead they continued up and around as he felt someone watching him. He could not see the person but felt the gaze which sent a shiver down his spine.

After getting all his paperwork from the office, a student was called down to walk him to homeroom.

"Ah, it is you?" he said, unsure of his comment until a faint memory popped into his head. This was the same male who was standing across the street from the house the day they moved in.

"Hmm," was what the male said.

"Do you two know each other already, Win?" the office clerk asked.

"No, Ms. Jo. We just happen to live on the same street," Win sweetly answered.

He jolted, surprised at this young male's sweet voice and when Win smiled at Ms. Jo, he felt like his initial assessment was completely wrong. This young male was more than good-looking; he was competition material. But he refused to show any emotion, not wanting Win to think he could not compete.

Damn! I would have to break his confidence first, he thought to himself, *how many more like him are here?*

He thanked Ms. Jo, but she only glanced at him quickly to nod before turning her attention back to the young male in front of her. "Win dear, make sure Pantu understands the rules, we don't want any incidents."

Win folded his hands and bowed. "Of course, Ms. Jo."

Win turned and headed out of the office holding the door open for him. He could not help but notice the smile on Ms. Jo's face as her eyes followed Win out the door.

What the hell!? He thought to himself.

Once outside the office, they made their way to the Advanced Honors Senior Learning Area. After badging into a building, and heading down an empty hallway, Win finally said more to him than just hmm.

"People constantly want to feed me so don't take it personal." Win stopped and looked at him. "You're really good-looking so you shouldn't have a problem making friends." After a chuckle, Win added, "But you still have to wait like the rest of us to say you're dating."

He looked at Win, startled by the comment, but kept his reaction in check. "Why would I have to wait to date?" he asked, ignoring the fact he did not know what the hell a "date" was.

By now Win's gait was light and he was skipping on his way to class. "You'll find out soon." Win smiled at him as he held the homeroom door open.

Walking into the classroom stunned him. As he looked around at all the students and even the homeroom Professor, everyone was bright and felt similar to himself. He was happy the Professor introduced him since he needed to use the time to adjust. Once the Professor asked him to say a few words, he was ready.

Keeping a calm composure, he spoke. "Hello, as Professor Tram stated, my name is Pantu. I am new to Sunset, and this is my first day on campus. If you happen to see me turning in circles, I will thank you in advance for any help offered."

The students all giggled or chuckled slightly at his words and he could feel it; they all held some sort of positive feelings towards him. He thought to himself, *they all seem nice enough, so this should be easy, but why do I feel unhappy about my plans?*

After having this thought, he felt like this was definitely the longest day of his life. How could everything go so wrong within only a few hours? He thought the day was starting well but slightly off. It was fine, he could moderate his plans as needed. He was able to make a "friend" in homeroom, but it was not Win, who was the most popular person in the class.

The young Women kept sneaking looks at him while smiling and giggling behind their hands. This made him feel a bit better, and he thought to himself maybe Win was trying to trick him into not approaching the Woman Win wanted to date.

He decided he would find out who Win liked and pursue her for shits and giggles. If things came to ahead, he was willing to sleep with her as well, once, just so Win knew not to mess with him anymore. He smiled at the young Women, and they squealed in delight. His new "friend" came up from behind and threw an arm around him.

His "friend" whispered in his ear, "*Wow, you will definitely be popular in no time.*"

He rolled his eyes and shook his head as if he disagreed with his "friend", but he was really thinking, *ah, duh!* He noticed Win was looking at him as if he was projecting his thoughts, but he just smiled back and took out his books as the bell rang for first period.

During lunch, he sat with his homeroom "friend" and his friends. *I should probably remember his name since he and his lame friends are perfect patsies for my fake friends*, he thought.

But these people did not feel lame to him. There was something about them which set off alarms in his head. Calling them lame was his feelings of superiority which he could not seem to shake.

"Oh yea! Remember, whatever you do, *never*, we mean NEVER touch Drum."

He snapped out of his thoughts and looked up to see a friend of his homeroom "friend" giving him the must-know information about the campus.

"My apologies...what? I do not play drums. I am not in a band?" The confusion on his face along with his response made his table and a couple of tables around them start laughing. His "friend", Dill, however, refrained.

"How adorably handsome!"

"You mean stunningly beautiful!"

"Pantu is definitely in the top 4."

"Oh, let's change it to top 5?"

"Pantu has a sense of humor also?"

"Just wait until Queen uploads a picture!"

"OMU[23]! It will get so many likes!"

"What I said was never touch Drum," the friend of a friend responded, and he remembered the male's name as Turn.

He was enjoying the small talk around him and the attention he was getting. "What drum should I not touch?" he asked, still confused. *Does this school have a sacred object that helps them, like where I come from?*

"That Drum," the friend of a "friend" named Jet nodded towards one of the cafeteria doors, which was swamped with young Women and males.

He couldn't see exactly who Jet or Turn was talking about, but the loud squeals and excitement made him pause.

He wondered, is *there someone here who can catch the attention of anyone?*

Never mind that, he pushed the thought to the side. *I just need to find one Woman who would be desperate enough to date me.* He knew he couldn't bring someone around his parents who did not fit with the type of Woman he was known to attract. His parents and Psychiatrist would not fall for it.

As his eyes wondered across the tables, he noticed a beautiful young Woman sitting quietly surrounded by her friends. In a sea of blond, brown and black hair, as the only student with vibrant, curly, red hair currently in the lunchroom, she stood out. Her skin, the color of dove feathers, made him wonder, *would she feel just as soft?* Her good looks would make her perfect and she was about the same stature as the type of Woman he was thought to be attracted to.

With her by my side my parents might just buy it.

"You would do better in life not to mess with her, Pantu."

He did not bother to take his eyes off her to figure out who made the statement. It did not sound like Dill, so he was uninterested in looking at whomever was speaking.

"Why not?" he asked, his eyes still on the woman.

---

[23] *OMU is short for Oh My Universe! It is a popular phrase amongst Beings.*

Dill leaned in and started whispering, to which he leaned over to hear better while keeping his eyes on her.

"Well, she's the reason no one messes with anyone from our campus."

Now Dill had his attention. *How great of a fighter is this Woman or is it because she could be considered the most beautiful on campus?* He patiently looked at Dill, waiting for more information.

Put, the last of Dill's friends, explained at the beginning of her first year some seniors from a nearby city's campus attacked her during a shopping trip to Hollis. When Drum found out, he went to the campus and beat every senior involved and anyone stupid enough to jump in. Put gave details about the viciousness of Drum's attack and how every one of them ended up in the hospital with at least one broken bone.

"That happened here?" he asked.

His question was answered by Dill. "Yep, and for six months, Drum fought any students from other campuses who would challenge him. But he never lost, and he never killed anyone. With so many of their kids in the hospital, it became a spoken rule between parents and other campuses not to mess with us."

He rolled his eyes and thought to himself, *my Universe! Have I isekai'ed[24] myself into a manga?*

Dill continued to explain during the Surf and Turf War, Drum found out she tried to kill herself. He and his best friends went to the hospital every day. They would light candles and place flowers under her window.

Soon everyone on campus heard what Drum and his best friends, called The Four, were doing and started coming to show support. The choir would sing songs outside her window, and the drama club would perform plays. The day she was discharged, students gathered to ask her to come back and said they would protect her.

"It was all over the news," Dill said. "Media ate it up and it went viral online."

Yes, I have isekai'ed myself into an action manga where the plot armor protagonist has a harem, while I am just a side character.

He remembered he might have read something somewhere about it but disregarded it because it was common for males to protect Women. That article did invoke unknown feelings in him, which he pushed back down. Besides, it was from a hick sounding town somewhere out in the boonies.

---

[24] *Pronounced ease-saw-kai-ed. Japanese anime/manga term for dying in your own world, only to be transported into another.*

He groaned and slid down in his chair. He leaned forward to rest his head in his arms and sighed. He did not have it in him to play with the Woman's heart after everything she went through.

Dill thought his sighing was due to the fact he could not date the most popular Woman on campus. Dill was right, albeit for a different reason. Dill wanted to offer him some words of encouragement.

"She's the one voted most likely to win Drum's heart, if she hasn't already." Dill patted him on the back. "But don't worry, once Drum asks who he wants to be his girlfriend—"

"Or boyfriend," a male walking by interjected.

"Once Drum asks someone to be his girl or boyfriend," Dill corrected, "it will free everyone else to openly date."

He lifted his head from the table. "So, no one will date until this Drum chooses? What the fuck kind of logic is that?" He ignored asking exactly what a girlfriend or boyfriend was and why the hell a male would have a boyfriend, since the information was irrelevant to him.

Dill's face never turned to look at him, but their eyes met as Dill whispered, *"No one will ever admit to dating you, but some still...you know."*

By now, he was over this crazy ass campus. He gathered up his trash and after dumping it, he went to the library for some peace and quiet. He was in a corner of the library with an open book trying to figure out this weird campus. He was not reading, just pretending to in case anyone wanted to bother him. Sitting on the floor between the aisles, he went over the information he received earlier.

Drum. Who is this male beating down schools and protecting his classmates? Why will no one date until this male does? How long will it take for him to date someone?

It was not a part of his plan to secretly hook up with someone. He needed to show he could have a healthy relationship. It was the only way he could convince his parents that after all these years, he was over her.

Hooking up would not be enough to fool his Psychiatrist either. Meaningless sex was, as she would say, 'Not a step in his right direction'. He would need to give her something to help him convince his parents he was getting better. Friends alone would not be enough.

He took out his phone and looked at it. *Why is everyone always checking these things? They are constantly on them.*

He groaned and the Librarian, who was a few rows over restocking books, heard him. The Librarian peeked around the rows of shelves until she found the source of the sound.

"Um, excuse me. As a student, shouldn't you be at the assembly?" the Librarian asked.

"An assembly!?" He was so deep in his thoughts he was struggling to focus on what was being said to him.

"Yes, the mandatory assembly is happening right now in the gym. Every student on campus must attend for moral support and to boost unity," the Librarian said, with a fist pump. "And you also receive extra credit points for any class you implement it towards."

Ah, the assembly! That is right! He thought to himself the homeroom Professor mentioned it, but he was not paying attention.

He jumped up, gathered his bag, and after putting the book back, he bowed respectfully to the Librarian and turned to leave. He did not notice the smile that brightened the Librarian's face upon seeing he placed the book exactly where it was supposed to go, even in a rush, but he felt it.

"What a thoughtful young person," he heard her murmur as he left.

He realized the Librarian was not lying about every student being at the assembly. The empty campus only helped to echo the noise coming from the gym. As he hurried to the gym doors, hoping to quietly sneak in amongst all the noise, in his rushed and confused state, he failed to process that several doors down from him, on his right, were his schoolmates in their team uniforms.

He opened the doors, and it was the moment he wished he would have just skipped the assembly all together and stayed in the library.

DRUM: A CLOSED INVITATION
WEEK ONE: MONDAY

The next day the campus was buzzing with the news of yesterday's events. Walking to his homeroom, the hallways and courtyard were filled with students commenting.

"*Apparently* it was a human tourist guy."

"Well, it couldn't have been a local."

"No one here would do something like that."

"Stupid fucking humans! Coming here and trying to ruin the atmosphere!"

"They're just jealous of us."

"Did you guys hear Queen and Win were there?"

"Yea, they're down at the police station now giving their statements."

"So, Drum had something to do with it?"

"Who knows but I heard the guy's balls were crushed."

"I heard his member was broken."

"They said online the human had to be identified by his fingerprints."

"He won't last long in prison under a Barrier."

"With the time he does have, he might like it there!"

Drum said nothing as he made it to his desk and sat. He also didn't mind the conversation shifted to talk about a new transfer student.

"The student is in homeroom 1-SAH[25], right?"

"I heard the Senior is totally hot."

"If Drum doesn't pick me, I would totally be interested."

"It's pretty late in the year to transfer to another Higher Ed campus, isn't it?"

"Especially as a Senior at the end of the year!"

"But who wouldn't want to come to our campus?"

---

[25] *SAH- Senior Advanced Honors*

"With Sport leading the team, we will win the championship this year for sure!"

"Which championship?"

"ALL of them!"

It seemed as if the laughter from his classmates made him smile as he looked out the window, but his smile was from the Being he was watching walking up the steps to the Admin Building. The Professor entered as students found their seats and homeroom started.

This had to be the longest day of his life. The anticipation was making him anxious. He was constantly checking where the new Being was and by the time the midday campus assembly happened, he was ready for his final class to start.

But this assembly was to announce the new varsity line up for the soccer team and since Sport was the captain, there was no way he wouldn't be here to support his best friend.

As he sat at the top of the bleachers in the last row with Queen to his left and Win on his right, they left ample space of six feet between them so no one touched him by mistake.

Their bags were piled on the row in front of them to keep anyone from sitting around him. Propping his foot up on the bleacher, he leaned back and closed his eyes, turning on his Enhanced Hearing[26].

He heard Queen stretch and yawn. "I'm exhausted."

"Me too,"—Win yawned— "but we have to support our bestie!"

Queen settled into his seat. "So, what do you think about the new student?" Queen asked.

Without opening his eyes, he replied, "Don't know. The student missed orientation, right?"

Win leaned back, folded his arms, and huffed. "Yea, Pantu has some Ability[27], since I was looked directly in my eyes and even watched me walk away. Pantu also definitely knocked me down to fifth place in looks." Without saying it, both he and Queen knew Win was telling them Pantu could see through Win's Barrier.

He knew Win frowned when the ladies a few rows in front of them aww'd. He also knew Win gave them a half smile when they squealed and his left ear twitched, hearing them quickly turn around.

---

[26] *concentrating Energy around one's eardrums, allowing a Being to hear conversations within a certain distance. See Universal Abilities #11.*
[27] *Ways a Being can use their energy.*

Win asked him, "So…when will your Dad let you date? I would like to at least SAY I had a girlfriend in this lifetime."

He smiled as he knew what he was about to say would make his best friends and the whole campus flip. But he himself was unsure of how to feel about this information.

He was nervous since no one on campus, in town or nearby cities, ever intrigued him. He wasn't willing to date someone he didn't want touching him, who couldn't touch him. As he twisted the ring on his right middle finger, he answered.

"As long as I'm still the number one student on campus, my Dad said I'm mature enough to date whenever I want," he replied, as he sat up and opened his eyes. "So, I guess I'm looking for a date to my birthday party next year."

The assembly was about to start but everyone around them was staring at him with surprise.

Because school in The States was slightly different than here, he was the only student who would spend his whole AH Junior year as a nineteen-year-old. Most of the Juniors in Advanced Honors classes were already twenty-one and with a little over a month and a half left in the year; there were only a few birthdays remaining. Some of his Junior classmates would start turning twenty-two before he reached twenty.

His birthday was in the second month of an eighteen-month year, but since the dates of the Saturday party changed around every year, no one other than his family or best friends knew the actual date of his birth since most of his information was registered private.

His birthday parties were always the Saturday nights of the Senior Graduation Ceremony at the end of the school year, and everybody wanted to go. Even those not from Sunset or the surrounding towns.

His birthday parties were some of the most viewed videos on the intranet and the internet. Every year it was something different. Always at a different venue in town, a trip to a different city or island, or on a yacht, all paid for by his family.

The one thing everyone also wanted from his birthday party was a chance to woo him or Justin, now known in Sunset as It-thipong, with his nickname being Pong. But that seemed an impossible task as he held firm to his Dad's rule of not dating until he was ready and the issue of touching. The swag gift bags were a great consolation and second to wanting an invite to his birthday party.

The Dean cleared her throat to gather the students' attention, but those around them were busy posting on social media the news they just heard. He felt a smile from Queen, and he cut his eyes away since he could only smile back.

Queen already planned something, and he figured Queen received some information from his parents, probably years ago. He chuckled and looked at the floor as students' phones chimed across the gym.

THE FOUR: MEET PANTU
WEEK ONE: MONDAY

"Calm down! Whatever it is can wait until after the assembly," The Dean, Mrs. Hu, relayed into the microphone. "We are here to welcome the starting line-up for our soon to be champions!"

After a short speech, the students cheered and held up signs, banners, and pompoms as Dean Hu introduced the coaches and support staff. As she called out the names of the team players, they entered one by one through the door to line up on the floor.

You could see the differences in the personalities of the three best friends sitting at the top of the bleachers. Win was happily cheering for the team between his mind wandering, while Drum sat quietly with a smile, watching the team enter. Queen on the other hand, was busy liking or commenting on social media posts in which he was tagged.

It was an unspoken rule if you posted something online and wanted it to be known as truth, you tagged Queen. If he liked your post, then it meant it was verified by Queen, himself. If it wasn't true, Queen would comment "R", which no one wanted.

A "R" comment from Queen was a social death sentence. You would be smart to delete the post immediately as everyone knew Queen hated rumors. If you posted something about someone and didn't tag Queen, you could bet someone in the comments would.

Midway through the celebration, Dean Hu called out a player's name, but instead of the player coming through the door, another student entered.

The crowd went silent as they looked at Pantu, whose face was now bright red with embarrassment. They whispered amongst themselves how the student didn't look anything like the player whose name was called, but there were not so quiet arguments on whether the student was unnaturally handsome, or incredibly beautiful.

Drum's eyes followed Pantu, who looked at the Dean and apologized profusely to her and the players on the team as he passed them.

Hurrying up the bleachers to the only wide-open spot one could see from a quick glance, Pantu apologized to the students as he passed, ignoring the whispers about his looks and his body as he made his way to the open seat.

Win, who looked confused as Pantu squeezed past his legs, could only watch as Pantu sat down and dropped his bag. Drum, whose eyes never faltered from Pantu's face, didn't react when the bag hit his leg. But when Pantu turned and quickly touched his leg, with an apology, Drum froze.

The whole gym was silent, and everyone's eyes were focused towards their area. Win quickly grabbed and pulled the back of Pantu's shirt, snatching him back into Win's chest. Queen, just as quickly, slid between Drum and Pantu while Sport was already standing behind Win.

As Queen was calmly and quietly speaking, slowly moving further and further away from Drum, Pantu held a look of confusion on his face of *why does it sound like Queen is begging for my life?*

Queen kept pushing back until there was enough space between him and Drum, who hadn't moved from his spot. Win went to the other side of Drum, who still didn't flinch or speak.

Pantu couldn't see Drum's face since Queen was blocking his view, so he shrugged it off. Pantu turned to face the front where he saw the Dean staring towards the area, pleading with her eyes.

Pantu didn't know what to make of this and looked at the ground. He didn't realize he was holding his breath until the actual player whose name had been called came into the gym to the cheers of his peers.

Queen turned to Pantu with sweat dripping from his body and his make-up ruined, and with a quiet, deadly voice asked, "Do you have a death wish?"

Pantu decided his best bet was to stay quiet and not ask questions about the white-colored Dome[28] which just disappeared from around them, while keeping his eyes glued on the Dean.

---

[28] *What those in The City call Barriers.*

DRUM: A FACE WORTH NOT BASHING IN
WEEK ONE: MONDAY

His first natural response to someone hitting him was to punch them down the bleachers, but when Pantu touched his leg, he only wanted to touch Pantu back.

He froze, not understanding why he held this feeling. He wasn't interested in relationships. He tried to encourage his schoolmates to date regardless of him being single, but no one wanted to take the risk of not being available.

He wasn't attracted to anyone. No one stood out to him or caught his eye. It wasn't because he was egotistical but because of his haphephobia. At least that's what his parents' thought was best to tell people.

Being in a relationship at his age meant there would be lots of touching involved and he wanted desperately to avoid that. He didn't have overly sensitive skin or a germ phobia. He had trust issues.

After the traumatic event in The States, his parents hid them in his Mom's hometown. The only people in town able to touch him were his immediate family. Everyone else was lucky to escape major bodily harm or worse.

Because of what happened when he first moved here, everyone in town knew not to touch him, and tourists who wanted to be handsy with him needed to get through his best friends first. It was a major reason why he was never seen in the busier parts of town and one of the reasons he went straight home almost every day after classes.

But he didn't want to punch Pantu, whose face was flushed with embarrassment the first time he saw him on campus. The thoughts in his head were never there before. He wanted Pantu to touch him. He wanted to do more to Pantu than just touching, but he was confused because he was still waiting on his Angel to come back to him.

He hadn't seen his Angel in so long, he thought maybe he really did imagine a Golden Healing Angel from that night to help deal with the trauma. But he remembered what the voice told him, and since the voice stayed true to its words for all these years, he was patiently waiting.

But he didn't hold any romantic feelings for his Angel, just a sense of friendship, so when the scenes of him and Pantu kissing and touching each other were interrupted by Queen pleading with him, it took him a second to realize the fear. He didn't know how to react, but his best friends immediately came to his rescue, giving him some time to breathe.

As Win quickly moved Pantu out of his reach, Queen was in front of Pantu unnecessarily trying to calm him down. He said nothing and after taking a couple of breaths like

Queen suggested, he turned and focused his gaze on the Dean, dropping a Barrier he didn't realize he created.

Dean Hu sighed in relief when his Barrier came down, and no one was injured. She shakily continued as Sport jogged down the stairs to re-join his team on the floor, making her realize he had no intention of retaliating.

ALEX: A PLAN RENEWED
WEEK ONE: MONDAY

He was sitting at the top of the bleachers across the gym from Drum. He was in love, dreamily looking at Drum as he waited for the assembly to start. He knew he wasn't the only Being on campus who felt this way about Drum, who held a Charm[29].

Ever since he first laid eyes on Drum during a joint middle school field trip, he'd become obsessed. He was trying to figure out how to get closer to Drum. He dumped his boyfriend and focused on how to catch Drum's attention.

Drum was pretty much always surrounded by his best friends and rarely went anywhere on campus alone. He figured it would just take the right moment, and he needed a way to make it happen. He sighed as the assembly started and cheered with his friends for the team while sneaking glances at Drum.

He was from the neighboring city, Hollis, and after a lot of begging, pleading, and fighting with his parents, he was able to travel to Sunset to attend the private middle school Drum was enrolled at. He followed Drum to the private high school as well.

He was a First-year Liberal Arts student but the same age as Drum, who was in his second year and a Junior by AH standards. There was only one reason for him to wake up earlier than everyone else...Drum. And after last semester's grades, he was getting an apartment in Sunset, to be even closer to Drum.

As he was sneaking a peek at Drum's profile, the crowd quieted down. He looked to see what was happening and his face showed shock.

It's him! The guy from Hollis. What is he doing all the way out here and attending my campus no less? Oh, this is perfect, he thought to himself. *I have information about the new student I'm sure no one else knows.*

As he became giddy, wondering if this information was worth a Favor from Queen, he watched the new student apologize and make his way to the bleachers. He turned away from the guy walking up the bleachers apologizing every inch of the way.

What an asshole, he thought to himself, *I wish he would do more than embarrass himself.*

After being threatened by this guy on their first encounter, he was all for telling his business to Queen. As complete silence filled the gym, he looked up and around until he

---

[29] *The Ability to force others to fall in love and/or force people into obsession. See Universal Abilities #17*

saw the empty space where three of The Four were sitting but could see Sport standing with his arms crossed, watching.

Haha! He got too close to Drum. Stupid fucker! Doesn't he know there are spoken rules in this town?

He giggled despite himself. He thought, *it's a good thing this guy is already on Drum's bad side.* He was disappointed Drum didn't destroy the guy's perfectly handsome fucking face but maybe this information was now worth a Favor for sure. This made him incredibly happy and as the assembly slowly started again, all he could think about was what to wear on his date with Drum.

As the assembly ended, he rolled his eyes at the new guy leaving the gym in a hurry. He looked over at Drum, who made no effort to move, and decided to follow the new guy instead. Quickly heading out of the gym, he kept his eyes on the new guy but followed far enough behind so it didn't look like he was stalking him.

The guy didn't seem to be paying attention to his surroundings as the guy entered the office building. He hurried to the door and peeked through the glass. He didn't see the guy anywhere. He entered the building and looked in the office windows.

He thought for sure the new guy entered this building so where could he have gone? As he slowly walked back towards the exit, trying to figure out where this guy was, the bathroom door opened. He turned, opened the nearest door to him, and entered.

Watching the guy from the door window, he shook his head. Using Queen's personal bathroom was highly frowned upon unless you needed help. It was a safe place for Queen to handle business or for Drum to get away from crowds.

He quickly moved away from the window as the new guy passed and with his back against the wall, he finally noticed he was in the Professors' Lounge. They were all staring at him wondering what he was doing. His face turned bright red, and he bowed deep as an apology before he slid out the door.

The new guy was in the office as he passed, but he didn't care anymore. He was headed to find Queen. He was sure he would get a date with Drum, and he couldn't wait. As he rushed to where one of Queen's offices was, he was snapped out of his thoughts by his friend throwing his arm around his neck and playfully jumping on his back.

"Where you headed Alex?" his friend asked him.

If it was one thing, he liked about those he considered his right-now friends, it was the fact that everyone accepted everyone else. His friend saw no problem being around him, even though he knew he was head over heels for Drum.

He was also one of the few who called him Alex. This was a feeling of peace attending this campus. In Hollis, once the other students found out he was gay, he could only hang out with the gay crowd. His middle school had their cliques and once you were labeled, you were stuck.

"Uh, class. I'm headed to class," he Lied.

His friend looked at him puzzled. "This isn't the way to our class though?"

That's right we have a lot of the same classes, he thought.

"Going to sneak one final peek at the love of your life?" his friend asked, with a smile. "Come on, I'll go with you. Someone must pick you up off the floor if Drum happens to look your way," his friend said, with a small laugh.

He shook his head and turned around. "Let's just go to class," he said, his face even redder than before.

His friend shrugged and turned to walk with him to their next class.

I'll wait to see Queen after day classes. See if I can get more information before then, he thought.

DRUMxQUEEN: TO HIT OR NOT TO HIT? THAT IS THE QUESTION

WEEK ONE: MONDAY

Drum stayed in the gym until everyone, but Queen left.

"You must really be pissed you couldn't beat the new student's ass," Queen commented, but the echo was loud.

He didn't want to beat the guy's ass in the way Queen meant, but he agreed anyway. He also thought he didn't know what to do with someone he liked. Other than seeing people kiss and hold hands, he didn't know if there was more to liking someone.

He wasn't interested and watching sex videos made him uncomfortable. All the touching sent him into shock, and he never made it past the first couple of seconds. Hence, his best friends never showed him again.

Queen looked at him as he spoke. "You must be smarter about this. We still have the city prosecution and the guy's defense attorney asking questions about yesterday."

"I know. I won't cause a scene," he said, half-heartedly.

"If the victim didn't say they woke up in my arms, you would be the one on trial right now," Queen said.

He stood up and stretched. "For not killing a predator. Would they have rather I finished it? Then what experience would they have without handling...cases...in...court?" he responded, but his words faltered as he realized Pantu's bag was still sitting where he dropped it. *"Pantu forgot..."* he whispered.

Queen quickly grabbed the bag without touching him. "I will find out what class Pantu's in and give it back." Queen opened the bag and found Pantu's schedule. "You stay away from Pantu."

Reading over the paper Queen pointed to a line. "Last class of the day is...Advanced Honors Calculus for Business and Social Sciences, Professor Tingyu. Hey that's your"— Queen looked up at him—"class."

He saw the worry in Queen's Tri-colored Energies as Queen looked at him.

"Drum! Don't do anything stupid!" And even though Queen whispered it, the echo in the gym yelled back at them.

He smiled his charming smile and took the bag from Queen without touching him. After getting his own bag, he headed out of the gym to his final class of the day.

Queen

Queen watched as his best friend walked off. He turned his head slightly as he looked at Drum and smiled. There was something different about his best friend. Others may not have noticed or shrugged it off, but he knew. He watched Drum carefully since first grade, so the smallest shift in Drum's personality was clear to him.

Hmm, I wonder what this new student is really like, he thought.

He got comfortable on the bench and pulled out his phone. He already knew the guy's name was Pantu, since they shared a class, and now his full schedule. At first, Win was bothered by the guy living on his street and sharing a homeroom, but when Win noticed Pantu staring intensely at the young woman he was in love with, Win instantly disliked Pantu.

He didn't blame Win for feeling that way, this guy was incredibly handsome, *but he hasn't shown the natural charm needed to be in the Top Four,* he thought. He was formulating a plan. Drum was going to be happy, even if it cost him his own reputation. If he had to move some Beings around, then that's what he was going to do.

A man with this much information should be able to use it to make my best friend happy, he happily thought. He decided to skip his last class as he had much to do in very little time, and he also needed to check a bathroom alert.

PANTU: IS MATH REALLY ALL THAT INTERESTING?
WEEK ONE: MONDAY

His day could not have gotten worse. There was no conceivable way things would continue to go downhill from there. One day, he would want to kick himself for challenging the Universe but right now, he wanted to kick the Universe's ass for accepting his spoken challenge.

When the assembly ended, he made a beeline for the door and left to go to the bathroom. After emptying his bladder and washing his hands and face, he looked in the mirror and told himself those precious words, "My day cannot get any worse than this."

Taking a deep breath and putting on a smile, he left the bathroom to go to his next class. As he looked to his right and then to his left, he stood unsure as to which direction to take before he remembered he left his backpack in the gym.

Ah well, he thought with a shrug, *there is no way I am going back for it, that crazy ass male might still be there, still as a statue.*

He shuddered as he remembered the male, whose leg he hit, did not move the rest of the assembly. He could only see the male's legs as he snuck looks out of the corners of his eyes, but they never once twitched. The male sat still, in one spot, until the end of the assembly. Even though everyone else got up and left, the male stayed right where he was.

He thought he would just have to figure it out, but luck would have his back today as the bathroom he was in was down the hall from the main office. He saw the door to the Professors' Lounge close and felt an unsettling feeling. He decided to ignore it for now and figure out his current predicament.

Yes! he thought to himself. *Score one for me!* After getting a copy of his schedule for the second time today, he rushed to his final class. He did notice the students seemed to be relaxed and not in a rush to get to their classrooms, but he was taking no chances.

He finally made it to his class and after asking about empty seats, he was directed to one in the back row. He did not care about the quiet laughter behind his back as he sat and placed his head down. He felt no need to conversate with anyone right now. He just wanted to catch his breath and stay far away from the crazy male from the assembly.

He did not hear any of the conversations as he text his Ma to pick him up on time, not wanting to be on this stupid campus longer than needed. He was also asking her to look up a nearby Higher Ed campus to transfer to when the atmosphere in the room changed.

Conversations became softer, but he wanted the noise. Not so he could listen to what was being said, but so he could drown out the thoughts in his head. He wanted to draw so badly. He texted his Ma to bring his sketch pad and pencils and if she forgot, he would not text her for a month.

It was then he noticed the room was silent. He slowly looked up and noticed a male's long slender fingers clutching his backpack. The brown hands were caught by the Omega Star[30] from the window, giving a warm glow to them. As his eyes travelled further up, he noticed the slender, tone but muscular build of the male standing in front of him.

His eyes continued up, and he caught a quick glance of flickering images of a slender Dragon and a paler version of the young male standing in front of him before clouds blocked his view. His eyebrows furrowed. He decided not to ask since his words were stuck inside his throat. But when his eyes finally landed on the face of the male standing in front of him, he froze as he came face to face with the most alluring person, he ever laid his eyes on.

The young male in front of him stood waiting, but he could only quietly gasp as he took in the young male's face. He stared into honey-colored eyes and noticed there were flecks of green dancing in the young male's irises. He felt as if he fell into a vat of warm honey, with only leaves to cover his most intimate places.

The young male's eyes stood out from his warm, smooth, light brown face and his shaggy, loosely coiled hair framed his face. He could not tell if the young male's hair was deep black since it seemed to shimmer blue at some times.

The young male was relaxed in front of him, still waiting. He could sense the regal personality rolling off the young male and was a bit intimidated, but he also felt a slight thrill from the eyes of this young male, which sent a familiar shiver down his spine.

He was silenced by the soft look on the male's face and his chest tightened, but every small, tight breath he took while looking at this male's face smelled clean with a slight scent of cinnamon or honey, maybe both? It was everything good about the world all wrapped up in this young male standing in front of him, holding his backpack.

Ah shit! My backpack!

---

[30] *Omega Star is what Beings called the smaller of the two nuclear fusion balls of hot plasma rotating around the planet. Humans used sun for both, distinguishing between them by using big or small.*

But he could only continue to stare into this young male's eyes, and his Mind[31] was emptied of all thoughts as he was hypnotized by a light. Set behind the young male's irises, it started to shine, brightening the colors in the young male's eyes.

It was as if his own Mind was a fresh canvas waiting to become one with assorted colors of paint. He did not move as the young male dropped the bag on his desk and slid into the seat next to him, but his eyes followed.

His heart raced when he realized they were in the same class and were now sitting next to each other. Everyone in class watched the interaction without a word but phones were pinging back-to-back. As soon as Professor Tingyu walked in, their phones were silenced; put away and the class focused.

He looked to his left at the young male sitting next to him diligently taking notes. He may have remembered some foreign words on the young male's paper, but it was only because his eyes followed every movement the young male's face made.

It was not until the young male next to him gathered his own backpack and stood; he realized class was over. He quickly looked around the room to see most students were already gone.

He looked down at his desk and accepted the fact he had not touched his backpack since the young male dropped it on his table. As the young male passed by; some folded papers were dropped on top of his backpack.

The young male walked to the front of the class and leaned on a desk as three other males came into the room from the front door and stood around the male, leaving space in between them.

"What's the plan for your birthday party next year?"

He was hearing the conversation but was not paying attention. He was trying to figure out if and why he spent the whole class staring at this young male.

"I was thinking of a house party."

He forced himself not to look up at the sound of the young male's voice. He felt his bones melt at the soothing sounds coming out of the young male's mouth. It was sticky sweet but with a slight deepness to it which wrapped him in warmth.

Wait? Why am I analyzing this young male at all? Why am I thinking about him? Is this one of the "know thy enemy" moments?

"We finally get to come to your house!?"

---

[31] *Also known as a Being's Conscience. This is the Energy Form surrounding a Being's human brain.*

"I've already posted it so you can't take it back!"

He felt like he was dropped into a manga panel, or the popular thriller book series, 'The Moonlight Sector'. He unfolded the papers and realized they were the notes from class, but they were written in his language. He was quite sure the young male wrote his notes in a foreign language, so why did he have notes written perfectly in Thaikoriense[32]?

When his phone started buzzing a ringtone, three of the young males in the front looked at him like he was interrupting the most important conversation about ending planetary hunger. It was his Ma telling him she brought his sketch pad and was waiting for him downstairs.

He realized they were the only people left in the room. He grabbed his bag, shot out of the room, and did not stop running until he made it to his Ma's car door. He did not bother to look back; too unsure of what he might feel.

---

[32] *An Eastern language spoken in certain regions of the planet. It is a mixture of different Asian languages from Earth.*

DRUM: FEELINGS OF HAPPINESS SURFACE
WEEK ONE: MONDAY

All he could do right now was hold Pantu's bag until he could catch Pantu's eyes. He wanted Pantu to look at him. So, he waited until their eyes connected before dropping the backpack on the desk.

He held in his smile and slid into the seat next to Pantu. He figured the class was playing a joke on the new student, and honestly, he felt affection for his classmates instead of being mad. They didn't know he was pleased Pantu was sitting next to him.

They wanted to see what he would do after the assembly. But he couldn't do what they expected him to do, and he couldn't do what he wanted, so he was at a stalemate.

He took his Calculus book and notebooks out of his backpack and after finding a pencil, he set his desk for class. Pantu turned to look at him and his heart started beating as fast as he could hear Pantu's.

His Mind was built differently than normal Beings. Multitasking was one of his Specialties. His Mind and body were completely synced, so doing a multitude of things at once was simple for him.

While he was sitting, enjoying the fact Pantu's eyes were only focused on him, he was taking notes in both English and Thaikoriense. He was also planning missions for his team, while completing unspoken plans to coordinate with Queen.

Pantu never opened his backpack and was only looking at him. He didn't feel like Pantu was staring at him the way everyone else gawked at him as if he were this endangered creature let loose. He felt like Pantu was gazing at him.

He thought about how much he would like to lock eyes with Pantu as they touched each other. He wondered what it would feel like to have Pantu touch his skin. The thought of Pantu running his hands up and down his back made him excited, and he felt heat in a part of his body never before heated.

As he was enjoying this new feeling, he was secretly upset when class ended. The whole class. That's how long he held Pantu's attention. It made him happy. He started packing up when Pantu realized class was over. The flustered look on Pantu's face made a small smile escape his lips.

He dropped the class notes on top of Pantu's still unopened backpack and went to the front of the class to meet his best friends. He stopped at the third row to lean on the desk as his best friends came into the class and hung out in the first row.

Sport lazily asked him, "What's the plan for the birthday party this year? I need time to prep."

With a shrug, he casually responded, "I was thinking of a house party." He watched his friends out the corners of his eyes as their Energies lit up.

Win's excitement was contagious, and he squealed. "We finally get to come to your house!? This is beyond exciting!"

"I've already posted it so you can't take it back!" Queen said as his phone was now on fire.

Queen's Energies was beyond excited, and he thought Queen would hurt his gorgeous face if he was smiling. His best friends' excitement over the news he was finally inviting Beings to his home, died when Pantu's phone started playing a weird tone.

His best friends looked past him to find the noise. Win's Energy lost its excitement when he saw who it was, Sport's Energy was trying to figure out why Pantu's ringtone sounded so bad, but Queen's Energies was neutral, and it made him pause for the briefest second.

He himself didn't turn because he knew he would stare at Pantu and Queen, well Queen would know, if he didn't already. Queen was the one person who watched him closely since elementary. Sport and Win knew him as well, but he and Queen's friendship was different. Deeper. There were things they never needed to say to each other, they just knew.

And so, he knew if he showed a glimpse of happiness, Queen would do anything in his power to make sure he was completely happy. He knew Queen possessed a lot of power, so his happiness up to this point was easily satisfied with overly complex puzzle boxes. Queen owned a small storeroom full.

He heard Pantu run out of the classroom while Sport and Win's conversation started about what the inside of his home looked like. As Queen slowly turned to join the conversation, he could feel the Energies of Queen's eyes briefly lock with his own. He lifted his head to join in the conversation. There was no doubt in his Mind Queen now knew.

QUEEN: A SMALL ANNOYANCE AND A TRUSTED SOURCE
WEEK ONE: MONDAY

Drum's look said it all. He knew the innocent looking smile which crept onto his best friend's face wasn't for them. Even though they were joking, Drum's eyes weren't in it. At first, he was trying to rationalize what happened at the assembly as Drum not causing a scene for legal reasons.

Everyone else on campus wrote it off as Drum staying calm for his best friend Sport's sake. A Junior playing the starting lineup as Varsity Captain was a big deal. This was the first time in the campus' history an underclassperson was leading the starting team two years in a row and Drum was not about to ruin it for Sport.

But now, he was sure. Why was Pantu sitting next to Drum when his desk was clearly marked on the other side of the classroom? There were no coincidences when it came to Drum. What you see is what you get. Drum never pretended to be kind or nice, he just was. He was respectful and intelligent. He just couldn't handle physical contact. It's been that way since they met.

But here this new guy, Pantu, was walking around with his beautifully stunning face not bashed in, after not only hitting Drum, but touching him as well. He knew none of the other students were talking about the fact Pantu touched Drum, only he noticed. He saw Drum unconsciously use his Energy to protect the new student from being seen around him.

Since anyone else who is around Drum would start to feel a heat which increased the closer you came to him, Pantu not only sat right next to Drum, but he was positive he'd seen Pantu touch his haphephobic best friend. He felt justified after doubting himself about the assembly, but he would wait until his best friend wanted him to know.

He laughed as Sport was describing a giant fifty-foot-tall statue of Jeffers, the greatest basketball player of all time that he thought was in Drum's home. After waiting until most of the students left the building, they made their way out of the classroom.

"I have some business I need to attend to. See you tomorrow!" he said, as he split from the group and made his way to one of his private offices.

He had several around campus. After Mr. Caleb donated money to build the Higher Education AH sections of the campus, he politely asked for a few quiet places for Drum, but instead, Drum gave them to him. He even had a private bathroom in the office building the other students respectfully gave to him and never used.

There was an office in every Level's AH homeroom building. The Junior building is where most of his business on campus was done this year. A private stairway leading to a room on the gym building's roof, a social media clubroom in a shared building for meetings and the gender-neutral bathroom.

It may have started off as a public gender-assigned bathroom but the atmosphere on the campus changed once they started attending. He could accept the fact their Higher Ed campus was different, and it wasn't because of the dating thing.

He shook his head as he thought, *it's because our campus has become relaxed.*

Their second year of Higher Ed was almost over, and the campus was different. There were no known bullies. If there were any before, he was sure they either changed to the night classes or left, figuring it wasn't worth being pummeled by Drum.

Drum's presence alone was enough to curb the bullying and with me next to him, everyone became way more open than I would have imagined.

He, himself, was gay and Drum's best friend. Somehow their childhood friendship leaked over into an open acceptance for the whole community. Anyone could be themselves and not feel judged or condemned.

Which was, in fact, how the Cleaning Club came about. Students who were germophobic came together to keep the campus clean. All throughout the day, they helped the Housekeepers and Janitors keep their campus spotless. No one cared about sexual orientation; they only cared you could clean.

He laughed to himself as he thought about how the gender-neutral bathrooms really turned into a free for all. If the gender-specific bathrooms were full, no one would think twice about finding a gender-neutral one to use. No one freaked out because a guy would be taking a shit next to a girl peeing.

It doesn't matter at all, he thought.

The staff also said nothing. Since the last school year started, they noticed the change in the atmosphere and the unity amongst the students. The students became calmer and helpful, assisting the Professors and office staff.

The school's grade also improved from a C to an A+ after their First-year final exams. This of course made the staff extremely happy as parents praised them for doing an amazing job with their children. Parents were saying the changes in their kids were a blessing and the staff ate it up.

It may be because I might have let it slip that Drum is attracted to intelligence and hates bullies, he thought to himself.

He stopped and raised his eyebrows in intrigue as he noticed a short, first year standing in front of his clubroom door. He turned off the phone alert used to inform him of a visitor at his closed offices.

Manpa is the name on his registration, but he prefers Alex, he thought to himself, *even though he lives in Hollis, he applied here because he's in love with Drum, followed him since middle school.*

He knew quite a bit about the guy waiting in front of his office and by the time he reached the door, a smile graced his face. He knew the first year would try and give him whatever he could to get a date with Drum. Maybe the first year could help him. He wouldn't make the decision until he listened to what the first year had to say.

Opening the door wide, he gestured grandly. "Welcome."

After he placed a cup of tea in front of the first year and one on the table for himself, he sat on the opposite couch. He took in the first year sitting across from him.

Short blond hair with deep black eyes and warm beige skin, the cute first year was on the shorter end of Beings at five-eleven. He was mixed. His mother, a Westerner[33], met his father, a Northerner[34], when he moved to Hollis to start a business.

"Well, what brings you here to see me? And the name on your registration says Manpa but do you prefer to be called by another name?" he asked, as he leaned back, sipping on his tea.

"Umm, Alex please, and I have information," Alex said nervously, his eyes darting around, taking in the room.

He didn't like the persona Alex was giving off, and it made him cautious. "Who doesn't have information?" he retorted.

"It's about the new student," Alex paused as he leaned forward. "I'm positive that he wouldn't want this getting out." Alex clenched his hands together and continued, "I want a Favor for this information."

"That's not how gold Favors work," he stated. He placed his cup back on the plate and leaned back, as he gracefully crossed his legs.

Alex squeaked, embarrassed. "Oh! How do they work?"

He took a deep breath and expelled it as if he was tired. "If you're a student here, you can ask for help with a problem you can't solve yourself. Completely free, no strings

---

[33] *Those whose lands have been invaded and settled by outsiders. It is sometimes used as an insult.*

[34] *Those whose family line come from the northern part of the planet. This term is also more commonly used for Beings from the northern part of The States.*

attached." He leaned his head back and continued, "But as a student, you can verify information for a Favor." He held his head up and looked at Alex, "But not all information is deemed important enough for a gold Favor."

"But the locals said —" Alex started.

He held up his hand and stopped Alex. "Let me explain clearly. Adults and those not on our campus can exchange information for Favors, as I can't be everywhere all the time. The information exchanged can only be about yourself.

"Students from our campus who have information, know I will approach them, *if there is a need*, in order to verify said information." By now he leaned forward, his voice holding a hint of a threat at the end. "No one assumes I don't already know."

The OH SHIT! look on Alex's face was enough to let him know his point was made.

"Queen, I'm so sorry!" Alex stood up and bowed as he apologized.

He waved his hand to dismiss the slight. As he started talking, he stood and went to the door. "There may come a day when I offer you a Favor in return for verifying some information, so I would keep whatever you know quiet until then, if others know, then I will just offer the Favor to them." He paused at the door and held it open for Alex.

Once Alex was gone, he sat at his desk. This Alex was going to be a tough one. He already knew the personality Alex had would never mesh with Drum. It was only Pantu's first day and Alex was already trying to sneakily give dirt on him.

He also knew this guy was trying to play stupid. Alex wanted him to believe that how he operates was unknown to the young man. When he told Alex he knew he wanted a gold Favor, not the regular green and yellow ones he normally handed out, Alex didn't question the color of the Favor.

Even though Alex never approached Drum before, they knew the level of lust this guy held for Drum. He assumed Alex wasn't happy about what happened in the gym and was looking to discredit Pantu, but he couldn't let go of a gut feeling Alex knew something important enough to probably ruin Pantu's life. So, until his best friend figured out what he wanted to do, he would keep Alex's mouth shut for the time being.

"It would only last so long before I have to bait him to continue being quiet."

He didn't care what the information was, everyone had secrets, but he needed to keep Pantu in town so Drum could figure out his feelings for him. He groaned, leaned back in his chair, and rubbed his temples as a knock on the door had him telling the Being to enter.

Sharon came in. "I have the information about the stolen badge," she said, as she dropped the papers on the desk.

"Umm, thanks doll," he said, absentmindedly.

"Humph, normally I'm Dollface." Sharon crossed her arms and pouted. "Did the beautiful new student steal your eyes too?" she asked, as she sat on the end of his desk. "Whatever you need, you know I will help."

Sharon was swinging her legs, looking at him. As he moved his chair side to side in rhythm with Sharon's legs, he thought to himself that he liked Sharon's personality.

She never asked about anyone's business, for Favors, or gave him false information. She never asked more of him than he was willing to give. It was one of the reasons why they first hooked up at the beginning of the school year, her tight opening was keeping him coming back for more.

He knew students on campus thought he was secretly in love with his best friend. No one knew Drum's sexuality because he never showed any romantic interest in anyone. Drum was kind to everybody, no matter their gender or sexuality.

But he wasn't romantically interested in his best friend. Although they shared the same problem, finding someone they liked while understanding it couldn't just be anyone. He knew he could be used to get closer to Drum or for information, so he also kept any romantic feelings locked away.

Besides, no one has THAT Scent, he thought. "Could you keep an eye on someone for me?" he asked her.

"Just say who," she replied, with a smile.

He knew he could trust her to keep quiet. "There is a first year named Alex. He's obsessed with Drum," he told her, while looking at her reaction.

"I don't know anyone in Sunset named Alex, but I will find him and keep you updated," Sharon said.

"He goes by Alex, but his name is Manpa, if that helps," he added.

"Ooooohhhh…Drum-Stanpa!" Sharon said, with a laugh. "You're right to keep an eye on him, he might fuck up and get his face bashed in if he's not careful," Sharon said.

He leaned forward and rubbed his hand on her thigh. He kept going higher until his hand was under her skirt and he stood. "You know what I'm really interested in right now? What's under this sexy skirt of yours."

By now his left hand was completely under Sharon's skirt grabbing her thigh. He waved his right hand and created a tree-bark brown-colored Barrier around the room, locking the door. He kissed and sucked on her Adam's apple.

His left hand moved her closer to the edge of the desk and his right hand slid up her back, under her shirt to release her bra hooks. He slowly pushed her down while unbuttoning her shirt and she took her bra off. He kissed and licked a trail down her body until his mouth found her left nipple.

She used her arms to hold herself at the right angle while he sucked and nibbled on her nipples going between the two. She groaned and rocked against his left hand.

"Queen!" Sharon whispered.

His left hand found the base of her member and glided up to the tip, making Sharon shudder. Using his other hand and his mouth, he ripped open a pre-lubed condom while she undid his belt and his pants.

Laying her back on his desk, he held her legs up and looked at Sharon's member, trailing his eyes down to her hole, he smiled. Sharon was watching him, and she shivered, while her hole tightened.

He Produced[35] lube in his hand and dripped it on her hole. His member was hard, so he needed no guidance to meet her opening. Sharon moaned as he slowly entered her. Her opening was quivering as he pushed deeper. He gripped her thighs as he stepped forward to go further.

Sharon's eyes were closed, and she was gripping his shirt tight as he went deeper inside her. He hit a spot, and it made her member jump in excitement while pre-cum leaked from the tip.

He wrapped his hand around her and started to stroke to the rhythm of him gliding in and out of her opening. Every time he went to pull out, her opening tightened as if it didn't want him to leave and when he slid back deeper inside her, she sucked him all the way in, to his base.

Damn, he thought, *I really like it when she does that.*

As she moaned, she moved with him. The louder she moaned, the faster he started to go, inside of her, and with his hand. Her arms reached above her head and gripped the edge of his desk until her knuckles turned white. She was almost there.

Shit! So am I, he thought.

"Ohhhh, Queen!" she shouted out, as she started to leak.

He didn't stop. He kept his rhythm as more continued to come out of her. Her opening tightened and he used force to go deep. He only needed two more strokes before he went deep and stayed. His stomach clenched and he came inside the condom just as Sharon finished coming.

"Oh, shit Dollface!" he said, as he gently pulled out of her.

---

[35] *The Ability to pull items from an alternate space. See Universal Abilities #16.*

Her legs were shaking, and he gently lowered them. He used warm wipes to clean her opening along with her stomach and member before helping her sit up. He fastened her bra after she put it back on and helped her button her shirt.

He knew Sharon was a Senior who was already hired by a company in The States, which was on the other side of the planet. There were no reservations about a relationship between them. They both knew this was just a hook-up, a stress relief for the moment.

"Damn Queen, I needed that," Sharon said, as her legs finally stopped shaking.

"Me too," he replied with relief, as he sat back in his chair. Sharon slid off his desk to leave. She walked to the door and with a wave behind her, she left him alone with his thoughts.

PANTU: DO NOT CRY OVER SPILLED MILK
WEEK ONE: MONDAY

He realized it at the worst possible moment. He did not speak to his Ma during the ride to their house and since texting while driving was a huge no in their family, there was nothing for them to talk about.

He stared out the window and cut his bad thoughts off. It was a good trick his Psychiatrist taught him, to find one positive thought and make connecting lines to other positive thoughts.

He noticed his Ma was looking in her rearview mirror at him. He felt whatever look on her face was fake so why bother wearing a Mask. He was fine with it though. If his parents could be fake to him, then he felt no guilt about his plan to leave them.

Besides, she really should be more focused on the road, the way she drives. He continued to stare out the window until they reached their house.

He did not bother to stop and take off his shoes as he went straight to his room. He slammed the door loudly, so his Pa knew he was there, and tossed his bag along with the things he was holding in his hands on his bed before stripping down to his boxers.

Getting into his bed, he pulled the covers over his head and waited for his Ma's routine of knocking on his door, asking if he wanted a snack. He texted her to leave him alone and tossed his phone somewhere on his bed. It annoyed him that his parents kept trying to talk to him.

He was not used to cellphones, so the ultimate parental lock did not bother him. He was only able to call or text his parents and his Psychiatrist. He always needed to have his phone on him, as it was GPS enabled, so his parents could track him.

There were no games, and the camera app was locked. He could not save anyone's number his parents did not approve of on their phones. Everything else was blocked. He had no clue what social media or the internet was, and he did not care.

The first day did not go as planned at all and he was frustrated. He was fairly sure somewhere during the day, he escaped death more than once. He took a deep breath and sighed.

This will all be over soon, he thought, as his hand slid down his stomach.

In a couple of months, just a few weeks, he will be back with her. *She is still waiting for me back home,* he told himself. His real home. The home where his Dream lay, not this weird, fake town his parents brought him to.

He moved his hand up and down over his boxers and felt his penis jump. It was not hard, but it did want to be touched. He moved his hand under his boxers and wrapped his fingers around himself. The coolness from his hand made it shrink back.

"My apologies," he said to his penis. "Let me warm you up." He moaned as he slowly started to stroke himself.

He let his thoughts loose as he pictured her in his Mind. Her small, perky breasts, her slim waist and her white, petal-tinted skin were always enough to get him hard. But today he did not get hard like he normally did at just the thought of her. He was unsure why as his body was trained to respond to her instantly.

Maybe I need to go further, he thought, *it has been a while since I last saw her.*

He pulled his covers from over his head and down past his knees. He started thinking about the hair covering her vagina and he wondered if the male in math class hair down there was slightly blue like the hair on his head.

His eyes popped open and looking at his ceiling, he rationalized his thoughts, whispering, *"It is only because he scared the shit out of me, that is all."*

His penis was hard, so he closed his eyes and continued to think about the Woman he left back home. Her slender legs wrapped around him and her round bottom pushing up against him until his balls smacked against it.

Yes! That is what I need, he thought, holding the memory in his head.

But his penis betrayed him. It did not go soft; it just became semi-hard. He never experienced this issue before. He trained himself to be instantly hard at the thought of her, so whenever she wanted him, he was ready to go.

"What in the Fuck!?"

He groaned out loud and repositioned himself on his bed. He was going to get one out, he needed to. It was the only way he was able to stay hard for a longer time when he was fucking her. She hated it when he came before her and the few times in the beginning of second training, when he did, she would punish him thoroughly.

He quickly figured out if he came before fucking her, he lasted as long as she wanted him too. He could also come on command. The punishment the one time he did not was worse than the punishment for coming before her. He kept up his training, even though it would be a while until they fucked, he was uninterested in being punished again.

He wondered what to do as the scent of cinnamon made its way to his nose. He breathed it in, and his penis was hard. He moaned as he stroked himself and thought about freshly baked cinnamon bread, hot out of the oven and that was all it took for him to come all over himself. He tightened his hold and felt good. He moaned deeply and rolled over to his left, his eyes still closed.

After the final shudder, he opened his eyes and looked at the objects on his bed to focus his eyesight. He noticed the folded papers the male in Calculus gave him. He picked them up and as he drew the papers closer to his face, he smelled it.

Cinnamon! Fucking shit, he thought, *is this why I became hard? Is this the reason I came?* He would not allow himself to just accept the obvious fact, staring him right in the face.

"Maybe I am just attracted to the smell of cinnamon. That is all. Do not overthink Pantu," he scolded himself.

He unfolded the papers and looked over the notes. The handwriting on the paper was exquisite. He stared in wonder as he looked at every letter on the first page. He sat up and slowly went through each page as if he was reading a masterpiece. With such picturesque, perfectly flowing writing, he was beginning to wonder what else this male could do with his hands.

"Like draw or something," he quickly added, out loud, to no one.

But he himself was an artist. And this was written artistry. Without thinking, he inhaled the scent. "Yes, I am only attracted to the scent." He nodded. "I should find some cinnamon scented items for her. She smelled like jasmines, no lilacs or was it roses? Is it even flowers?"

He could not remember, but he knew it was nowhere close to cinnamon. He told himself it was fine if he did not remember what she smelled like. He would soon be holding her and smelling her scent for the rest of his short life.

He got up, dropped the notes on his desk, and went to shower. After, he sat at his desk and using the notes, he completed his Calculus homework quickly. He started the heavy load of missing work for all his other classes when his Ma came and knocked on the door, telling him dinner was ready.

He left his desk and found his phone on his bed. Texting his Ma, *'not hungry'*, he went back to studying. He knew she texted back saying she was leaving his food in the oven without looking at his phone. He continued studying, and when his Ma knocked on his door to tell him they were going to bed, he finally stopped.

Giving himself some time to stretch, he gathered the Calculus notes and placed them under his pillow. He waited until he heard their bedroom door close before leaving his room. He went downstairs, grabbed his food, and sat at the table. He had plenty of time to think while he was eating.

This male with the beautiful handwriting is the same male who wrote his notes in both another language and Thaikoriense.

As he was thinking, he went to get a drink. *He sits in the last row, but was the chair in front of him and to the side of him always empty?*

As he reached for a glass and moved over to the refrigerator, he continued to think, *was he the same male I hit at the assembly?* He opened the fridge door and took out a jug of chocolate milk. *Is he the same male whose leg I touched?* As he poured a glass, he thought, *why did people react in such a way?*

Somewhere in his Mind what his friend, or his friend's friend, said popped in, "NEVER TOUCH DRUM!"

And Drum was a person, right? A person who did not like to be touched or he would bash their face in, right? He took a drink of milk and added more to his glass before putting the milk back to walk to his seat.

A person who always kept space around to keep others from accidentally getting free plastic surgery, courtesy of Drum. As he made the connection of who the male from Calculus was and who Drum is, he froze and the glass of milk he was holding crashed to the floor, echoing through his quiet house.

His thoughts about his situation changed. He decided on a different plan. One much more daring and dangerous than his simple plan to lie low until graduation. There was something different about this town with the people in it and if it was a lovely place, his parents could finally stop running.

PANTUxQUEEN: HOW TO WIN OVER THE QUEEN OF SOCIAL MEDIA, COMPLETELY
WEEK ONE: TUESDAY

Ahhh...I am finally going to have a normal day, he thought as he sat in his homeroom. *If I can just avoid Drum, then everyone will forget what happened yesterday and my face will stay handsome.*

It was only the second day for Pantu, but his mini plan made him smile to himself while making doodles on his paper. He noticed the students in class staring and whispering but it didn't bother him. He wanted the attention, needed it for his actual plan. The more popular he was, the more friends he could easily make.

Once Dill entered the classroom and saw him sitting at his desk, the young male hurried over. When Dill's hands slammed down, he lifted his eyes in annoyance, calming Dill.

"You haven't followed Queen yet?" Dill asked, throwing his hands up. "Pantu, it's been like forty hours[36] since you started on campus!"

"Why would I need to follow Queen?" he asked. "We only have one class together."

He felt inner relief when Dill didn't laugh or poke fun at him as some of his classmates were doing. He listened as Dill explained everyone on campus, including staff, followed Queen on social media.

"Everybody keeps talking about it but what is this social media? Where is it?" he asked.

His classmates went silent and stared at him as if he was a bug alien from another planet. Dill didn't seem to notice, or act shocked he was so clueless and immediately went into explaining.

"Social media is basically webpages on the net which let you create your own profile to connect with people all over the planet," Dill said, as he scrolled through his own phone. "Queen is the most popular from our town as anything he posts gets hundreds of billions of retweets, comments and likes." As Dill was speaking, he turned his phone.

He refused to look at the screen and pushed Dill's hand away. "I have nothing like that," he stated, matter-of-factly. "I do not know what a webpage is or where this net is located."

---

[36] *One planetary rotation is 80 hours. Due to there being two Stars and two Moons, a full day is halved with there are 20 hours of starlight and 20 hours of moonlight.*

By now Win was interested in the conversation and was looking intensely at him, which made him uneasy. He learned the Top Four were best friends. Queen, Win, Sport, and Drum were almost always together.

He is going to tell Queen, he thought to himself.

It didn't bother him that he didn't have social media or know what the net was. Where he was from, only two people secretly owned computers, all other information came from books and verbal knowledge. He never heard of a cellphone before leaving his hometown, much less owned one. He felt his city may have been behind in the evolution of society and technology.

But when his parents said no internet or anything related, he listened. Not because it was the right thing to do, but because he wasn't ready to go back yet. He did *not* want them finding him again so soon.

He would at least make his ungrateful parents proud before leaving them disappointed. Dill was looking at him waiting for an answer to a question he hadn't heard asked.

"What was that again?" he asked.

"Do you want me to make you a page on your phone?" Dill patiently asked again.

"Ahh, no, I am good," he said as he sat up straight in his chair. Professor Tram came in, and homeroom started.

Win is still staring at me, he thought, *that may not be a good thing.*

Lunch was finally here, and Queen was beside himself with anticipation. He was giddy as he sat in his chair waiting for Pantu to come in. Checking the door constantly, he turned and glared at Win.

"Did you scare Pantu away by staring daggers?"

"What!" Win looked indignant. "I barely stared at Pantu." Win's guilty face was showing.

"If Pantu doesn't show, I will have you owe me a Favor," he lashed back at Win.

"But I confirmed Pantu didn't have any social media, and doesn't know what or where any net is," Win whined back at him.

He wasn't mad at Win; in fact, he was excited to finally meet someone who wasn't socially driven. *Drum is hardly ever on his phone, and he only posts or likes what I tell him to*, he thought, while looking at Drum sitting two chairs over. There was an empty chair in between them and plenty of space between Drum and Sport, who was to Drum's left.

"Pantu's here," Sport stated, with a nod at the door.

"At least let Pantu sit down and eat before you pounce," Drum commented, with a heavy tone.

"Of course," he responded. Waiting patiently, he watched as Pantu ordered, sat with his friends, and started eating.

"Now?" He looked anxiously at Drum, who gave him a quick, barely noticeable nod.

He was immediately in the chair beside Pantu. "Oh! I see the new student is getting along well here," he said. He gracefully leaned into the palm of his hand, resting his elbow on the table.

"It is Pantu, not New Student," Pantu responded, with no emotion. Pantu watched as he crossed his legs, sitting comfortably in the chair.

"Are we ready to try it out?" Pantu turned, speaking to Dill.

"Uh, no. I need the parts to fine tune it," Dill answered cautiously, while looking past Pantu and at him.

He noticed Pantu watched the interaction carefully, without looking.

"Could you be a doll and verify some information for me?" he interjected into the silence.

Pantu turned to look at him.

Watching as Pantu's eyes searched his face, he continued, "I hear you don't have any social media profiles?" he asked, tapping the table with his well-manicured nails.

Pantu started to eat.

Dill nudged Pantu to answer. Moving closer to Pantu, Dill whispered, *"If you verify information for Queen, he'll give you a Favor."* Dill implored with his eyes.

Pantu glared at Dill out the corners of his eyes while continuing to eat.

"You want a Favor from him," Dill quietly pleaded.

"Why would I want a Favor from someone, if they do not care to call me by name?" Pantu asked, uninterested.

Listening to Dill and Pantu, a sly smile creeped across his face.

Dill started to panic as Pantu still refused to verify anything. Grabbing Pantu's arm, "Queen is not just *anybody*. He can do things or *GET THINGS* for you," Dill pleaded, hanging off Pantu's arm. "Things you would need to upgrade..." Dill trailed off.

Pantu raised his eyebrows, thinking about it. "Well, seeing as how he did not bother to inform me, how important can the information he wants, really be?" Pantu asked, turning to look at him. "It is not as if we are friends for you to just ask about me," Pantu ended.

He couldn't help but smile. "Pantu, it's common knowledge," he said, sweetly. "You moved here at the end of last month, right Pantu?"

"Yes. I did Queen," Pantu answered.

"Pantu, you have no social media?"

"No, Queen. I do not."

"No internet either, Pantu?"

"No. I have never seen the internet before, Queen."

"No intranet, Pantu?"

"I have never heard of an intranet before, Queen."

"Pantu, are you going to make a profile?"

"No, Queen."

"Never Pantu?!"

Pantu sighed and looked at him as his eyes traced the structure of his face again, Pantu blurted out, "I know you are a male, so I am not trying to be silly with you, but your bones curve in such a natural way, it softens your face. I would love to sketch you."

His face and ears went red from the compliment. "Oh my!" was all he could reply with.

He felt the hard stare filled with jealousy from across the lunchroom and gathered himself to stand. Reaching into his bag, he pulled out four, thin, gold-plated cards. He placed all of them down and moved them in front of Pantu.

"What a doll. I simply adore you Pantu!" he said, with glee.

Pantu

Pantu felt Drum standing close, so he chose to examine the cards left by Queen instead. He didn't know when Drum left his seat to stand behind Queen or how Drum was there so fast, but it was probably best if he didn't look at Drum. He wanted to keep his face intact for as long as possible.

The cards were gold in color, thin and lightweight, with a black circle surrounded by black initials of D, W, Q, and S on both sides. Slightly bigger than a business card, it was simple but elegant. He smiled and handed one to Dill, who looked at him with wide eyes.

"Umm? You're giving me a Favor?"

"Yes. I would have never known about favors if you had not told me," he said. He cut his eyes at Queen to counter.

Laughing Queen replied, "You would have been given a Favor for the information whether you knew about it or not. The other three are bonuses."

"HMPH!" he pouted back, still refusing to look further behind him.

Queen squealed in delight. "Ekkkk! How adorable!" Queen leaned down, closer to his face to whisper, *"You're quite Special, aren't you?"*

It felt as if his face was full of heat, but the hottest areas were around his cheeks. He slowly turned to catch Queen's eyes. "I am only special because you think I am."

Queen stepped back, placing his hands over his chest, Queen looked at Drum. *"Oh my!?"* Queen said. Smiling as he twirled his way to the door, Queen looked as if he was high on the strongest Moon Blossoming flowers possible.

He was internally happy as he thought about a list to give to Queen. There were things he couldn't find in Dill's Pa's junkyard, and he COULD NOT ask his Ma to order. He needed to replace the parts soon, so he could call her again. If he skipped a week, he knew she wouldn't be happy.

He smiled as he thought about his plan. First, he had to keep her off his parent's trail, second; was to graduate Higher Ed, so his parents would at least have a happy memory, and third; was to get his trust fund then leave.

What she said would happen when he came back to her was roses and cupcakes, but he knew it was a Lie. And even knowing that, he still had to go back.

I hate the smell of roses and cupcakes make me fat. He shook his head to clear the thoughts.

"Not now, just be patient. Everything will work out," his Mind told him.

The rest of his day was normal. *Well, I guess this is normal for a town like this,* he thought, as he sat in his chair. It was the last class of the day, and he could finally go to his house. He was proud of the fact he didn't openly look at Drum once. Still sitting, he gathered his books and packed his backpack.

He sighed loudly. *I am so behind in my work. Maybe I should not have missed the first week. Advanced Honors classes are no joke. Besides homeroom, lunch and a free period, I have the same five core classes every day for five straight days. Twelve-hour days for two months before exams and new classes after break. This is supposedly what gifted people use to graduate within three years instead of five.*

He was lost in his thoughts; leaning back in his chair, his eyes closed towards the ceiling. He felt someone sitting in front of him.

"I need you to sign this," Queen said, with glee and he jumped at the sound of Queen's voice.

"Sign what?" he asked.

Queen pushed the paper on his desk towards him. "It's a release form for Private Citizens. It allows...people to put your photo online or post personal information about you."

Queen went off lost in his thoughts which he vocalized. "If you had a profile, I could have just DM'ed you the paperwork and you could have electronically signed it, but since you don't have one, I need your permission, in writing, or else no one will be able to post a photo, video or any identifying information of you online, even by accident," Queen finished.

Looking at the paper, he pushed it back towards Queen. "No thank you. I would rather not," he said. Zipping his backpack and standing to leave, he added, "I do not want photos of me placed on something I am not interested in participating with or on." He smiled at Queen. "Thank you for respecting my privacy!" he said, brightly.

Queen gracefully slid out of the chair in happiness. "Oh! My!" Queen said and looked at Drum with pleading eyes. Win and Sport were holding back laughter, Drum said nothing, and he refused to look at Drum before leaving.

QUEEN: A PLAN OF INVITATIONS
WEEK ONE: WEDNESDAY

The next day on campus was pretty eventful for him. He learned even more about his best friend Drum, and it sent a thrill of excitement through his Energies. Of course, it didn't start off that way, in fact, it seemed like a regular day.

By the time lunch came, he was ready for some fresh air, so they agreed to meet at the top of the outside bleachers. He knew Drum would be happy about it, and sure enough, Drum was the first to lounge on the bleachers with a huge smile on his handsome face, as he basked in the Omega Star's light with his eyes closed.

Drum's skin just seemed to soak up the star and in return for the gift of warmth, Drum's skin glowed. He sometimes wished his skin would shine brightly under the stars, but he knew only Drum would be able to maintain decorum.

He swore he would have a hard time controlling himself if he shined like Drum, so to keep others safe, the Universe denied him the warm, beautiful, brown skin It blessed Drum with, but still gave him a nice sized member, so he shrugged and accepted the fact the Universe knew what It was doing.

He gracefully climbed up the bleachers while making as much noise as possible to annoy Drum but only received a smile that reached those honey-mint eyes. He smiled back and sat down to the left of Drum. With his back facing the field, he got comfortable and took a deep breath.

"Freedom!" he exclaimed, with his arms spread wide open.

Sport and Win came around the bleachers to jog up.

"This does feel good," Win added.

"I'm way too big to be kept inside all day," Sport said, as he sat down to the right of Drum.

Win sat next to Sport. "Is that why you're always pulling your member out and showing it off? Is it too big to be kept inside your pants?"

Drum was trying hard not to laugh but his repressed facial expressions made everybody else laugh. Drum put his head down on his knee and joined. He knew Drum was uncomfortable thinking about touching, or at least Drum was before.

He could see Drum's response was slightly different and when Drum put his head down, it was to hide his thoughts. They ate and talked about Drum's party announcement which went viral.

"Students from the other campuses want an invite and people want to know if we will live broadcast the event," Win said to him.

"They also want to know the theme of the party," Sport said, looking at him. "Still need to prep."

He was overwhelmed with so many questions, and it was barely two days after the announcement. He hadn't even started his section of the guest list.

"So far I have planned for the list to be six hundred Beings. One hundred and twenty from Makis Ridge Higher Ed and Hollis campuses, one hundred and fifty from Sunset Town and three hundred and twenty from our campus, not including us, will get an e-invite." He read off his phone.

"No need to send my brother one or the last five guests he's bringing," Drum added.

He nodded. He knew the number might change so he left room for an increase. After checking with Drum and him not flinching at the number of guests who would be coming to his home, he thought, *his home must be fucking huge!*

It was a fact Drum never invited anyone to his home, including him. Everyone knew where it was, but it was surrounded by a huge forest and out of respect, no one approached his home. It may also have something to do with six-year-old Drum getting lost in the woods around his home for over a week.

The huge search party was called off after his parents said they found him. No one knew where Drum was, how his parents found him or what happened to him during that time, but everyone avoided inviting themselves to his home. And with Drum's disposition, along with the Park on their property, his home hidden in the forest was mysterious.

It only took thirteen years to get an invite, he thought, as one of his Bees approached.

Speaking only to him she started, "Here is the current guest list, organized, typed and printed." She smiled with pride.

"Thank you, Faith. You know you didn't have to type the list or print it, right?" he questioned, with a soft voice and his eyebrow raised. He took a quick glance over the list and innocently placed it closer to Drum. He turned his attention back to Faith, who was pouting.

"I wouldn't have to type it up if it wasn't so sloppily written and I wouldn't have printed it out if I didn't need to personally air my grievances," Faith whined, as she plopped down next to him and hung off his arm. She shot death looks at Sport and Win, who together, avoided her line of sight.

When he blew a sigh, Win immediately pointed and shouted, "Sport did it, it's his fault!"

Sport jumped away from Win's accusing finger and shot back. "You wrote one name and left me to fill in the rest, as you daydreamed about her." As Sport was justifying his horrible handwriting, Win could only look guilty.

"Do you know how fast I had to write thirty names and emails with no help?" Sport pretended to swing a hammer down on Win's head, who pretended to be hit and passed out.

Drum picked up the papers to look over the list and his face showed a quick look of disappointment as he finished scanning through all the names.

He reached inside his bag and offered the Bee a yellow badge with the green initial Q on it. He was quickly coming up with a plan as he scanned the Bee's Energy thumbprint to register her with the badge when Drum spoke up.

"What about Pantu?" Drum tried to look uninterested. "Pantu didn't ask for an invite?"

Win immediately frowned and waved a hand in front of his face. "Not Pantu!"

Rolling his eyes, he sighed at Win.

Sport, on the other hand, was confused. "Why not? Pantu's new here and it would be rude not to extend an invitation. That's not like you Win." Sport finished with disapproval in his voice.

Win looked like a chastised toddler but kept his mouth closed in agreement.

"Well, since Pantu hasn't asked for an invite, we should extend one, shouldn't we? What should we give as a reward?" He winked at Drum, who was pretending not to notice he had already caught on to Drum's plan.

Win perked up at the mention of a reward. "OOHHH! Twenty minutes in Heaven with the Being of your choice!" Win shouted out.

Faith immediately looked at Drum and blushed.

"Sure. But it needs to be willing participants," he said, pretending to be lost in thought. He was waiting on Drum to speak up.

Drum offered, "How about twenty minutes in Heaven with your Being of choice and Pong will oversee or five minutes alone with me?"

He smiled, knowing this would light the campus, hell, the whole intranet on fire. He would narrow the field down to day students and only on campus, not to overwhelm Pantu.

"Why do they only get five minutes alone with you?" Faith asked.

"Well, they see him more, but Pong is making himself available for the party," Sport answered instead.

Win begrudgingly agreed. "Ugh...I guess. But Pantu better not accept an invite from Kat."

He knew Drum was not at all interested in having five minutes alone with anyone...else. Everyone on the campus thought Kat was a shoo-in to win Drum's heart, but it was Win who ignited the events that happened at the beginning of their first year. Win was in love with Kat since middle school, but only his best friends acknowledged his affections for her.

"I know you will set boundaries, so I'm leaving this to you," Drum stated.

He nodded. "Sport. Win. Can you make sure they are followed? Faith, can you ask your sister Sharon to inform the AH Senior Bees, please? Slow to bring Pantu around, rigggghhhhttt?" His last word held a hint of knowledge as he looked at Drum, who avoided his eyes but answered with a hint of a smile.

Walking to their next class, his phone beeped. "Oh, there's someone in the private bathroom," he said, checking the alert. He looked over at Drum. "We should check it out, in case someone needs help," he implored.

"Yeah," Drum replied. "See you in class Sport."

He and Drum broke off from Win and Sport to head towards the office. They chatted about what the party theme should be and decided on a concert festival. They entered the bathroom in the office building he used to talk to students from all over campus who needed help.

They quietly looked around. His eyes widened while he quickly and quietly locked the door. Drum stood there listening, trying to figure out what the sound he was hearing was. Motioning to Drum, they went to a closed stall and peeked over.

Pantu was there, sitting on the toilet, pants down with his member in his hand. His eyes were closed, and he was masturbating, fast, while moaning and whispering *please*.

"Need a hand?" he asked Pantu, brightly.

Looking up to find the voice, Pantu looked at him and then Drum before coming over his clothes. The stunned revelation made him back up from the door and smile, but Drum looked confused.

"Drum!" he called, sitting on the counter. His best friend, who was still looking over the door trying to figure out what was happening with Pantu, jumped at the sound of his voice.

"Back up and give Pantu some space."

Drum stepped away and nodded while taking off his clothes, only to hang them on the stall door.

He watched with a grin on his face. "What-cha doing?" he asked louder than needed, knowing full well what Drum was planning.

"Giving Pantu my clothes," Drum stated. "I doubt anyone would wanna walk around like that."

Clapping his hands together, he excitedly commented, "Oh wow! That is an EXCEPTIONALLY LARGE member!"

They heard a short, scared *ahhh* come from the stall and he silently laughed while making a motion with his hands to say it happened again. Drum shook his head but couldn't hide the smile on his face.

"What are you going to wear?" he asked, filling the silence with noise.

"I have gym next, so I'll just wear these," Drum stated, as he held up his gym clothes. "I also have an extra uniform in my gym locker, so I'll be fine."

Since Drum always wore pants and a long sleeve under his uniform shirt, no one has ever seen more than his face, neck, and hands. But now, Drum was completely naked from the waist down. He couldn't help but admire the lower, scarred, and tattooed physique of the beautiful man in front of him. Drum could Seduce[37] him or anyone he wanted into liking him, even Charming them to fall in love. But they both knew; Drum was not his type.

"Well, we should give Pantu some privacy to clean up," he said, as he jumped down from the counter. "AH Political Analysis is calling my name!"

---

[37] *Increasing the natural scent Energy gives off to control others. See Universal Abilities #9.*

PANTU: A HELPING PAIR OF EYES
WEEK ONE: WEDNESDAY

Just when he thought he could have a normal day in this weird town, he embarrassed himself yet again. Day three of making a complete fool of himself. He had a free period after lunch, so he decided to get one out.

He went into the student bathroom by the office, which always seemed deserted. Getting comfortable in the stall, he pulled out his penis and started rubbing to get himself hard. He thought about her but that just made his penis soft, so he let his Mind wonder to land on the scent of cinnamon, and he immediately became hard.

Ahhh, that feels so good, he thought. He set his rhythm and moaning from pleasure, he failed to notice anyone entering the bathroom.

"I am getting there, I am so close," he pleaded to himself, but it wouldn't come out. *"Please!"* He started whispering to himself when he heard Queen's voice.

Startled, he looked up at Queen and then over at the stunning face of the young male he was trying to avoid, only to come.

Ah shit, it is leaking out!

He went to cover himself, causing it to get over his shirt. He was trying to stop it from coming out, but his penis wouldn't listen. It continued to leak, relieving him of so much pressure and easing his tension.

Finally! He silently sighed as his penis started to calm down.

He watched as Drum's clothes landed on the stall door, but when he heard Queen talk about the size of Drum's penis, an *ahhh* escaped his lips as more came out.

Holding his head in one hand while his other held his penis in a death grip, he lifted his legs, so his shoes rested on the seat of the toilet and putting his head down, he silently prayed for a time machine or a spaceship. He wasn't being picky, either would do.

He was lost in his own thoughts but the sound of the bathroom door closing and the click behind it brought him back. He stood up to take in the mess he made all over himself before opening the stall door. He checked the main door, making sure it was locked.

He went to the sink and started taking off his clothes to wash them but became unhappy with himself. He threw his shirt into the sink and started running the water. Tears started coming out, but he ignored them and stripped down to his boxers. He closed his eyes and wished he wasn't on campus right now. His boxers were just as bad as his outer clothes.

Texting his Ma to come and sign him out, he washed his boxers and hung them upside down on the hand dryer before starting it. Cleaning the rest of his clothes, he turned and took Drum's down from the door.

The scent hit him so fast, he became lightheaded. He caught himself to keep from falling. Cinnamon wasn't the only thing he smelled. There was a hint of honey, like the bread his Ma used to make when they lived in The Slums and were happy.

They used to live in the poorest part of The City. Located on the outskirts, the citizens live there in poverty. Fresh baked cinnamon bread, hot out of the oven and drizzled with honey is what he smelled as he inhaled Drum's scent.

There was something else he just couldn't put his finger on. Another scent, stronger than the cinnamon and honey, but he ignored it and started getting dressed. He found Drum's boxer briefs and blushed. He folded them and placed them in his backpack.

"I cannot wear another male's undergarments, can I?"

He wrung his clothes out and placed them under the dryer. He put on his own boxers before putting on the long pants left by Drum.

Well duh, he is taller than me. I guess I would have to stand on my toes to...stop it Pantu! You do not like males. You have her waiting for you back there. Besides, it is not like you can stay in this town for too long.

He finished getting dressed and looked at himself in the mirror. Drum's clothes swallowed him up and he smiled. He realized he wasn't crying anymore but didn't know when he stopped. He looked at the two-tier embroidered name, *DRUM* was above *Suppade XC Santiago.*

He traced it with his fingers. Taking a label out of his bag, he printed his name and placed it over Drum's. After a text from his Ma, he gathered all his stuff and shoved it in his backpack. Unlocking the door, he ran out to her car.

DRUM: A DAY WITH NO FINAL ANSWERS
WEEK ONE: WEDNESDAY

He didn't understand what happened in the bathroom, so Queen explained it to him as they walked towards the gym.

"So, guys milk themselves every day?" he sincerely asked.

Queen giggled into his hand. "It doesn't have to be every day, Drum. But sometimes guys use others to milk them." Queen glanced at him to see his reaction, but he was lost in thought.

They came up to the gym and Queen bid him goodbye before turning to go to his own class. He entered and after climbing to the top of the bleachers; he sat and watched his class play basketball. His eyes followed the game, but his thoughts were on how adorable Pantu would look in his clothes. He couldn't wait until Calculus.

He remembered how Pantu's face looked when his member started squirting and leaking white stuff. He wanted Pantu to make the face again, but he wanted to be the one to make his face like that. He wanted to touch Pantu there and watch his reaction. He didn't know if Pantu liked guys since he was staring so intensely at Kat.

So why does Pantu have that Scent?

He knew this Scent was driving him crazy, but he was also confused. As much as he wanted his Angel back, his Angel only held one scent which was soothing to him. His thoughts were filled with Pantu, while trying to figure out why Pantu held the scent of his happiest memory along with the same scent as his Angel.

"I can't rush into this," he reminded himself. "I need to be patient or Pantu might freak out."

He understood Pantu may have lived his whole life without knowing what he really is and to offload everything at once could possibly break Pantu. He didn't know what Pantu experienced in life, but he wanted to make him smile, make him happy.

His phone went off, and he checked the message. '*Pantu signed out for the day*'.

He sighed and leaned back against the cold, brick wall, closing his eyes. *I guess I will have to wait a little longer to see him in person*, he thought as he smiled, opening his eyes to look at the photo of Pantu leaving the campus in his clothes.

PANTU: HOW TO TALK YOURSELF OUT OF COMMON SENSE
WEEK ONE: WEDNESDAY

He didn't stop moving until he was undressed in his room. He took everything off, tossed the clothes in his basket, and set it out front of his bedroom door. He threw himself on his bed, covering his eyes with his arm.

He muttered to himself, *"It is not what happened."*

He started rationalizing his actions which conflicted with his emotions. He'd never been so out of control of his body, and it was starting to make him tremble worse than his Pa. His penis shouldn't have come the moment he saw those honey eyes. The green flecks in Drum's eyes seemed to dance and was definitely NOT the reason he made a fool of himself, yet again.

This is not how things are supposed to go, he thought. *I keep having to change my plans and I have only been on campus for two and a half days!*

He didn't know what to say to himself, so he repeated over and over that it was not because of Drum. But it only made his penis hard, and he was not going to touch himself if it meant he would come thinking about "him".

"Ahh, what am I doing? I am not into males! She is waiting for me back home. It is just the scent. Yes, I like the scent. It reminds me of a happier time. That is all."

He forced down the doubt creeping up in his head. There was no way he would ever like a male more than a friend, even a best friend. His Ma knocked on his door to tell him dinner was ready. He was so busy thinking; he was surprised time passed so quickly. At least his Ma stopped asking about a snack.

He sat up, but his penis was so stiff, he arched his back to try and help. He looked at his door, and his eyes went wide. Grabbing a pair of sweatpants, he hopped into them and flung his bedroom door open.

"Ma! Where is my basket?" he asked, his eyes searching the hallway and down the stairs.

The inside of the house was open. As he leaned over the banister, to his right were the stairs leading up to the three main bedrooms with walk-in closets and bathrooms. Between the three rooms was a quiet sitting area with several bookshelves, couches, and a recliner.

The ceiling to floor crescent moon bay windows in the sitting room were his favorite thing about the house. Next to the sitting area, there were stairs, leading to an attic. On the left side of the house was his parents' room, which took up the whole side.

Downstairs, the kitchen was the first thing his eyes landed on as he went right to left scanning the open interior. The dining room was next, followed by the front hallway and door. He kept going, checking the living room, and finally leaning further over the rail to check the hallway beneath him.

"Pantu! Be careful!" his Ma shouted, as she walked towards him from the kitchen. His Pa was sitting at the dining room table but was staring at him.

"Where is my basket?" he asked again.

"It's in the washroom. I put it there..."

But he was no longer listening. He ran down the stairs, jumping over the hated step and continuing into the laundry room with his parents following.

His Ma asked him, "PanPan, what's wrong?"

"My clothes! Did you burn them yet?" he asked, searching through the baskets.

"No. I haven't started yet. I was going to—"

"Well, where is my basket then?" he interrupted, throwing his hands up.

"Ah! I set it towards the back of the dryer," his Ma said.

He brushed past her and dug through his basket. It was still there, Drum's clothes, unburned. They still carried his scent. He gathered the pants along with the shirt to turn and see his parents staring at him like he lost all common sense.

"They are not dirty," was all he could mumble out, as he looked everywhere else but their eyes.

He stood there for a moment as he was trying to understand and name what he was feeling. He decided he didn't like the unnamed feeling and turned, dropping the clothes back into his basket.

But after another moment, he decided he liked the feeling of saving the clothes from being burned, so he took them out again. He paused when he went to drop them back in before his Ma caught his arm. She took the clothes out of his hands, hung them on a hanger, then handed them back to him.

He went to leave the room. *"Thanks,"* he mumbled, and stopped to quickly glance at his other parent. "Pa." He left to go back upstairs.

"Would you like dinner Pantu?" his Ma asked, with a smile.

"Not hungry," he said, before he closed his door to lean against it. He held the clothes to his chest. He couldn't understand why he'd saved the clothes from being burned and he wasn't trying to. He took the shirt off the hanger and placed the pants in the back of his closet.

He gathered both the notes from under his pillow and the boxers from his bag before he placed them inside the shirt. He folded the shirt into a square, showing his homemade nametag and placed it inside his pillowcase. He didn't question why he did it, he just did.

PANTU'S MA: SKY KNOWS BEST
WEEK ONE: WEDNESDAY

She smiled at the retreating image of her son. She knew it wasn't her son's uniform he grabbed, and it was why she hadn't burned the clothes in his basket yet. When he came running out of the building in a uniform way too big for him, she said nothing.

When she saw it sitting in the basket outside his room, she peeled the nametag Pantu stuck on to read Suppade's name. She didn't know what happened, but Pantu's uniform was nowhere to be seen, so she assumed the young man gave her son his own uniform in a gesture of kindness. She took a deep breath and tilted her head to follow her son up the stairs, she asked about dinner.

It was the first time Pantu spoke to his Pa in over five years and two years since he quit speaking to her. He wouldn't speak in their presence, touch them, or even look at them. If it weren't for the cellphones Doctor Robin sent to them and suggested they use, there would still be no communication.

She understood he was upset, and that was putting it mildly. Over four years ago, they drugged him and fled The City, the only place they ever called home. They left the rest of their family behind and ran.

Pantu wasn't willing to accept the truth about The City, so they couldn't explain anything to him. She knew he was looking for a way back, but she was trying her hardest to find a home for him that would show him what The City truly was.

This town seemed like the perfect place. She didn't know what to expect when they first arrived. She and her Husband lived in hiding with other people the first few years after leaving The City, while Pantu received "help".

They ended up moving several times, always running. It's been a few months since the last incident which caused them to run. After saving Pantu again, they slowly made their way across multiple countries, using sightseeing as an excuse why they were on the road so long. They used the route given to them by someone helping and they finally ended up here, at the edge of the land.

Everything was paid for. The home and cars were given to them. No bills came to their home, and the utilities were on and working when they moved in. Whenever she went grocery shopping, she never had to pay at checkout. She tried today and was impolitely reprimanded.

Her Husband already received an onboarding bonus check long before he started his new job at The Headquarters' building last week. His Boss wanted to give him time to adjust with his family to the town.

That was nice of him, she thought as she moved back into the kitchen. *So that's his name, Suppade.*

She knew who he was now. The young man who helped them was him. She was taken aback when her son drowsily said the young man who carried him to the van over four years ago, smelled a certain way.

She knew exactly what the Scent meant. Her Pa told her if she ever met a person who carried that Scent, marry them, be it Other or human. Which she did. She never thought they would meet the young man again, but years later, they were living in the same town as him.

Pantu told her himself this was the same young man. He never wore the clothes of another person, not even Coin's hand-me-downs. Pantu always refused, threatening to walk around naked before wearing the clothes off someone else's body.

She turned to her Husband and asked, "You feel it too, right?"

He nodded. *"This is not the same Pantu from The City,"* he whispered back to her.

"It's for the best. Maybe he can protect this Pantu better than we can," she said. "Maybe he can help this Pantu realize the truth about The City."

PANTU: GETS WHAT HE WISHED FOR, IN THE WEIRDEST OF WAYS
WEEK ONE: THURSDAY

"Today will be normal!" he said to himself, before climbing the stairs to the AH Senior-Level building.

It was one of the things he liked about the campus. Each Level came with its own buildings and areas. Only those with Level classes were able to scan their badge to get in. There were shared areas in which any student could go without a scan.

There were exceptions, for example, the Cleaning Club. The president was granted access to all buildings and could assign badge access for a certain amount of time. Running an errand for staff would also grant a student a temporary scan.

He didn't get far before a cute giggling Woman approached him.

"Hi! You're Pantu, right?" she asked, with a huge smile.

"Ah, yes. That would be me," he responded, unsure of the young Woman's intentions.

She giggled back at him. "So incredibly handsome!"

He smiled at her and moved closer. Before he could take more than two steps, Dill hooked his arm around his neck, smiled and waved at the Woman, then dragged him towards the front doors.

"Ignore everybody," Dill told him.

"Why? She could have been asking to be my Woman…or something," he responded, unhappy Dill just ruined a potential moment.

"You don't want that ask," Dill said back to him.

Everybody was looking at them as they went into the building and up the stairs to their homeroom.

"Dill, what the fuck is going on with you?" he finally asked, as they stopped in front of his desk.

"Pantu, you need social media. It's open season on you!" Dill told him, with a look of a sick baby bird. "Who did you piss off?"

He looked unsure of why this was happening to him and shrugged his shoulders. "Nobody? Everybody! I do not know."

Dill shook his head. "Find the safe zones. It's all I can tell you without..." Dill trailed off and cut his eyes at Win, who was watching them.

"Right!" he said as he sat. "Well, at least now I know who is upset."

A young male came up to him and tapped his fingers on his desk. "Pantu!" the male said, reading off his nametag with a smile. "Damn! YOU ARE HOT!" The male leaned down, closer to his face and lowered his voice while staring into his eyes to ask, "Do you want to go—" But he didn't get to finish.

A "NOPE!" came from the other side of the room. Win was shaking his head, and the male left the classroom with an embarrassing look on his face while an overly sweet scent followed him.

He is not even a student in my class, he thought. He spent the rest of homeroom deep in thought. *At least I now know classrooms are safe spaces.*

Since he had the same Professor for homeroom and second period, he could safely stay in the room without being bothered. Second period was Dill's free period, so there was no one to give him more information about what was going on.

He spent the day mentally mapping out the campus and testing out safe spaces. The library was a given, wherein the cafeteria was not. He was immediately bombarded as soon as he walked through the door for lunch.

He quickly made his way into the library and decided to spend the rest of lunch and his free period here. He would plan routes later tonight and test them out tomorrow. He also found out everyone was trying to invite him to Drum's birthday party. He turned down so many people he'd lost count.

He wanted to be popular *but not like this*, he thought. *I am seriously not even the main character of my own life*. He sighed.

He realized he shared homeroom and second period AH Renaissance and Reformation with Win, third period AH Special Topics in Chemistry with Queen, fifth period AH Foreign Language with Sport and seventh period AH Calculus with Drum.

Besides lunch, his fourth class being a free period, and sixth period AH Fabrication Design II were the only times he wasn't around one of "The Four". And that depended on whether he chose to eat in the lunchroom.

He would have to wait until Design to speak to Dill without Drum or any of his best friends being around. He decided instead of thinking about safe zones; he would catch up on some of the work he still needed to submit.

He was suspicious of the fact Dill was missing during Fab Design. Since he hadn't painted anything in years, he used the time to think. It felt like he was being tested.

The invites could be seen as targeting him, but they weren't overwhelming. There were places he could go to avoid being asked. No one was mean or vicious when he didn't accept their invitation or ask him multiple times in a row. There always seemed to be someone around him to make sure he was safe.

Wait! Do I feel safe with them around? Not safe, no that cannot be it. They are just making sure whatever rules they placed are being followed. He could respect that. If this was payback for touching Drum, he'd take party invites over crushed skull any day.

It wasn't as if he would even go to the party. He wouldn't be here after exams, so maybe he could accept a random invite and the whole ordeal would be over. But something felt off about accepting any invite. There had to be a catch. The reason why most of the campus wanted to go to this party with him. A reward in return for getting him to say yes.

And I was going to randomly give it away, he thought. *I will have to find out what the reward is first. Maybe I can use it to my benefit.* He smiled to himself.

I wonder about Dill. No, Dill approached me in homeroom, long before I made a fool of myself. Besides, he could have refused to upgrade it when he knew what I was doing with it. He couldn't bring himself to think badly about Dill. He liked him and they were friends. *I am sure whatever Dill is doing, it is important.*

PANTU: LETTING YOUR ACTIONS SPEAK FOR YOU
WEEK ONE: FRIDAY

The next day he was proud of the fact he trusted his friend. Dill left campus early to help his Pa with a large order that came into their junkyard.

He didn't think Dill's home being called a junkyard was the proper use of the word, having lived in The Slums before. It was entirely too clean and well-organized. Dill's Pa named his shop, "Junk N My Back" and they lived above and behind the shop office.

Dill told him his Pa liked Women with big butts, but he had an issue with believing his friend since Dill's Pa was married to a flat ass woman. But Dill showed him photos of his Birth Ma and said his Pa was paying homage to her memory.

Dill and his Pa possessed a Talent for building things. Dill's Pa really enjoyed melting diverse types of metal and reshaping it, his nickname being Metal. He was quite Talented and he, and eventually Dill, built several amusement parks, which Metal's wife, Lyra, managed.

"New rides for a park?" he asked Dill in homeroom.

"No. It's for other things," Dill answered, uninterested in finishing the conversation.

He could respect that. There were things he couldn't talk about, things he didn't want people to know about him, so he let the conversation go.

"If you are free Saturday afternoon, we should meet in Hollis. Hang out," he offered.

He texted his parents days ago, telling them he made a friend, and he should be allowed to go to Dill's home. He added if they didn't trust him to hang out at Dill's then he shouldn't be allowed to go to school. He was sure after a lengthy chat with his Psychiatrist, his parents finally agreed.

"Can't. It's a huge order and I have to help my Dad. I'm probably going to be busy after classes the next week," Dill apologetically said. "We can still hang out at night though."

With a sigh, he nodded. "I will make some new sketches for our next project."

Dill looked at him. "You should get the layout of the town. Take a walk, so you can find your way around. Don't stay inside all weekend."

With a nod as his response to Dill, his friend went to his seat as homeroom started. After verifying the map in his head was the same as the one posted by the front office for fire escapes, he spent the rest of the day avoiding Drum and his best friends while testing out routes.

He used the time to also find more safe zones. By the time Calculus class was over, he was satisfied with most of his routes. He didn't notice Drum was looking at him with a smile, but he felt it. When Drum dropped the class notes on his desk, he realized he hadn't been paying attention in class, again.

"I am too far behind to lose focus," he scolded himself. He looked up and jumped a little as several notebooks landed on his desk. "What are these?"

"Notes dating back to the previous Monday. One notebook per class. It should help with homework and classwork," Queen replied happily. "But projects are not included," he added, darkly. Queen started laughing when his face showed he was unsure of Queen's intentions.

"You're a gem," Queen stated.

He was wondering why they would help him. Were they not upset with him? He was sure they set the campus up to invite him to Drum's party. He almost thought the notes were fake, but he knew Drum's notes were better than any he could have ever written. Besides, he learned how to work out the problems precisely and received a perfect score on his homework using those notes.

"Why would you help me?" he asked, completely lost.

"Because you're Special," Queen responded, with much belief behind those words.

He rolled his eyes away from Queen. He was told his whole life he was special, but by now, he didn't believe it. He just wanted to survive.

"If wanting to live makes me special, then everyone is," he said. He rose from his chair and packed his bag.

As he picked up the books, Queen touched his hand. "I like you Pantu."

He slowly moved his hand back and took a deep breath. "I do not mind if you do, but I have only been with Women. I am...I cannot." His breath came out slowly.

Queen was taken aback by his reaction. "Oh!? Do you not like gay...men?" Queen asked, politely.

"I have never met...gay...men...before, but I do not think one person should speak for all. I will decide whether I like YOU or not based on your own personality," he responded.

Queen was at a loss for words and could only stare at him. For longer than a moment, Queen sat still with wide eyes and a gaping mouth.

"Wow! That's the first time Queen has ever been speechless," Sport said, making Win and Drum join his laughter.

"All it took was a Pantu!" Win added, and the three of them fell out laughing again.

The sound of Drum's laughter made him smile, and he held up the notebooks.

"Do you mind?" he asked, and Queen nodded. He packed up and turned to walk into Dill.

"I've finished upgrading it, and it works perfectly," Dill said and handed him a small black box which he quickly stuffed into his pocket.

"Your hands are a gift from the Universe," he responded. Throwing his arm around Dill, they left the classroom while Dill was turning his hands over and staring at them.

"I think you might..." Dill's voice trailed off as they walked away.

PANTU: FINDING A SAFE HAVEN
WEEK ONE: SATURDAY

Every Saturday, Pantu and his parents went into Hollis since he had a standing appointment with his Psychiatrist. He knew his Doctor wanted details about life in The City, but he wasn't ready to talk about it.

His parents made The City seem like the worst place on Torven and previous psychiatrists kept calling his birthplace a cult. But it was all he knew. He was born and raised there for seventeen years before he was drugged and kidnapped by his own parents.

One of those years running was spent in a mental hospital trying to "un-indoctrinate" him, but The City found him, "she" found him there. When his parents learned the doctor at the first hospital started working for "her", they snatched him and ran again. He knew Doctor Robin spoke to his parents after his sessions to update them on his progress, so he had to give her something, or he would never be off the medications.

Every week he needed to have a blood test to monitor the levels of medicine in his system. Even though he was starting to feel unhappy about everything, he admitted he was granted more freedom now than ever before, even in The City.

His parents decided not to restrict his movements inside the town, as long as he carried his phone with him and responded to every text they sent. He still needed to let his parents know everywhere he was going outside of their house, campus and now Dill's home.

He sat on the couch and put his face in his hands. Sighing deeply, he waited. She was sitting in the chair across from him. He thought Doctor Robin was beautiful.

Her deeply tanned skin with a golden undertone fits perfectly with her tightly coiled, deep red hair, mixed with random blond curls, he thought.

Her soft blue eyes threw him off when trying to figure out her family line. There was something about her which felt different to him. She was able to tell when he was purposefully leaving out details.

"Well, your friend"—she looked at her notes—"Dill. Can you tell me what he's like?"

He explained the differences in their personalities, the way Dill was patient and never laughed at him because he didn't know what seemed to be normal information.

"I feel like I could trust him and talk to him," he said.

She nodded with a smile. "Anyone else you feel comfortable around?"

"NO!" he immediately responded. He didn't want to get close to anyone else unable to last a day in The City. "There is someone who is watching me," he said, thoughtfully. "I feel someone lurking, but I do not know who it is." He wasn't sure if saying this would make him look paranoid, but it was seriously bothering him.

"I don't think you are paranoid," she responded. "Most patients are careful of what they say so they don't look a certain way. Your face showed concern." She smiled at him.

"But I'm glad you have the courage to speak about your feelings. You've suppressed them for so long." She folded her hands and leaned forward. "This is a step in your right direction."

He smiled to himself but the feeling he experienced on campus of someone secretly watching him made him quickly lose his smile again.

"Maybe I am going crazy," he irrationalized.

"You should think about not talking yourself out of your feelings, Pantu,"—she leaned back and continued— "if your feelings are telling you something, you need to decide whether you should trust them. If you start to doubt yourself just because these are emotions you haven't felt in a long time or at all, you could possibly fall right back into your former self.

"Your returning emotions and any new emotions you feel, there is an option to explore them. Rationalizing them or disregarding them because you don't understand them or you are afraid of them, wouldn't be a step in your right direction," she finished, as she jotted down some notes.

"I thought you would have asked me about The City by now," he said. He looked around her office.

"My responsibility is to you and your well-being. If you're not ready to talk, then for now, pushing you would be a step in my wrong direction." She wrote notes as their conversation continued. "I would hope to work on you feeling comfortable in a new town before opening up that discussion."

He looked at her questioningly. "Not safe?" he asked.

She paused her writing. "The only place I can make you feel safe is here, in my office." She folded her hands. "It's up to you to find a safe haven for yourself."

The ride home was filled with his parents' praise. They were happy he'd found an actual friend and was smiling, even if they still hadn't seen him smile in years. He said nothing as they pulled into the driveway.

He lazily got out of the car and walked into the house. He didn't know what he was going to do, probably sleep. He threw himself on the living room couch and closed his eyes as his Pa turned on the television to watch a documentary on narwhales.

He was drifting off to the monotone voice from the show when his Ma called him to the front door. "Pantu, there's some young men here to see you," she unnecessarily yelled towards the living room.

"Ahh!" was his response as he forced himself off the couch and to the door. He stopped when he saw Sport, Queen and Win all lounging on his front steps.

Sport nudged Win to speak, which was done with little enthusiasm.

"Do you want to walk with us around town?" Win asked.

He rolled his eyes at Win and replied, "I move slowly, and I am allergic to exercise." He turned away. "No thanks!"

His Ma caught him. "You should go," she said.

He looked at her, knowing she was giving her permission without it being obvious to anyone else.

"Ma!" he half-heartedly protested.

"Maybe you can find the rest of the series you like to read at the town's library," his Ma said, softly. She looked at her husband who came to stand behind them.

"It's good to get a sense of where you live," his Pa added.

He cringed at the sound of his Pa's voice. "Yes," he said to the young males standing on his doorstep. "As long as we stop by the library."

The walk was pleasant. The town smelled clean and depending on where he was, different scents would fill the breaths he took. All the scents he inhaled were nice and relaxing. It was peaceful and quiet as they walked.

No, it wasn't complete silence as if no one spoke, but the laughter of children and the happy conversations with neighbors was a stark difference from where he came from, and it made him smile.

He could have only imagined this in a dream. He painted a happy scene like this before, but it was destroyed by "her" when she found out he was the one who painted it. He made her look like a fool for not knowing about his Talent, and his punishment was so severe, he lost the joy of painting and never wanted to make another friend. It brought her pure happiness but at the cost of his own peace.

If they find me here, I can talk my way around knowing anyone, he thought to himself, *this way no one gets hurt.* He put his hand in his pocket to rub the words on the coin he always carried with him. One side read, "Positive Thoughts" while the opposite stated, "Good Vibes Only". He decided to have both on this walk.

After showing him the library and walking past a high school, they came to a wooded area. It was gated with a sign which read, "Park. This Way" and a hand pointing into the woods.

"There is a park here?" he asked, intrigued by the fact it was surrounded by woods.

"Yea, but no one goes there," Win answered.

But he was already inside the gate walking along a narrow cobblestone path. When the path ended, he came upon a large field, *or is it a meadow*, he thought, *or is it both?* The vast sea of green and gold tall cattails seemed to call to him. He noticed a shimmering royal-blue Light and went to touch it.

Sport grabbed his hand. "We should go. It's getting late."

He turned slowly to look at Sport and nodded, allowing himself to be pulled away from the captivating Light. Once they were back on the open sidewalk, he felt it. Malicious Intent and it was strong. With a quick blank, he turned on his True Vision to pinpoint the source of Intent. His eyes went wide, and he stumbled, feeling someone catch him.

Closing his eyes and taking several deep breaths, he stood and tried again. Turning on his True Vision, he was able to see the Light flowing throughout everything his eyes landed on. He kept taking deep breaths as he looked at the bright, starlit, Light-filled town. From the buildings to nature, there wasn't anything existing here without Light inside it.

Neutral Light, he thought. *A whole town made of pale violet Neutral Light. The abundance!*

The vivid colors around him forced him to turn off his True Vision, since the brightness was straining his eyes, but not before he caught a quick glance of Drum's best friends' Lights.

Sport finally helped him find his balance and explained, "It's why no one goes there. It makes people lightheaded."

He only looked at Sport, unwilling to tell why he almost passed out and decided to continue the walk instead. On the way back, he was disappointed he didn't find the source of the Intent and pulled out his cell phone when the alarm went off.

"My apologies. I must make a phone call," he said, before turning away to put some distance between them.

After feeling like he was far enough away for them not to hear him but where he could still see them, he pulled the box Dill gave him out of his pocket. Plugging the black box into a port on his phone, he turned it on and waited until the light changed from red to green. Dialing "her" number, he waited until she answered in her usual annoyed voice.

"Took you long enough." She huffed into the phone.

He rolled his eyes, but his voice didn't match his face as he replied, "My Sweetest Heart, I stepped away just for you."

She giggled into the phone. "Of course, you did. I am still your Owner after all," she said, with pride in her voice. "Did you find it?" she asked.

"No, and I am still looking. It has been very well hidden. But none of it will matter once something called final exams are over and I graduate from a school," he told her. "I will be a legal adult and entitled to it anyways."

She laughed. "Make sure to do what I told you before you leave."

An unhappy feeling rose inside him, and he knew it showed on his face. "Yes. I know," he responded. "Bad Pas should not be allowed to live," he added, while holding back tears.

His voice, however, didn't waver at all as he quickly moved onto the only reason why he called her. He knew she claimed to not be able to orgasm without him and the threats to his family still in The City ensured he would continue to follow her rules. After talking her into an orgasm, he hung up.

He felt dirty and disgusted with himself. In such a clean town he felt like crawling out of his skin and starting over. As he walked back to join the males patiently waiting for him, well at least Sport and Queen were, he realized his body reacted differently to her. Hearing her voice did nothing for him. He trained his body to respond to her commands, so why wasn't it listening?

He could excuse it away by thinking he was in public, and since *no one here just pulled out their penises and jacked off*, he thought maybe he shouldn't either. But he didn't even get hard. There was no reaction down there while he was talking to her. It was if his penis went beyond REM sleep. As he joined them, his face didn't show how upset and unsure of his future he really was.

"Convo not go the way you want?" Win still asked him.

He shook his head and shrugged his shoulders at the same time.

Queen said nothing, just looked at him as if Queen knew something about him that he didn't know himself.

"It does not matter as long as the conversation was had," he said, ending the conversation.

PANTUxDRUM: BREAKING DOMES
WEEK ONE: SUNDAY

The next day, Pantu decided to go back to the park he'd seen. He wanted to know why he felt drawn to the place and, well, to touch the blue Light. He texted his parents that he was walking to the library and left in the late morning.

He'd checked the times and knew he could get there before closing to check out a book. Walking up forty-two steps to the main, red-brick, small, castle-style library in Sunset, his eyes caught sight of a group of people hanging around a low-setting wall to his right. He felt eyes on him but couldn't see pass the people standing together and cooing over someone.

Shrugging his shoulders and feeling no Ill or Malicious Intent, he continued up the stairs. After asking for a temporary card that required no information, he checked out a book he'd already read and left out the huge, glass, double door library entrance.

Halfway down the stairs, he felt the same stare from before. He looked around and his eyes stopped on a white, red-eyed, long-eared rabbit, sitting on the brick ledge, watching him. Or at least he thought the rabbit was. Continuing down the stairs, he kept his eyes on the rabbit, whose head turned to follow him down the steps.

The rabbit only jumped lightly to turn its body to face him at the bottom of the steps, but stayed where it was, it's cute nose wiggling. He shook his head and took off in the direction of the park.

He was happy his assumption was correct; most people would be in their homes by this time. The streets were quiet and glowed softly from the hanging lanterns as he came closer to the gate.

It was when he felt it again. He quickly looked around and saw the rabbit sitting across the street, watching him. Without hesitation he went down the path, walking faster than his normal speed.

He didn't stop or look back until he came to the beautiful blue Dome of Light blocking him from the field meadow. Quickly turning, he could only see two red glows, sitting at the darkened entrance of the path. He immediately turned and reached out to touch the Dome.

As the tips of his fingers connected with the Light, he could only gasp as where he touched shattered in the most amazing way. The Light popped into tiny blue sparkles, which tickled his face and his body with heat, making him giggle as the Dome slowly opened a door for him at the same time.

He stepped inside the Dome and was overwhelmed by the rush of happy feelings attacking him. He needed to take more than a moment as the scent he inhaled while also taking deep breaths, settled into his body. *Safe.* It was the word which came to Mind. He felt safe here. As he walked further into the field meadow of cattails, he brushed his hand along them, wondering how marsh plants could grow on such dry land.

Lifting his head to feel the starlight, he walked until he found a place to sit. Not far from where he opened the Dome was a small, circular area made of black marble. The design of the tiles reminded him of a black hole and even though he knew it was marble and solid, he still tapped the tip of his foot on the tiles, for his own peace of Mind.

After ensuring his footing was solid, he walked up to an oversized bench, which was not only off the ground and connected to what he assumed were poles, but the whole thing was made of royal-blue clouds.

He tilted his head and stared at the hanging bench before he touched the swing to test its solidity. When the clouds didn't disappear at his touch, he sat down. Between the softness of the clouds and the heat coming from them, he found himself lying down.

Taking out the book, he laid on his back and started reading. It wasn't until his Ma texted him that he realized he was there for hours. He lazily left the field meadow and went to the opening he'd made. Taking a longing look back at the hanging bench, he left and walked back to his house.

After spending the weekend working out of town, Drum was finally back. He hadn't talked to his best friends yet and he'd just entered his room when he felt Pantu touch the gate again. He was there before Pantu made it to his Barrier. Standing on the other side of the field, amongst the trees, he watched as Pantu broke his Barrier.

Not break, he thought as he realized Pantu made a door for himself. *He opened my Barrier.* He was stunned. No one was able to open his Barrier before, much less break or even crack it.

His heart started racing as he watched Pantu enter. He quickly used his Energy to create a sitting area for Pantu, while not only being playful about it, but testing a theory as well.

He was unsure if Pantu knew what he was doing, since Pantu seemed to have no idea, he was different. His body warmed up as he took a step towards the edge of the trees. When Pantu laid down on the swing, he leaned against a tree, pulled his right leg up, stuck his hands in his pockets and closed his eyes.

He stayed that way until Pantu left the field. Closing his Barrier after Pantu, he looked at his watch and understood Pantu could handle the Energy in the field for over five hours. Other than him, no one else could come close to the field for longer than a few minutes.

"But Pantu just did," he whispered to himself. *I guess if he smells that way to me, he has to be powerful*, he thought.

He was, without question, the most Powerful and the Strongest Being living. His Father, the Emperor, was at one time considered the Strongest, in and out of his Being Form and he was lucky enough to have inherited his Father's physical strength. What made him Powerful was his possession of an unknown number of Abilities, more than the average amount most Beings held, and it led to discord.

He was considered Special since birth, but the more he tried to downplay or ignore it, the more Beings pressed the unwanted word onto him. He was slated to rule after his Father, but he still wasn't feeling it.

Emperors were chosen by their most important Ancestral Artifact as its Protector. If you could touch the Artifact, you were chosen to rule. If no one living is chosen, the title goes to the Being family who protected the most Barrier Towns. Since it was dangerous for a Being to use their Abilities around humans, they found safe places on the overpopulated planet where they didn't have to worry.

He shook his head as he Instant[38] back into his room. Falling on his bed, he closed his eyes. Pantu made it clear and honestly, he wasn't attracted to anyone before, so his own sexuality was always in question.

He himself didn't know, since he never thought of anyone the way he thought of Pantu, but he knew his Heat would Flare and his heart would race whenever Pantu was close while his thoughts would be full of them touching.

---

[38] *The Ability to teleport. See Universal Abilities #5*

DRUM: A WELL-KEPT SECRET
WEEK TWO: MONDAY

He always woke up at o'four-thirty sr (star-rise) for exercise and training. He finished and came back to get ready for classes. Eating breakfast with his Mom, Dad and younger twin siblings was necessary in their home. There were always random family members to join them as well.

Kitten, the nickname he gave her at birth, was the loud and outspoken older twin. She was feisty with a slight tendency for violence. The younger twin, Pup, was quiet and reserved. He would go weeks without speaking.

They were both highly gifted when it came to their studies, but because of what happened during the attack on their family, they couldn't be far from each other without having seizures. And even then, with Kitten's slightly violent nature and Pup's severe inability to talk to strangers, school and the town were out of the question for them.

He knew their property felt like a plush prison for his younger siblings and he wished he could change that for them, knowing he was responsible for them being trapped. It was why he mostly came home after classes, and why he never invited his best friends to his home.

He normally arrived on campus ahead of everyone else but found Pantu was going over routes again. He smiled as he scanned his badge and entered the AH Junior-Level building.

"Pantu is adorable," he said to himself.

He knew Pantu was actively avoiding him, refusing to talk to him since the assembly incident or look directly at him since the first day of Calculus. He needed to find a way to get Pantu to do both.

Even if Pantu didn't want to be romantically involved with him, they could at least be friends. He wanted Pantu around because he liked the feelings he was experiencing for the first time, and Calculus was now his favorite subject. He was surprised to find his best friends spent time with Pantu.

"Leave it to Queen to open a door," he said to himself, with a smile. He sat thinking of how he could get Pantu to talk to him but ultimately decided to leave it to Karma. "The Universe gave Pantu that Scent for a reason," he said to an empty room. Taking a deep breath, he smiled. He felt good about today.

He decided not to go to lunch and instead headed to the Manga Room. Materializing[39] a table, he set himself up in the far back end of the room with a chair and his gaming laptop, knowing Pantu would come into the library during lunch and stay during his free period.

No one in the library, other than the Librarian, Doctor Faye, or whichever Aide was working, knew he was in the room. He had a private entrance from outside which could only be unlocked with his Crystal. There was one student key, and it was first come first served, or so it seemed.

Students could request the key for the door to the room's entrance inside the library, but he knew the Librarian and her Aides would decline their requests if he was in there, unless it was one of his best friends. He stayed in the room just enjoying the fact Pantu was this close to him.

---

[39] *Turning Personal Energy into a solid object. See Universal Abilities #15.*

DRUMxPANTU: IT'S NOTHING BUT A NAMETAG BETWEEN THEM
WEEK TWO: MONDAY

Drum's Foreign Language class ended, and Calculus finally came around. He was excited and he knew Queen acknowledged the silent change with brighter Energies. He headed to the Senior-Level math building for Advanced Honors Calculus with Queen and Win breaking off for their own classes. He entered as the Professor was calling attendance. He was either early or late for his classes to avoid crowds.

He made it to his seat and took his materials out. He didn't look at Pantu, but felt him, making him smile. After the hours long lecture, it was time for classwork. He already completed everything on the syllabus for all his classes during the break. He only showed up for notes to use on quizzes and tests, and attendance points. His best friends started doing the same thing in middle school, hence it freed them up to focus on other things.

He watched, out of the corners of his eyes, as Pantu got the first question wrong. He pulled out a small note pad and wrote, *"This is the equation for #1-3"*, before adding the formula. He folded it and tossed it onto Pantu's desk. He received a surprised look and after unfolding and reading the note, Pantu used the formula to come up with a different answer.

He noticed Pantu took the note and added it to his own. He wrote a formula for questions four through nine and tossed it on Pantu's desk. He avoided looking at Pantu and was simply happy his presence was even being acknowledged.

Once Pantu finished his classwork, he relaxed. His day was going well and his routes to class worked, since he was only asked to Drum's party a few times. He was able to feel less stressed, and it allowed him to notice other things.

It helped Drum just gave him the formulas for the problems, as his notes were not the best, since he hated taking them. Trying to find the most important things being said and writing them down fast enough to not miss the next important thing was not fun for him. He was a self-learner.

He could normally remember what was being said, but with his Mind distracted with rationalizing his new-found feelings and his brain focused on his ever-changing plans, he was having a challenging time focusing on his Professors talking for hours straight.

As he looked around, he noticed the desk to his right had three nametags on it, while his was empty. A quick glance to his left let him confirm what he knew, only Drum sat there. He took out a label to print his name, adding decorations using honey-brown and green colored pencils before he placed his nametag on the left side of his desk, close to Drum.

Out of the corners of his eyes, he could see Drum was trying not to smile at the fact he claimed the desk. As he secured the tag with tape, Drum could only stare at the small slip of paper.

His heart was already beating like he'd run a hundred miles without stopping, while his body kept feeling flashes of heat. When Drum turned from the tag to stare out the window, he felt the heat disappear and his heart start to calm. He took a quick glance at Drum and saw the young male still couldn't contain his smile.

He found himself staring until he heard the bell ring, but he didn't get up to leave, nor could he take his eyes off the young male's smiling face. Once Drum slid out of the chair and leaned against the desk to pocket his hands, he found his sanity as Drum stood staring at his custom nametag.

He didn't know what to do after seeing Drum smile so brightly. What was he supposed to do when this male's warm smile could stop and start his cold, uncaring heart?

"It's beautiful," Drum said out loud, never once looking away from his tag. "Can you make me one, please?" Drum asked.

He went to stand. "May I know your favorite colors?" he inquired, accepting Drum's request.

Drum, still staring at his nametag, responded, "Blue."

"Just blue?" he asked, leaning his head to the side while looking at Drum. This exchange felt familiar to him, but in the haze of new-found feelings and experiences, he couldn't focus his Mind enough to figure out where he'd heard these words before.

Drum's long curly eyelashes slowly lifted, giving access to the hidden honey-green eyes which refused to focus on him during class. Their eyes met and holding each other's line of sight, Drum nodded.

"Okay," he agreed, with a slight smile.

His response caused Drum to smile, deepening his own smile. He turned away when Drum's best friends entered the room and picked up his bag along with his classwork. He dropped the work in the basket in the back of the room and went to leave.

"PANNNNNTUUUU!"

He heard Queen shout out. Giving a wave and a smile to Queen, he continued out of the classroom, glancing back to see Drum again staring at his nametag.

PANTUxDRUM: A GIFT GIVEN
WEEK TWO: TUESDAY

The next day went even better for Pantu. Switching up his routes made it harder for the other students to track him, and he planned a different route for every day.

Next week, I will mix it up!

He was confident he would survive until he found out what the reward was, or Drum's party happened, whichever came first. He entered Calculus and left a small box on Drum's desk, before sliding into his chair.

Yesterday, he stopped by the campus library and asked one of the Aides to look up the definition of Suppade. They looked at him oddly and he guessed they thought he could do it himself, but it would be a violation of his parents' rule of no internet.

Although Drum's first name meant powerful in Thaikoriense, he needed to paint the rest of the name in another language as that part was from a different country.

Even remembering Drum's name after glancing at the desk tag, still didn't stop him from spell checking himself with Drum's shirt, which he hid in a new place. SUPPADE XC SANTIAGO.

He practiced saying the name several times until it sounded right. X-CEE SAN-TI-A-GO.

A long, royal-blue Dragon was painted above Drum's name, with clouds on each side. He added a three-limb branch under the first and last name, with different Moon Blossoming flower designs.

Between the branches, he painted Rig Fifth-Moon Demon TiKa. He was unsure if Drum knew the manga existed, but since it was his favorite and he was the artist, it's what he painted.

He hoped Drum would like the designs since he didn't know Drum's personality. *A blue star just does not feel right*, he thought. He exhaled a deep breath and prepared for class.

He watched as Drum sat and picked up the box to turn it over several times before putting it in his backpack, becoming more interested in what was outside the window. Drum made no effort to even acknowledge his Gift, more than a quick glance.

He, on the other hand, was experiencing an incredibly elevated level of unhappiness after Drum disregarded his Gift. The arduous work he put into finding the right shades of blue to make the colors fit together meant nothing since all Drum did was look at the outside.

"Maybe I should have painted the box," he said to himself. He blew out his breath and saw Drum quietly laughing, so he shot daggers out of his eyes, but the young male refused to look at him.

A folded note landed on his desk, and he glanced at it before looking back up at the Professor. A second folded note landed on his desk but had writing on the outside. *"#1"*, with an arrow pointing down to the words, *"this note"*, and *"#2"*, with an arrow pointing perfectly to where the first note was sitting. He shook his head but stopped as an unfolded third note with the word, *"Please!"*, and a frowning face with a single tear, slowly inched its way onto his desk.

Instead of acknowledging Drum, he focused on the lecture, wondering if the Professor could distract him from smiling. After confirming his Professor was of no help, he picked up the second note to read it. All it said was, *"read the first note"*. He dropped it back on his desk and bit his lip to stop the grin his smile was turning into. The silly way he was feeling brought him happiness, so he opened the first note.

"I want to open it after class, undistracted", was what Drum was trying to tell him.

He looked over at Drum and slightly nodded his head, which made the young male give him a smile that crushed his heart.

Drum had no idea what he was feeling, but seeing Pantu's cute lips pout was the most tantalizing thing he'd ever witnessed. He relented and gave in, tossing notes until Pantu opened the first one.

OMU! He will have me burning down the planet to see him pout, he thought as Pantu smiled at him. *Yep, I don't think I can tell him no. Or should I, just to see him pout?* He smiled back at Pantu, making Pantu blush and look away.

He wanted to be the one to make Pantu blush, smile, laugh and even pout. If he had to do it as friends, then he would be willing to stay by Pantu's side with the lesser title, but even that thought made him happy. *Thank you, Karma*, he mentally vocalized, as he looked out the window and into the clear, bright sky.

He was, however, trying to hide how excited he was to see his nametag. So much so, that during class, he kept having to stop his leg from shaking while silently berating time for being so slow.

Class was finally over, and Pantu packed while glancing over at him. He made no effort to move, and Pantu looked dejected, maybe thinking he wouldn't like the Gift. Whatever undelightful thoughts were in Pantu's head showed vividly across his face.

He could only assume Pantu was mentally cursing him, and even though his heart ached, he couldn't help but smile at receiving another pout from the stunningly beautiful young man next to him.

"Pantu?" he softly called, making Pantu stop mid-slide to take a deep breath.

When the most beautiful, light-filled brown eyes lifted to look directly into his, he could only force the air out of his inflated lungs passed his tightened chest to fall right into them.

"Stay?" he asked. "Please?" he added.

When those brown irises landed on the desk, he gave a goofy smile to his questions being non-verbally answered by Pantu, whose butt found the chair again. Pantu's arms were calmly folded on the desk, but his eyes jerked towards him when he took the box out of his bag.

Pantu finally looked around to notice only five Beings were left in the room. Three didn't have Calculus last period but it was the smile Pantu gave Queen which made him jealous. He still hadn't opened the box, since he was now concerned with whether Pantu was more interested in his best friend.

"Never mind, I will just throw burn it," Pantu said and reached for the box.

But Pantu only grabbed the top as he was staring at the nametag with a small smile which continued to grow as he took in every detail. His finger traced the blue Dragon, and he lightly laughed at TiKa being one of the decorations. He couldn't help but affectionally touch every part of the painting, hypnotized by the kindness he felt while staring at his tag.

"I love it!" he whispered. *"It's perfectly me,"* he added, as he continued to admire the first Gift he'd ever accepted outside his family and best friends.

Pantu dropped the top back on his desk, grabbed his backpack, and hurried out of the room. Queen went to call out to Pantu, but his slightly raised hand stopped his best friend.

"Pantu painted it."

His best friends' Energies were confused, but he could see the painstaking details Pantu put into his tag. For the long, small Dragon to be as accurate as it was, he knew it must have taken Pantu hours.

The curve of his name was written with such care and every decoration fit him perfectly. Pantu managed to make every shade of blue individually stunning while blending them together to make the whole tag breathtaking. He was in awe at Pantu's talent.

"You should add giclee gloss coating to it and frame it," Win offered.

"Then add it to your keychain," Sport added.

"So, you always have it close," Queen finished, and his brightest smile shined through as his best friends accepted his acceptance of Pantu's Gift.

Pantu's face was flushed red, and he was riding high on his feelings. Drum loved it, or he thought Drum loved it. *He did say he loved it, but was he just being nice? He at least liked it…right?*

It was a big step for him, since he lost the joy of his Talent when his owner destroyed all his paintings, except for the one she forced him to paint of her. He stayed up late making sure his Gift was as perfect as could be.

Was this the new feelings his Doctor was talking about? Every day after Calculus, he would return to his house stiff and use Drum's shirt to help him come.

He didn't like that his body didn't listen to him as he was worried about re-training, but at least for now, he was still able to get one out. He smiled as he lay in the mess from his masturbation.

He felt good and unhappy at the same time. He didn't know how long these feelings would last, so maybe he shouldn't get attached to feeling them so often. *I cannot stay here long. I cannot become attracted to males. Maybe I should keep my distance from Drum.*

PANTUxQUEEN: THE KEY TO FRIENDSHIP
WEEK TWO: WEDNESDAY

The next day, Pantu decided to skip lunch again and focus on some of the past due work he still needed to finish. He was in the library doing his assignments when Queen slid into the chair across from him.

"Wow Pantu! You still use books to do your research?" Queen asked.

He looked up to see Queen's voice match the look he was being given. "Yes Queen. It is easier for me to cite my work this way," he said, looking around.

He felt it again. Someone was watching him. If he could find a better safe zone during lunch where he wouldn't be bombarded with the same question asked multiple ways, he would go there. But for now, it was the library.

"What's wrong Pantu?" Queen asked.

"Just a feeling Queen." He shrugged it off and went back to his work.

"So, Pantu…how are you getting along on campus?" Queen interrupted his train of thought.

He put his pencil down and giving Queen his eyes, he told the truth. "Besides the fact I have a weird feeling someone is watching me, I am behind in all of my Advanced Honors classes, and I am pretty sure I have isekai'ed myself into a manga."

"You read manga?!" Queen asked.

"Yes, they were always available in any library I went to," he casually said, waiting for Queen to question his past. He wasn't going to answer and prepared himself to navigate the conversation around the topic.

"Hold on, be right back."

It wasn't the response he was expecting, and he watched as Queen spoke with the Librarian. She handed him something and Queen gracefully and happily walked back.

Maybe he would have lasted at least a day in The City. His thoughts were interrupted as Queen slid back into the chair, *and he is more graceful than any Woman in The City.*

Queen smiled as he slid a key over to Pantu. "Here you go!"

"What is this for?" Pantu asked, calmly looking at the silver key with a small, wooden label attached.

"It's the only student key to the Manga Room," he whispered to Pantu. "It's rare anyone gets the key, but I'm friends with Doctor Faye, the Librarian. You might be able to find a manga to read in there," he ended, with a knowing smile on his face.

"Why is there a locked room full of manga in a school library? Is a scary ghost in there? Are you pranking me?" The sound of Pantu's voice was the only indication this calm-faced young man didn't understand why the room needed to be locked.

He didn't take offense. He felt Pantu wouldn't question things unless he honestly didn't know or was confused.

"It's locked because it's also where the school keeps the banned books," he informed Pantu.

"Why keep them here if they are banned?" Pantu asked.

"It's the contract the school, students and parents agreed too. At first, the school removed the books from the curriculum, but students argued online availability, public library access, and bookstore purchases, so limiting our accessibility only on campus was fruitless.

"Parents compromised by allowing the books, but their child would need a signed note on file to check out anything from the room. Hence, the locked room compromise," he said. He looked at Pantu like he was speaking to the most precious child ever.

"By students...you mean..." Pantu trailed off.

"Sport," he quipped. "Sport is an avid reader," he added.

Pantu's face showed the quickest flash of surprise as the information registered.

"What's on your mind?" he asked as Pantu went quiet.

"I am trying to figure out what to give you for verifying some information for me. You already have Favors cornered, so what do I have, that would be worth you informing me of what I want to know?" Pantu asked, with a beautiful, but soft, knowing smile.

"A custom nametag please!" he immediately and happily answered.

Pantu's small laughter of agreement was too high-pitched and sweet to be a chuckle.

When he felt himself blushing, he instantly agreed. "So, what would you like to know? If it isn't the personal business of someone else, I can answer it," he said, quietly cheering at getting a nametag from Pantu and calming his enflamed cheeks down at the same time.

"If I were to accept one's invitation to Drum's party, what would they receive in return?"

He looked surprised and answered without asking the question he so desperately wanted to know. "A choice at his birthday party between twenty minutes in Heaven with the Being of their choosing, with assistance from Drum's older brother, Pong, or five minutes alone with Drum." As he said this, he carefully watched Pantu's face, but he was given nothing. *Was earlier a fluke? He's good at controlling himself,* he thought, *when Drum's not around.*

PANTUxDRUM: THERE IS A MEETING IN THE MANGA ROOM
WEEK TWO: WEDNESDAY

"Hmm," Pantu said.

He looked at the key and decided to do what Queen so obviously wanted him to do, go into the Manga Room. He assumed Drum was in there, and he wanted to prove to himself it was only the cinnamon-honey scent, not the male who aroused him.

He stood and placed the books he was using back into their correct places. He noticed the Librarian smiling in kind at him. He packed his bag and headed up the stairs to the locked door.

Using the key, he entered and looked around. The door closed and locked automatically behind him. He dropped his bag by the door and started looking through the rows of books.

He passed the banned books and arrived at the manga section. Looking at the titles, he started talking to himself out loud. "I have read this one, so it is not what I am looking for. 'The Second Time I Relived My Life as a Slime?' Well, that will not work since I am not a slime.

"Berserker sounds like how my life is going right now." He picked up the book and flipped through it. "Nope! That is not it, but it is graphic and intriguing. I am adding it to my list to read."

As he moved up, down and around the shelves, he was actively looking for a manga to solve his problem. "I am not even the main character of my own life. Who has a harem of Women and males? There must be one which is at least similar."

As he came upon the last row, he walked around it and was startled. He jumped as he noticed Drum sitting silently at a desk, watching him with a smirk. Drum had a book opened which was quickly closed and stashed in the backpack on the table.

"You read manga as well?" he asked.

Drum nodded. "It's how I know you painted The Moon Demon TiKa on my nametag." Drum pulled out his keychain. The tag was now glossed and inlaid on a small thin gold slab attached to the keychain the young male carried with him.

He smiled and looked away while biting his lip. "So, *he does like it,*" he softly said.

Drum tried to hide a smile, but a bit of it slipped out, making the young male turn from him.

"Was it a manga you were reading?" he asked.

"No. It's a manhwa."

He looked at Drum with a raised eyebrow, asking the question with his face.

"It's another form of Eastern manga. Written in Hangul," Drum explained.

Both his eyebrows went up with respect Drum was able to read Earth's Korean language, which was seen as dead, because it was no longer fully spoken on Torven. He was wondering just how much this young male in front of him knew about the true history of this planet and their people.

"Hmm. Have you read a lot of them?"

"Naturally."

"Maybe you can help me?" he asked.

"Maybe," Drum answered with a shrug.

"I am looking for a manga, or manhwa, where a character has isekai'ed themselves into another world where the main character has a harem of Women and males but the isekai'ed person is just a side character," he said in one breath.

"That's oddly specific," Drum said, with a light, but slightly deep, laugh.

"Yes, well, I need a guidebook," he said, and slid into the chair across from Drum.

The young male raised his eyebrows; crossed his ankles; folded his arms across the table and leaned forward. "A guidebook? Have you been isekai'ed?" Drum asked. A huge grin graced Drum's face and he needed to look away from the reason his Light was flowing faster due to the increased beat of his heart.

"It feels like I have. I am wondering why I do not even feel like the main character of my own life anymore," he responded, looking around the room.

"So, make yourself the main character," Drum stated.

He waved off the comment as he spoke. "It is impossible. The main character is actually not a bad person. And there is no way I would ever be able to outdo him. He is everything good about life all wrapped up in a perfect person." He rolled his eyes. "Besides, it sounds *exhausting* being the main character and I have exercise-induced allergies," he added, meekly.

Drum laughed. "Oh. If that's the case, what's the guidebook for?" Drum inquired.

He was still not looking directly at Drum. "I want to know what to do when I am no longer the main character of my own story...I mean life." He shook his head and started over. "I just need to know how to survive until I graduate."

"Oh. Only until then?" Drum asked, but the tone of the words were heavy and unhappy, causing him to look directly at the young male.

"Well, I am unsure where my life will go after that," he said, quietly.

Drum nodded and looked away from him, which made him feel unhappy. He ignored the fact he enjoyed when Drum's eyes were focused on him and decided to only give way to the unhappy feeling of Drum's eyes ignoring his face.

"Hmm. I have an idea of something but it's not a manga," Drum told him, still not looking at him.

"What is it, a manhwa?" he asked, trying to catch Drum's eyes, but Drum avoided him.

"It's called a donghua."

"A what?" he asked.

Drum leaned back and stretched, causing him to take a slow deep breath as he watched, and he released it just as slowly. Even if it was the scent which invoked feelings inside him, the young male sitting in front of him was covered in it.

He understood he would have been killed if Yolk was Drum and the realization shot him back to what he considered was reality, The longer he sat there, the more a second scent was becoming prominent in his nostrils.

"Donghua. It's another version of Eastern animated shows. It's in Mandarin," Drum said, after he finished stretching.

"Ah. I do not watch TV," he said, with an ah well, I tried, kind of attitude. But really, he was trying to hide how impressed he was.

Drum was able to read two "dead" languages, and he wondered just how intelligent the young male sitting across from him was. *That would make four languages which can be understood by Drum. Thaikoriense, Korean, Mandarin and the one I cannot wrap my tongue around, English.*

"It's also a novel," Drum added.

"I do not read Mandarin," he said, defeated and unhappy he wouldn't be able to read the one story which could possibly help him. He put his face in his hands, unhappy.

"It's a pretty popular novel so it's been translated into almost every language on this planet," Drum said, completely defenseless against his pouting face.

Drum's reaction to him made his face light up at the new information. "Aaaahhh! What is it called?" He looked at Drum with a giddy smile and Drum smiled back, while turning away.

"I don't know if it's the right genre for you though. I don't think you would be into Danmei."

He pouted again. "Is it about a person who is not the main character of a story they isekai'ed their way into?" he asked, with an unhappy look on his face.

"Basically." It was all Drum could get out, and he watched as the young male opted to pocket his hands instead of touching him.

"Does the main character have a harem?"

"Yea, at first."

"Does the person find a way out?" he asked, leaning forward.

"You could possibly say that, depending on how you read it," Drum said.

"Then I want to read it. I do not care about the genre if I can find some tips on how they survived," he said, with confidence.

Drum smiled and shook his head. Looking down at his nametag and running his fingers across it, Drum quietly gave the title of the novel. "'The Reverse Hero's Self-Serving System'."

He repeats the name and gets up to look for it.

"It's already checked out."

"Then I will try the town library after classes," he said, and sat back down.

"Not there either. Do you really want to read it, despite the genre?" Drum asked, and opened a silver, square laptop with stickers all over it.

"Well, yes. It sounds like it will help," he said while identifying all the stickers he knew.

"I ordered the book. It will be at the Little Shop of Books Friday by o'ten sr and you can pick it up any time after," Drum told him, after typing a few keys on his laptop.

He looked at Drum but didn't say anything as his Light started to become frazzled. *Maybe this was not a promising idea*, he thought, unsure of the repercussions.

"I ordered it under my name," Drum told him.

He calmed down and nodded. "I should expect nothing less from the MC," he said.

"I'm the main character of YOUR life?" Drum asked, with wide eyes and a small smile.

He said nothing as he realized what came out of his mouth. *I have never slipped up like this before*, he thought to himself, looking down to hide his overheated face. Drum's happy face made him smile despite himself.

"Wait! I don't have a harem!" Drum said, looking off to think.

He laughed at the look on the young male's face. "You most certainly do. Almost everyone on campus wants to be your One."

"OH!" Drum said, looking questioningly at him. "Almost everyone?"

He nodded. "I am not sure about straight males wanting you, but you have all the young Women and...gay...males wanting to be your One and Only."

"Oh," Drum said while staring at him.

"Thank you for the book recommendation, but do you not have a class after lunch?" he asked, changing the subject as he leaned back in the chair.

"It's cancelled," Drum said.

"Ah! That is why you are here. By the way, what were you reading?" he asked, leaning forward.

"Something you wouldn't be interested in."

He huffed at Drum. "How do you know?"

"Because I listen when you speak," Drum told him.

The shock his Light gave him was quick to appear and the same to leave. He avoided Drum's eyes but still smiled. "Are you embarrassed by the genre?" he asked Drum, in a teasing voice. "Is it romance?"

When Drum didn't reply but looked away, he clapped his hands together and squealed. He quickly looked around since he was being rather loud, but Doctor Faye had yet to come in and tell them to be quiet.

"You read romance books?" he whispered. "I thought you did not have those types of feelings?" he said. He was completely interested in the path of this conversation.

"I never did...before," Drum said back, while refusing to look at him.

"It is Kat! Is it not?!" he asked before a laugh. "She is a shoo-in to win your heart, so, did she?" He lowered his long eyelashes to softly eye Drum.

"I don't think Win would like me making a move on his girlfriend," Drum casually said.

His long lashes felt like they were touching his eyebrows as he looked directly at Drum. "I thought no one on campus dated," he stated.

"Not openly, so if you say anything, Win will kill you," Drum whispered. "Literally kill you."

He looked up. "I heard nothing. Who am I to tell the business of another?" he said, finally noticing the sparkling royal-blue Light covering the ceiling.

Drum laughed. "I see why Queen likes you."

He was really enjoying the game of eyes they were silently playing. If Drum looked at him, then he would look away. When he looked at Drum, the young male tried to hold his eyes but when he smiled, Drum would smile back before looking away.

"So, who do you have those feelings for?" he asked, quietly.

He didn't know why he wanted to know, and he didn't know exactly how he would feel if it wasn't him. He could accept Drum was now the main character, but he felt self-entitled to Drum's attention.

He was accustomed to being the number one adored person in The City. His G-Ma was the third most powerful Woman in The City and Indria was the second, so is that why he felt he deserved Drum's full attention?

He lived what people called a spoiled life in The City, but they didn't know what happened behind closed doors to make him into the spoiled number one. The mental, physical, and emotional abuse he had to endure. Drum didn't answer but just looked him directly in the eyes. His Mind went blank as he looked back into Drum's eyes, before rolling his own.

He huffed. "Fine, do not tell me. It is not like we are close or anything."

Drum looked down and smiled.

"May I see the book?" Pantu asked, politely.

He smiled and frowned at the same time while shaking his head. Pantu stood up and went for his backpack.

"You really don't want to do that," he stated.

Pantu paused, eyeing him suspiciously. When Pantu opened his backpack, he suddenly placed his hand on the bag close to Pantu.

"Understand you decided to be nosey," he said, before removing his hand.

Pantu rolled his eyes and sucked his teeth while pulling out the book.

He looked at Pantu surprised. No one outside his family ever openly invaded his privacy or his property like how this young man just helped himself.

As Pantu flipped through the book, he landed on a page and froze to stare for quite a bit of time, definitely longer than a minute.

"I can take a photo and frame it for you if you like?" he told Pantu, as he stood and closed the gap between them.

Pantu snapped back with a quick shake of his head. Blushing, Pantu quickly closed the book and put it back in his backpack, zipping it up.

He stepped forward until Pantu backed up against the wall. He placed his hands on each side of Pantu without them touching.

As he moved closer, he could hear both their hearts speeding up. Their breaths came quietly from their parted lips as he stared into two beautiful, bright, light brown eyes. Unable to handle the intensity of his gaze, Pantu's eyes closed.

"Pantu," he whispered, close to a darken red ear.

Pantu's whole body shivered, and his eyes snapped open, to slowly raise those adorably long lashes to look him in the eyes. Pantu slowly stretched his hand but stopped when a thought flashed across such a stunningly beautiful face.

This made him step away and move to sit back in his chair. He folded his arms on the table and thought he may have pushed too hard on Pantu, who would probably leave the room. But when Pantu sat back down in the other chair, he looked up in surprise.

Pantu blushed, quickly looking away to hide his face. "I thought there was only one student key, so how did you get in?"

"There's a private entrance only I can access." He waved towards the direction it was in.

"Is this your private room?" Pantu asked, while looking around.

"Not exactly. If a student wants to check out a book from here, they can ask the Librarian. If I'm not in here she will give them the key." He watched Pantu's reaction to the information.

"And if you are?" Pantu inquired, with a tone stating he knew Queen got the key with the knowledge he was already in the room.

"Long as there's a signed consent form, they can request the book, and she will have it available by the end of day classes," he said.

Pantu didn't say anything, just looked in his general direction without looking into his eyes. Whatever Pantu was thinking, stayed unsaid as the bell rang. He was visibly upset at the interruption, which for some reason made Pantu add a smile while standing to stretch.

Pantu walked to the door, and he listened as Pantu picked up his own bag to wait for him. Pantu jumped at his use of Instant, but he only gave Pantu a half smile as he removed his Barrier when he opened the door so they could leave together.

Walking through, Pantu mumbled a *thanks Drum* and was shocked to see Queen still sitting in the same chair, reading a book. Queen closed the book and gracefully stood, and he was sure the swaying flow of Queen's happy Energies was due to assumptions about what happened in the room.

"How can a male be more graceful than a Woman?" Pantu asked quietly, as they descended the stairs.

He answered from behind Pantu, leaning in close to whisper, *"It's his natural Ability."*

When Pantu shivered and looked around the library, he immediately turned on all his Enhanced Senses along with his Awareness to find what or who was making Pantu feel uneasy. The only thing he found out of place was a small snake with a weird Energy signature inside the library.

"Are you okay?" His soothing voice pulled Pantu's attention away from finding who the feeling was coming from to have Pantu look him in the eyes and smile.

"Ah? I will figure it out," Pantu responded.

Queen sucked his teeth and stood right in front of them with his hand out. "I'm checking out this book and returning the key, so wait for me," Queen said to him, and he nodded, trying to figure out why the Energy signature of the snake wasn't normal.

"Do you always have an escort to class?" Pantu jokingly asked.

"We have the same class fifth period," he replied, smiling at Pantu while they waited at the bottom of the stairs for Queen.

Pantu looked away with a roll of his eyes.

"What class do you have next?" he asked.

"Advanced Honors Level Six Foreign Language," Pantu said, with little enthusiasm. "It is not like I will ever visit another country to use the language, nor do I plan on being employed by an international company, so it is useless to me," Pantu added. But as he was talking, he was holding his arms, and his eyes were scanning the library again as if trying to find the source of an uncomfortable feeling.

He gave Pantu a puzzling look, but it went unnoticed. "Do you feel uncomfortable here?" he asked, concerned.

"Hmm," Pantu said, with a nod.

"I can have a key made for you to the Manga Room," he offered, and his response garnered a stare from the young man.

"Hmm," was all Pantu said again before Queen joined them.

"I should go." Pantu said and walked off.

ALEX: ONE PISSED OFF SASAENG
WEEK TWO: WEDNESDAY

Alex thought he knew Pantu's schedule but after the post from Queen about the reward for Drum's party, he was having trouble keeping up with the elusive student. He spent last week following Pantu, but Thursday and Friday were impossible as the routes changed between classes.

He was trying to find a time when both Drum and Queen were around to "run" into Pantu. He wanted them to know he knew the new student, since it seemed Queen didn't want any information from him.

"Maybe Drum would want to talk to me then," he said and smiled to himself.

But Pantu avoided being around Queen and Drum in the shared areas. He couldn't access the AH Levels for Juniors or Seniors as a First Year Liberal Arts student. Drum's homeroom class was in the AH Junior-Level area, and if he was fast enough, he could catch a glimpse of Drum moving from one area to another.

He didn't know what to do Saturday past, when he saw Pantu and his parents in Hollis, where he currently lived. He decided to follow Pantu back to his house using his motorbike while keeping his distance.

He was really surprised and upset when Queen, Sport and Win went for a walk with Pantu around town. He followed them, of course, and noticed they went into the forest area behind Drum's home.

"Are they sneaking Pantu to see Drum?" he asked himself but angrily dismissed it, since he knew Drum always left for the weekends.

They quickly came back out and when Pantu moved to make a phone call, he made sure he was close enough to hear what was being said without being seen. He looked at the black box connected to Pantu's phone and raised his eyebrows.

"Upgraded it huh?" He followed them back to Pantu's house and realized Win lived on the same street.

"The fucking convenience of it all," he said, pissed Fate gave this asshole everything he wanted.

He hated Pantu's existence. Ever since the first day they met in Hollis, he felt an anger settle in his chest. Pantu was taller than him, way too handsome for a man to be all by himself, a soft voice able to get Pantu anything he wanted, and the same scent as Drum.

He prepared himself to drip malice on every word to Pantu before he even talked to him, but when Pantu turned those soft brown eyes on him, he forgot he needed to breathe. He wanted Pantu every which way from the moons, but he was in love with Drum, right?

He hated Queen seemed interested in Pantu but didn't want any information from him. To hang out with any of "The Four" was already a huge accomplishment.

"Maybe Queen likes him?" He laughed out loud.

Pantu was straight and he knew this based on the first conversation he eavesdropped on in Hollis. He verified it with the second conversation, so he felt Queen was wasting his time. But he didn't care, Pantu was starting to get too close to Drum and he couldn't have that.

"Drum is meant to be with me and me only," he reassured himself. "I just have to find a way in," he said to himself as he watched Pantu's house.

He came back Sunday to see Pantu leave on a walk. He waited and his patience paid off when Pantu's parents also left. He let himself into the house and looked around. He took videos of the whole house, including Pantu's parents' room. He saved Pantu's room for last and he took a deep breath before going in.

He wasn't expecting Pantu's room to be so bare. There was nothing on the walls and no pictures of anybody in his room. There was a bed, nightstand, a computer desk with no computer and half of a bookshelf with hardly any books on it. There were a few clothes in Pantu's closet but that was it.

The scent was so sweet and delicious; he touched himself while trying to breathe in every particle inside the room. Before he took videos and pictures of the minimal room, he filmed himself masturbating on Pantu's bed. He couldn't find any dirty clothes in Pantu's room, so he submerged his face in Pantu's clean boxer briefs.

He went into the bathroom. There was nothing in Pantu's medicine cabinet and the bathroom only had one of everything. The bare minimum.

"My Universe is he living in a hotel?" he said out loud, unable to hide his disgust. He opened the drawers in the bathroom to find a hairbrush and a container of floss. After taking some of Pantu's hair, he left.

He looked around the room again and shook his head. "I guess he's not staying long so what's the need for material things."

He couldn't help himself though. He started touching Pantu's items on his nightstand, turning them slightly. He laughed, thinking Pantu would never notice he was here. He heard the garage open and running downstairs, he turned into his Form to slither out through the side door.

Monday and Tuesday, he was able to watch Pantu in the library. It was the only place he knew Pantu would be that was a shared area for all students.

When Queen showed up and started having a conversation with Pantu, he moved closer to listen but quickly realized he would be spotted if he came too close. When Pantu packed up to leave, he smiled.

Did Queen piss you off? Poor little Pantu. Always pouting, never getting your way, he thought. *And here I thought you were going to ruin MY life, but it seems like you can't keep yours together.* He snickered.

His smile was quickly lost when he realized Pantu was headed into the Manga Room. It was Drum's private room. The only one on the entire campus and Pantu went right in.

He was confused but reassured himself Drum wasn't in there. If he was, Pantu wouldn't be in there long, since Drum didn't like anyone other than his best friends being around him, in case of accidental touching.

He was stuck. He couldn't get to the stairs without being seen by Queen. To his surprise, Pantu stayed in the room throughout lunch. Now, he wanted to stay to be among the first to see the damage done to Pantu's body. But Queen also stayed in the library, reading.

Skipping his next class, he was livid when he saw Drum and Pantu leave the room together. When Drum whispered in Pantu's ear, he became enraged. For every breath which was hard to take, he wanted to bash Pantu's face in himself.

He couldn't hear what they were saying, and he wished he possessed Enhanced Hearing but when Drum smiled at Pantu, he started plotting Pantu's immediate departure from the town and this lifetime.

He ducked behind an aisle and turned into his Form as Pantu looked around again. It was only when Pantu left without Drum in tow, could he breathe again. "Son of a weak-willed bitch." He cursed Pantu and spat venom on the carpet.

"Ruin my life? I will end yours, socially, then physically," he quietly said.

He wanted to wait until Drum and Queen left the library, but when Drum's beautiful eyes stared directly at his hiding spot, he nervously backed away. When Drum walked towards him, he ducked the cameras and Beings, to slither out of the makeshift hole he made days ago.

"No one has done more than me to deserve Drum's time and smile." Using his Energy, he closed the hole behind him.

PANTU: READY TO LEAVE
WEEK TWO: THURSDAY

Today, he decided to skip the library altogether. The Malicious and Ill Intent he felt leaving the Manga Room with Drum, ignited a feeling of being unsafe inside him. He didn't appreciate the feeling, and since he didn't know who was targeting him, he became even more aware of his surroundings.

He didn't know if The Cloakless found him and was watching, waiting. But he wanted to leave Dill, Drum and Queen out of it. It also didn't help knowing someone was in his room.

When his parents came home Sunday and saw he wasn't there, his Ma sent him a text. His bedroom door was opened, alerting his Ma's phone. He excused it as not properly closing his door and ended the conversation. When he went into his room, he didn't notice anything missing, but there was a faint smell that wasn't his, or Drum's.

Items in his room were moved just slightly, and it bothered him, but he knew if he said anything to his parents, they would move again, possibly off the continent. They had gone as far as they could go.

He felt the only option left was to leave his parents here and go back. If his parents took him off the continent, he didn't know if he would be able to fund his way back to The City.

"I may have to leave earlier than I thought," he said to himself in Calculus class. *At this point, fuck the trust fund!*

As much as he tried to rationalize the feelings of people watching him, he couldn't rationalize someone being in his room. He pushed off the feeling of being watched until his room was violated. It was enough to make him ready to leave.

He didn't want to involve anyone from the town in his personal problems, so he was trying to figure out a plan, but his Mind kept coming up Drum. He knew Drum would be a treasure in The City and definitely knock him out of the number one position, but he also knew what came with the title and he didn't want Drum to have any part of it.

He was having a tough time paying attention in his classes and skipping lunch every day didn't help. He decided his plan now was to figure out how he could leave. His parents monitored everything about him.

If he missed a class, his Professor would text his parents. If he opened his window or bedroom door at home, an alert would be sent to his Ma's phone. The only money he could use was on his bank card, which his parents also monitored. He never managed his own money before, and he wasn't sure if there was enough to get back to The City in one trip.

He wouldn't use Dill to make his getaway, and he genuinely couldn't ask Dill to Lie on his behalf. His stomach growled and he was fighting to keep his eyes open. He was mentally exhausted and wanted to turn both his Mind and brain off. He was so wrapped up in his feelings and thoughts he didn't notice the look Drum was giving him.

DRUM: HOW TO PISS OFF THE MOST POWERFUL BEING
WEEK TWO: THURSDAY

He was upset. Not at the fact Pantu didn't come to the library for lunch or even look at him during class, but at the look on Pantu's face during Calculus. Pantu looked distracted, scared, confused, tired and hungry.

When Pantu's stomach growled, he took out his phone and using their group chat, asked his best friends to bring food for the hungry young man next to him. He didn't know what else to do since Pantu wouldn't talk to him about what was going on.

He wanted to be the one to console the absent-minded Being igniting these new emotions inside him, but he knew Pantu was still afraid to touch him. He thought they would be able to talk to each other after yesterday, but there seemed to be even more distance between them.

He wanted to know what was happening so he could fix it. It was making his heart break to see Pantu like this. The more distraught Pantu was, the more he felt the hurt coming from the young man.

When class was finally over, he spoke to a sluggish Pantu. *"Can you wait a moment, Pantu?"* he asked, gently.

Pantu seemed out of it, and he watched as tears formed in the corners of Pantu's eyes.

If he cries, someone is going to get hurt, he thought to himself. He was trying his damnest to control the Heat rolling off his body, but the angrier he became, the hotter his Heat.

His best friends entered and headed directly to Pantu's desk. Sport opened the food containers while Queen placed them in front of Pantu. Win sat on a desk out of the way to cross his arms and stare at the food.

When Pantu looked up surprised, then over at him, he was already staring out the window, avoiding Pantu's eyes and any questions. His best friends could feel his Heat and knowing he was pissed, they said nothing.

When he saw Pantu was eating, he left the room. He felt everyone's eyes on him, but he was helpless. He didn't know how to make Pantu smile, and it was killing him, literally. He went to the library and walked around the main floor searching for the weird snake his Awareness sensed yesterday.

There weren't any snakes in the library today, so he tried to smell any overwhelming scent, but it had already been a day, and he knew the Cleaning Club took their activities seriously.

When he couldn't sense or smell the snake, he searched for abnormal Energy and found some. A tiny patch of it hidden in the non-fiction section, a corner of the library where there were no cameras. As he leaned his head back in frustration, Queen was there for support.

"Pantu won't talk to me Panya and I don't know what to do?" He was trying to keep it together. His emotions never became unstable since the incident. Not like this. "I know someone was making Pantu feel uncomfortable yesterday. It's why Pantu didn't come back today. Someone else is stalking Pantu. But there are so many smells, and I don't know if the Being came back today either," he rambled to Queen.

"You are the number one student on campus for a reason," Queen replied, telling him what he needed to know without saying it directly.

"Who wouldn't want to stalk Pantu?" he asked, confused. "They like Pantu!?" he added, in anger.

"Suppade, you're about to go off the rails," Queen said, quietly.

"Why not? Why can't I be pissed off?" he asked, refusing to look at Queen's Energies.

"You're not one to half-ass anything." Queen told him what he already knew. "If you go off the rails, the whole town would be destroyed. If they run, you would burn down the whole planet."

"Would it help me find who's stalking Pantu?" he asked. His tone was deadly serious as he read Queen's Energies, hoping for a yes, but he knew he wasn't going to get one.

"It would kill everyone, including Pantu," Queen told him, knowing he wouldn't want to hear or do it.

"Suppade, if you care about someone, you can either be supportive or stay away. Trying to fix every trivial problem will only cripple the one you want to protect. Whoever sits *there*, must become strong.

"We can only support and encourage the Being to stand. A weak Being in *that* position is *not* the best idea." Queen knew he understood what was being said and everything that wasn't.

He nodded, knowing and trusting Queen already planned his future to include Pantu.

"Drum?" The soft sound of Pantu's voice made him turn away from the direction it was coming from.

He couldn't look behind him right now. He needed to find the other Being who was stalking Pantu. He went to walk away but Queen stepped in front of him. He stopped. He could and would never hurt Queen, he loved him like a brother. He stood there trying not to feel Pantu behind him.

"Can we talk?" Pantu asked him before walking to the Manga Room.

Pantu went inside and holding the door open, he followed. Pantu let the door close, watching it lock. As he walked up and down the aisles of books, his hands were in his pockets. Pantu didn't follow but walked along the side of the shelves looking at him.

"Are you unhappy with me?" Pantu asked, softly.

"No, Pantu. I'm not mad at you," he said, gently.

"I would rather you were mad right now, but you seem unhappy?" Pantu asked.

He stopped and tilted his head at Pantu. "I'm unhappy I can't do anything," he said, leaving out the obvious.

"Win told me you asked them to bring food. Thank you. I have been out of it with schoolwork and not eating properly."

He stopped walking and looked down at the ugly carpet. "Pantu," he said. "Are you Lying to me?"

Pantu looked down as well. "No. I cannot Lie." Pantu looked up at him. "I always needed to look a certain way where I am from, so I am not used to being able to eat what I want, when I want. I am also learning how to balance having a social life which does not include death behind every corner with physically attending classes. It is a lot."

"Your face yesterday was of someone being stalked," he started. "You were frightened. What am I supposed to do? *Let someone scare you away from...?"* he whispered, trailing off.

"I do not know for sure if it is the case. It is only weird feelings I keep having," Pantu told him and moved closer towards him. "Maybe I am overwhelmed?"

"Are you going to leave?" he asked.

"I—" Pantu stopped.

"Pantu?" he asked again, his eyes pleading for an answer.

"Could you just be my friend?" Pantu asked.

He looked into Pantu's eyes for the longest moment before nodding.

"Can you let me handle this myself?" Pantu asked him, softly pleading.

He refused to answer while continuing to hold Pantu's eyes and was given a weak smile as Pantu accepted he wouldn't handle this alone.

"Pantu."

"Yes Drum?"

"Just to clear the air, I've been stalking you as well."

"I figured, but I have never felt any Ill Intent from you," Pantu said, giving him a small, tired smile.

"I won't stop…even if you leave," he added, before turning to exit out of his private entrance, leaving Pantu standing in shock by what he said.

QUEEN: THE BEST WAY TO PISS OFF A QUEEN
WEEK TWO: THURSDAY

He wasn't expecting the day to end like this, but it helped to add an 's' to his perspective when it came to making his plans. He never had the pleasure of experiencing even a minor change to his plans before and it caused the right side of his Mind to throb a little.

He was always so confident, it felt natural to be set in his ways when it came to the Beings in town. He knew the disposition of everyone who lived here, but Pantu was throwing him for a loop. He couldn't get a definite read on Pantu and now he needed to find who was about to have Drum burn everything down to the ground.

He felt a heavy weight on his back as if the whole of the planet settled right between the curve of his shoulder blades. He knew his best friend was experiencing new and unknown feelings, so if Pantu left, Drum would follow.

It became a bit harder to breathe as he went over everything from the last two weeks of Pantu being in town but stopped when he realized Drum's affections for Pantu might already run deeper than he thought.

Drum only accepted individual gifts from his family. Even as his best friends, Drum would only accept a collective gift from them, and only on his birthday. Drum turned down every Gift offered to him…before.

The nametag was a Gift for Drum, and I just asked Pantu to make me one! His thoughts made him a bit scared his best friend might also be pissed at him, thinking he was trying to flirt with the one Being Drum was ever interested in.

But he could only calm his best friend down enough to let Pantu talk him out of going nuclear. At this point, whoever this stalker was, they would be used.

"They're obviously obsessed with Pantu. I have to make them show themselves to me," he said, as Win and Sport looked at him, concerned on their faces at his stooped body. His tight shoulders pulled closer to his face, and his right middle finger was pressed into the side of his temple.

He was thoughtful. "Have you noticed Pantu looking around in class?"

"Nope!" Win said and Sport shook his head.

"So, it's probably not someone who has easy access to Pantu. We also don't know when Pantu started to feel like this. Pantu has been coming here every day, yet no one approached Pantu while alone," he thought out loud.

"Do you think they may be waiting for a certain moment?" Sport asked.

Win nodded. "Like when Pantu is around certain...people?"

"Common areas could include a Liberal Arts student," Sport added.

"Hmm," he agreed.

"Let's see if we can trigger the stalker," Win said.

He stared at Win as the right side of his Mind throbbed harder. "Are you willing to put your life on the line if said stalker goes crazy and harms Pantu? The lives of the people you love, everyone in town and on the whole planet?" he asked, seriously.

"Yes," Win said, confidently. "If we can't protect the only one Young Master has ever liked, then how are we qualified to stand behind him? To even be considered his best friends?"

He looked at Win with so much affection, Win foolishly grinned back.

Sport smiled and nodded at Win. "That's the Win we know and love."

The compliment from Sport made Win blush.

"You are absolutely right Win, my dear," he said, as he regained his confidence and Grace. He realized he lost it after Drum was so distraught.

"Let's find and use this bastard until we've dried them up. They fucked around and made Pantu scared which set Young Master off." As he gracefully and confidently straightened his spine, Win and Sport smiled, nodding in agreement.

"The bastard who made me doubt myself and almost lose my Grace; my confidence; I will have their life ruined. They will never get what they want"—he looked at Sport and Win—"we will make sure of it."

SKY: HOW TO LAND A JOB WITH NO FORMAL INTERVIEW
WEEK TWO: FRIDAY

She arrived right as the person was unlocking the door.

"Ah! HI! My apologies!" she exclaimed.

"It's okay!" The older Woman laughed. "The store opens at o'ten sr on the dot every day." The Woman smiled at her.

"My child sent me here. I was told there's a package I needed to pick up, and it would be ready at o'ten o'clock. I didn't know you also opened at o'ten sr," she said, apologetically.

The older Woman just smiled and let her through the door. She had to pause as she took In the store. It was spacious, with three levels of shelved books covering the sides and the back of the store.

There was a staircase on the right side leading to the second floor, which was the only level to have bookshelves around the whole floor. On the first and third levels, there were oversized windows in the front and back of the store.

The left staircase led to the protruding third floor. Wider than the second floor, only the sides of the level were filled with bookshelves. This left the circular middle free for customers to lounge in comfy sofa chairs on the first floor. Or they could relax in one of the bar's highchairs at the tables surrounding the sofas.

Standing in the middle and looking up, was like looking through a telescope. There was a circular hole with a glass roof showing the bright sky. There were posters of what she assumed were the more popular titles, hung behind the register on the first floor.

The barista stand was made for one, maybe two if they worked well together, to make drinks and serve food. She realized the bookstore was much bigger on the inside than the tiny three-story building showed on the outside.

The smell of freshly brewed coffee and baked goods made her stomach growl, and her smile widened. She never felt so at home. She loved the layout of the store, and the smell relaxed her. The older Woman was still smiling as she took in the store.

"Have a seat! I will get you a drink and a pastry," the older Woman offered.

"AH! Thank you, but I'm just here to pick up a book for my child," she said, continuing to turn in circles to look around the store.

"Okay. Just give me your child's name and I will look up the order," the Woman told her.

"It's not the name on the order."

"Then your name?"

"It's not under my name either," she said, embarrassed. She stopped turning and took out her phone, looked up the text message, and gave the name of the book. "It was ordered by a young man named Drum," she told the Woman.

"Drum?" the Woman asked her.

"Yes? My child said, *Drum ordered this book at the 'Little Shop of Books' for me. It will be there Friday at 010 sr,*" she read the message.

"Drum ordered a book for someone?" the Woman said out loud to herself. "That's a first!" the Woman added, then laughed.

"Ah, do you know Drum?" she asked politely.

"Yes, he's my grandson. I was hoping to find the book before today, but the last employee I hired rearranged all the book genres and added call numbers. Now it takes days to find a book I have stocked. I don't know why they used the library system in a bookstore but didn't update the computer?

"Let me get the author's name and call number for the book and take another look around. The rush won't be here until o'twelve, so I have a little under two hours to find it." The Woman went off towards the register, comfortably talking to her.

"Is it just you here?" she asked, looking around at the empty store.

"Yes. I run it by myself until I can find someone else." The Owner winked at her.

"I could help you look for the book as well. I might find a book or two to read myself," she enthusiastically offered.

"Oh! That would be great dear!" the Owner accepted.

She quickly found the book, picked up a book for herself as well and went back to the register.

"This book is a series; would you like to order the second, third and fourth one as well?" the Owner asked her with a smile, as a cup of coffee and a bakery treat moved towards her.

"That would be great! My kid loves reading and once my child starts a series, the kid reads it all the way through," she told the Owner. She was happy she might get a smile out of surprising Pantu and the taste of the baked treat.

"There are also two other series, written by the same author, do you think your child would be interested?" the Owner asked.

"I can have it as a surprise. Our bookshelves at home are pretty empty," she said with glee, as she clapped her hands together.

"I have the first book in each series in stock here but will have to special order the remaining." The Owner gave her the books' names and call numbers, watching as she headed off to look for the other two titles which she finds easily.

"Wow! You have a talent for this!?" the Owner praised her.

She blushed. "Well, my Pa is amazing with numbers, and I was supposed to follow after him, but I wasn't good with them the way he needed me to be," she said.

"Maybe because you were meant to use your Ability another way?" the Owner asked, looking directly at her. "Like working here," the Owner snuck in, with a chuckle.

She could only stare at the Owner.

After a moment, the Owner continued, "This is a very popular author, for both women and...men," she commented, as she scanned the books into the computer.

She looked at the front of the three books and noticed each one had two young men on their covers. One cover looked as if they were getting married, but the guy was drawn so beautifully, she almost couldn't tell it was a man. She flipped one over and read the synopsis.

Doesn't seem bad, maybe it's about best friends, she thought.

As she scanned over the back of the book, the 17+ rating stood out along with the word Danmei. She took out her phone to look it up. It was a word in another language for a man-to-man romantic relationship. She flipped over the other two books and her eyes got wide. She bit her lip unsure of what to do. He told her to pick up this exact book.

"Just get the books. If your child doesn't like them, you can bring them back," the Owner offered to her.

"Ah okay. Thank you?" she said, with uncertainty.

"I needed to order these books anyways, I can hardly keep them on my shelves," the Owner spoke as she wrapped the books in nice paper and set each in the same decorative bag, before handing the items to her.

"I need to pay. How much do I owe you?" she asked, with her wallet in hand.

"How about you come tomorrow morning at o'eight sr and help me get the store ready for the weekend rush?" the Owner asked her.

"I would love to!" she answered, elated. She took another look around the store. "I really don't have much to do today." She looked back at the Owner. "Do you mind if I hang around?" she shyly asked.

The Owner smiled. "Not at all. By the way, call me MawMaw. Everybody does," MawMaw told her.

"Ah, hello MawMaw. I'm Sky," she said, as she held her hand out to MawMaw.

"It's nice to meet you Sky. Hang around and get a feel for the store. The elementary students should be coming around o'twelve o'clock for their weekly field trip," MawMaw informed her, after shaking her hand.

She nodded, face full of wonder as she slowly walked off, checking out everything in the store.

QUEEN: EASY LIKE SUNDAY MORNING
WEEK TWO: FRIDAY

He spent the first half of his day in his office in the AH Junior-Level building. He didn't have a test until AH Political Analysis, so he was moving Beings on campus and in town around where he needed them.

Gathering information that seemed unimportant to everyone else was how he was able to piece things together. Placing nature where he needed it was another way he gathered information without anyone knowing. It was how he knew who he could trust and when someone was withholding information.

He'd subtly and naturally infused nature underneath almost every Barrier Town belonging to The Royal Family with his Energies since Young Master taught him how in the second grade. It was an Ability he'd kept from everyone who wasn't his best friends.

Even his Adoptive family didn't know his full Abilities. He was able to communicate with Nature. Trees, minerals, plants, and the animals that needed them to survive, he could freely talk to them. He was able to ask for their help when needed, and in return, his or Young Master's Energies would be given as a thank you.

Young Master thought it best not to reveal all their Abilities, making their Level unknown and harder to counter. He knew what Young Master was up against and he was determined to make sure Drum came out on top. He wouldn't allow anyone else to stand above him.

Now since their Young Master found someone he was interested in; it was up to them to make sure Pantu was safe. He understood Sport and Win would follow his plans absolutely, as they always trusted him to guide them.

Young Master also trusted him, and it was a huge responsibility on his shoulders. But he wouldn't have it any other way as his life was made much better by just being around Young Master. Drum was more intelligent than all of them, so Drum knew he couldn't do everything himself.

"He really made sure to have the best around him," he said as he thought about their group.

He was the Planner, the Information Gatherer. He made sure Young Master didn't have to worry about logistics or his image on social media and was the buffer when Beings needed assistance.

Win was Young Master's Personal Accountant. He handled any and everything finance related. Young Master never needed to worry about whether he had money. Win was unnaturally talented when it came to numbers and investing was like an easy game of Janggi[40] for him.

Sport was Young Master's Bodyguard, or rather, everyone else's Bodyguard. Sport was also the Peacemaker for disputes in their friend group. In elementary school, when he first proposed no one call Drum Young Master, his best friend wasn't sure about asking his schoolmates to change their way of speaking to him. Even though it visibly annoyed Drum that everyone treated him differently when it came to the moniker he didn't ask to have, his only response was to ease Drum's displeasure.

He continued to press and finally the issue was resolved in middle school when Sport stepped in. Sport thought the locals, especially those in their age range, should get to know Drum, not Young Master. But only if Drum really wanted to be able to relate and show them who he truly is.

Sport said the next generation of Beings should feel comfortable around him, and Drum agreed. Sport was able to relate to both sides and find common ground. He knew the three of them altogether made it easier for Drum to breathe.

So, he knew what Drum was feeling when it came to Pantu. Wanting to fix every problem and make someone happy was what he'd been trying to do with Drum since they met.

Drum appreciated it but didn't want a problem fixer, he wanted a friend. He resolved to work behind the scenes of Drum's life and to be a best friend to the first Being who ever acknowledged his Abilities and accepted him for who he was.

He was able to be himself because Drum told him in the first grade, "I only want to be best friends with the you that makes you happy."

It was if Drum could see he was hiding and when he told Drum he liked guys, Drum encouraged and supported him through everything.

"How could I not wish for your own happiness?" he said, with a smile.

His plan was already in motion to draw the stalker out. Win informed Dill before homeroom, Pantu almost passed out from hunger yesterday. He knew Dill's disposition and could see how much Dill valued his friendship with Pantu.

He could see the instant connection between them, and felt Dill would be a great best friend for Pantu to have. If Dill was the Being he thought, and he couldn't remember the last time he was wrong about a Citizen, then this would work.

"Well, it's not today either," he said, as he sat at the lunch table with his best friends.

---

[40] *The Korean game of chess.*

Sure enough, Dill was coaxing Pantu into the lunchroom to eat. A scared Pantu looked around, and he smiled when he saw Pantu relax after realizing even though everyone looked at him, they didn't bother or approach. He watched, without looking, every move Pantu made and how the random group of Beings in the lunchroom reacted.

Pantu must have figured out Dill's a safe haven for him. He's more intuitive than I've given him credit for, he thought with a smile.

He's harder to figure out than I thought. Just because he seems like an Amish Romani, doesn't mean he doesn't catch on quickly. He was starting to like and appreciate Pantu more and more every day.

Hmmm, it seems like Drum's able to find the most extraordinary Beings and bring them together.

ALEX: THE STENCH OF INTENT
WEEK TWO: FRIDAY

He waited in the library but when Pantu didn't come again today, he went searching. Looking around the shared areas, he found Pantu in the lunchroom eating and laughing with his friends. It pissed him off.

How could he be so happy after making Drum smile at him?

He heard what happened after classes yesterday and it made him feel better. One of his "friends" happened to see Pantu headed to the library. His "friends" kept him updated on the happenings when he wasn't around.

It lightened his heart to know Pantu looked horrible and weak, but here Pantu was, having fun and being out in a shared area without being pestered by invites.

"Did someone win the reward?" he asked himself, as he watched Pantu through the window. He noticed Pantu started looking around again and smiled to himself.

"No one's won yet, or it would've been trending. But, if nothing else, his pain brings me comfort," he said to no one.

When he saw both Drum and Queen were in the room, he decided this may be his only chance to show Drum he knew Pantu. Hopefully, Drum would approach him and talk to him. If they knew what Pantu was planning, maybe they would leave Pantu alone or better yet, stop him.

"The spot next to Drum belongs to me," he reminded himself as he entered through the doors.

Making it look like he was casually headed to the lunch line, he walked as close to Pantu as he could. When Pantu turned with a look of disgust on such a handsome face, he was taken aback. He raised his eyebrows and decided to stick to his plan. If he made it seem like he and Pantu knew each other, he would have a way into the group, through Queen's crush.

"Pantu?!" he exclaimed.

But Pantu didn't answer. Instead, Pantu turned; shook his head and wiggled his nose, as if he was an adorable bunny trying to get rid of a horrible smell.

The whole lunchroom was watching as they still held their own conversations. Even Drum's eyes were looking in his direction, but he couldn't feel the intense gaze on him. He needed to make himself the focus of the conversation.

"It's great to run into you again. I didn't know we went to the same campus. How do you like it here?" he asked.

But Pantu's hand was over his nose and mouth. "You. Back up!" Pantu said, forcefully.

"Huh?" he asked, confused, and offended.

"You stink to low hell! Do you even know what a bath is?" Pantu asked, while trying to breathe through his mouth.

"YES! I TAKE ONE TWICE A DAY!" he shouted, upset Pantu was insulting him in front of Drum.

Pantu stood and walked the opposite way around the table to avoid him, but he stepped in front of Pantu, who went to throw his half-eaten food away.

"What do you want, you little snake?" Pantu loudly asked, while covering half his face with an arm.

"I wanted to say HI?" he said, mad Pantu was still implying he smelled.

"AH! NO THANK YOU! I do not need a conniving little snake like you being friendly to me," Pantu blatantly said.

He was so taken aback; he paused before whispering to Pantu. *"If you think you are going to ruin my life just by being mean to me on campus, you should know The Four hates bullies so much they end up in the hospital."*

Pantu moved his arm and after forcing himself not to breathe deeply, responded, "Is that why they are friends with you? Ah wait, I did not know you existed at this campus before now."

Pantu went to move around him, but he blocked Pantu's path again. "If I were to tell them what I know..." he said, with a friendly smile to fool those he thought couldn't hear the conversation.

Pantu whispered back, *"Keep your mouth closed before I tell everyone you like to fuck old men for money."*

His eyesight flashed red. *How the fuck does Pantu know?* He was so used to extorting those he thought could be used for information, or to get closer to Drum for so long without being caught, he assumed he was safe from his own actions.

"Kindly take me off your fucking list of friends!" Pantu expressed before leaving the lunchroom after dumping the trash.

He decided his only option was to cry and run out of the room. He entered Queen's bathroom and waited for them to check to see who needed help. But instead of Drum coming with Queen, it was Win. His disappointment showed on his face.

Queen looked at him for a moment before asking, "Do you need help?"

"Yes. There is a student who just threatened my life," he Lied to them. "I don't feel safe on campus," he added, making tears fall.

It was okay Drum wasn't here. Queen was really the one he wanted to get away from Pantu, and he knew Win wasn't fond of Pantu either, so maybe he could use Win's dislike of Pantu to get Win on his side, even if it meant breaking up The Four.

Queen gracefully slid onto the counter and swinging his legs, asked, "Who is this student?"

He started openly crying. "It's...the...the...new guy...Pan...Pantu."

Queen tilted his head. "Do you even know Pantu?"

He wiped his tears and snot on his sleeve as he continued, "When we first met in Hollis, I didn't know he wasn't gay. I tried to ask him out because well, he's extremely handsome, but he threatened to shove my own penis up my ass.

"I didn't know he went to this campus until the assembly, and I just tried to apologize to him, but he said he would end my life if I opened my gay dick sucking mouth to speak to him again."

"And who did and said all this?" Queen asked.

"Pa-Pantu," he stumbled out.

Win looked confused for a moment before he sucked his teeth. Win looked at Queen. "See, I told you."

By now Queen's face was full of surprise and Win looked disgusted.

"What do you want to do Queen?" Win asked, obviously pissed.

Queen shook his head and let out a breath. "Keep away from Pantu for now. I have to let the staff investigate this," Queen told him.

"You don't believe me?" He was indignant. *I even used human words to make it more believable,* he thought.

"We have no room on this campus for bullies. I will have Dean Hu speak to Pantu as an impartial party. Until then, stay away from Pantu and Dean Hu will make sure Pantu stays away from you." Queen slid down off the counter, and taking out his phone, started texting.

"What happens if he comes after me?" he asked, his voice trembling. He held himself, hoping his tiny frame and shivering body would invoke sympathy.

"Who?" Queen asked.

"Pantu!" he answered, dropping his arms in frustration.

"You said it yourself, as long as you don't talk to Pantu again, Pantu won't touch you...right?" Queen asked.

He froze. Did he say that? *Fuck, I should have used a different Lie. I thought since Queen was gay, he would immediately side with me.* He thought as he nodded.

"That shouldn't be hard to do since Pantu is an AH Senior and you're a Liberal First Year," Queen added.

Win didn't look pleased. "That's it!?"

Queen expelled another breath. "It's he said, Pantu said, so both sides are needed."

Queen said himself, he helped students on campus with any problem they had, but to him, it seemed like Queen was uninterested, passing his problem off to Dean Hu.

Maybe Queen really has a thing for Pantu? Someone as handsome and mysterious as Pantu would be able to entice Queen. But he felt a little better. He was right about Win not liking Pantu.

I might be able to use Win to get closer to Drum, he thought to himself.

"Win, can you walk him to his next class? I'm going to have a conversation with Dean Hu," Queen asked, sweetly.

"Yea," Win mumbled back and walked out the bathroom with him in tow.

He glanced up at Queen as he passed, but Queen was busy on his phone as it was pinging back-to-back.

DRUMxPANTU: THE RELEASE OF FEELINGS
WEEK TWO: FRIDAY

Queen's look let him know exactly what to do after Pantu left the lunchroom. Waiting to see the first year's reaction, they split as soon as the crying student left. He knew where Pantu was headed, and he was there, waiting in front of the Manga Room door. Pantu was so upset, he didn't notice.

"Pantu!" he said, softly.

The surprise on Pantu's face made him smile and when Pantu walked towards him, he was elated. They went into the room and headed to his desk.

They sat across from each other, and he didn't say anything for a minute while he let Pantu gather himself. He now knew who was also stalking Pantu, but he wasn't sure if Pantu put it together.

"How do you know Manpa?" he casually asked.

"That is his name?" Pantu asked, confused.

"He prefers another name, but I can't call him by it," he explained.

"Why not respect his choice?" Pantu questioned.

"Because he chose the name of my childhood best friend from my hometown to get my attention, but he doesn't know the full story behind their disappearance," he said.

"Ah! I never knew his name, and I never gave him mine, but we met in Hollis the weekend right before I started physical classes," Pantu told him, while looking at the desk.

"Did you talk to him then?" he asked, as he leaned forward.

"He overheard a conversation I was having and threatened to tell Queen, who I knew not at the time. But I mean honestly..." Pantu started, looking up at him, "who threatens to tell someone they do not know...business to everybody?"

He raised his eyebrows at the pause but decided to ignore it. "Pantu, did you threaten him back?"

Pantu took a tired breath and let it out. "Well, yes. I threatened to ruin his life if he fucked with me," Pantu answered, looking away, embarrassed.

"You might not know, but he's obsessed with me. He's been trying to date me for years," he said, with a smile.

Pantu eyed him, leaning forward. "Then date him Drum, so he will leave me the fuck alone. He will be so distracted; I could live in peace."

He laughed. "You think he wouldn't rub it in your face?"

Pantu looked confused. "Why would he care what I think about his relationship?"

Leaning back, he answered, "Well, you did say you would ruin his life, but if he gets what he wants..." He gestured to himself.

Pantu rolled his eyes.

"Would you really subject me to dating him?" he asked. "I will if it helps you feel more comfortable," he added.

Pantu looked at him, then turned away.

"Interesting way to tell someone you don't wanna be friends," he stated, a half-smile on his face.

"He threatened to tell my...business again. And I do not want to be friends with someone who has a permanent stench." Pantu looked lost in thought. "I swear I have smelled it before."

He nodded, understanding Manpa was slipping into the shadows of Pantu's life, while thinking Pantu wouldn't notice.

"What did you say back to him?"

Pantu looked away from him again but didn't answer and instead started playing with his nails.

"Pantu?"

The soft sound of his voice made Pantu look at him and pout.

"I told him if he says anything, I will tell everyone he sleeps with old men for money," Pantu answered, with an innocent look on his face.

"Pantu, it has to be true. Queen won't tolerate rumors being spread, no matter who starts it or who it's directed at," he said, softly. "He deals in truth."

"It is true," Pantu said, unwillingly. "I have proof," Pantu added.

Making a tent with his hands under his nose, he commented, "OH. You would have me date this kind of snake for your peace of mind?" He hid his smile. "I guess he would be able to teach me how to do it, for a price," he added, looking directly at Pantu, who had good enough manners to look ashamed.

"You're beautiful!" he said, after a long silence between them. He didn't mean to blurt it out, but Pantu was making him want to do things he wasn't even sure how to do.

"What? You know I am a male, with a working penis," Pantu said, moving back from the table and pointing both hands down to his genitals. "I am incredibly handsome, not beautiful," Pantu said, moving back up to the table.

It took so much willpower not to look where Pantu was pointing, since he knew he would be showing his obvious interest, but he wasn't ready to find out if he affected the young man the same way. He didn't know how he would feel if Pantu showed no interest in him.

"OH, then you are handsomely beautiful," he said.

Pantu looked confused. "Can someone be both handsome and beautiful?"

"I guess if you have a working member, you can." He shrugged.

Pantu laughed. "Well as long as I am not ugly, I will take it."

He looked at Pantu sideways. "You've never been ugly before, have you?"

"Nope!"

"You're so proud of that," he said, laughing.

"What! These are great genes. But I mean, it does me no good here. Everybody is waiting for you to pick someone. If not Kat, then are you going to randomly select someone? Pick a name out of a hat?" Pantu leaned forward. "I cannot get a Woman to talk to me for longer than a couple of seconds without an invite to your party. They refuse to be seen as a couple," Pantu said, dejectedly.

"I mean, you can hook-up, right?" he asked.

Pantu shook his head. "I would rather not hook up. It is much like sharing and that..." Pantu trailed off.

"*Relationships matter to you?*" he asked, gently.

"I have never been in what you would call a relationship, if I understand the sense in which you mean," Pantu answered confidently. "What about you?" Pantu asked back.

Shrugging his shoulders, "I don't know. I have never been in a romantic relationship before either," he responded.

Pantu looked shocked. "NEVER!?"

"No."

"What about a hook-up? How many of those have you done?" Pantu asked, with a mischievous smile.

"None," he answered seriously.

"AH! SWEET UNIVERSE!" Pantu shouted in surprise. "Are you a *virgin?*"

He laughed for a moment as he leaned back into the chair. "Why are you surprised? That must be the word you use where you're from. Everybody knows already. It's not a secret."

Pantu was stunned. "AH WOW! What do you call it here?"

He leaned onto the desk. "Depends on your Level of Comfortability. My Level was always Complete Abstinence, so my sexuality has always been a guess." He chuckled. "Have you never met someone like me before?"

Pantu's face was still reeling from shock. "Not at your age. I mean...once I...then I was not...now it feels like I am again."

He reached his hand across the table. "Hello Pantu. I'm Drum, Level Outercourse," he started, then smiled. "Nice to meet you."

Pantu stared at his hand and asked, "If I shake your hand, are you going to rearrange my face?"

He patiently responded back, "Are you going to leave me hanging?"

Pantu looked skeptical. "I thought you did not like people touching you?" Pantu asked, eyeing his hand suspiciously.

"I don't mind when you touch me," he said, softly.

Pantu looked him in the eyes and tried not to smile. "Hello Drum, Level Outercourse. My name is Pantu, Level Unknown," Pantu responded, as he reached out his hand.

The coolness from Pantu's hand calmed and soothed his Heat. It was refreshing. Being around Pantu, his body would always heat up and run hotter than what was normal even for him, but Pantu's touch was able to satisfy his Heat.

"You are really warm and inviting," Pantu said in a hushed voice while taking small breaths, as if trying not to smell too much of his scent.

"You have a cool, soothing touch," he said, trying to also control his breathing.

Pantu pulled his hand back slowly. He didn't want to break contact, but he also couldn't sit there just holding Drum's hand. As he looked into the young male's eyes, the green flecks started dancing as a smile lit his face and he was tempted to touch himself. He was trying to rationalize what he was feeling but couldn't, for the life of himself, think properly.

Soon as he could no longer feel Drum's hand, he immediately touched his own face. Rubbing his hands across his cheeks, as if he was trying to make sure it was all there, was only the second reason why.

"Thank the Universe, my face is still intact." He breathed out. But the first reason was him wanting to cool his own face as he felt his cheeks were enflamed.

"How could I destroy someone so handsomely beautiful?" Drum gently said.

His body reacted without a thought in his Mind or his brain. The warmth from Drum's handshake still radiated on his own and when the bright-faced young male said those words so softly and truthfully to him, his Mind, brain, and body disconnected.

What just happened? He knew the answer, but he couldn't admit to it because he couldn't even form the sentence in his brain, much less his Mind. His Light started ringing from the discord happening inside his body.

"Ahh...I have to go to my next class," he said.

"The bell didn't ring," Drum said, with a slight smile on his face.

"I...I thought I heard a bell?" he questioned himself. His nerves were clearly not responding to his Mind telling his body to calm the fuck down. He was looking around as he couldn't remember where the exit was while trying to quiet the ringing in his Light.

"If you're uncomfortable..." Drum trailed off.

"I do not...I just—" he started as the bell rings. "Ah class," he said, but made no move to leave.

"I thought you had free period after lunch?" Drum asked.

"Yes!" came his absentminded answer.

He was trying to figure out how to check his clothes without being obvious. He couldn't stand up and have a huge stain on his pants right in front of Drum. He was also trying to figure out why and how this happened. He couldn't decide which problem to solve first while trying to avoid Drum looking at him with a half-smile.

It is as if he knows, was the only clear thought in his head.

When he looked at Drum, his whole body tensed up and this time he was certain. He couldn't stand up. He may have been uncertain before, but he knew now there was definitely a stain. And a big one at that.

As he tried to hide what happened under the table, Drum smiled at him. He was sure Drum knew he just did the same thing in the bathroom, right here. He was feeling the release of all the tension which wound his muscles tight trying to figure out who was Maliciously stalking him with Ill Intent.

Finally, coming face to face with the stench, which was in his room, he used his True Vision to see what he was dealing with and was disgusted by the sight of the first year. But Drum was showing he was a man of his word. Just as quickly as Drum figured out, he was being stalked, Drum and his best friends showed him the stalker.

He was trying to name the emotions coming from his body after his Mind and brain refused to rationalize his feelings for him and instead, compounded everything to add to the stain on his pants.

When he opened his eyes, the first image he saw was of Drum's lowered eyes watching him. He saw the rise and fall of Drum's chest and wondered if Drum could smell him. He meekly looked at Drum and breathed out a quiet, *ahhh.*

The feelings in the locked room were heavy, and when Drum's eyes closed, he could tell the young male was trying to hold it in, but was unsuccessful when Drum's body slumped, giving up the fight. Drum's eyes opened and slowly looked at him. He could only hide his smile as the room smelled more of the field meadow than cinnamon and honey.

He could feel a heat cascading off Drum, which randomly flared hotter, but the more he paid attention to the heat, the more he sensed a pattern. Drum was trying to suppress his heat to keep him from feeling it. If Drum was aware of his Talent for reading Intent, what else was Drum aware of?

As he and Drum held each other's gaze, neither of them verbally admitted what happened under the table nor did they verify by looking. It was as if they silently agreed to challenge each other to see who would leave another stain on their pants first.

They both filled the room with emotions, trying not to be the first to cave. Their intense gaze was broken when Drum's phone went off, playing a beautiful but erratic song.

Answering it, "Queen," Drum said, still looking at him. "Uh huh...that's not good...okay...that was nice...I will tell Pantu." Drum closed his flip phone and placed it on the table. "You have to go sit in the Dean's office for a meeting," Drum said casually to him.

"What?" he asked, still caught up in the scents, emotions, and Drum's eyes.

"There has been a bullying complaint lodged against you," Drum told him, unbothered.

"Why would someone..." He trailed off, quickly realizing who did.

"Dill and everyone at your lunch table went to the office and gave their recorded statements," Drum added, watching his reaction.

But he didn't know what to think and it showed on his face. "Dill knows I am not a mean person," he said, sure of his best friend's thoughts of him but unsure of whether anyone would believe Dill.

"You're right," Drum said, waiting until their eyes found each other before continuing, "their statements were given on your behalf."

He felt inner relief and happiness, which he was sure showed all over his face and in his body.

"He's a good friend, that Dill. He had the whole table go to the office right after the incident to give statements," Drum told him. The look on his face for trusting his best friend made Drum smile in return.

"The complaint was filed after the statements were given," Drum said.

He rolled his eyes and his head into his hands. His phone went off and after he checked it, he exclaimed, "MY PARENTS HAVE TO MEET WITH THE DEAN TOO!" He groaned and slid down in his chair.

This is simply great, he thought, *where to next?* Off the continent was the only other place he could think of where his parents could hide him. He couldn't afford to get in trouble but as he slouched in his chair, with his hands over his eyes, he peeked and checked his pants.

He sat up, completely accepting he may have to move again and now concerned by the fact his pants were clean. He was certain he came at least once, but his pants showed no evidence of the deed.

Was it not a lot that came out? His thoughts contradicted themselves. *"I am pretty sure it leaked quite a bit,"* he mumbled so softly, it seemed it was still only a voice in his head. He looked at Drum who was smiling to keep from laughing.

PANTU: TRIGGERED
WEEK TWO: FRIDAY

He sat in the office; unsure while also fighting the trembling of his body as he thought he was about to be expelled or worse. He heard what the first year said to him, *"The Four hated bullies"*, and now he was being labeled as one. He didn't know what a bully was since they didn't have or use that word where he came from.

"We also did not use gay to describe male to male relationships," he said to himself.

"What's that sweetie?" Ms. Jo asked him.

"Ah, I was just saying the word gay is a new term for me." He shrugged as he commented.

Ms. Jo asked, "Well, what did you call a man in love with another man?"

"I would rather not say. Thinking about it, it is a derogatory way to describe a person," he said, unhappy he even knew the saying. He looked up as his Ma walked into the office and hurried to him. He refused to look her in her face or talk to her.

"PanPan? Are you okay? Are you hurt? How are you feeling? Do you need some water?" Her questions flew out.

He huffed out a breath. His Pa came in as his Ma was still looking over his body to make sure he was unharmed. His Pa didn't look at him, and he didn't acknowledge his Pa's presence. His parents waited with him in the office, and he listened as the end of six period bell rang.

He was silently praying his parents didn't have to move again because of him. He tried to think about how he could change his plan, again by the way, because of the slimy, two-faced, snake.

He sat quietly until Dean Hu's door opened and she invited them in. He went in last and noticed Doctor Robin was already sitting in the office. He looked around at the adults, assured with the knowledge he was about to be locked inside a mental hospital again.

I know I cannot survive in a place like that again, he thought, as he came close to tears.

He didn't want to sit down, but he didn't want to stand up. He didn't know what to do. Like his Pa, his body started to tremble, and he was holding back tears. There were too many unnamed emotions flowing through his body, so when his Ma took his arm and led him to a chair, pulling him down to sit, he was a robot. Gripping his hands together, he stared down at them until his Doctor spoke.

"Pantu, we are only here to hear your side of the incident," Doctor Robin said, gently inviting him to speak.

He looked at her, then Dean Hu and back to his Doctor.

"All she told and showed me was what was given to her as evidence. I would never violate your privacy," Doctor Robin said to him.

He nodded, trusting her.

"When did you first meet this student?" Dean Hu asked him.

He glanced quickly at his Doctor. "In Hollis, the Saturday before I started on campus, after our session," he answered honestly.

"Did you two have an altercation?" Dean Hu inquired.

"Not anything physical. He threatened to tell a conversation he overheard to Queen. I threatened to ruin his life," he answered, looking at his Doctor out the corners of his eyes.

Doctor Robin's raised eyebrow let him know she understood he'd left out some things but was still being honest. When she didn't press for details, or ask who he was having the conversation with, he took a calming breath.

"And that was the end of that meeting?" Doctor Robin asked.

"Basically. We exchanged words, but I never once touched him or said anything worse than ruining his life."

"What happened after that?" Doctor Robin asked.

"He ran off," he said, cutting his eyes at his Ma. "And I followed him."

"You did what Pantu!?" his Ma asked.

He looked down at the hardwood floors and became quiet. He missed the look shared between Doctor Robin and his parents as he closed his eyes, thinking his parents were probably going to tighten his restrictions.

No more going to Dill's home or being able to walk around town freely, he thought.

Dean Hu asked him, "When did you meet said student here on campus?"

He took a deep breath; let it out and answered, "Today. At lunch. I had no knowledge of him attending this campus. He told me the first time we met no stranger would be able to ruin him because Hollis was his home turf. So, I assumed he lived there, and I would never see him again."

Doctor Robin was taking notes while nodding her head.

She knows I am telling the truth, and that little bit of knowledge made him feel better.

"Pantu," Dean Hu started. "You have been here for two weeks, and you never saw him at this campus? Nowhere in the shared areas?" she asked.

He looked up at her. He felt something different about what she was asking, so he stayed quiet.

"I understand asking this when our campus is over twelve hundred acres sounds off, but I'm only asking because it is well known the student likes a particular...person who you..." Dean Hu stopped herself. "Queen is best friends with the...person this student likes, and you have been seen talking to Queen," she reworded.

"Before today, I have not seen him since Hollis," he answered honestly, which made Dean Hu accept his answer.

Whether or not she believed him, he was still unsure. His parents were quietly listening to the conversation, and he took a deep breath. He didn't want his parents to be upset with him. The mask he wore to cover himself and keep his parents out, was slowly cracking.

Just like Sakikuro Ichi's final form, he thought to himself. *I am quite sure I am in a manga now. It is gonna suck not having MC plot armor though.* His thoughts made him unhappy.

Doctor Robin asked, "Why did he say he approached you two weeks after you started here?"

"I'm wondering that as well," Dean Hu interjected. "I checked, and the student was present your first day on campus when you —" she stopped, looking at his parents.

"What happened on your first day PanPan?" his Ma asked, turning to him.

As he turned red and looked away from her, he noticed Doctor Robin was trying not to smile.

"Pantu was slightly embarrassed in front of the whole campus," Dean Hu answered. "But the students found Pantu's personality to be quite endearing," she added, with a smile.

He put his head in his hands and groaned.

"Ahhhh! My poor PanPan!" his Ma said, while rubbing his back.

He almost cried in his hands. He refrained from talking, looking at, or touching his parents for years and didn't realize how much he missed her touch. He didn't want her to stop, and was happy she continued, even after the answers and questions started again.

"He wanted to say hi. He wanted to know how I liked the campus," he told them.

"What was your response to him?" Doctor Robin asked.

His nose scrunched up as he responded, "I called him a conniving snake and told him he smelled bad."

"Pantu, do you know what a bully is?" Doctor Robin asked.

He took a guess. "A mean person who threatens someone else?"

"Not exactly," Doctor Robin said, as she wrote some more notes.

Dean Hu's face was trying to understand why he didn't know the meaning of the word.

Doctor Robin continued, "What else was said between the two of you?"

He thought for a minute and responded, "He said The Four would not allow bullying on the campus, so I needed to be nice to him, or they would put me in the hospital. He also said he would tell them what he knows," he told them, as he wanted to go back and avoid ever meeting the little snake bastard.

"So, he threatened you by using them?" Dean Hu asked, with a smile on her face, but her eyes held a bit of hardness in them.

He could now tell Dean Hu was not happy about this situation, but he was still unsure of what she would do, especially if he had to continue. Which, to his distaste, he had to.

"What else was said," Doctor Robin asked, after finishing her notes.

He looked down and behind him as if he didn't want to say.

"Pantu, being honest is the only way we will be able to handle this situation properly," Dean Hu kindly told him.

"I told him...I would tell everyone...he...fucks old men for money," he whispered.

"PANTU!" his Ma shouted. "How could you say that out loud about somebody?!" his Ma asked. "I'm so sorry, Pantu has never spread Lies about someone," she said, looking at Dean Hu. Turning to Doctor Robin, she continued, "Pantu has never Lied."

He took a breath and blew it out. "And I have yet to." He pouted, thinking his Ma didn't believe him.

"I know PanPan," his Ma gently said. "They don't know your personality."

"It's what you saw when you followed him that day?" Doctor Robin asked.

He nodded at her, happy someone understood, and his Ma believed him.

"This has become an even bigger issue," Dean Hu said. "If this is true—"

"I have proof," he interrupted and every adult in the room stared at him like he just confessed to being a serial killer.

"Pantu, where is it and have you shown or sent it to anyone else?" Dean Hu asked.

"It is on my phone, and I have not informed anyone but you all, and..." He stopped, not wanting to drag Drum into this. "I have not shown or sent it to anybody. *I forgot it was there until I saw him today,*" he mumbled, obvious to the atmosphere in the room.

"Pantu, I need your phone. And I can't give it back to you," Dean Hu said, calmly.

He fidgeted in his seat, unwilling to give up the one thing which was secretly keeping his family in The City alive. "Why do you need to take my phone? I will not be able to go anywhere without it."

"Pantu, what you have on your phone is sexual acts done by someone underage. A minor. It's called child pornography and it's illegal to be in possession of it." When Doctor Robin said this, he understood why he received those looks and why the snake felt safe enough to file the report.

He put his head in his hands and stumbled out, "I...I...I did not know." His Mind flipped so fast through every moment of torture, his brain couldn't keep up. "I am going to the cells for re-training. I will not last long there. I am too handsomely beautiful to survive. I..."

"PanPan, it's okay. We will stop by the store on the way home and get you a new phone," his Ma said, gently holding him.

He took his phone and placed it and the black box on Dean Hu's desk and backed away. "In order to see the video, the control box must be connected with a green light," he explained. "I am going to get in trouble for that, am I not?" he asked, nodding his head towards his confiscated items.

"As long as you didn't send, post or show anyone else, I will keep your name out of the police report," Dean Hu said to him.

"But they will know it once belonged to me," he said.

"I will have it cleared and untraceable before it's sent in as an anonymous source," Dean Hu said, mostly to his parents who nodded back.

"I do have one more issue we need to clear up," Dean Hu said to him.

He blew out a breath, wondering what other Lies the snake came up with. "Other than the fact I told him we are not fucking friends, that was all."

Dean Hu looked directly at him. "That was the whole conversation? You didn't threaten to, and I quote 'Shove my own penis up my ass or kill me if I ever opened my gay dick-sucking mouth and talk to Pantu again?' Did you threaten him because he is gay?" She placed a sheet of paper back on her desk.

"WHAT?!" he asked. "NO!" he answered, to which his parents looked lost.

"What's gay?" his Pa finally spoke and everyone except him looked at his Pa.

His Ma shrugged her shoulders and looked at Dean Hu for help.

"It's when a...person is attracted to someone of the same sex or gender," Dean Hu answered. "It is popularly and mostly used for men who like men."

His Pa turned to him. *"Are you one?"* his Pa softly asked, and he responded by rolling his eyes and turning his body away from his Pa.

"Darling, Pantu doesn't even know who *he* is right now, so how could he possibly know that?" his Ma asked, making both him and his Pa slowly turn to look at her.

"Wait!" his Pa said. "There are...*gay people* here?" his Pa asked, with a wavering voice.

He froze at the sound of his Pa's voice, knowing while everyone else heard the trembling, he heard a bit of happiness in his Pa's undertone. *My Pa has found a male he likes here?*

"Yes Darling. Gay people live here and it's okay. Nobody will be put to death." His Ma patted his Pa's trembling folded hands.

I have to find out who it is, he thought.

By now Dean Hu was looking at his parents while she spoke to him. "Pantu. I need two essays completed and on my desk by next Friday, the end of day classes.

"One will be on the definition of a bully. How to stop others from being bullied should be included in the essay. The second will be on Gay Rights. I will need three papers on the topic. Completed by you and your parents," she ended, looking at his Pa with a raised eyebrow.

His Pa nodded and looked down, but his face was still processing the idea two males could freely love each other in this town. Dean Hu turned to Doctor Robin, who nodded.

"I have received verbal statements from those around when the incident happened, and your account matches with theirs. I believe you didn't say the things the complaint said you did as you didn't have further contact with the student after the lunchroom," Dean Hu said as she organized the papers on her desk.

"These are the parameters of the complaint until the student can produce physical evidence or witness statements for Hollis. Follow them closely. That will be all for today. I will see you Monday Pantu." Dean Hu smiled at him.

He couldn't believe the outcome. He was fairly sure he was going to be expelled or placed in an underground cell, but he was given a chance to state his side. He didn't Lie about the incidents and even though he left out unnecessary information, they trusted him to tell the truth.

It did help everyone sitting at the lunch table heard the exchange, but how did Dean Hu know he didn't have contact with the snake after the incident? He was deep in thought when he bumped right into Dill.

"Ah Dill! You are still around!?" he asked, so caught off guard, he hugged Dill.

"Yeah Pantu, had to see what the verdict was," Dill answered, and hugged back.

"I have to write two essays and stay away from Mansna...the first year," he said, and his shoulders slumped.

"Yo, you are so behind with your late work! How are you going to fit two more essays in?" Dill asked him.

"She did give me till next Friday, so I guess I will spend this weekend researching and writing," he said, pouting.

"I will help you with the research!" Dill happily said.

He smiled big and laughed a little. "Wait! Do you still have to help your Pa?" he asked, losing his smile.

"Nah. We were almost finished so my Dad said he will handle the rest," Dill said, nudging him. "He likes to put his signature touches on orders like this."

His smile returned. "Nice! Thanks Dill!"

His best friend looked at him. "What's the essays about though?" Dill asked.

He held up one finger. "Bullying, and how to help others being bullied," he said, before holding up a second finger. "Gay Rights."

"Bullying I get, because of the type of complaint filed, but Gay Rights throws me for a loop," Dill said, scratching his head.

"Even though he said he was bullied for being gay, it was more for my parents," he said, casting a quick glance their way. "My parents were introduced to the word in the Dean's office, so she wants to make sure WE ALL understand and are RESPECTFUL of OTHER people's LIVES," he said, casting the louder words towards his parents.

Dill nodded. "Got it."

He pulled out a piece of paper and a pen. "I am going to need your number again," he said, as he waited to write.

"Did you break your phone?" Dill asked.

"As many times as I have dropped it, one would think," he said, meekly.

"Pantu, you suck at loopholing." Dill shook his head at him.

"It is not broken, but my connection to it is. I no longer have it," he said, hopeful Dill would let it go.

Dill started saying his number and he started writing, happy Dill understood him. After getting Dill's number, they started walking towards his Ma's car.

"So, did you meet him before? It seemed like he knew you," Dill asked, looking at him.

"Remember the little snaaa…male I met in Hollis?" he corrected.

Dill nodded. "Wait! That was him?" Dill pulled him to a stop. "The guy who threatened you when you first met?"

"One in the same." He smirked.

"He obviously knew you went to this campus since last week, why approach you now?" Dill asked.

He looked at Dill and shrugged. "Just to say hi."

Dill on the other hand, didn't look so sure.

"Yes, I think so too," he said.

Dill looked at him and nodded.

DETECTIVE LOCK: A MADE ASSET
WEEK TWO: FRIDAY

Queen was in the lobby of the police station asking to speak to him. He thought since Young Master and Sport were also with Queen and Win, they were coming to fill in some gaps he personally had with the Cove case.

Anything Young Master said would be strictly confidential, so no cameras or audio devices were on, and the two-way mirror was blacked out. He knew Sport's clasped hands meant there was a Barrier in place to keep anyone from trying to listen or see what was happening.

Once he was sitting in front of them, Win pulled out a phone, added a black box to it, waited a moment until a green light appeared, pulled something up and slid it across to him. He was confused, wondering if they recorded what happened.

"What's this?" he asked. "Evidence?" he answered himself. He looked up from the phone directly at Queen.

"Play the video, Detective Lock," Queen said.

He pressed play on the phone and took in the details. Set in a motel room, two Beings were talking while undressing each other. One was a well-known politician and the other he didn't know.

"Wait till the end," Queen said.

He let the video play, listening, more than he was watching. When it ended, he looked confused again. "He paid him?" he asked no one in particular and shrugged. Since sex work wasn't illegal in Sunset, he was wondering why he was being shown this.

"The shorter Being is a first year who attends classes on our campus," Sport stated.

His face showed immediate disgust. The legal age in Sunset is twenty-two, so one of the Beings in the video was underage.

"The phone is clean. When you trace it, you will come to a dead end," Sport stated plainly, letting him know to trace the phone for investigation purposes, but he would never know who recorded it.

He nodded.

"This happened in Hollis, but the Being has also rented rooms here," Queen added.

He took a deep breath; he knew how Young Master felt about a situation like this and he was honored to be trusted to handle it.

"Underage sex worker. Multiple johns. Here and in Hollis. I will check surrounding cities as well," he stated.

"This has to be done properly and handled quietly. We think he may have extorted others into this, so we don't want the workers to know what's happening." Drum finally spoke up.

"I have Beings here on the force who I trust with my life and a couple of private detectives still left in Hollis, Young Master," he assured Drum.

The four young men stood up and walked towards the exit. Win disappeared before he reached the door, followed by Queen, then Young Master. He couldn't see the Portal, but he knew Young Master made it. Sport paused and looked at him.

"Take your time." Sport continued to walk as he spoke, "Make sure to get them all," the young man added, before disappearing through the Portal.

He knew who Sport's foster parents were. They both worked and lived in the country's capital as High-Level Officials for the government.

Queen's Adopted Mother worked as a Diplomat in another country, while his Adopted Father was the Lead Advanced Honors Professor and the Head of the History Department at S.H.E[41].

Win's Adopted Father was the Chief Financial Officer of Sunset Town before recently being promoted to CFO of The Santiago Family Trust, while Win's Adopted Mother is the Elder Judge of the region. All decisions made in any courtroom in Sunset Country and all other Barrier Towns protected by The Royal Family, were finalized by her.

And then there were Young Master's parents, who are, well, the most important Beings on the planet. But most Beings, and even less humans, didn't know Young Master's parents' Energies were holding together the Sphere, keeping it from exploding, destroying the planet and everyone on it, Being or human.

Humans only knew Young Master's Father as the wealthiest man on the planet. He owned multiple five-star resorts and restaurants across a multitude of continents. He owned a successful world-wide music company and a private security firm used by the richest of Beings...and humans.

Being the Owner of the planet's first private, luxury, nonillion enterprise producing cars, yachts, jet planes, and homes also helped his bank account. The vast amount of investments Mr. Caleb made was handled by the eighty-storied-tall Headquarters, here in Sunset. He also owned several championship sports teams for fun.

---

[41] *A nickname for the university school of Sunset Higher Education.*

Young Master's Mother was the Empress of them all. She made sure all Barrier Town Citizens were happy and felt safe. She was a bright light to the town, and Citizens adored her. She's called "The Light of Sunset".

He knew she was involved in the country's only non-profit organization for the education system. She spread the organizations across the Barrier Towns, affording more Beings the opportunity to attend private institutions, and was on The Board of Directors for the Barrier Town Orphanages.

He took what they were asking him to do seriously. "I refuse to fuck this up. Not after what they did for my daughter, Kat," he said to himself, confident he would be able to repay them.

DILL: THE SCENT THAT BRINGS YOUR FATE
WEEK TWO: FRIDAY

Pantu's Pa left as Ma Sky went to introduce Pantu's Doctor to him. "Doctor Robin, this is Dill. Pantu's best friend." She motioned to him.

"So, you're the infamous Dill. It's nice to meet you," Doctor Robin said, as she held out her hand.

He politely shook the beautiful Doctor's hand. "And you would be?" he asked her, while looking at Pantu.

"My Psychiatrist," Pantu responded, not bothering to look ashamed, scared or upset.

"Wow! You're right Pantu!" He smiled at Doctor Robin as he inhaled her Scent. "But she is way out of your league," he added, then laughed at the shock on Pantu's face.

Ma Sky laughed along with him and even Doctor Robin let out a small laugh, although her mesmerizing blue eyes held confusion in them.

Pantu blushed. "I may have told him you...look good...are beautiful but, I meant it...not in a bad...nor in a romantic way." Pantu stumbled over the words, while playfully trying to hit him.

He was skillfully evading Pantu, while laughing. "Hey Pantu," he said, suddenly stopping to catch Pantu's swinging hand. "I'm your best friend?" he asked, smiling crazily from the revelation.

Pantu lost his smile and looked at Ma Sky before quickly looking back at him. "I never said that!" Pantu said, with an almost straight face.

"Okay then, fine. I will help Ma Sky with her paper. Since she knows what a best friend is," he said, and went to move towards her.

Pantu grabbed him from behind and jumped on his back. He grabbed Pantu's legs and bunny-hopped down the steps to Ma Sky's jeep.

"Now, you can claim the title of my best friend!" Pantu said loudly to him, and they fell out laughing.

As he sat on the steps, he watched Pantu join him. He felt a connection when Pantu first walked into homeroom and immediately started talking to him.

He was glad he did. Pantu was an awesome Being...a bit spoiled, but still caring and considerate of others' feelings. Pantu also opened up to him about his past and his thoughts now.

He was the only student whose number was in Pantu's phone, and they talked every night. His best friend hated texting, since he didn't want his parents to see what they talked about. Pantu said his Ma Vowed not to listen in on their phone conversations and he trusted her as Pantu told him things he never told his parents.

But Pantu also listened to him and would engage him in conversations about himself, retaining everything he said, as if it was the most vital information his best friend would ever know.

Yea, I have friends, he thought, *but I've never had a best friend, until now*. He smiled. "I think my first time will be with Doctor Robin," he said.

"You are sure?"

"Surprised?" he asked, laughing a little.

"I really should be," Pantu said. "No one wants to be my Woman until Drum chooses." Pantu huffed out a sad, pouty look, which made him look away.

"But I still could have hooked up?" he said, indignantly turning back to his bestie.

"Yes, but then we would not have become friends if you just offered your penis all over town," Pantu said and playfully shoved him. They both laughed.

"That's true!"

"How do you know she is your Match?" Pantu asked, and he heard the serious tone underneath.

"She smells like my favorite memory," he said, dreamily.

"HUH?!" Pantu asked him, confused and surprised.

"Not everyone with a pleasant smell is meant to be married or anything, it just means that they may have a special role to play in your life. You have a pleasant smell for me as well. It's how I knew we would be best friends."

Pantu looked at him weirdly. "So, *how do you tell the difference?*"

"Towns like this brings those meant to be together and sets them up right in front of each other. If someone smells like your favorite memory, it means they're extra special to you," he said, as he looked at Pantu, who wasn't saying anything but also didn't look at him.

"Some...people just have a pleasant smell you don't mind being around. They don't come with a memory, only a scent. Those are family, friends and...people you can hang out with.

"The...person will start off smelling like the one memory where you were truly the happiest but there's also another scent, it gets stronger the more you connect with each other, a certain, mutual scent shared between only the two of you. If you find them, marry them," he explained to Pantu.

"So, did you smell a double scent on her?"

"Yes. Faintly. It's how I know," he said, happy he finally found his Scent.

"What does the certain scent smell like?"

"It's different for everybody, but you will know when you smell it," he said.

Pantu stared at him, taking in his features. Apparently Pantu's eyes found his thick, tightly coiled, light auburn hair and lapis-colored eyes, paired with his natural, deep brown skin with a warm undertone pleasing since Pantu smiled.

He also told his best friend about his parents. His Dad was from the Southern States, which was sometimes seen as less cultured than its Northern counterpart. His Birth Mother was a banished Northerner, who died during childbirth, so not only was she kicked out of one of the wealthiest and influential parts of the planet, but she was also seen as weak by her family for not being able to accomplish the one thing most "natural" for women.

He wondered how Doctor Robin would respond to his past while imagining what hers was like, but he was pulled out of his thoughts by Pantu.

"Is there a reason I have yet to meet a human in Sunset?" Pantu asked. "They are some in Hollis, but none I have seen here."

His eyebrows went up. "I vaguely remember humans used to live here when I was younger, and we quietly lived with them until The Royal Family came. Weeks later, a Barrier was over the town. Sunset, Makis Ridge, and several places to the east of us, are underneath The Royal Family's Barrier. But the air is toxic for humans, so they left, and more Beings moved in, making Sunset grow from there."

"Royal Family?" Pantu asked.

He nodded. "The Royal Family expanded the Being Community by creating Barrier Towns. They protect Beings unable to fend for themselves or who just don't want to live around humans."

"What are they like?" Pantu asked, staring intensely at him.

"Well, the Emperor is big, and most find him intimidating, but he really cares about Beings. He improved the quality of life for those under The Royal Family's Barriers. Our Empress is kind. She's the reason most Beings around the planet can afford a quality education." He was hoping Pantu wouldn't press the issue.

"You keep saying Beings. Is this what you all call yourselves?" Pantu asked, relieving his body of stress as he nodded.

"What did you call yourselves where you're from?" he asked.

"Others," Pantu said, looking away. "Do you think The Royal Family would be able to protect my family, if we needed it?"

"It's what they do best," he answered, making Pantu look at him with a sad face.

"They're already protecting you," he told Pantu, who perked up.

"Why would they care about one family when they have so many more to protect?" Pantu thought out loud.

"You're a Private Citizen, which means no one can take a photo or video of you without your consent or unless they're authorized to do so. No one can put your information online. No one can force you to leave from under the Barrier," he explained.

"If they aren't The Royal Family or someone authorized, they won't even be able to see your first name on your student records, much less, your Citizen record without clearance from The Royal Family."

He watched as relief flooded Pantu's face, so he decided to ask. "How did you know there's no humans here?"

Pantu looked at him and smiled. "When I walked around town with Sport, Queen and Win, I saw only those with Light inside their bodies. All around campus, there are only those with Light inside them. Is it not a common Talent? It is how you know who is like us and who is not."

He shook his head. "We can feel the Energy others give off, it's a Universal Ability called Aura Radar, but very few of us have Enhanced Vision, or the Level needed to see Energy."

"Enhanced Vision..." Pantu said, looking up at the sky. "There is a shimmering white Dome over Sunset."

He shrugged. "We call those Domes, Barriers and I've never been able to see Energy, but like most others, I can feel it. I know as long as it's there, I will have Purified air to breathe, Purified food to eat and Purified water to drink. I also know if I use my Energy under this Barrier, I can replenish it just by breathing."

Pantu's eyes slowly lowered to meet his face while widening from the information.

"You mean all the food and water under this Dome is Purified!?" Pantu asked, his voice going up an octave.

He smiled at Pantu. "Yep, and the air you're breathing right now." He pulled his Energy from his body and created a small, mini, working microphone.

Pantu pulled Energy out of his body, and it turned into a small, chestnut brown butterfly with random black markings. The butterfly fluttered about until it dissipated.

"Are The Royal Family descendants of Phoenix to do something on a scale this massive?" Pantu whispered.

"I don't know. Phoenix is a myth in our community and a fantasy story amongst the human population," he answered.

He watched the expressions across Pantu's face as he took in the information. He knew his best friend was planning a way to avoid meeting The Royal Family. He decided to steer Pantu another route.

"The Empress is in town sometimes, but the Emperor hardly comes around. He travels a lot for business, but the Empress' Mom runs a bookstore in town. Maybe we can stop by there one evening and you can talk to her?" he offered but the polite smile Pantu gave wasn't in agreement.

PANTU: AH! FOR THE LOVE OF READING
WEEK TWO: FRIDAY/SATURDAY/SUNDAY

On the ride to their house, his Ma handed him the bag sitting in the front seat. "I've picked up the book you requested and a couple others by the same author."

He hurried and pulled the first book out. It was wrapped nicely in thin decorative paper. He didn't want it to tear, so he unwrapped it gently. It was the book he'd told his Ma to get.

Brand new and crisp, he was in love. The artwork on the front made him smile. As he flipped through the book, the inner artwork also caught his eye. He turned to the first page and started reading.

He didn't realize they were at their house as he still had his face in the book. He made it upstairs with minimal tripping, to his bed where he plopped down and kept reading. He skipped dinner and ignored his phone the rest of the night as he was caught in a world that felt oddly similar to his own.

"I wish I had an Interface helping me." He pouted, then laughed. "I guess Dill would be my Interface."

He checked his phone after he finished the novel and noticed it was after midnight. He texted Dill back to reschedule. He reached into the bag and pulled the next book out. It was a different title, but he liked the cover artwork and opened it to read.

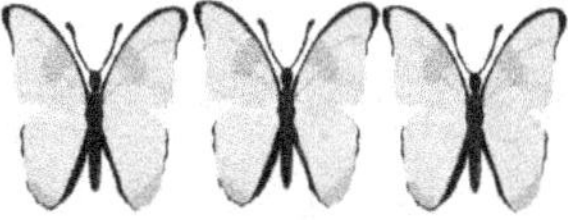

He was reading since Friday afternoon and halfway through the second book, his Ma knocked on his door to tell him it was time to leave for his Saturday session. He found his phone and texted, 'reschedule', to his Ma.

He also sent a text to Dill to cancel the library trip again as he just wanted to read. He went back to the world of "Grand Shifu of Angelic Cultivation'. When he finished, he texted his Ma for the remaining books in the series.

She texted back that she already ordered them, and they would be in the bookstore next week.

He thanked his Ma and went to take the last book out of the bag. He paused as he looked at the cover and realized the two males were dressed in traditional Eastern red wedding clothes. The artwork was beautifully drawn, making one of the males on the cover so handsomely beautiful, he almost couldn't tell.

He drew in a breath, as he remembered what Drum called him. He couldn't bear to open the book. He just wanted to stare at the cover. His mind went back to the picture he saw in the manhwa Drum was reading. As he traced the image of the taller male, he pictured him and Drum in the same pose as the males in the manhwa. His whole body shivered.

"That would be impossible," he said, out loud to himself. He couldn't afford to live in a fantasy world where he was happy, but he could read about them. He opened the book and was almost finish reading when his Ma knocked on his door.

"Pantu, it's time for us to leave for your session," she called through the door.

"Okay! Let me shower!" he responded, not wanting to look for his phone.

His parents brought him a smart flip phone just like Drum's, and he was happy. They also let him download a ringtone, so now he had a song instead of a weird stock tone. He placed the book faced down but then thought better of it and found a bookmark. He hopped in the shower and after hurrying to get dressed, grabbed the book to finish on the drive.

During his session, they talked about the incident on campus. She still didn't ask who he was talking to, and he didn't offer the information. He also talked about the books he was reading and why he was reading a particular one.

He talked about his friendship with Dill some more, leaving out what Dill told him, but she seemed to know and jotted something down. He talked about physically attending campus and his classes.

He planned with her to finish the essays by Wednesday and turn them in. She also challenged him to make a choice between making a new friend or painting a picture to show her. He agreed to the challenge, thinking a friend would be the easiest route.

They talked about his medicines, and she explained she was planning on lowering his doses even more; by decreasing the number he took a day, and the strength of the pills until he was completely off the medicines.

Freezing, he stared at his Doctor, wondering why she wanted to stop his medications so soon after they started physical sessions. The thoughts in his brain were unhappy with the idea, but his Mind was sending happy pulses to his Light.

He was unsure, since the medicines kept him from having another episode, like the one that resulted in them leaving their home. But this was what he wanted since he couldn't be on medication living in The City. A crazy pet was a dead pet.

They finished their session, and he waited in the café across the street as his parents talked to her. He ordered a drink and when he went to pay, he found his tab already settled. He looked around, trying to find who he needed to thank.

But the barista whispered to him, *"You're Pantu from Sunset Town. Anything you want here is free."*

He looked at her and after stumbling over thanking her, he sat next to the window where he could clearly see Doctor Robin's office. He sipped his drink, waiting for his parents so they could leave. He saw the snake sneaking to hide between the buildings. He watched as the snake kept checking the door to his Doctor's building, waiting for someone to come out.

The snake's darting eyes, and impatient attitude made him chuckle to himself. He sent a text to his parents to pick him up at the café as he continued to enjoy the crazy snake show with a drink.

When his parents exited the building, the snake's mouth dropped open. When his parents stopped the car in front of the café and he exited the store, he smirked at the snake before getting in the car. He didn't bother to look back.

That evening, he went for a walk. He couldn't call her since Dill was building a new box to connect to his flip phone. He decided to walk to Dill's home and see if it was ready. As he passed Win's home, he noticed Win lounging on his porch watching him walk by.

"Hi, Win!" he called out.

A crisp, "Hi Pantu," came back.

He decided to keep walking and a loud, exasperated "UGH" came from Win's direction. He heard Win stomp down his stairs, and he slowed his walk as Win caught up.

"You do not have to walk with me."

"Yea I do."

"Why? Did my parents ask you to watch me?" he teased.

Win answered, "As if I would do this because YOUR PARENTS asked."

He stopped and stared at Win, who asked him, "Where you headed?"

"Dill's home," he said, deciding not to overthink it and continued walking.

"Is it far?"

"It is a good distance."

"GOOD! I need to stretch my limbs anyways," Win said, as he took a good, long stretch before walking alongside him again.

Along the way he learned things about Win he assumed would never be an issue for the handsome, skinny male next to him. He learned Win was graduating a year early and already had a job set up for him by his Pa, which he refused.

He also found out Win was the Valedictorian for their class. He thought about asking Win for help with his schoolwork but decided against it, since at times during their conversation, he was sure Win wanted to punch him in the face.

It was only after he apologized for staring at Kat, making her feel uncomfortable and promising several times he would never make a move on her, that Win forgave him when he said, "Kat deserves better than me."

Win smiled with approval and after that, Win's cheerful personality showed through. They connected, talking and laughing about how their Pas were both amazing with numbers, but they each took their own routes.

His feelings were honest. He thought if he had been a better friend to Yolk, maybe he would still be alive. By the time they reached Dill's home, he felt comfortable with Win and like Dill said, Win now held a pleasant scent which made it nice to be around him. He didn't notice the scent until after he assured Win of his lack of interest in Kat. He also noticed Queen and Sport always gave off pleasant scents.

All four smelled pleasant, with one having a stronger scent, carrying his favorite memory. There was a scent he couldn't place if or where he had smelled it before, and something was tugging at the back of his Mind.

He was trying to think of what the scent was when he accidentally said out loud, "Whatever is that scent?"

He didn't notice Dill was standing in front of him when he heard, "What scent?"

He jumped and Win was looking at him with a questioning face. "The scent the first year had. It was so strong in the cafeteria. I faintly smelled it before, but I do not want to believe it," he said, as he was technically still trying to place that scent as well.

"He didn't smell like that when you met him in Hollis?" Dill asked him.

"No, he did not smell like that there. He had an odd odor coming from him, but it was not this scent," he answered.

"Where else did you smell it?" Win asked.

"It was faint, but I think...in my room," he answered.

Win went off deep in thought and Dill handed the black box to him.

"Do you need to make a call?" Dill whispered to him, and he nodded.

"Go between those stacks over there and I will keep Win here," Dill told him, in a hushed tone.

"Thanks Dill!" he said, appreciating his best friend even more.

The conversation went the same every time. He would soothe her displeasure and make her orgasm. After he hung up, he blew out a deep breath. It happened again. His body no longer responded to her and now, his Mind wasn't in it.

"Thank the Universe my voice still listens to me, or my family would be fucked," he said to himself, as he went to rejoin Dill and Win, who was still deep in thought.

He was only in town for three weeks and already he was feeling different. It made him hesitant, going back with no control over his body, knowing she would "train" him again.

"I learned quickly the first time, maybe this time it will be over after one training." He tried to reassure himself.

They stayed at Dill's until late in the evening and Dill's Pa offered them a ride. He was headed to pick up his wife from one of their amusement parks, with their street being not far off the route. Dill rode along with them, and they talked about the amusement park rides. Well, Win and Dill told him about the rides, which only made him want to go more.

PANTU: AN UNAVOIDABLE CONVERSATION
WEEK THREE: MONDAY

He knew he needed to speak to Queen. After talking with Dill, and sometimes Win, Sunday evening and into the night, he adamantly didn't want any misunderstandings between them. He liked the scent Queen gave off and didn't want it to change.

He realized Win didn't hold a scent until after he made things right between them, so his train of thought was they themselves could control their own scents, based on how they felt about him. He wasn't sure as he also thought he might be going insane again.

"What if I am still in the mental hospital, drugged up, and imagining all of this? Worse yet, what if I never left The City and this is my happy place while being tortured for what I did?" he quietly asked himself.

There was no way the Universe would allow him to be happy after all the years he spent in The City, trying to survive. He moaned. "No one escapes the grasp of The City. They will find me one day."

Queen didn't acknowledge him during class, other than a quick smile at the beginning. He decided third period was not a proper time to talk since there was a test and Queen left, right after finishing.

Dill was waiting for him downstairs, so he turned down some more invites as he made his way to his Safe Haven. They entered the cafeteria, and he immediately noticed The Four were not at their usual table.

"Sometimes they go out to the bleachers to eat," Dill whispered to him.

He nodded and after getting his food, which he noticed he didn't have to pay for, he looked around at the other students, who placed their phones up to a machine, which dinged. He glanced back at Dill and noticed he did the same thing.

After leaving the line, he whispered to Dill, *"Why am I the only one who does not pay for lunch?"*

Dill looked at him and smiled as an *oh, so he finally realized* thought crossed his face before Dill explained. "Your lunch is paid for through a special account. You know...with your phone the way it is."

"That makes sense," he said, relieved there was a reasonable explanation for his lack of having to pay for things.

Dill didn't head to their normal table, but instead headed outside, and he rerouted himself to follow.

Catching up to Dill, he asked, "Are we not sitting inside?"

Dill stopped and looked at him. "You said you wanted to talk to Queen," Dill said. "There he is." Dill pointed to the bleachers.

He followed Dill's arm, to his hand, past his finger, to look in the direction in which it was pointing. His eyes caught Queen's, and he swallowed whatever was pushing its way up his chest.

"Is it my nerves or did Queen take his scent away? *I really do not want Queen to smell like Mansnake,*" he mumbled to himself, while Dill patiently waited for him to move.

He slowly ascended the bleachers and The Four's conversation died down. His body was definitely aware Drum was looking at him with a raised eyebrow and a slight smile.

He looked to Queen and started. "I wanted to let you know..." he paused and took some breaths, "I never said what he accused me of," he ended. But he felt the need to continue. "I said things to him yes, but I never said..." he trailed off, cursing his nerves.

"You never said you would kill him if he opened his dick-sucking mouth and spoke to you again?" Queen asked. "When all he wanted to do was apologize for hitting on you the first time you both met?" Queen pouted.

"WHAT?! He never *hit* on me. EVER! My Ma would never allow it!" he said.

"Not *hit* on you, hit *on* you. He told Queen he likes you," Dill explained.

Everyone looked at him, and he closed his eyes. *Well, they probably think I said it now,* he thought to himself.

"We know he Lied on you Pantu," Queen said, with a smile. "We *knew as soon as he started explaining, everything coming out of his mouth was a Lie,*" Queen said, gently to him.

He opened his eyes and looked so gratefully at Queen, that Queen's cheeks turned bright red.

"Thank you for believing me. I would not insult or threaten a person based on their..." He looked at Dill.

"Sexuality," Dill helped.

"Yes! It is okay to say that word here. Based on their...sexuality," he added.

"We know Pantu," Queen told him.

He took a calming breath and turned to leave.

"If you didn't call men who like men gay where you come from, what did you call them?" Sport asked.

He froze, his body trembling ever so slightly. After a moment, he turned and looked at Dill, whose head shook.

"Ah, it is a rather derogatory phrase, so I would much rather not say it," he answered. He was unsure if Queen would slap him dead, but he knew he didn't want that to be the outcome.

"Well, NOW I have to KNOW!" Queen shouted.

He turned around to look at Queen. "Please do not ask me to say it," he pleaded, with unhappy eyes.

He didn't want to lose what little cordialness they had between them. A small slip of paper and a pen appeared in Queen's hands, and he tilted his head as Queen handed the objects to him.

He looked unsure of Queen's Talent Level but placed his food down; took the items; wrote the phrase; folded the paper and handed it back to Queen. He was praying Queen would understand he now knew to never say the phrase or associate it with anyone.

The laughter that came from Queen was unexpected and his look changed. Queen handed the paper to Win whose reaction was the same and when Sport looked over Win's shoulder to read the words, he laughed as well. There were only two who didn't bother to read the paper. One was Drum, who never took his eyes off him.

"You know anyone who does anal sex could be called this, not just gay men," Sport said, giving him a full smile.

"Besides there are some steps one could take to not do what you wrote on the paper," Queen added, doing a little head dance.

"Sit down," Win commanded. "*Your food is getting cold,*" Win softly added.

He looked unsure but when Dill sat down, he followed. Only then did Drum's eyes leave him to look around. He felt Light being used and quickly turned on his True Vision to see a sparkling white Dome over them. With another quick blink, he turned his Vision off.

"You said you never met a gay man before where you lived. Why is that?" Sport asked.

"Because, for several generations no man or male has ever declared himself as such. The last male who made his declaration, was killed several hundred years ago," he casually said as he started eating. The look on their faces made him pause, and he felt the need to clear up his statement.

"He was brutally tortured, mutilated and executed, all publicly. So, there has not been a man or male to CLAIM he is gay where I come from, in over several hundred years," he said, calmly explaining to them. But his explanation just made their faces contorted further to add open mouths and wide eyes.

"There have been men or males ACCUSED of being gay, but it was mostly to remove them out of someone else's way...or because they seemed too close to someone important." He shrugged. "Or both" he added, hoping it helped.

It didn't. Now even Drum's face was scrunched up in deep thought.

"Why do you keep saying or males?" Win asked.

"Where I come from, a male is an unmarried person with a penis. Once a male marries, he would then be considered a man," he said, shrugging.

"Is that what happened to your best friend Yolk?" Dill softly asked him.

"Not exactly," he said. He blew out his breath. "They said he killed himself because graduation broke him." He started pinching himself, but when Dill touched his hand, he released the pinch.

"I was...well, I still am, the most celebrated...person there. When he started rising in the ranks so quickly, others took notice. Coming from the lowest ranks and breaking top ten at an incredible speed, made certain people feel as if he was a threat," he said, talking to the bleacher seat.

"Was he?" Sport asked.

"Yes."

"Pantu!" Win exclaimed.

"Not the way you are thinking," he said. His look between Sport and Win, was with pleading eyes.

They looked back at him, expectedly.

He looked down at the bleacher seat and continued, "To me, there was no threat to my position, he would never be able to catch up to my numbers. They were the highest ever recorded," he confidently and indignantly remarked, which made everyone smile and raise their eyebrows.

"He was a threat to my life," he started. "We were childhood friends. And when he entered..."—he took a deep breath—"training," he pushed out. "We met again. He was the lowest in the ranks and it is a dangerous place to be.

"I thought if I taught him how to turn off his emotions and how to...complete certain tasks, he would be okay," he carefully said. "When he broke the top ten..." He paused for a long time, his thoughts finally catching up to him.

He assumed the only way for his plans to work was to not upset these four, but now he was believing everyone would think he was a bad person. There were things he wasn't ready to expose, which might lead to them misinterpreting his words.

He was thinking Dill wouldn't want to be his friend anymore if he knew the full truth behind Yolk. He talked to Dill about his late best friend, but he never shared the details.

And now, he wanted them to try and understand him more than he cared about being hated. He would never say the things he was accused of, and he never threatened to kill anyone in his entire life.

He had people punished but no one ever died. Then there was the incident, but no one died from that either. But if trying to explain to them meant he would have to spend the rest of his short-lived, physical Higher Ed campus life as an outcast and shunned, well, he felt as if he deserved it.

He knew he couldn't go back and live as carefree as he was doing now. He still needed to keep on his toes because accusations where he came from could mean death without proof.

Maybe I can go back to online classes, he quickly thought. "When he broke the top ten," he started again. *"He confessed his feelings to me,"* he whispered. "He told me how he did anything he could, to be closer to me. How he loved me since we first met. I lost it and told him; I had no feelings to return."

He'd stopped trying to suppress his emotions with Drum around. It was easy for his brain to know what to do, but his Mind and body stopped listening to him weeks ago.

"The male who died for being "gay" was from my Ma's family, so it was deeply instilled in every generation after him, the consequences of being..."gay"...health and social wise," he informed them.

"Did you really not have any feelings for him?" Sport asked, softly.

"Not romantic ones. He was supposed to be my best friend. That was all. I have always wanted a best friendship like what my G-Pas have." He wrung his hands together. "I thought if I stopped helping him, he would not climb any higher.

"But when he broke the top five, we saw each other more as the top five would host...parties together. The top three were still held in a different, more private regard. I was still able to avoid talking to him and since his numbers were not top three, me snubbing him was normal.

"I tried to get him to control his emotions and kill his feelings, but when he told me he would die for me, just like my ancestor did for his lover, I told him his stupidity would get us both killed." He put his head in his hands. "But...but...then he...he became number three in the ranks, and I needed to figure out how to avoid him."

His breaths were coming quicker and when Dill touched his arm, he was so grateful, he took the deepest breath, smelling the scent of the field meadow, which calmed his emotions. He raised his eyes to Drum then quickly looked away.

He didn't know where to look or what to do with his hands as he continued. "But by then, we unknowingly caught the attention of a person who was heavily financially invested in me staying number one.

"They wanted to split us up, so they pushed him into final education and rushed his graduation. They broke us both during his ceremony," he ended, taking a deep breath.

"How did they do that?" Queen asked.

"They made me watch," he said, but there was nothing casual about the look on his face.

"Why would making you watch him graduate, break both of you?" Queen asked.

"He failed," he said, praying to the Universe they didn't press the issue. He noticed the look Drum gave Queen and when no one asked, he continued.

"They were going to re-educate him, until he graduated." He felt weak, and didn't realize he was shedding tears, until they dropped from his face.

"I went to see him. See if I could convince him this time to kill his feelings, but there was only a note left for me. By the time I made it to where he was, they were putting his body under a sheet. They said he jumped." He was wiping away tears that were falling uncontrollably, unable to stop them from leaving his eyes.

"So, he was the first man or male in over a hundred years to be killed for being gay?!" Win said, the look on his face made clear Win was unsure of his own comment.

"Not according to the records," he told Win. "He never declared himself, nor was he ever accused, so his cause of death was listed as a mental break due to educated-related stress. Had he made his declaration, I would also be dead," he told them.

"Do you remember what was written on the note?" Sport asked him.

He turned and opened his backpack. He noticed Sport didn't say planned in front of the note, and there was a glimmer of hope. Taking out his sketch pad, he flipped the cardboard back around and pulled a perfectly preserved piece of paper from a small cut between it.

He smiled at Win's honesty and handed the note to Sport, who read it out loud, "My death will be your fault. My blood will be spilled because of you. We should have stayed in The Slums where we belonged. Remember your place or everyone you care about will die like me." Sport looked up from the note.

"What a weird suicide note?" Win said, after hearing it.

"The last line sounds like someone killed him and will continue to kill," Drum said, with a raised eyebrow.

"It is not his writing," he said.

"So, Yolk didn't kill himself. He was murdered to keep him from making his declaration!" Queen said what was silently written on everyone's faces.

No one other than Sport looked at the note to see if it was his handwriting and it wasn't, but he knew who wrote the note. It was the fact they trusted what he was saying was truth, which made his heart hurt. It was as if something in him cracked. He was beside himself. No one, outside his G-Pas, ever acknowledged his feelings about Yolk's death.

"Even as the number one celebrated person, with my G-Ma and grandma being the third and second wealthiest Women, I was powerless. Within two hours, his body was stripped and burned while his death was labeled as planned. I was told by a family member invested in my position, if I made a fuss, I would be accused as his lover, and they would see to my public death."

The tears flowing out of his eyes wouldn't stop. He hadn't cried this much since he was eight years old and everything he'd suppressed kept coming out. While he tried to wipe them away, Drum came closer to him and held out his hand. Without thinking or hesitating, he laid his hand inside of Drum's and the warmth was soothing as it spread over his body. He couldn't help but smile at Drum.

"Where I come from, I have always needed to be steps ahead of any accusations. It can mean death without proof, no matter your status. I was normally ahead of most accusations and my G-Pas helped.

"This is the first time I have ever been caught off guard. I do not like the feeling, so I shall return it tenfold." In those honey-green eyes, he didn't see sympathy, he saw appreciation.

The group understood how he was feeling. To them, it was just a bullying complaint they easily handled to put more space between him and his stalker, but to him, it was an accusation which was triggering, heavy and life-threatening.

The snake hit a nerve in him, and they all saw it. They also saw the fight in his eyes, which made them all smile at him. He was willing to fight when so many others had given up. But he wasn't going to end up like those before him.

"I get why now you told Queen you like people based on their personality, not what gender they love," Win said, with a smile on his face.

Drum gave him a smile, and he was still as the loudest sound in his head was from the crack coming from around his heart.

"Thank you. Thank you for surviving...for living," Drum said, softly to him.

PANTU: HOW HIGH CAN ONE GO?
WEEK THREE: TUESDAY

He spent yesterday evening being fussed at by his parents. Well, his Ma fussed, while his Pa only nodded and grunted in agreement. He talked on the bleachers, right through three classes, and his Professors informed his parents. It was also then, he learned Win would be driving him to campus in the mornings, as his Ma was now employed at the local bookstore.

Even though it seemed like he wasn't listening or didn't care as he rolled his eyes several times, nodding while looking away and acting like he was exhausted, he was trying to hide the smile that came with remembering.

They lived in the outermost area of The City, called The Slums, until he was seven. They were poor, but happy. He remembered when he fell into a mud puddle that was deeper than he thought and came home to their little shack, filthy.

He ran around their eating room table, splashing mud everywhere as his Pa tried to catch him for a bath. His Ma was fussing and laughing at the same time. He was finally caught and given a bath by both his parents. When his G-Pas came for their weekly visit, he told them the story, which made them laugh as well.

He picked up his phone and sent one text to his Ma.

> As GLou would say, "It is a kindness from the Universe I have someone to fuss at me and you have someone to fuss over."

He left the table as they were reading the text on his Ma's phone and went to his room to call Dill.

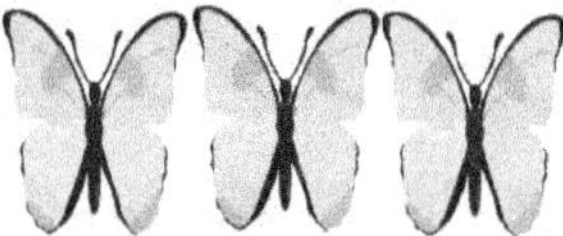

He was now in the passenger seat of Win's car, headed to campus. Win was playing music, which he was bobbing his head too.

"It's the number one song on the planet, by the current number one star, Bianca B. It's the first time she has ever sung a song written by someone else," Win told him. "She's Queen's favorite singer, so be careful what you say about her," Win warned.

He smiled. "There is nothing bad I can say about her voice," he agreed.

Win nodded. "You catch on quick!" Win said, with a quick glance at him, before focusing back on the road.

"Why do you say, the planet, instead of Torven?" he asked, realizing no Being under the Barrier ever referred to the name of the planet.

"Because we believe this isn't our planet to name," Win answered.

They made it to campus before the first bell rang. After thanking Win and complimenting his driving, he ran over to Dill, who was even earlier than him.

"We have to test it first; we do not want a fiery repeat of the space shuttle," he warned Dill, who nodded in agreement. They went off to find a quiet place to test their invention.

At lunch, both he and Dill hurried to their table without grabbing food. They were greeted with dead stares and scoffs as they sat. The inquisitive look on his face was clear and as he looked at Dill, he knew they were on the same page.

"What's with the attitude?" Dill asked, sitting a medium size box on the table.

He added another box and folded his hands, while pouting at their friends.

Unable to withstand his pouty face, Jax spoke up quickly, "We just thought you would be sitting at another table from now on."

"Yea, since Win is driving you to campus," Put added, looking away from his puffy cheeks.

Turn tried to close the conversation while staring at the tray in front of him. "And since you BOTH hung out with them yesterday."

He turned and looked at Dill with a smile. "I guess we should show them first then."

"If they don't want to see our newest invention, then—" Dill started but was interrupted by the three males' excitement.

"Holy shit!"

"You two built something else?"

"I want to see it!"

"It's not a shuttle again, is it?" Put asked, unwilling to engage in another one of their fiery inventions.

He and Dill laughed while shaking their heads.

"The shuttle had some issues with wiring," he said, eyeing Dill.

"Well...SOMEONE drew the wiring wrong," Dill shot back.

"SOMEONE did not explain the wires PROPERLY and REFUSED to notice when he was the ONE who built it," he ended, looking directly at Dill, who shrunk every time he became loud.

"Well show us!" Jax said, leaning onto the table.

Dill opened a box and took out the invention. Their friends looked at it weirdly.

"It's a ramp?" they finally asked after inspecting it. They were wondering why he and Dill were excited about this invention.

"Yes!" he said. Opening his box, he started laying down tracks, which Dill connected. He pulled out a miniature motor bike, handing it to Dill. After backing up the bike while counting the clicks, Dill locked the bike at the beginning of the track.

"Press the button," Dill said to Jax.

Jax shook his head. "Too soon after the shuttle."

Dill blew out a breath. "But we tested it already!"

To which he quickly smashed the button. The motorbike took off fast, but when the rest of the table was anticipating the bike shooting off towards the wall, and looked in that direction, he and Dill were looking up.

When the bike crashed, their friends stared at them before looking down at the table. The bike was sturdy and still intact, but everyone else was trying to figure out what just happened.

Jax reached over and grabbed the bike. After setting it back up, Jax pushed the button, and they watched as the bike reached the end of the ramp to spring up, almost to the ceiling of the lunchroom.

The sound of the crash was mixed with sounds of excitement as more Beings gathered around to watch. Everyone wanted to push the button to make it spring the highest.

His table was now so crowded he couldn't see Drum anymore. As a student pushed the button, they watched again as the bike went higher than before, but this time as it came down, there was a soft sound as the bike landed in a hand. Looking at the hand and following it up, his eyes met Dean Hu's.

He quickly turned to Dill, with his hand covering half his face. "I shall slide under the table and make a break for the door," he faked whispered to Dill.

"You're just going to leave me here?!" Dill asked with a high-pitched tone.

"We shall meet again. One day. On the other side," he replied to Dill. He tried to slide out of his chair and under the table to the giggles of everyone else.

"Pan-tu!" Dean Hu said, trying not to laugh as well. "Meet me in my office, Dill you too." She placed the bike down. "And every piece of your contraption as well," she ended.

He hadn't looked in her direction again, so he whispered loudly to Dill. "She is going to call my parents, is she not?" he asked, trying to control his nerves from making his body visibly shake.

"Yes. Yes, she is," came an answer from behind him.

DILLxPANTU: SHOWING ONE'S POTENTIAL
WEEK THREE: TUESDAY

As Dill and Pantu sat in the office waiting for their parents to get there, he was freaking out. "My Dad has never received a call from the Dean before," he said, looking around and fidgeting with everything he could touch.

Pantu nudged him gently. "My apologies." Pantu looked at him sadly.

But he refused to look at Pantu. He knew it wasn't Pantu's fault, but he was too deep in his thoughts about how his stepparent, Lyra, would react.

Their parents arrived at almost the same time and waited with them in the front office. While Lyra was openly flirting at, but being ignored by Pantu's Pa, Ma Sky was busy looking over every inch of Pantu's exposed body parts to make sure her child was unhurt.

His throat tightened at the motherly love he'd never experienced. The breath he took hurt, and his mouth twitched, holding back his tears. His Dad came, stood silently beside him, and placed a comforting hand on his back.

His tears dried up and were replaced by surprise and affection as Ma Sky moved over to him, inspecting him the same as Pantu.

Pantu looked surprised when Doctor Robin arrived but before he could say anything, Dean Hu's door opened.

After everyone sat down Dean Hu started. "I was informed Pantu and Dill were using this inside the lunchroom without authorization," she said, as she gestured towards the ramp set up on the table behind them.

Both sets of parents turned to look, igniting their Dads to stand and inspect their invention. After testing it and watching as the bike crashed into the ceiling, they started talking about specs and the inner workings of the ramp.

His Dad, talking mechanics and Pantu's Pa, talking numbers. Everyone else in the room, but Pantu, was looking at their Dads, talking about their invention like two excited kids. Lyra rolled her eyes and bounced her leg, impatient with the conversation.

"Are you finished?" Dean Hu kindly asked them.

They both looked embarrassed and meekly returned to their seats. Dean Hu laid three large sheets of paper at the edge of her desk and their parents leaned forward to look.

"It's the schematics of the ramp!" his Dad said.

"Drawn to scale," Pantu's Pa added. "But these numbers on the side suggest the ramp should be a lot larger?" he said, more a statement than a question. He looked over at Pantu, who avoided his Pa's eyes and innocently looked everywhere else in the room.

"It seems Pantu drew these, and Dill built the ramp," Dean Hu said.

"Pantu also helped build it," he mumbled.

"I only sketched what you described and cut the wood to the size you said. You did everything else," Pantu retorted.

"You painted it," he reminded Pantu.

Neither of them wanted to take full blame, but they also didn't want to diminish each other's efforts. They were proud as they looked at each other and smiled. Both were okay with the fact they would get in trouble for an awesome, and finally working, invention.

"I see," Dean Hu said, raising an eyebrow. "I noticed neither one of you has applied for employment yet," she said. She opened one of her desk drawers and took out two packets.

"Dill!" Lyra started, honey dripping from his name. "First, you embarrass me by having your Dean call me at work because you're playing with toys when you're supposed to be learning, and now I find out you haven't turned in any of your applications?!

"We worked on those together. Why haven't you turned them in?" she asked, her face red with anger by his actions. Lyra was clutching her purse, making her knuckles turn a lighter pale shade.

Together was a loosely used word for his stepparent. She filled out the applications herself since it gave her access to his personal information. She also only applied to jobs in remote areas.

"Because I know what Pantu wants to do after graduation," he said, looking at the pattern in the hardwood floors.

His stepparent was in complete shock and couldn't get anything out as his Dad was trying to console her. Pantu was looking at him with surprise as well.

Dill continued, looking up at Pantu. "We just became best friends. If it ended so soon, it would be tragic."

He tried not to smile. He hadn't thought about employment, since he wasn't planning on being here after graduation, nor did he want to work for other people. As the thoughts hit him, he couldn't meet Dill's eyes anymore, but instead of questioning him, Dill grabbed one of the packets to look over.

"Well, this is one of the top companies on the planet. They only accept a certain number of our graduates, and the company guarantees a starting pay well above the maximum range," Dean Hu said.

"And luckily, it's located close to us. You both should apply. I think Dill would be great in the Engineering Department with Pantu in the Art Department, and if you graduate in the top five of your class, a sizable employee sign-on bonus awaits. Anyone I personally recommend is automatically hired," Dean Hu finished.

While his parents and Dill's Pa held smiles on their face at the news their sons could be employed at one of the top companies on the planet, Dill's stepparent's face didn't look pleased at all.

"Dill already filled out his applications, and I will make sure they're submitted." Dill's stepparent snatched the packet out of Dill's hands and tossed it back onto Dean Hu's desk.

He hung his head, refusing to stare at Lyra's face again using his True Vision. She was testing his patience when it came to Dill, and since he refused to have a repeat of Yolk, he was tempted to leave a small surprise for her inside her weak Mind, knowing she wouldn't be able to counter his Talent, since she heavily relied on her brain.

But when a soft hand landed on his back, he knew Dill was asking him to let it go. Instead, he waited until everyone calmed down, before he spoke.

"I do not want to paint because I am required too. I want to paint because I feel like it," he said, softly.

His parents looked at him, his Ma with understanding and his Pa with a slight nod. They knew what happened to him to make him not want to paint in years, so they silently agreed with him.

Doctor Robin paused while writing and suggested, "Then what about a self-employed, freelanced architect? They make good money, and you could take on a project whenever you felt like it."

He looked back at her with wonder on his face. *Is she telling me I have options? But I have none here, I must go back?*

"It's your choice Pantu," Doctor Robin said, jotting down more notes.

He looked at his packet, still sitting on the Dean's desk and slowly reached for it. His chest felt heavy, and his nerves were making his hands shake worse than his Pa. When Dill reached out and steadied his arm, he quickly grabbed the packet, holding it to his chest.

Stop asking for the impossible, he silently told himself while giving Dill back the other packet, to Lyra's hard stare.

DRUM: A PLAYFUL LITTLE ONE
WEEK THREE: TUESDAY

As Pantu and Dill left the Dean's office, he heard them joke about finding a good paying company as far away and as north as they could go, hoping he wouldn't be there so they could date.

"You mean the Neizberg Research Facility? They scouted me already," he said, surprising both Dill and Pantu. He was waiting in the office, and they looked at him weirdly.

"Why are you here?" Pantu asked.

He smirked. "I go to classes here."

"No. Why are YOU in the Dean's office?" Pantu clarified.

"I'm in trouble...again," he said. A full smile on his face.

Both Pantu's face and Dill's Energy looked as if they didn't believe him.

He straightened up to look behind them. "Mother. Father," he said to the two figures who appeared out of a Portal behind Pantu and Dill, in the now crowded front office.

He saw the changes Pantu's face went through as he took in the two standing behind him. Pantu looked at his Mom with admiration but when Pantu saw his Dad, Pantu's face went into shock.

He knew his Dad was bigger than most, with broad shoulders and a thick muscular figure, his six-foot eleven-inch-tall Dad was quite imposing. He held back a smile as Pantu took a loud, scared gulp and slowly turned around to look at him.

"Beautiful, kind, understanding, loving Mother of mine! Listen. What had happened was—" He started.

But his Mom cut him off. "I don't want to hear it mister. How many times does this make?" she asked him, moving closer to poke him in the side.

"This year or all together?" he asked her with a goofy grin on his face.

"Drum!" His Dad's deep baritone voice filled the room and made him try harder not to laugh at Pantu's reaction.

"Father, I was practicing THE JEFFERS DUNK!" he said, while acting out the motions.

His Dad's Energy showed he was impressed. "Did you perfect it!?" his Dad asked, almost shaking the room with his voice alone.

Pantu was stuck between scared and shock whenever his Dad spoke, making Pantu fall deeper into confusion.

"Too much force," he said, shrugging his shoulders and giving his Dad a full smile.

His Dad's Energy held a pleasant color, so he knew his Dad smiled back. "It's definitely a game ender," his Dad said, with pride.

Pantu noticed this exchange and raised an eyebrow. Looking at him, Pantu spoke with a sly smile. "Ah! So that smile works, even on your Pa?"

He looked at Pantu with a questioning face. "Huh?"

Both of his parents paused for a moment in thought.

"Drum! Did you just Charm your Father?!" his Mom asked, with surprise.

"What?! No Mom, I wouldn't..."

But his answer came too late as a grunt from his Dad let him know he was again in trouble. He took a deep breath and looking at Pantu, he stuck his hands in his pockets, waiting.

"The repairs are coming out of your bank account," his Dad said.

He snapped his neck to look at his Dad in surprise. Pantu and Dill were now both trying not to laugh as they went to sneak out from between him and his parents.

"Pantu," he stated, to which he received the most innocent look and a reason.

"It is only what you deserve for taking the option of the Neizberg Research Facility away from me," Pantu stated plainly while smirking at him and being loud enough for his parents to hear.

His parents held back laughter at the look on his face stuck somewhere between impressed and shocked, as Pantu and Dill left the office.

After what he did, he had no choice but to agree to remodel the whole gym before he and his parents left the office. Pantu and Dill would also be helping as restitution for using the ramp indoors.

He walked out of the office to Pantu and Dill having a conversation on one side of the hallway with Pantu's parents speaking softly to Doctor Robin on the other side.

"Hello Doctor Robin!" he said, with a smile. "Long time, no session," he added, with a small wave.

"That would be a good thing, is it not?" Doctor Robin asked, and he could tell by her Energy, a mutual smile graced both their faces.

Pantu's parents' Energies turned towards him.

He does have great genes, he thought seeing where Pantu received his incredibly good looks.

Pantu's Mother's light pink Energy was extremely beautiful, and it was genuinely playful but strong, which could only come from having a matching personality.

Pantu's Father, although timid looking, Energy was a glowing, sky-blue color, and he glanced at the man, knowing there was more to him than he was showing.

"I've been and am the psychiatrist for many students in town and the surrounding areas," Doctor Robin explained to Pantu's parents.

"It's because she's the best!" His Dad's voice shook through the hall.

"She can connect and relate with our kids, so we only go to her. Youngest in the country to get her Ph.D. and start her own practice!" his Mom said, with pride in her voice.

Doctor Robin's Energy blushed and Pantu looked at his Doctor, impressed. Dill's Energy, on the other hand, made Pantu nudge him.

"Dill, stop. I still have to see her every week." He heard Pantu whisper to Dill.

"So, we have to work together to remodel the gym," he said, turning to give his full attention to Pantu.

He was mostly speaking to Pantu, since Dill was still focused on Doctor Robin, who was now having a conversation with both his and Pantu's parents. Pantu didn't respond or look at him.

"I guess Dill and I can get it done ourselves," he jokingly said.

When Pantu rolled his eyes and leaned against the wall, he fought hard not to wrap his arms around the handsomely beautiful, pouting, young man in front of him. So, he stuck his hands in his pockets. He also felt the bulge in his pants, but instead, he bit his bottom lip, looking away.

"AH!" Pantu shouted before running back into the office.

PANTU: A RIFT IN NEED OF REPAIR
WEEK THREE: TUESDAY

When he came back out of the office, everyone was looking at him with questions on their faces.

"What? I decided to turn in my essays. Better time than any, since I am already here." He shrugged.

"Ah! I have mines in the car!" his Ma said, and she looked at her husband.

"Mines is still sitting on the printer," his Pa said, looking down at the floor.

"PanPan, can you drop your Pa's essay off tomorrow?" his Ma sweetly asked him.

When he rolled his eyes, folded his arms across his chest, and huffed out a breath; his Ma came to hold his arm. Everybody's faces wore different expressions, but no one spoke, waiting to hear his response.

He looked at his Ma, and although she was smiling, her eyes held a stern look in them. He knew this look. It was the eyes she gave to inform him not to publicly disrespect his Pa, or he would physically feel the consequences.

His eyes found the floor, not knowing how long it would take for his body to heal from his Ma's punishment, before he responded, "If some papers happen to be in my backpack tomorrow, I will stop by my new best friend's office, and leave it on her desk," he said, agreeing to his Ma's request, without acknowledging his Pa.

But even without looking, he could still see his Pa nod and smile while looking at the floor. His Pa trembled while shifting on his feet, trying to make himself invisible while his Ma was smiling brightly at her husband.

He didn't like the smile his Ma was giving his Pa, wanting her to look at him instead. When she turned to smile just as bright at him, his lips twitched as he pressed back his own smile, and he bounced a little on his feet.

He told her, "Turn it down Ma, I cannot see."

It was the joke they shared every night in The Slums when she tucked him into bed as a child. She would smile brightly at him as it was his request for her smiling face to be the last thing he saw before closing his eyes. He would pout and complain her smile was so bright, it was blinding him, which always made her laugh.

His Ma looked like she was going to cry from the memory, and he cut his eyes away from her, trying to hide his face, which felt heated, as if Drum's slender, warm hands were caressing his cheeks.

Drum's Pa was watching his Pa's reaction, or him trying not to have one, while Drum's Ma was smiling at their interaction. Dill was still entranced by his Doctor, who was taking notes, but Drum was looking at him with no expression.

When Drum turned to walk away, his Mind raced a mile a second. He felt Drum was unhappy with the interaction between him and his parents. Drum was the only one to understand, but not accept his answer, or his disposition towards his Pa.

Too many things have happened for me to let go, he thought as he accepted Drum's feelings but was unwilling to let go of his own.

As Drum passed his own Ma, she grabbed his arm, and Drum stopped to calmly look at her.

"Stop by the market after classes and grab dinner for tonight. Your turn to cook," she told Drum, who gave his Ma a heartbreaking smile, or at least his heart was broken, because Drum didn't direct the gorgeous smile his way.

"I get to make dinner tonight!? Nice!" Drum's sweet laughter filled the hallway. "Taco Tuesday it is."

He looked at Drum's back with wide eyes. "YOU...YOU can cook?" he asked.

It felt like time slowed as he was able to see the details of every movement each Being made. His Ma's surprised face was turning to look at Drum; his Pa's face froze but his wide eyes moved to look at the young male not far from him.

His Doctor was writing but stopped mid-stroke when she heard the tone of his question. Drum's Pa face held pride, but Drum's Ma's stern face was turning to look at him.

Dill's smile was slowly fading from also recognizing the tone in his voice. The only eyes on him were Drum's. How Drum moved so quickly, he had no idea.

He blinked and it seemed like time started to flow again. Drum's Ma walked towards him with a gentle, but stern look on her face, dragging a backwards Drum with her.

"What's wrong with him cooking?" she asked, matter-of-factly.

Dill was by his side, trying to explain. "Both men and women cook here, Pantu. There are even famous chefs all around the planet who are men," Dill said, without judgement.

"Men are not supposed to be in the kitchen," he said, without emotion, looking at Dill.

"Well, who IS supposed to be in the kitchen?" Drum's Ma asked.

"Women," he stated. The looks on everyone's faces, except his parents, made him want to explain. "Where we come from, it is law forbidding men from stepping foot in any kitchen to learn how to cook."

His Doctor stepped in. "It's a difference of culture," she said, looking between the parents.

"Pantu, it's cool. I can kind of cook," Dill said.

"Are the Women here not concerned their men would poison them?" he asked, not understanding how to trust anyone outside his own G-Pas.

"Did something happen over a hundred years ago?" Dill asked softly.

"Couple of hundred. Women say a husband poisoned his Wife, so no man or male is taught how to cook," he stated, with a look on his face saying it's a normal way of life.

Dill chuckled. "If you can't cook, just say so."

"He cannot either." He motioned towards his Pa.

Everyone turned to look at the shaking man, who responded while looking at the floor and holding his left arm, trying to make himself smaller. *"I would never poison her. She is my Love."* His Pa's quiet voice was filled with affection and for some reason, it pulled at the unhappy feelings he held for his Pa.

The looks shared between his parents made him question the way he saw their marriage since the Yolk incident. He didn't understand why his Ma would still hold such feelings for a spineless, disrespectful man.

He didn't like it. It made him unhappy, knowing what his Pa did while still being married to his Ma and claiming to love her. He believed his Ma deserved better than his Pa.

"You have at least barbequed, right?" Drum's Pa's deep voice sounded out, shaking the building and his nerves.

"What is a barbeque?" Both he and his Pa asked at the same time.

"Oh! My man!" Drum's Pa started walking towards his Pa but turned his head to speak to him. "You still have classes, so I will introduce you to the wonder later."

Throwing his arm around the much shorter man, Drum's Pa started to lead them away. "Let me introduce you to the thrill...that is the grill," Drum's Pa continued as they walked out of the front office building.

But he caught the quick look of happiness in his Pa's eyes when Drum's Pa's arm landed on his shoulder. He realized the man his Pa held feelings for was no other than the giant who helped create the particularly, intriguing, young male he was trying to control his own feelings for.

As his eyes went wide with the current information, he was trying to figure out if he could stop his Pa from disrespecting his Ma again. His small quiet breaths while he was mentally planning what to say to his Ma to get her to leave his Pa were interrupted when Drum's Ma pulled his Ma from off his arm.

"Oh, we should grab some frozen mimosas!" Drum's Ma said to his Ma.

"I actually should go back to work," his Ma apologetically said, but he could hear the unhappiness in his Ma's voice.

His Ma liked Drum's Ma! What the hell was happening right now? He knew he missed way too much in the few weeks they'd been here. He was so caught up in his own head, he ignored what was happening to his parents.

"You will, right after a couple of drinks. Your coworker will be understanding," Drum's Ma said, as she led his Ma away from the group.

"That's my cue as well. I will...see you all around," Doctor Robin said, as she closed her casebook and put away her pen.

"Let me walk you to your...vehicle?" Dill offered.

Doctor Robin looked at Dill and after a quick look at Drum, she accepted Dill's offer, leaving the two of them alone in the hallway.

He put his head in his hands. "He is going to make a move on her," he said to no one in particular.

"More than likely. The way he was focused on her, I think he likes her," Drum answered him, smiling.

"I still have to see her every week." He moaned into his hands.

Accepting all this as reality was draining for him and he leaned against the wall. He didn't look but felt Drum's eyes on him. It made his face warm every time Drum would focus on him. He liked it. Drum moved closer to him, and his breaths came faster. His heart sounded as if it was the loudest noise, even after hearing Drum's Pa's voice.

"We can meet tomorrow...after classes..." He paused as Drum came so close to him; he could feel Drum's warmth radiating over his skin. *"In the library?"* he whispered out. His knees felt weak, and he was grateful the wall was holding him up.

"Okay!" Drum responded and stopped moving closer.

He slid around Drum and headed towards the back doors of the building. He decided to bypass the bathroom, since it was more private than an empty, open hallway. He needed fresh air. His chest felt heavy and every breath he took around Drum smelled faintly of cinnamon with honey but mostly of the field meadow.

He knew he was aroused without needing to check himself. He also knew he wouldn't be able to masturbate while on campus. The unhappy feeling of being caught again, made sure his hands stayed off his penis during school hours. Not after what happened the first week.

PANTU: A CHALLENGE NOT ACCEPTED
WEEK THREE: WEDNESDAY

"It is going to be a normal day," he said to himself. He smiled as he stood on the bottom steps of a Senior-Level building.

But his face darkened when he realized he just challenged the Universe to make this day even weirder than all the others. He silently kicked himself and began begging the Universe for forgiveness. He never prayed or talked to the Universe before coming to this town, but his G-Pas secretly did in The City.

"Our Governess is the Goddess who stands tall; without her, our lives would fall; she gives our needs and answers our prayers; her word is law," he said, reciting the mantra which must be said before every prayer in The City.

The Governess wasn't here to hear his prayer, but the Universe was, so he asked to please be given a normal day. His wish was granted as his routes allowed him less than five invites, the entire day.

When he was in Calculus class, besides the small box Drum tossed into his opened backpack, it was an easy, stress-free day. When class was over, he sighed, happy.

"Thank you, Universe!" he said, out loud to a classroom of only him and Drum. "We are meeting in the library, right?" he asked. He watched as Drum nodded before leaving the classroom.

He sat in his chair, wondering why Drum seemed to be unhappy…well not unhappy, but more nonchalant than usual. He remembered the box and quickly grabbed it out of his backpack.

He opened it and was glad he was sitting down. The smell of freshly baked cinnamon honey bread hit him, and he relaxed. It was a handkerchief with the words, "For MY Dumpling" sewn along the edge. He noticed Drum's writing under the lid of the box, "Keep it close. For whenever you smell anything unpleasant-X," he read out loud. It made him smile.

Besides his G-Pas, no one had ever given him a gift meant for his own personal use. Grandpa Mack gifted him with a love of painting and rare flowers, while Grandpa Lou gifted him a love of reading and acting. Both their gifts were meant to help him mentally escape the stress that came along with living in The City.

Mostly, he was used to gifts adorning him for the pleasure of other people. To his knowledge, no one else ever gave him a personal gift, right? But racking his memories made his brain hurt, so he discarded the thought.

He neatly and carefully folded the monogramed handkerchief before tucking it in his shirt pocket. Drum believed him when he said the snake smelled horrible.

He was smiling and slightly skipping as he walked to the library. He entered to find Drum and Dill already sitting at a table, one on each side, neither of them speaking to the other. Drum was reading a book and Dill was on his phone.

Dill's eyes saw him first and waved him to an empty chair, to which Drum smirked when he sat next to Dill but didn't glance up from the book. Once he settled into his chair, Drum put away the book and leaned onto the table.

"I'm just the bankroll for ya'll ideas. You two can do whatever you want," Drum said.

He was trying to adjust to Drum's attention only being locked in on him and he felt not just his face, but his whole body heat up. His eyes found Drum's soft smile too much to handle, so he leaned back in his chair and stared at the designs on the ceiling.

Speaking while his eyes were still on the historically incorrect painting on the ceiling, "Yes, because we both know so much about sports and what a basketball court is supposed to be like."

He leaned forward, his eyes finding Drum's face. "You take the court, and we will handle the fans' area," he said. While he was lost in Drum's eyes, the full smile Drum added made his heart race.

Drum leaned back, breaking his trance, to pull papers out of a tube. "This is how the current gym was constructed," Drum said, standing up to spread blueprints on the table.

"Yea, before you performed a slam dunk and brought down half of it," Dill commented, making Drum chuckle.

"Most viral video online right now," Dill added, re-watching the video.

He stared at Drum in awe as he stood, wondering how physically strong Drum's slim, but toned body was. He leaned across the table to look over the papers, to which he felt Drum also lean in.

"What if instead of general benches, we do individual seats?" He looked over the size of the gym. "There is additional space to expand, but I am unsure if a basketball court always has to be this size?" He looked up at Drum, who was incredibly close, but uninterested in the papers on the table.

"Ninety-four by fifty, standard Higher Ed court. Center line at forty-seven feet. There is still a need for locker rooms with showers, coach's boxes, and scorer's tables," Drum informed him, holding his eyes hostage and heating up his body.

"Maybe we can add indoor food stalls along the side?" he asked, gazing into Drum's eyes. He already knew he was hard, and he was praying he didn't come. *Not right now. I will cut you and my balls off if you dare leak,* he thought.

His penis seemed to understand he was serious, and it shrank back down. His balls seemed unhappy they were included when they didn't do anything.

My Universe, I am threatening my body to not come! This is a first, he thought while staring into Drum's eyes.

His heart, on the other hand, wouldn't listen to his threats and seemed to say, *you know you will die if you cut me out, so go ahead.*

"You and I will scale the court, while making sure there is space for what is needed. Dill and I will work on the aesthetics of the extras. We will all decide how the outside of the building will be structured based off everything we fit inside," he directed.

Drum's slow blink and smile in response to his plans sent his heart, which laughed at him, into overdrive. There was nothing he could do about his heart turning traitor to his brain, the last body part to still listen to him, so he excused himself to find books on architecture.

"Oh," was all Drum said, but the feeling of Drum's eyes on him as he walked away made his Light tingle.

ALEX: A PLAN WORTH ITS WEIGHT
WEEK THREE: WEDNESDAY

After hearing about and seeing Pantu spend three classes talking with The Four, he was determined to keep Pantu, who was now getting rides from Win, away from them.

"I thought Win didn't like him?! Why are they riding to campus together? Is Queen really trying to make him a member of their group? Is Queen trying to make Pantu his boyfriend? Why is he here with Drum if Queen is the one who likes him?

"Maybe Queen is trying to get Pantu to get along with all his friends. So, of course he would start with the friend who dislikes Pantu the most. I don't like Queen's plan. He's too close to Drum," he said to himself, as he watched from his little corner of the library.

Drum and Pantu were physically getting closer to each other. He didn't know why no one could touch Drum, he only knew it became hotter the closer one was, and if you touch him, you burned.

"How is he able to stand the heat?" he asked, quietly. "Doesn't matter, here he comes," he said, a sly smile on his face.

He hid behind a shelf of books and waited until Pantu was directly on the other side to slowly make his way around to peek at the man whose face he wanted to personally carve off. But Pantu didn't seem surprised, just annoyed.

"WOW!" he whispered. *"You're doing a fantastic job of ruining my life. Guess your beautiful, sandy brown eyes are bigger than your appetite, huh?"* he asked, a sweet smile on his face.

Pantu said nothing and continued to search for books.

"Public embarrassment, constant harassment from invite requests, the lunchroom ramp and you have a bully complaint to deal with," he said, covering his mouth to giggle.

Pantu stayed silent but the look on his handsome face, which could also be called beautiful, was one of dislike at his words.

"Seems like I'm winning this game," he said, as he leaned his head to the side to look at Pantu seductively.

Pantu rolled his eyes and shook his head, and his light brown hair, which was loosely hanging down Pantu's smooth, unmarked neck, gently moved as well before Pantu let out a deep sigh.

He stared up at Pantu and when he didn't see a protruding Adam's Apple, he wondered if Pantu was really a lesbian tomboy. Pantu was as pretty as a woman.

He raised an eyebrow. *"I thought you couldn't stand to smell me?"* he asked.

Pantu refused to speak or look at him, but he wanted those gorgeous eyes on him. He never thought he would feel this way about anyone except Drum, so he decided to go all in.

"If I tell everyone you accepted my invite to Drum's party, I can make the harassment go away"—making an explosion motion with his hands—*"Poof!"* he said.

Pantu turned to look at him and his heart leapt for joy. He knew he was blushing as he enjoyed Pantu's eyes on his face.

Finally! A reaction! He smiled, while shyly looking down at a book he didn't care to read the title of. *"And who would believe you didn't?"* he asked. *"No one can see or hear us right now,"* he informed Pantu.

When he felt Pantu's eyes leave him, he glanced up to see Pantu looking around. Pantu's eyes found him again and nodded. Sure enough, no one could see them, much less hear them.

"So, you are after the reward. Which one do you want? Five minutes alone with Drum or twenty in heaven with his brother's help?" Pantu asked him, with no emotion.

"Why would a straight man care about the business of a gay one?" He shrugged at Pantu, wishing Pantu would give him any small indication of his sexuality.

"I can make your life easier before you leave and go back to your girlfriend," he said, pausing to give Pantu a chance to deny the relationship.

When Pantu said nothing, only looked at him, he felt conflicted. Since Pantu wasn't gay, he didn't need to worry about him and Drum being more than potential best friends. But it also meant he and Pantu wouldn't be anything more than friends.

"You accept my invitation, and the harassment will stop. I'll also clear up the complaint against you," he offered to Pantu. He thought he backed Pantu into a corner enough for his offer to be accepted to calm his life down.

"You filed a false complaint against me, Lied about what was said, informed Dean Hu about the ramp and now you are threatening me again. Did you file the complaint to use against me?" Pantu asked.

"It doesn't matter that the complaint is false, nor does anything else I did. All that matters is everyone saw me running out of the lunchroom, crying and distraught. And since you seem adept at avoiding invites from Liberal students, I had to think of something," he said. A victory smile lit his face.

"I will slowly carve out my eyes and run into the same wall repeatedly, thinking it will move out of my way…before I accept anything from you," Pantu said, grabbing a book and turning away.

"If I say it, everyone will believe it anyways. It's easier to agree and get something out of it than to be used and cast away. Once I tell everyone, no one will care about you and your silly little problems. You will be labeled a bully, and forced to leave the school an outcast," he quietly threatened.

Pantu turned and looked at him with a bright smile which sped up his heart and made his eyes flutter, unable to take in the radiance of such a beautiful face.

"Make sure your Lie holds weight," Pantu happily said, before walking off, leaving him in a stupor.

When he regained himself, he cursed Pantu into the depths of the planet as he fumed with so much hatred for that asshole's existence, his feelings spread throughout the library.

As the Librarian started loudly complaining about opening windows because of a stench, he secretly made his way out of his new, discreet exit, unseen.

PANTU: POSSESSIVE ABOUT HIS PAIN RELIEVER
WEEK THREE: WEDNESDAY

He had a problem. He couldn't fall asleep. His penis was hard, but it was painful to touch. He tried masturbating every day this week but couldn't come. Any time it became hard, he would double over in pain.

This led to him constantly threatening his penis to calm down. He flipped his pillow over and smelled it, looking for Drum's scent, but it was fading as it started to smell more of his room than Drum.

He moaned in frustration and forced his eyes to close so he could Sleep Think. He wanted to feel like he was in space, walking amongst the stars. It was an open dark space, littered with dull brown stars. He used his Sleep Think in The City to survive.

As his body rested, his Mind was carefully analyzing everything he'd seen and heard during the day with everything he knew previously. He was able to plan without losing rest while figuring out how to live through prolonged periods of time without incident.

He hadn't dreamed since he was eight and concluded his life was never going to be a happy one, so why dream of better days or places he would never have a chance to see? But as he walked around his space deciding which problem to handle first, he stopped at painful balls and groaned.

"This happened because I became so wrapped up in the scent. Maybe I should buy some cinnamon scented items to help ease my tension," he said.

"But it is more than just cinnamon, I would have to find the right amount of honey to mix in to get the scent just right," he said. "I could ask Drum what..."

At the mention of Drum's name, the scene inside his Mind changed, and he was in the private field meadow. He felt warmth spread over every inch of his skin and it's when he realized, the scene didn't change, he was moved.

"Am I dreaming?" he asked himself, not believing where he was. "AH! My Universe!" he exclaimed. "I am actually dreaming!" he said, happy to finally take a break from Sleep Thinking. "I wonder what soap Drum uses?" he asked, still trying to figure out his most pressing problem.

He was enjoying the sensations running across his hairless arms and legs, giving him goosebumps. Still dressed in his cotton boxers and short-sleeved, yellow T-shirt, he learned how to take deep breaths while smiling. It felt peaceful and safe, so the thought just slipped away without him noticing.

When he lifted his head and closed his eyes to feel the starlight on his face, a voice from behind made him jump.

"You called?"

He yelped in surprise. Drum was standing behind him wearing a long-sleeved, thin black shirt and grey sweatpants. Hands in his pockets, Drum looked at him with a smile. He was stuck wondering why he was dreaming of this young male.

"How could I possibly dream of you?" he whispered. "Why are you in my dream?" he asked, more of himself than what he assumed was his mental image of Drum.

"You're quite possessive, aren't you?" Drum asked him, with a chuckle.

He has the nicest physique I have ever seen, he thought as he looked Drum up and down, multiple times. He doubled over, grabbing his stomach and breathing deeply, he tried to lessen the pain.

Drum leaned over sideways to look at his face. *"Are you hurt?"* Drum gently asked.

"It is okay. I will make it go away," he answered, unwilling to tell the reason for the pain.

"If it's your back, I can give you a massage?" Drum straightened and moved closer to him.

He held up his hand, stopping Drum and responded, "It is not my back, so there is NO need for a massage." He was finally able to stand up.

"Oh?" Drum asked.

He was so stiff, he internally grimaced in pain as he ignored Drum's question and moved, while pretending he was fine. His penis wasn't listening, even under the threat of being chopped off. He walked around Drum to move towards the middle of the field meadow.

I need to get away from him, he thought to himself as he stood in the middle of the field meadow. He closed his eyes but was shaken when he felt Drum's warm arms wrap around him.

His eyes went wide as he tried to keep his knees from buckling, his heart from racing, his penis from leaking and his head from spinning. But all common sense came back to him when Drum's hands moved down into his boxers.

"I cannot be gay!" he blurted out.

To which Drum responded, "Oh?!"

Drum paused, waiting for him to do something, but he was frozen and his thoughts in disarray. After a moment, he felt unhappiness as Drum's hands slid off his body, and he found his own hands stopped Drum, craving the warmth.

He slid Drum's hands down towards his throbbing penis. The instant he experienced Drum's warm, slender, calloused hands wrap around his cold, hardened penis, he felt himself leak again.

Drum was stroking him slowly and his whole body tensed up. The multitude of amazing feelings running through his body as his penis refused to stop leaking, occasionally squirting, made him melt into Drum's chest, the release of pressure making him weak.

Drum held him up with one arm while easing a week worth of frustration with the other. He couldn't help it; he moaned so deeply it vibrated in his stomach. Clenching his hands to hold on to Drum's strong arms, he ahhh'ed and moaned so many times, he lost count.

He is so strong, he thought, as his body let go of the final amount of tension it was holding, shooting out multiple times. His breathing matched his racing heartbeat while adding to the rhythmic tingling of his Light as he was satisfied. His penis flopped over, happy and content, and he felt the small, quick change in the rhythm of his Light.

"Pantu," Drum whispered in his ear.

"Huh?" he drowsily responded, unable to focus his half-closed eyes, or control his overly relaxed body.

"Wake up."

His eyes opened and he was back in his room, in his bed. "What the hell just happened?" he asked himself out loud. He felt wet under his covers and lifting them up, he saw he soaked through his boxers, his covers and after removing the sheets, his bed.

"Why was it so much?" He groaned into his hand. "Why was it him?" he asked. He ignored the faint answer from somewhere inside him and pushed it back down into the depths of his body.

"A Woman has not touched me in a sexual way for so long, my body is only reacting to being touched," he explained to himself. "It could have been anybody."

His irrational thinking made him feel better about the dream. He cleaned himself up; laid on the unmade bed, away from the huge wet spot; covered himself up with a blanket and fell into a dreamless sleep.

PANTU: HOW TO STOP A LIAR IN ITS TRACKS
WEEK THREE: THURSDAY

As the day progressed on campus, he noticed that even though he was walking alone, Beings would only look at him and whisper. He decided not to use his routes, and no one bothered him. The whispering, together with the lack of invites, let him know the snake indeed held to his word to spread his Lie.

He quietly laughed. "So quick with it. He wasted no time. How obsessed with Drum is he?"

The closer it came to lunch, and the more he avoided commenting on the obvious whispers, students started to congratulate and praise the snake. He understood as he avoided Queen's probing eyes during third period.

He realized he didn't have time to properly cement his plan and would have to enact it with the foundation being hope instead of verified information. When the realization of how much he missed his G-Pa's hit him, he took a deep shaky breath and let it out, holding back his tears. His plan depended on Drum's willingness to read his intention and Queen's reaction.

Drum said Queen hated rumors, but how good is he? It could all go to shit quickly if Queen misunderstood or worse, was outwitted.

That would never happen, he thought as he rolled his eyes.

The closer it came to lunch, the calmer he felt. He skipped lunch and headed straight for the library. After asking the Librarian for the Manga Room key, which she gladly gave him in return for always placing the books back exactly where they were supposed to go, he went into the room.

He could hear Drum's voice talking to someone, but no one was answering. He could wait. As he walked along the shelves absentmindedly reading titles, he jumped a little when he saw Drum sitting at his desk, alone, with his laptop open and a black contraption over his head.

Drum was quickly pressing buttons, telling someone to move to the left and fire something. He stood there looking at Drum quietly, who only glanced up once, while continuing to talk into the black thing.

He patiently waited until Drum's shout of victory was followed by instructions on what to do to get ready for another fight they would have later. After closing his laptop and taking the black thing off his head, Drum looked at him warily.

"What were you doing?" he asked.

"Playing a game online," Drum answered, emotionlessly.

"With other people? It sounded as if you were talking to more than one person?" he asked.

Drum nodded; packed his laptop into his backpack and stood up to leave. It seemed Drum wasn't interested in talking to him.

"Thanks for calling off the invites to your party," he said.

Without looking at him, Drum answered, "I didn't call off anything."

"Well, maybe Queen did, since everybody stopped asking. It is quite a relief!" he said. His voice sounded happy to be left alone.

"Because they heard you accepted an invite already," Drum told him and looked at him as if he knew.

"Did I? That is weird? Well, anyways, people are leaving me alone and I do not have to attend your party. It is a win-win for me!" he said, with a smile. He started to turn and leave.

"*Come again? You accepted the invitation but never planned on going? Isn't that a Lie?*" Drum asked, with a gentle voice.

He turned his head to glance at Drum with a blank look on his face. "I do not show up to one's event without an invitation or dateless," he said, waving his hand to dismiss the conversation. He started to leave.

He heard the deep breath Drum took before speaking, "I guess until the reward is claimed, the invites are still valid."

He paused and quickly smiled, happiness settling inside him, before straightening his face to turn and meet Drum's smile.

Making it look like he was unhappy, he crossed his arms and stomped a foot on the ground, pouting his face for good measure. "That is not fair!"

But Drum was no longer listening, leaving the room through his private entrance. Waiting a moment before exiting out of the same door and running down the steps, he didn't mean to, but he tripped on the last one, falling face first into Drum's backpack. He backed up, unsure if Drum was going to hit him.

Possible Reality Drum and Dream Drum are two different people, he thought to himself. His feet touched the stairs, and he stopped.

Drum turned around to look at him along with the gathering crowd.

"It is obvious no one wants to go to your party with me, since they stopped asking on their own," he said to Drum. "Who would want to go on a date with someone accused of being a bully?"

"I'm not going to repeat myself," Drum said, before turning away.

"It is your party. Why have YOU not invited me?"

Drum's slow turn to face him was the longest five seconds of his life. He refused to back down and stood looking directly at Drum, who stared back at him with a raised eyebrow. Drum walked towards him, but he couldn't move without going back up the stairs, so he stood there, barely breathing.

Drum stopped before getting too close and tucking his hands in his pockets, Drum asked, "Pantu, would you like to go to my birthday party with me?"

Silence filled the outside as the crowd, now grown to include those in the lunchroom, became quiet, all waiting for his answer. He saw Queen, Sport and Win standing by the lunchroom door, but made no effort to stop Drum or him.

"Yes!" he rushed out, feeling elevated levels of happiness inside him. Silently clearing his throat, he tried again. "Yes. I will go to your birthday party, whatever it is," he answered, leaving out the "with you" part.

Drum smirked, turned, and walked towards his best friends with everybody giving Drum wide berth.

Standing as still as the statue he thought Drum was during the assembly, he was jolted back to this plane of possible reality when out of nowhere, Dill came and hung an arm around his shoulder.

"Pantu! Are you okay!?" Dill asked, while shouting in his ear.

He ignored Dill's question, since the most important action now was him touching his face to make sure all his bones were still intact.

"My face?" he sincerely asked Dill.

"Still too handsome for one person alone to own, and too gorgeous for a single person to possess all to themselves," Dill answered back.

He released the stress in his body.

"Pantu, walk with me to lunch and tell me, WHAT THE FUCK JUST HAPPENED!" Dill exclaimed.

QUEEN: SO MANY PLANS, SO LITTLE TIME
WEEK THREE: THURSDAY

He couldn't believe it. He stood admiring a pro at work. Watching Drum and Pantu's interaction, he was feeling like Drum's proud Papa and enamored with the way Pantu was handling the snake. He chuckled to himself.

Win was upset at being so far away from the situation. "What's so funny?"

"Pantu is a master!" he answered, with awe.

Win was anxious, and it sounded in his voice. "Pantu's face is about to get bashed in if we don't stop Drum."

"Calm down and watch the actions of an expert at work. See if you can tell why Pantu is the number one celebrated person from there," he offhandedly said to Win, his eyes never leaving the interaction.

Win was impatient and didn't want to wait. "Just tell me please!" Win whined, using the only voice known to make him relent.

"Pantu is asking Drum to publicly call Manpa a liar," he whispered.

Win looked surprised. "Explain, and I thought his name was..." But he covered Win's mouth before he could finish.

"Never say *that* name around Drum," he warned. "And when the first year started spreading statements of Pantu accepting his invite, the longer Pantu went without confirming it, the truer it sounded," he started, turning to watch the interaction.

Sport jumped in, "By asking Drum for a public invite to his party, Pantu is saying OUT LOUD and to everyone the first year's invite either wasn't accepted or is a Lie, a rumor."

He started up again, "And since there is a crowd of people to see and hear Pantu accept an invite from Drum, when no one has proof Pantu even accepted the first year's invite..." He was too excited to continue explaining.

Sport finished with a smile, "If Drum asks, it means HE believes Pantu never accepted ANY invite."

Win was covering his mouth, trying not to laugh. "My Universe, Pantu's good. But this only works if you..." Win turned to look at him.

"I know. Pantu hedged a bet I would see or hear about this and understand. Which is why it's being done publicly, knowing Drum would never hit Pantu.

"Everyone else assumes Pantu is lucky to escape possible death every day. Pantu might be testing me. Seeing if I truly hate a rumor or if we trust Pantu not to Lie to us...to Drum. Maybe both."

No Being ever made him theorize before, so the look of awe on Win's face was rightly deserved. "This is definitely going to make Pantu the most talked about Being..."

He nudged Win, nodding to him to be careful with his words and Win corrected himself.

"Person on campus and the most anonymous one online," Win finished.

He wiggled his nose as Drum walked up, telling Drum how adorable he thought the interaction with Pantu was. Drum answered with his heart-stopping smile that was endearing to him.

"Should I go next?" he asked by only raising his eyebrows.

Drum said nothing and left the decision up to him, so they headed to their classes.

He decided to give Pantu a gift, mostly in return for the beautiful nametag Pantu sketched for him. Blending green, brown, and yellow together to make a tag fitting of him and decorations describing him perfectly. Pantu hand drew his tag and colored it beautifully but didn't paint it.

Drum was still the only one with a hand painted tag from Pantu and as he thought about it, he couldn't help but smile. Pantu wasn't willing to give his all to just anybody, and the realization made him feel better about Pantu's personality while easing the tension within Drum.

He asked Pantu how he knew those were his favorite colors and Pantu shrugged, saying he seemed more a nature-ish type of male.

He wasn't one to jump to conclusions, but his gut feeling was never wrong, Pantu figured out more about their town and the Beings in it, than he let on. But Pantu was standing behind Drum's affections, so he wouldn't come right out and say it, knowing his best friend was in a delicate place with his feelings.

He decided to give it a day for the news to spread throughout the campus and online, reaching the first year. He would normally see or be told by nature when the guy was on the fringes of circles around them or hiding behind someplace.

Since the rumor, the first year kept his distance. He knew the Lie was spread in order to make him verify the information for a coveted gold Favor.

The first year is probably surrounded by Beings ready to record the interaction and post it.

Whatever the plan, he knew Pantu just gave him the perfect opportunity to make the first year come to him instead. He would refrain from labeling this a rumor until he spoke to the first year, face to face. Until then he would proceed as if Drum won his own reward, pissing the first year off even more.

Pantu gives gifts differently, depending on his relationship with you. If you aren't able to intellectually understand, Pantu's gifts would just pass you by.

Pantu gave Win the gift of friendship, instead of becoming a devastating romantic rival, and Win accepted. And although it did take a moment for Win to agree, Pantu was patient.

Pantu gave me a gift of excitement. Drum liking someone I can't get a read on is the most exciting issue I have ever come across. My anticipation is through the roof trying to figure out Pantu's personality.

Sport and Pantu haven't been around each other enough for Pantu to give a gift to him, but I can tell Pantu will. Sport will get a gift because of the way he was honest and supportive of Pantu while he was telling us about this asshole Yolk.

The first gift Pantu gave was to Drum. It wasn't the nametag, but the touch. Pantu showed Drum, someone outside his family can touch him. It was the best gift anyone could have given to a man who hasn't been "touched" in over thirteen years.

He smiled to himself. *This is a dangerous plan you're executing, Pantu.*

DRUM: WHAT A YOUNG MASTER WANTS
WEEK THREE: THURSDAY

He was full of new emotions, and he was welcoming them all, excited about finally being able to feel this way about someone. He left Queen to his own devices, but he could read Queen's Energies and knew any plan would come out in favor of Pantu.

He tapped his right foot slightly on the ground and sent out his Awareness. Subtly, sending white Energy across the ground, he saw Pantu freely walk the halls without any invites.

He could hear the whispers of the student body, confused as to who won Pantu's invite, and he chuckled at the beauty of it all. Pantu's plan wouldn't be finished until Queen closed it and the thought made his smile bigger.

His invite assured Queen would talk Manpa right into a corner without giving the snake the reward. He could also tell Queen's Energies was impressed but not satisfied with the way Pantu ended the invite requests.

He was proud of the way Pantu handled it, but even he was feeling greedy and wanted more. Reading Queen's Energies told him his best friend was going to give him what he wanted. Queen would use this to keep Pantu and him trending online.

Since Pantu's first day, students have been speculating about what happened behind his Barrier. Since Pantu's status as a Private Citizen barred anyone from posting any personal information about him, Pantu was only known to Beings on the intranet as #AnonB, short for Anonymous Being. On the human internet, Pantu was known as #AnonB, with no explanation.

If you went looking for Pantu, you wouldn't know who he was, even if you held a conversation with him. Because of Pantu's distinct way of speaking, even his words were instantly changed to keep the personal fact about the Private Citizen hidden.

No one on the intranet could point out the fact Pantu used human words or didn't conjugate his verbs online without receiving a huge warning flash across their screens, before it was posted with huge gaps of information, making the post incomplete.

If the Being kept trying to upload personal information, they would be blocked from both the intranet and internet. If the Being left his Barriers and tried to post on human electronics to the internet about a Private Citizen's information, they would meet a special team.

With the number of quiet whispers about what happens if one was to be persistent about posting privileged information, very few Beings cared enough to find out the repercussions of breaking The Private Citizen Act.

But Queen would have to cause more public interactions between him and Pantu, to have posted online and he was curious to see what Queen planned. His smile was bright as he was the first one to Calculus. He sat in his seat and leaned back while looking out the window, he was in good spirits, his Energy tingling with excitement.

He stopped smiling when Pantu walked in. He didn't look at or acknowledge Pantu as he pretended to obliviously stare out the window until class started. He was taking notes and would catch Pantu sneaking looks at him. He acted unbothered by what happened earlier, but the feeling of pride was still there.

Pantu didn't feed me to the snake. He almost smiled at the thought. He did say he would date Manpa if it gave Pantu some breathing room, but he'd only said it to make Pantu pout.

He was honestly scared when Pantu walked into the Manga Room. Was there a chance Pantu was coming to tell him there was nothing he could do about Manpa's invite, even though Manpa was Lying on him? Again. He was scared Pantu would want nothing to do with him, but Pantu always seemed to exceed his expectations, and it impressed him.

He tossed a note onto Pantu's desk and watched as Pantu opened and read it. Pantu looked confused for a second before glancing down at his shirt pocket. When Pantu blushed, he turned to the window and covered his face by placing his smile into his hand. He was grateful to his little brother for giving him the idea when he didn't know what to sew on the handkerchief.

"Just choose one of your favorite memories," Pup said, walking by.

After class ended, he waited. Pantu slowly got up and left the room, constantly peeking at him with a look he could only describe as a mix between innocent and sad. When Pantu added a look of confusion, he couldn't hold it back.

He tensed up and when his body slacked, he knew he released. As the last bit added to the already large stain on his uniform pants, he silently thanked the Universe Pantu's back was turned, and he was sitting down.

He quickly waved his hand, using his Energy to clean his pants, boxer briefs, and member. He stood in the empty classroom, looking out the window until he saw Pantu walking down the steps.

When Pantu turned and looked up at him through the window, he couldn't help but smile and was rewarded with a genuine smile back. Once Pantu was in his Mom's jeep, he turned, gathered his bag, and left the classroom.

He wasn't headed home, but to The King's Lounge. It was a room on the roof of the gym. There was a private enclosed stairway accessible by a locked door, which only opened with a registered Crystal.

The room itself covered half of the gym's roof and the other half was once set up like an outside entertainment area. Tables, chairs, hanging lights and lanterns once decorated the side of the gym he brought down. It was the one place only The Four held access to.

The other areas of the campus were for Queen to handle business. They were open for students to access, albeit, his offices were mostly handled by his Bees, and nothing of importance was kept in them. Even the Manga Room had a student key.

This was the one area Queen set strictly off limits and for only them. The students dubbed it "The Queen's Hive", which made them laugh, as no other student was ever inside to see the huge sign in the room.

He could have been there in an Instant or even created a Personal Portal. But he wanted to think and there was a ban on using Abilities on campus. He would only get in trouble if caught, so he casually walked through the almost empty campus. The day students were leaving before the night students started arriving.

As he passed, he was polite to the Cleaning Club members, throwing smiles, compliments, and gratefulness their way. Their dedication was always impressive to him, and he let it show on his face.

Walking across campus, he was wondering what and how much to tell Queen. He knew if he told Queen too much, Queen would become obsessed, but he still wanted to be as honest as possible with his best friend.

If he told Queen Pantu was more than just a crush, more than a first love, Queen would understand and would be willing to force Pantu into his arms, and he knew it would cause Pantu to push him away. Pantu and Queen would be at odds since each held an elevated level of stubbornness.

Checking the door closed and locked behind him, he slowly climbed the stairs. When he finally arrived at the door of the room, he paused. He could see Queen's Energies was already in the room, making cold drinks and snacks for them. He asked to meet Queen privately in the lounge, with just a look.

That was enough to let Queen know this was a best friends talk. He needed Panya. Panya told him the truth, even when he wanted to twist it or didn't want to hear it. Panya would give him advice along with choices.

Setting a white Barrier around the outside of the room, he entered and sat at the table in the kitchen, patiently waiting while Queen served the food and drinks.

They started eating and he asked, "What do I do Panya?" He looked directly at Queen with what he could only assume was a confused but happy expression on his face.

"Well now, what exactly is the conundrum which has you both happy and confused, Suppade?" Queen asked, happily.

"He's powerful, Panya. Just as powerful as probably me," he said with a shrug.

Queen's Energies became excited at the news. "There isn't another Being on this planet equal to you in power. Or at least, there never was before," Queen said, happy at the news.

"He created a RMD and pulled…"—he said, looking down at his food—"not pulled, more like connected it to me. We share an RMD."

Queen went quiet for a moment, and he paid attention to the flow of Energies inside his best friend's body, being careful not to overwhelm Queen, but he knew Queen was amazed.

"A Realistic Mind Dream is thought to be a fictional Ability. No one has documented an experience inside one in centuries. All the recounts are so old, they're written more like a horror fantasy story," Queen said, elated their research wasn't in vain. "So, that means there are Beings able to have Personal Abilities thought lost to us," Queen added.

"Yea," he started. "I also milked him while we were in there," he added, embarrassed, but the smile which laced his face was one of pride. Pantu could resist his natural charms, and the thought only made his body increase his Heat index.

Queen freaked out. "OH MY!" It was all he could say in the moment.

"But he said he cannot be gay," he sadly said. "I can't get a read on him or pinpoint how he feels because his feelings are everywhere and so strong. I don't know if he realizes I was there with him. He thinks it's his own personal dream. He doesn't seem to realize it's our Shared Space. Even after what happened there, he still approached me. He asked me for help?

"But when we touch, he cools down my body. He disturbs my emotions and calms my Heat. Panya, it's driving me crazy. I didn't want to wake him, but it took everything in me not to go too far. Panya?" He paused.

"I want him," he said, knowing the full weight of those words. "I want him to be mine. I want to give him every reason to stay. I want him to choose to stay." He was scared Pantu would become afraid of him and run. "To choose me," he added.

QUEEN: THAT'S WHAT BEST FRIENDS ARE FOR
WEEK THREE: THURSDAY

As Drum sat across from him, he listened as his best friend poured his heart out. Seeing Drum's emotions in disarray made him seem like a normal Being. Unlike the rest of them, he knew Drum wasn't. He squealed in delight as Drum outright asked him for help.

"The Mother Knot Tree could only wish her Humanoid Form looked this good!" he said, as he was mentally solidifying his plans.

Once Drum personally invited Pantu to his party, it was never a question of whether he would believe the first year and give him the reward. The questions were when and how. When would he call the first year out on his Lie and how would he do it? It was obvious Pantu was standing his ground against the first year and if Pantu was willing to fight, he would fight with him.

He knew Drum trusted him to handle it; thus, details were never discussed between them. He and Drum came to an agree-to-agree moment in elementary school. Since their morals lined up with each other, the problem was how the power would be handled.

They each came to the same conclusions, just by different avenues. So, Drum agreed to be hands-off and let him handle the power information provided, using it to help the Beings living under Drum's Barriers feel safe. He agreed to handle the power using Drum's values.

He knew his actions directly influenced how other Beings perceived Drum and the responsibility came with a heavy weight. The Citizens all loved, respected, and trusted Drum to keep them safe, no matter what the residents whispered in their ears.

After everything you have done for us, how could we not want the best for you, he thought, as he responded to Drum. "We need to find out what will keep him here. It seems like where he comes from is quite a harsh place. Is he looking for safety? Is he looking for love?" he said, slyly. Drum looked embarrassed and he giggled at his best friend's cute response.

"It does seem like he's afraid of something or someone outside my Barrier. He's holding on to laws and ideology which confuses me," Drum admitted.

"It doesn't SEEM like he knows what he is, and it could be a major factor in getting him to stay," he thought out loud. "Living as a human this whole time, then seeing us use our Abilities freely, MIGHT freak him out and make him run, so we should hold off doing any over the top Abilities in front of him," he stated.

"It seems he's comfortable with this Dill guy. He trusts Dill completely," Drum mentioned. Drum ignored his implications as he suspected Drum was starting to agree with them.

"Do you think the experience with Yolk makes Pantu protective of Dill?" he asked Drum, watching his reaction. If Drum thought of Dill as a hindrance, it would be better to have the Being removed.

"Yes. I also think Pantu is learning and trying to be a better friend. I feel like he needed us to know why he wouldn't say what was stated in the complaint, and why it triggered him. But he really wanted to be honest with Dill.

"Even if he exchanged some words or left out some information, he was truthful with what he did say. We can't force him to tell us more than he's willing to," Drum said.

He was caught staring at his best friend looking extremely handsome in such a thoughtful pose. Drum smiled at him, and he shook his head, not clearing it, but to bring his lost thoughts back.

"He may have said more to Dill later since he wants a friendship with him. But after what he explained about Yolk, it seemed to only make Pantu and Dill's friendship much stronger."

"They're like us Panya," Drum said, with a smile. "He found someone who would give him the friendship he wanted but never found with Yolk."

He agreed with Drum's assessment, while catching on to Drum telling him to leave Dill alone. He added, "And Dill is exactly the solid Being I think he is, so we won't be able to get any information about Pantu from him."

"He opened my Barrier Panya," Drum softly said. "It was if he could see the color of my Barrier. When he touched it, it fell open as if it was inviting him in. He stayed in the field for over five hours, and he probably would have stayed longer if his phone hadn't gone off."

As Drum was telling him this information, the look of surprise and shock was constantly switching, until they merged on his face.

Drum continued, "The RMD is a detailed reconstruction of the field, and the Energy held there."

By now, his confusion showed clearly on his face. "I thought the field made Pantu light-headed?"

Drum shrugged. "I'm not sure if the field had anything to do with that, but the next day, he was unaffected."

He was trying to piece it together in his head but there wasn't enough space. "A Full-Core Being, born to a Half-Core and Quarter-Core Beings, can open your, once, unbreakable Barrier and stay in a field holding the Sphere's Energy longer than a few minutes?! He can also make a detailed RMD, smell Malicious Intent, see the color of Barriers. I—! Who is he? What Level is he?!"

He was so excited; he was up and moving as he was talking. He couldn't stay still, but the next thought made him freeze and stare at Drum with a look of admonishment.

He said, "Pantu also has the Ability to raise the dead!"

Drum looked confused. "What?!"

He looked down at Drum's member area and back up to Drum's face.

Drum could only put his head in his hand and laugh. Making a tent with his hands, Drum agreed, "That's true."

His mind was in overdrive. Pantu wasn't completely oblivious to the Abilities Drum used to move quickly or to clean them up after their chat in the Manga Room.

"If the Elders—"

But Drum cut him off. *"You know we can't tell them this,"* Drum said, gently.

He knew how Drum felt about some of the elders. Being families who created "safe" places for their kind to live freely. The more towns a family protects, the greater opportunity to become an Elder.

Although Drum's Grandma threw all the Elders for a loop when she announced her engagement long ago, the law of 'There must be ten Elders at all times' was voted on by the Ten Elders and approved and set into law by The Royal Family.

"Right!" he said, understanding they would have to move differently to keep Pantu off the radars of those elders. His plans would become difficult if Pantu wasn't willing or didn't trust him.

"He never told Win he knew about him and Kat," Drum added.

"Wait! He knew about that when he and Win went for a walk?" he asked, and Drum nodded.

It helped him get a better picture. "Pantu used the information to make a relationship with Win. Instead of threatening him or becoming a rival, Pantu praised Win. He must have known the information would have disrupted the whole student body.

"Pantu could have used it to stop the invites, but instead, found a way to handle the situation without Malicious Intent to anyone." The picture in his head was becoming clearer.

"He dealt with public embarrassment…multiple times, invite requests, a bullying complaint, using powerful information without Malicious Intent, all while using Abilities thought dead and having an unnatural Ability for details.

"Pantu received a recommendation from Dean Hu herself, to one of the top companies on the planet. Is currently handling a rumor with adorable grace AND has the FULL protection of Young Master himself, all within the span of…what? Two and a half weeks?"

He was impressed, and that didn't come easily. He was rearranging the picture in his head. "You need information. And I think I know just how to get it from Pantu himself," he said, looking at Drum expectedly.

"HUH!?" was Drum's scared response.

They would normally move in tangent without cancelling out each other's plans and since Drum never pried, he was sure Drum's fears were valid.

He smiled to himself and bobbed his head at the newest Bianca B song playing in his Mind, he informed Drum. "Everybody dreams about their hopes and fears. Their wants and their needs. In the RMD, you can get Pantu to open to you," he said, while still jamming out to a song only he could hear.

"That would be…" Drum started, but a look from him made Drum trail off.

"You would never Lie. You will try to tell him. I think it's how Pantu will use this information is why you will be able to do it." He didn't say anything else. There was no need since he knew Drum would agree as it didn't break with his values of Lying.

He knew how much Drum hated liars. He hated bullies. Most of all, Drum hated those who would use information to subjugate, threaten, or hurt innocent Beings.

Drum hates everything the first year has shown himself to be, he thought to himself. *I was right, yet again.*

DRUMxPANTU: ONE SPOILED DUMPLING COMING RIGHT UP
WEEK THREE: THURSDAY

Drum was anticipating tonight. He wasn't sure if Pantu would show up, but he trusted the Universe wouldn't fail him. His little brother helped ease his nerves and rile them up with one sentence.

"We can't wait to meet your Fated," Pup said to him, in passing.

Being Fated wasn't a guarantee he and Pantu would end up together, but it was a sure thing Pantu would meet his younger siblings. Pup was talking more than usual. Normally, he wouldn't say anything for months and would give Kitten a look to calm her down. But lately Pup seemed to be antsy and would verbally tell Kitten to cool it. Chastising his older twin in front of everybody was unheard of.

Before Pantu showed up at the end of last month, Pup would walk around him saying, "Why so late? What's taking so long?"

Only he and their older brother Pong knew who Pup was talking about but since he only responded with a pat on Pup's head, the rest of their family waited for the mystery Being to show up. Pup was also the one who suggested a house party this year for his birthday. One of Pup's Personal Abilities is to see glimpses of the future.

As Pup described it, "It's a still photo of what will happen." Since Pup didn't want a lot of those scenes to change, he never told anyone exactly what he saw but would give out clues whenever Kitten would okay it.

He was actively trying to keep Pantu from living in this town, but after what happened, he knew the safest place for Pantu was here.

"The Universe refused to let me out of my Fate," he said, laying down on his bed.

He completed the twin's bedtime routine and was now thinking about Pantu. He didn't know when he drifted off, but he was standing in a forest like the one around the Sphere's field. He heard Pantu call his name and was immediately standing behind Pantu with a half-smile on his face.

"Then do not ever show up. Dream Drum is mean!" Pantu pouted.

He came close enough to whisper in Pantu's ear, "Who's *mean?*"

"YOU!" Pantu responded loudly, as he jumped. *"Dream you is mean,"* he said, softer, while moving away.

He noticed Dream Drum's clothes were different from last night. The young male wore the same type of clothes, but in distinct colors. A thin white, long-sleeved shirt with black sweatpants is what draped Dream Drum's nice physique.

Okay, it is more than nice, he thought to himself.

Toned, tall and athletic, a six-foot-four and a half Dream Drum was standing in a relaxed pose, watching him.

I wonder if he is flexible? He would have to be if he is based on my thoughts of Drum. Did I really notice that much about him? His mannerisms, his tone of voice, or is this how I perceive him? His thoughts were interrupted by a gentle voice.

"Pantu," Dream Drum said, calmly. "I'm real."

He looked at Dream Drum. "Well, everything here feels real. But this is a dream. I have not dreamed since I was little. All I did for twelve years was Sleep Think or Think Sleep," he said, walking amongst the field meadow. He began touching the cattails moving gently in a wind coming from nowhere.

"What's think sleep?" Dream Drum asked.

"It is when my body is unable to rest because my Mind and brain are overwhelmed. There is no calm trying to figure and plan everything out," he said. He took a deep breath to enjoy the scent of the air.

"So, what were you thinking about yesterday before I showed up?" Dream Drum asked.

He didn't notice the smile, but he felt it as he started. "How to..." he paused, thinking. As he reflected on his thoughts, the unhappy feelings he felt were not strong enough as he was still unwilling to say everything. "Mix cinnamon and honey together to get a certain scent," he finished.

"Oh?"

He looked at Dream Drum and knew his whole body was redden by the sight of the small smile on the young male's face. Dream Drum's penis jumped and his quick glance away, let the male know he noticed.

After chuckling at his shyness, Dream Drum took a deep breath and started to inform him, "This place, this space, is unique, Pantu. I have never met anyone who—"

He cut Dream Drum off. "I care not." He turned to look towards the young male. "This is my dream, and I want to have it." He pouted, crossed his arms, and refused to look directly at Dream Drum, who was unable to continue explaining or look at his sensual pouting.

"You're quite spoiled, aren't you?" Dream Drum asked, without looking at him.

"Yes!" he said. "And since you are MY Dream Drum, you have to spoil me," he said. "If you are unwilling, then there is no need for me to dream again," he said, sure the young male would agree.

He heard soft laughter as Dream Drum was right beside him and wrapped one arm around his waist while using the other to grab his arm to pull him closer.

"You never need to persuade me Pantu. You only need to ask," Dream Drum gently said, looking down at his face, which was still turned away.

"I was not persuading you; I was only voicing my option to Think Sleep instead," he said. He turned to look at Dream Drum with the softest look, complete with unhappy eyes, and placed his hand on quite a solid chest.

Dream Drum tensed up, and he could hear the hard breaths while feeling the thumps of racing heartbeats and knew he and the young male were both aroused. As Dream Drum gripped him, pulling him closer, he made his request.

"Dream Drum? Will you spoil me?" he quietly asked.

"Is it what you want?" Dream Drum asked, looking directly into his eyes.

The soft whisper of a *yes* from him made Dream Drum's stomach tighten.

"Then I will spoil you," Dream Drum whispered back.

He couldn't believe asking worked. He pocketed the bit of knowledge; now happy he would be spoiled. *If I cannot be spoiled in the real world, I might as well be spoiled in my dreams,* he thought happily while he was in Dream Drum's arms.

Liking a male or man was a deadly thing in The City but here in his dream, he could like this young male all he wanted. He was used to catering to "her" every whim and desire before she even asked.

For once, he wanted someone who would focus on him, what he wanted, how he felt. Someone who would listen to him, someone who would let him decide what he wanted. Choice. He wanted someone who wouldn't deny him a choice.

He turned to hug Dream Drum and felt the hardened bulge through the sweatpants. It matched his own but felt way bigger and longer than his. He knew he was a solid eleven inches, but Dream Drum's penis unnecessarily exceeded that. His face registered pure disbelief.

Dream Drum responded, "Oh. So, you realized?"

He was so caught off guard; he had no idea what to think. He was unsure if the smile on Dream Drum's face was silently asking outright about the size of his bulge.

"Since I'm spoiling you and you've laid claim to this Dream Space, it means whatever happens here, is because you wanted it to happen, right?" The half-smile on Dream Drum's face only widened as the realization was slowly transmitted from his Mind into his brain.

He froze. Whatever he was trying to think about ended there as Dream Drum came close to his ear to whisper, *"So, if I nibbled here,"* nibbling on his ear, *"or kiss here?"* Dream Drum moved down to kiss his neck and a quick *ah* slipped from his lips.

Dream Drum paused for a second before continuing, "That would mean you want me too."

The soft, warm kiss on his neck made every part of his body shiver. He was quite sure he came but his brain hadn't made it to that part of his body to check if it was okay.

"Or is he the only one to enjoy it?"

Dream Drum's hand slid down into his boxers, finding him already hard and leaking. His cool penis was gripped with such a warm hand, his body slacked against Dream Drum, who *ohhh'ed* from his chest.

He was shaking and his whole body felt the vibration from Dream Drum. He didn't realize his eyes were closed, until he opened them and saw they were lying down in the field meadow.

Dream Drum laid slightly above the ground, and he was on top. He didn't know when they were moved into this position but when Dream Drum grabbed his butt and pulled him closer, he gripped Dream Drum's neck and buried his face into it.

"Pantuuu," Dream Drum moaned, trying to move him into a different position.

He was moving in rhythm with Dream Drum's stroking, and his leg was right on top of this male's penis.

"Your thigh. It's going to make me release," Dream Drum got out, as they both let go of their built-up tension.

He felt his body slack from the absence of stress and was fairly sure red was tinting his olive skin as he looked down to see he ruined Dream Drum's shirt, entirely. He also happened to notice; he had no clothes on!

"WHAT THE HELL HAPPENED TO MY CLOTHES?!" he shouted, as he sat up. He looked down at a fully dressed Dream Drum who was silently laughing.

"You're the one…being spoiled…so I have…to make sure…I can spoil…all of you," Dream Drum managed to get out, between the laughter.

"See! You are mean!" He pouted as he playfully pushed Dream Drum away, but felt warm arms wrap around him to pull him close. He didn't feel naked at all.

"Pantu, I don't know if you know but I work far away on the weekends," Dream Drum stated.

"No, I did not," came a drowsy reply from him.

"I can't be here to spoil you, if I'm not close to you," Dream Drum said, quietly waiting for his acknowledgement.

He lazily replied, "Okay."

Dream Drum smirked and shook his head. *"You wouldn't invite anyone else into your Dreams, would you?"* Dream Drum asked him softly, unsure of the answer.

He dropped the idea he might be able to create multiple Spaces because he didn't want to share this experience with anyone else. Looking up at Dream Drum, he asked, "Do you want to be the only one in my dreams?" with a longing smile.

"Yes!" Was Dream Drum's immediate, gentle response.

"Then I dub thee, The Mighty Dream Drum, Only Spoiler to His Highness, Thee Great Pantu," he theatrically said, holding back his laughter with a smile.

Dream Drum was staring at him with wide eyes and a frozen smile. He covered his face and laughed at the young male's inability to speak, but his laughter broke through Dream Drum's smile.

While looking him directly in his eyes, Dream Drum asked, "That was great, His Highness. I love my moniker. Would you mind if I give you one?"

He responded with a dare, "Only if you make it better than yours."

"How about, Our Highness, Thee Great Pantu, Dumpling to the Only Dream Spoiler, The Mighty Drum?"

He felt his cheeks share the warmth they were generating with the rest of his body. He covered his face with his hands and nodded. "I like my moniker better," he said from behind his hands.

"I like my Dumpling better too," Dream Drum responded by saying the same thing Possible Reality Drum wrote on the note, while pulling him closer as they laid down.

Lying naked on top of a very firm chest and toned body belonging to Dream Drum only increased his happiness. *Universe, I know this is just a dream, but if this was my reality, I would want nothing more.* He didn't think the Universe could hear his prayer, inside his dream, inside his Mind, so he asked.

Dream Drum response of "Yes," was exactly what he wanted to hear. The next words though, he didn't.

"Pantu," Dream Drum said, with an unhappy look on his face. "Wake up."

QUEENxALEX: HOW TO STOP A LIAR IN ITS TRACKS; LESSON TWO
WEEK THREE: FRIDAY

Queen knew from his Bees, the first year was upset. He already gathered the information he needed to give Pantu a gift. He wasn't going to use all of it; he didn't need to. Some simple questions were all he needed.

I wonder if the first year will call Drum a liar? The feeling was a little thrilling and he silently thanked Pantu. It was the most exciting three weeks of school, and he was living for it.

The story on the intranet was #AnonB was personally asked to Drum's party while #TheComp said he won the invite. The drama of two Beings going head-to-head for Drum's attention was the juiciest news. A Senior and a first year competing for a Junior.

He shook his head, knowing Pantu wouldn't be happy about being tied to the first year, but ecstatic about being the number one choice.

Beings used a different system than humans to communicate. This system united Beings from other Barrier Towns under Drum's family authority using Energy to connect everyone within their own intranet. Beings living under Drum's Barriers didn't use electricity for power like humans, but Sphere Energy.

Very few Beings knew Drum was the one to create the intranet. It can still be accessed outside of Drum's Replenishing Barriers, but only those with Energy can access or understand anything on the intranet. Using the intranet outside a Replenishing Barrier also requires using Energy you won't get back just by breathing.

They could still connect to the internet humans used on their own technology, but any information related to their world wouldn't compute or was immediately scrubbed.

Those Beings who found a way to post any Being information on the internet were immediately blocked from the intranet or worse. Human made technology couldn't be used under any of Drum's Barriers as the Neutral Energy disabled all non-Energy devices.

The thoughts in his head were pleasant as he knew he was about to make Drum laugh. He was hoping Pantu would help him give Drum a little gift later, but for now, he would give Pantu a gift. The thought Pantu understood how he gave personal gifts, as opposed to everyone else, made him smile.

His gifts were not physical. Information came with knowledge and there was a lot he knew. He knew the first year was trying to replicate his information system.

The first year needed more Beings willing to be his eyes and ears, so he was going to use the invite reward to make himself popular. The first year wanted to stand out as a possible, viable choice for Drum's affections. He also knew the first year was using information in a way that pissed Drum off.

Pantu showed them, without even knowing it, he was different from the first year. Drum purposefully told Pantu. Without informing Win, he asked Win to keep an eye out in case Pantu left his home. Drum wanted to see how Pantu would use information which could bring the whole student body to its knees.

But Pantu used what he knew to honestly gain a friend instead of subjugating those he had information on. Pantu knew they were behind the invites, but he never confronted them and found a way to control how much he was asked and when. He could have threatened Win to stop the invites, but Pantu chose friendship over comfort.

By lunch, #AnonB was still trending at number one on the intranet as everyone was trying to figure out who won the reward. He knew Drum refused to open his phone or respond, Drum's face unhappy with one hashtag and what it implied, that the first year stood a chance.

But it was what he wanted. #AnonB trending at number one would only help to break the first year's emotional state. He informed his Bees to question the validity of the first year's request online.

He smiled at the second trending topic, #AnonBxDrum, while the third was #AnonBxTheComp. The fourth trending topic was #BrokenHeartedKat and his tag of #VerifiedByQueen was fifth trending.

He was checking his makeup as the first year walked up to their table. Sport was sitting directly next to him. Win sat across from Sport and next to Drum, with plenty of space between them.

There was an empty chair between him and Drum, who was to his left and uninterested in the conversation as he was eating while looking over a new puzzle box given to him. The first year was standing between Sport and Win at the opposite end of the table.

"Queen?" the first year asked, his eyes locked on to Drum's face.

The cafeteria became dead silent as the students looked on, excited to see the results which divided the campus firsthand. They were anticipating watching the exchange, so no one spoke or made a sound, even staff were engaged in the conversation taking place.

"Yes…Manpa?" he answered back, reading off the first year's monogramed shirt. "Oh, you go by another name, don't you?" he asked, trying not to laugh at a Liberal student wearing a required AH uniform.

"I told you before it's Alex. I'm still waiting for my new monogramed shirts. I wanted to let you know I already invited Pantu, and he accepted," the first year said, confidently.

He saw Drum freeze at the name Alex. Everyone felt Heat when Drum's eyes flashed in anger before he took a deep breath to steady himself, releasing the Heat wave. Everyone else realized Drum wasn't fond of the name or upset about being challenged and looked away from the first year.

"OH! You did? Are you? Did you? Did Pantu?" he asked, as he packed his makeup, placing it back in his bag. He took out a small, forest green notebook. "Do you mind verifying the information for me? I was there to see Drum's invite, but I have only HEARD of yours," he asked, politely. He phrased the sentence to imply a Favor for the information. *He wants me to start calling him Alex because it will catch on quicker.*

"Um, yea, that's no problem," the first year said, already distracted by the thought of a black and gold Favor.

"Okay. Drum invited Pantu yesterday, when did you invite Pantu?" he asked, waiting to write.

"Before Thursday," the first year answered, waiting for more questions.

He thinks he can do what Pantu did. He failed the first time with the complaint, probably thinking his excessive amount of talking fucked him up. Does he really think he can be as charmingly adorable as Pantu and control the conversation? It's like the first year is testing my patience for rumors. I should show him how to properly control a conversation, he thought, nodding while writing down the first year's answer.

"Okay, what day did you ask Pantu? Was it the day before? Several days ago…?" he asked.

"It was the day before, Wednesday," the first year stated.

"Wednesday…" he said as he jotted it down. "What time Wednesday did you have this conversation? Was it before, during or after day classes?" he asked, looking up at the first year. He saw the slight signal from Drum. "You know, this would be easier if Pantu was here with you," he said, as the lunchroom door opened and Pantu walked in.

"Speaking of…" he said.

He turned to see Pantu enter the lunchroom, scrunch up his nose, turn and walk out, without ever once looking in the first year's direction. He watched through the windows as Dill stopped Pantu to run back into the cafeteria, buy two lunches and run back to Pantu. They walked in the direction of the courtyard before he looked to the first year for an answer. He could see on the first year's face he didn't expect Pantu to come to the lunchroom.

"After day classes, I mean Wednesday after day classes. We met in the library, after day classes, on Wednesday." The first year was focused on watching Pantu walk away with Dill.

"In the library? Drum? Didn't you spend Wednesday after day classes with Pantu?" he asked.

"Hmm!" and a nod was Drum's reply.

"Were you in the library with Pantu?"

"Hmm!"

"Did you see him there?" he asked, pointing to the first year.

"Ohm," Drum said, still engrossed in the puzzle and his mouth stuffed with food.

"Drum didn't see you there. I can't ask Pantu right now, so did anyone else see you and Pantu in the library?" he asked.

"I think so. I was looking for books on airplane engineering for a project and Pantu was looking for books on architecture," the first year said. "We met when he bumped into me on the same aisle."

He looked at Drum, who ignored the comment.

"Did Pantu leave the table at any point during your time in the library?" he asked Drum.

He needed to make sure the questions flowed the right way. If he asked the wrong one, all this would have been for naught. Drum wouldn't Lie, but if he phrased his questions incorrectly, he knew he would expose Drum's Abilities.

Drum nodded. "Twice. The first time Pantu left alone."

The first year smiled in agreement.

He was anticipating the first year trying to use Drum to verify the claim since Pantu asked Drum to publicly call the first year a liar.

"So, what was the conversation?" he asked.

"Pantu apologized for being a bully," Alex said, to remind them Pantu still had an open complaint. "He apologized for the things he said to me. Like threatening to shove my own dick up my ass for being gay," he added.

He wanted to validate his complaint statements by informing the other Beings listening. They would believe Pantu was a bully and guarantee the FreeLove and LiL (Love is Love) communities would side with him.

"OH! After supposedly saying something so harsh, it was kind of Pantu to apologize. Did you forgive Pantu?" Queen asked, interested.

"Yes," came his quick response.

"Who started the conversation?"

"Pantu."

Queen nodded while writing and continued, "So how did the conversation about Drum's party come about?"

"I didn't know Pantu is straight, so I apologized for complimenting him when we first met in Hollis. I told him how deep in love I am with Drum, who was in the library with Pantu AND Dill, but I couldn't go to his party since the list was full. I suggested we go together. He said sure, he would go with me!" he ended, knowing his story sounded believable.

Everyone on campus knew he was in love with Drum. By stating Pantu sexual orientation and Dill being in the library, it would erase thoughts of Pantu and Drum being alone and kill the trending #AnonBxDrum, maybe even replace it with #Drum-x-Alex. It would also further solidify his claim of meeting Pantu.

He figured some would think Pantu used the invite to gain his forgiveness and get out of the complaint, but he didn't bother with the thought. They would believe he won the invite and Pantu was an asshole.

"Was Dill also in the library with you and Pantu?" Queen turned, asking Drum, who nodded, never looking up from his puzzle.

He was close to victory, and it felt so good. *Not only will I win the five minutes alone with Drum, but I will also get a Favor from Queen. This has to be my lucky day. I knew Drum wouldn't Lie, so if I just continue to frame my story around set facts, it will be hard to deny my story and Pantu will look like a fool and a liar. He really should have taken my offer.*

"Was that all you and Pantu spoke about?" Queen asked.

"We did talk about his first day, and I told him since he's a senior, he would be graduating and already had plans of leaving soon, so not to worry about it, most everyone forgot already," he said with confidence. He hoped it would make him look like a nice Being and he dropped information about Pantu's plans to escape the Barrier.

Queen knows I have information on Pantu. Since he didn't outright ask for it, I will drop him a bone and make him come to me. Two Favors will make it hard for him to turn down my request for a date with Drum, even though he gave Pantu four when he verified less information.

Right now, I need to get my reward and the first Favor. If I show I'm a forgiving Being by offering kind words to the one who threatened me, it will make others feel like I'm kind-hearted.

The slight smile which graced his face from seeing everything he wanted was close enough to grab with his own hands, relaxed him. He didn't feel the slightest bit of remorse, since Pantu chose not to accept his offer. He could imagine the look on Pantu's face as he and Drum became the "it" couple. His thoughts were interrupted by Queen's voice.

"So, you handled the bullying complaint?" Queen asked and he wondered if Queen was actually smart enough to read between his lines. He didn't want to outright tell Queen; he needed the Favor of verifying information.

Queen continued, "Pantu's a Senior, graduating this year, having a bully complaint on record would bar Pantu from the employment Dean Hu herself, recommended."

He smiled at Queen's stupidity, thinking Pantu would go off to work after graduating. Of course, Queen was showing him why he didn't qualify to be Drum's best friend, or around him, once he secured Drum's affections.

"The parameters of the complaint you filed, clearly state the two of you shall not be in the same space, at the same time, nor converse with each other, since YOU were worried Pantu would physically hurt you for being gay? It also states the two of you shall respect each other's space. If ONE of you is already in a shared area, the other MUST leave.

"It seems PANTU is still holding to the parameters of a COMPLAINT filed by SOMEONE who said they forgave Pantu TWO days ago ANNNDD accepted your date invite," Queen explained and smiled at the confusion on his face.

Queen kept going, "Did Pantu offer the invite acceptance in exchange for you dropping the bully complaint?"

He started to tremble, and his eyes darted around. The moment it registered with him he should have been concerned about how being alone with the Being he was afraid of, and asking them out with no witnesses, would look; it was too late. Especially without dropping the complaint.

"We didn't talk about the reward. No one mentioned it."

"It was a requirement no one mentions the reward in exchange for anything. I didn't bring it up but since you offered, Pantu asked about the reward last Wednesday. I told Pantu myself!" Queen paused to let the memory of last Wednesday show on his face. How Queen figured out he was in the library was a new mystery to him and it disrupted his thoughts.

It was the realization Queen so obviously wanted before continuing, "So, you're saying Pantu DID NOT offer to give you the reward NOR ask to drop the complaint in exchange for said invite. Pantu only asked for your forgiveness, which you stated..."— Queen flipped back through his book and read—"you gave." Queen looked up from the book directly at him.

"I just want to understand, so I can verify your information. A Being, you accused of bullying you to the point where you told *me* you feared for your life, after *bumping* into you, whom the Being can tell, by scent, is in a room, apologizes without asking *anything* in return but forgiveness. And *then* accepts a date to an infamous party from said accuser, knowing the accuser would receive the reward? Did I get that correct?"

He couldn't control his breathing as Queen spoke and was already upset Queen didn't just accept his words. They were both gay, so Queen should be in his corner. "If you don't believe me then fine! But I was in the library first and I didn't approach him, we ran into each other," he huffed out, indignantly. Forgiveness without asking anything in return would make Pantu look like a good Being, while he would be criticized for not dropping the complaint.

Queen smiled. "Hmm. You saw Pantu, Drum and even Dill, but if no one saw you in the library speaking to Pantu, it is going to be hard to verify your claim. And since you did say you forgave Pantu, why is the bullying complaint still active?

"There is STILL a set of parameters which *strictly* state the two of you shall have no interaction, on or off campus. Don't you think it'll be hard to attend a party with someone you can't be in the same room with?" Queen asked him, curiously.

"I haven't gotten around to closing it," he said, meekly.

"You've had a day and a half while you were running around telling anyone who would listen, you won the coveted invite, but well, I guess the reward was much more important," Queen said and turned to Drum, who slid his hands up his face to hide his amusement.

"I know *I'm gay* but since Pantu has been nothing but kind to me, even hand drawing me a beautiful custom nametag, I think I can ask Pantu personally, or would you like to be there with a Professor? Dean Hu would be better, then we can clear up the invite, date, and the complaint altogether!" Queen said, with much joy.

Drum outright laughed in his hands, and he took a step back to finally look at Win, who was not holding back and laughing heartily, while Sport's head was shaking back and forth. When he glanced around the lunchroom, he could see distrust and disgust in the faces of those watching. He noticed only three Beings were recording the interaction, all from strategic vantage points. And he could also hear the whispers were no longer in his favor.

"Why have you all allowed a bully to stay at our campus?!" he cried out. "I thought you hated bullies? Is that a Lie or can only the *BEINGS* you want to FUCK, be bullies?" He clenched his teeth, staring daggers at Queen. If he couldn't get the Favor or the reward, then he would force them to oust Pantu and turn him into an outcast.

Queen's slow turn to acknowledge him made his Energy cold as a glass of sweet, iced tea on the hottest Southern day and when Queen's eyes landed on him, he could feel prickles of his cold Energy poking right under his skin. He could only stand, visibly shaking.

Win stared at him as if he'd lost his mind while Sport looked down at his food. Drum turned away from the table and excused himself, with one finger up, from the conversation.

"You're *accusing* me of *letting* Pantu bully you *because* you think I want to *fuck* Pantu?" Queen asked in a dangerously deep voice. "Besides the fact no one at this table has the authority to expel any student, you are purposefully omitting information in order to Lie. Do you want to pretend you don't know I'm on the fucking WELCOMING Committee?

"It is my chosen responsibility to make sure new students are adjusting to the campus. The same way I welcomed *you* this school year, I welcome all. Just because Pantu missed the new student orientation, doesn't mean I neglect MY RESPONSIBILITY.

"Or are YOU the one who decides who I should or shouldn't welcome, for fear I would FUCK everything with a got damn hole?" Queen's voice was laced with dislike.

Sport stood and moved his chair next to Win, giving Queen a clear line to him. If he felt Queen's anger, then he knew everyone did. The accusations he was openly stating to Queen's face were immediately shot down.

He slowly took another step back, his Mind too preoccupied with the latest information, while replaying his conversation with Queen and trying to piece together how this was going in Pantu's favor, for his lips to stumble out a response.

"You want to claim a reward no one else has been able to claim for weeks, with no fucking proof and a mouthful of stank ass Lies. Go get Pantu, let's talk right here, since you said you and Pantu are on good terms.

"I mean...you claimed you had a cordial conversation." Queen spread his arms wide and looked around. "Pantu even accepted a DATE with you, so you *must be* friends, or are you still too fucking scared to talk to Pantu without staff present?" Queen asked, leaning forward. He felt Queen's eyes piercing right through him.

"Fine. I will close out the complaint. Would that help?" he asked, his voice holding a pleading tone.

Queen ignored his question and asked, "Do you think I only speak to hear the sound of my own voice!? I told you, never assume I don't already know. I watched the library surveillance tapes. I saw Dill, Drum, and instances of Pantu being there. But your ass was nowhere on the tapes, inside or outside of the library.

"Pantu left the table the first time for less than two minutes, and the second time Pantu left, Drum went along. Now, unless you want to call Drum a liar to his face, he stated he didn't see you in the library at all. So, when did you have time to chit chat as much as you say the two of you did?"

He was utterly confused. He was sure he and Pantu spoke for longer than two minutes. He realized learning to duck the cameras didn't work to his benefit.

"A word of advice which the FreeLove and LiL Com will cosign, unless Pantu declares a gender or sexuality, don't assume just because Pantu isn't interested in *fucking you.*" Queen stood and looked at the rest of the room.

It hit him. Not once during this conversation did Queen ever state Pantu's gender. He looked down, even more lost in confusion. What was Queen thinking? Queen should be his ally or under his heel. He was...He was... But he didn't get to finish the thoughts as Queen made an announcement.

"I will make a post, asking if anyone saw him in the library on Wednesday and/or speaking with Pantu. If there is an answer back by the end of day classes, I will consider giving him the reward, AF-TER verifying their information. If not, I will label this post as...a rumor," Queen said, with no emotion, looking directly at him.

He shivered. He knew having a rumor post from Queen would ruin his social media presence. He worked hard to build his following but one word from Queen and his couple thousand followers on the intranet would drop him. He might be able to salvage his human following on the internet, but Beings were not so easily swayed against Queen.

"Ask Pantu if we met in the library," he defiantly stated.

"I can do that, but I will inform you, Pantu will also need to verify the conversation. But you don't seem to appreciate how nice I'm being, offering you the reward with verified information, seeing as how you claimed to have asked Pantu in a Safe Zone." Queen's slow smile when his face changed at the realization, not only did he break the rules, but the possibility of Queen learning about the real conversation was something he didn't want. His eyes fluttered with tears and fear.

"I'm working on a fifty slot V.I.B list for Drum's party. This will be an extra list with exclusive passes. Regardless of whether your name is on the invite list, everyone will have a chance to be onstage with the hottest names in music and passes to the after party," Queen stated, smiling at the crowd and those recording.

The whole lunchroom erupted in screams and phones started pinging. He slowly backed up, his eyes on the ground, his breaths hard and difficult to take in and let out, he silently accepted Queen was no longer willing to speak to him.

"I MAY open this list up internationally and add six hundred more invitation slots," Queen added, making the students and staff scream, again.

He clenched his fists and stormed out of the lunchroom.

PANTU: A LITTLE TRUST GOES A LONG WAY
WEEK THREE: FRIDAY

He heard the screams from the lunchroom as students were rushing out.

"I need my name on that list!"

"OMU, I wonder how Queen is going to fill the slots?"

"I can't believe we'll be on stage with the planet's top performers!"

He also heard the whispers.

"I can't believe #TheComp would Lie about the invite."

"He took the opportunity from the whole campus!"

"I see why Pantu can't be in the same room with him."

"I wouldn't want to be either if he blatantly Lied on me."

"Queen more than made up for his Lie though!"

"Queen is really amazing!"

"Six hundred more invites?!"

The talk of the V.I.B list quickly drowned out the whispers. It was the first plan he enacted here in town, but he wasn't even close to being finished. The first year started it, but he would end it.

I wonder, what is the punishment for filing a false bullying complaint? He thought, eating contently while Dill was away from the table getting information from the other students, about what happened in the lunchroom.

I know it is not death, but this stupid snake still would not last ten minutes in The City.

He was approached by a male who leaned on his table. He looked up at the male and raised his eyebrows in appreciation. The male was quite handsome, and his makeup accentuated his features.

"I'm so sorry Pantu. I can't believe I believed that asshole. If you are good with Queen, then you're good with us!" the male said, gesturing to the group of seven males, who all waved and smiled at him.

His smile and redden cheeks as he slowly lowered his long lashes made the males all giggle and squeal in happiness.

"Pantu's like the main character in a romance anime," one of the males said.

"Anime?!" he asked, unsure of the term. He racked his Mind, recalling the dictionary he memorized to help him understand the difference between the meaning of certain words he used, verses how Beings use them.

The males all melted with a collective "OOOOHHHH!" By the time the Leader went to speak to him, he already understood what the word meant, but chose not to stop the male from explaining.

The Leader informed him, "Anime is the animation of manga. It's a T.V. show." The Leader's smile deepened while leaning closer, pulled in by the happy feelings leaking from him.

His face turned a light shade of red, and he let out a small giggle accompanied with a slight smile and sent the males into a frenzy again. But he needed to take another look, because the crowd had become bigger and mixed in gender. So, he just sent Women and males into a frenzy.

"I do not watch T.V." he stated. He was unhappy he wouldn't be able to experience anime and all its wonder.

The group "Aww'ed" at his unhappy confession just as Queen walked up. Everybody was now whispering for a different reason. They hoped they would hear more drama direct from Queen's mouth and their eyes were glued on him. But they were hit with other news instead.

"We should hold a PSPSA (Parent, Staff, Professor, Student Association) Anime Night fundraiser, right here in the courtyard. There will be an admission fee, but everyone can bring their own seating, and the school will provide the food, free of charge, of course."

The students went into a frenzy again, walking off while posting and calling their friends, not caring if they were still in class. He faced Queen with the most grateful eyes, making Queen redden and look away from him.

Queen regained himself before leaning closer to whisper, *"I know you aren't finished. Do you at least trust me a little now?"*

Which made his smile wider. "I do," he said, as he secretly slid Queen a recording device Dill made for him.

ALEX: JUST A TOUCH
WEEK THREE: FRIDAY

He was in his own private room in the First-year Liberal Arts building, fashioned to mimic Queen's personal office. There was no door yet, as he was still working on perfecting his own Favor cards and adding more Beings to his information system.

Staring at the Favors he created, small black cards with a gold A above an ouroboros dragon in the shape of a small gold heart and a gold S under, he knew he needed Beings to speak more favorably of him and Drum for these to mean anything.

"It seems as though Queen has chosen a side," he said to himself, in his hidden office.

He couldn't believe what happened. He was so close to getting the reward. He thought just saying Pantu accepted the invite would be enough as no one else claimed it yet.

Others knew he and Pantu had history so it wouldn't seem unbelievable that they talked. He didn't expect Queen to know the parameters of the complaint, much less expose them to everyone.

"Useless," he said, as he threw the Favor cards at the wall. No one other than a few Beings called him Alex, so the cards would mean nothing and since Queen refrained from calling him Alex during their conversation after seeing Drum's reaction, he knew Beings would also avoid calling him by the name.

He thought he could use the complaint to discredit Pantu and make him lose his social standing. The thought of Pantu being extremely popular online irked him. Labeling Pantu a bully should have killed any social media presence or at least turned the attention negative. He believed Pantu hanging out with Dill and his friends would give more credit to his complaint and have The Four run Pantu off campus.

"But even after labeling him a bully, Pantu became even more popular!" He was beside himself.

#AnonB was always trending on the intranet as Beings constantly posted updates on Pantu. And he knew other Beings made #AnonBxDrum an imaginary relationship. The fanfiction for Drum and Pantu were the most popular online right now. He posted his own fanfic of him and Drum, but the reviews on it were so bad, he deleted it.

There was a lot riding on the invite request. It would have made his complaint more valid, replace him as the possible to win Drum's heart instead of that bitch Kat, who refused his offer several times, and would have made him look like a decent Being so he could recruit more eyes and ears.

He set up his own small information team, but they were mostly Beings he extorted into helping. There were only a few he considered in a friendly light. *When I sit next to Drum, I must make sure I have the right Beings around me.*

He knew no one saw him in the library, he made sure of it. So, whoever vouched for him would have to be willing to Lie and after Queen's announcement, he knew then, no one would be willing to stand in front of Queen. Not after what just happened to him.

"Ugh! I would have been able to rival Queen's information. Maybe Drum would have given me access to the damn golden badges, or we could have started our own," he fantasized.

It took years to learn about gold badges and Bees, so when there was an opportunity to snatch one, of course he did. He had no luck in figuring out how the badge worked, since cracking an Energy code is difficult to do. He smirked, thinking all these years of research and experimentation wouldn't be in vain.

I'm so close to cracking Beings' Energy code. I need to find him and gather some more of his Energy. I'm not sure if killing him would deactivate the badge, so it's probably best not to.

He kept it in a Barrier box made of several different Beings' Energies, as he was sure it was GPS enabled. He was still working on crafting a badge which worked the same as one of Queen's gold badges.

"Dill would be a perfect fit on my side," he commented.

He knew how talented Dill was when it came to building any order someone wanted, no matter how complicated. Dill was also amazing at repairing any electronic. For some reason Energy didn't seem to resist Dill. He knew Dill helped his father with the rides for their family theme parks.

When he found out Dill also upgraded a lot of the systems to better use the Energy powering the campus, he was conflicted. He wanted to befriend or extort Dill into helping him with the badge, but he also knew the truth behind Drum and Dill. He knew Drum wouldn't accept Dill as a friend, so he stayed away from Dill and the rest of his bully friends.

"But now it seems like Drum doesn't care about Dill hanging around him," he said, tilting his head to think.

When he first saw Drum, he was enthralled by the overly handsome, tall, star-favored boy. All the middle schools in the surrounding areas attended a free day at the new museum in Sunset Town. Drum, whose smile and eyes were the most beautiful things he'd ever seen, was the main attraction during their joint field trip.

When he found out Drum was next in line to rule, he immediately wanted to be the one standing next to Drum, he wanted the title of The Emperor's Husband. He evolved his plans over the years to make sure it would happen.

Slow and steady, while keeping others away from him. He will see me and realize I'm the one, the only one for him.

He was sure it was working. He was looking for a way to get close to Drum. To achieve that, required him to do things others wouldn't see in the same light.

I have to be the one standing next to him. Who else would be worthy of him? After everything I've done, just to get to this point, I will succeed.

He could use multiple Abilities, which he believed qualified him to stand next to Drum. He knew Drum used them as well. Most Beings could use their Personal Energy for one elemental base Ability and any related sub-Abilities.

If a Being could control air, they would also be able to move items with wind, use air bubbles or pockets, and could use the wind to help them fly. But they would be restricted to using only air.

There were Universal Abilities, every Being learned as a child. Creating Barriers was one of them. Most Beings could create a Barrier, but none could make one as big and indestructible as Drum, or as many. Drum could also break all other Barriers with a flick of his wrist.

He, himself, could evade Barriers. He found a new Ability when Drum placed a thin Barrier over Hollis. He wasn't sure if The Royal Family monitored their Barriers, so to keep his actions secret, he found he could mask himself when coming and going.

Moving faster than the normal human eye was labeled Ground-step. Most could Ground-step and cover a short distance; hence they would need to continue until they reached their destination. Drum's movements seem instantaneous, no matter the distance.

Portals were another Universal Ability. But over time, it became harder for Beings to conjure using their own Energy. Since there were still a few who could do them without using electronics, the Ability stayed on the list. Kids were deemed Special if they could self-create Portals.

There were more Universal Abilities, and he could do most of them, but he hid the fact ever since he was little and his older sister stressed not telling anyone, not even their parents.

He didn't want anyone to know what he could do as those kids deemed Special were taken away, never to be seen again. He also didn't want anyone but Drum to know he had a Form. He wanted to have it be their little secret. He hoped Drum would see him as Special and protect him.

"Fucking Pantu! Literally told the whole lunchroom what I am. I had to file the complaint, or they would have thought I was an actual snake. No one knows what Pantu can do, but he knew I was a snake when that information isn't even registered." He fumed as he swiped the items on his desk onto the floor.

Most Beings were born with a Form; it was considered a disability if you didn't have one. The difference in Forms was the Ability to either release your body into the full Physical Form, or the Energy-based image which covers your physical Humanoid Form. The latter was commonplace, so a Being able to complete the former, was seen as "extra" Special.

He knew everyone thought he was Formless and disabled, since he registered himself as such and it allowed him to be content while using his Abilities without being caught.

They heard him. He knew Queen would be interested in the reason why Pantu called him a snake.

Yeah, he could have meant I'm conniving since it doesn't seem like Pantu knows about Beings and Abilities, but Queen is by no means stupid.

"Queen wouldn't go into a conversation unprepared. The way he crafted his questions made me relax and drop my guard. The more Drum agreed with me, the closer to victory I felt. Queen used it to make me comfortable and to take my mind off where the conversation was going. He seduced me, without even using his scent, into talking too much.

"I don't think Queen believes Pantu and I held a conversation. I know he was telling the truth about the video since I didn't smell any Lies from Queen. I thought since Pantu wouldn't show up on camera, I could craft my story around Drum. How did he see instances of Pantu?

"UGH! Why would he side with that fucker? Queen turned the whole conversation in favor of that motherfucker. He never said he liked him, but it seems he is trying to get Pantu and his friends to get along. Does Pantu hold Queen's Scent?

"Is that why Win is driving Pantu to campus, and he pushed Drum to have a conversation with Pantu? That can't be right." He shook his head. He was trying to understand what was happening.

"It's as if Drum likes Pantu. Drum was okay with Pantu staying in the Manga Room for two whole periods. They sit next to each other in Calculus. He even personally asked Pantu to his own birthday bash.

"He can get really close to Pantu, closer than he has ever gotten with anyone. Does that mean Pantu might be able to touch him? No way! The only Beings able to touch Drum is family, and absolutely no humans can stand his heat," he said to himself.

"But I found a way to be touched by Drum," he said, with a shy smile. "I just have to get close enough to show it!" His smile widened. "Seems like I need information." He turned and worked on questions he needed answered to continue his plan.

DRUM: A DEEPER CONNECTION
WEEK THREE: SATURDAY

He was in a business meeting with his Father, Caleb, and older brother, Justin, when he heard Pantu calling for him. He looked off to his left as if he was deep in thought and peeked at his watch.

Pantu's asleep right now. He's in the RMD. But why can I hear him, this far away? His thoughts quickly returned to the part of his Mind still listening to the proposal.

He already knew it would be turned down. Humans. They were trying to offer his Father an investment on land owned in several other redeveloping countries. Humans would cover the cost of construction, and they all would reap the benefits on land "currently" empty.

The humans were focused on the money aspect, since they assumed his Father was more concerned about keeping his status as the wealthiest person alive. But every non-human in the room knew what value those seemingly forest filled, small, country-sized plots of land held.

His Father held up his hand; handed the papers to the man standing next to him and stood. Every Being in the room who wasn't already standing, stood, and bowed as his Father and the man standing next to him, turned to exit the room, leaving the humans confused. Before exiting the door, his Father cast quick glances at both Justin and him, and they nodded their heads in understanding.

Justin took control of the meeting, while he gathered his papers and left. When he entered his Father's office, the doors locked behind him, the windows and blinds were closed, and his Father set a thin Barrier using his crimson red Energy.

His Dad asked, "Xavier, what was that?"

His Dad used his birth name, Xavier, while in The States, and his nickname, Drum, every other time. His Father used his given name, Suppade, while handling Beings' businesses outside The States. When they moved to Sunset, his name was legally changed to Suppade Xavier Carlito Santiago, be he was only registered as Suppade Santiago.

No one used his State's name unless they were family or remembered him from The States as a child. Everyone else knew him as Drum, Young Master, or Suppade. He knew his Dad immediately sensed what was happening during the meeting, it was why he ended it so quickly.

"Someone was calling me. I could hear them even though they're far away," he said, knowing he couldn't Lie to his Dad or the man standing next to him.

"Did you get a new Ability?!" his Dad asked, excited.

Although he never Lied and would never Lie to his Dad, there were things he never told him. His Dad was kind enough not to pry unless necessary and left it to him to talk when he was ready.

"I'm not sure," he answered. "It was fleeting," he added, confused.

He wasn't sure if it would work with anyone other than Pantu, and he was thinking now would be a great time to test it out again. His Dad already knew he was actively pursuing Pantu, but he felt he needed to secure Pantu's affections before he spoke with his Dad again. He never said anything to his Mom, but he already had a feeling she caught on.

"Okay let's test it out. Your Momma back home. I'll call her, and tell me what she's saying, as much as you can, with ease. Don't push too hard and overload," his Dad said. The man standing next to his Dad dialed his Mom's number and handed off the cellphone.

He held up his finger, asking for a moment. Planting his feet firmly on the floor and closing his eyes, he sent out his Awareness. His eyelids rapidly moved as he used his Enhanced Vision to follow his white Energy across continents, then across oceans before he locked on to his Mom's Energy. Focusing, he sensed her emerald Energy in their kitchen at home. He relaxed his focus and calmly opened his eyes, bringing her into view.

"Dad, can you ask Mom if she's wearing her yellow sweater, sitting on the counter, eating my homemade lactose-free raspberry gelato?" he asked, with a tiny bit of defiance.

"Babe?" his Dad asked, into the phone.

He heard his Mom shriek and saw her jump off the counter to turn around in circles, looking for a camera.

"How did he know that?!" his Mom asked, breathlessly.

"We think he may either have new Abilities or received a boost to the ones he already has," his Dad told her.

"OMU! You mean..." his Mom trailed off.

"Yea but that wasn't the Ability I'm trying for," he said, deflated. "Dad, can you go into the other room? We can video chat so you can tell me if I'm hearing Mom on my own or through the phone," he said, holding the connection to his Mom's Energy.

His Dad went into a connecting room and placed another Barrier, this one thicker than the one around his office. After confirming he couldn't be heard, even with Enhanced Hearing, his Dad connected to the computer in his office.

He asked the man still in the office with him to put headphones in and a Barrier around himself so he couldn't hear the phone conversation. He was honest and didn't peek behind their Barriers. He really wanted to know if his Abilities had become…more.

He could do that, peek behind Barriers without anyone sensing him. His hearing was beyond amazing as he could eavesdrop on any conversation he wanted, if he wanted. He could also locate any Being if he focused, and it would be easier if he recognized their Energy.

He never tried all of them together outside a Replenishing Barrier as the amount of Energy it required should be draining to him. It did before when he and Queen tried it in elementary school. And right now, he wasn't under a Replenishing Barrier, giving him the perfect opportunity to try again, since he wanted to test this Ability, knowing the man in the room was watching him with Enhanced Vision, to make sure he didn't use all his Energy or overload his damaged Core. This time, it worked, without draining him.

His Dad listened as the man repeated everything he heard his Mom say, word for word. His Dad was stunned into silence as he searched for the words to explain to his Wife, their son's Energy was powerful enough to hear and see Beings who were halfway around the planet.

"*We can't let the Elders know. They will only see this as a threat to their privacy,*" his Mom said, in a quiet, dangerous voice.

"We have to let two of them know, Babe, they family!" his Dad pleaded.

"They will bring it to the others. Even if it's out of pride, it will only place a larger target on our son's back," his Mom said, starting to cry.

"*We will tell them in time as family, not Elders,*" his Dad said, gently.

"Okay! But know I'm prepared for war if they come for our family again," his Mom said, defiantly.

"Babe, I told you I would kick-start the zombie apocalypse, just say the word," his Dad said, with a pleading voice, to which his Mom laughed and relaxed.

He decided any conversation from there on was private and let his connection to his Mom go. The man closed the computer; dropped his Barrier and poured a glass of Purified water, before kneeling in front of him. He read the worry in the silver Energy of the man in front of him.

"I'm a'ight Major!" he said.

Major nodded and handed him a glass of water. "How much that took from you?" Major asked, in a deep, southern drawl. "It didn't seem like a lot?"

Major was only a few inches shorter than his Dad, but at six-foot, eight and a half inches tall, Major was just as imposing. He only knew from photos what Major looked like. Major's broad, wide shoulders were thick with well-defined muscles and his body filled with tattoos. His mahogany brown skin and beautiful face was from his Desertlander Momma. Major's loosely coiled hair was a mixture from his Momma and Islander father. The silver color of Major's hair and rain cloud-colored eyes were from experimentation.

He nodded. "Quite a bit doe," he said, before downing the water. *What did you do Pantu?* He thought, as he sat the glass down. He told Pantu he worked too far on the weekends for him to be there in the RMD, but Pantu found a way to contact him, and he forced himself not to disappear right in front of the humans to answer Pantu's sweet voice calling out his name.

Major refilled it. "You need mo' Energy?"

"No. There ain't no missions today, so I'll be good. Dont'cha think you need yo own Energy? If this here is enough for you to win against me tonight, I'mma need more training!" he said, jokingly to Major.

DRUM: FROM THREAT TO ASSET
WEEK THREE: SUNDAY

He was happy to be back in his own room. After doing the twin's bedtime routine, he went into his connecting game room and sat. He wasn't going to game tonight; he needed his brother; he needed Major.

He knew he'd shown new Abilities to his Dad. These Abilities weren't new to him; he just hadn't shown anyone other than Queen, Major and Pong or tried them all together outside of his Barrier.

But his Dad pointed out being able to locate a Being is still a separate Ability from seeing or hearing them. He knew the rest of the Abilities he'd shown were left out. His Dad wasn't stupid or ignorant, and he never treated his Dad as such.

He appreciated his Dad knowingly deciding not to mention everything in the moment, but he knew they would have a conversation soon. If he left it unresolved for too long, it would cause a rift in their trust.

As he was lost in thought, Pong walked through a Portal and collapsed on one of his couches. Propping his feet up on a coffee table and with his hands behind his head, his older brother looked at him.

"Something on your mind little brother?" Pong asked him.

"Pong...I used my Awareness...across continents," he said.

"Um, Drum? You can't use your Awareness further than the continent you're standing on," Pong said, sitting up. "Even trying to do something on a scale that big would deplete you."

"That's why you use yo Awareness within a certain range," Major said, coming through another Portal. He sat in a gaming chair and leaned forward. "That way, they still don't know what you can do."

It was because he showed multiple, powerful Abilities at an early age. The second child to be born with a Full-Core to the same Being couple, was a miracle since Beings could normally only have one Full-Core child. Their ancestors tried to co-exist and procreate with humans, hoping to produce more than two children, but their bodies now functioned more like actual humans.

Some Beings tried to wait to find their Scent to have a child, but there was no need to wait to have sex and same gender couples were infertile. Their Entity Forms were weakened, so having one Full-Core Being child was a feat.

He nodded. "I'm not really worried about Mom," he started. And he wasn't, knowing she would be playfully oblivious to everything. She wouldn't say a word and would wait for him to tell, ask, or show her.

"But you don't know how long you will be able to keep Pantu's shown Abilities from Pops," Pong finished.

He groaned and slid down in his chair as he nodded.

"Pops will tell NanaPoo and she will tell MawMaw," Pong listed.

"And they both gone tell my grandma, the third elder," Major continued. "That's three Elders already."

Several of the Ten Elders were not at all happy about his talent for gaining new Abilities and saw his family as a threat ever since the Sphere chose his NanaPoo as its new protector.

When NanaPoo married Abuelo, she gave him the title, authority, and power of Emperor while she continued to make music, tour and become an actress. NanaPoo took on the title of First Elder when his Dad became Emperor. Abuelo's family went from being the Tenth Elder Family, to the First Elder Family under his NanaPoo.

The previous empress received an elder title from his NanaPoo but was moved to third elder when MawMaw joined as the Second Elder, after his parents married. It ruffled a lot of feathers since it moved some Elders down and previous Elder Families were removed from the list.

"You know *those elders* won't be happy with you showing off." Pong's head rolled and he knew Pong overdramatically rolled his eyes. "They're really not happy your Form is a Dragon and mine is a Phoenix."

Those elders first snubbed their noses at his brother's mythical Form, revered by their people as a sign of the most powerful ancestor to ever live. When his Form showed as a Dragon, a Being Form never seen on this planet; those elders took greater offense. The elders started whispering about how children would destroy them all. That he and his brother were too powerful to live. They would be exposed to humans.

"You thinking Pantu increased yo Abilities and if they find out, they gone want him," Major said, shaking his head. "And we know what they gone do to get to him," Major warned.

"We still have a big ass target on our backs and all it took was Momma being pregnant with four Full-Core children," Pong said. "You know what they will do to Pantu and his family."

The elders were already upset his NanaPoo had five children, with three of them being Full-Core. The elders were shouting about the unfairness of it all when other Beings could only have one Full-Core child.

When his Mom became the only documented Being to become pregnant with four Full-Core children, this pissed those elders off to their breaking point. They wanted to get rid of him and his Mom, who was pregnant with the twins.

Those elders wanted his brother and Dad, who were doing missions with Major and In, Major's younger brother, to save Beings oppressed by those elders and humans, out of the picture, so they could continue to enslave their own people.

When he was six, he and his pregnant Mom were attacked in their home while his Dad, Major, In and Pong were ambushed on a fake mission. It caused his Energy to implode within him, enhancing a new Ability given to him for protection.

He no longer trusted anyone who wasn't his family and even with his Energy thrown out of peace, he felt his Energy still understood him. The Heat came from within to keep anyone who wasn't his family from touching him, so what happened that night would never happen again.

"I'm thrown for a loop when it comes to this family. It's like his parents let him do whatever he wants but he follows their rules. Whenever Pantu's Dad is around him, he's this cowardly, timid man, who is afraid of his own son.

"His Mom does everything she can to appease Pantu, almost like she's barely holding on to a fragile peace treaty." He was up and walking around. "Queen just threw his hands up since he's walking on eggshells around my feelings."

"We need to know where Pantu stands. His Dad is invaluable to us. He's Pops' best friend and he has proven his loyalty to our family and our company. His Mom seems harmless and fun, plus she's best friends with our Momma," Pong said while walking towards him, ready to calm him down.

He stopped and glanced between Major and Pong. "Ya'll haven't met her yet, have you?" he cautiously asked.

Major and Pong shook their heads, looking between themselves.

"Yea, she appeases Pantu, but she's nowhere near harmless. She'll break every bone in Pantu's body if he disrespects his Dad," he said, scared for Pantu.

"Then it's not Pops you need to be worried about," Pong said.

"You know what Auntie will do to him if he becomes a threat," Major said. "She willing to throw away her own happiness to keep us safe."

Pong held him by the shoulders. "Eventually you're gonna have to give Momma more than just your feelings. I really don't wanna see my Momma cry, Drum."

He understood what they were saying to him. After the attack, at only six years old, he decided to play their game. They called him a threat; he showed them he was an asset. Only the Beings in the room knew he could communicate with the Sphere.

He asked to use the Sphere's Neutral Energy with his own Personal Energy to erect Barriers over the Being Communities his family had already established across the planet. At the time, Major was only sixteen, but nonetheless, Major purchased more land around the Communities for him, since he didn't want anyone to know he was behind the idea, allowing him to increase the size of each Barrier.

This caused already established Communities, not under any direct leadership, to ask for Barriers as well. Together, he and the Sphere protected over several hundred Barrier Towns. The rest belonged to four elders he knew were trying to replace him with their own puppet, and two he was unsure of.

The Sphere also spoke to him, or rather, he felt what it wanted. By the time he was eight, he, Pong, their parents, In and Major, finished planting Knot Trees in every Barrier Town protected by The Royal Family.

Knot Trees were what Beings used to either find their Fated, or to traditionally marry each other. They also connected the other places to the main Mother Knot tree in Sunset Town and the Sphere. They provided the clean air Beings needed to restore their Energy. It also fertilized the land.

This made even the elders who hated him and the ones he was unsure of allow him to plant a Knot Tree in their towns, but they had to strengthen their own Barriers as well, since the output of Energy was too much for humans to handle.

"There's something else on yo mind," Major said.

"The Sphere. I think there might be a way to increase the Energy inside, maybe even heal it," he said. He knew they would understand.

"You think Pantu can increase the Sphere's Energy like he does Abilities?" Pong asked, not expecting an answer. "His parents know about this town and Beings. Even though they were raised hidden amongst humans, they know what they are and what they can do." Pong looked at him, catching his eyes until he stared at Pong's dual Energies of orange and red. "Does Pantu know what he is and what he can do?"

He shook his head and shrugged. "I don't know. He doesn't say anything when I use my Abilities and he thinks our RMD is a dream," he said.

Major stood. "What you need?" Major asked, relenting.

"Any information on Spheres and mystical orbs," he said. "And time. I need time to pursue Pantu."

"I can give you until yo birthday for the Sphere," Major told him. "I will gather anything I can find in my grandma's library and make a copy, so you good."

"I can probably get you three weeks for Pantu," Pong said. "And that's min and max. Momma's not gonna be happy with any of us past that."

Major and Pong left through a Portal, and he dropped into his chair and sighed.

He set an internal deadline to find a way to fix the Sphere by midnight on his birthday. The Sphere was already cracked when his Dad took over as protector. But without his Dad and eventually his Mom placing their Energies around the Sphere, it would have imploded, killing everything on several different planets. But he knew much more would have been lost.

The Sphere chose him at birth, but he was a stubborn little one. He chose education, wanting to be more like his Mom, over learning to be its protector and fighting, like his Dad. After the attack, a chunk of the Sphere broke off. Now it was his Energy holding the Sphere together.

He felt what happened then was some of his fault, but he was smart enough to know there were other Beings and humans to blame and would one day get his revenge. He was asked to be patient, and he listened.

He was finally ready for bed. He'd gotten what he needed out of his Mind. He laid down, wondering if Pantu was waiting for him. He closed his eyes and was instantly pulled into the woods. He saw Pantu sitting in the field but didn't approach, since Pantu wasn't calling for him. He only stood in the forest nearby, giving Pantu his space and privacy.

PANTUxDRUM: AN UNFINISHED...
WEEK FOUR: MONDAY

Pantu was frustrated. He missed Dream Drum. As he sat by himself under the outside bleachers eating his lunch, he contemplated going to the Manga Room. *I am probably already too late.* He didn't know how to act around Possible Reality Drum. *As long as I can stay away from Real Drum, I should be okay just dreaming about him. This way I can still go back.*

As he tried to agree with his own thoughts, his penis wouldn't get on board. *Ahh, just because Dream Drum spoils you, does not mean Real Drum will,* he pleaded with his penis. But it wouldn't listen. It kept jumping and twitching.

He waited until the second bell rang before standing and stretching. *Drum should have class, so I should be able to go to the Manga Room undisturbed.* He slowly made his way into the library. He found Doctor Faye at the front counter and received the key after asking politely.

He went up to the Manga Room door and unlocked it. Once inside, he closed the door and waited to hear the lock click automatically before moving towards Drum's table. He rounded the corner and saw Drum, relaxed and reading a manga or a manhwa. He wasn't sure which one, but he thought Drum would be gone.

He turned away. "I thought you had class?" he asked.

"Canceled," was what he got back.

He turned to leave but Drum's voice stopped him.

"The Phys Ed Professors and Coaches are so engrossed by the new gym designs, there won't be any classes until after the construction is finished," Drum said.

Instead of replying, he started walking towards the door but froze at the softness of Drum's voice.

"Pantu? You don't want to talk to me?" Drum asked, gently.

There was no pleading in Drum's voice, but Drum asked a question he didn't want to answer. He was actively trying to avoid Real Drum for this very reason.

Well, one of the reasons, he corrected himself. He stood there, frozen, unsure of what to do, so he looked down and clutched his hands together in front of him.

"How's it going with your make-up work?" Drum asked him. "You have about two weeks to turn everything in."

"Two and a half weeks," he corrected. "And it is why I came here. I need to work on a shit-ton of assignments. Advanced Honors is no joke. I hate taking notes, but I need the notes in order to help me with the work because I am so distracted during class." He went off on a tangent.

He turned because he felt Drum smiling at him and sure enough, Drum was sitting there with a huge grin. His "tsk'" was followed by a pout, accompanied with crossed arms as he leaned on his left leg.

"To semi-quote a wise Headmaster of mystical arts, "Help is freely given, to those who ask"," Drum said. "First," Drum added.

He looked around while he thought about it. Dream Drum told him he only needed to ask, so he decided to do so while almost looking into Real Drum's eyes.

"Drum, will you help me with my makeup work?" he asked, politely. "Please?" he added.

"Yes," Drum replied.

"Thank you," he said, as he moved closer to slide into a chair. There was a happy feeling he never felt from anyone not his family. This feeling was directed at him, and since he wasn't used to feeling such strong positive emotions from someone not in his family, he was at a loss.

He was able to get a better look at the book. It was the latest official color edition of his favorite manga. He read about them in the official uncolored books, but never ran across them in person, until now. He wanted to know what would happen, but he hadn't gotten as far as the color manga Drum was reading. He was feeling beside himself with the urge to peek.

Drum looked at Pantu eyeing his manga. "Pantu, are you okay?" he asked, trying not to laugh at the looks of restraint flashing across such a beautiful face.

"Ah. That is my favorite manga. I have never seen a color edition, but I have not read this far into it yet, so I cannot ask to see it. I want to but just like on the island before the plunge, the freedom of adventure is the real treasure, just like reading it for yourself," Pantu rambled.

His amusement showed on his face. Pantu unwittingly Charmed everyone he met but never showed any interest, as if he didn't realize how enticing he could be. He understood he wasn't the only one to notice.

I wonder if he's interested in me outside of the RMD? He smiled. "Would you be upset having to start from the beginning?" he asked, watching Pantu react to the realization of what he didn't say.

"I would *love* to start over. Maybe I can catch something I missed the first five times I read through to the last volume I could find!" Pantu said.

He forced his ass to stay seated as he smelled Pantu's excitement while seeing it settle onto such a bright face.

"I can bring the first three, custom-made, colored omnibuses to our first tutoring session," he told Pantu, as he stood, unable to withstand the excitement leaking off the young Being in front of him. He chose not to suppress Pantu's Scent, but left the manga, knowing Pantu wouldn't look inside. He started gathering certain manga books as he walked along the shelves.

Pantu watched him before standing and following him down the aisle, wondering what he was doing. He cracked a smile at Pantu's accelerated heartbeat.

"What are you doing?" Pantu asked louder than needed and nervously looked around to see if Doctor Faye would come in and shush them.

Stopping to look Pantu in the eyes, he answered, "I was trying to get away from you."

His smile was wide as Pantu's only response was his cheeks flushing. He moved closer, making Pantu back up towards the wall by the desk.

"Or did I get up on purpose, to make you stand up?" he asked.

Confusion showed on Pantu's face. "Why would you want me to stand up?" Pantu asked, continuing to back up.

"Pantu. There's a wall there," he said, quietly as he used his Sender[42] Ability to place the books on the table.

Pantu's back hit the wall, and the only means of escape were to the left or right. Moving slowly, he continued to step closer to the young Being, who didn't know what to do with his hands as he nervously looked everywhere but into his eyes.

"Why space? Why up?" Pantu asked.

"Well, I know how I'm feeling right now, but I was unsure when it came to you. I wanted to check and that's difficult to do sitting down," he answered and smiled as he placed an arm on each side of the wall, blocking Pantu in.

---

[42] *Using Energy to send an object or person a certain distance away. See Universal Abilities #14.*

He gave Pantu time to move while taking the questions and lack of evading him to heart as he proceeded. He enjoyed watching the thoughts laced with confusion flash across each shade of brown, perfectly melded together to form the eyes he loved staring into.

He looked down at his own member and back up at Pantu, who looked down at him and then at himself. The light pink color which started to spread from such plump cheeks only deepened when the embarrassment reached Pantu's ears, which were the cutest shade of strawberry red.

He leaned in, whispering, *"Pan-tuuuu,"* he sang into the reddened ears.

His words sent a shiver throughout Pantu's body, and it made him happy, seeing this effect outside their Shared Space. Pantu's body was naturally sensual in the RMD, but out here, he held less control. Pantu clutched his hands together between them.

"Are you cold, Pantu? Shall I warm you up?" his husky-sweet voice mumbled into Pantu's ear.

Unclenching Pantu's hands, he took the right one and held it against the wall above their heads with his left hand. He slid his right hand down while moving closer until their bodies touched.

His right hand landed on Pantu's tucked shirt right at the waistline. He slowly moved, giving Pantu a chance to stop him. He kissed right behind the blushing ear and the vocal response he received back made him unintentionally moan and release.

When his hand reached Pantu's member, he rubbed through the clothes. He felt a stain increase in size and wetness while Pantu was trying not to let his knees buckle. The reaction he received made him tense up again.

"Pannn-tuuuu!" he sung into Pantu's soft smooth neck.

But his eyes, which were closed and enjoying every moment of this, snapped open as his Enhanced Hearing was triggered. He pulled back from Pantu's neck and looked around slightly, listening while sending out his Awareness.

When he realized what was happening, he took a step back from Pantu, who looked upset he stopped, but unsure of what to do or what was now happening. He looked down at their clothes. Both their pants held large wet stains on them. When Pantu looked down and closed his eyes in confused embarrassment, he waved his hand to clean them up.

As he slid their hands down off the wall, he reached into Pantu's left pocket and pulled out the clearly labeled student key, making anger flash across his face.

It was quickly replaced by sadness as their hands unhooked from each other. He moved the key from Pantu's left pocket into the right one and pressed the record button on the new device he knew Pantu received from Dill.

Pantu didn't have a chance to fully feel the emotion of surprise as seconds later, the door to the Manga Room unlocked and his expression switched to shock, looking down at their clothes.

But the stains on their pants were gone, which shocked the young man even more. He didn't move from in front of Pantu, just gave a bit more space to stand up without them touching each other.

"OH DRUM!"

The voice he knew Pantu hated sounded out and the anger the Being felt beautifully showed across his face.

"I was wondering if you would be able to tutor me after classes!? I really need some help..." The voice started off excited but died down as he moved to sit on the table, exposing Pantu was already in the room.

He was waiting to see what the first year would do, since the bullying complaint was still active.

"Pantu!? You're here!" the first year said, with forced excitement.

He stared at the first year, wondering why all he could see was a blob of black. He could only feel the first year's intention was laced with malice, since he couldn't read the first year's Energy.

He looked at the first year's head, wondering why there was a new color and what it meant. He decided he would have Cyber send an alert to those who needed to know about a new color popping up. He would text his Mom, so she could help him figure this out.

Pantu rolled his eyes and looked away from both of them. A stench must have hit Pantu like a semi-truck when he clutched his chest, trying to breathe, forcing the scent out of his mouth like he was suffocating.

"Pantu!" he said.

Pantu turned to look at him, and he nodded towards Pantu's shirt pocket. Quickly grabbing the handkerchief, Pantu took several deep breaths and relaxed. Calming down enough to roll his eyes again while he folded his stench saver, so the monogramed words were clearly visible, Pantu took care placing it back inside his shirt pocket.

He cracked a smile as he looked at Pantu. *He really can smell Intent like we smell Lies.* He was impressed. He kept his focus on the pouty Being, who was refusing to bless him with a glance, until the first year started again.

"I could really use some help. I know you're the number one student on campus and you have already taken first year classes at the Advanced Honors level, so I was hoping to reach top five, only with your help, of course," the first year said to him, while focused on Pantu.

He didn't like the way the first year's body was reacting to Pantu. He understood what happened that day in Hollis, when Pantu and the first year met.

He was certain the first year hit on Pantu, who didn't acknowledge what he couldn't understand, so the first year resorted to extortion, which to Pantu, seemed like it came from nowhere.

Pantu didn't seem to understand the first year liked him, a lot, and since he turned the first year down without even knowing it, the first year's feelings turned into jealousy whenever he saw the two guys he liked, together.

He understood all of it from just a quick assessment, and he was beginning to smell the scent the first year gave off, the one Pantu was the first to smell. He put an internal Barrier around his sense of smell to block it out. He looked back at the AH Senior and waited.

Pantu looked at him and told him in a tone which said, 'I do not care', but his body language said, 'Don't you dare'.

"If you want to cancel, it is fine. I can ask someone else," Pantu said, looking to the left and staring at the wall. *"It is not like you made a Vow or anything,"* Pantu added, speaking softly.

"I have to decline your request, since I already agreed to tutor a student," he said to the first year, both still watching Pantu's reaction.

"OH! Um. Okay. Thanks for listening to my request. It was truly kind of you," the first year said, while hoping to invoke a response from Pantu, who said nothing and didn't look at either of them.

"What time works best for you?" he asked as he grabbed his manga and placed it in his backpack.

"I normally get home around five," Pantu said, softly.

He moved closer to hear, even though he didn't need to, his hearing was amazing, he just used it as an excuse. "Why does it take you an hour to get home from campus?" he inquired.

"My Ma still picks me up, so we stop and eat together. We share a different item on the menu every day," Pantu whispered.

"That's adorably sweet of you," he said, with a smile. "Your place at five it is then," he agreed, before turning and walking towards the main library entrance doors.

"You like dumplings, right? I can pick some up on the way home. As a thank you," Pantu called out to him.

He stopped and turned. "Ebi. I like Ebi dumplings," he said. With his back towards the first year, he waited with a smile while Pantu realized he wanted shrimp dumplings.

Pantu nodded, understanding, until he looked at Drum, who looked at his shirt pocket and up at him. He made the connection Drum was calling him Ebi Dumpling and closing his eyes, he took a deep *I cannot believe this male just said that I am going to go off* breath, while Drum quickly exited the room, laughing. He went to gather his backpack when Alex stepped in front of him.

"I thought you couldn't stand to smell me. Is that how you block out my scent?" Alex asked, glancing at his shirt pocket.

He didn't respond.

"Is it a gift from The Four? Was it your birthday?" Alex asked. "I would have gotten you something, had I known you *Lied* about the day you were born," Alex added, looking for a reaction.

"You are blocking me from getting my things, so I can leave the room," he said, with no emotion. "Please move," he added.

But Alex made no indication he was going to move. "The words on that makes it seem like a personal Gift?" Alex questioned. "Why would a straight man accept a personal Gift from another man, if it isn't their birthday?" Alex asked.

When Alex lifted a finger to try and touch the side of his face, he sidestepped Alex and grabbed his bag. He went to leave the room, but Alex stepped in front of him again and he knew Alex was using Light.

He quickly blinked, turning on his True Vision to see Alex's body covered in ever-moving black lines. But he could see a bit under it, to Alex's coal-black snake Form, staring back at him, ready to strike. He quickly turned his Vision off.

"Move," he spoke but Alex only crossed his arms and sneered at him.

"You do know WHY no one openly accepts Gifts OR flaunt around Gifts given to them, right?" Alex asked, with raised eyebrows. Getting no response, Alex continued, "I don't know where your human acting ass came from, but in this town, things are different.

""There are spoken rules, like don't touch Drum. There are also unspoken rules, such as what happens when you accept a personal Gift. It means you accept the feelings of the Being giving the Gift and they know what they will get in return." Alex paused, looking at him.

"If you two aren't friends, and it's not your birthday, then that Gift would mean you're okay with giving Drum want he wants," Alex said with a chuckle, and a glance down at his butt. "Queen will bend over for you, but I really doubt Drum will, so that means..." Alex said, laughing.

He closed his eyes and took a deep breath. He was trying to regain his Calm, to remember his G-Pas' teachings.

"I'm glad you like my scent now, Pantu," Alex said, standing closer.

"I cannot smell you at all," was his reply and he saw red flash across Alex's black-colored eyes.

"Let's see how long you can hold out before Drum comes calling for what you Promised him," Alex said, with a smirk. "Is that how you got Queen to side with you? Pretending to like him and giving him a custom-made nametag, all while accepting Gifts from his best friend?

"Will Queen still side with you or let you bend him over if he knew you were inviting his best friend to your house? You're straight, so will you give up your ass willingly? Or will Drum have to take it?" Alex asked, laughing into his hand.

"Goodness Pantu, way to stir a pot. Pitting two of the most powerful Beings against each other? Did an *Elder* send you here?" Alex asked, in a sing-song voice. "If so, I vote for Drum taking it without the lube.

"Just imagine. Drum holding you down until he rips you open! The thought of you screaming in pain, excites me!" Alex exclaimed.

As he stood there, his Light didn't want him around this snake and was buzzing with dislike. Alex noticed his shaking body; his clenched hands at his side and became happy at the look on his face.

"That's what's going to happen, all because you went against me and accepted his Gift. I guess Drum wanted to have a taste of you before throwing you out to everyone else. Or maybe it's payback for what happened on your first day?" Alex happily informed him.

"I wasn't going to use my secret weapon against you, but it seems like you just won't listen. Most bow out after I ruin their social image, but you don't give a shit about that, so I guess I shall have some "friends" get your hole prepared for Drum's probably MASSIVE penis."

Alex loud laughter at the tears he was holding back made his Light wince at the sound.

"Haha! Are you going to cry? Are you feeling how much pain your asshole is going to be in? Don't think about running away so soon. I want you to be here, where I can hear you scream. I doubt "pure" Drum will want such spoiled, damaged goods, but he might still track you down somewhere else for his payment.

"So, you should stay here Pantu. Stay close to me." Alex ended in a whisper, *"Afterwards, you can take all your anger and frustrations out on me. However, you want. Whenever you need."*

He bolted. He didn't know how fast he was going as he was out the door and down the steps, trying to reach the main library entrance. Once he could see the doors, happiness started to form inside him, so he didn't feel the hand which grabbed his arm even as he was swung around to face the interior of the library.

Rapidly blinking his eyes to adjust to the feelings he was experiencing, he was also trying to figure out how he was stopped and why he couldn't see the doors anymore, but a quick snap of someone's fingers helped bring him back into focus.

He realized it was Dean Hu. He was so overwhelmed by what Alex said to him, he needed fresh, clean air. He turned around to walk back towards the doors but was stopped again by Dean Hu.

"Pantu. Show me the key you used to get into the Manga Room," Dean Hu said, calmly.

He pulled the student key out of his pocket and that's when he noticed Doctor Faye nodding her head in agreement.

"Was anyone else up there with you?" Dean Hu asked him and while watching the door they saw Alex come out, happy and in good spirits.

ALEX: A LIFE NOT WORTH RUINING...YET
WEEK FOUR: MONDAY

He watched and laughed as Pantu fled the room. "If you think I will allow you to have Drum, you must be fucking crazy!" he called after Pantu. He waited until the door closed and locked before turning around to pull the handkerchief out of his pocket. He deeply inhaled the scent and instantly became hard.

It's the sweetest thing I ever smelled, he thought to himself as he pulled his member out and started stroking. His Mind was trying to place what the exact scent he smelled from both Drum and Pantu was, but he didn't have Enhanced Smell, and this scent felt familiar as something was also tugging at his confused brain.

The sensual scent was intoxicating, and he felt himself about to come. He quickly wrapped the handkerchief around his member to catch himself. His body didn't care what the scent was since it was happily wrapped in pleasure. He felt good.

I may have lost the reward from Drum, but you have now lost something from him as well, he thought. He drunkenly smiled while stuffing himself back into his pants, handkerchief and all. *This is the softest thing I have ever felt. Seems just like Pantu, soft and sweet. I wonder what Pantu tastes like?*

His head was filled with images of how he thought Pantu's naked body would look and how it would feel to touch Pantu's soft looking skin as he left the Manga Room. Between the new Bianca B song playing in the background of his Mind and his singular point of thought being Pantu, he failed to notice, until it was too late.

He froze. He didn't expect the Dean to be here. If she saw Pantu leave the room, it means she saw him walk out the door. She held her free hand out, and he looked confused.

Dean Hu glanced up at the room door and back at him.

Oh shit! I have the universal key, he thought. He shrugged his shoulders and shook his head.

He knew the Dean wouldn't frisk him, so if he stayed quiet, he might have a chance to hide or dispose of the key. He really wanted to hide it so he could make a copy but was willing to dispose of it if he had to. He saw the librarian shake her head.

"My office. Both of you. NOW!" Dean Hu said. She released Pantu to walk off and walked beside him as they followed. He knew she was watching him out the corners of her eyes, so he refrained from putting his hands in his pockets.

They made it to her office, and he was starting to get nervous. *They can't frisk me without my parents' consent* was the only comforting thought in his Mind. He remembered the complaint was still active, so he would find a way to place the blame on Pantu. *If they talk to us separately, I can make this work.*

The Dean directed them to sit on opposite sides of the office. He was quietly trying to find a time to hide the key without Ms. Jo noticing. He was looking around as he had already slid the key out his pocket and into his sleeve when the Dean's back was turned.

They waited in the front area of the room while Dean Hu and the librarian spoke in her office. Pantu's parents both rushed in, and his mom went to hold on to Pantu, while his dad stood by the door.

Pantu's parents passed their best genes to him. They made him too perfect.

"Ah, my PanPan! Are you alright?" Pantu's mom asked, full of concern and worry, looking all over his exposed limbs.

"Yes Ma. I am not physically hurt," Pantu replied, sounding like an overly heckled son, tired of being questioned.

Pantu's mom hugged him, and he watched Pantu breathe in his mom's scent. Everyone looked up as Drum walked into the office, pass everyone and straight into the Dean's office without knocking, speaking, or looking at anyone.

Closing the door behind him didn't stop anyone from feeling the rush of heat coming from the room. Drum was upset. He didn't know exactly what about, but he figured it was about the keys. When Ms. Jo's back was turned, he disposed of the key by sending it through a small Portal to his office.

A young woman about his age came in and nodded to everyone in the room as she also made her way to the office door but knocked before entering. The heat trapped in the room rushed out. He could feel the sweat beads already formed and dropping from his body. He used his shirt to fan himself, as did everyone except Pantu, who looked unbothered by the massive heat wave.

The young woman calmly closed the door after entering. After about five minutes, Drum left without speaking and the young woman invited Pantu and his parents into the room. They came out awhile later, being escorted by her.

The young woman turned to him and gestured towards the door. "My name is Doctor Robin. After you," she said.

He rose and walked into the office. He'd noticed Pantu's mom's disgusted look on her face and Pantu's dad glared at him like he would do more than hit a child, just this once.

But his head tilted as he tried to understand the look in Pantu's dad's eyes. That man looked like he's killed before and would definitely do it again, to protect his child. There was a feeling of seeing the last bit of life leaving a person's eyes which Pantu's dad and him both understood.

He didn't understand how such a timid man could invoke such a shared feeling, but Pantu's dad's eyes unsettled him. Like the man was able to see everything he so carefully hid from the world. He felt this way before, several times, around Pantu. There was something different about the men in this family and he was intrigued.

Once everyone was seated, Dean Hu asked him, "I can't seem to get in contact with your parents. Neither of them is answering their phones. Is everything okay?"

He didn't know who in the room could smell Lies, but it was all he had to go on. It he could keep it to a minimum; he might be able to slip out of this. *If I can mix the truth with Lies, it might confuse whoever can smell them*, he thought to himself.

He nodded. "They're on a cruise vacation out of the country and don't use human phones. You have to email them, and they will contact you, when they have a chance," he half-Lied.

Kicking his feet, he noticed Doctor Robin writing in a notebook. His Mind flashed back to Queen, but he tried to dismiss it. He knew it was an uncommon Personal Ability to smell Lies. So uncommon, that after Lying so much and never being called out on it before, he was sure Queen could smell Lies, since Queen was the first to tell him his Lies stank. And if Queen could, of fucking course Drum would as well. He realized how stupid he was, not to assume at least Drum would know. How did his Mind not process it?

This is all Pantu's fault! He's way too distracting. My focus has never been so split before. I need to get him out of the way quickly or my whole plan will go to shit.

"Is it really okay to speak to me without my parents here?" he asked, shifting in his chair to move his hands under his thighs, while his eyes darted to each of them, untrusting of the Beings around him. Of course, he was only pretending. How fair would it look if they questioned him without his parents when Pantu was able to have his present. He could use this. Doctor Robin stopped writing and was looking at him curiously.

"It's okay for you to speak with us. It is clearly written in the student handbook you received during the Welcoming Orientation. Both you and your parents signed this paper,"—Dean Hu held up the Student Contract—"stating you received the handbook and will be responsible for reading and understanding campus rules. Since I'm here, Doctors Faye and Robin are also here, and Ms. Jo, we can resolve this without your parents present," Dean Hu stated.

He didn't know what the fuck was in that handbook because he never bothered to crack it open. Hell, he didn't even know where his handbook was.

"Alex. How did you open the Manga Room door?" Dean Hu asked him.

He already hid the key, so he was unafraid of being frisked. "I was going to knock on the door, since the library aide said someone already had the key, but it was cracked, so I walked in," he half-Lied, looking at the ground. He cut his eyes to see Doctor Robin again writing in her book.

"Did you know Pantu was in the room?" Doctor Robin asked, tapping her pen against her notebook while waiting to write down his answer.

"Not at first. I saw him only after speaking with Drum," he answered.

It was a partial truth. He didn't know if Pantu and Drum were even still in the Manga Room. There was a back exit they could have used, so technically, it wasn't a full Lie. Doctor Robin didn't bother to write anything, only continued to tap her notebook.

He knew he had to keep both his Lies and his intent in check. He saw Drum flinch when he released his feelings, and after Doctor Faye complained about the smell in the library, he knew she would remember.

She could have vouched I was there, but she would also be calling me smelly.

He was going to make this work in his favor. With him already having an open complaint against Pantu, he only needed to play the victim. He needed them to think about his fear of Pantu, to add value to his false claim. He tried to think of some Lies to say Pantu threatened him with, but with more than Dean Hu in the room, he needed to be careful.

When he first gave his complaint, Dean Hu didn't seem bothered by his Lies and easily filed the complaint, so he was sure the Dean couldn't smell Lies. When he had the conversation with Doctor Faye in her office, she didn't seem to notice the Lies coming out of his mouth. He'd constantly Lied to Ms. Jo, who believed everything he'd ever told her.

But with this new Being, Doctor Robin, he didn't know if she could. This Doctor reminded him of his conversation with Queen, and it made him pause. *She didn't call me out on my half-Lie, so maybe she can't as well. When I'm finished here, Pantu will be more understanding of just who I am and more inclined to listen to me from now on,* he thought. He was laughing internally and finding pleasure in the things he would make Pantu do.

"I'm asking because Pantu produced the student key and Drum has already given his statement,"—as Dean Hu spoke, she pulled the key out of her desk and placed it on top—"while Doctor Faye stated she personally handed the student key to Pantu, when the master key was reported stolen from her office.

"I just wanted to check how you, based on the testimonies of Doctor Faye, her Aide, Drum and Pantu, were able to enter a locked room without a key?" she asked again. "The Aide stated they told you the key was given to Pantu. And I've had the door checked, the lock isn't broken," Dean Hu added, looking between the written statements on her desk.

He couldn't say anything. He didn't understand what was happening. He took a deep breath. "I think I should wait to have this conversation with my parents around," he said. Tears welled up in the corners of his eyes. "You can check me all you want. I told you the door was cracked!" he Lied, his voice cracking with the pain of their disbelief in him. Doctor Robin said nothing, only wrote in her notebook.

The Dean waved the comment away. "I'm not going to frisk you. It's unnecessary. Per your complaint parameters, you should have never entered the room at all, even cracked. Although both Pantu and Drum have given statements that the door was locked," she informed him. "But I will ask if you and Pantu exchanged words?"

He froze, being put on the spot. It didn't matter what he would say Pantu said, Dean Hu already believed their testimonies. He was so busy trying to keep his Lies and intent in check, he forgot to find a way to call everyone else Liars. Since he wasn't sure of Doctor Robin's Abilities, he tested her. But even after he realized Doctor Robin never called out his Lies, he'd still absentmindedly neglected to think up anything. So, he kept it simple.

"No, I only spoke to Drum, asking him to tutor me, but he said he was already tutoring a student. Drum left first and Pantu left right after him," he said, thinking he would cover his Lie with truth and then a half-Lie.

He knew Pantu spoke to him, which was a violation of the complaint, so Pantu wouldn't want to get in trouble either. As the aggressor, Pantu would be held responsible. But Doctor Robin started writing again and he couldn't understand why it was bothering him.

But before he could figure out what was so disturbing about Doctor Robin, Dean Hu slid a small device out of her desk drawer and showed him.

"What's that?" he asked, looking at the slim, thin, circular, white, metal device.

"It's a recording device. It was recording since before you walked into the Manga Room," Dean Hu answered calmly. "The sound of a door unlocking can clearly be heard, right before you speak. This was given as evidence of you having the universal key. We have yet to listen to the rest."

His Mind went numb, and he started to panic. He didn't know if it was Drum's or Pantu's recording, but as the Dean pressed play, he knew he didn't want anyone to hear past him talking to Drum.

"NO! STOP!" he shouted, unsure of everything on the recording, he lunged. But he was met with Dean Hu's invisible Personal Barrier and bounced back from her. He flew back into the bookshelf beside the Dean's desk, knocking down several shelves of books and awards.

Dean Hu leaned back and looked at him weirdly. She continued to let the recording play, and as the conversation started, he went to run out the door. The secretary, Ms. Jo, was waiting by the door, stopping him from leaving.

"It's in the school contract you and your parents signed, all parties involved in a campus investigation must fully cooperate or be expelled while the school enlists the help of the police from there on out," Ms. Jo said, looking down at him with dead eyes.

He stood there, listening to the conversation over again. He refused to look at the faces of the Beings in the room because he didn't want to see their eyes. He turned and sat in his chair as Doctor Faye was picking up the items he knocked down and putting them back. He knew he needed to handle this here since he couldn't afford to have the police in his business. If he was lucky, the recording would stop after Drum left the room.

He was in his own world and didn't realize his intent against Pantu was leaking until the comments about his scent became louder. Ms. Jo opened the windows as everyone in the room couldn't take what they called, his stench. He thought about the Gift Drum gave Pantu that cancels out his scent, and it made him even more upset at Pantu.

It's because he got too close to Drum. Queen should have just taken my information on him. He even accepted a personal Gift from Drum, while giving Queen Gifts. No one is talking about that. It's all his fault.

Tears started streaming down his face as the conversation between him and Pantu sounded out. He was fucked and he knew it. The recording proved he violated his own complaint, held Pantu, someone he was supposedly scared of, against his will, wished and threatened sexual assault on him, all while offering himself to Pantu.

After the recording ended, Dean Hu placed it on her desk with a lost look on her face. She leaned back as she thought about how to handle this new situation. No one has been expelled from the school since Mrs. Hu became Dean, but he knew there were students who transferred out or just quit altogether. He wondered which one he would have to do. If he was forced to leave the school, it would only give him more time to make Pantu's life a living hell before killing him.

"Let's pause on that as it will be handled as a complaint violation. Speaking of, Alex, would you like to explain why you filed a false bullying complaint?" Dean Hu asked. She didn't bother looking at him but reached into her desk to pull out another recording device.

"This was dropped off at my office minutes before the call from Doctor Faye about her key. Oddly enough, I was looking for you to explain this. You weren't in class, so imagine my surprise when I went to the library to investigate the key and you walked out of the Manga Room." She pressed play and the Wednesday library conversation sounded out.

He could clearly be heard admitting the complaint was invalid and threatening Pantu. He refused to look at anyone as he cried.

"Alex, do I even need to tell you the complaint is invalid. Now, for filing a false complaint, threatening a student, stealing, harassment, and bullying, you are suspended for two weeks. You may not step back on this campus until you have completed these requirements.

"First is the full two weeks, ten school days, suspension. The second is four psychiatrist sessions, by a school approved Doctor, who will clear you to come back. The third is a meeting with you and both your parents, in my office with the school appointed Psychiatrist and these papers, signed.

"Once those are completed, you may go back to classes. If you would like to continue being a student here, you will give proof of weekly sessions with a Psychiatrist approved by Doctor Robin.

"If these steps are not completed, or you opt not to have weekly sessions, I will take that as your *withdrawal* from the school," Dean Hu said. She filled in the paperwork needed to be signed by his parents.

He was shocked. *I'm not expelled!? Why aren't I expelled? They have all the proof they need to file both a bullying complaint and a police report.* He was trying to piece it together.

Doctor Robin said, "Both Pantu and Pantu's parents have declined filing a report on you."

He couldn't believe it! Why wouldn't Pantu file a report? Wait? Why did no one here gender Pantu? It's the same as Queen. Why would Pantu get a report while his was a complaint? He asked the difference.

Dean Hu explained, "A complaint means you said someone did something to you and an investigation is held to find proof. Had you read the paperwork, you would know the lunchroom conversation was not included in the complaint you filed, since there were statements contradicting what you said.

"You made a claim you feared for your life, so the complaint was about the contact in Hollis, which we couldn't confirm or deny. Your complaint is only valid for thirty days, which gives you time to give the school evidence or you can give us a restraining order from Hollis police which has evidence of the contact in Hollis.

"A campus report is filed if you have proof of said activity and/or there are matching witness statements," she ended. She handed a stack of papers to him, outlining and explaining the details of his suspension.

"You have a list of Psychiatrists, approved by the school. I suggest your parents contact them as soon as possible to set up the appointments. You will be escorted to collect your things and off the campus grounds by Ms. Jo. The campus' Barrier will also restrict your

Energy until we have set the return meeting. I will see you, your parents, and your Doctor in two weeks," she said.

Ms. Jo gestured for him to leave the office.

He was glad the day classes were long over, so he wouldn't be paraded around in front of the students he shared classes with. It also gave him time to think. Had he read the complaint, he would have known to have one of the police chiefs he was extorting to file a fucking report for him. He could have been done with Pantu with just that.

He checked to make sure it was still safely tucked away. He looked at his watch, seven thirty ss (star-set). Drum was with Pantu for two and a half hours and he wasn't close enough to receive the signals from his pets inside Pantu's house. He still needed to grab some things from his home, so he headed to Hollis on his moped.

Fuck you Pantu. I've got something for you. You should have filed the fucking report, then at least you would have had some peace. You fucked up. Don't touch what isn't yours. Not without my permission.

PANTUxDRUM: LOST AND FOUND
WEEK FOUR: MONDAY

Pantu was disgusted, but he still needed to teach the conniving snake a full lesson on how to ruin someone's life. Many owners fell from grace because he punished their pets.

By his third year, being number one, he punished both owners and pets. No one ever died by his word or his hand, they would just be demoted to the Outer Ring, The Slums or tortured. It became a rarity for anyone to challenge him.

He possessed what his G-Pas called Talent. Several of them in fact. One of them was smelling and feeling people's evil emotions and ill intent. It was how he was able to stay ahead of those who wanted to ruin him.

He was thinking as he prepped for Drum's arrival. It took a lot of coaxing from his Ma for him to openly go into the kitchen. He adamantly pleaded with his Ma to believe he would never poison her.

Her laughter and simple, "I know" was enough to stop his nerves from vibrating his whole body.

He decided to learn how to reheat food already made. He was applying the knowledge to heat up the shrimp dumplings he asked his Ma to buy on the way to their house. He looked at the clock and four fifty-eight ss flashed into four fifty-nine ss.

He didn't know if Drum would be on time, but when the doorbell rang at exactly five o'clock ss, he smiled. He set the plate of dumplings on the table next to drinks, along with his piles of make-up work and went to answer the door.

Drum was leaning against the handrails with his hands in his pockets, wearing loose blue jeans, a white shirt with the logo of his favorite manga over a black, thin, long-sleeved shirt. He looked closer at Drum's shirt and saw the signature of the manga creator, Eiichi Goda. Drum looked up at him to smile, and his heart stopped for a moment, with a familiar shiver running down his spine while his Light tingled, before he could only look away.

Drum was sexy in anything he wore without trying. Even the campus uniforms only AH students were required to wear looked perfect on Drum. He'd never seen the young male in casual wear, but Drum made the clothes feel expensive.

He felt naked and underdressed in a light brown T-shirt with *Seize Your Life* across it and khaki shorts. He never felt so beneath a person in his whole life. It was the first time he ever thought of these words, *I wish I was Special.*

He was pulled out of his thoughts when he heard Drum's silky voice.

"Are you going to invite me in?"

It was the only way he could think of to describe the voice which reached his Orb. How could a person's voice be so light and sweet, with a deep undertone that pulled him in, making him hear and cling to every word?

He looked at Drum, unsure of how to react. "Yes, come in."

Drum reached the top step but was stopped by him planting his feet and crossing his arms in front of the handsome young male.

He needed to look up into Drum's face, which soaked up the freely given rays of starlight and send it back out into the world brighter than what was given. The person standing on his steps was a most particularly annoying person. He wanted to know but Drum seemed impossible to figure out. There was a sense of Drum being more than what he could see, a complex puzzle he couldn't figure out from just a glance.

I have never met someone who could command my attention or incite my curiosity for longer than a few minutes. It annoyed him for sure, but he would figure out how this young male could resist his Charisma[43].

"Wait! Are you a vampire who needs an invitation in order to come in and suck my blood?" he asked Drum, his head tilted to eye the tall, handsome male in front of him.

Drum's smile widened. "Actually Pantu, I prefer Energy over blood."

He felt his Light rushing throughout his body faster than he ever felt it before and as he tried to ignore it, he replied, "But starlight does not burn you?" He didn't smell a Lie, and it intrigued him.

Drum raised an eyebrow. "You know how you can see vampires, but can't see a reflection?"

His Mind instantly connected the dots. "You can stand the Stars because it is a direct light. The Moons reflect the light of the Stars and since you are cursed with no reflection, you also can not tolerate anything which reflects." He nodded in acceptance of this latest information. "Makes sense."

Drum's slight chuckle sent out a feeling towards him of pure appreciation and admiration. His G-Pas would feel this way whenever he won a debate, and he didn't realize how much he missed the few happy feelings he felt in The City.

"Tick-tock, tick-tock." Drum clicked his tongue, marking the seconds. "Are you resending your invite?" Drum asked him.

---

[43] *Term Others in The City used instead of Seduction.*

He was too busy trying to ignore the feelings rushing through him, along with his body reacting, on its own, by the way, while keeping his voice steady and his face from heating up. But it was all for naught, since as soon as Drum spoke, he needed to start all over again.

"Ah! No! My Light is not healthy. It tastes like how the first-year smells," he said.

"How would I know, unless I've tried?" Drum asked, giving him a full smile.

Sadly, while accepting his fate, he relented. "Just agree...that you will not suck me dry." He pouted in defeat.

Drum looked at him with a smirk, glanced down at his shorts and back up to his face. He watched Drum and understood what was being said before his whole body felt the way he did when he touched his face in the Manga Room with Drum's heat still on his hand.

Drum's raised eyebrow at his body turning a deep red, had him at a loss for words. He turned and walked back into his house and instead of closing the door in Drum's face, he didn't know why he left it open.

He couldn't believe what he just said. What was even worse was Drum's non-verbal reply. He was sitting at the eating room table with his face in his hands, trying to cool himself down when Drum came and sat, right next to him. He sat straight up, his eyes darting around, trying to figure out what was happening. He set the table up so they would sit across from each other. But Drum made no effort to move and started to unpack.

Chill out Pantu! He is only sitting next to you. No need to get all riled up. Real Drum is your friend, so be friends. Do not confuse him with Dream Drum. His Mind was telling him, and he was listening. *Friends.* He could work with that. He stood and moved Drum's table setting closer.

"Where are the assignments you have completed? Have you turned them in yet?" Drum asked him.

He snapped out of a trance he didn't even realize he was in. "Ah! I left the completed work upstairs. It is finished so I do not need help with those," he said, not looking at Drum and trying to figure out what in the hell was happening to him.

"You don't want me to check them? Better to know they're correct before turning them in?" Drum asked.

He nodded and went upstairs to his room. Leaving the door open, he started to gather his completed work. He was taking and releasing so many deep breaths to Calm himself, he was starting to feel light-headed. He could do this, figure out this male without becoming attached. But Drum wasn't Yolk. There were things happening to his body he couldn't medically explain, and it was making him feel unhappy.

"Your room's pretty bare?" Drum asked.

He jumped in shock. He looked at a calm, relaxed Drum, leaning against his door frame. Drum's eyes circled the room, coming back to meet his. He turned away without saying anything and continued what he was doing.

Drum went over and opened the floor to ceiling curtains covering the sitting bay windows. He ran over and quickly tried to close them.

The look Drum gave him made him mumble, *"It feels like someone is watching me."* He kept trying to close the curtains.

Drum stepped behind him and in one quick movement, closed the curtains with a wave of a hand, before wrapping him in warmth.

"Drum. I...I..." Was all he could say as he turned to face the male holding him. If this were a dream, it would be okay for him to live how he wanted. If this were reality, well, it would mean he was really out of The City. He was free.

Drum waited a moment and when he became quiet, the handsome face responded with a slight smile, which made his penis twitch. When warm hands moved to possessively grip his butt, he gasped at his penis leaking. As he was being lifted, his legs and arms wrapped around Drum, allowing himself to be carried towards his bed.

He felt himself falling backwards. Drum was now half laying on him while smothering his neck with warm kisses which made his back arch, his body reaching to soak up more warmth. When Drum's hand finally found his penis, his boxers were already destroyed.

When sweet, deep moaning joined the small, high-pitched noises he never knew could come from him, he came all over Drum's hand and his clothes. As Drum continued to stroke him, he felt Drum's Light spread throughout his house. He wasn't paranoid. He felt the warm Light collide with six other Light-created things in his house before they were burned away.

Once the Light dissipated, he soaked up warmth from the blast of Light Drum then sent out to cover the whole property. He became even more aroused, finally able to feel comfortable in his own house. His body trembled and wiggled so much, the male on top of him let out a deep moan.

"Pan-tuu!" Drum pleaded.

When an "AAAAH!" from his lips made it to Drum's ears, the young male's whole body went stiff, and it was when he smelled even more of the field meadow.

His penis jumped and when the vein on the back of it twitched, he came again. He laid there for a brief second before he rolled away from Drum and curled up in a ball.

"I have to clean up," he explained.

"Okay," Drum said, and rose to leave. "I will wait for you," Drum told him, and he could sense honesty behind every word.

He was waiting for Drum to finish, but Drum didn't have anything else to add as he unlocked and opened the door to leave. His thoughts were now focused on when the door was closed, much less locked. He sat up and watched as Drum walked away.

"There is no way Real Drum would say that to me and mean it in that way," he said, out loud to himself as he moved to the bathroom, but Drum already cleaned them both up.

"This has to be a torture dream." He stared in the mirror. "It is your dream, go for it!"

He went back downstairs and sat next to Drum, who was trying not to smile. When he noticed Drum was eating the dumplings along with the kimchi, he placed the completed stack of work in front of the male and pouted.

"You like kimchi?" he asked.

The look on Drum's face upon the realization only the dumplings were for him, made him happy, but he decided to cover his smile by pouting. When Drum decided to offer a sign of peace by picking up a dumpling with kimchi and holding it out for him to eat, he thought about it for a moment; knowing that in The City, accepting an offering from someone meant you were open to their advances. He shrugged and ate the food.

Drum's smile at him eating the food only grew wider at his enjoyment of the delicious combination. Drum pulled out the first three books and sat them on the table. His eyes went wide at the beautiful, thick, wooden-covered, colored omnibuses in front of him.

He went to pick up volume one but was stopped by an "OH" from Drum, who leaned on the table, watching him.

"What?" he asked, pausing his reach.

"Ten pages," Drum said and smiled.

"Drum. What ten pages?" he asked, wondering why Drum was so short with his answers and explanations.

"You have to have ten pages of assignments completed," Drum answered. "And by completed, I mean correct."

He eyed Drum while continuing to slowly reach for the first volume.

"Confident huh?" Drum said with a chuckle.

He just smiled at Drum, ignoring the fact he wanted this male to kiss all over his flawless body. Except for the hair on his head and his long, curvy eyelashes, there wasn't a single hair anywhere else on his body.

"I would not be, except someone and his best friends gave me their notes, sooooo," he said, as his hand landed on the volume.

He gently pulled back, clutching the book. His deliberate movements as he turned to look at the manga while opening the book to the first page were overexaggerated and he was sneaking glances at Drum's reaction.

Whatever Drum was in the middle of doing before he dropped his completed work in front of him, stopped. Now he was watching his work being checked. Drum laid several papers down in front of him and one page off to the side.

He hadn't read past the first page as he watched Drum separate his pile of completed assignments. The stack in front of Drum was increasing while he was counting the pages being laid off to the side and when the amount reached five, he became excited.

I am halfway there, he thought.

He put the book down and turned to face Drum. He gave a full lopsided smile, making the male take shallow breaths as his eyes closed. He wondered if he smelled like anything to Drum, who never mentioned he held a scent.

He asked, "Do I smell to you?"

To which Drum's eyes opened and turned to look at him.

"Yes," was all Drum said.

"Is it a bad smell?" he asked, unhappy Drum could resist spilling everything. In The City, the simple words of his questions could Entice[44] anyone into telling him everything without him having to probe deeper. How the young male in front of him could pull anything more out of him, was deeply bothering him.

"No."

"Well, what does it smell like?" he asked, moving closer. Maybe Drum just needed to smell more of him in order for his Charisma to work. If he could get Drum to spill on just one simple question, then he could get Drum to tell him everything, so he could finally put an end to this unnatural curiosity.

"Pretzels."

"Ah? Then why do you call me Dumpling?" he asked. He moved back to increase the space between them. It was a simple answer to his simple question. Why did his Charisma not work on Drum?

"Because"—Drum smiled at him—"I like to eat dumplings."

---

[44] *Term Others in The City used instead of Charm.*

He looked at Drum, tilting his head as his Mind and brain tried to understand, making a small frown pull at the corners of his mouth. "You do not like to eat pretzels?" he asked.

"Not anymore," Drum replied.

"Ah!" he said out loud. *I smell like something he does not even like.* He was feeling like this was what people called a mistake. He wasn't used to publicly making those. *We are just friends. He smells like he means me no harm. So just be friends Pantu. Stop thinking too much about this. You can go back straight. Why care what you smell like to HIM?* His brain was trying hard to calm his emotions, his Mind, and his body, so he accepted the reasoning.

Drum turned to finish checking his work.

"That would be six!" he said to Drum with happiness laced in his voice. He would win this little bet, and he didn't know why it made him happy, but it did.

Drum smiled in response but kept focus on the paperwork. Drum put more pages in the front pile, to his dismay and when Drum laughed before placing another paper in the side pile, he didn't understand but bounced with happiness anyways.

"That is now seven!" he exclaimed, moving to rest himself on Drum's armrest.

As he came closer to Drum's face, he started bouncing faster in anticipation. Drum seemed unable to focus, since he decided to use his Charisma, his facial expressions, and his body language to distract the young male. It must have worked because Drum placed the papers down without looking at him.

"I can't concentrate."

"Why not?" he asked, batting his long lashes at Drum while slightly frowning up his face. He could have sworn he saw the male's pants twitch, but he kept his focus on the incredibly handsome face next to him.

Drum turned to look him directly in his eyes, coming close enough to make their noses touch. "You.Are.Distracting.Me," Drum stated, each word holding such happy emotions within them.

He stared into honey eyes and saw the tiniest, dancing, green, leaf shaped specks in Drum's eyes. But the longer he was enthralled by these eyes, the brighter the light behind them shone. This was the first time in his entire life; he was happy to be held captive.

"WHAT!" he exclaimed, giving his brightest smile. "Fine. Then I will not be excited at all anymore," he said, teasing.

"Is that a challenge?" Drum asked back, with a smirk.

His mouth fell open, and his face froze. Drum was quick-witted and he was enjoying it.

"I will just stay on my side of the chairs," he said, backing up, hoping to pull Drum to him.

But Drum turned and finished checking the rest of the papers without adding any more to the correct pile and he couldn't understand! He'd pulled out more than he'd ever had to use on a person before and it didn't seem to work on Drum. He was sure if it were anyone else, they would be soft molding clay in his hands, ready to be shaped to his liking.

"I know there were at least ten completed." He pouted, sincerely. Not only did he lose the bet, but he also couldn't get Drum to tell him much of anything.

Drum looked at his pouting face and spoke, "You're correct Pantu." Drum leaned closer to him and smiled. Drum picked up the side pile of papers and placed them in front of him.

"You only have seven incorrect assignments." Drum grinned at his happy reaction.

"You should have more confidence in your intelligence. It takes a near perfect score to get a limited seat in an Advanced Honors homeroom," Drum told him.

He was frozen, trying to understand again what was happening to his life. He completed half of the assignments, but wasn't ready to turn them in. *"I do not feel very intelligent,"* he mumbled.

"I guess I would feel that way too if I missed my first week of classes," Drum said, teasing him.

"I—" He stopped, unwilling to make another mistake.

"Wanted to be the main character?" Drum teased again.

He felt his face heat up and refused to look at the male causing such an emotion.

"What is the difference between a homogenous and heterogeneous mixture?" Drum asked.

"When the substance is evenly distributed throughout the mixture it is homogeneous. If the varied materials can be easily distinguished, then it is a heterogeneous mixture," he replied, absentmindedly, happy to distract both his Mind and his brain from trying to understand his feelings.

"Which is faster, gravity or vacuum filtration?" Drum asked.

"Vacuum filtration," he answered.

Drum looked at him with a raised eyebrow, waiting for him to explain a question only asked with his eyes.

He ignored the fact Drum so easily did to him what he was known for doing in The City and continued, "If the product of interest is a solid, a vacuum is connected to the flask to pull the solvent through more quickly. Using filter paper with a funnel into a beaker to separate mixtures when your product of interest is a filtrate, is gravity filtration." He stared at Drum, unable to believe what was being said, since these were such simple questions.

"Bonus question," Drum started, "name the atmospheric levels and their distance from the ground."

He held up a finger while looking at the table and accessing the information inside him. "The Breathable Ozone level is sixty-eight miles from the ground." He held up another finger. "The Tropicalsphere starts at sixty-eight point two miles from the Breathable Ozone layer with the Nexusphere starting at three hundred and forty-one point two miles."

With three fingers up, he continued, "Middlesphere starts at five hundred and eighty-three point two miles. Hell starts at three thousand four hundred and twenty-one point two miles, while Heaven is the largest and starts at six thousand eight hundred and thirty-one point two miles away but less than two million ninety thousand miles before the vacuum of space is reached."

He turned to Drum so he could see Drum's expression first-hand instead of feeling them as he stated his next words. "There is a thin unnamed layer which is point two miles thick between each named atmosphere. The thin layer is included by human scientists to keep what they consider mythology out of their work."

He smiled as he watched Drum's eyes flicker slightly and at the same time, there was a slight jerk at the corners of Drum's lips. He couldn't help but wonder if Drum knew the name of the thin layer and was feeling a bit indignant at being tested. It felt too much like a City debate, but he knew it was the only thing he could use to relate. He was racking his Mind but all he knew was The City.

"Do you have a name for the thin layer between each atmosphere?" he slyly asked while holding a small, soft smile on his face. If Drum didn't realize there was even an extra layer, he wouldn't have a name for it nor be educated in his history. *How could he be the most intelligent if he knew not the history of his people?*

Drum, however, gave him a full smile and answered, "Our human ancestors worshipped them as The Protections of Phoenix, but now Beings just call it Phoenix's Barriers." Drum turned from the wide-eyed look on his face with a slight chuckle and went back to his work.

"I looked at the dates of the incorrect assignments, and they are from after you ran into Manpa," Drum told him.

He was slowly coming back to this possible reality. The classes were hours long and required concentration as the assignments were extremely difficult and numerous. The

Advanced Honors courses were compressed into two months with classes every weekday, if he was distracted dealing with the first year, his grades would suffer.

"Do you like the gift? Does it work?" Drum asked Pantu.

"Yes, it did," Pantu said, avoiding his eyes.

"Oh, did you like the scent?" he asked, with a smile.

"Yes."

"What does it smell like?"

"Cinnamon and honey."

"Oh!" he said, before turning to focus on dividing Pantu's work into classes.

He was really enjoying his first day as Pantu's tutor. Other than being tone deaf in his essays; writing like asshole humans from earlier centuries, his facts were concrete, his grammar was decent, and Pantu's citing was precise. He took folders out of his bag and placed the separated completed work into their own class folders before Pantu said anything else.

"I did not mean to, but I lost it," Pantu said, quietly.

"Lost what?" he asked.

Pantu looked around. "The Gift you gave me. I lost it somewhere between the library and Dean Hu's office. Or maybe on my way home. I know not where it is," Pantu said, holding back tears.

"Pantu. It's okay..." He started.

But Pantu was visibly upset, gripping the armrest tightly and slightly shaking. "No, it is not, Drum. It was a Gift you gave me, *for me,* and now I no longer have it. Losing a Gift where I am from is the BIGGEST insult. I cannot ask my Ma to help me look for it. She would be so disappointed," Pantu said as tears started to fall. "It was the only thing that kept Mansnake's stench away."

He came close to gently remove Pantu's hands from the armrest and held them. He figured the first year correctly assumed Pantu's handkerchief was a Gift from him and stole it off Pantu. He didn't say anything about it in the office because he doubted Pantu would even want it back at that point.

"Want to learn something cool?" he asked instead, hoping his Mom would figure out the snake's forehead color soon.

Pantu bounced in the chair, hoped laced in those beautiful multi-brown eyes.

He nodded towards Pantu's chest. "May I?" he asked.

Pantu's head tilt and questioning look made him smile and continue, "I need to look at your Energy to see if this will work. If you're able to do it, I will monitor your Energy while showing you this Ability."

Pantu's eyes looked over to the left, thinking for a moment before looking back at him with a smile and a nod.

He increased his Enhanced Vision and looked inside Pantu's body. The Energy swirling was a deep brown color, but he could tell it was because of something else flowing inside Pantu's Energy, which gave way to such a deep brown color. He would need to clean those impurities from Pantu in order to Purify and increase his Energy.

Pantu's body was having a challenging time replacing the small amount of Energy that was used during their conversations. Pantu was partially blocked, or his Energy was being restrained, he wasn't sure which one it was, but he knew he would figure it out.

He could see Pantu would still be able to do this simple Ability, and it would help him get a better read on the Energy by watching Pantu use it.

"Think of your favorite memory, the one that makes you the happiest," he instructed.

Pantu's eyes closed, and he watched as the Being relaxed and smiled. He saw the Energy soften the swirling force inside Pantu.

"Take a small amount of your Energy and wrap it around the scent from the memory. Carefully hold it and bring it to the forefront of your Mind," he instructed. He watched carefully as Pantu completed each step naturally.

"And slightly push it out to cover your skin, so all you smell is..." He trailed off as the scent of cinnamon and honey did more than cover Pantu, it filled the room.

His chest tightened as he stared at the handsomely beautiful Being. He was sure the Being in front of him said his Gift smelled like cinnamon and honey and now Pantu was releasing the same scent from his happiest memory.

When Pantu's eyes opened, the brightness of the light brown eyes added to the full smile on his face. The whole house was filled with the light scent of cinnamon and honey, and Pantu was so happy, he smiled and bounced in the chair, while still holding on to his hands. "Will this work around Mansnake?" Pantu asked, still bouncing in the chair.

"Yes," he absentmindedly answered. "But you need to practice containing it, then I can teach you how to focus it."

"Okay!"

Pantu's bright response made his Heat Flare up more than he anticipated and when Pantu turned to look at him with such an innocent look, in response to feeling the Heat pouring off him, he stared back while watching the bright light flicker and dance, making the different shades of Pantu's brown eyes melt together.

He wanted Pantu in his arms and when he felt the cooling Energy coming off the Being in waves, he responded by pulling the only Being he's ever wanted closer. But he didn't stop there, as he pulled Pantu onto his lap.

Pantu held his face, and he moaned at the coldness spreading over his body as their eyes were locked into each other, both unwilling to release the other. The moan he received when his hands grabbed onto Pantu's butt and member, encouraged him not to start out slow. He moved Pantu with one hand, to match the speed and rhythm of the other hand, stroking him.

Pantu felt his hardening member through his jeans and rubbed against it before he smelled Pantu coming while staring into his eyes. He tensed up and moaned in response, refusing to even blink.

"Is your Ma in the driveway?" he asked.

Pantu, who scrambled to climb off him, exclaimed, "MY CLOTHES!?"

He held on to the soft, squishy Being on his lap and laughed. "Just teasing," he said as he made new clothes appear on Pantu.

Pantu looked down at the soft, ambiguous clothes, but didn't say a word as he was carefully helped back to his own seat.

"What assignments do you have due tomorrow?" he asked, deciding not to say anything about the adorably confused look on Pantu's face.

"Let's work on those first so you don't fall further behind and then we can practice."

But Pantu wasn't listening, still looking down while wondering where the clothes came from.

"Uh huh," Pantu agreed, deciding to also leave it alone. *"I am still not sure which of the two options are worse,"* Pantu mumbled instead.

"Are the other options worse than here?" he asked, making Pantu turn to stare at him.

PANTU: A UNIVERSAL FRIENDSHIP
WEEK FOUR: TUESDAY

He had to admit, Drum was an amazing tutor, and very well organized. He was able to complete all his current assignments and correct the seven pages quickly as he had time to concentrate and feel at ease in his house.

Drum separated the remaining work into piles for the next three days and left the essays for next week. He wouldn't be overwhelmed, and he could keep up with his current schoolwork.

He'd asked Dill in homeroom who the number one student in their class was and Dill said, "Drum."

He asked if there was a number one student on campus and Dill told him, "Drum."

"The school updates the list every Monday morning and it's posted online and in all the homeroom classes," Dill told him.

He knew the first year wasn't lying about Drum being number one, he just didn't trust anything about the snake. When he looked at the list by the door of their homeroom class, Drum was number one in the Senior Class with scores which raised his eyebrows in respect.

Win was next and listed as the Valedictorian, which confused him. Dill was seventh and he was listed as sixth. He noticed next to his name, was a small drawing of an apparition with the word ghost next to it. Someone also wrote #AnonB on the other side of his name.

"Dill, why is there a ghost next to my name?" he asked.

"Because no one knew who you were for years and you still can't be seen online," Dill said, smiling.

"We should have lunch outside today. We can test the new and improved shuttle after we eat," he said, overly happy they finally completed it.

He finished painting it last night after Drum left and was wishing lunch were here already. He was trying to avoid seeing Real Drum after what happened several times yesterday. He was still trying to rationalize this as a dream in his Mind, while everything else was telling him, this was reality.

He was failing to understand if his feelings for a male were based on his feelings of guilt about Yolk. He could honestly say he was never physically or sexually attracted to any male, but his guilt about abandoning Yolk as a friend made him a bit more attached to Dill than what was allowed in The City.

They would have been put to death the way he clung to his best friend. He called Dill every night, even if they spent the day together, making sure he listened to Dill, and validated Dill's feelings. He was trying to make sure Dill never felt abandoned or alone. There wasn't a good balance, and he understood that.

He was trying to find one since Doctor Robin and Dill were currently seeing each other. They were honest with him, and he saw no problem with it since he trusted them. Besides, he knew how intoxicating the scents could be.

He would rather his best friend be happy and not make Dill choose between the once in a lifetime scent or their friendship. It made him unhappy to think either choice would leave Dill unable to cope with the decision. He wanted to do whatever he could to keep a smile on Dill's face, which meant he needed to accept their relationship.

Since neither of them seemed to discuss him as Dill never spoke about his sessions and Doctor Robin still didn't know the things he told Dill, it gave him comfort and peace while strengthening his trust in them.

It helped Drum was tutoring him after day classes, so now Dill had the weekdays free. He was trying to find other things to do on the weekends so Dill could have more time with Doctor Robin, but Dill insisted they continue their crazy day inventions and movie nights.

He spent so much time with Dill, he was quite sure Dill could read him like a book, so when he mumbled, *"I guess it is just repressed feelings about Yolk."*

Dill immediately understood and looked at him. "Oh please, if that's the case, just avoid me as well," Dill said, with a roll of his eyes.

He sighed and looked away. *Yes, he knows me way too well. It is just like GMack and GLou,* he thought with a smile.

He always wanted a best friendship like what his G-Pas had with each other. He thought he found it in Yolk, but there was no sexual attraction in his G-Pas' friendship, so he was confused.

Dill continued, "After, or even before Yolk, did any other pets try to be your friend?"

He responded with a yes look.

"Did any of them like you as more than a friend?" Dill questioned.

He just shrugged, not wanting to think about his lives in The City right now. Dill's eyebrows were raised at his lack of response.

"I find it hard to believe Yolk was the only man or male attracted to you in all The City. Yolk was just the only one with enough balls to verbally and directly tell you." Dill stated.

He was thrown off by Dill's blunt statement, making him think about his interactions with the men and males in The City.

Dill asked, "Did you accept any of their affections?" and he shook his head.

"What about the women? Did you accept their affections? One would think after Yolk, you would openly delve into the affections of a woman," Dill commented but he denied those words with a quick shake of his head.

"Not even "her"." Dill said it as a statement since there wasn't a need for it to be a question because Dill knew he never had feelings or felt affection for his owner. No person in his family could ever be with someone who owned a pet or slaves. His owner possessed both. Dill also knew why he called her every week.

"Hmmm, so you chose to deny the feelings of everyone before and after Yolk. If this was repressed feelings, don't you think you would have accepted someone's affections in the year after Yolk, woman, male or man?" Dill asked, while tinkering with the control. "What about the years you spent away from The City? You didn't accept anyone's affections, instead you hid yourself away or covered yourself up so no one would have any for you."

He lay back on the grass and looked up at the sky.

"Did you accept Mansnake's affections for you?" Dill asked, and he felt the smirk from Dill in the question.

"Um, eww. I would never because he never hit on me," he said, remembering the black markings on the snake, moving around like the snake was covered in worms.

Dill's eyes rolled at his enjoyment of being oblivious. He knew Dill accepted his obsessive friendship but also knew he was trying to find a balance. None of his behavior or past bothered Dill, who kept his secrets.

"The conversations with Mansnake in both Hollis and the Manga Room, the guy threw himself at you. He likes you Pantu, in a creepy, weird way, but did you accept his disgusting affections?" Dill asked.

He felt sick to his stomach. "NO! I could never like someone like him. It is for the same reason I cannot get along with your Pa's wife," he said, truthfully.

"Yet you accept Drum's affections. His Gifts, his help, his touch, you accept them all, but then try and rationalize The City's laws in a place where they don't exist," Dill stated.

He knew Dill wasn't upset with him. His best friend was always truthful and would gently tell him what he thought or felt. Dill also didn't know how much of Drum he really accepted. He hadn't said a word about the intimate touching or the dreams.

Dill only seen him touch Drum once, but he wasn't ready to try and explain. He knew his best friend would tell him the truth he was successfully pushing down and quieting within himself.

"Do you know Drum never tutored anyone before? He's never been to anyone else's home. He never touched anyone in years who wasn't his family, not even his best friends. He only gives gifts as part of The Four. He's never given anyone a personal Gift?" Dill informed him.

He turned and looked at Dill. He didn't know that. He assumed since Drum was popular, he would be a Community Male[45]. He really couldn't believe it when Drum told him he wasn't.

When he asked Dill about it, Dill responded with, "Yea. He has a reputation to uphold but I think it's more because of his own personal values."

It was then he found out Dill's Level was also complete abstinence. As his Mind was sorting through the information, he felt his Light start to tingle when Dill jumped above his face.

"By the way, he's here!" Dill said, with a smile.

His eyes went wide at the news and the tingling increased, as if his Light could feel Drum's eyes on him, even if he couldn't see the male. He continued to lay there for a while, using the time to Calm himself, since Dill was still working on the shuttle control. When he heard the click of the controller being put back together, he sat up. Drum was a lot further away than he thought as The Four were by the fence.

Drum was comfortably leaning against it, looking directly at him. His heart started racing in harmony with his tingling Light as Drum walked towards them. He turned away in a hurry to talk to Dill but was distracted by Drum picking up their shuttle.

How the hell did he get so far so quick? He thought, as his eyes returned to Drum, to stare. "What are you doing?" he asked, unhappy with the multitude of emotions coursing through his body. His feelings weren't directed at Drum, but at his own inability to be honest with himself.

---

[45] *Community Male- a term in The City for a male who sleeps with multiple women. Some males were denied marriage and turned into community males so women would have more options.*

"I know you and Dean Hu are new best friends, but I don't know how happy she would be if you blew a giant hole in the field," Drum plainly stated, looking directly at him, making him turn away.

After fixing a few wires and explaining to Dill what he did, Drum replaced the shuttle and put his hands in his pockets. "Are you avoiding me?" Drum asked.

"Yes," he responded, refusing to glance Drum's way.

He heard footsteps after an "Oh!" escaped Drum's lips.

When he turned to watch, he was confused how anyone could move so fast, as Drum was back to his best friends. They were leaving the field and as he watched, his heart ached, and his Light slowed its flow inside his body.

"Dill," he said, "it hurts. Why does it hurt?"

To which Dill responded by rubbing his back and telling him, "You know why Pantu."

PANTUxDRUM: A MEMORY RECALLED
WEEK FOUR: TUESDAY

Pantu sat in the field meadow in his dreams and waited for Dream Drum. He didn't remember how many times he called out before he realized he was being avoided, the same way he avoided Real Drum. He didn't like it, it made him unhappy, and he started to feel tears form.

Real Drum still came over and tutored him but sat on the other side of the table, only focusing on work. Drum refused to banter or even smile and looked sad whenever he tried to make what Dill called a joke.

He rested his head on his knees. He didn't realize how many thoughts were overflowing out of him and he was unconscientiously saying his thoughts out loud, but he couldn't go to his Think Sleep.

It wasn't as if he were a prisoner here, but this was the safest place he'd ever experienced, in or outside himself, and he didn't want to leave. So, he sat there, his words spilling out of him.

"Is Real Drum and Dream Drum both upset with me? You said you would spoil me. Do you hate me too? Why does it hurt? Is this my punishment for Yolk?"

As he was saying his thoughts, the field meadow fell away, and his surroundings were replaced by a giant indoor coliseum.

Drum, who was in the RMD, just refusing to approach Pantu, out of respect for Pantu's wish to avoid him, registered pure shock at his new surroundings.

He watched as a young, scantily clad, Collared Pantu led a woman to an overly jeweled and bulky chair in the middle of the huge room. She sat down on a pillow Collared Pantu fluffed on the seat for her.

He glanced at the extravagant woman and thought she was overcompensating for something. It wasn't until he really looked at her, he understood.

She wore such heavy, powdery makeup you couldn't tell what her real face looked like underneath. Her clothes would have been expensive if they lived a couple millennia ago. Her movements were over the top and clumsily done.

His face twisted; trying not to think about how Queen would react to this woman's graceless movements. This woman was the type to flaunt her wealth but left her class in the womb. Her grace was forced and unbelievable. He could also tell she was more than several years older than Pantu.

Which wasn't difficult to tell, since Pantu's smooth, plump skin made him look younger than twenty-one. But Pantu wasn't twenty-one here, he was even younger than him.

His eyes were pulled to the stage when they dragged a young man, kicking and screaming, onstage and started to strap him to a mattress on top of a table. The man was screaming for someone named Oryn to help while looking at Collared Pantu.

His eyes were pulled to the stage when they dragged a young man, kicking and screaming, onstage and started to strap him to a mattress on top of a table. The man was screaming for someone named Oryn to help while looking at Collared Pantu, whose face showed he wasn't expecting this, but it passed so quickly, even he was unsure of what he saw, since Collared Pantu's body did an excellent job of not reacting.

Collared Pantu's calm face held as the young man on the table screams were ignored and he continued to serve the woman sitting comfortably in the chair.

He was confused as a sour smell entered his nose. The stench made him focus on the woman and for the first time, he was starting to understand Pantu's Personal Ability.

The woman was looking at Oryn, hope on her face for a response or for Oryn to act in a certain way, so she could publicly justify her punishment.

He could feel the sadist pleasure this woman craved from punishing Oryn. The woman enjoyed the sounds Oryn made. The cute, high-pitched sounds made her wet between her legs, and she never left a mark. It made her look like the kind, loving, caring Owner which every other Owner strived to be like.

She was lucky to have found Oryn, so she needed her pet to know he couldn't have anyone else in his life except for her. She would finally break Oryn today and use that stupid pet Yolk as the nail in the coffin.

She was highly upset when she found out Yolk thought he was important to her Oryn. She was the only one Oryn would love because she was the only one worthy of his affections.

She'd found a secret painting her Oryn did and it incited anger inside her. Not only did Oryn manage to hide such a talent from her, but she was also fuming about the amount of money she could have made off this talent. She burned every painting she found throughout The Center and forced Oryn to paint her portrait, leaving it as the only painting in the entire City from Oryn.

His heart hurt and he realized if he could understand everything this woman was feeling, then His Pantu could as well. He looked around unbothered by the woman's feelings of superiority as he found His Pantu curled up into a ball and silently crying on his knees.

He went over to His Pantu and hugged him while telling him, "Give me your emotions."

But Pantu wouldn't listen. "I cannot see this again." Pantu shook his head.

"Pantu please!" he begged.

Pantu refused to even raise his head. "I have no feelings. I already gave them away," Pantu repeated to himself, over and over.

He looked at Collared Pantu, still serving the woman. When Collared Pantu looked directly at him and slowly down to the ground, he was taken aback.

Can he see us!? He was impressed. This was a memory, right? They shouldn't be seen, but if Collared Pantu could see them, maybe he could help. He needed to help. He couldn't leave either Pantu like this.

He slowly walked over to Collared Pantu, who refused to verbally or visually acknowledge him. Collared Pantu kept focus on the woman, but he could see Collared Pantu's eyes cutting to the ground in front of him.

The woman's attention was on the stage as she heartily laughed. When the woman abruptly stood and raised her glass, he froze his body, waiting for the woman to look at him.

But instead, the woman shouted out in a nasally voice, "This is what happens when you come for my pet, the number one pet!"

There was a roar of applause and it's when he closed his eyes and sent out his Awareness. He could feel four thousand people inside the full indoor coliseum and some of those people were Beings. The woman's slimy smile as she bathed in the fake and forced admiration was redirected to the stage.

When the woman sat back down after Collared Pantu fluffed her pillow again, the wide swing of her leg to cross it over the other would have made Queen die in embarrassment for the woman, only for Queen to force himself back to life just to teach this woman True Grace.

He continued forward, moving one step at a time, not to startle Collared Pantu. They both realized the woman Collared Pantu was serving couldn't see him standing right in front of her, and Collared Pantu slowly looked back up, into his eyes.

"Let me take your emotions," he gently asked.

Collared Pantu agreed by looking up and down several times using his eyes without the woman noticing.

He moved behind Collared Pantu and pulled his own Energy out of himself; he exchanged it with the emotions Collared Pantu was suppressing.

He felt anger, betrayal, fear, hurt and sadness from Collared Pantu, but he didn't feel love. Pantu really didn't have any feelings for Yolk other than friendship, and he felt it. He could also understand Collared Pantu never held any feelings for the woman sitting in the ugliest chair he'd ever seen.

His Pantu stood. "It was you!" Pantu said, as he Instant back beside His Pantu, who watched him take the emotions from Collared Pantu.

When Pantu's arms wrapped around his neck and hugged him, he felt it in his heart more than his pants. He was feeling elated by Pantu expressing any emotion towards him.

"Let's go back," he said to Pantu.

Pantu nodded but before they could leave, the men taking part in the graduation came out. Both Pantu's heads snapped over to the line-up.

He slowly turned and looked. His stomach twisted in disgust, and he felt confused by what he was seeing.

The young man was now completely strapped to the mattress table, with his member hard and in the air, along with his legs. The men lining up had a clear view to the young man's hole.

The first man took off his cloak and was naked underneath, his own small, human-sized member hard and standing at attention. The man laughed and said out loud, "Well, let's see if you can get the highest score."

As he went to turn away, he noticed Pantu's Father in the line. Covering His Pantu's eyes, he whispered, *"Pantu."*

They were back in the field and Pantu collapsed to the ground.

He sat down in front of Pantu. *"So, that was Yolk's final graduation?"* he asked, gently.

Pantu nodded.

"It's to see how many men you can have sex with?" he asked. He kept his voice soft and gentle while speaking. He could see the trauma it left, and he didn't want to agitate Pantu. But to his surprise, Pantu opened up to him.

"The number to graduate is ten. You must make ten males come without showing any reaction and you can graduate. They want to make sure you are not at all attracted to males or men after going through final training, which involves male trainers.

"Not every male in The City becomes a pet. There are not enough owners for it. And while having multiple pets is seen as wealthy, it is also seen as foolish if they are not professionally trained.

"So, hundreds of years ago, the Minister approved male trainers to help the wealthy women who wanted multiple pets but did not want to train them on their own," Pantu explained.

"Did you graduate?" he asked.

"No. I left before entering final training. I know it upset some of the trainers who bid for my education," Pantu said, with a sad chuckle.

"What did they give him?" he questioned.

Pantu looked up, with a face scrunched in thought. "What?!"

"Someone gave Yolk something before his graduation. He was drugged and hard before they even strapped him down," he said.

The realization hit Pantu. "It is not like drugs are hard to come by in my family. My Senora Madre is over the only pharmaceutical company in The City," Pantu said.

"You know who wrote the note?" he asked and Pantu nodded.

"You know who drugged him?" he inquired and Pantu's eyes found the ground to nod again.

"So, you know who killed him." He ended his questioning, letting Pantu know they were both having the same thoughts.

Pantu took a deep breath and exhaled. He could feel the coolness wafting off Pantu, asking to be held. He was Instantly behind Pantu, covering his Dumpling with his Heat. Pantu looked up at him with such sad eyes, it softened every part of his body.

"You would still touch me? Even after seeing...that?" Pantu asked, surprised.

"I like you Dumpling. Nothing's going to change that. Everything you experienced in life has made you the person you are today. The person I'm holding in my arms, the one I Promised to spoil," he said, meaning every word. Nothing in Pantu's past was enough to drive him away.

Pantu's forehead was against his chest as he cried. "She will never let me go. I was the only pet she had no desire to kill after a couple of days. I was her status. She will find me," Pantu whimpered into his chest.

"Then let me protect you."

Pantu looked up at him. "You can only protect me here, in my dreams." Pantu pouted.

"You know that's not true Dumpling. I can protect you...in here and out there. Just ask me too," he softly said before kissing Pantu's nose.

PANTU: TRUSTING THE PLAN
WEEK FOUR: WEDNESDAY

He knew something was wrong when his Ma said she would drop him off at campus. His alarm bells continued to ring as he was walking up the steps only to be engulfed in a sea of students. As everyone was talking at once, his Mind separated what each person said and he realized what was happening, again.

Queen started a V.I.B list and he was the one to decide which fifty names went on the list. He made his way to his homeroom, declining to comment.

He felt like Queen was up to something when Win didn't show up for homeroom, and Queen wasn't in Chemistry, his alarm bells felt justified. He also learned there were no safe zone places, only people, and there were only two, Drum and Dill.

Ah, he is definitely up to something, he thought. He smiled while walking to lunch next to Dill.

No one bothered him, just looks of anticipation and rosy cheeks from those who caught both his eyes and his smile. He made it to the cafeteria and when he noticed The Four sitting at their table, laughing and joking, he smiled. He would play along as he was interested in seeing what Queen planned.

He grabbed his tray and acting as calm as possible, he went through the lunch line, but after leaving the line, he detoured and went straight for The Four's table. Dropping his tray in the empty space between the two best friends, he leaned against the chair and turned to look Queen directly in the eyes.

"Call it off," he demanded, adding a small amount of force behind his words.

"What?!" Queen's question and innocent look made him soften. He could feel Queen asking more than one question with just one word. A small smile graced his face, seeing the similarities between best friends.

"I won nothing, call it off," he said, gently but with a tired undertone. "I did the party invites, now this Queen?" he said, asking for an explanation.

"Well, Pantu, seeing as how Drum won his own prize, it doesn't seem fair to everyone else, who was duped out of the reward, does it?" Queen asked, smiling at him.

AH! My Universe, he is good, he thought, giving a full smile to Queen.

"Then punish the one who cheated everyone by making him do it," he said, understanding Queen was asking his permission to put some information out.

"I would, except #NoComp hasn't been on campus since Monday, so I'm at a loss. I don't know when he will be back!" Queen said sweetly to him, while moving ever so gracefully to rest his head on his hand. "Let's compromise on this, shall we?" Queen asked, with soft, kind eyes.

He enjoyed the way Queen phrased the words and thought to himself he was right in a few of his assumptions about the handsome young male. With intelligence, grace and overall looks, Queen would be a treasure in The City, but there was one assumption he held which would have this male naked and chained in the middle of The Center and he wouldn't wish that kind of hell on Queen.

"Hashtag NoComp?" he asked, deciding Queen could last at least a day in The City.

"Yep! Everyone online has changed the cheater's hashtag from The Competition, #TheComp, to No Competition, #NoComp. They all know you were Lied on, and they were misled," Queen explained, smiling at him.

"Fine. But only if I agree to the terms. If I do not like them, we can wait for hashtag NoComp to come back," he said, with a slight smile.

Queen's cheeks turned a light red color at his teasing. "And if he never does?" Queen asked, with lips forming an oh and wide eyes.

"Then you never get your list," he said, shrugging.

Queen gasped. "Then is Drum supposed to take the twenty minutes alone with his own brother?" Queen asked, holding back a smile.

"There is always the five minutes he could spend with himself," he said, with a teasing smile. They both looked at Drum as Beings in the cafeteria laughed at their jokes.

But Drum was expressionless, never taking those smoky, honey-green eyes off him. His breaths were short and shallow, trying to remember if behind Drum's eyes; there ever sat the color of smoke from a billowing campfire.

He quickly turned away from Drum, trying to regain his own composure.

"OH! I like you!" Queen said, gracefully leaning back and crossing his legs, Queen made himself comfortable.

Queen was sending out positive, happy feelings along with a pleasant scent. He pulled the chair out and sat down in it facing Queen. He read the male quite easily as he knew Queen left himself open on purpose.

Sit down, get comfortable, is what Queen's body language and Intent was telling him, but there was a teasing undertone to it which made him interested in finding out.

"You gather the names," he said to Queen, starting negotiations. He'd already figured out a way to give Queen what he wanted in exchange for everyone leaving him alone.

He was going to use his skills of debate and the Talent for reading Intent his G-Pas taught him.

"Wait? Why do I have to?" Queen asked, with a pout.

"Because you would have a better system for collecting names. You could extend the invitation on that net thingy as well," he said. He praised Queen while giving him a way to open it up internationally, like he originally wanted.

Queen smiled in agreement and leaned forward. "You would still have to choose the names. How will you decide that?" Queen asked him. "It would be too many requests to go through individually before the party," Queen added, and glanced at Drum the same time he snuck a pouty look.

So, Drum is popular online, he thought. But the look Drum was giving him made him freeze momentarily, before slowly lowering his eyes to look away, trying not to spread the heat further than his already enflamed cheeks.

"You collect the names, put them in the same-colored balloons, and I will shoot them!" He was proud of his idea, and he gave Queen a bright smile, making Queen's cheeks flare up again as Queen leaned back, accepting his proposal.

"Wait, so you wouldn't even know who submitted their names?" Win asked.

"Nope. I care not whose name goes on the list, but it gives everyone who submitted their name a fair chance of luck to be chosen," he explained.

Sport smiled at the proposal. "I like it. What are you going to shoot the balloons with?"

"It is perfect timing. Dill and I are crafting a bow. I will use that!" he said, happy they would have a way to show off their invention, even start having Dill receive orders for the bow he designed, and Dill was building.

"Nice! You can show off the bow and pick names at the same time!" Win said, grinning.

He softened his eyes as he glanced at Win, who was now lost in an ocean of thoughts filled with profits. He could see the numbers running through Win's head, even without his True Vision.

"Ooooh!"

"I want to see that!"

"That sounds fair!"

"I like that idea too!"

"Anybody can submit their names!"

The excitement was starting to build. The feeling of happiness was starting to overwhelm him. The more excited Beings were for an event this big, the more potential customers he and Dill would have from what he now knew would be quite the audience. If any of The Four complimented their bow, they would have to mass produce it.

"We would have to do it off campus though. Our inventions work...sometimes," he said, lowering his eyes away from Queen. If he downplayed the bow now, everyone's anticipation would be through the roof about whether the bow would work.

Queen waved it off. "It will take a while to gather all the names, so we will use that time to request permission to use the field on the weekend from Dean Hu, and you and Dill will have time to perfect your bow," Queen said, quickly putting it all together before standing to make an announcement.

"The cutoff date to submit your name online will be the fifteenth day of next month. And since picking names like this sounds exciting as hell, we will set a date and hold it in the field here on campus, so anyone can come watch. Oh, and Drum will also be shooting fifty names, so the list has now grown to one hundred," Queen said, with a smile and a look over to him.

He smiled back; now certain Queen would last at least a week in The City as an uncollared male.

PANTU: BE-FORE I HIT A WALL
WEEK FOUR: WEDNESDAY

The nod in return was cut short by his phone dinging. He glanced at it and saw Dill text him several times, but he only just heard his phone go off. He opened it and as he read the messages, his brows furled and his lips turned into a slightly downward frown, trying to understand what Dill was texting about.

Ah! The schematics for the bow. Maybe Dill wants to go over them before the end of lunch, since I just offered to shoot it in front of the whole campus. He rose to leave with his food and Queen looked at him with furrowed brows.

"Dill needs to talk to me, see you later!" he said, with a smile. He made his way over to his table and slid down next to Dill as the whole table turned to look him in his face.

"WHAT!?" he asked, wondering why the whole lunchroom was silent.

"My Universe! Why would you do that?" Dill asked, looking like a baby bird alone and lost in the woods.

"DO WHAT?" he asked. He was now a lost baby bird in the woods right along with Dill.

"Sit in THAT chair?" Put asked. Both of Put's eyebrows were as far up as they could go on Put's face, but there was a look of respect in Put's eyes.

He was looking around, fairly sure his face matched what he was feeling. "Because it was there to sit. Was I supposed to stand the whole time?" he asked indignantly. "Sounds like exercise to me," he added, feeling highly unhappy by the thought.

"It would have been better if you did," Jax said, shaking his head.

"What. The. Hell." was all he could get out. He put his head down and took a deep breath. "Dill?" he asked, looking up at his best friend. "Did a person die who only used to sit there and now I will be forever haunted by their apparition for sitting in *their* chair?" he questioned, innocently accepting his fate.

"What?! No. Our campus isn't haunted Pantu," Dill said, looking away from him.

"Is the chair infected with an experimental virus and now I will be patient zero of a massive planet-wide zombie apocalypse?!" he asked, bouncing at the thought. "Do not worry, I will not bite you, I will only scratch. Better hygienically for all those involved!" he said, happily accepting this fate as well.

Dill only took a deep breath as the other students in the room giggled and stifled laughs at his assessments.

Dill slowly looked at him, who was looking back expectedly, along with everyone else in the room.

"That chair is symbolic," Dill started.

"Sym-bolic h-ow D-ill?" he asked.

"Well, you know how nobody will "date" until Drum has chosen someone?" Dill whispered, in a quiet room.

"Ah. Yes," he stated.

"At every school we've attended since middle school, there's always an empty chair next to Drum, to symbolize he's still single. That chair has sat empty for years," Queen said, appearing next to him to sit on the table.

He jumped and looked at Queen with wide eyes. He didn't notice Queen until he spoke.

"HOW—?" He stared at Queen, who was sitting on the table, swinging his crossed legs. He was still staring at Queen but the slow realization of what the chair meant made his mouth fall open and his eyes even wider.

"And you just sat in it," Dill said, softly.

He turned to slowly look at Dill. "BE-FORE DILL!" he said, forcefully stressing each sound. *"You tell me things..."* he whispered, "BE-FORE" he stressed, "I hit the wall, Dill!"

He put his head in his hands and groaned as the lunchroom erupted in laughter. He moved his hands to let his head drop to the table, but Dill caught his forehead.

"I didn't think you would ever sit there!" Dill tried to explain.

He blew out his breath. He knew it wasn't Dill's fault, but his, for not being honest about him and Drum.

"What else should I know Dill?" he asked, gently letting his best friend know he wasn't upset.

"Well, not much else, there is a room called The Queen's Hive you won't be able to enter without a special key, so no worries you might accidentally find your way into there.

"Queen also runs the campus's social media site, so that's his club, but you're welcome to go there. His offices as well, oh, except the bathroom on the first floor of the office building. That's used if a student needs to speak with Queen privately."

As Dill said this, he lifted his head and looked at Dill, who understood his bathroom mishap happened in THAT bathroom and his best friend's eyes widened.

I have got to be more honest with Dill, he thought as he returned his forehead to Dill's hand.

"In the town I would suggest staying away from the tourist side of it, since you could be seen as a tourist hunter. Other than that, the town is quite open, although I would also suggest staying away from Drum's home and the area that says 'Park, This Way'," Dill ended, confidence in his voice that everything was explained.

He lifted his head to look at Dill. "Why do I need to stay away from parks?" he asked, tired.

"Not every park, just this one. The air there is different. And it's on Drum's family property," Dill said, not knowing he already spent several hours there.

"Got it," he said, as he laid his head in his own hand and gave a thumbs up with the other.

His thoughts were distracted by several Women arguing. He lifted his head and realized Queen was still beside him. As he watched a group of Women argue over who would sit in the chair he just sat in, his heart hurt, and he felt his lips starting to pout.

If anybody could just sit in it, would it really be so symbolic? He didn't want anyone else's ass to sit in the chair and as his eyes met Drum's, it was as if Drum understood.

Drum nodded slightly while still looking at him, and Sport stood to walk around the table between the Women. Sport gently pulled them back from each other and moved forward to the metal chair. He happily watched as Sport picked up the chair and started folding it into a square shape to leave it on the table.

Sport looked at the Women and asked gently, *"Aren't you all best friends?"*

The Women's cheeks flushed at Sport's kind smile to them, and they went to each other; quickly apologizing. Grabbing their trays, they walked off determined to submit their names for the list.

He was really trying not to smile. His Light was buzzing on the inside, and he smelled his excitement filling the room with the scent of cinnamon and honey. When everyone started commenting about how good the lunchroom smelled, his cheeks felt warm, realizing it was him. The bell rang at the end of the period, and the lunchroom sprang to life as AH students moved on to their next class.

"Are you headed to the library?" Queen asked him.

He nodded after taking a moment. He wasn't sure if he would go into the Manga Room again, but he was going to check out a book for his Fabrication class.

"Let's walk together," Queen stated.

PANTU: A CHAT AMONGST FRIENDS
WEEK FOUR: WEDNESDAY

He said bye to Dill before they split. The look his best friend gave him was a bit unsettling, but Dill refrained from speaking. He and Queen walked in silence for a bit while the students they passed by all held questions in their glances at him and Queen.

"It doesn't bother you that people assume things about you?" Queen asked as they walked.

"Not at all," he replied, not caring about the indescribable feelings he received from the other students. "Until they have the courage to say it to my face, here, the whispers mean nothing to me," he stated.

He was used to whispers about him for years throughout The City. No one, except Yolk, as Dill so recently pointed out, had the courage to say anything to his face. And no one ever outright accused him of much as he was adept in handling it before it came to that point. If he didn't feel Malicious or Ill Intent from the other students, he didn't mind the wild assumptions about him. Some of them were quite intriguing.

They made it to the library and walking off to the side of the steps, Queen twirled to look at him. "Why haven't you asked?" Queen inquired.

"It would kill the intrigue," he responded.

The fact he would answer and know exactly what was being asked, made Queen pause for a moment. "So, are you mad?" Queen questioned, wanting his honest feelings.

"In your sense of the word, no. Your personal Gifts are different from everyone else's. I realized it was a quiet Gift you gave to Drum." He acknowledged Queen's assumptions.

"It's like a fantasy to you?" Queen asked.

What he felt from Queen was the same feeling he would experience whenever he received something new from his G-Pas. He would open the box, and his eyes would go wide, with happiness filling him at the sight of a new gift.

"Yes, and I know it is selfish of me—" He started but was cut off by Queen.

"What the fuck Pantu! Then be as selfish as you fucking want!"

"I will have to wake up eventually," he mumbled, an unhappy feeling settling inside him. He was unsure of where he would be when he woke up and the feeling of being unprepared to face his reality, caused him to tremble at the thought.

"If I was in a world that felt like a Dream, I would be selfish as hell too. Until I either woke up or was slapped in the face by reality, I would live to my heart's content," Queen said, with a look of happiness shining brightly on his face.

He was slightly thrown off by Queen's reaction. He didn't expect this kind of response from Queen, of all people. He thought Queen was all Graceful business, but he was seeing a side he doubted many were able to see.

"Thank you!" he said. "Is it just me or do all of your quiet Gifts come with an added bonus?" he asked as he winked at the perfectly put together male standing next to him.

Queen was beside himself with a lost baby bird look on his face. "Whatever do you mean my dearest Pantu? What gift could I have possibly given you this time?" Queen asked.

"You helped me realize I need to be a hell of a lot more honest with Dill," he stated.

Queen perked up. "Dill's a good friend. It seems like he can be honest with you, so I think it would hurt him to find out something about you, from someone else," Queen said, eyeing him. "Just like Drum and I," he added, letting him know he knew what was going on between him and Drum, as Drum's best friend.

He smiled at Queen with meek acceptance of the news. *If Dill has not stopped being my friend yet, knowing what he does know, why can I not be open with him about everything?*

He asked for this. His G-Pas told him if he asked the Universe, it would answer. He wanted a friendship like his G-Pas' so badly he slipped and thought Yolk was the one.

He never imagined he would ever meet someone like Dill, much less leave The City, so even though his G-Pas told him to be patient, he rushed. Now his chance, which he thought he no longer deserved, was here and he was about to fuck it up.

"So, thank you for the gift!" he said, with a smile. "I can ask Dill to spend the night, so we can talk."

PANTU: A GRADUATION REQUIREMENT
WEEK FOUR: WEDNESDAY

The conversation with Queen brightened his mood as he walked into the library.

"OH! Pantu! There you are. I've been waiting for you," Doctor Faye said. She led him past the checkout desk and into her office. "Have you completed your volunteer hours yet?" she asked, with feelings of worry wafting off her.

His crazed look was followed by his response, "Huh? Volunteer?"

"Yes, every graduating Senior must provide one hundred hours of volunteer service in order to graduate. Most Liberal students do about twenty to twenty-five a year so they will be completed before graduation. The Cleaning Club is the quickest way to get all your hours in a year if you're Advanced Honors, but if that's not for you, *could you help here instead?*" Doctor Faye gently pleaded.

"Yes. I will. Do you need me to put the books back? I can work alongside your Aides until I can understand checking out and returning books," he offered back. He liked Doctor Faye; she was kind and always spoke softly. She smelled good and would offer a smile to everyone.

"Oh, thank you but the Aides will focus on the front desk and helping students. I will be busy putting the books back and keeping records. *I would just need you to handle the requests for the Manga Room,*" Doctor Faye said, softly, while looking at him.

He froze. He wasn't sure he was ready to go back in there after the incident with Mansnake. His chest tightened, and it was getting harder for him to breathe.

"The lock has been changed, so instead of keys, there are only Crystals. One Crystal for each lock. One would be for you," Doctor Faye said, letting him know another crystal was not around for someone to steal.

He knew who had the other one and the thought calmed him. No one other than him and Drum would be able to go inside the room.

Unless someone steals my crystal, he thought.

"You would keep the Crystal with you, and it will only respond to you," Doctor Faye said, as she held out a small red crystal attached to a clip.

He didn't smell any Lies from Doctor Faye, and he really wanted to know how a crystal would react to him, so he held out his hand. Doctor Faye placed the crystal into his palm and closed his hand over it. He felt the crystal heat up before cooling off and he opened his palm to see the crystal was now deep brown in color. He looked up at Doctor Faye, who was nodding happily.

"Great! I will leave this basket..." Doctor Faye started speaking as they moved out of her office and back towards the front desk, "right here, so students can place their request for manga or banned books. You can pick the requests up here and bring them down before you leave.

"You can get several hours a day or more if you have the time. And I know it may seem like it will take forever, but you will have all your hours before you graduate in about three months!" Doctor Faye said, happy he seemed to have agreed.

Doctor Faye placed three papers with written requests in his hand. She also gave him a kit to separate and label the requests by student and shooed him away towards the Manga Room stairs while she went off to reshelve books.

PANTUxDRUM: A TOSS OF A COIN
WEEK FOUR: WEDNESDAY

Pantu stood, looking at the door to the Manga Room. He took a deep breath and held it as he slowly climbed the stairs. He knew Drum would be in there, but he didn't know how to apologize for being an ass to him yesterday.

Yes, Dream Drum saved me, but Real Drum is still upset with me.

He didn't know what to say as he made it to the top of the stairs unprepared and let go of the breath he was holding. Taking the crystal, he worked out that by putting it against the smooth black part of the door, it flashed a deep brown before it unlocked. Slowly, with no words in his Mind or brain, he walked in, making sure to push the door close behind him to watch and hear it lock.

He shuffled his feet as he made his way back to the table. Real Drum laughed and he peeked around the corner. Real Drum was on his laptop playing a game and talking to other people.

He quietly placed his items down, and taking the papers, he looked for the books on the list. He found the books quicker than he would have liked and went back to the table to sit. He separated the books while sneaking glances at Drum from behind his long lashes.

When it came to labeling the stacks, he decided to make collectable nametags for the students. He pulled out his colored pencils and based off the student's name; he drew whatever came to him. Drum was now watching him style a label and attach it to a stack.

He didn't look at Drum, he just spoke. "This crystal key is quite unique."

Drum put away his laptop and earpiece. "It stores the Energy of the Crystal's Owner. Placing it against a lock reads the Energy to see if the Owner is authorized to enter. Even if the Crystal is lost or stolen, no one else will be able to activate it," Drum said, looking at him. "I heard the recordings," Drum added.

He looked up at Drum, and quickly back down at the items in front of him. Everything was blurry and he knew there were tears in his eyes. He didn't know how to respond.

"You know if you ever feel uncomfortable or there is something you don't want to do, you can say stop, you can say no," Drum said, softly to him.

But instead of calming him, it made him tremble to hear Drum's soft voice. "Ahhh," was all he said.

"Pantu?" Drum asked him gently. "I don't want you to be upset with me for overstepping your boundaries. I will respect whatever decision you make," Drum said, and stood to leave.

"I just wanted to let you know; I will leave you alone, so you don't feel like you need to hide to avoid me. You can have the Manga Room to yourself, and I will move my seat," Drum said, softly, before turning to leave.

"Drum," he whispered. *"I like when you touch me,"* he admitted so quietly, he was unsure if he heard it himself.

Drum heard him and stopped, with his back to him, so any expression was hidden but he felt Drum's heat. It was what calmed him down enough to form a thought.

"Can we talk?" he asked.

Drum dropped his bag and moved to sit back down. He used the time to think of how to proceed. Drum wasn't a typical person; it was what made the stunningly handsome male so intriguing to him. But as he waited until Drum became comfortable in the chair with folded arms resting on the table, he knew he didn't want a debate.

"How about, you can ask me any question, and I will answer if I can. If I cannot answer, you can ask another question until I am able to. Then I can ask you any question and if you can answer it, we will go back and forth?" he asked.

He wondered if Drum would turn this into an interrogation or a debate. He really just wanted a friendly conversation without feeling like he needed his guard up. Drum was always so comfortable around him it put him at ease.

Drum avoided his eyes and nodded with a quiet "yea".

"How do we decide who goes first?" he asked, looking at Drum with a smile. His Light was quietly humming, waiting along with him to see where Drum would lead the conversation. He was allowing someone other than himself to control the flow of a conversation involving him, and it made his Light vibrate throughout his body.

Drum shrugged and looked away from his smile. Drum seemed unhappy but he was sure it was because of the way he treated him yesterday.

"Let us flip a coin," he said, pulling out a thin gold coin. He showed Drum his coin with *Good Vibes Only* minted on one side and *Positive Thoughts* on the other.

"Which side would you choose?" he asked, leaning forward.

"Good Vibes Only," Drum mumbled.

He laughed. "You seem like a good vibes kind of male," he said. "I like Positive Thoughts, so I will go with this one." He held the coin out to Drum. "Would you like to flip?"

Drum shook his head.

"Okay. I will do it, since you are too scared," he teased.

He could feel Drum's heat flaring up, and he didn't know why it made him smile. Drum watched as he flipped the coin onto the table. It landed on Good Vibes Only and he looked at Drum expectedly.

Drum looked away. "Where did you get the coin?"

"Grandpa Mack and Grandpa Lou!" he said, with a bright smile. "They were two coins my G-Pas treasured and kept with them from an early age. When I was born, they pressed the coins together to make this one. I have had it ever since," he said, leaning back in his chair while spinning the coin on the table.

"This town is different. The air smells clean, the food tastes delicious. It is calm and peaceful here. I have also seen and heard things that make me question my sanity," he said. He didn't bother looking at the young male, since he could feel Drum was now staring at him.

"It reminds me of the fantasies my G-Pas used to tell me when I was little. I believed them when I was younger, so they only became fairy tales when the harshness of real life placed a collar around my neck," he explained.

"My G-Pas would tell me I am different. Special. At first as a child, I believed them, but the more I experienced, the less I believed." He shrugged. "I am now beginning to think the fairy tales were in fact stories.

"Stories about Entities, who can do things humans cannot. Entities who have Talents and live together freely using their Light. Entities who can make the impossible, possible," he said, watching his still spinning coin.

"Not every Entity, or Being, can make the Impossible happen," Drum replied.

He could feel Drum's eyes on him, and he knew not once while he spoke, did Drum look away. His Light could feel Drum staring at him even if his eyes were focused anywhere else.

He finally calmed his Light down enough to look up. But when his eyes caught Drum's, he felt his penis twitch with excitement making him jump a little at the impromptu reaction. "Can you?"

DRUM

"Yes," Drum responded, without hesitation.

"Then why would anything else matter to me?" Pantu asked, looking him directly in the eyes.

The different browns in Pantu's eyes seemed to flit around, making him hard. What Pantu said to him made his member excited and it twitched. He took a deep breath to calm himself, but the Scent Pantu was giving off made it worse. He put his hands in his lap and closed his eyes to steady himself instead of suppressing the Scent. He felt Pantu smile.

"I have asked you two questions, and although you only VERBALLY responded to one, you can ask me two," Pantu teased.

He opened his eyes to look at Pantu and received a playful smile. *Does he honestly not know how enticing he is?* He thought as he tried to think of two questions which didn't involve his hands on Pantu's smooth, soft, skin. "What stories did your G-Pas tell you?" he asked, instead.

"Stories about Phoenix, her husband Wolf, and their enemies," Pantu said, nonchalantly.

But his surprise showed, and he was very much interested. "Would you tell me the stories if we had enough time?" he asked, anxiously, since he was looking for any information about Phoenix.

"It is a pretty long story. Or maybe I think it is long because my G-Pas were only allowed to visit me for a few hours once a week?" Pantu asked himself, placing his hand under his chin while looking off, thinking.

He really wanted to hear about Phoenix, but his excitement about it seemed to make Pantu a little jealous. In the stories he read, Phoenix was gorgeous, but every story touted Phoenix as being from a different region. Phoenix was called something different by those regions who still held the mythical bird in their mythology. Apparently, his thoughts and facial expressions made Pantu's eyes roll.

"Allowed?" he asked while doing a horrible job of trying not to smile at Pantu's pouty face. Pantu's cheeks were filled with air, plumping those pretty, pink lips to poke out. The reddish hue on Pantu's cheeks wasn't from blushing, it was from anger.

"Yes!" Pantu said, releasing the air in his cheeks. "My G-Pas are married to two of the most influential and wealthiest women in The City. But my parents, Coin and I, lived in the poorest part of The City called The Slums. I was born and raised there until I was seven. Being seen in The Slums was not a good social look for my G-Ma and Indria.

"My G-Pas on the other hand, did not care. They would outright come to see us once a week for a couple of hours. Of course, they also snuck some hours in here and there." Pantu's bright laughter at the memory widened his own smile. Pantu's eyes held love for his G-Pas.

While he was thinking of which folk story Pantu would tell him about Phoenix, or if this one would be different from the many versions he'd heard, he glanced at Pantu and what he saw made him pause. There was a look of confusion as their eyes met again. He could read the question in Pantu's eyes, but he wasn't sure if Pantu would understand his answer.

But Pantu was pouting again, and he knew it was his fault. He didn't know what he did, but he wanted to do it some more. He smiled as his member stretched towards Pantu, wanting to help console him.

"Pantu?" he asked, gently. "That was three. It's your turn," he said, quietly fighting his urge to wrap Pantu's soft, squishy body in his arms.

"Do you remember in the mornings?" Pantu asked, still upset with him.

"Yes," he answered, quietly. He knew Pantu was trying to hold on to the Dream while accepting the fact he was actually there.

"Then I will tell you there."

"Okay."

"Drum. Do you think we could cancel tutoring tonight?" Pantu asked. "I will still have the stack you separated completed before tomorrow and will make sure I have all homework done as well," Pantu compromised.

"Come to campus early tomorrow and I will check your work here. Your Crystal also works on the side door," he responded.

Drum's response sent a jolt through Pantu's Light. Drum didn't ask why or deny him.

"I—. I did not think it would be this easy?" he mumbled as he tried to accept the response.

"You only have to ask Pantu," Drum gently said.

So gently, he couldn't stop his Light from sending out his desire. The table and chairs disappeared, and he was about to blink to clear his eyes, so his brain could register the missing items that were right in front of him, when his falling body was quickly wrapped in Drum's arms. He used a string of colorful words to describe Drum's warm kisses on his neck, which sent shockwaves of happiness through his Light and body.

Yes, it felt good in his dream world, but nothing compared to Real Drum's touch on his skin. It sent a heatwave over him, warming his cold body and making something inside him crack. What sounded like cracking ice was drowned out by the waves of Light crashing against his skin, trying to escape his body to also experience the inviting heat sending goosebumps over his entire existence.

He knew all his clothes were gone, but instead of landing on the hard carpet of the Manga Room floor, he felt cushioned and safe. He opened his eyes to look around in amazement at their unique environment and wondered if he fell asleep in the Manga Room while Drum was still playing a game.

"We...we were just on campus! How—?" He couldn't get his words out as he was kissed down his body until Drum reached his nipple. He arched his back trying to push and pull Drum at the same time.

"Mmmmm," he moaned, trying to be quiet. He felt his penis squirt and his whole body turned bright red. *All from him kissing on my nipple?*

He couldn't believe it until Drum moved to his other nipple and flicked it with a warm tongue. Drum gently nibbled on his hardened nub, before covering his whole nipple to gently suck. The warmth from Drum's mouth, the heat Drum's body was expelling, and Drum's touch was mixed in with this intoxicating scent, making it impossible for him to form a complete thought, much less a coherent sentence.

His Mind, Light, heart and body were doing whatever they wanted, and his brain seemed to have given up trying to regain control. His body never responded to anyone the way it reacted to Drum. He felt himself come again and his nails held on for dear life to Drum's shoulders. When he felt Drum kissing further down, his grip became tighter, wanting to stop Drum from going any further.

"AH!" he said, unsure of how Drum would react.

He possessed the biggest penis of all the pets in his generation, and he was proud of it, but against Drum, he felt small and inadequate. He never seen Drum look at his penis, and he didn't want Drum to laugh at how small he felt.

Eleven inches should not feel as small as it does around Drum, he thought, as he looked down at Drum looking up at him.

Drum understood and he released a shaky breath as Drum moved up to his neck. He felt Drum's warm hand slowly stroke him with a tight, possessive grip. Drum moaned into his neck, but he felt the vibrations all throughout his body.

He wrapped his arms around Drum's neck; linked his legs around the leg where Drum's penis was and started matching Drum's stroke. The low, deep moan which came from Drum made his whole-body shiver and come, again.

"Dummmmm-pling," Drum's deep, sticky-sweet voice called into his neck, and he felt Drum's penis twitching before Drum's pants were soaked with wetness.

One instant they were in the field meadow and the next, they were back in the library's Manga Room, standing up, clothed and clean. The table and chairs were back, along with everything on them.

He didn't say anything, just softly smiled. *GLou and GMack were right. I wish they were here to experience this. I will get them out of The City. I Vow;* he told himself.

Drum was sitting on the desk and as soon as Drum's arms reached out to him, he moved without thinking, right into them.

"Why didn't you file a report?" Drum asked.

"Because I am not finished with him. This is not near enough for me to keep my word to him," he told Drum honestly, while wondering why his Light responded to this male in such a way.

"How do you plan on doing that?" Drum asked.

He didn't feel like this was an interrogation, but Drum trying to seriously understand how he thinks and feels. "His social standing, his mental, emotional, and physical state. I will take out each one individually, so by the time I get to his last state, he will not have the other three to fall back on." He proudly told Drum while smiling.

Drum smiled back at him with a raised eyebrow. "You have already hit his social standing, but Pantu, if he hurts you, I will kill him," Drum stated, with an even tone.

He leaned back to look Drum in the eyes. The smile on Drum's face didn't match the tone and he couldn't understand why. "You cannot just kill people, Drum. You would go to prison!" he said, his eyes wide and his Light still tingling from Drum's words. He didn't want to admit it, so he was trying to push down the feelings of happiness at Drum's words.

"Depending on who I kill, I would be imprisoned, but I wouldn't go to prison," Drum said, giving him an unreadable look.

He shook his head to clear away all of his half-thoughts to allow his brain to irrationally explain what was happening between them. "You said you would be my friend! Besides, I have never killed anyone. I am not allowed," he said, giving a soft look to Drum. He felt Drum's heat and tried not to smile. "Vow to me!" he pleaded.

"I Vow," Drum immediately answered.

The quick response made him happy, and without thinking, he hugged Drum, who laughed at his giddy reaction.

"You're going to kill Queen with overexcitement. I think you're the first Being to make Queen worry about his plans having an uncommon variable," Drum told him, shaking his head.

"Huh? Who is the variable? Uncommon? Me?" he asked.

Drum's sweet laughter sounded out, making him try to hold back his own laughter, but a giggle slipped out, making him fully laugh with Drum.

"I can talk to Queen. Maybe he could give me some pointers when creating the perfect plan?"

He was happy he could talk to other people without it being a mental fight for superiority. Drum showed him he could be comfortable enough to have fun conversations without someone trying to trip him up or it being worth points. He only felt Ill and Malicious Intent from the snake, since he still used his routes to go to his classes.

"My turn, and that was five questions you left unanswered," he said, looking at Drum while batting his long lashes to give Drum quick glimpses of his brown irises.

"Okay. Go for it," Drum said. He was smiling while hugging a soft and sweet Pantu. This felt good, holding, touching, talking, and laughing with Pantu.

"Why do you say I smell like a pretzel?" Pantu asked.

His face lost its smile as he looked away from Pantu.

"Drum?" Pantu asked, softly.

"Yes Pantu?" he asked back.

"Am I ugly?" Pantu asked, sad and pouting.

His eyes snapped towards Pantu, and he held Pantu's face close to his. *"No Pantu. You aren't ugly. You're too handsomely beautiful to put into words,"* he expressed to Pantu, gently and truthfully. "You smell like my favorite memory."

When he blatantly told Pantu this, he heard Pantu's heartbeat speed up.

"I was born on a different continent called The States. We lived there until I was six. Every year around my birthday there is a travelling event called a State Fair. My family went every year.

"At first, I ate everything I could eat as a baby at the fair, but when I turned two, my older brother snuck me a freshly baked pretzel. It became the only reason for me going and the only thing I would eat at the fair for the next four years," he told Pantu.

"Then why do you call me Dumpling?" Pantu asked, gently.

"Because it was the first and only food I ate when we came here. I ate about ten baskets before my Mom cut me off," he said, with a sad laugh.

"You don't seem very happy about either one," Pantu said nervously, and he could feel the slight trembling of Pantu's body.

"Because even though those were happy memories for me, one was followed by tragedy and the second was proceeded by an unwanted announcement," he quietly said. He looked at Pantu with a sad smile.

"Why would you want to be around me if I smell like memories which make you sad?" Pantu asked, close to tears. Pantu leaned away from him, looking for an escape from his arms.

He pulled Pantu close and whispered, *"Because you're the first and only person to make me have glimpses of a feeling I haven't truly felt since I was six,"* he said, before looking Pantu in the eyes. *"Happy."*

DILLxPANTU: NO MORE HALF-TRUTHS
WEEK FOUR: WEDNESDAY

Dill came over, packed with snacks and ready to get some schoolwork done. They went into Pantu's studio, which was just the attic set up for Pantu to paint. It was rather dark, so Pantu hung tiny, sparkling lights all around the ceiling and down the walls to brighten up the place.

He knew how much Pantu wished he could remodel the room, but it would require speaking to his Pa, so Pantu had to deal with this for now. He was worried his best friend didn't consider this his home and made no plans to stay. They sat on the floor doing their work and sharing the snacks they brought for each other.

"Ah, Dill? How unhappy would you be if I told you Drum and I are closer than you know?" Pantu started off, looking down at the floor.

"What do you mean CLOSER? You guys touched once? I mean, Drum's been making it obvious he likes you," he said.

Pantu whispered, *"Well, it is true we touched once in front of you and his best friends, but we have touched a lot more in private."* And even though Pantu thought he didn't hear, when his best friend looked up, the look on his face showed every word was heard.

"PANTU! WHAT! THE! UNIVERSAL! FUCK!" he shouted and clutched his heart, pretending he couldn't breathe. "I—, I—, I'm going to die. I've lived a good life. I have some good friends and the best friend I have wanted my entire life. I even have a girlfriend," he said, and slowly laid down on the floor.

Pantu clapped and smiled. "Wow! That was way more believable than last time. You are getting better at this!" Pantu praised him.

He sat up and looked at Pantu. "I must be up to par so GLou will let me join his plays. I hear he's a tough critic," he said, smiling. "Now, explain from the beginning," he said, shifting his butt to get comfortable while snacking.

Pantu started from the first day, when he touched Drum at the assembly, embarrassed himself by staring at Drum in class, the class notes, when he was caught in the bathroom and what actually happened. Pantu came to the part about wearing Drum's clothes and he cut him off.

"Hold up! You mean to tell me you wore another man's clothes, even though yours should've been dry by then?" he asked.

The realization hit Pantu that his own clothes were in fact dry by the time he left campus.

"Wait. You came without even touching him?" he slowly asked, realizing what was being told to him.

"Yes. It is weird because my body has never acted like this before, so I am unsure of what to do?" Pantu told him. "There is more," Pantu added.

"OH, MY, UNIVERSE!" he said, excitedly.

"He...um...well...he, he masturbates for me." Pantu tried to explain but his confused look made his bestie try again.

"He strokes my penis until I come," Pantu said, bluntly.

He sat unmoving and in complete shock. Pantu went on about the notebooks from Drum's best friends, finding the park and sitting in it, to which he gasped.

"What? Because it is on Drum's family property?" Pantu asked.

"No. Pantu. It's because no one can take the Energy Level there. Well Drum can, but no one else will go there because they will die. No one wants to," he said, in awe of his best friend. "You were there for about five hours? Pantu it's a miracle you aren't dead!"

Pantu looked confused. "It was calm and peaceful there. I was able to open a door in a beautiful royal-blue Dome of Light and walk right in," Pantu said, nonchalantly.

He looked at Pantu and quietly pleaded, with fear in his voice, *"Pantu. Never tell anyone you did that. Do you understand? They will take you from me."*

"Drum knows," Pantu said. "I think it was his Dome. He put one around my house."

"That's why you can never tell anyone other than me and Drum. If others found out you can open a Barrier made by Drum, they would hunt you down, worse than The City and they would use you against him," he pleaded.

"Ah!" Pantu said, nodding. "I will stay quiet to anyone other than you. Why would people use me against Drum?"

"Not people, Beings. Others like us who hate how powerful Drum is," he told Pantu, a determined look on his face. "Keep going," he said, satisfied with the look of agreement on his best friend's face.

Pantu mentioned being followed by a red-eyed, long-eared rabbit and he interrupted.

"That's Mr. Floppy Ears, The Royal Family's pet bunny. He goes wherever he wants and as long as you don't attack him, he's pretty chill," he informed Pantu, who was both right and wrong when it came to fearing Mr. Floppy Ears.

"Dill, Mr. Floppy Ears is obviously a rabbit, not a bunny," Pantu countered, looking confused.

"Yea, well, the last Being to call him a rabbit lost a bottom lip," he warned.

Pantu's shocked face didn't disappear until the conversation started back up. Pantu told about Drum's painted nametag and the look on his bestie's face was of one waiting for his expected commentary.

"YOU MADE A GIFT FOR DRUM, GAVE IT TO HIM, AND HE ACCEPTED!?" His voice echoed through the attic. "Oh Pantu, you know you gave the first Gift, right?" he teased. "Not to mention, Drum helped you the first day you met, even after hitting him with your backpack, he let your flawless face stay intact?"

"Do you want to know or not!?" Pantu asked, trying not to smile.

He gestured. "My fault, carry on."

Pantu told him about the book order, The Four giving him food after Calculus, the Dumpling notes and then about the Dreams. As Pantu explained, he listened, his expression going from sad to scared.

"Pantu. You cannot invite anyone else into your Dreams," he stated. He knew his best friend didn't understand Universal Abilities verses Personal Abilities and Pantu's Personal Abilities were outrageous, possibly Furtive List insane.

"I cannot even if anyone else wanted me to. I told Dream Drum he would be the only one," Pantu said, confidently.

"Do you know what those Dreams are?" he asked.

"No. Dream Drum was trying to tell me, but it was my first time in years having a dream." Pantu pouted.

"So, he didn't shatter your Dream?" he asked, with a knowing smile. He knew his bestie understood from the little Drum was able to explain before being cut off by a spoiled Pantu. But his best friend was also very playful and was great at using his playful nature to get what he wanted without outright having to state anything.

"It is my dream, so Dream Drum said he would spoil me!" Pantu said, defiantly.

His sad smile and chuckle at being right about Pantu's personality, made him wonder just how far his best friend was willing to go with this plan. *Pantu. I know how much you want this whole thing to be a dream or a mental escape from being tortured, but you need to know this. You cannot show your Talents to everybody. You cannot let them know what you can do,* he told Pantu quietly.

"But Drum knows. I think he knows I can do other stuff as well," Pantu said.

"You mean like smelling Intent?" he asked. He was surprised, but it quickly faded. "Of course, he would. Drum is one of the most intelligent Beings on the planet. He's the only one powerful or smart enough to help someone as Talented as you." He approved with a nod.

"You trust him?" Pantu asked.

"With my life. Do you know he could have had me removed away from you?" he asked, looking sideways at Pantu.

"Why would he do that!?" Pantu asked, upset.

"Pantu. You can touch Drum, the only Being outside his family who can do so. We both know Drum likes you and we're close, so he has to know you tell me things you haven't told him. I could have been seen as a threat, especially with you having the type of Talents you have. But it seems like Drum doesn't like to see you upset, hurt or in pain," he explained.

"It does seem like he has no Malicious or Ill Intent towards you," Pantu thought out loud.

"I wouldn't be upset if he did," he said, sadly.

Pantu looked at him, waiting.

"I've known Queen since our preschool days and Drum since he moved here in the first grade. Drum was bullied by everyone in the school except Queen. We would throw things at Drum, sharper and sharper items, but Queen would block them.

"We would tease Drum about his skin's reaction to starlight, his hair and his accent while Queen would be the only one to defend him. Even the teachers and staff ignored our actions.

"But Drum never retaliated. He never said a word or ducked. Drum has never not been handsome. The girls bullied him because he refused their Gifts. One day a girl tried to give a Gift to Drum, and he turned her down in front of a huge group of students.

"The girl was so embarrassed, she transferred schools. An E-Level Five student, who had a huge crush on the girl, found out and was angry at Drum. The boy was bigger and heavier than Drum, so everyone thought it would be an easy fight.

"But when Drum finished with him, the boy's hand was burned off and if it wasn't for Mr. Caleb, Drum's dad, chopping off the boy's arm, it would have burned away the boy's whole body. The boy's face was unrecognizable from the amount of flesh he lost. With each gloved punch Drum gave, the boy's body melted.

"I was standing in front. I saw everything. The hand the boy used to hit Drum in the face started slowly burning away, but anywhere there was a barrier of clothes, yes, the boy burned, but the burning stopped when Mr. Caleb yanked Drum off the boy. Drum verified the rumor of what would happen if you touched his skin, or he touches you.

"Drum also unnecessarily broke the guy's spine. Even after all of that, Drum was never mean to us. He helped us and was kind. He made our town cleaner and safer. I decided then I would never follow a crowd again, only Drum. But my damage was already done. I was a bully. We all were, but Drum..." He hung his head, unable to properly express his remorse.

"I don't know any six-year-olds who would have handled that kind of situation with reserve. He never yelled at us; he never bullied us back. We all knew he could if he wanted to. He was able to get us to like him," he quietly said to Pantu. He knew his face was filled with guilt about what he did as a kid.

"Wait, so if you touch Drum, your skin melts?" Pantu asked, surprised, and started checking himself to make sure none of his skin was burned off.

"That's why I'm telling you not to tell anybody. Don't show other Beings you can touch Drum. Not until you are sure about your feelings for him," he explained. "Drum has a reputation, a flawless one. If you flaunt you can touch him, but..." He trailed off, not wanting to hurt Pantu's feelings.

After thinking, he continued, "If you don't want to be with Drum, that's cool. Drum is the type to respect other people's boundaries. But please, please Pantu, don't play around with his feelings. He's never liked anyone before and there are others who would see him ruined and dead. They will use you to get to him," he pleaded.

"Why are you telling me this? I have never liked anyone before either?" Pantu asked, turning away from him to pout.

"Because Pantu, you have plans that are dangerous. I will help you, stand next to you no matter what. But understand you can get close to Drum. Are you only going to like him for now or are you planning on liking him past that?

"He likes you Pantu. How much more is he going to like you until you execute your plan? Others will start to notice. He's being polite by not touching you outright.

"I'm not rushing you to figure out a label for the two of you. I'm saying, be careful as you decide," he said. "If anything happens to you Pantu, know Drum and I will set this planet on fire, and we will bring it down."

They continued talking, with Pantu completely opening up, including his reactions to Drum and everyone else. He listened and commented on everything. He was able to get Pantu to laugh and seriously contemplate the plans they made.

Whatever questions he asked and Pantu was able to answer, Pantu did. But there was a lot Pantu was unsure about, hadn't thought of, or couldn't tell him. He also teased Pantu could make his Dreams a reality, which only made Pantu turn bright red.

"Whether you want to admit it or not, there is something between you and Drum. It's your choice to pursue it FOR YOU, or to leave it alone. Drum isn't going to hate you because you don't want to date him. He isn't the type. Also, never ask him to Promise anything you don't mean."

Pantu looked at him, scared.

"You asked him to Promise you something?" he asked, putting his face in his hands and groaning.

"What is so bad about wanting to handle Mansnake on my own?" Pantu asked, indignantly. He handled a lot of pets and owners in The City, so one slimy snake wouldn't be a problem. *"Besides, who keeps all their Vows anyway?"* he mumbled.

"Pantu, we aren't fickle like humans. We don't Vow or Promise things easily, because when we make Promises, we're compelled to hold to them. Queen's Favor cards are his Promises and incredibly hard to get.

"If your request doesn't go against the morals of the Being Community or Drum's values, Queen will do it." Dill paused and looked at him. "If it's someone we really like, someone who holds our Scents, we will Promise anything," Dill stated, expressing the amount of power he was holding.

But it took him a minute to understand the look on Dill's face. "I—!" He stopped himself. A denial would be a Lie, and although he could use creative ways to see a different viewpoint, his G-Pas taught him to never Lie.

"Drum is rumored to be the most powerful Being in existence. And since no one knows for sure exactly what he can do, the speculations in the Being Communities have a lot of Beings split.

"But even still, everyone expects a lot from him. Don't complicate either of your lives for shits and giggles. Oh, and you can never let others know Drum made a Promise to you," Dill told him.

"After your takedown of Mansnake, everyone thought they were trying to recruit you to join their group. But after the exchange between you and Queen today, *everyone* knows Drum likes you," Dill informed him.

"What!?" he asked, his eyebrows raised at Dill constantly telling him, Drum liked him, without a Lie being smelled. Dill genuinely believed Drum was interested in him and the confirmation from his best friend made a smile tug at his lips.

"They are the most handsome and charming Beings, not just on campus, but all over the intranet and the human internet. Everything they do and say in public is posted online. And it's not like Drum's been subtle about his feelings.

"Drum announced he can date and set his sights on you. The invite requests? Never been done before. Personally, inviting someone to his party? Never been done before. Someone sits in THAT chair and has a personal Crystal to the Manga Room. NEVER. BEEN. DONE. BEFORE!" Dill stated.

"I just received the crystal today!" he whined, impressed by how quickly information spread throughout their campus. He would roll his eyes at hearing the word-of-mouth information finally reaching The Outer Ring weeks after it was already old, dead news in The Center.

"And everyone knows! You, Pantu, most certainly have the looks. Your Charm is you're innocent, cute, and funny. Not to mention, since you, me, nor The Four have confirmed your gender, everyone is wondering about you. The theories and fanfiction online about you are wild!" Dill informed him.

He stayed offline, so all his information came straight from Dill's mouth. But this time, instead of ignoring Dill's comment, he really wanted to know.

"What are they?" he asked to Dill's overly happy expression.

"Well," Dill started, "one theory is that you're a tomboy."

"Huh?" he asked, tilting his head to remember the word from the dictionary.

"They think because you're a Private Citizen, you're dressing as a guy to keep your identity a secret. Beings also post theories of you being the first woman to ever join The Four. Theories that you're a masculine-leaning lesbian, or an unnaturally, incredibly beautiful guy are all floating online. And since no one can tell just by looking at you, it sends Beings into a turbulent tailspin trying to figure you out." Dill grinned hard at him, knowing he would use this information to his benefit.

"But you can also be...alluring to any gender," Dill said, laughing at the scrunched up look on his face.

He didn't want to be alluring to anyone who wasn't Drum. He couldn't afford to split his focus, nor was anyone else particular enough for him to do so. "Dill, I am really not trying—" He was cut off.

Dill looking at him, a knowing smile on his best friend's face. "I know Pantu. But you draw others to you. Whether it's with good or bad intentions, you attract others.

"Those with good intentions, like me of course, will only want to be your friend, best friend, to help you. Those with bad intentions see you as a sexual conquest, someone they want to dominate, like Mansnake. Like her," Dill said.

"And there are those without a scent, wondering what to do with themselves when they're around you. You confuse them." Dill laughed. *"But you are also kind-hearted and nice,"* Dill said softly, with a smile.

"Ah, how?" he asked. Dill knew his plan for Mansnake wasn't exactly brief.

"You befriended me," Dill said, looking away.

He said nothing but the look he gave Dill was one of trying to understand what Dill wasn't saying.

"While I may have started out following the crowd, I soon became the unelected leader. I was the one who instigated the fight between Drum and the E-Level Five student. Jax, Turn and Put helped. A boy was almost killed because of us.

"But now we live with the guilt of knowing the guy will never walk, talk or eat on his own again. The Being who tried to heal his arm and face, could only do so much," Dill said. There was a look on Dill's face of deep unhappiness, and it hurt him to see his best friend suffering.

"Yes. That sucks dirty nut sacks, but you know I have done worse things, and yet you are still my best friend," he said, encouraging Dill.

"Yours was to survive, ours was for the shit and giggles of our parents," Dill said, hanging his head, and the feelings leaking off Dill reminded him of the first day he walked into homeroom. The feelings of uncertainty divided him, and he felt unhappy about being so callous and mean to people who were innocent and unknowing about the life he lived before coming here. He didn't want them mixed up in his business and it created holes in his plan.

"Well, Drum and Queen have never spoken badly about you. In fact, they both have told me you are a good friend," he happily said, hoping to cheer Dill up.

He tilted his head, using his Talent to read people. Dill was trying but was held back from a full smile due to the thoughts still in his head. Even if it was never stated it was his plan, he could see on Dill's face, Drum figured it out but refrained from retaliating. Dill was unsure of how Drum would react to being best friends with the Being Drum liked.

He thought about how Dill said Drum could have removed him but didn't. He didn't know if Drum would one day make the decision to take his best friend from him, but the thought made him unhappy.

Going through his memories of Drum and Dill's interactions, he realized Drum didn't seem to notice Dill was around, since Drum's focus was always on him. Dill also seemed to shrink into the background and said extraordinarily little around Drum. It appeared Drum only recently semi-acknowledged Dill's presence.

Dill was deep in thought about Drum, of all Beings, saying anything nice about him. He knew Dill was trying his hardest to be a more accepting and open Being. In the years leading up to now, he wondered about Drum and Dill's interactions.

"And you are a good friend," he said, happy. "The bestest!" he exclaimed.

"That is...not a word?" Dill said, starting to laugh.

"It is now," he said, his voice even. "Besides, Drum told me everything I went through made me the person I am today. Do you not think the experience changed you and made you better?" he asked, before continuing.

"You are the only person who never laughed at me when I did not know something. You helped me understand, even though some of that knowledge came late as hell." He jokingly pushed Dill.

"Yea. Sorry about that. Your scent kept wavering, so I was scared you didn't want to be my friend," Dill told him.

His eyebrows shot up, and his eyes went wide. "And now?" he asked, seriously wanting to know. He knew Dill's loyalty to him never faltered, and it made him unhappy that his scent wavered with his best friend. He didn't want to be unhappy and cry from losing his best friend, and he knew Doctor Robin would be as broken as him at the loss of Dill. He needed to find a way to protect Dill.

"It's just there. Solid. Steady," Dill said, looking at him.

He smiled and felt his body release tension as his shoulders sagged. Only Dill knew his plan and was helping him. He was thrown in disarray when Dill found his scrambler and offered to upgrade it, so he could better use it on his cellphone. He could have called her every day, but he didn't want to talk with her more than he needed to.

He was only calling because she threatened the lives of his family still trapped in The City. He was going to go back and help his G-Pas escape. He wanted to bring them here, so they could see their stories were real. It's why Dill was telling him not to play around with his own, or Drum's feelings, if he didn't plan on giving them a try. There was no guarantee he would be able to come back.

He cleaned up their mess, while Dill moved the oversized bean bag to the middle of the floor and took a projector out. Setting it up using his phone, Dill started a movie he downloaded.

Dill stuck to his rule of no intranet/internet and would download videos and movies to show him. Dill would clean up the videos so he wouldn't see anything related to the intranet while watching them. They sat on the beanbag together to watch the movie.

"Do you think Drum would kill someone?" he asked, quietly.

Dill responded, "Yes," without hesitation.

He pressed his lips together and looked around. "So, if say, we went to The City and rescued my G-Pas, but I was caught and collared, *Drum would not be unhappy or anything, right?*" he asked, softly.

Dill turned to look at him. "Besides the fact that if you were collared, then we're getting collared together, how am I supposed to come back here, look Drum in the face and tell him the one person on this planet who he likes and can also touch him was collared, so I left him behind?" Dill asked, looking like a baby bird unsure of whether the person holding it would kill it or feed it. "He would kill me Pantu."

"But we saved my G-Pas!" he said, with a small smile meant for encouragement.

"So, Drum could have the satisfaction of killing us all. Then, he would march into The City and would make your owner un-collar you before ripping her in two, only to bring the whole fucking thing down after killing everyone else there," Dill said, staring wide-eyed at him.

"He...he would not..." he stumbled out.

"Drum didn't say he would hurt, harm or break Mansnake, he said he would KILL him," Dill stated.

He knew what Dill was saying was true. He could feel Drum's feelings and when it was said, he felt Drum meant it. And after telling Dill everything, his best friend said exactly what he felt from Drum. He realized then just how dangerous his plan really was.

PANTU: THE DEADLY SIN OF GREED
WEEK FOUR: THURSDAY

If I knew my days on campus would be this peaceful, I would have gotten rid of Mansnake sooner. He was able to focus on his classes, he and Drum enjoyed privacy in the Manga Room, and no one threatened or bullied him.

He made acquaintances with quite a few who smelled nice. He also found out Dill was right about others not liking Drum. He could smell the Intent against Drum the more he was around The Four.

Those Beings never did or said anything to him, but when the light scent of cinnamon and honey filled their noses, Dill or one of The Four would realize someone's Intent was strong. He only released his scent if the Intent was against him, Dill or one of The Four. This happened in the shared areas, so he assumed most, if not all the AH students held positive feelings towards The Four.

It wasn't that he didn't care about other Beings' disputes, but he really didn't care to announce his Talents when Dill made him agree not to let anyone other than Drum know what he could do.

He figured Drum's best friends were smart enough to catch on and Queen outright knew, so he wasn't surprised when Drum asked him about it. He thought he would have been asked in the Manga Room, but the male kept his hands to himself.

Drum seemed distracted but whenever he sent out his desire, he would watch Drum fight not to touch him. He turned it into a little game, getting pleasure out of Drum's restraint.

He didn't know why Drum was refusing to touch him, or what he and Dill talked about when they left together in the middle of lunch. He didn't ask why Drum showed up late to the Manga Room, or why Drum was now sitting across the dining room table from him. He didn't question any of it. He completed his homework and the two packets. Drum checked them and left before his parents came home.

His Mind was a jumbled mess, and his brain was laughing at him, giving him an unhappy feeling. He was taking a shower, constantly frowning as he was thinking, *is Drum no longer interested in me? He did say he would wait for me, but am I taking too long and telling too much, so Drum decided I am no longer worth the wait?*

Am I such a weird Being, that Drum is trying to distance himself from my crazy? My Ma did pass down her amazing looks to me, but I also received her crazy. Does Drum think I am as weak and useless as my timid Pa? The man did manage to pass his best genes to me, maybe he also passed his personality as well. Maybe Drum figures I am not good enough for him because he believes I am my Ma's crazy son and my Pa's useless child?

He was hoping he could show Drum he could be of help, that he could be useful. But all Drum told him during tutoring was to continue practicing on focusing his Ability so he didn't fill the whole area, it would start to become too obvious. He was confused as Drum said it so gently and caringly, he couldn't do anything but agree.

Drum wasn't upset at him, and he thought it was all he cared about, until now. Now he was worried Drum didn't like him or was tired of him being so different. He was passed out when his Ma opened his door to let him know dinner was ready.

He was planning on Sleep Thinking. He didn't mind his body being a little restless since he figured Dream Drum would probably not touch him or worse, ignore him. But when he opened his eyes to look around, he was in their dream space. He plopped down to the ground and sitting cross legged, he put his head into his fists and rested his elbows on his legs.

"AH! I was trying to avoid being here. HE would not want to touch me if REAL HIM does not care to. Maybe it is better this way." As he said this, there was a cattail which leaned forward towards him.

He absentmindedly started to pet the cattail. "Maybe Drum can find someone with less issues to give his affections to," he said to the cattail, which was more interested in him petting it then listening to his problems.

"Would you really be okay with me giving my affections to another?" Drum's voice quietly whispered near his ear.

He jumped in surprise with a yelp exiting his mouth as he almost fell over, but Drum's strong arm caught him around the waist. He stared up at Drum with wide eyes. He didn't think Drum would show up or touch him. He couldn't understand why his Light didn't warn him. But the more he thought about it, the more he realized it wasn't a warning, but anticipation.

His Light was anticipating the amazing feelings Drum was giving him. Since he fought so much against his feelings, his Light was now at a stalemate, wanting to listen and follow him but unhappy with the decisions he was making. Drum pulled him up and taking his arm back, placed his hand in his pocket and stood up, looking down at him, a sexy, half smile gracing such a handsome face.

The starlight radiated off Drum, and the brightness from the young male standing next to him was visibly noticeable, even without his True Vision turned on. He'd never met anyone in The City who shined so brightly.

He could tell this young male was pure in his intentions and Drum followed the second law of his family, never kill an innocent person. There was no mask when it came to

Drum, nor any blemishes. He was so intrigued, he couldn't stop thinking about everything he'd learned so far living in this town.

Drum was dressed in a thin, midnight-blue, long sleeve shirt and white sweatpants. He didn't know how many combinations Drum owned but he could look amazing in anything. The color of the shirt only brought out the shimmer of blue within Drum's jet-black hair.

He looked at the shoulder length hair on top of Drum's head and smiled at the shimmering pattern, which oddly calmed him down. He noticed Drum was wearing black socks, which he'd never worn before. He looked up into Drum's face before turning back to the cattail.

Drum sat down beside him and crossed his legs. Taking his hands out of his pockets and leaning back on them, Drum made himself comfortable. He looked at the male and smiled.

Drum was the only person who was always so relaxed around him. He didn't look threatened, uncomfortable, or nervous whenever they were around each other. Other than Malicious or Ill Intent, those three emotions were the ones he felt the most from other people in The City.

He realized how much he appreciated and liked how Drum never once felt those feelings towards him. So much that every time he saw Drum relaxed, he would get hard. He focused on the cattail and leaning his legs up; he wrapped his arms around them and hugged.

"You never answered my question," Drum told him, giving him a full smile.

"Well, if it makes your life easier, then why not?" He shrugged, not feeling like trying to change the subject or talk around it. He still didn't feel his Light reacting to Drum and he was trying to figure out why.

"Would it make you happy?" Drum asked him. "For me to spoil another? Touch another? Hold someone else…"

As Drum was saying this to him, his Light started to cause tiny sharp pains right underneath his skin. His Light was obviously against him agreeing to Drum's proposal. His Mind was sending out unhappy images showing him Drum's words, so he knew his Mind also didn't want Drum to do the things they did together with anyone else, in his dreams or reality.

His heart was beating fast and off rhythm. The lack of a pattern with his heartbeat was making him feel unsure of what was happening to him. He closed his eyes and focused on calming his heart down. He felt a small crack and slowly shifted his body to adjust to the foreign feeling, which was quickly becoming a natural occurrence.

"It is not fair to want everything, I should just be happy with what I do have," he said, unwilling to ask for the impossible.

He was having intense feelings of unhappiness cause by the possibility of getting everything he wanted and then being forced to wake up from his dream when he was the happiest. He wanted to keep his eyes closed forever and live in this dream, but reality would find a way to slither back into his conscience.

"When has life ever been fair to us?" Drum asked.

He knew Drum was already looking directly at him with a smile since his Light was back to flowing unnaturally happily inside him. His Light was happy, his heart was back to its mundane pattern, and his Mind was now sending out images of him and Drum, entwined in each other's arms. He turned to lock eyes with Drum and knew the words came from experience, a shared hardship of life.

"I am already being greedy wanting your time, attention, and affection in my dreams. It is quite selfish of me to want you to spoil me in here and out there," he told Drum. He was fighting himself. Of course, he wanted Drum to only focus on him, both in his dreams and reality, but with the way his body was reacting to a male, he knew he would need to train himself while she re-trained him to respond to her.

Drum moved closer to him, and he felt wrapped in warmth. One of Drum's arms was casually thrown over his right shoulder, and the other was around his waist. Drum's connected hands were right in front of where his Orb was inside his body and he felt an inner vibration, making him take and release a calming breath.

As soon as Drum hugged him, he fell back onto Drum's warm, sturdy chest. His head rolled back and forth a bit as he was trying to remember what he was so urgently thinking about.

Drum whispered in his ear, *"Then let's be greedy and selfish together."*

PANTU: A CAN FULL OF WORMS
WEEK FOUR: FRIDAY

He woke up feeling unsure about how this day was going to progress. He didn't know why even Dream Drum wouldn't "touch" him whenever he was hard. He was used to coming every day, now, several times a day.

His body felt a little uncomfortable, but he could deal with it. Besides, he would see Drum in the Manga Room. It would be his last chance before Drum left for the weekend. He couldn't get himself off anymore. His penis only responded to Drum's warm touch and would shrink back; unhappy he even thought to touch it with such cold hands.

He looked down at his penis, semi-hard from his dream. "Traitor," he said, and his penis shrunk back. He shook his head and got up to get ready for day classes.

He'd missed spending time outside of school with Dill. Yes, they still spent the weekends together, but he and Dill used to spend every day around each other. So, he was making the best of Dill's first and only relationship. He didn't want to be the reason they ended things or to lose his friendship with Dill.

Balance is key. The thought popped into his head.

Dill switched his seat in homeroom to sit in front of him. They were talking about the movie saga Dill was making him watch. He loved action movies, but this saga was grating his nerves. Dill was explaining the remaining movies, but he'd already checked out.

"Pantu? You really fell asleep during the fourth movie, so now we have to watch from there, that way the next movie makes sense," Dill explained.

He groaned and put his head in his hands. "I beg of you to release me from this torture," he said, whining.

Dill stared at him with a comically wide-eyed look. "You don't like the saga? It's one of the most popular action series. It's why there are nine of them and more on the way," Dill said, chuckling.

The over-dramatic roll of his eyes made their classmates snicker.

"Five more. There are five more movies of him crying about his family while racing cars, breaking out of prison transport, and two of the movies you showed me had nothing to do with that main character." He threw his hands up, while groaning and leaning back. "I am over it," he said, shaking his head.

Their classmates started laughing and talking about all the things which annoyed them about the saga.

"But I thought you have a compulsion to finish what you start?" Dill teased.

"You, my bestie, have finally broken me. All it took was a saga which makes no sense," he said, crossing his arms and looking away from Dill. "I refuse!" he said, determined not to sit through another no plot, absent storyline movie.

Dill laughed and agreed. "Okay I won't show the saga about the cars who can transform into robots, the storylines for those are non-existent," Dill said, pretending to be unhappy and frowning.

He held back his smile at Dill, understanding his different definitions of plot and storyline. The storyline was the essence of the movie, but a good plot would keep him watching. A good plot was someone he found attractive in the movie, so that meant there was no one he would stay to watch and no rhyme or reason for him to become invested in the story. It may have good action, but he wanted more from his movies.

"Ah," he said, his face mimicking Dill's. "At least I do not have to sit through FIVE more movies about doing crazy shit in the name of your family then crying about it," he said, turning his frown upside down. "If they make movies about manga, surely, they make movies about comic book superheroes?" he asked.

Dill's frown disappeared as Dill's mouth dropped open. "Pantu, you just opened a can of worms," Dill said.

The room erupted into which universe was better, WonderVEL or Twisted Comics.

He looked around, hiding his smile behind his hand as students pleaded their case for their favorite universe. He smiled and giggled when his eyes turned back to Dill. *"Oops!"* he whispered.

Dill leaned in, close to him. *"Whichever universe you choose, will greatly affect our friendship,"* Dill whispered back. "Don't judge them based on the comics though. Watch the movies, then choose," Dill said. "We can go through them during winter break," Dill planned.

The room suddenly became quiet. He sat up in his chair, thinking the Professor entered the room.

Dill leaned even closer to his face to whisper, *"He's here."*

His eyes went wide when he felt the tingling sensation in his Light return. But Drum wasn't even in the room yet. It was if he could feel a familiar shiver travel down his spine and sense Drum's Light, focused on him. His eyes darted around, trying to find a safe place to settle as Win walked into their homeroom, followed by Queen, Sport and finally Drum.

The Four entered through the back door of the room. Even though Drum entered last, he was the first to the window and leaned against it while his best friends gathered around, talking quietly amongst themselves. His classmates, who were already in the room, were taking photos and videos of The Four while posting them.

He knew better than to turn around, so he leaned closer to Dill, their foreheads almost touching. He could see in Dill's eyes; his best friend was experiencing the multiple ways his life would come to an end. He knew Dill was willing to face death for him, so he added a smile to his face and saw Dill die inside.

"We have the shuttle and ramp completed, so we should work on the spaceship next," he said.

His Light was sending goosebumps across his skin as it happily flowed inside his body, and he knew Drum's eyes were on him. But this feeling also interrupted his breathing along with his heart rate, and he cut his eyes to the side to see Drum leaning against a now empty desk. He assumed the Being sitting there moved to allow Drum the space, and also so they wouldn't melt. Dill immediately jerked back from his face and his eyes turned back to Dill with a question in them.

"Oh! You're building an actual spaceship based on the models you're making?" Drum's smooth voice sounded out right by him.

He slowly turned to Drum, relaxed and leaning against the desk next to him. The smile on Drum's face was directed at him but Drum's eyes, which were focused on Dill, caused his best friend to shrink back from the invisible, murderous daggers stabbing every one of Dill's vital points.

"That's dope," Drum said, with a smile while slowly moving those honey-green eyes back to him.

Hearing those words made him want to jump up, wrap his arms around Drum's neck and kiss Drum's full, plump lips. He felt his body warm up at the happy thought, but instead of acting on it, he turned away from the urge while mumbling, *"As if you think any of my ideas are dope."* He was trying not to be unhappy, but his arms crossed his chest, and his lips were playing a game of whether to poke out in disappointment or for a kiss.

Drum leaned forward, keeping a relaxed nature, and loudly whispered, *"If I knew praising you would make you blush this much, I would've done it sooner. How adorable!"*

When Drum said these words, he felt his penis stiffen, as if reaching for Drum's warm hands. He knew he was fighting a losing battle of control when his penis leaked a bit, making him close his eyes and focus on unusual ways to remove his penis without losing too much blood or Light.

He felt warmer and knew Drum leaned so close to him, he could feel the warm breath on his ear, so he sat as still as possible, not to accidentally touch Drum, while he was praying his ears were the same color as the rest of his body.

But Drum stopped before touching him and whispered gently, *"I guess I will spoil you with praise more often."*

His body felt every word Drum said, and he was sitting as still as he could, silently praying to the Universe, no one looked at the large stain he felt on his shorts. Drum smiled and glanced at Dill as if to say something without dagger eyes, but left it unspoken before looking back at him.

"Don't worry," was all Drum said to him before standing to leave with the sound of the bell.

He knew without looking, Drum cleaned him up. He could feel the dryness of his boxers, and he felt so good and at the same time unhappy, because he wanted more.

"Your #AnonB conversation with Drum has gone viral," Dill said, looking at his phone.

His face scrunched up, and his lips pouted out with him trying to understand what Dill meant by viral. "Why would anyone post that?" he asked.

"Because anything about #AnonB and Drum, or The Four, immediately trends," Dill told him.

He rolled his eyes and leaned back in his chair. He was uninterested. Dill told him any personal information about him wouldn't be uploaded to the intranet. Even the way he spoke was translated differently, so most Beings paraphrased what he said.

Beings could only use their own technology inside of Domes, since human made tech wouldn't work, it was equal to paperweight and the reason he needed to toss his first cellphone once they crossed the white Dome.

The cellphone started to erode after only a few days under the Dome. Beings were still able to access human internet on their own tech, but it also restricted any information on him or any Being related information.

He was wondering about Mansnake, who lived in Hollis, but he noticed there was a thin, barely noticeable Dome around Hollis and his thoughts about the snake quickly dissipated. With Dill's assurance of him being a Private Citizen working all over Sunset Country, not just Sunset Town, he was cool with the, as Beings called it, hashtag.

Queen and his Bees were also strict when it came to personal privacy online. Queen's Bees were Beings he trusted and worked with him. There was no age range or gender requirement to be a Bee, and he found out Queen's Bees were all over the town and surrounding cities. He didn't know how to spot them as Dill told him not to bother, there were more than even he thought.

His day was going well, and he was smiling and laughing with other Beings who didn't yet know he understood the town and the "people" in it. He enjoyed their play on words to avoid letting any information about Beings slip.

He felt happy they hadn't sprung this information on him as he would have thought he was in the mental hospital having a delusional episode again. There was no telling how those delusions would have played out in this reality.

Even though he had almost every class with one of The Four, they never bothered him. They did, however, move their seats closer to him, or in Win's case, right next to him, with the argument he and Dill always had the most interesting conversations early in the morning.

PANTUxKAT: A NEW FRIEND AND A DEEPER UNDERSTANDING
WEEK FOUR: FRIDAY

Lunch, however, was different. Dill needed to convince Pantu to eat, which was more difficult now than before. He believed he was gaining too much weight, and it was why Drum wasn't interested in touching him anymore.

The food here was so delicious, he was eating a lot more than ever before. He held the perfect male body in The City. With smooth, hairless skin, his body curved softly with a subtle scent which couldn't be denied. Women would clamor to get as close to him as possible, just to touch his cold, marble-like skin.

He searched the town desperately, but no places here sold diet pills. He still refused to exercise more than a walk around town, so his next option was to regulate his eating.

Since he'd never seen Drum's body, he imagined how perfect Drum would look undressed, while at the same time imagining himself as a blob of frozen choco-chip cookie dough. Drum's toned stomach was blessed with abs to match the solid chest, which brought him happiness every time he laid his head against Drum.

He only knew because he could feel Drum's body through the thin shirts in their shared space. The strong arms which were able to lift and hold him up while pleasing him only made him want to hold on to them forever.

As they entered the cafeteria, he quickly noticed Kat was standing by the door waiting. Kat called out and walked towards him with a smile so bright and beautiful, he stared. He was frozen, realizing Kat was calling for him. His Mind was funneling through every thought but was unable to focus on one as Kat continued to come closer.

The only passing thoughts he could understand sounded like *do not look at Win, do not look at The Four's table, do not let anything slip*. He stood there, unmoving. Kat waved her hand in front of him and looked up, slightly giggling at the unnamed expression on his face.

When he heard Kat's giggle, he snapped out of his trance and stumbled across his words. "Ah...hi...Kat. Nice...to see...you."

Kat giggled. "Would you like to join me for lunch outside?" Kat asked and held up a layered basket. "I've gotten enough food for the both of us," Kat said, brightly smiling at him.

He couldn't respond, he was stuck on stupid which was slowly turning into him slightly trembling. *This is how my life would end when I was so close to twenty-two. I have never ridden a roller coaster, but I have made a best friend. I have never been on an airplane, but I have learned to swim. I have never...* His thoughts were cut off by a warm feeling next to him.

"Are you coming to Anime Night tonight?" Drum asked, casually, standing with both hands in his pockets.

He turned to follow the voice which warmed and calmed his body. "Yes," he responded, slowly starting to breathe normally again.

"Dope. I will see you there," Drum said.

Drum's smile brought the color back to his face and his heart started beating faster than normal again. When Kat tugged on his arm, he moved with her but took the basket and her backpack to hold them as they walked.

Kat led them out of the cafeteria and across campus to the middle of the empty field. She pulled a blanket from her backpack and spread it out for them to sit. After getting comfortable, Kat waved her hand over her head, and a beautiful ocean-blue Dome appeared over them. Kat only smiled at him before opening the trays and their focus shifted as they started eating and complimenting the food.

"Holy Universe! This is delicious!" he said, completely forgetting his diet. Each piece of food he placed in his mouth, just dissolved, leaving the flavors of the dish to dance across his tongue.

If the dish was a mini meat bun, the savory taste of the beef used would be accompanied by the slightly, buttery flavor of the crispy bread. If the mini bun was sweet, he was at a loss trying to understand how the food melted like heated caramel but still held the designated sweetness for each treat. He loved the guessing game of figuring out if the bun would be sweet or savory.

"OOOOOHHHHH! I'm in heaven. This just melts in your mouth!" Kat said and shoved a piece of what she was eating into his mouth.

"Did you make this?!" he asked, with wide eyes and a mouth full of food.

"Oh, Universe no! I can't cook! Sport made this for us," Kat said, with a longing smile.

They finished all the food quicker than they would have otherwise as they praised each bite. Once all the food was gone, Kat leaned back and smiled at Pantu.

"I know you heard what happened to me my first year," she started.

Pantu looked at her surprised.

"I felt it from you," she quietly said, and received a questioning look from Pantu.

"I sensed you experienced the same thing. I know Dill gave you the watered-down version your first day on campus, but I saw it in your eyes; when you looked away from me, you knew how I felt. And it was from experience, not empathy," she told him.

"I was sexually assaulted by five seniors from Hollis Higher Ed while shopping with my Mom for a birthday gift for my Dad," she said. She felt her smile disappear. "They waited for me to be alone before they snatched me," she said with large tears forming in the corners of her eyes.

Her Energy was buzzing, scared to recall what happened to her, but she wasn't about to let another Being fall into the trap she did. If she could help Pantu understand, even a little, she would open herself up, so there would be one less victim.

She could smell a light, pleasant scent coming from Pantu and it gave her hope he would listen without judging. She felt safe enough to tell Pantu this and held no fear about seeing the hated look of pity cross Pantu's face.

"I fought as hard as I could, but there would be others who held me down and soon I just gave up. It was a losing battle for me, and I was tired and in pain. It felt as if my Mind, body, and emotions were all disconnected and I was outside of myself, watching. My Mom has the track your kid app and she found me, naked, curled up in a ball and covered in their scent and cum."

As she was saying this, the look on Pantu's face was one of shock and disbelief. It was like Pantu couldn't understand how she could ever be put into a violent situation like that. She also realized Pantu didn't know about the sexual part of her attack.

"I never wanted it to happen. I didn't know those guys for them to attack me. I felt worthless. If anyone could have me, what would ever make me special again? Why wait to make my own decision when someone stronger could just take whatever they wanted from me? Why would anyone ever want to touch me again?" she asked. She leaned up to look Pantu in the eyes.

Pantu moved closer and hugged her. She experienced a slight cooling sensation running all over her skin. Every inch of her was slowly and softly being covered. The Energy she felt was calming and conveyed a sense of resolve. Yes, this happened to her, but this wasn't everything about her. There was so much more to her and sensing the happiness in the Energy of her willingness to share, pulled her lips into a soft smile.

"It may seem like our experiences are different, but the common factor is neither of us wanted what happened to us, to happen. It's called sexual assault. Here, and most everywhere, it's against the law for someone to force, coerce or drug another for any type of sexual act," she said, as she watched the realization crawl over Pantu's face.

She only held on to her soft smile as her eyes told Pantu, she knew. She saw it in him. The same feelings, of weakness and hopelessness mingling in with fear and anger to cause despair, she saw them in Pantu's eyes.

"I never wanted to do any of those things. I was seven years old. I could not fight back, say no, or stop. They threatened to kill my family in front of my eyes before keeping me as a slave forever. How could I possibly fight?" Pantu said, taking deep breaths and his face said there was an understanding of why they were having this conversation.

"You were a child Pantu..." she started.

Pantu cut in. "So were you." Pantu looked directly at her, and they hugged each other for comfort.

She really didn't want to let go. Pantu's body was cold, sending goosebumps over her, but it was a calming chill which radiated from his body. She didn't know any man who could be as smooth and soft as Pantu and she sat there happily still hugging Pantu, who hadn't released her, making her smile brighter.

"You should know Manpa or Alex, is the reason I tried to kill myself. The reason I gave up on life," she stated.

Pantu pulled back and looked at her in surprise. Her smile drooped into a frown at the loss of comfort. She wanted more but when she felt a Heated gaze from clear across the campus, she composed herself. She realized Pantu's scent and touch was an incredibly High-Level of Seduction and the only way she could hold her own was because of the Heat from the stare.

"He wanted a date with Drum and somehow found out about Win and me. He asked me to set up a double date, but I refused to be used for someone else's obsession. After I was assaulted, he came to my home to tell me he had someone record it and if I refused him again, he would send some more to get a taste and upload it to the dark net," she explained.

"What is the dark net?" Pantu asked.

"It's a part of the human internet where a lot of bad things are uploaded, brought, sold and laundered," she answered. "He was going to post it on a site where those less than human pay to see people get assaulted. He was going to make money off my trauma, repeatedly," she said.

What she didn't want was for this video to find its way onto the screens of her fellow classmates. She was a Liberal Arts student, having given up her seat in AH after the attack. If anyone on campus found out about the video, if Win saw it, she knew she wouldn't be able to deal with the different looks on Beings' faces. The whispers, which only recently died down, would spring up again and she was confident she wouldn't be able to deal with them. She knew she would snap, if only to protect her Bubbly.

Sitting here next to Pantu, she realized she didn't have any more tears to cry about this, in fact she felt confident about her resolve to not let it control her life. She was sitting next to a Being, who not only cleansed her Mind, but he also gave her clean, fresh, unviolated skin. Her body felt unused as if Pantu healed her there as well.

She and Win were having issues when it came to touching. They would spend time together, but she wouldn't let Win's hands touch her. She felt used, unclean, and unworthy of her Bubbly, but now, she longed for Win's touch again.

Somehow, she felt she could finally open to Win about what happened. Her Bubbly patiently waited for her to talk about it and now she felt confident enough to express herself.

And these feelings were thanks to the Being sitting next to her, who healed, not only her body, but calmed her Mind. She felt brand new, her skin fresh and smooth. She didn't know if Pantu knew what he did, so she would inform Drum first and let him handle it.

"I was so scared he would find a way to me when he started coming here this school year, I never went anywhere on or off campus by myself. But then you came to town, and I saw you getting close to The Four.

"I was scared the same thing would happen to you, but I saw you stand up and not bend to that fucking despicable first year. I saw you take him down," she said, smiling brightly at Pantu. "It was the best feeling I'd had in a long time," she said, joyfully shaking her head.

"Would Win not protect you from Mansnake?" Pantu asked Kat, wondering why this male didn't protect his Woman. Something like this happening to a Woman in The City was mostly unheard of but fuck if he didn't do something just as bad. Even if it was to survive, he realized he was starting to sound similar to Mansnake.

"Yes, but he doesn't know who was behind the attack and I refused to verify anything. You're the only Being I've told. Mansnake has his foot on a lot of our necks that way. It's why we won't verify what he's done, and how he's never gotten in trouble for anything. We're afraid of the information he has on us," Kat said, happily looking in the trays, searching for more food.

"Win would have killed him?" he asked, joining Kat's search through the baskets.

"No. Drum, Sport and Queen would have because Win would have cried," Kat answered. "Queen, Sport, and Drum are all over-protective of Win. They are all protective of each other, but Win is more fragile than them. He's like their baby brother. It's what drew me to Win. He's sensitive and caring with a good heart, but he isn't the type to physically fight," Kat said, smiling while thinking about Win.

"Win's Mind wanders off and he doesn't care enough to pay attention to most of what is happening around him. Win doesn't do anything for himself and if it wasn't for Sport, Win would wear the same clothes and not bother to bathe and eat whatever, even if it's spoiled. Win's home would also be condemned by now." Kat giggled at the thought.

He returned Kat's cute actions while he thought about his interactions with Win and nodded in agreement.

"The guys who attacked me all died of suicide," Kat said, with a knowing smile.

He knew Yolk's death wasn't as simple as he tried to make it sound. "I think the people I love killed someone to protect me, so I understand," he said, smiling back at Kat.

He now understood the feelings of restraint from Drum were because Drum felt uncomfortable touching him in a sexual way. He was ignorant of the laws here since he adamantly refused to accept anything new and not of The City as unrealistic. He understood why this conversation was necessary.

Drum knew he didn't understand boundaries because he never knew they existed for males. The words no and stop meant nothing to him since he was never given a choice. But Drum was giving him one. It was his decision how much they would do and how far they would go. He realized Drum could have gone all the way in his dreams but didn't. He didn't know his own boundaries.

Drum was giving him the kind of respect only shown to Women in The City and it made him want Drum to touch him even more. All the cascading thoughts about Drum not wanting him, after meeting his parents and seeing his past, settled in his Mind, allowing space for troubling new thoughts to roll in.

Kat interrupted these new thoughts. "But haven't we both met Beings who respect and care about us and our feelings?" Kat asked.

He smiled and nodded. "That battle was not meant for you to fight," he said to Kat. He didn't know why he said it, but he felt it.

Kat looked at him, a huge question written all over her face.

"It was Drum's battle with those assholes and my battle with Mansnake. My apologies, you were caught up in it," he said, feeling unhappy someone else again suffered because of him. If he could have just come here sooner, Kat wouldn't even be a thought in the snake's Mind or brain. He closed his eyes and let out an unhappy sigh.

"Pantu! You didn't even know Mansnake before all of this!" Kat exclaimed, shaking her head and holding on to his arm.

"It matters not. Drum was never his to begin with," he said. *Drum is way too particular a Being for this dumbass snake to understand.*

The snake thought of Drum as this towering mass of brute force, willing to take everything from someone, even without consent. He frowned, wondering why after knowing Drum way longer than him, the snake would think of Drum in such a manner. Drum was kind, but not kind-hearted. Drum was patient, calm and relaxed around him.

Kat looked shocked at what he didn't say, but she could obviously and easily read whatever look was on his face. Kat grinned and giggled. "Oh really? Then whose is he?" she asked, looking at him out of the corners of her eyes.

He just smiled in return, releasing his thoughts and neutralizing his face. His back jerked as a now familiar shiver went down it. Warm and inviting, he didn't fight the feeling, since his Light started tingling, splitting his focus.

"Oh! I guess he can answer for himself!" Kat said, with a giggle.

He felt his whole body heat up and he could only stare down at his redden thighs poking out of his shorts. He stared at the strawberry color of his arms and legs, and his eyes went wide. He'd never been this color while living in The City.

He turned and saw Drum standing relaxed behind him with a smile that stopped his heart from beating for the briefest of moments, while his pants tightened at the curve between his legs. He heard the bell ring and suddenly Win was there looking through the empty trays.

"There's no leftovers," Win said, a pouting frown on his face. The look Win gave and the unhappy tone in the words made him feel bad about eating at all.

"Ahhh, I was hungrier than I thought on this diet," he said, taking full blame for the food eaten. Even outside of The City, he wouldn't dare embarrass a Woman.

Kat looked at him with a bright and knowing smile. He blinked and Sport appeared.

Looking at the trays, Sport nonchalantly asked, "Was the food decent?"

He decided to play with Sport, just to see his reaction. "I skipped my morning meal and was so hungry; I ate more than I thought I would. Thanks for feeding me Kat!" he said, ignoring Sport's question.

It left Sport to tilt his head and purse his lips. "But was the food at least decent?" Sport asked again, looking between Kat and him.

Kat's look said she knew what he was doing and wanted to play along. They both stood and started making small sounds of pleasure as they stretched their bodies.

"I am so full after lunch, I should take a nap," he said, not paying any attention to Sport and trying not to laugh at Kat, who was holding in her laughter, which was turning her face red, making her light freckles darkened. Sport, on the other hand, couldn't get a full sentence out and was turning back and forth, throwing up his hands. Win was trying to calm Sport down as there was no verification of whether they liked the food or not.

He felt a little bad but at the same time, completely okay with freaking Sport out. He didn't forget Sport had a hand in the invites and he smiled at Kat. *"I think I broke him,"* he whispered.

Kat bent over, holding her stomach while laughing. Kat's laughter sounded like a small, but fast flowing creek. He couldn't help but laugh along with Kat's soothing laughter, freaking Sport out even more.

"Are you going to do your volunteer hours?" Drum asked him, ignoring Sport's breakdown and Win's attempt to bring him back around.

"Yes," he answered Drum, while keeping his eyes averted. He turned to Kat. "I will walk you to class," he offered with his tone and a smile.

Kat nodded and gathered her backpack which he again took from her to carry while they walked.

"We should clean..." he started, looking at their mess still on the ground.

Kat shook her head, happy and smiling brightly, she linked her arm around his and pulled him off. He looked back at Drum apologetically and received a smoky-eyed, half-smile which made him shiver.

DRUM: UNREMEMBERED PROMISES KEPT
WEEK FOUR: FRIDAY

He turned from watching Pantu and Kat disappear around a building, well, he only paid attention to Pantu walking away from him, to laugh at Sport's meltdown. He bent down to clean up the picnic area and told Sport, "I'll ask Pantu in the Manga Room about your food." He calmed Sport down with just one sentence.

"O-Okay," Sport said, and reached in his bag to bring out a small notebook and a pen. Sport placed it close to him. "Can you write down any suggestions or comments Pantu has?" Sport asked, hopeful.

"Yes, and Win will ask Kat in their next class together and take notes from her as well," he said, agreeing and dragging Win into his solution.

"You will have honest critiques by the end of day classes!" Win said, patting Sport on the back.

Sport nodded and reached into his bag; he slid another small notebook to Win with a pen. Win blew out his breath as if he was over it, and looked at Sport, whose Energy was tingling from whatever look Win was giving. He shook his head at his best friends' Energies reacting to one another and let them be.

After putting the basket back together, he finished cleaning and folding the blanket. He knew Win would take the blanket and Sport the basket, so he left them there before grabbing the book and pen. He opened a royal-blue Portal into the Manga Room and two white ones for Win and Sport to go to their next class.

He stepped out of his Portal and sat in his chair. The bell hadn't rung yet for the start of the next period, so he knew Pantu wouldn't be here for a while. Pantu always stopped and talked with Doctor Faye and her Aides, before coming up to the room, so he took the current manhwa he was reading out of his backpack.

It was about a guy who could shoot pearls out of his member and the man he fell in love with. He didn't really get how they could have fallen in love so quickly, but he assumed the amazing sex helped.

He didn't want that with Pantu. He wanted Pantu to love him before they decided to take that step, not because of it. And that was only assuming they made it that far. Everyone thought due to his status, he refused to have sex before he was legal or married and wore a self-imposed Promise ring on the middle finger of his right hand.

Everyone had their own guesses. Beings and humans theorized he would take the ring off if he had sex, signaling he was involved with someone. Beings thought it would disappear forever while humans thought he would give it to whomever he was dating. Both groups thought it was a sign of his complete abstinence, or it was for show since he couldn't touch anybody. But it somehow gave Beings his age a glimmer of hope.

He didn't care to correct them. He twisted the only jewelry he wore on his body, tracing the impossible words to read wrapped around his ring. Not impossible for him, but anyone nosey enough to try. This was his own language he used to keep anyone from knowing what he didn't want known. He personally crafted this ring, and it was the only hint to the knowledge of the hidden language.

Four simple words which only he could understand. He also never spoke his language out loud. He knew how talented his brother, Dad and NanaPoo were at translating languages, so to keep them from breaking their Minds trying to figure it out, he kept it to himself.

But things were different now. There was someone who could touch him. He met Pantu years ago at the age of fourteen. Before the start of his High School life, he helped Pantu and his parents on their way away from The City. He, Sport, and Pong were their transportation. He never told details to anyone not there that night.

He was at a loss as to why the boy thrown into his arms didn't burn away to nothing. He made Sport Promise not to say a word to anyone, including Win and especially Queen and Major. He told Major what he could and never let Major on any missions which involved meeting Pantu. Only he and Sport went on those missions and Major directed.

He knew if Queen knew, Queen would spin the planet to find and bring Pantu to Sunset, but he didn't want Pantu here. He wanted to stay as far away from Pantu as possible. Given what was expected of him, he couldn't be in love with a guy.

When he showed his best friends Pantu could touch him and not burn, Queen was amazed, but also saw Sport was unsurprised. Queen didn't ask questions, nor reveal any assumptions. He only knew because of the connection he and Queen shared.

But now, he wanted to be with Pantu. He wanted to be just as greedy and selfish. He didn't want to be forced by The Elders to marry anyone who wasn't Pantu, nor did he want to touch anyone else the way they touched. He needed to protect his Dumpling like he Promised years ago.

Pantu didn't remember, but he did. He remembered the night vividly every day since. For years, he forced himself to push it down and tried to forget about Pantu. But their connection was different than his and Queen's. Outside The City, whenever Pantu was panicky and filled with fear, he felt it, every time.

He was still trying to figure out how to tell his Dad, his Elder Grandmothers and his older brother he was refusing the throne...again. He didn't want to be Emperor. He knew Queen didn't know about him, never wanting to be the next ruler and already made several plans for his future. He understood Queen didn't want to follow anyone but him and he was unsure how to break the news. Not unsure, he was scared.

Scared of what Queen would do to make sure he sat on the throne. He'd given Queen a lot of power, not just online and in The Royal Family's Barrier Towns, but also physically. While Queen was always respectful of his values and never abused power, he knew how Queen felt. Queen was absolutely sure he was the only one who could lead him, all of them, to a better life. Sport and Win did as well, but Queen was fierce when it came to his loyalty.

He was so distracted he didn't notice when Pantu entered the room until his name was softly said. He looked up in surprise. He was never caught this off guard since he was six, but the idea of telling Queen about his plans to decline the throne clouded up his head. He smiled at Pantu and glanced at the requests in his hands.

"Those are only going to increase every day," he told Pantu, who looked at him with a pout. He closed his eyes for the briefest of moments to gather himself. Pantu was intoxicating and when his member jumped at the sound of Pantu's voice, he couldn't help but smile brightly.

"Why would they increase? Are manga and banned books popular here?" Pantu asked, sitting his stuff down.

"Somewhat, but it's your custom hand drawn nametags they want," he said. "Ever since Queen has been showing off his tag, the students have been trying to find a way to ask you for one. They're slowly making the connection you're over the Manga Room and make custom nametags for those who request a book," he said. He smiled at Pantu's surprise and dismay.

"I just did them to pass the time, since there were only a few requests," Pantu said and sat down, upset.

"You can start your own business with this. Sell them planet-wide!" he said, with a small laugh.

Pantu, on the other hand, looked disgusted by the thought. "I am unwilling to work after graduation!" Pantu said, with a pout. "There will be no time for me to achieve my Dream if I am busy making other people money."

"OOOH!?" he asked. He rested his chin in his hands and smiled knowingly at Pantu. He could smell Pantu's member leaking from the sound of his question. Of course he used his sweet voice with Pantu, but he added his deep tone, making Pantu's pants wet.

"Am I going to have to find a job to pay bills!?" Pantu asked while ignoring the stain. Pantu's eyes were full of tears and a pouty frown pulled at two cute, pink, pouty lips.

He could tell Pantu wasn't used to handling or caring about money. Pantu lived the life he wanted and everyone else took care of every need. He couldn't help but rest his cheek in his hand as he softly laughed at Pantu's facial expressions of fake pain. He thought he was doing a fantastic job of ignoring the massive amount of Heated Energy trying to push its way through the tiny hole at the tip of his member.

"You wouldn't have to work if you just ask for what you want," he told Pantu, with a raised eyebrow and a half-smile.

Pantu looked at him for a moment and then rolled his eyes, refusing to ask. It only made him more excited Pantu could resist him. Anyone else would have given in to him before he finished his statement, but Pantu made him work for everything he wanted from him, and he loved it. One could say, he craved it.

"You're a stubborn one, aren't you?" he asked, laughing. Pantu gave him a mean pouty face and then refused to look at him.

"You are just as stubborn," Pantu said, quietly back to him.

"Am I?" he asked, teasing Pantu. "I give in most every time, how does that make me stubborn?" he asked, enjoying the conversation and the Scent of their Energies filling the room.

"Then give in now," Pantu said, using a sweet, whining voice.

He tensed up and looked away from Pantu. When he regained his composure, instead of admitting what just happened, he teased Pantu. "Give in to what, exactly?" he asked, ignoring the stain on his pants.

Pantu looked at him with frustration and shock. He smiled at Pantu's slightly gaping mouth and wide eyes at his teasing. *Pantu must be used to people giving in to him,* he thought.

"It is fine if you are stubborn and unwilling!" Pantu said, with a fake tantrum.

He leaked again, this time not caring enough to fight it. "You know...I will, if you ask," he said, with a soft smile, "until then...well...how am I to know what you want?" He threw his hands up and sighed. He leaned back in his chair, comfortably.

The stare he received from Pantu was like those shimmering, light brown eyes were imagining bringing him to his knees, while he begged for a denied sweet release. He raised his eyebrow as Pantu decided to look for the books instead. He put his head down and laughed quietly, while waving his hand to clean them both up.

He followed Pantu down each aisle, never touching, just watching. He was relaxed with his hands in his pockets, leaning against the shelves while Pantu found the books.

Once all the books were collected, Pantu went back to the desk. Still not asking anything of him, he quietly watched as Pantu sat the books on the table. When Pantu turned to face him, he stood still, waiting. He held his breath when Pantu moved closer to place both hands on his chest, slowly moving them up to his neck, making his body stiff, but he never removed his hands from his pockets.

Cold, soothing hands wrapped around his neck and leaning up while pulling him closer, Pantu whispered, *"Real Drum?"*

"Yes, Real Pantu?"

"Will you spoil me?"

"Yes, Real Pantu," he quietly answered back as he clenched his hands into fists inside his pockets.

"Forever?" Pantu asked again, softer than before.

"Yes, Real Pantu," he whispered while forcing his knees to lock to keep him standing.

"Vow that you——" Pantu started.

He interrupted. "I Vow. I Promise."

Pantu pulled back, surprised he Promised so easily.

"I did not finish what I was about to say!" Pantu said.

"It doesn't matter Pantu. I will Vow anything, and I will always keep my Promises to you," he stated. He took his hands out of his pockets and wrapped them around Pantu's waist, pulling his soft, cold Dumpling back to him. The feel of such a cooling body was addictive and his enflamed Energy wanted to Heat every part of Pantu while enjoying the cooling sensation lowering his own temperature.

"Drum, I know why Kat talked to me." Pantu started looking away while taking a step back to leave his arms, but he held on firmly and waited until Pantu was ready to continue.

"I understand now I can say stop, and I can tell you no. But I have never needed to use those words with you. You have been respectful of me, and I want you to touch me. I like it a lot when you hold me and kiss on me. I like that you still want to be around me and touch me, even after what you do know about my past." Pantu paused and took a deep breath before continuing. "But it does not get better Drum. My past does not get better and the more you know about me, I am sure you will walk away from me," Pantu said, almost crying at the statement.

"I Promised you Pantu. I have and will continue to keep my Promises," he said, gently, as he moved Pantu's face so they could lock eyes. He gently wiped the tears falling from Pantu's eyes and softly kissed each eyelid.

"You have only promised to spoil me?" Pantu asked.

"I Promised you more," he said, holding Pantu's eyes hostage with the dancing green in his irises. *"You don't remember?"* he whispered.

Pantu shook his head and looked sadly at him.

"It's okay Dumpling. I will just have you ask me again," he said, with a mischievous smile.

Pantu tried to pout but ended up with the sweetest look of appreciation and a smile which buckled his legs, and he quickly locked his knees again.

Before Pantu could gloat about the obvious win, he Instant them back into the field. The cattail from their dream seemed to notice Pantu was around and started stretching towards him, to which Pantu's hand glazed by it as he moved them closer to the middle of the field.

Pantu didn't realize his clothes were missing until he gripped on a bare bottom, making Pantu gasp in excitement from leaking. He flipped them, having Pantu's back facing the ground while he was on top.

Pantu must have thought he was going to hit the ground, but fell on the softest feeling, better than pure bamboo sheets, and he gasped, opening his eyes to realize he was on a royal-blue cloud. An actual cloud was holding them up off the ground and Pantu's face was astounded. Pantu gasped again, looking directly into his eyes and the fire lit in them.

He looked at Pantu for a moment before the urge to kiss on the handsomely beautiful young man under him became too much and he broke, kissing his neck. He moved down to kissing across a hairless, smooth, cold, solid chest before sucking on harden, brown nipples while his hand found Pantu's stiff and leaking member. He started to slowly stroke and watched with enjoyment as Pantu's body wiggled and trembled, coming after about three slow, possessive strokes.

He didn't stop as he kissed and sucked on each of Pantu's sides, leaving red marks. He didn't miss any part of Pantu's stomach, leaving as many hickeys as he could kisses. He went back up to Pantu's collar bone and sucked just under it. He didn't miss a spot as he greedily licked, kissed, and sucked all over Pantu's torso.

Pantu was weakly trying to handle the feelings he was releasing. Every part of Pantu he kissed, sucked, or touched, was already warmed from his Heat, but this was as if he was sending electric currents throughout Pantu's body, which contorted as if shockwaves ran through it. His free hand was switching between gripping and massaging a thick, soften thigh, and he moaned every time he squeezed.

As he flipped Pantu, his hand never stopped stroking. Pantu was now face down in the cloud while he was kissing, licking, and sucking all over his back while still gripping

Pantu's member, never wanting to let go. He felt his bulge through his pants part Pantu's butt cheeks and moaned deeply as his member settled against Pantu's hole.

As he moved up and down Pantu's back, making sure every spot was caressed, his bulge was rubbing between two, plump butt cheeks, and he loved it, along with the sounds of light, high-pitched pleasure, which came deep from inside Pantu.

He felt Pantu's member veins move every time he came, which only excited him more. His pants were a sticky mess, and he didn't bother to try and control himself. He didn't care that he released so much Energy to leak down his leg or stain his pants.

Pantu's moans of pleasure were like the sweetest music to his ears. The way the soft body was putting up the weakest of fights against coming so much, wiggling under him, and the way Pantu was grabbing the cloud for dear life, was starting to overwhelm him.

He felt the buildup in his member but didn't know what was going to happen. He moved down to Pantu's butt, and both their moans became louder. He noticed Pantu's arched back, and he squeezed his stomach muscles to keep from exploding at such a beautiful offering. He slowly lowered his mouth as his hands rubbed and gripped Pantu's soft, bubble butt before he licked the right cheek.

All he wanted was just a nibble but when he bit Pantu's butt cheek, he heard the loudest, "AHHHHHHHHH, DRRRRUUUMMM!"

Pantu moaned and at the same time, he felt Pantu's member explode into the cloud while his whole body arched in the weirdest of ways as Pantu continued to let loose from his member.

He understood as his own body responded to the overwhelming feelings and he himself moaned, *"PAANNTUU!"* as his member shot out so much Energy, he thought he broke it, and it would never turn off again.

He collapsed on top of Pantu's trembling body and lay there for a moment, holding on to Pantu to calm them both down. Neither of them wanted to go back to campus but somewhere in his Mind, he knew Pantu still needed to finish the nametags and classes.

"At this rate, you won't have enough time to finish all the tags," he joked as he laughed. He rolled off Pantu, satisfied with life. He lay on the cloud next to Pantu with a lazy smile on his face and half-closed eyes.

When his words registered, Pantu jumped up and looked concerned. "I need those hours! What if she comes into the room and I am not there?" Pantu asked, looking at his relaxed face and raised eyebrow.

"She doesn't have a Crystal to the room," he said, calmly.

Pantu was still panicking. "She could knock on the door!" he said, looking distressed.

He grabbed his Dumpling and gently pulled to rest Pantu's head on his chest. "She won't bother you while you're in the room. No one, other than the two of us have Crystals and whenever you come inside the room a light comes on which says, "Do not disturb", at the checkout table," he explained to Pantu, who relaxed and laced their fingers together.

"I still have time to do the tags," Pantu said, happily.

"Do you want to keep doing them?" he asked.

Pantu nodded and they were back in the room, dressed and cleaned but still holding on to each other.

PANTU: A NIGHT AMONGST FAMILY AND FRIENDS
WEEK FOUR: FRIDAY

His Light was happily buzzing and flowing inside him, and it made him bounce a little to feel it flowing so peacefully in his body once again. It was Anime Night, and he and Dill would meet at the entrance. He knew Drum would be there and the thought made him smile.

His parents were going and most of the students' parents were also attending to socialize. Dill told him the other students' parents heard Mr. Caleb was going, so they wanted photos for their social media profiles as Mrs. K was at all campus events, but Mr. Caleb was as elusive on social media as his sons.

He knew Mr. Caleb was going because his Pa was trembling even more than normal about attending his first campus event that didn't involve his son in the Dean's office. Either way, he assumed having a photo with Drum's Pa was on the top of most every parent's to-do list.

He was okay with going with his Pa. After the second time he was kidnapped, they were able to be in the same space without him throwing a fit. His parents found their own best friends, and it made him feel better.

His parents were just as closed off to Others as he was and knowing they found people they could be themselves around, while not worrying about being used to target their son, made a happy feeling bubble up inside him.

As he searched through his closet, he lamented his lack of clothes and, right after, heard the doorbell ring. His Ma called him, and skipping over the hated step, he went down to see Queen and Win standing inside his house with a large bag. As he reached the last step, Queen walked up to him and handed him the bag before shooing him back upstairs.

"We'll save a spot for you and your parents in the courtyard," Win said. They said their goodbyes before leaving.

He opened the bag and saw new clothes neatly folded. He hurried back to his room and changed into clothes that fit him perfectly and comfortably. Nice black, thigh-hugging pants with side pockets halfway down his legs, an oversized, long sleeve, white tee shirt with his favorite anime logo on it, a soft undershirt, which only came down to his belly button and new tennis shoes to match his white tee shirt.

He smiled as he appreciated Queen and Win dropping these off, but he was sure Drum brought them. He liked the open thumb holes in the shirt and how the material felt so soft against his skin. He didn't know if he was comfortable with Drum choosing his style, since he was unsure of exactly what he liked. He shrugged it off as much as possible and headed out.

They arrived with time to spare. His parents walked in to find a spot while he waited patiently at the entrance for Dill to show up. The shiver which went through his spine caused him to slightly adjust his body to handle the sensation. He knew his Light would start tingling and sure enough, once the shiver faded, his Light started singing.

The huge smile on his face caused everyone who walked into the area to speak politely to him as they passed, returning his smile. Dill was right, most of the Beings who passed by him didn't know what to do with themselves, so they could only express their desires through a questioning greeting, which he kindly turned down with an even tone greeting back. When Dill and his parents showed up, he waved his arms in the air while bouncing on his toes.

Dill's Pa, Mr. Metal, was a naturally, ruggedly handsome man, while his wife, Lyra was busy trying to mimic his Ma's fun style. Although his Ma didn't wear make-up, Mr. Metal's wife played around with hers, making her face bright and wearing short shorts and a barely there top while she was smiling and laughing at the attention she received. He didn't like her and barely looked at Mr. Metal's wife, but he was as polite as possible. He and Dill bumped their elbows and slid their hands into an upside down high five.

"What's up?" Dill asked before laughing.

"The Universe," he responded, laughing along.

His parents were polite with Dill's because of Mr. Metal's face but never spent time together. Mr. Metal was always working in his shop and his wife worked directing their family amusement parks from early until late.

He led Dill in after Mr. Metal paid for his family's tickets. He saw he was let in with no ticket, and he turned around to pay but stopped when he realized he didn't have his wallet or his cellphone.

Ah! Maybe my parents have my ticket, he thought, as he turned around to Dill's amused face.

"What?" he asked Dill.

"Oh, nothing," Dill said and grinned so big and bright, it went from ear to ear.

He scrunched his face in annoyance. He knew that face from Dill. "Go in and ask my parents if they have my ticket," he huffed out.

"Sure, just walk with me to the area and point your parents out in the sea of Beings," Dill joked with him.

But he didn't realize it was a joke until he was ushered in, still without a ticket. His look at Dill hushed any jokes he knew Dill would make, was itching to make.

"Fine but don't blame me when they get randomly blurted out," Dill said, with a shrug.

"PAAANNNNNTTTTUUUUU!"

He heard Queen call him, as only Queen ever did. His face lit up as he searched the crowd to see his parents set up their chairs close to where The Four were sitting and was already talking with Dill's parents. He grabbed Dill's arm to hurry over and Win and Queen pointed out their parents.

Sport didn't bother to point out his parents and was talking to a young girl about seven or eight, who was calling Sport big brother. The young girl was telling Sport about the first big kid rollercoaster she was finally tall enough to ride at one of Dill's family theme parks.

His parents were watching the interaction between Sport and the young girl, as was he. Both his parents held small smiles on their faces and Lyra must have thought those smiles were for her. They weren't, and he rolled his eyes at Lyra laughing and constantly touching his Pa's arm while she still hung on to Mr. Metal, who ignored his wife's actions.

Most parents were interacting around the fringes of the courtyard, which was completely cleared. Large tents with characters from the anime covered the food tables and were placed closer to the covered walkway. The tables from the courtyard were moved under the walkway for Beings to sit and eat.

He sat down in front of his Ma's chair, and she patted him on the head and motioned they were going to mingle with the other parents. He smiled and nodded before turning back to the group, knowing his parents couldn't take Lyra's face and annoying voice for too long. But Lame Lyra followed after his parents, dragging an uninterested Mr. Metal with her.

Drum was sitting off from everybody, and he looked over shyly, wanting to thank Drum for the clothes. Drum smiled, motioning with those honey-green eyes to an empty spot. He moved to sit in the middle of Drum and Dill. The rest of the group tried to hide their smiles, which made his body heat up when Drum didn't try at all. He was feeling his thoughts of thankful prayers to the Universe, his body was completely covered.

"Nice kicks Pantu!" Dill said, looking at his shoes. Dill just noticed and took a full look at his outfit.

"That was never in your closet, when did you buy that? Did you go to the mall without me?" Dill asked.

"NO!" was all he said while refusing to meet anyone's eyes.

"You look stunning in your new outfit," Dill teased, nudging him.

"A handsomely beautiful Being," Drum said.

His face felt hotter than a star and by now, The Four couldn't hold back, even the young girl seemed to understand and laughed along. He dropped his head in silent acceptance of their laughter. It only took Dill a second to realize who purchased his clothes and raised both eyebrows to nod in approval at Drum.

"Nice moves," Dill complimented with a muffled voice while still using him as a shield.

Drum smiled without acknowledging Dill and he knew the smile was for him. He wanted to crawl in a hole somewhere and hibernate for life, but instead he commented, "We really need to finish the spaceship or build a time machine. Either one would work."

To which everyone around them fell out laughing. He was politely interrupted by a student who asked him about their nametag.

"How did you know coral was my favorite color?" the student asked, kindly and with joy in her eyes.

"I did not know you had a favorite color. It just seemed right," he said to her, with a small smile. He felt this student's underline Intent in his Light's cold reaction to her. He didn't let his worry about the conversation show on his face. Being so close to Drum, he tended to forget himself and go crazy with his thoughts and feelings. He needed to Calm and control himself.

The student shyly smiled back and speaking in a demure tone she thanked him. He could smell a light scent coming from the young woman, but he wasn't pleased by it at all. He wondered if anyone else around him could smell what this young woman was doing, but he decided to keep his eyes on the student.

"You are welcome!" he replied, not reacting to the Intent the woman was giving off.

The young woman's eyes fluttered, and she hesitated a moment before she spoke. "Coral is the color of my Energy!" The young woman revealed, her cheeks flushing at stating the information, like a secret was exposed and he was the lucky one to know.

The young woman tucked her hair behind her ear and continued, "We've never met before, so how would you know my favorite color is also the color of my Energy?"

He gave a full, closed lipped smile and responded, "I read the way you write your name and sketch what comes to me."

"You're a psychic!" the young woman loudly exclaimed.

He knew the young woman was being loud to draw attention to the fact she was, not only around The Four, but also speaking to #AnonB. He would allow this young woman to dig her own social grave, since she was bold enough to try and trap him into Lying or revealing his Talents. He kept what Dill told him close to heart, so he wouldn't let other Beings know what he could do before informing Drum.

"I do not know the requirements for being psychic, since we do not have any with those Talents where I come from." He was starting to get mixed feelings from this young woman. He was trying to understand why the young woman's Light was so unstable towards him. She wasn't talking to him because she wanted to, but because she had to. Like a pet being forced by his owner to debate him.

The young woman was thrown off by his answer and let out a small, forced sound, somewhere between a gasp and a giggle. The young woman decided to continue and turned her sound into a forced giggle. Covering her mouth with her hand, she answered back, "You're really funny and adorable. I'm Bi, so I'm totally into either, but I've never met someone who can seem like both without even trying." She didn't give him a chance to react to her comment and proceeded to ask him, "Are you doing anything tomorrow night? There is a new movie in town, and we can go together to see it."

His face froze. Everyone around them was paying attention to the conversation, posting everything they could online. The only reason he froze his face was to garner a multitude of thoughts inside the heads of Beings watching.

The woman asking him was physically beautiful, hell most everyone in town was, but he was sure Drum was sitting right next to him, and he thought nobody openly dated until Drum chose. This woman was willing to risk it all by asking him in front of everyone. Dill nudged him and when he looked at Dill all he received as help was a smile.

Worst interface ever, he thought. He looked back at the girl nervously. "Ah...I...ahhh..." was all he would say. He let the tone of his few words encourage the young woman. But he didn't feel bad for what he was setting her up for.

His back was to a wall multiple times in The City, but he never went against his morals, no matter the threat. He wanted to live his life without it being dependent on the death of another, so he never broke, never faltered.

"I will wait for you at the entrance of the theater at six-forty ss, the movie starts at seven ss, so we will have time to get food and drinks." The young woman smiled as she touched his shoulder. The soft feel of his clothes made the young woman's smile deepen and her cheeks a light pink color.

The young woman skipped off, and he could only lower his eyes to look at Dill with his mouth open. Dill's fingers snapped several times in front of his face before he came back from death, and he swallowed so loudly he was sure everybody heard him.

"What just happened?" he asked his best friend.

Dill leaned closer. "You, bestie, have a date tomorrow night at seven. I would suggest being there at about six-thirty so you can buy the tickets." Dill finished in a whisper. *"I don't think THAT'S going to be free."*

His eyes opened wide. He looked at Queen, whose face couldn't believe he accepted a date right in front of Drum. Sport was shaking his head in disappointment while the pretty young girl next to him was giggling. He still hadn't turned to look at Drum, but he figured he would watch the whole movie by listening.

"NOBODY DATES UNTIL DRUM HAS CHOOSEN. YOU TOLD ME THAT, WIN TOLD ME THAT. DID YOU BOTH LIE TO ME?" he whispered, loudly enough for those sitting around them to hear.

He knew saying these words out loud were truth and would inform those Beings smart enough to understand, that Drum still hadn't asked anyone, not even him. It would keep Beings guessing and he was thinking Monday would be an enjoyable day to end his impromptu plan against the young woman controlled by a snake.

"What!? Pantu? I would never Lie to you!" Dill said, hurt by the accusation.

Win was looking pleased by whatever interaction was going on in his own head and wasn't paying attention to what was happening around him to respond.

"You are just too, how did Drum put it, handsomely beautiful, and Talented, you make Beings want to know just how good you are with your hands," Dill joked.

His best friend was trying not to laugh at his facial expressions changing so much, he looked ready to overload and explode. When his Ma came back to her seat, he scrambled to her; pulled her back up and started walking as fast as he could manage towards the entrance.

"PanPan! What's wrong?" his Ma asked, as she let herself be dragged away by her unstable child.

His Pa appeared in front of him, and he abruptly stopped, his Ma running into his back. He was looking everywhere around him, wondering how his Pa could reach them so quickly after still being on the other side of the courtyard when he started dragging his Ma. He wasn't planning on his Pa leaving with them and huffed out a breath.

His Light was buzzing but it wasn't a happy buzz, and it was making his Mind disconnect from his brain since he still didn't know how or what Drum was feeling, and it made him unhappy. He didn't want to see a movie with someone who wasn't Dill, maybe also Drum, but he tossed that thought to the side as his Ma asked him again.

He mumbled out a response. *"I just want to leave town for a couple of weeks. Nothing too long, just until after graduation,"* he mumbled, into his chest.

"Seriously, why do you always try and leave without me?" Dill asked, throwing an arm around him.

"Dill!" was all he could say.

"Look don't worry about it. She is obviously after something else," Dill said.

He snapped his head to look at Dill. *"I am not fucking her!"* he whispered, harshly.

His parents were confused until he told his Ma he was just asked out on a date, which neither of his parents understood until he stated, *"Courtship"*. His Ma giggled and his Pa's eyes went wide while still staring at the ground.

"I will explain in the car after we have packed and are a good distance away from here," he said, as he continued to walk, moving around his Pa and still pulling his Ma with him.

Mr. Caleb stepped in front of the entrance, his voice boomed out, making the ground quake. "The movie is about to start; we should all get to our seats."

His arm went numb, and he had a mild stroke.

When Mr. Caleb added, "Since we all paid to watch the movie, we should enjoy it, right?" Mr. Caleb was looking down right at him.

He was doing a horrible job of keeping his knees from folding under him and was clutching onto Dill for dear life to steady his shaking legs. *Both Drum and his Pa can make my knees weak, though both for vastly different reasons*, he thought, as he was dragged back by both his Ma and Dill.

He kept his eyes away from Drum and looked for a place where Drum wouldn't be in his line of sight, but the only place left was right next to him. He wanted to cry but sat cross-legged on the ground while everybody was chatting and finding their way to their seats.

Dill leaned over and rubbed his back. He looked at Dill with a small frown and furrowed eyebrows.

"I wouldn't read too much into it," Dill said. "She's not even your type!" Dill smiled as his face changed. His best friend knew what he was doing and was helping him.

Once everyone was settled, the head of the PSPSA made announcements and introduced the movie. He was looking back at the ground when Drum said his name.

"Pantu?" Drum whispered, the sweet voice calming his rattled Light.

He looked up at Drum, but only out the corners of his eyes.

Drum nodded towards the screen and asked in a normal neutral tone, "Haven't you read this one already?"

He looked up as 'Fiend Killer: The Final Train', scrolled across the screen. He started bouncing his legs. "Fiend Killer?!" he asked, "there is a movie about it?"

Dill leaned over and looked at him. "It's a whole anime," Dill replied.

He turned and slowly looked at Dill. "Remember the one word precious to us as best friends?" he asked.

Dill searched his head, trying to remember.

"BE-FORE!" he said to the laughter of the surrounding students.

"Worst interface ever," he said before slumping his shoulders in defeat.

When Drum's sweet laughter filled the air, everyone was up, looking around for the source of such an inviting, warm laugh, which was sending shivers through Beings' Lights. He didn't like the feeling Drum was giving off to others but like the majority of Beings around him, he was shivering at the warmth being released from Drum's laugh.

Dill looked at him and grinned before they both started laughing as well. Mr. Caleb, however, didn't laugh, but was staring at his son as if it was the first time Mr. Caleb ever heard Drum laughing.

PANTU: ANOTHER VOW
WEEK FOUR: FRIDAY

As the movie progressed, his Pa became more emotional, encouraging, out loud, for the heroes to win, which incited his Ma to encourage her husband's passion. Mr. Caleb and the other Pas around them also joined in, which had their wives laughing and supporting them. This caused the parents to start a rally section for the heroes, and their kids joined in.

His face was flushed with a warm heat, which didn't come from Drum, and he buried his head in his hands. But then he felt it. Intense Malicious and Ill Intent. He looked up, his eyes widened, and his mouth dropped open at how strong it was, and it was directed completely at him.

Quickly regaining himself, he closed his eyes, searching the area to pinpoint the direction of the source. He was so caught up in finding the person with such Intent, he didn't feel Drum looking at him.

Without opening his eyes, he raised his head, looking up and around, trying to pinpoint the Intent in a crowd of Beings. However, he paused when he realized this didn't feel like Light, it felt the way it did in The City.

His body ran cold, and he needed to force his frozen lungs to take a breath, while he clasped his hands together tightly in his lap, praying to anyone who would listen that when he opened his eyes, the feeling would be gone.

Luck was not on his side today as he still felt it. He slowly looked around and in between his cheering parents, he saw him. An asshole who hated him and tried to ruin him several times but ended up being kicked out of The Center and into The Outer Ring. The young male became one of The Cloaked, quickly rising to become Cloakless.

Their eyes locked and the male made a gun out of his hand, placed it under his chin, and pulled a fake trigger before moving his hand in a slicing motion across his throat.

He was so still even his Ma noticed, but when she looked behind her, the male was gone. His thoughts ran so quickly through his head, he couldn't keep up. He only knew he couldn't let the male get out of town. If the asshole hadn't already told "her" where he was, he had to stop him. He turned and told Dill he was going to be back.

He stood, and walking as calmly as he could manage, he headed out of the courtyard and around the office building. He didn't see the male and his Light was sending tiny needles into his skin. He was searching while walking further and deeper down the unlit road, away from campus, when Drum's warm hand on his arm stopped him.

"Pantu, what's wrong?" Drum asked, turning him around.

"I will handle this Drum!" he said, pushing Drum back towards campus. He continued to look around for the male, his Light now pricking his skin even faster at the thought the male was leaving town.

"Pantu?" Drum asked, softly.

"Hmm?" was his response as he continued to look, avoiding Drum's line of sight.

If the male was using human tech, he knew it wouldn't work under this Barrier. How long was the male searching around town for him? If it was close to a week, he knew the tech would be rusted by now. The buzzing of his Light was only increasing the feelings of pain from the needle-like pokes.

"Are you scared?" Drum gently asked.

His whole body went silent, making him stop and look at Drum. "It felt like my Light wanted to run away from my body. It was stabbing my skin and buzzing so much, I needed to force myself to think," he replied.

"Ask me now, Pantu," Drum told him, grabbing his arm and pulling his body closer to the warmth he craved.

This sent his Mind and his brain on separate missions to figure out Drum's simple words. "Huh?" He managed to get out.

"You know what I'm asking, I don't like to repeat myself," Drum said, holding him hostage with those dancing eyes.

"Drum?" he asked, quietly. "Will you protect me?"

"Yes, Pantu. Always!" Drum replied, with a full smile and he felt another crack inside his body.

"Vow?" he added. He was unsure if Drum knew all the trouble he would bring from The City, Drum wouldn't want to deal with it.

But Drum's response was swift and strong. "I Vow Pantu," Drum said, and erected a pale violet Barrier around the courtyard, so others wouldn't get caught up in what was about to happen.

DRUMxTRACEY: A SOUND MOST HATED
WEEK FOUR: FRIDAY

Someone scared the life out of his Pantu, and they were going to die tonight. Drum was annoyed by the Being trying to Seduce Pantu, and he figured it wasn't really a date, but a way to establish him and Pantu as friends while trying to figure out Pantu's sexual orientation. Queen confirmed his suspicions with a quick look.

He wasn't upset with Pantu, who never agreed to anything, and it seemed like Pantu and Dill had a plan to deal with the Being, so he wouldn't get involved unless Pantu asked. Using his Enhanced Vision, he stared into the wooded area where the guy was hiding, waiting to ambush Pantu. Taking in the weapons strapped to the guy, he pulled Pantu to stand behind him.

With no emotion, he asked, "Pantu. Do you know him?"

He could see the guy was a Rock-Core human, which meant this guy could stay under his Barrier for about a week before becoming violently sick. Eating the food here would have turned this human into a sex fiend, so he knew there must be a base somewhere outside his Barrier, but still close enough for the guy to search the areas under it. This human knew about them.

Pantu nodded in return.

He stared until the guy came out with a sadistic smile on his face. The guy was dressed in all black, with a hooded, black trench coat. He felt Pantu tightly grip his right arm and tremble a little at the slow walk from the guy.

"PANTU?" the guy finally asked after making it to the middle of the road. The guy laughed loudly, obviously hoping to draw a crowd.

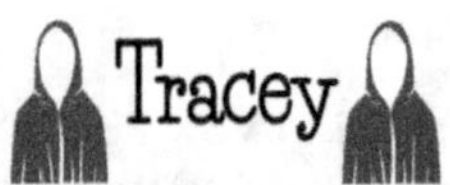

Tracey wanted to embarrass this Pantu before dragging him back for definite torture. He was peeved because even though this Pantu escaped a while ago, he was still number one. No one could come close to this Pantu's numbers, and it upset him more.

Since this Pantu male was declared on break, the only pet in history to be given one, his standing would stay until he was outranked or died. With the numbers of this Pantu, and two High-Level Madres, no one would demote him publicly. Plus, his Owner was still the Governess' Daughter.

This Pantu was protected from being tortured or killed on their way back to The City. The Governess' Daughter did not want anyone to touch her precious pet. And since this Pantu was wanted alive, he decided he would start this Pantu's Final Training on the way back, as punishment for Pantu mentally and physically breaking his Owner. He was willing to accept torture or death to be the first to publicly and truthfully lay claim to Pantu's Final Training. When he saw Pantu shiver, it made him bolder.

"Young Lord, you changed your name to Pantu? What are you...five?" he asked, laughing.

He looked around confused for a moment as a tall, big, strong, and handsome male walked up. He stopped for a moment before gaining his confidence back. There was backup so he was not concerned. He was, however, interested in the male standing in front of Pantu.

"Did you start Final Training without permission or a proper Trainer? You know how much she likes to see you in pain. Why deprive your Owner of such a delicacy?" he said, with an evil smile. "And so much money?" he added, chuckling.

"I am not going back with you, Tracey," Pantu said to him from behind the male's back.

"What authority do you have to use that name?" he asked, turning red from anger.

"Am I still number one?" Pantu asked, leaning around the male with the same knowing and enticing smile which would bring people to their knees in The City.

He clenched his hands as anger boiled up inside him, using the pain from digging his nails into his palms to stop his penis from swelling. "It will not matter. Once you are back, you know what will happen, right?" he goaded. "I will do to you, what you did to my Owner."

"Ah! So, I AM wanted alive. Nice to know. And we both know your owner deserved much more," Pantu said.

He flinched, realizing he let the information slip. As Pantu turned away from him, he reached inside his coat and pulled a collar from his belt. He smiled as it clicked open. Pantu heard the sound of the collar opening and froze for a moment before his hands quickly moved to his neck, his grip so tight, he was almost choking himself.

His laughter was brought to an abrupt halt as he watched the male gently remove Pantu's hands from around his neck. The look the male gave Pantu made his own stomach clench.

He wanted that look. He wanted the male to look at him like that. He was also thinking about all the sadistic things he wanted to do to the male while making Pantu watch, just like Yolk.

But when the male's eyes turned to meet his, he froze. He knew this male, did he not? He would have remembered seeing two-toned eyes this gorgeous, but he was sure he never did. This male felt familiar. He was scared and it excited him. His penis was itching to fill this male up and his ears were longing to hear this male's cries of pain.

"You know this collar was made especially for you. But alas, it seems you have become a fat-ass. Will it even fit your once smooth, soft, slender neck anymore?" he asked. He looked into the male's eyes while he talked. The calmness in them was terrifying and it excited him even more, making him bolder.

"We can even bring your false trainer back. I can have one made for him, with my bio code of course." He smiled while biting his bottom lip. His penis was rock hard, but his hole was quivering as if it wanted the male to fill him up while he Trained this Pantu. As the images of him enjoying the naked attention from the two males standing in front of him crossed his brain, it made him more restless to start the journey back to The City.

"It might not fit your neck anymore, but your false trainer would be a perfect fit," he goaded again, trying to push the always calm, cool, and collected pet into anger.

To which the male only gave him a calm half smile, and he shuddered, in shock and disbelief as he felt himself come. He was confused. *Did this male make me come with just a smile?*

Pantu turned to face him and stood in front of the male, who was several inches taller than Pantu, meaning the male was even taller than him at only five-eleven.

"Do. NOT. Even. Think. About. It." Pantu said through clenched teeth while spreading his arms wide.

The male looked down at Pantu and smiled. "Aww. Are you protecting me?" the male teased.

"Drum, you should leave. If Tracey attaches that collar on you, the only person able to take it off is the owner," Pantu tried to inform Drum.

He watched as Drum held Pantu's waist and kissed Pantu's neck, which made Pantu drop his arms and turn to smile at Drum.

He was disgusted by the exchange, and it showed on his face. "His name is Drum? What? Are *all* your names chosen by a fucking five-year-old?" he asked. "And when did you become an outright sh…?"

But it was the smile in which Drum looked at him with, before looking down at his pants and back up at his face that made him pause. He took a deep, hard breath since he did not know whether there was a stain on his pants, and he refused to look down to check.

He heard the big, handsome male behind Drum and Pantu laugh, and it was then he remembered the big male was there since before their conversation, right? How could he forget a male that big was standing there?

QUEEN: AN UNSEEN FAVOR
WEEK FOUR: FRIDAY

Certain Beings felt Drum's Barrier going up and came to see what was happening. Mrs. Sky already followed Pantu, which caused Drum to leave after her. As he, Sport, Win and Dill decided to leave, Drum's Barrier was completed, blocking them in.

Only Sport was able to walk through, shrugging at the rest of them before jogging off to find Drum. This caused some of the other students to wonder what was happening as he became frustrated Drum was keeping something from him.

Pantu's Pa walked through the Barrier, and it frustrated him even more. But he stopped as he recognized the calmness in which Pantu's Pa gait held. The man wasn't a trembling mess, and it made him pause, rethinking the situation.

When Mr. Caleb walked by, he casually said, "If you already know everything Queen, how can life be as exciting as it is right now?" before stepping through Drum's Barrier.

The fact Drum adjusted his Barrier to allow certain Beings through, while keeping everyone else away was not a new Ability to him; Drum keeping him and Win at bay, was.

"What the fuck happened to where Drum wouldn't want us to see?" Win asked. Win's Mom side-eyed him for rudely cussing in front of her.

"Sorry Mom," was all Win could say looking away.

"A Personal Favor," was his answer, and Win understood.

Drum was about to hurt someone, and he wanted there to be as little witnesses as possible. He broke up the small crowd and sent everybody back to watch the movie, to their disappointment.

He knew no one would get through Drum's Barrier or hear what was happening out there, so why bother? He sat next to the exit and nervously waited. His frustration was gone and now he was just worried. He was praying to the Universe; everybody made it back safe and unharmed.

When he felt a Portal open in front of him and he heard Drum say, "Only you," he stepped through.

SKY: NEVER AGAIN
WEEK FOUR: FRIDAY

She was scared. She knew the look on Pantu's face. The City found them. She was surprised it took them this long, since they learned not to stay in one place for longer than a couple of days, max. They slipped, becoming too comfortable and now, she was worried they would collar her son again and torture him.

She watched Drum instantly appear behind Pantu to grab his arm. She stayed behind Pantu and Drum looking around for any signs of The Cloaked. Instead, a young boy about Pantu's age walked out of the wooded area in front of the campus.

He was most definitely from The City. He was only made a Cloaked because he challenged Pantu too many times and lost everything, so he found another way to have as little authority as males were allowed.

Although he was young, he rose in the ranks of The Cloaked by being ruthless, quickly earning the title of Cloakless. He was no longer required to wear a cloak and cover his face. He was free to travel, to hunt and lead his own team of Cloaked.

She stopped, focusing her Mind and brain together to analyze the situation as Sport jogged up. Her weapons were with her Husband, so her eyes looked around for the heaviest object she could find. They landed on the thickest tree off the side of the road. She was ready to leap towards the tree to rip it out of the ground, but when she saw the Cloakless pull out the collar, she was taken back. Her Mind replayed when Pantu was seven.

She told him to never go to the parades that came through The Slums. She knew they were coming to look for pets, and she didn't want Pantu to end up like Coin. His Pa instilled this in him, or so she thought.

When she heard the parade music, she called out to Pantu, but he was nowhere to be found. She became frantic, searching for him everywhere around their little shack in the woods. When she reached the area outside of the woods, one of the kids Pantu thought he secretly played with told her he and Yolk went to the parade to see Pantu's brother. She never ran so fast in her life.

The landscape was a blur as she headed towards the only sound she could hear, the parade music. Her thoughts sung along with the terribly off-beat music, signaling who was leading the parade, *no, no, no. Pantu, please!*

She made it to the parade and began to search desperately for her son. She pushed, shoved, and even elbowed her way to the front of the desperate parents, willing and ready to sacrifice their own children at a chance for a bit of Foil. It made her not care enough to be gentle and she knew she left bruises on every parent she touched.

When the parade halted, she heard him. Her Mind focused on her son's voice and when she finally made it to the front, she saw him. Pantu was hanging onto Coin's arm with a pleading look, begging Coin to come back. Telling Coin in the most adorable voice how much he missed him and tugging at Coin to follow.

She was frightened as she ran to him with enough fear spilling out her heart to fill her entire body. *I can save him! I can stop our parents' words from becoming truth!*

The governess' daughter was already at Pantu's side patting his head. *I can still make it*, she thought as she was running to the front of the parade.

The governess' daughter bent over and looked at Pantu. "How adorable are you!? You would make an excellent pet!" she said, placing a collar around Pantu's neck. The shock of the collar connecting with his spine made Pantu faint.

She slid and caught her son before he hit the ground and screamed as her and her Husband's parents' words hit home. "He is only seven! How could you be so cruel as to collar a child not old enough!? TAKE IT OFF!" she yelled at the young girl.

The teenaged girl laughed and kicked her, while Coin stood there, not moving or reacting to anything happening to them.

"I can do whatever I want, and I want him as a pet. Now take your hands off my brand-new pet before I have you publicly flayed, BITCH!" the governess' daughter spat out at her.

"The law says ten is the age a male can become a pet. Do you not know the laws you force everyone else to follow?" she asked, never releasing Pantu.

"I will make the laws, you dirty whore. Now release my pet or should I have you flayed right here?" the governess' daughter asked, with a sadistic smile.

"You are not the governess, only her rotten, over-dried egg," she answered back.

"What the fuck! You bitch!" the governess' daughter shouted.

The young girl went to slap her, but her Husband came between them, taking the slap. He kneeled in front of the young girl and bowed his head.

"You know who he is and where he is. He will become your pet at the legal age of ten, as the law states. So, will you please un-collar my son?"

By now, this gained the attention of the governess herself, who left her seat and walked down the stairs to them. The governess smiled at her and her Husband on the ground protecting and holding their collared son. When the governess realized exactly who they were, she became excited.

"Ah! You made one you claim?" the governess asked in a nasal voice. "He will be an exception to the law. He will remain collared and enter training at the appropriate ages.

"Until then, why not come back to The Center. I am sure *both* your Senora Madres miss you dearly, and I know they have yet to meet this little one," the governess said, as she turned to walk away. "It will be the only way you will ever see him again," the governess added, before she re-entered her float.

As she came back to reality, she knew she couldn't let it happen again. She refused.

Holding up the collar, Tracey asked, "This is the one day in your life you get to choose. Who will it be? Will this Drum be your Owner's new Pet, or will you take the tight-ass collar and your place back at her feet?"

She ran in front of her son, arms spread. "Hey motherfucker! The only way you will ever have a chance to collar my child again will be over my cold dead body," she said, with a fierce anger in her voice as she eyed the tree, she was now closer to.

Tracey laughed at her. "Would you wear the collar instead? I wonder how much the only daughter of the Second High Lady of The City would fetch? Ah! Wait. This one is for males only. So, that means you are worthle..."

Tracey didn't get to finish as Drum's fist connected with his face, sending him flying back to flip over several times before landing on his back. She could tell Tracey was out before he even connected with the ground.

Her expression of shock matched Pantu's but Sport just folded his arms and smiled. Drum calmly walked back, taking gloves, which weren't on his hands a second ago, off. She was shocked at the speed in which Drum moved and at the fact he knocked someone out over her.

"Why would you...?" she asked Drum, surprised.

"Pantu, Sport and I are used to people talking about us. They are hollow, empty words of a coward. I would treat you as my own Mother, so I refuse to let someone disrespect you and think I won't rearrange their face," Drum stated, to Pantu's bright smile, her admiration and Sport's crazy grin.

PANTU'S PA: SHOWING A DIFFERENT SIDE
WEEK FOUR: FRIDAY

He and Caleb came up from behind the group. His eyes downcast, he watched Drum try to refrain from touching Pantu in front of them, but Pantu didn't seem to care and hugged Drum. His quick glance let him know Caleb was just as surprised as he was, but for different reasons.

He knew Caleb was surprised to see someone other than family could touch Drum and not burn, but he was surprised at the boy on the ground. He understood what was happening between Pantu and Drum, so the thought was left alone. He used his True Vision to look in the distance at the body lying in the road.

"That's Tracey!" he said, in a scared, trembling voice as his shaky hand lifted to point. "We're behind a Barrier! How did they find us? Wait? What happened to his face?" he asked, looking at the Beings standing around, his eyes skipping over Pantu.

Skylove and Pantu turned on their True Vision to look at Tracey's face in horror as half of it was burned. He watched Tracey's face, still slowly burning away and falling off.

"And you thought he could collar me," Drum said, with a laugh.

He watched out the corners of his eyes as Drum smiled at Pantu, fighting to keep his composure while touching Pantu in front of Caleb, but Pantu was oblivious and chose to hang on to Drum's arm, even linking fingers. Drum couldn't stop smiling but also didn't look at Caleb and held Pantu's hand as well.

He held back his smile at Drum and Pantu, and instead, looked away, scared. He was thinking. They couldn't let Tracey or any of the other Cloaked leave the Barrier. He was unsure of how Caleb would handle this. When Tracey started to regain consciousness, he turned to Caleb.

"He is the Cloakless leader of a group of Cloaked. They travel in packs of six," he informed Caleb.

"What you wanna do?" Caleb asked Drum.

He was confused why Caleb was asking his son for leadership. He thought Caleb would handle the situation and capture the group. He was holding on to hope Caleb would kill Tracey or call Major for The Warehouse.

Drum finally looked at Caleb, who nodded and Sport, who bowed his head. Both their clothes changed into black as they turned and left without a word to find the other five, leaving the rest to watch Tracey.

Skylove looked at him, and he gave her a confused shrug back. He was piecing it together in his head but there were too many holes. He realized things here weren't as they seemed. Drum held more authority in this situation than his own Pa.

It took Tracey longer than a moment to come back to reality, and he struggled to stand up again. When Tracey touched the side of his face Drum connected with, Tracey screamed in horror as he pulled chunks of his face off.

"MY BEAUTIFUL FUCKING FACE!" Tracey yelled. He looked up at the group. "WHO DID THIS? I WILL FUCKING COLLAR YOU AND FUCK YOU UNTIL YOU BLEED. I WILL SHOVE MY KNIFE IN EVERY HOLE AND MAKE YOU SCREAM FOR MY HEARING PLEASURE!" Tracey shouted.

Drum raised his hand. "First off, your face has been greatly improved, if I do say so myself. I'm quite proud of the work I did," Drum said, his calm voice amplified.

Tracey stared hard at Drum. "I am going to make you my own personal play toy, you fucking night—" But Tracey was cut off by a sword being shoved through his right shoulder.

He didn't see Drum move. One second Drum was standing beside Pantu and the next, he was stabbing Tracey. Drum removed the sword and held it to Tracey's throat even as Tracey dropped to his knees.

He motioned for Skylove, and they moved closer while Pantu followed. They came close enough to hear Drum and Tracey's exchange.

"Would you care to finish that sentence?" Drum asked Tracey, never breaking his calm demeanor. Drum stood with one hand in his pocket while lazily holding the sword to Tracey's throat.

"How? When? Where...did the...sword...come from?" Tracey asked, shocked, and confused. "You are like them. You are an Other!"

"I thought not. The sword came from my right pocket, and I prefer the classification of Being," Drum said, as he turned to walk away.

"You know we will obliterate this poor ass place to get him back. We will make Pets out of all of you, Woman, or male. There is a new Minister, and he has more authority than any man or male has ever held in The City. Poor or denounced Women are now allowed to be Pets." Tracey laughed but was cut off by coughing up the rest of the blood leaking from his mouth.

Drum paused in front of him and stuck the sword clean into the road, hilt up. Drum locked eyes with him and smiled before walking back to Pantu.

He asked, "What good would it do if she already knows where we are?" His body was trembling.

Skylove moved to stand beside Pantu to watch him think. He was encouraged by the bright smile on his Wife's face.

"She does not know yet. This fucking town does not have any got-damn service. I was the only one to recognize this Pantu's plump fat-ass, yet I cannot even turn on my phone to take a photo.

"But she will know. If I disappear, she will know. My last check-in was a place close to here. They will send Cloakless Others. You know how much she values your son. And not just because he is the highest-ranking pet but because he is YOUR SON!" Tracey spat out blood as he spoke.

He started talking, releasing his Calm to straighten his body and hold his head high, looking down at the disgusting pile of kneeling human. "I know she is still obsessed with me. She cannot let go of the fact I never loved her. Never wanted her. How could I love a woman who smelled like shit re-digested and shitted out again in a sewer pile of rotten dead animals."

He wasn't asking a question, just stating facts as he took the sword out of the ground and slowly walked up to Tracey, while respectfully examining the sword.

While the sword was plain without any decorations, he could see the quality of materials used to make the sword were the second best on the planet. The balance was even, and it was lightweight.

The thinness of the blade should have made it flexible or easily breakable, but he could feel the sturdiness of the sword. This could have only been crafted by a Talented Being.

"I thought you learned your lesson when Pantu sent you to The Outer Ring, but your pencil-thin, five-inch cock thought the better of itself. Or maybe my son is just too fucking kind-hearted." He stood in front of Tracey.

He wasn't trembling like he normally did; in fact, he stood tall and showed a little of what made him the number one pet of his generation. He was confident in his pose, and it showed on his face as he sliced Tracey's head clean off in one stroke.

"Oh! That was dope!" Drum said, with praise in his voice.

"It's a high-quality sword that's been well maintained," he said, examining the sword again while cleaning it with a napkin he pulled out of his pocket. He tossed the bloodied cloth on Tracey's headless body.

He walked up to Drum and handed the sword back, hilt first. "What's going to happen to me now?" he asked, looking Drum in the eyes. He read up on every law in Sunset, so he knew he would be jailed for his actions until his trial. He sighed, hoping to get a chance to ask Caleb to protect his Wife and son.

"Nothing," Drum said, snapping his fingers. "There's no proof he was ever here."

He turned to watch and saw Tracey's body and head starting to burn away to nothing. He turned back to Drum in surprise.

"You're not going to turn me in?" he asked with wide eyes.

"Over a human?" Drum scoffed. "Anyone who tries to force a Being from under the Barrier will be killed. So, as long as Pantu didn't want to leave with him, he would've died anyways."

He nodded. "Thank you." He looked at Pantu holding on to Drum's waist and Drum's arm around Pantu's shoulder. He looked away. *"Are you okay?"* he quietly asked Pantu. He was back to trembling while waiting to see if he would receive a response from Pantu.

"Yes...Pa. I am fine," Pantu mumbled, not looking at him.

"Good," was all he said, and went and hugged his Wife, releasing the built-up tension in his body.

"What about the other ones?" Skylove asked Drum.

"My Dad and Sport have taken care of them, and we have a team retracing their steps to find their hideout, somewhere outside my Barrier," Drum responded.

He felt Skylove's Energy tingle at the mention of a team, and he lightly squeezed her slender waist.

"The movie is almost over. We need Queen." Drum waved a hand, and with his True Vision still turned on, he could see a large, Being-sized, white shimmer.

"Only you," Drum said through what he now knew was a self-made Portal.

The shock appeared on his face as another riddle was solved. "Wait, so my Pa wasn't being crazy with his multitude of riddles?!" he asked. He looked at his Wife, then his son and back to his Wife before looking at Drum and back to his Wife. Pantu misread what he was asking his Wife.

"No! GMack is not crazy!" Pantu said, indignant of his accusation against his own Pa.

Queen stepped through and took in what was happening. Without saying a word, Queen looked at Drum and waited.

"Take them home," Drum said.

"I will make sure Dill spends the night while Sport and I will stay the night at Win's," Queen answered with a slight bow.

Drum looked distracted and Queen nodded.

"We will also spend the night at Pantu's," Queen changed. "Your Barrier is still up, so we will have our Energies on alert outside of it."

Drum relaxed and nodded, placing Pantu into Queen's hands, literally, before walking off.

"Drum!" Pantu's panicked voice rang out. "You are leaving?"

It made Drum freeze, but he didn't turn to look at Pantu. *"I have some business to take care of with the captured five. Queen will make sure you all make it home safely. I will come see you when I'm finished,"* Drum told Pantu gently.

Pantu nodded and grabbed onto Queen's arm.

"I will wait for your text," Drum said, before making another Portal, but he could see this one was royal blue.

"Make sure Pantu eats," Drum added, before disappearing.

He whispered to his Wife, and she nodded, both of them turning off their True Vision. Skylove went to Queen and Pantu to pull them back towards the campus. He quickly found the collar in a ditch on the side of the road and picking it up, it disappeared from his hands.

PANTU: WAITING PATIENTLY FOR HIS PROTECTOR
WEEK FOUR: FRIDAY

Queen did, in fact, make sure they made it home safely. But first, they returned to the campus parking lot where Win and Dill were waiting with their parents to leave.

The movie was still playing, so most students and parents were still enjoying the show and food. A few were out in the parking lot since Drum's Dome disappeared, and some were leaving.

He ran to hug his best friend. As Dill was consoling him, they leaned against his Ma's car. Their parents talked for a little. His Pa told the other parents there was someone trying to kidnap his child and both Queen and Win looked surprised. They turned to look at him, but he refused to answer.

Dill stepped in front of their questioning looks and shook his head. Some Beings walked up with the young girl who was sitting next to Sport and introduced themselves as Sport's foster parents. Mrs. K appeared, followed by the Beings Queen pointed out as his parents.

His Pa explained they escaped from their homeland, but someone immensely powerful wanted to kill them and kidnap their child. They were constantly running and hiding for years.

The parents started to exchange numbers. They would all meet and set a plan to keep his whole family safe. Tears came from his Ma's eyes at the amount of support from Beings they didn't really know, and he went to hold and console her.

On the drive to their house, in which they were proceeded and followed by some of the other parents, he realized he was mentally exhausted, and Drum was right, he was hungry. When they made it to his house, his parents invited everybody in for food and drinks. Sport's foster mother turned her nose up at the simple house and made the excuse of having to put her daughter to bed, then left.

Dill, Win, Queen, and him all went upstairs into his attic studio, and their Pas brought food, drinks, blankets, and pillows for them. After everyone set up their own sleeping space, Sport popped his head in.

"Any room for one more?" Sport asked and the daggers he received from Queen and Win made Sport nod his head in acceptance, but he quickly ushered Sport in, and a sleeping spot was made for Sport on the floor as well.

"It looks like some of the parents aren't leaving either. They seem very worried," Sport informed everyone.

He started crying. "My apologies! This is all my fault. I never wanted this to happen. I should leave, so no one gets hurt. She will destroy everything and everyone to get me back," he said, between his sobs.

Win came and hugged him as Dill patted him on the back.

"Where should we go?" Queen asked him.

He looked at Queen, his Mind not understanding what was being asked and still crying.

"If you leave, Dill and Drum will leave. I, Win and Sport will follow Drum, Kat will follow Win. So, I ask again, where should we go?"

He shook his head. He couldn't understand such kind words coming from someone not his family, so he asked, "Why would you all leave? This is your home. It is nothing like where I come from." His cries now just sniffles. He didn't understand why so many Beings he didn't know well would do something like that for him.

"Then why not make this your home," Dill said to him.

"We cannot stay in one place for too long. You see they have already found us!"

Sport smiled, looking at him. *"Are you or your parents hurt?"* Sport asked, gently.

He shook his head.

"Does anyone else know you all are here?" Queen asked.

"He said he did not have a chance to contact her, so if they were all captured before leaving, our whereabouts are still unknown," he answered.

"Do you feel you and your parents are safe?" Win asked.

He meekly nodded.

"Do you trust Drum will protect you and your parents?" Dill asked him.

His eyes took in the Beings sitting around him and he wished he could turn his True Vision back on. But instead, as he thought about what happened tonight, he lowered his head and nodded.

"Do you trust we will protect you as well?" Sport asked him.

He felt more tears coming out. They were nothing but kind to him, a bit playful as only Queen could be, and they never did anything which would endanger him. They gave him his space; his privacy and they didn't let anyone bully or mistreat him.

He hadn't known them for long, but he already felt a connection to everybody in the room. He didn't want to leave them. He didn't want to leave Drum. His Mind registered his brain finally agreeing with an idea which was making his Light happy. He nodded and cried in his hands.

"If they hurt you..." he started.

Sport clasped his hands together and a beautiful purple Light formed around his hands. Sport spread it out and laid it across the floor.

He was looking at Sport's Light, enjoying the color of the flowy, wavy, almost transparent light hovering slightly above the floor. "Your light is a beautiful, pale iris color," he said, staring at the Light.

When he touched the Light, it shattered into tiny iris sparkles. He meekly looked at Sport. The breaking of his Light caused Sport to look at him while forcing back a smile, but it also made Sport nod in appreciation.

"If they try to hurt us, then you will protect us," Sport told him.

His nose scrunched up, and his eyebrows furled, since he knew he wasn't strong enough to lift the sword Drum, and his Pa used tonight. Sport laughed at his face, and he pouted his lips while puffing his cheeks. When he looked at the Beings sitting around him, Win's thoughtful looks at him made him want to know what was on Win's Mind.

"How much did you eat?" Win asked.

"Very little. I am much too tired and uninterested in eating," he replied. He didn't know if he had the strength to lift silverware to his mouth.

"Nope. That won't do," Win said, and went downstairs.

"So, how long have you known about our town?" Queen asked, sitting up, both legs to the side with one arm holding him up and the other hand lightly gracing Queen's knee.

He was more interested in Queen's Grace, but since answering a question with another question was rude, he was forthcoming. "About one week after we moved in," he responded. "It was when I woke up."

Queen's head tilted towards him, and he could see the questions passing quickly across Queen's face. "How long were you asleep?" Queen decided to ask.

"Years," he said, with a small smile.

Win came back with a lot of food and Sport helped him carry it in, while lecturing Win about not asking for help. The look Win gave, quickly shut Sport up. Once they finished all the food, the doorbell rang and they froze in unusual positions, trying to listen to what was happening downstairs. When they heard Mr. Caleb's booming voice, all their shoulders released tension at the same time, since they felt even safer.

But his back spasmed at the now familiar feeling of knowing Drum was here and watching him. His Light started to tingle, and his chest was tight, counting down the seconds until he would be back in Drum's strong, warm arms and able to lay his head on Drum's broad chest.

"If Mr. Caleb spends the night, no one will dare approach your house!" Dill said, and they all laughed.

"We should post a sign saying Mr. Caleb is here, to deter people," Win added, his face holding steady to the thought. It made the rest of them laugh at Win trying to figure out where to properly place the sign, so it can be seen by all.

"OH? And is there a sign for me?" Drum asked, popping his head in from behind the door.

Win answered, "We should place that one by the Barrier, then no one in their right Minds would even enter."

To which everyone laughed again. His elation was spread throughout the room, filling it with the scent of cinnamon and honey. He ran to Drum and hugged so tightly, it was as if this was his last night in town and he would be leaving back to The City tomorrow. Drum hugged him back just as tight. When he finally let go, his eyes held grateful, happy feelings towards Drum for everything and for coming back to him.

"I know," Drum told him with a smile.

It was only two words and a smile, but it was the steady feelings coming off of Drum which made his Light send goosebumps all over his body, while going crazy from the amount of warmth his Light was soaking up. He knew every part of him was again red and his penis was hard, so he laid his forehead on Drum's sturdy, toned chest for a moment, willing his Light to calm the fuck down, before leading Drum to the sleeping mats.

Drum looked around and asked, "Where am I supposed to sleep?"

To which everyone rolled their eyes and some even sucked their teeth in response. Drum snapped his fingers, making sleeping clothes appear, so everyone could bathe. He stood there for a moment and stared at the pile of clothes.

Queen's smile to him, informed him that he verified information for Queen about how long he knew this town was different. Even so, he was still enthralled at how Beings were able to do such amazing Talents and used their Light without reserve here.

"It's one of Drum's Personal Abilities," Queen answered without him asking. He was sure the look on his face told everyone what he was thinking.

"The air one breathes will naturally replenish one's Light," he reminded himself, out loud.

He held up his hand to form his Light, but Drum quickly grabbed him and spun him to ask, "Which bathrooms can we use?"

They were using his room plus the second empty bedroom on the same floor. Queen went first to shower in his bedroom while Win used the spare room.

When Queen came back, he asked, "Not planning on staying long?"

He felt even more heated than feeling Drum's Light and he knew his face was a deep red color. "It is difficult to move fast with a lot of items, so some things get left behind. I found it simpler not to become attached," he meekly said, avoiding Drum's eyes.

PANTU: A GRIM CITY LIFE
WEEK FOUR: FRIDAY

While everyone showered and changed, Dill set up his phone for a movie marathon. Win wanted a romantic movie, Queen wanted horror, but he and Dill wanted action.

Drum was too busy nibbling on him to care, and he was trying to control the jerking of his spine from the heated sensations of Drum's mouth on his neck. When Sport recommended the Carrie Trotter series, his full body turned to stare wide-eyed at Sport, while pulling away from Drum's overwhelming kisses.

"There are movies for the books?" he asked, his elation again spreading throughout the small room.

Everybody except Drum and Sport moaned with uninterested looks on their faces.

Sport straightened his back, eyeing him with a singular raised eyebrow and a puffed-out chest. "Have you gained the highest level of comprehension for the literature Young One?" Sport asked, as if he was a centuries-old, pompous, Higher Ed Professor, who thought himself more knowledgeable than the planet.

"One may only gain true comprehension by dissecting all the books, Oldest One!" he answered, challenging Sport with disinterested eyes and a haughty face.

"We shall ascertain your Level of Discernment with the differences between literature and live action, Youngest One," Sport said back, stretching his neck to try and look down on him.

Win was laughing at the absurdity of it all while Queen looked between Sport and him, wondering why they were both joking in such a way.

"Well, it does have horror, romance, action and what no one asked for; mystical god magic," Queen said, shrugging his shoulders to give up and let the thought out into the Universe.

Dill found the movies and started downloading them.

"Why can't we just stream them?" Win asked.

"Pantu isn't allowed online," Dill answered, softly.

He noticed how quiet Dill became in Drum's presence and he assumed Drum and Dill didn't interact after the bullying incident. Even though Dill was trying to shrink back into the shadows, Drum didn't seem to notice or hear Dill speak.

"Why?" Sport asked. He wasn't there when they were told, so he still didn't know.

"Because some powerful person in his home country is trying to kill Pantu's parents and kidnap him. It's why Pantu doesn't have a lot of stuff and why they always had to run," Win simplified for Sport.

"The easiest way to find a person is online, so if Pantu never goes on it, it makes it harder for him to be located," Queen stated.

A look quickly passed Sport's face but was only seen by him and Drum and he had no idea what the look meant, so he just blinked his eyes at Sport. When Sport looked at Drum, he felt Drum nod and Sport let out a sigh.

He decided to give details, wishing to ease Sport's shaking body. "The powerful person is the governess, who rules The City with an iron fist," he started. "Her shitty daughter was my owner and she and her ma are trying to drag me back."

"Is where you're from called The City? The whole country?" Win asked.

He nodded. "I was born and raised there. There are different areas of The City. The Slums is the poorest part, where we lived until I was seven." He looked up at Drum, asking with his eyes for paper and a pencil. Drum understood and a new sketchbook with colored pencils appeared in Drum's hands in front of him. Laying the sketchbook on the floor, he started drawing, enjoying Drum's lazy way of resting a chin on his shoulder to watch him.

"Then The Outer Ring. It is better than The Slums, but not by much. Pets in the top one hundred families could live there closer to the border of the next section of The City, or if you were skilled enough, you could earn a place there.

"There is The Inner Ring, which housed those rich or the families of pets who were in the top forty and over five hundred thousand points. Then, there is The Center. The governess lives there and those wealthy enough to afford it.

"Any pet in the top three could move their families there as long as they were over one million points. Those in the Top Ten Families of The City and any with high family status could as well. The closer you are to the governess, the more prestige you can claim," he explained and held the book up for everyone but Drum to see.

"So many questions!" Queen said, with wide eyes.

"Ask away," he said, his Light slowing the flow inside him.

"If you don't want to answer you don't have to," Queen said.

"Thanks," he said.

"I thought your Grandmothers were number two and three, why did you live in The Slums?" Sport asked.

He shook his head and lowered his voice. "I have a G-Ma and an Indria. My G-Ma is my Pa's Ma and Indria is my Ma's egg donor. I call her grandma here, around you all because it was easier than explaining, but in The City, she would only be called Indria. I can never call her family in front of my parents and definitely not in public. She was denounced long before I was born," he explained.

Sport nodded, taking in the information. Queen and Win waited until he continued.

"I think us living in The Slums had something to do with my parents falling out with the governess. She could not kill the only children of the two Women who controlled access to The City's money, food, and medicine," he theorized. "My parents never told me what happened, and my G-Pas always told me it was not their business to tell," he added.

Queen looked at him with happy eyes. "I like your G-Pas already!" Queen said, and everybody laughed.

"A pet? So, owners of popular animals can live in better parts of the country?" Win asked. "But how would the governess' daughter be *your* owner? You aren't an animal?"

He took a deep breath. He tried but the answer was stuck in his throat. When Drum softly breathed out on his neck, he felt his muscles slack and his Light flow return to normal as Drum's breath travelled over his body to equally spread heat.

"Did you eat?" Drum asked, interrupting the feelings of happiness running through his Light.

It gave him a moment to collect his thoughts and himself. "Hmm. Win made sure to overfeed me," he said. He turned slightly to speak and smile at Drum, who kissed his nose, making him giggle when another heat wave washed over his body.

Everyone smiled at their display of affection. Drum smiled at his best friends in appreciation and mouthed a thank you, to which their faces turned red as they smiled back.

"Only birds were domesticated and allowed to be kept in The City. Here I see cats, dogs and pet stores selling all unusual types of animals. It would have been burned down in The City along with the person and their family being killed.

"A pet is a collared male with an owner. Only males could become pets and only women can own a pet. After they turn ten, males can choose to become a pet, which most in The Slums and Outer Ring do to increase status or to bring in points for their family.

"If they are chosen, a collar is clasped around their necks which connects with their spinal cord. The only person able to take it off is the person who put their bio code in it, their owner.

"If they are not chosen, the law states they can always keep trying until the age of thirteen. After that, they no longer have the option of being a pet," he explained.

"Remember how I told you; I was the most celebrated person? It was because I was the number one pet in the whole country."

"Why did it connect with the spinal cord?" Win asked.

"It is to keep the pet in line. The owner could kill the pet at any time, so to stay alive, the pet must be obedient. If only the owner is able to remove it, there is a less likely chance of the pet killing the owner.

"This also means an owner can treat a pet however they want with no fear. And if the owner neglects to send a live bio signal to the collar, the pet will die, and then well, their whole family line could be executed," he explained.

"Did you choose to be a pet?" Queen asked him.

He shook his head. "If a woman is wealthy or powerful enough, they can collar whoever they want, whenever they want," he told them.

Everyone paused to digest this information. For Beings who lived peacefully under a Dome for so long, he could only imagine they were trying to figure out how such a place could exist. The picture he was painting of where he was born was filled with dark colors.

"How did you get collared?" Sport asked.

He looked at the floor and swallowed hard.

PANTU: AN UNTRUE FRIEND
WEEK FOUR: FRIDAY

"Pantu, if you're uncomfortable, we can stop," Drum softly offered to him.

He shook his head. His Mind was, for once, aligned with his brain. Dill wanted him to be open, but he was shivering at telling these people, no, these were Beings, so much about his life. He felt like the more he spoke, the darker the colors he added to his painting. But Dill asked him to try, so he would be as open as he could be.

"When I was seven, Yolk told me Coin was in the parade coming to The Slums and he would take me there to see him. I went, even though my Ma told me to never go to any parade and my Pa stressed coming home.

"I was to come into our home if I ever heard the music. But I really wanted to see Coin. He left when he was twelve and never came to visit. I did not know why he left but I just wanted him back.

"Yolk took me to the parade, and I saw Coin. I ran up to him trying to convince him to come back home. I even told him he could have the crispy end pieces of the cinnamon honey bread my Ma always made for my G-Pas' visit.

"This woman comes up to me and pats me on the head, tells me I am adorable, and I pass out. When I woke up, we were living in Indria's house in The Center, and I had on a collar," he said, shivering at the memory. He pulled his legs up to wrap his arms around them, consoling his freezing body with his cold arms.

Drum hugged him from behind and he held back his tears at the soft kiss to the back of his neck, right where his collar once connected with his spine. He was growing his hair out to cover the only mark on his body. Not a physical one but the mental and emotional scar which was left.

Relaxing against Drum's chest, the heat spreading over his body was warmer than ever before and he knew Drum increased the heat. He smiled and felt several cracks inside his body but ignored the feeling to focus on the more pleasurable warmth.

"Holy Karma Pantu! I thought you had to be ten to be a pet?" Win said.

"That is the law, but I was an exception. I was *special*," he said, with disgust.

The looks everyone else gave Drum was one of collective understanding, But Drum's face was busy burying itself in his hair for Drum to say anything or react.

"Hmmm. No wonder you two fit so well together," Queen said, with a soft smile.

"Is Coin your older brother?" Sport asked.

He blew out his breath. "Coin was a child born in The Slums, whom my parents raised before I was born, but he was denounced when I was five. I was told he was using the fact my parents took care of him in The Slums to give claim to our family name, so he was not acknowledged as family."

"It's so weird Yolk was the reason you were collared," Queen stated.

He looked at Queen's eyes holding questions, but his unhappy feelings around Yolk kept him from asking. "I should have just returned home like my Pa said," he stated back.

"How old were you when Coin left?" Queen asked.

"Ahhh, about five?" he answered.

"Were you friends with Yolk before he left?" Queen asked.

"No. I only started secretly hanging out with other kids in The Slums after Coin left." he answered.

Queen nodded. "Did you tell them about Coin?" Queen asked, with a raised eyebrow.

He looked at Queen and went quiet at what was being implied was what Dill was also alluding to. Queen understood things he didn't say, like the fact his parents kept him, and at one point Coin, close to home.

They didn't let them interact with the residents of The Slums. As the grandkids of the number two and three Women, they would be used against their Grandparents to leverage power. Queen understood and the knowledge made his eyelashes flutter, not wanting to accept this as his reality.

"I'm asking because you don't strike me as the type to tell anybody anything unless it's necessary. How often did the parade come through?" Queen asked.

He thought for a moment. "About every three months."

Win's head tilted, but instead of Win going off into his own head to think, he spoke out loud. "The numbers aren't adding up. That means for two years, the parade came around twelve times. Why would Yolk wait so long to tell you about Coin?

"How did he even know who Coin was, what he looked like and that he was going to be in the parade? Was there a special announcement? How did he know for a fact Coin would be there?" Win asked, more to himself, as the numbers were making Win's face twist from having so many unanswered questions.

Sport patted Win on the head and received a happy look from Win. He was adding it together as well and he looked at Queen, whose eyebrow hadn't gone down.

"I wish I could say I'm sorry, but I'm not. From the moment you first mentioned Yolk to us, I had an unsettling feeling," Queen told him.

"When I snuck back to The Slums a few months later, Yolk and his family already moved to the Outer Ring," he said, understanding what Queen was getting at and confirming Dill's suspicions.

He put his head in his hands. Yolk set him up as a child and was so successful, he came back to do it again as teenagers. He just let the tears fall at his stupidity. It made sense to him now. Why Yolk was killed. They knew. They knew and they protected the stupid decisions he thought he could make on his own.

"I did not want to see it. I did not want to fucking believe it!" he cried. "Did I really want a best friend so badly to where I would endanger my whole got-damn family?" He was beside himself, feeling like a disgrace to the high status of his family.

"Dumpling. Come, let's lie down. This is enough for the night," Drum said, not caring to look at anyone for confirmation.

Queen and everyone else moved to get comfortable on their mats. Dill waited until he was calm, then started the first movie. He moved to lay his head on Drum's chest to see the movie better. He saw Dill give a nod to Queen and received a wide-eyed look back.

Dill was also the one who convinced him to be more open and honest with The Four. Queen called it, he wasn't the type to express his feelings or thoughts to anyone, freely. He was dealing with emotions he wasn't used to having, so Dill spoke his Mind, but was gentler about it than Queen was.

Dill went to use the bathroom and after a moment, Queen followed. He decided to eavesdrop on their conversation to get a better understanding of the looks Dill and Queen gave each other, so he stood at the top of the stairs, just outside the attic door. When Dill came out of his bedroom, Queen was waiting by the door.

"You knew or you assumed." He heard Queen say.

He didn't hear Dill say anything and leaned forward to peek at them.

"You're a good friend Dill. Pantu is lucky to have you in his life," Queen added.

Dill looked down, took a deep breath, and asked, "Is it selfish that I don't want him to leave? I've never had a best friend before and Pantu is the only Being I can tell anything to, who will listen and support me.

"He doesn't judge me or my past. When I told him what I did, he encouraged me to continue to be a better person. Even after all he has been through, Pantu still is so sweet and kind-hearted." Dill looked so unhappy; Queen hugged him.

"We're all being selfish wanting Pantu to stay. Even though our reasons aren't evil intentions, it's still Pantu's choice whether he stays or not." Queen pulled back to look at Dill. "But we can't force him to stay. *It would be the same as putting a collar back on him*," Queen said, gently.

Dill nodded. *"I know,"* Dill replied, softly.

"All we can do is give him one thousand reasons to stay," Queen said, with a smile, which made Dill smile in return.

"Now move. I have to pee!" Queen said, with a laugh.

He quickly returned to laying on Drum's chest and received a warm, soft kiss to the forehead, making him smile.

DRUM: UNDER A BARRIER
WEEK FOUR: FRIDAY

Drum was feeling happy as he held Pantu in his arms in front of their best friends. He was surprised and shocked his Dumpling was so touchy in front of their parents, but he refused to pull away, knowing it would hurt Pantu to deny his touch.

He felt Pantu had a hard battle with himself when it came to his feelings, but Pantu was doing in a couple of weeks what it took him years to do, come to terms with liking a guy.

Even if it was for varied reasons, neither of them was ever encouraged to live or love freely. They each had "responsibilities" which required them to place others happiness above their own.

He was still unsure how his Dad would react to his announcement of declining the throne or waiting to see what will happen with Pantu, a man who couldn't produce an heir.

He knew claiming a man would cause the elders who hated him to try and deny him the throne, so why even fight for it? If he could be with the only Being he's ever liked and travel, he would be happy.

The first movie was over and Pantu, along with Sport, were talking about the differences between the book and the movie. They were extremely detailed in their discussion, which pulled everyone else in, except him.

He was content just holding Pantu and listening to the sound of such a soft and sweet voice, but the way this light voice flowed throughout his body made him hard.

Anything about the young man in front of him, excited him and the elation which came with knowing Pantu chose to be right here with him, caused his member to twitch. Pantu's back arched just a little and he growled softly into a smooth and squishy neck. He knew only Pantu, along with Win heard him and when it was suggested they throw on a movie to fall asleep to, he was grateful.

Everybody got comfortable again as Pantu's earlier excitement about the Trotter movie engaged the others, who already seen the movie multiple times, into praising or criticizing their favorite parts. This Ability was handed down from his Pa.

He saw it in action during Anime Night. Pantu's Pa was able to sway the emotions of the whole crowd, and his son possessed the same talent.

Pantu, however, was also able to incite a human, and apparently Beings, sexual desires. He knew Pantu wasn't doing it on purpose, so he wasn't jealous when others blushed or looked away, because he was the one holding and touching his Dumpling.

He also wasn't jealous of Pantu and Dill's friendship, in fact, he thought this Dill helped Pantu in ways he couldn't, and to be upset, would mean his and Queen's friendship meant nothing. There were so many new feelings and emotions he was trying to understand, and he welcomed them all.

As he and Pantu laid wrapped in each other's arms underneath their shared blanket, his hand caressed Pantu's back.

"Can I squeeze your butt?" he whispered.

Pantu gave him such an innocent look, he moaned and squeezed Pantu's thigh.

"You can touch and squeeze wherever you want," Pantu quietly informed him. *"But only if you mean it,"* Pantu added, pouting up at him so sensually, he leaked.

He knew Pantu could tell when he released, even if he tried not to show it. The smile he received was followed by a kiss on his neck, which took him by surprise. Sure, Pantu's face was buried in his neck or chest, but Pantu never outright kissed on him. Feeling such cool and titillating lips made him quiver with excitement, which reached every part of his body, making him squirt out.

"This is how it feels whenever you kiss on me," Pantu said softly, and so sweetly, he had no other option but to put a royal-blue Barrier around them, signaling to his best friends, not to get close. Even Dill stood and moved behind his best friends, while wearing noise-canceling headphones.

He knew everybody wasn't asleep, but his Barriers were top tier, so he was unworried. When Pantu looked around, confused, their eyes found each other as those beautiful, multi-colored brown eyes widened with surprise, making him lose the will to fight just by looking into such bright, innocent eyes.

He kissed Pantu's forehead as he felt a hand slide under his shirt. He froze, waiting to see Pantu's reaction to the multitude of scars on his stomach.

The soft look to him as if Pantu didn't know if he wanted the touch, made his stomach clench up. After a soft, winning smile graced his Dumpling's face, he knew Pantu understood what just happened. Pantu was happy and giggled, which made him hold on tighter. But instead of Pantu's hand going up, it turned and slid down.

He moaned while watching Pantu shiver and wiggle from the sensation. Adding more Heat, he wanted to keep Pantu as warm as possible but when his hands found Pantu's cute little round bubble butt, he didn't want to move them.

He didn't squeeze, just kept caressing Pantu's smooth, soft skin. It took Pantu a minute to realize there was no blockage to his roaming hands and his eyes popped open to see he was the only one still fully dressed, again. The pout he watched grace Pantu's face at being the only one naked, made him pull his Dumpling closer into his embrace.

Pantu's cool hands slid up his back and over his clothes, reaching his neck, which Pantu stopped to caress, as a thank you.

He lowered his head to make it easier for Pantu to massage, but when the hand kept going and reached his hair, he froze again. He allowed Pantu's hand to slowly and carefully glide through his hair while laying quick kisses on his neck, timing them to be two seconds apart.

He was feeling overloaded. Coupled with the fact Pantu was playing with his hair above his member, the hair on top of his head and landing soft kisses on his neck, how could he not release?

"So *soft*," Pantu moaned.

"*Pannn-tuu*," was all he could moan as Pantu's hand slid below the hair above his member.

"*So warm*," Pantu moaned into his neck. Pantu licked and kissed his neck gently. "*So tasty*," Pantu whispered.

He growled and his hand found Pantu's member. He felt everything leaking and he moaned as he squeezed Pantu's butt while playing with the tip of Pantu's member. But Pantu couldn't fully grasp his member and was getting frustrated, thinking his sweatpants were in the way and when his pants disappeared, Pantu looked up at him, and he smiled back.

"When did you learn how to do that?" he asked Pantu, with pride in his eyes.

"I do not—." Pantu tried to say.

"*My Dumpling is so talented,*" he whispered. "*Could you leave my shirt?*" he asked, softly.

Pantu nodded and tried to grip his member, but when he looked down, Pantu could only stare at how thick and long he was. It was also a lighter brown color than the rest of his body. Pantu looked confused.

"Pantu, you don't have to..." He started.

Pantu ignored him and wrapped both hands around his member. He switched between moaning and growling as Pantu slowly went from tip to base.

"So *big!*" Pantu moaned. "*How would it ever fit?*" Pantu quietly thought out loud.

He exploded out the tip of his member, and he felt Pantu quiver at the sight while Pantu's member squirted as well. They were both spent after pleasing each other. Their breaths were heavy and their hearts racing as they looked into each other's eyes. Pantu smiled sleepily and moved closer to him. Even after all the work they put in, neither were sweating as Pantu's body kept his Heat from increasing.

Pantu still had both hands around his satisfied, limp member, and he was still gripping Pantu's bottom with one hand but moved the other from his Dumpling's member to clean them up.

"You don't have to hold it. It's not going anywhere," he whispered.

"Hmph!" Pantu pouted at the comment of letting go of what he now claimed as his, before closing his eyes and resting on his arm, moving closer to fall asleep on his chest.

Pantu was wrapped in his arms and his warm member wrapped in cool hands. Pantu refused to let go and he smiled but didn't push. He could never deny the pout which made him weak.

And he calls me stubborn? He chuckled as he closed his eyes and fell into their Shared Space.

DRUM: LEFT BEHIND
WEEK FOUR: SATURDAY

Drum and Sport were up at o'four-thirty sr (star-rise). He took down the Barrier after cleaning them up from their Shared Space and bringing back Pantu's clothes, along with his own sweatpants. He opened a Portal for him and Sport.

Pantu held on to his member the whole night and when Pantu sleepily pleaded, "Five more minutes!", he immediately gave in.

He looked at Sport apologetically and held up his hand, indicating five and Sport nodded, before stepping through the Portal.

He replaced the Barrier to whisper, *"Dumpling, he's hard."*

Which made Pantu wiggle against his body and whine.

He bit his lip and moved his closer while removing his pants and Pantu's clothes. He held on to his Dumpling's member and while he stroked the top, he rubbed his own member against the vein on the underside of Pantu's.

The leaking of pre-come made his body shudder. He was trying to wait until Pantu came first but between the wiggling, moaning, the feel of Pantu's butt, and the coolness made him release. He tried to hold in his response as Pantu sleepily whimpered and came, but what came out of him was a weird, deep growl.

"Four minutes left," he teased a sleeping Pantu, who only smiled and snuggled closer to feel his Heat.

"Okay. Why are you getting up so early?" Pantu asked.

"Exercise and training. I've done it every day since I was six," he informed Pantu.

"Okay. Are you coming back to me?" Pantu asked.

"Always," he said, softly.

"Ah. Okay," Pantu said, stretching and rolling over to snuggle his butt close to his member, which jumped in excitement as it settled between Pantu's cheeks.

He just held on, praying to the Universe for restraint. *He's going to make me go back on my Promise,* he thought as he fought the urge his member was giving to just put the tip in.

It was the longest four minutes of his life as he held a soft body in his hands. He closed his eyes and caressed every part of Pantu.

He knew Pantu's body from memory, but he was exploring which parts of Pantu's body were the most sensitive. He wanted to know exactly where to touch, lick or kiss to elicit certain responses from Pantu.

When his alarm went off signaling the five minutes were up, he reluctantly replaced their missing clothes. Kissing Pantu's neck and behind his ear, he squeezed his bottom one more time before covering Pantu back up with the blanket and removing the Barrier. He disappeared through the Portal.

After a few hours, they stepped out of a Portal back into the attic. He didn't want to be disrespectful and just Portal anywhere in Pantu's parents' house. He was contemplating opening the Portal on the steps, but Sport told him Queen said they would be coming from the attic later than everyone else.

They were already showered and changed when they came back, so they walked downstairs. He immediately looked at Pantu, who was sitting on the living room floor with the others, while their parents were all at the dining room table. It was loud as everybody who stayed over was eating breakfast and conversations were mixed.

He smiled at the relaxed atmosphere and sneaking up behind Pantu, he whispered, *"Did you miss me?"*

Pantu yelped in surprise, while everyone around them blushed and laughed.

He felt his Dad's eyes on him as he sat next to Pantu, who left plenty of space for him to get comfortable.

He heard his Mom whisper for his Dad to *"leave it be"* and he smiled with love for her.

He knew his Dad was uptight when it came to their businesses and the Beings' side of things but always deferred to his Mom and followed her rules unconditionally, so he knew his Dad let it go, for now.

Queen looked at him. "Are you wearing that to the mall?" Queen asked, with Energies that clearly said, 'change your clothes'.

"I guess not, since I didn't know that's where we were going today," he said, with a smile.

His red sweats and long-sleeved, light pink shirt with white socks and slides would embarrass Queen, who would keep plenty of distance between them as to not be associated with the style.

He noticed Pantu was wearing a thin, light yellow, long-sleeved, half shirt with a soft, skin-tight, white tee underneath along with deep brown, baggy pants. Pantu looked enticing and he smiled and winked at Queen, who he knew picked out Pantu's clothes. He took a look at what everybody was wearing and looked at Sport confused.

"It's V.I.B Day at Makis Ridge's upscale shopping center," Sport told him.

"They only hold it once every six months!" Win said, excitedly. "Only those with V.I.B status cards can shop today, unbothered, no cameras, and no crowds!" Win added, bouncing up and down from excitement.

"Mrs. K and Mrs. Sky are going with us while the rest of our parents figure out what to do about last night," Queen informed him with a look.

Drum nodded and he and Queen stood up, but Pantu's hand on his arm stopped him. He looked gently at Pantu.

"I'm just going to change. I'll be right back," he said, as Pantu looked embarrassed to be holding on to him.

He smiled, feeling just as elated as he did when Pantu stepped in front of him to protect him last night.

They went upstairs and once the attic door was closed; Queen's Energies became frantic.

"Do you know how worried I was about you all! My heart was beating so fast, it was in overdrive! I was praying to the Universe everybody would come back without a scratch, or I would have gone nuclear!"

Queen was rushing to get everything out and he could see his best friend's Energies shaking Queen's nerves, which finally snapped after holding it in for so long. Although he couldn't see his best friend's eyes, he could see the tears, and Queen's body was shaking, which made him look down at the ground.

"I'm sorry Panya. I wasn't sure how it would go since I didn't know how many there were. It's harder for me to sense humans, since their Energy is non-existent and I could really care less about them." He shrugged. "I didn't want to endanger you or Win," he explained.

"BUT ENDANGERING YOURSELF AND SPORT IS OKAY!?" Queen shouted, his nerves made him unable to control his emotions or Energies. Queen never snapped on him before, but he assumed the prospect of losing two best friends made Queen irrational.

He could only look like a chastened child, unable to look at his best friend's trembling Energies. *"Sport can hold his own,"* he said, quietly.

"SUPPADE SANTIAGO, IF YOU EVER LEAVE ME AND WIN LIKE THAT AGAIN, I WILL SLAP THE HEAT OUT OF YOU!" Queen shouted at him, finally reaching a breaking point to allow the tears to fall. *"If you go, we all go. If you die, we all die. You are more to me than just Young Master. Why can't you see that?"* Queen softly told him.

He felt like whale shit falling slowly to the ocean floor. He nodded, tears falling out of his own eyes. He'd hurt his best friend, scared Queen and there was no one to blame but himself.

"I'm so sorry Panya. I will never do that again, but you have to give me your word, whatever you see or learn about me, won't change your feelings for me. I couldn't live without you by my side. I know that. I feel that. So please don't hate me." He asked so sincerely, Queen almost hugged him.

"It's not like you kill Beings or anything," Queen said, slightly laughing and wiping the tears away.

When he didn't respond, Queen looked up at his face, his best friend's Energies held shock at what he didn't say and his sad expression.

"I give you, my word!" Queen said.

He sadly nodded; making several outfits appear on the bedding he and Pantu used with just a wave of his hand. Queen picked out dark blue, slack, jean pants, with a collared, button-down, long-sleeved, white dress shirt. He put on a blue tee underneath. He switched into his clothes while Queen went to fix his make-up.

After Materializing fresh socks and Producing a new pair of shoes, he smiled, looking down at his fresh kicks. He placed moisturizer in his hair before using a pick to detangle his curls. Making sure to spray a little seduction-blocking cologne, he felt and looked good, leaving his shirts untucked.

They went back downstairs, and everybody turned to look at them, having heard Queen yell at him. Queen showed no signs of remorse, and he looked like he was right to be yelled at.

"He has some pretty damn good best friends!" His Dad's booming voice sounded throughout the house.

Queen was trying to hold back joy at being praised by his Dad, but couldn't, which made everyone laugh and the mood became easy-going again.

DRUM: SPOILING HIS DUMPLING
WEEK FOUR: SATURDAY

They didn't Portal directly to the mall, but instead he drove everyone in a large passenger van. Pantu was amazed when he stepped inside. It was spacious and luxurious, with soft, cushioned, cream-colored seats, a mini refreshment bar, a bathroom and several T.V.'s set up for gaming and streaming.

When he sat in the driver's seat, Pantu came and joined him in the front passenger seat. It was just a seat right behind the driver, with enough room where they could communicate and Pantu could see where they were going.

"Are they going to let in my Ma and me? We are not V.I.B," Pantu asked him.

"You're with me, so yes," he said, smiling as he took off and headed out of Sunset Town after getting the shout, "Seatbelts!".

Pantu's head leaned on the top of the headrest and his arms were wrapped around his neck. Pantu's hands rested on his chest, and he sighed, happy.

"How far is it?" Pantu asked, making conversation.

"It's in Makis Ridge several hours away, so we're going to Portal once we get out of town," he replied, enjoying Pantu's lazy way of touching him.

"Why wait until we are out of town?" Pantu asked, curiously.

"Because I would like to confuse the snakes following us," he said, nonchalantly.

Pantu perked up at the mention of snakes. "Wait! What?" Pantu asked, confounded.

"Dumpling, you were right when you said you felt someone watching you. It was him. He's been in your home, your room. I killed several of his snakes the first time I went to your home. I'm sure he has a clear view of your window as well," he told a shocked and upset Pantu.

"WHY DID YOU NOT TELL ME THEN?" Pantu asked, indignantly.

"Would you have completely believed me *then* if I told you there were Beings able to control Energy snakes?" he asked calmly, and with a knowing smile.

Pantu pouted and he felt it, in his pants.

"*We never knew he had a Form before you told us, Dumpling,*" he softly added. "He's registered as disabled, meaning he said he doesn't have a Form."

"Form?" Pantu asked, completely over the fact the first year violated his privacy.

"Yes. Almost every Being has a Form they can release. We cover our human bodies with Energy, which is called Energy Forms, or you can turn your physical body into your Form. Either way, it makes us even more powerful. And it's seen as a threat to some Beings if your Form is...unique.

"Energy Forms are seen as an immediate threat to the humans who have populated the majority of this planet. They don't understand and they don't try to. For a Being able to change into a Physical Form, it's worse. If humans find out you can, then we're either killed, collected or used for their amusement, since they see themselves as the highest life form on this planet," he stated.

A bewildered Pantu understood what he meant. They made it through his white Personal Portal, closing it behind them right before the snakes could slither through. He parked close to the main entrance in a private parking spot reserved for The Santiago Family.

"You have your own parking space, in a whole different city?" Pantu asked him.

"Uh huh," was all he said with a smile.

At the doors of the mall, they were greeted by staff bowing in respect. He smiled and nodded his head in response, but he could tell it made Pantu uncomfortable.

With a quick look to his Mom, she politely asked for an undisturbed shopping trip, and they would inform someone when they needed help. She was handed a small, royal-blue box with a button to push to call for assistance.

They entered the mall, and he noticed Pantu held on to and walked with Dill. Pantu refused to meet his eyes, so he nodded in respect of Pantu's decision and walked with Sport. They talked about the upcoming games at school and planet wide.

They were making plans to go to the next championship game together with the best seats in the house, since sport announcers were slating this to be an injured Jeffer's return game. When they walked into a skincare store, he and Sport hung back while his Mom and Mrs. Sky walked off to shop.

Queen and Win pulled Pantu and Dill with them. He pressed his lips together in a suppressed smile at Pantu's lost look while being dragged deeper into the store. Queen and Win started talking with an employee.

Sport shook his head. "Pantu's a goner. No one should ever show Queen they don't have any Starscreen."

He laughed. "I remember being six and Queen bringing me here to buy everything I would need to keep my skin to the level of his viewing pleasure." Sport laughed at his comment.

He walked into the store, lazily looking around while picking up items to buy. Dill returned to Sport's side and stayed by the entrance talking, occasionally glancing to see if anyone needed help carrying anything. He casually walked closer as Queen and Win were explaining Pantu's lack of skincare items.

"Pantu needs everything from scratch," he heard Win start off saying.

"Yes! And Starscreen, plenty of Starscreen!" Queen added, touching Pantu's soft baby face.

"HUH?! What is Starscreen?" Pantu asked to the amusement of the employee.

"It protects your skin against the harsh rays of that big hot star in the sky," Win told Pantu.

"And helps to prevent wrinkles before you're old," Queen interjected.

Pantu's hands went to his face. "I have wrinkles?!" Pantu asked, horrified at the thought.

"Nope, you have baby soft skin," Win said to Pantu.

"So, let's keep it that way, as long as possible," Queen added.

"It also helps protect against human skin cancer," the employee said.

"I agree with Queen on this; I need a lot of that!" Pantu agreed by nodding enthusiastically.

He smiled at the exchange between his best friends and the man he was already head over heels for. Once everyone was at the checkout counter, he came and placed some items on the counter as well.

The employee rang the items up and placed them in separate bags for each customer. Once she was finished, Queen presented a loyalty card to be scanned while he placed his phone to the black payment box, and they all heard a ding of a completed transaction.

Pantu looked lost as everybody, his Ma included, grabbed their bags, and turned to leave the store. He paused, watching Pantu have an internal struggle on whether to take the bag.

"Pantu, your bag," he said gently, but Pantu just gave him a lost look.

The employee was confused as well. "Excuse me, did I do something wrong?" she asked, looking at Pantu's face.

Pantu looked at her so lost and confused; her Energy started to blush.

Dill was there with an arm around Pantu's shoulder. "Listen, the transaction is complete, take your items or you'll have wrinkles before your twenty-second birthday," Dill said, joking.

Pantu looked at Dill while avoiding his eyes, before bowing politely to the cashier, thanking her.

She looked stunned and quickly came from around the register to bow deeply to Pantu. "Thank you for shopping with us. Your business is greatly appreciated," she said, before rising from her bow. She took a quick glance at him, and he nodded before she moved back behind the register.

This only confused Pantu more.

Dill whispered to Pantu, *"Are you going to lose this too?"* Dill asked, prodding Pantu to snatch the bag.

Pantu held the bag close, thanking the employee again, this time without bowing and quickly turned to walk out of the store.

PANTU: A CONFUSING AND STUBBORN DUMPLING
WEEK FOUR: SATURDAY

The next place they entered was a shoe store. Pantu stayed away from everybody other than Dill, who clung to his side. His Ma and Mrs. K immediately went to start checking out all the shoes and it made him smile.

His Ma's high-pitched voice while looking at all the assorted styles, brands and colors of shoes reminded him of the innocence they still held about the planet outside of The City.

He, on the other hand, was only casually looking. He wasn't planning on trying or buying anything, so he walked slowly, listening to Dill talk about the unique styles.

"What's your favorite color?" Drum asked from behind him.

He jumped. "Is there really any reason for you to know?" he replied, moving away from Drum.

When he looked back, Drum was again with Queen and Sport, picking out shoes. He blew out his breath and looked back at the different shoes, walking until some caught his eye. He paused and looked at them. He liked the style or at least he thought the style looked nice.

He didn't want to focus on the shoes for too long, so he kept moving, listening to Dill talk and checking out the rest of the other shoes, until another pair caught his eye. He forced himself to keep walking, while ignoring the internal battle he was having.

When his Ma squealed at a pair of pink, pearl heels, he quickly went over to her. His eyebrows went up at the beautiful style of the shoes while they talked fashion choices.

"You should buy these and a plunging neckline dress, preferably in a fuchsia color," he told his Ma, to Mrs. K's small squeal and light hand clapping.

"Why plunging?" his Ma asked, her head tilted, thinking.

"Because your breasts are small, perky and would sit nicely in a dress which shows off the soft curvature of your bosom," he said, shrugging his shoulders.

Everybody but his Ma looked at him in silence. He held no sense of style when it came to himself, but he was deeply knowledgeable when it came to women's fashion.

"Wherever would I wear a dress and heels like this?" his Ma asked him, not caring enough to mention the looks and stares they were getting.

"For a night together with Pa. You should get some sexy panties as well. Ones that do not leave lines but cups your bottom nice and tightly. That way you can also show off your firm, toned butt. Or a dress tight enough where there is no need for panties," he said, nodding and smiling at his Ma, who was deep in thought.

"It's been years since we have enjoyed a night together," his Ma said, thinking.

He noticed the looks crossing everyone else's faces ranged and changed so much, even the employees at the store were having a tough time keeping their faces straight.

Mrs. K ended the silence and dispelled the looks with her words. "Well then, it's settled, these are the shoes for you. I know the perfect place to find the type of dresses Pantu mentioned and sexy lingerie," she said, smiling. "For that option, I would suggest the open toed pearl heels," Mrs. K added, looking at him for approval.

"AH! That would be so enticing. You never show off your slender, well-manicured feet, Ma. Pa would love it!" he agreed.

By now, everyone else was looking around, obviously not understanding the conversation between his Ma and him. Everybody but Dill and Drum was trying to find if anyone else understood the conversation that just transpired. Drum was only looking at him with a smile before appearing next to him, without touching.

"Maybe you should buy a pair as well?" Drum asked with a chuckle.

He turned to Drum with a bored and uninterested look, as if Drum were ignorant of the fact he was about to state. "I have a working penis DRRUMM. Wor-king pe-nis," he said, with a small shake of his head.

Drum's eyebrows shot up while taking a deep breath before turning to walk back towards the group. Queen was quietly laughing, Sport looked embarrassed for him while trying to hold back laughter, while Win looked lost inside his own Mind and not at all interested with any conversation.

Only Dill looked at Drum with furrowed eyebrows and hard eyes. Dill whispered, *"You of ALL Beings should know how well it works. The only one, by the way,"* Dill's arms crossed in defense of him.

Queen's tears were falling from his eyes as he fought off the overwhelming urge to fall out in laughter. Sport jerked his head back, trying to understand this conversation as well and Win still didn't care.

"May-be...Pantu...doesn't...know?" Queen said, between the silent laughter.

"Pantu has a thing about heels," Dill said, to which the rest of the group, except Win, looked at Dill.

Dill shrugged it off. "This is progress," Dill added.

Now the group, minus Win, collectively turned to him trying to picture all the reasons he hated heels.

"Don't bother, you'll never guess," Dill said and grabbed his arm to lead him back off to the men's section of the store.

"Pantu is the only Being ever with the Ability to resist your natural charm," Queen said to Drum, rather loudly while smirking.

"I know. It's annoying, but so satisfying," Drum stated, with a relaxed smile. "I have to work for every little thing!"

When they were ready to check out, everyone who wanted shoes placed their items on the counter. He was the only one with nothing to place. When Drum again paid for the full purchase, he grabbed his Ma by the elbow.

"Do you know how much all the shoes you want cost?" he whispered into her ear. He jerked her back before she could grab her bag and walked off with her in tow.

"PanPan. What the hell is wrong with you?" his Ma asked, her voice laced with a feeling he wasn't used to receiving from her.

He didn't leave the store, just pulled her far enough away to talk without being overheard. *"Ma, Drum brought your shoes!"* he said, quietly to her.

"AH!? That's so kind of him!" his Ma said, a bright smile on her face. "He brought the skin stuff too!"

"I know Ma. We have yet to pay for anything. What would Pa say if he knew *a male* was buying you things?" he scolded her.

"First off, the male isn't trying to get between MY legs. And second, he would be happy to know I'm not destroying our bank account?" she said with a question. *"PanPan...what's really going on?"* she asked, softly.

He turned red from his Ma's implication. "Ma! Just leave the shoes," he told her.

"Third, K and you picked those pearl shoes out for me. Fourth, I haven't had a night together with your Pa since Coin was born. Fifth, if you dance around the truth to me again, I will get angry," she said to him, threatening to put her hands on her hips.

He looked away and took a deep breath, blowing it out, but he knew better than to turn this into a mental debate with his Ma. "Fine, do whatever you want," he said to her.

He turned and walked out of the store, lost inside his own head, he didn't stop until he was outside. He found a bench to sit on away from the entrance and placed his bag next to him. He dropped his head into his hands and closed his eyes. He didn't want to think.

PANTUxSPORT: BRASH WORDS
WEEK FOUR: SATURDAY

Dill was next to Pantu. "Whoa PanPan. You alright?"

"No Dill. I am not okay," he said, his voice still soft but laced with unhappiness.

"Oh. Is it because Drum is paying for everything?" Dill understood why he was feeling this way, even if he couldn't put a name to it.

He turned to look at Dill. "So, you knew?" he said, wondering why his best friend didn't inform him of this before even leaving the house. If he knew, he wouldn't have come along.

"Everybody except you and possibly Ma Sky," Dill said, with a shrug. "Whenever anyone goes somewhere with Drum, he pays for everything."

"But why would he pay for everybody's stuff?" he asked, unsure of exactly why he was having these feelings.

"Are you upset he's paying for everybody or that he's paying for you?" Dill asked. "Maybe he didn't want you to feel weird about him only paying for you, your Ma's, and his Mom's items. Maybe he's also thanking his best friends.

"I don't know, but what I do know is I don't have enough money to buy anything in this center today, so I'm happy to be getting some free stuff, courtesy of my best friend," Dill said, with a smile and small nudge.

"It is not funny Dill" he said.

"Wait, so you're both mad and upset a guy who likes you is also spoiling you?" Dill looked like he could accept the explanation, but he knew his best friend was leading to something.

"I can buy my own stuff," he said, knowing he held his own money, in his account from his parents, although he hadn't checked it, ever. He also understood Dill was using the word in The City sense. To be "mad" where he comes from meant to be turned on. He didn't bother denying his Ma's or Dill's implications.

"Have you? Have you brought anything you would need to live in one place for longer than a few days? You have been here for how long? Yet your room still looks like you could run at any moment.

"And I know I'm going to sound like an ass but it's not like Drum can't afford it," Dill said. "Drum's Father is the wealthiest man on the planet. Drum works directly under him, so he has his own money," Dill added.

He turned to stare hard at Dill. "Say that again."

Dill rewound the conversation back. "Drum has his own—?"

But he cut Dill off. "Further back."

"Drum works under—"

He cut Dill off again. "Further back."

Dill looked at him. "Mr. Caleb is the wealthiest man on the planet?" Dill asked, hoping he didn't have to go back further.

His wide-eyed stare at Dill became even harder. "You mean to tell me; I asked the son of the wealthiest man on the planet to spoil me?" he asked as his breathing became unstable.

"It was in your Dreams Pantu. Calm down," Dill said, rubbing his back.

"Not just in my dreams Dill. I asked him yesterday. In...person. I asked...him...to Vow." He was now standing up to help with the hyperventilation he was experiencing.

"Wait, what?!" Dill asked, standing up with him and trying to help calm him down.

"I...was...going...to...tell...you...but...kid...nap...per." He lifted his arms up and lowered them, trying to catch his breath but he felt like he was suffocating.

"Do you know what it feels like, when a Being can't keep their Promise?" Sport's voice came out of nowhere. He looked at Pantu with disappointment and regulated Pantu's breathing.

"What!" Pantu said, looking over his body.

"I placed a Barrier inside your lungs to help regulate your breathing," he stated.

"When did you get here?" Pantu asked. "And you can do something like that?" Pantu added, looking at him, confused.

"Yea, I can, and I've been here. Did you honestly think you were just going to walk off, and nobody was going to protect you? I was outside before you even made it halfway to the main doors," he informed a bewildered Pantu.

"I did not see you?" Pantu said, looking around.

"You weren't paying attention, so no, you wouldn't have seen me," he calmly said. "Here's a heads-up Pantu, stop asking Drum to make Promises, you, yourself aren't willing to keep. Promises go both ways," he stated, before turning his back to lean against the bench. "If you think this is fun and games, your finicky nature will end up getting him killed," he ended. He felt Pantu staring at his back.

"Let us go back in," Pantu said, pouting at him while grabbing his bag.

He chuckled as Pantu licked his tongue out, being childish, for good measure. He shook his head at Pantu while Dill held back laughter in his cheeks.

"I will let Drum know to make a Portal," he stated, but Pantu was already dragging Dill to the entrance.

"Young Master was right, stubborn," he said, with another chuckle.

PANTU: HURTS TO THE ORB
WEEK FOUR: SATURDAY

They met up with the group, but he dragged Dill to walk behind everybody. When everyone else walked into a clothing store, he stood outside. Dill was about to go in, but noticing he wasn't headed inside, stayed with him.

"You can go. I shall wait here," he said, not looking his best friend in the eyes.

"Yea right. You don't go, I won't," Dill said, and stood beside him.

"Go get your free stuff." He shooed Dill away.

"I told you, it's—" Dill was cut off by Drum's presence.

"Pantu, are you going in?" Drum asked softly.

"No." came his short reply and refusal to look at Drum, who just nodded before entering the store.

"You're an ass Pantu," Dill said to him. "How can you be so sweet to him yesterday but ignore him today?"

They stood in silence until everyone came back out, happily talking. Everyone except Drum, who was quiet and wouldn't meet anyone's eyes.

"Let's stop and get something to eat," Mrs. K said and led them to a restaurant in the center of the mall.

They were escorted to a sectioned off table and he grabbed the chair next to Drum to move it far away, sitting next to Dill. Drum said nothing but also didn't look at him as he moved his chair to the head of the table and sat down.

Mrs. K sat down to the right of Drum with his Ma next to her, followed by Queen and Win all on the same side. Sport sat opposite of Drum at the other end of the table, while he and Dill had the whole left side of Drum to themselves.

Their server came to take drink orders, and she quickly showed a yellow and green badge to Mrs. K and Drum. Mrs. K raised an eyebrow, and the server nodded. Mrs. K smiled but most at the table missed the quick interaction. Only he, Queen and his Ma cared to notice.

"What can I get you to drink?" the server asked him.

"Just water," he answered.

He watched as Drum laced his fingers together and sat with his forehead leaning against them. Drum's head was facing down to the table, and he said nothing as everybody ordered. When it came to Drum, the server went to get his attention.

"Young—," but the server was cut off by Mrs. K ordering for Drum.

"He will have a large, hot, chamomile vanilla chai, with two lemons slices and a side of honey," Mrs. K said, looking at the server with a smile.

"Yes Ma'am. I will be back with your drinks," the server said politely, and with a bow.

By now, everybody was talking about the selections, but he said nothing and didn't bother to open his menu. When the server came back, she served the drinks before taking their orders for their meals.

Mrs. K set up Drum's tea. Measuring and cutting a lemon into small pieces, she added them and the honey. The other lemon was squeezed in as she stirred. Mrs. K placed it, so Drum was inhaling the scent, but he didn't move to drink.

The server started with him again. "And what would you like to order?" she said, with a smile and sweet demeanor.

"Actually, I am okay with just the water," he told her, handing his menu back.

Dill closed and dropped his menu on the table.

"What?" he asked Dill, emotionless.

"Are you really not eating?" Dill asked, turning to look at him.

"Pantu, why aren't you eating? Do you feel alright?" his Ma asked him.

"I am okay," he told them. "I am on a diet, and I ate too much at breakfast," he added, not looking at anyone.

Mrs. K, Queen, Win and Sport all looked at Drum, whose head was still down. If it weren't for the slight movements of Drum's shoulders from breathing, one would think he was a freshly carved statue. Drum said nothing as Dill also declined to eat. Win looked ready to cry, and Sport's menu was back on the table but now Sport's eyes were on him.

"Win," Drum said, reaching under the table to pull out a custom, leather, anime wallet and slid it down the table to him. "Make sure everybody's good," Drum said, before getting up and walking off.

Mrs. K called out, "Suppade!"

Drum stopped but didn't look back. Mrs. K stood up and walked to Drum, grabbing his face to lock eyes. Mrs. K gently asked a question in another language.

"I'm going home," was all Drum said.

Mrs. K spoke softly in what he was now beginning to understand as English, the same language his G-Ma would speak when she didn't want him to know what she was saying.

Drum responded back in English, before he switched to Thaikoriense. "I will put your bags in the van before I leave, and Win can drive everyone back. Let me know when you need a Portal," Drum said, before walking out of the restaurant.

Everyone else still at the table looked directly at him, each with their own opinions written all over their faces. He refused to look at or acknowledge anyone.

"I am living a minimalist life," he said out loud to himself.

"Hmm?" was all Sport said, looking at him with the past brash words written all over Sport's face.

He reluctantly stood and grabbed his skincare bag, going after Drum. Maybe he could find a way to get out of Real Drum's Vow to spoil him.

If I do not want or need anything, how can he be unhappy? He is having an attitude for nothing, he thought to himself as he went to find Drum. When he reached outside, he saw the door to the van closed. He walked in, leaving the door open and stood close by it.

Drum didn't bother to turn around or acknowledge him and continued to put the shopping bags away. When the last bag disappeared into the overhead compartment, he felt Light being used. He knew Drum opened a Portal and was going to walk through it.

"Drum!" His voice made the male freeze. "Are you really unhappy I am on a diet?" he asked.

Drum said nothing but after taking a breath, moved closer to the Portal.

"DRUM!" he shouted, coming fully into the van. "*Wait...please?*" he asked quietly. "*I am okay with not getting anything. And I am on a diet, but I gained so much weight, and there are no diet pills here or anywhere nearby, so I cannot keep eating,*" he whispered.

He looked at Drum's back and went to touch him but lowered his hand. Drum's hands went into his pockets but still didn't move to look at him.

"You are upset I do not want anything?" he asked, pouting.

"*Pantu,*" Drum finally said, barely above a whisper.

"What? Am I not Dumpling anymore?" he asked, with an unhappy voice.

Drum lowered his head. "*It hurts!*"

He couldn't see Drum's face and could barely hear him.

"What hurts?" he asked.

Drum didn't want to face him. Every time he tried to catch those honey-green eyes, he would be denied, and he was trying not to turn it into a small game, but the jerking of his lips to stop his smile felt unknown to him. When Drum spoke, the tone of the words used made him pause.

"It hurts, Pantu. When you're willing to touch me in front of my parents, but ignore me in front of strangers," Drum started, but as much as Drum tried to mask it, he could hear how deep the pain ran.

"It hurts when I talk to you, and you stare daggers at me as if you hate me. It hurts when I want to spoil you, but you won't let me. I feel it, Pantu. When you really want something but deny yourself, I feel your sadness," Drum softly said.

"I'm not upset Pantu, I'm hurt," Drum added. Turning to face him, Drum's eyes were leaving streaks of tears down his handsome face. It was a scene he never imagined he would see.

"You do not have—" he started but was completely caught off guard by Drum's demeanor. He felt no feelings from Drum, not even Drum's heat. He realized Drum was holding everything inside, not to share the pain he was experiencing which was enough to make tears fall.

Drum shook his head, and with a wavering voice, tried to explain, "We aren't fickle like humans Pantu. We can't decide to not hold to the Promises we make, nor can we take back what's been Promised." Drum doubled over in pain, his fist slamming into his chest. He could only stare since he was at a loss for words at the sight which was making his Light stab his heart.

"It feels like a knife twisting through my Core," Drum said.

He went to Drum, wrapping his arms around Drum's shoulders. "I will let you spoil me!" he said, now crying. "I Vow," he added.

Drum immediately pulled out of his arms to stand back from him. *"You don't need to Promise me Pantu!"* Drum said, his tone was low and soft.

"Why is it fine for you to make Vows, but I cannot?" he asked. He was unhappy. He couldn't feel anything from Drum or himself. His Light stopped stabbing him and went silent, making him wonder if his own Light was unhappy and unresponsive because of the way he was treating Drum.

"Because it's too much like putting a collar back on you," Drum said, touching his neck. Drum's fingers lightly trailed down to his collarbone, making his skin tingly and his Light sing as it flowed.

"I want you to choose. It's your choice if you don't want me to spoil or touch you," Drum said, dropping his hand.

"But it is hurting you!" he cried out.

"It's your choice whether or not it stops," Drum said, gently.

"But I made a Vow, why does it not stop hurting?" he asked, looking all over Drum's body. He wanted to turn on his True Vision but knew he couldn't without getting into trouble with his parents.

"It doesn't work like that. A Promise is only held if you are asked," Drum informed him.

"Then ask me!" he pleaded, slightly bouncing, hoping for a Vow. It would make things a lot easier for him if he was forced to hold to a Vow, rather than figuring this out on his own.

"Dumpling," Drum said softly. "I won't ask you to Promise me, not for something like this," Drum said. "If you don't want anything, then there's no reason for me to be here," Drum added, and turned to leave.

He grabbed Drum's arm. "Let me show you," he started. "If you will not ask me to Vow, then let my actions speak for me," he said to Drum, who said nothing, only closed his eyes to take a deep breath.

"Please!" He pouted, knowing Drum would give in.

Drum nodded and turned back towards him, making him smile brightly. But his smile was quickly lost as Drum shared his heat...and the pain, which was sharp and piercing. He shuddered, trying to accept the pain which he caused, but the tears wouldn't stop flowing, and his breaths were broken into unrhythmic gasps. He lived his whole life with humans and their fickle personality trait; it was why Drum never asked him to Vow.

He guessed Drum knew he wouldn't be able to take the pain that came along with having a fickle personality. Humans didn't have the same consequences Others, or Beings, experienced when it came to Vowing or Lying. Still holding on to Drum's arm and finally being able to wipe his tears, Drum let him lead them out, but not before he grabbed his bag with all his skincare items in it.

"Do you want me to put it away for you?" Drum asked, but he shook his head and clutched the bag tighter and closer to his chest. Drum weakly smiled at him and waved a hand.

PANTUxSKY: A POINT TUTORIAL
WEEK FOUR: SATURDAY

Pantu walked forward in the van and his eyes widened as a small gasp slipped out of his mouth when they appeared in the restaurant right by their table.

"Ah!" he said with a start. Using Portals still surprised him, but he didn't let go of Drum's arm as he moved his chair closer to the head of the table.

Once they were seated, Drum raised his hand, and the server came back.

Starting again with him, the server looked unsure of whether she should ask before she just went for it. "Would you like to order?"

He nodded. "But I will need a moment to look over the menu," he said, with a smile.

As he was busy pointing and ordering items, Dill moved closer to him so Win could move to their side of the table. Everybody finally chose what they wanted, with Drum requesting two orders of Lobster, Lamb, Field Hen, and Vegetable dumplings, one steamed and the other fried. Drum and his Ma also ordered kimchi and seaweed sides.

"You really like dumplings, huh?" he said, with a small smile.

Drum nodded weakly and smiled back.

"Zay, sweetie, what's wrong?" Mrs. K asked, as she rubbed Drum's back. "You don't look good. Are you sick?" she asked.

Drum answered his Ma in English.

Their food came and while eating, they shared amongst each other, as Queen started up a conversation.

"Hey Pantu, you didn't see any shoes you liked?" Queen asked, smiling at him.

He looked at Drum out the corners of his eyes but quickly looked away.

"There were a couple of shoes that looked nice," he responded, not catching anyone's eyes or their smirks.

"Oh! Because you have those shoes, in your size, already paid for," Queen said, smiling brighter as he leaned his chin on a fist.

He looked at Queen and back at Drum, who ordered more dumplings. He slid a dumpling off Drum's plate and started eating it, while Drum avoided his own Ma's eyes.

Turning to meet Queen's eyes, he plainly stated, "By now you should know there is no need to butter me up." He smiled at Queen's gracefully fake, O-shaped mouth and wide-eyed face.

"Does this mean…we're friends?" Queen asked, with glee.

"Go ahead and ask," he said.

Drum just shook his head.

"You do know anyone can wear heels, right?" Queen asked.

His expression as he thought about it lasted for a minute. "Now I do," he stated, accepting the details of the many different outfits he saw Liberal Arts students wear, versus the uniforms the Advanced Honor students wore. This was the most colorful and outrageous dream he never remembered having, but it was feeling like anything he dreamed could happen.

Sky

Sky looked at Pantu inquisitively, wondering how much he told them. Her child never mentioned what really happened to him during his years as a pet and she never asked. He also never talked about the laws of The City with anyone, even in the years after they left.

She knew Pantu never opened up to any other doctors before Doctor Robin or made any actual friends before Dill. She would see Pantu keep to himself, not talking or interacting with anyone.

She smiled. This town and the Beings in it were already a miracle to her family. Her child was talking to them again, making friends and speaking openly about his place of birth.

She never thought she would ever see this day. She blamed herself for her son getting collared. She blamed herself for not doing enough to stop what happened to make them run for their lives, even though she still didn't have a clue why they needed to run.

But here, Pantu was expressing his emotions and making his own choices. Even though she knew Pantu would always sneak into the kitchen as a child, she never saw him openly walk into a kitchen around other people before. She was praying to the Universe Pantu would find peace to make his own decisions, about life and about love.

"Well, is there a reason why you don't like heels?" Queen asked Pantu. "I've racked my brain since the shoe store and for the life of me, everything I think of, doesn't come close to what I assumed happened," Queen stated, breathless.

Pantu looked wide-eyed at Drum before taking a deep breath to blow out. She said nothing and only watched out of the corners of her eyes. She could see the connection between Pantu and Drum went farther than friends, hell even best friends. Although she knew who Drum was to Pantu, it seemed her child was being playful and was either ignoring the signs or fighting against his Fate.

"I am okay around heels…now," Pantu whined at Queen, pouting and looking completely innocent.

She couldn't help the small smile which graced her lips as Drum looked away and closed his eyes, a slight smile on his face, which he openly showed everyone.

Queen blushed at Pantu's innocent face and quickly looked away to gather himself. She said nothing but smiled knowingly.

"Fine!" Pantu said. "There are ways to increase your points as a pet," Pantu started, to her horror.

"PANTU! How much have you told them?" She gasped.

She knew what pets were made to do. She knew from her Husband. She never owned a pet, but seeing how women in The Center treated their pets, just for show, made her sick to her stomach.

The trauma her Husband suffered was enough to make her want to kill every woman who ever owned a pet. It was what she and her Husband fled from, hiding in The Slums.

Meanwhile, the treatment of pets sharply declined after they left The Center. She realized just how open Pantu was with the young men sitting around the table. Whatever he told them wasn't enough for them to stop being his friends or protecting him.

Pantu looked at his Ma and continued, "There are a lot of ways to increase your points as a pet. The most unpopular way was mental debates. If you lost the debate, you lost major points, and it did not take long for me to be the top debater.

"Another way is to style an owner or trainer for a major event, no need to be your own. The person styled would give extra points if they received a certain number of compliments, or based on the type of compliments, larger bonuses would be given. If you fucked that up, you lose points. The most fashionable way was to offer yourself up as a bid," he explained.

"What does it mean to bid yourself?" Win asked.

He answered, "You are placed on a stage and the women bid on you. Unless you are in final training, then women and trainers bid on you. They offer up point amounts and the one who offers up the highest amount wins. Then you spend time with whomever won," he stated, with no reserve.

He'd become used to the feelings which dug deep inside his stomach and would dig deeper every time he would tell them about his past. He wasn't sure if they would stop talking to him and he didn't know if what he would say would be what drives Drum away.

But the more he told them, the less he felt the digging sensation. They never held looks of superiority on their faces, only listened to the experiences he lived through, so those feelings of digging became fleeting moments.

"Have you ever bid yourself out?" Sport asked.

He shook his head. "But my owner would," he told them. "She was already the top owner before I even started my second level of training. The margin greatly increased her lead by bidding me out," he said, feeling a moment of digging. He knew they would be able to read between the lines, especially Queen.

"*You don't have an owner anymore Pantu,*" Drum said softly.

"Right. I am no longer collared," he agreed, while reminding himself that in any dream he would have, he would never be happy wearing a collar. "I was not placed up for bid much, as the number of points given was the highest recorded. I was also an exclusive pet," he said, with a full smile on his face. He was the best, number one and perfect. Although he was highly unhappy with what he went through, he couldn't help but feel a bit of happiness that he earned and kept his spot.

"But there was one woman, who would outbid most other women, to the point where she became a regular outside of the bidding," he explained.

His Ma interrupted, "Pantu, that's padding the points and against the law," she informed them all.

"And the governess' daughter cared not. We both know she and her family stopped following their own laws generations ago," he said, with a disinterested look and a wave of his hand.

He looked directly at his Ma. "Besides, there were plenty of points she never reported," he added to his Ma's lack of expression. "She would have someone bid outrageously for me with some of the outside points at the next bid," he told everyone.

His Ma placed her head in her hands while Mrs. K rubbed her back, and he felt the console of one Ma to another. He liked the comfort Mrs. K brought to his Ma and he didn't feel any ill intent from Mrs. K when it came to his Ma. It made him smile a little to see his Ma with someone she could trust.

She must have experienced something just as bad to understand how my Ma feels, he thought to himself while sneaking a glance at Drum.

PANTU: LET ME INTRODUCE YOU TO MY NUMBERS
WEEK FOUR: SATURDAY

"I am, of course, the top pet and my numbers are untouchable," he said, with a shrug.

"What *were* your numbers?" Drum asked.

He looked at Drum and smiled. "How about I tell you second place's numbers, and you all try and guess mines?" he asked, teasing Drum.

"Okay! What's the prize for the correct answer?" Drum asked, teasing him back.

He thought for a moment. "I will paint a portrait of the winner," he stated, and everybody but his Ma agreed.

"You're painting again?" his Ma asked him; her eyebrows raised at his offer.

"I...only painted...one...small thing since, but a portrait...would not break me...I think?" he said, thinking about it.

"Too late, you already agreed," Queen said, clearing the air.

He gave a knowing smile, while Dill pretended to exit the conversation, looking around and playing with the small amount of food still left on the plate. His Ma also said nothing as the rules were set. He noticed Drum stared at Dill with a face full of unanswered questions. When Drum turned his eyes away from Dill to look off in thought, he released a quiet breath.

Drum must have realized Dill knows my numbers, which means I have told Dill more than I have told Drum, even in our dreams. Drum's feelings still do not feel Malicious towards Dill, just unsure. He didn't want to pretend like he and his best friend weren't close. He genuinely cared for Dill, and he was racking his Mind trying to figure out how to protect Dill from Drum, who was showing some rather particular signs when it came to his best friend.

"You can only guess once and you must be within a five-point range, either way," he stated, happy his brain was able to help him move the conversation along. The Four and Mrs. K all agreed, while thinking of numbers.

"Do we get hints if we get close? Like hot, lukewarm, or cold?" Sport asked.

"Ah! That would make the game more interesting?" he stated. Thinking for a moment, he added, "Deal, but only if you all tell me one crazy fact about yourself before you answer."

"Sounds fair and makes sense," Queen agreed for all those playing.

"Okay…well, second place points, when I left, was at…" he paused, looking at everybody's faces of anticipation, "five hundred and sixty thousand points," he ended with a smirk.

"So what? You were in the millions!?" Win exclaimed.

"Wait, so you were the only pet whose family could live in The Center?" Sport asked, with a slacked face and raised eyebrow.

"The closest number two could live would be The Inner Ring!" Win exclaimed. "Holy shit Pantu!"

His face showed his unhappiness, mostly at the stupidity and greed of the owners and some pets. "Owners would often push their pets to challenge me, hoping they would gain prestige for defeating me, along with the points I would have lost.

"It would have increased the pet's standing and made the owner more popular, while I would lose points and demon spawn would lose face. But so many lost major points and were moved to The Outer Ring, even pets in the top forties.

"Some lost everything and were sent back to The Slums to start over. Tracey and his owner were a constant thorn in my side until I ultimately destroyed his owner, leaving them with nothing. So, Tracey decided to become one of the Cloaked to earn a living for them."

No one said anything, just silent stares towards him. He could feel the same feelings his G-Pas would have when he completed a painting, finished reading a book, or his herb harvest was plentiful.

His G-Pas would tell him they were proud of him and the happy feelings from them felt pleasing. He was exactly what he said he was, the most celebrated pet, the most exclusive and the only one whose family could live in The Center, even without their already given status.

Everyone realized they were staring when he lowered his head and started rubbing his arms, feeling too much pressure from the Beings sitting around him. They each looked away, their faces red while they started thinking and planning together what numbers they would say to get as close to the answer as they could.

Drum said nothing but the look on Drum's face softened, and a small smile was added. He was taught to be resilient, but his Ma and Dill knew he went through a lot worse than what he was carefully telling everyone else.

He was wondering why Drum's best friends still liked him, even after what he already told them. He knew they understood what he left out, so why not dislike him? Why not use the things he told them to dissuade Drum from even talking to him, much less, liking him.

They accepted him, even though they didn't know everything he needed to do to survive. He knew one day it would come out, but he was hoping it would come out later rather than sooner but mostly, he was praying he never needed to bring it up.

He knew his Ma caught on to there being something more than a friendship between him and Drum. Even after last night, his Ma still said nothing about his interactions with Drum.

Since it was her family's story which was taught to every pet in The City as a warning, he wanted to know how she truly felt about male relationships.

Last night he didn't care enough to try and hide it from her, or his Pa. He was also in such an alarmed state, maybe his Ma mistook Drum for his comfort person since Dill wasn't around. But his Ma was now best friends with Drum's Ma, and he didn't know how much his Ma told Mrs. K about The City, so he knew to be careful with his words.

Sport went first. "Crazy fact about me...I don't want to play professional sports after I graduate," he stated to everybody, but Drum, looks of rapid unanswered questions. Queen and Win looked at Sport like they were just now seeing their best friend's True Face after all these years of best friendship.

"WHAT ARE YOU GOING TO DO AFTER YOU GRADUATE?" Win said, rather loudly and with a high-pitched tone.

"So, I get to guess, right?" Sport said directly to him, ignoring both Queen and Win.

He nodded while trying not to laugh at Win's face.

"One hundred million points," Sport started out with.

"Why so cold, Sport?" His response to Sport's number made everybody but his Ma and Dill freeze while staring at him again. His Ma and Dill just shook their heads in disappointment, making everyone go back to thinking.

"It is a lukewarm, hot, cold, cold though?" he added, remembering the rules and wanting to help.

Everybody except three Beings went back to discussing numbers. He looked at Drum who was listening to Mrs. K but not answering any of her questions. Drum's eyes were on him.

"Let me try!" Mrs. K said. "Something weird about me is...whenever Drum leaves for the weekend," she paused before continuing, "there is a camp-out party in your bed with snacks and a martial arts movies marathon," she quickly finished, while turning her head away from Drum's reaction.

"*Say what now?*" Drum asked softly, folding his hands together while looking at Mrs. K.

"So, I'm going to guess two hundred billion points!" Mrs. K said, smiling brightly at him while ignoring her son's reaction of polite, silent laughter.

His eyebrows went up at Mrs. K's guess. "You are lukewarm, hot, cold, hot." He smiled.

Win's eyebrows furrowed and he knew Win realized his points may not have been points but instead, money. Win obviously remembered the conversation from last night and when Win looked at Queen, who silently confirmed Win's thoughts with a neutral look, Win looked back down at the table with closed eyes and hard-pressed lips.

"I like to dress up as Bianca B while singing and dancing to her songs," Queen said, ignoring everybody's different looks and continued talking. "My guess is three hundred and fifty billion," Queen stated, looking at him for confirmation.

"Wait! Bianca B is a Woman! Do you dress as a Woman? You can do that here and wear heels?" he asked, and he knew the heat in his cheeks was turning them red at the thought.

Queen looked between his Ma and his expressions, and light laughter flowed out of Queen's mouth. "So how close am I?" Queen asked him.

He stared at Queen for a moment as he tried his hardest to push down his own thoughts and feelings to bury them in the pit already in the bottom of his stomach. "Hmmm...it is a hot, hot drink leaning towards a lukewarm, hot," he carefully said.

"So, it's more than that!?" Win asked as his eyes popped open. "I would've loved to invest your points!" Win said, making his thoughts about the points clear.

He looked at Win, with a smile. He'd already playfully cracked Sport, and he decided to play with Win, to see if Win would crack. "Are you going to guess a number or dream about what should have been?" he asked, much to Win's happy face.

His Ma looked at him. "There's still your trust fund when you graduate. I will speak to your Pa about it, unless you...have other plans?" she carefully asked.

He shook his head. "I have searched for years, but you and Pa are great at hiding things, so I have given up."

"You would let me invest your points?" Win asked, biting the corner of his lip, while his fingers tapped on the table to wait for a response. When he nodded, Win went off inside his own head.

"Oooh! The amount on the returns would have been..." Win trailed off, lost in calculating.

Queen shook his head and waved his hand in front of Win's face. "He's out!"

Sport's face dropped once the realization hit. Queen was unaware of what he did, and Dill looked at Win with a sad face, wondering if Win would make it out, Mind intact. He knew Win would. But what he didn't understand was why he was reacting this way.

In The City he did much worse to keep his status, but here, he didn't want to destroy anyone, he wanted friends. But somewhere inside of him, it was ingrained, he would hold his own.

He would show he wouldn't break easily and can easily break others. He glanced at Drum, who only glanced back with a quick smile before Drum's attention went back to Win. Everyone turned and looked at Drum, who gave them a half smile, making them smile back, except Win, who was still smiling, happily calculating inside his head.

"I guess I will go last," Drum said. "Crazy fact about me, I'm a nineteen-year-old Higher Ed Junior with three bachelor's degrees, two master's and one P.H.D.!" Drum said, complete with a full smile.

He didn't know if he paused or completely froze at Drum's statement, all he could understand was his body wouldn't move, and he couldn't speak. His Mind went back to the student rankings list, now understanding the reason behind the vast number of points Drum possessed.

"I'm going to go with three hundred and eighty-five billion points!" Drum stated, with full satisfaction.

He still said nothing, just stared at Drum, unable to believe what Drum was telling him but not once smelling a Lie. *He would have survived The City, become Minister and taken over as the new Governor, he thought to himself. At nineteen, no doubt, he would have complete control over everybody. Even my Talents would not have compared. Wait, he is only nineteen and a Junior?! I am twenty-one, about to turn twenty-two next month and he is only nineteen? How in the hell does a nineteen-year-old become a Junior with six Higher Ed degrees already under his belt?*

His Mind couldn't function as well as it normally would because Drum was so close to him. Drum disrupted his senses and his calm, cold demeanor which helped him survive The City, by filling him with warmth. He both liked and disliked this about Drum. No one else could ever get him to falter, or to have feelings other than survival.

"Three hundred and eighty-five billion points," Drum stated again.

His mouth finally dropped. "You are only nineteen? And a Junior? In Senior Advanced Honor Classes? The number one student in the whole school? With six degrees already?" he asked Drum, still not believing him.

"Three hundred and eighty-five billion points," was the only thing that came out of Drum's mouth.

"Both Sport and I are Juniors," Queen said to him.

He looked at them, wondering why he couldn't smell any Lies. "But you are taking Senior Level Advanced Honors classes, how could you both be Juniors?"

He realized just how intelligent the Beings outside The City were. He only thought them quick-witted, but how could he possibly dream of multiple people more intelligent than himself? If this was his dream, why did he not feel like the main character?

It was not just the fact three of The Four were only Juniors, but even Win was graduating a year early and at the top of their class, meaning Win was younger than him as well. Drum was only nineteen and already accomplished so much.

He felt like he shouldn't even be sitting at the same table as the young males around him. The only difference between him and Mansnake was he was an unwilling party. He needed to tell himself that in order to keep himself above Mansnake and after the conversation with Kat, he understood himself better. It still didn't help at this moment.

He dropped his head in his hands. *At this point, the son of the wealthiest man on the planet is choosing between a sex slave and a sex worker, and it is not a good look for him. Ah, I should shut up about my life there, it is only making me look worse.* He was so deep in thought; Drum's voice made his butt jump out of his seat.

"Three hundred and eighty-five billion points," Drum said again.

He raised his head. "Ah, yeah. You got it exactly right," he stated, uninterested in the shouts which came from everybody.

PANTU: A BROKEN SPACE
WEEK FOUR: SATURDAY

He was thinking, planning. He needed to rearrange his plan so many times, now even he was confused about where this would end. He was overly confident while living in The City, as his G-Pas taught him how to use his Talents to make himself untouchable, but here, it was different.

Yes, his Charisma worked *but this is a natural reaction to my looks.*

He was able to do much more than Seducing people, but these were not just people, they were Beings. He couldn't respond to them the way he did feeble-minded humans or Light-restricted Others. He didn't want to. He wanted to live together with them and his family.

It was the first time he held to the thought of making a life here and his Light started to flow against itself, crashing inside his Light veins. He knew he wanted his G-Pas here, but he wanted to come back with them knowing someone would have to shoulder the responsibility of six Others escaping The City.

He would have to go back to give up his life to free his family. They would stop looking for his parents and his G-Pas if they had him. He was the reason behind all of this. Because of the one mistake he made, he broke his own family.

The governess' daughter refused to give up on me like her ma gave up on my Pa. He thought he could just live happily and freely, *completely under the radar until I go back.* He most definitely didn't plan on making friends and having all these emotions he wasn't used to feeling.

Whatever happened to having a fake Woman and fake friends to get off the medicine, so I could go back? What happened to keeping my parents at a distance so they would continue to not care about me? He asked his Think Space.

He watched as every plan shattered inside his Mind, making him numb. He was externally and internally unable to scream to release himself from the number of emotions weighing him down. Everything went completely black as all the stars went out inside his Mind.

He sat still in the darkness. As he listened, he could hear all his problems continue to crumble and fall apart in the vast, empty, dark space. The crashing sound as his internal world collapsed on itself was giving him a lobotomy.

*Mental hospital, that is where...*but he couldn't finish what he believed would be his last thought as a light so bright, made his internal self, cover his eyes with his hands.

But it still wasn't enough. He tightly closed his eyes and when the light seemed to settle, he was in the field meadow, with Drum standing in front of him, blocking the starlight.

Drum was watching him as they celebrated getting the correct answer. They were deciding on which clothes Drum should wear and if Queen would teach him how to apply makeup to Drum for the portrait painting.

Drum saw the moment the light went out in him and reached out to gently cover his hand. His face registered the slightest look of happiness, and he quickly looked at Drum to smile. He relaxed and joined the conversation, without speaking.

Drum raised a hand, and it went quiet. "We all worked together to figure out the number. Pantu, what do you think about doing a group portrait to remember today?" Drum asked.

He nodded. "But my Ma and Sir Dill shall be left out, since they did not participate," he said, eyeing the face of Sir Dill, who was trying to hide his expression by looking at Win.

"They didn't say anything, but they told quite a bit," Drum stated, without outing both his Ma and Dill's real contributions.

"Fine. They shall join the festivities," he agreed, after casting a suspicious look at Drum. *See, I am not so stubborn,* he thought, happy at his small win over Drum.

The most difficult of The Four to break would be Drum. Sport went first due to opportunity and whim. Win was harder since Win's Mind wasn't always with them. He needed to wait for the right moment. He was understanding how to break Queen, but there was no way he could set up the perfect situation without alerting Queen. He could wait; there was still over two months until graduation.

"So, is that lady the reason you hated heels?" Sport asked.

He shook his head. "She was tamed compared to the crazy things other women wanted." He continued his story. "There were the women who bid the extra points. She was one of the ones who wanted me instead of money as compensation. She always made me put my penis in a black pleather, fake gem, encrusted boot, with a custom twelve-inch heel and fuck her with it," he spoke.

Queen looked weirdly at him. "That's not that bad, and besides, your member never actually touched her, so..." Queen shrugged.

"Double penetration," he responded back to their looks of what he was hoping was what he felt, disgust.

"And some fake gems fell off in the process," he continued. "Demon spawn knew I hated the dirty-foot demon-whore and would use her as a mental punishment. Something always fell off, every time." He felt sick, his stomach churning from the bile disturbed by his digging.

"She would try and force me to back up her claims of her vagina and ass being worth more money than anyone else at parties. She made my stomach turn and her bone structure was not worth drawing," he said, his nose trying on its own to close up at the stench of the memory. "She wanted me to be passed to her when my own—, the demon spawn Intended Announcement came out," he ended, now with his whole face scrunched up.

Win was now out of his trance. "Intended?"

He looked at Win and smiled. He noticed he was seeing their personalities. Win was so innocent and pure hearted towards those he felt comfortable around. Win's appetite was even bigger than his and they both shared a love of delicious foods. Win could, of course, incite the whole school to rally in support just by being unhappy. He understood Win was behind what happened their first year. He could put that much together.

Sport was a sweetheart, and he was also one hell of a chef. Despite his size, he was never rough with anyone. He was popular as a Talented sports player, but it never seemed important to Sport, who observed more than he spoke. Sport chose to be quiet unless he was around his best friends or it concerned Drum, then he freely spoke his Mind to anyone.

Sometimes pretty brashly, he thought to himself.

Queen was a dreamer but unless one was deemed worthy, you would only see the business side of him. Queen's Mind was filled with unlimited possibilities to explore. He could also tell if you upset Queen, more than your social life would be ruined.

He knew he needed to handle Mansnake quickly and carefully after the second recording. Had Queen heard it before Mansnake was suspended, things would have gone differently for the stupid little idiot, and he felt that.

He only wanted to ruin Mansnake's social standing and to kill the hashtag with the invite request. He was happy Drum let him handle it and Queen understood him. But what he wasn't happy about was Mansnake insinuating Drum was a rapist and said it as if Drum possessed a record of doing this to anybody, Being or human.

He knew there were plenty of opportunities from the Gift to the Manga Room key incident for Drum to take from him, in his dreams and what he was now slowly accepting as reality. He knew Drum's personality was nowhere near how Mansnake imagined, so he deemed Mansnake unworthy of any hashtag related to Drum.

"Intended is closer to the meaning for fiancé, that you use. Marriage is different in The City," he replied.

"Oh! So, you can't own pets once you're married?" Mrs. K asked.

"Not the same pets you owned as a single woman. It's against the law and put in place to keep owners from falling in love with their pets. A woman can't have a child with her pet. The pet would have to kill the child before possibly being killed themselves," his Ma answered. "It's how I and Pantu's Pa were able to get married before his final training!" she added, with a smile.

"What the fuck!" Queen said and he felt the sharpness of Lights from Queen.

"They really made the women carry to term, have the baby, only for the pets to kill...their..." Queen trailed off.

"Most owners were high-born women from The Center and The Inner Ring, and most pets were from The Slums or The Outer Ring. Most males in the Inner Ring or The Center are never pets unless they want to try for the position of Minister or someone in their family upset someone in a more powerful family. So, a low-born male having a child with a high-born woman was seen as tainting the family lineage," his Ma explained.

"So, has any male in your family gone through final training?" Sport asked, glancing quickly at Drum.

"AH!?" He and his Ma both said, before sinking deep into thought.

PANTU: A LUCKY COIN
WEEK FOUR: SATURDAY

He finally looked at his Ma and the expression he received back made him lower his eyes, while his Ma answered.

"Coin. He became a pet at twelve, but his numbers were not the best—" his Ma started to explain, but he abruptly cut her off.

"They were shitty numbers. He was so bad, he could not break the top one hundred, even *if* he had guidance from GMack and GLou!" he said, as he rolled his eyes.

"Who is Coin?" Mrs. K asked.

"He is a child born in The Slums. I and my Husband raised him until he was ten. It was when he decided to leave and try to become a pet," his Ma said, looking down at the table. "He finally became one when he was twelve with the help of my bitch of an egg donor." The look on her face was the same one his Ma would have about someone in The City before he would hear of their death the next day.

Just from his Ma's look, The Four finally understood why he could never relate to Indria as family in front of his parents.

"I quickly surpassed his points and became the number one pet within months of being collared." He gave a slight, uncaring smile and a quick puff of a chuckle. "Pathetic," he added, unmoved by his Ma's look.

"Pantu! Coin made his decision and tried his best!" his Ma said, trying to end the conversation.

"No other male connected to our family ever went through final training. He is a stain on our legacy," he said.

"Well, there is much you are ignorant of when it comes to "family". Besides, do not think you are blameless. No other male in the family has ever done what you—" his Ma cut herself off and gave him the look he knew should shut him up, but he wasn't feeling it today.

"YES!" he said, with fake happiness. "If it were not for me and the terrible mess I made; we would all still be living so happily in The City. In Indria's multi-million Foil mansion. I would be gem-puss' husband and a Pa by now, while you and my own Pa would ignore me like usual!

"There would be no need to run and hide. YOU would be free of me." He leaned forward. "But all that being said, I still would not have to go through final training," he said, an unhappy feeling making his lips curl at his Ma.

Nobody said anything as they let how and what he said to his Ma sink in. The elevated levels of unhappiness were leaking off him, even though he was trying to act nonchalant and uncaring. His Ma took a deep breath to calm down before she excused herself from the table and Mrs. K followed.

"Pantu, that was harsh!" Dill reprimanded.

"Is it?" he asked. "Does not feel harsh enough," he added, trying not to let the tears even form.

Dill looked at him. "Why are you so upset with her? I thought you two were in a good place?" Dill gently asked, while rubbing his back.

"It still makes me so unhappy!" he said, holding back the already formed tears. "It makes me unhappy that she could still protect and vouch for him. After everything he has done, she has always looked the other way whenever I tried to tell her about him. I make one mess, the only one I have ever made, and I am forced to leave while he stays." He closed his eyes.

"He did nothing to stop me from being collared. He just stood there, would not even spare me a glance. His only thoughts were to become Minister and to marry the governess' daughter. He cared not what he had to do to achieve his goal.

"He killed so many people using my status and she never once acknowledged his wrongdoings. Even when GMack and GLou helped me clean up his obvious messes to keep him from being killed, all she would say is he was lucky.

"What makes it hurt harder is my parents would publicly ignore me. Since I was seven, my parents distanced themselves from me, as if they were ashamed of me for becoming a pet. As if I knew what it meant and wanted it.

"He left us in The Slums to become a pet of his own free will, but she never spoke badly about him." By now the tears were falling from his eyes. *I never knew I would cry so much in so little time,* he thought.

Win looked at him. "But he *is* lucky," Win said to his bewildered thoughts expressed on his face.

"He was lucky to have a little brother who still protected him, even though he's a dumbass," Win added.

Now this was a statement he really couldn't believe. "I did not protect him because I liked him," he responded.

"Doesn't matter why you did it, he was just lucky you did," Sport stated to him.

His realization of this gave him another outlook on the Beings sitting around him. He was so grateful his G-Pas stripped Lying out of him. He knew he could never Lie to any of them. They saw between his words, and they listened while retaining everything he told them. He wondered if they could smell Lies.

If they really knew what I could do, would they hate me? Would they think this is forced?

He was so intrigued by the assessment, he realized he didn't ever feel the need to Lie to them, nor had he ever wanted to. He still hadn't told Dill the most important thing about him that he kept hidden safely away.

It was the one thing his G-Pas stressed to be silent about to both Others and humans or he could lose his life. He just needed to be quiet about it until he was able to go back. He was deep in thought when his Ma returned.

Looking slightly apologetic about what she was going to do next, his Ma spoke, *"PanPan"* she whispered. *"I am——"* but she was cut off by a wave of his hand.

"It is fine. Although I pushed, no physical harm was done, displaying great control of oneself. Next time, I will be more considerate of your thoughts and say my words carefully, in order to keep my bones and Mind intact," he apologized. He understood his Ma's tone and knew he was two seconds away from having a broken bone, one which would take longer than normal to heal, his tibia. He also wanted to be careful and not ruin his Ma's friendship.

"Was that an apology?" Sport asked, obviously not satisfied with his flowery words and compliments.

Win shrugged his shoulders. "I wouldn't be alive to make an apology if I said something like that to my Mom, so I don't know?" Win asked himself while looking at Sport with wide eyes.

Drum and Queen were quiet the whole time, and both stared at the table. Queen seemed to be filling in gaps inside his head to get a better picture of his Ma and him, but he didn't know if Queen would understand the customs of The City. He could tell Drum was unhappy with him.

"Even after last night, you would still feel the same way?" Drum asked, turning to look at him. Drum raised an eyebrow at his slight frown and feelings of ignorance he released about no one understanding his lived experiences.

His face softened and he looked away. He didn't know the emotion he was feeling was shame. He never remembered feeling these emotions before as he was well trained within three months of starting his first training. He knew he was unhappy at himself for looking at Drum in such a way.

He never needed to experience being humbled before, he never had to be in The City. But with just one look from Drum, he felt like a regular human. He understood this as he made many a pet and their owner give him the same look. He didn't like the feeling, and he was unhappy Drum was the one giving it to him.

Why is he the only one to get under my skin? I cannot even think clearly around him. I slip up so much that I feel like I have fallen to the two hundreds.

But he also knew Drum wasn't wrong.

I have not seen my Pa with that much resolve ever. He was a kind and loving Pa when we lived in The Slums but turned into a sniveling coward when I became a pet. And it was the first time I remember my Ma standing up for me.

He understood he was so focused on the fact his parents left his G-Pas in The City, he held on to all the feelings he had while living there. He anchored his mentality there to hold on to the connection of his safe place, his G-Pas. Which is why up until the last incident, which ended with them here, he never learned anything about the outside world which was different from his upbringing.

This will not make all the hurt and pain go away. Am I just supposed to forget how they treated me? That they yanked me away after just one mess? They left the only people who loved me unconditionally since the moment I was born. As he meekly ran all these thoughts through his head with no answers, Queen spoke up.

"So, I have decided. I will get the shirt!" Queen said, aloud and completely to himself. Queen looked at Drum. "Can we go back to the clothing store? I have finally made my decision," Queen asked.

Drum smiled and nodded. "I have to make a stop, but I will meet you all there."

KANNIKA: AND YOU WOULD BE?
WEEK FOUR: SATURDAY

She didn't say much to Pantu, who looked perplexed. On their way out of the restaurant, she only observed the young man lost in thought. While she may not understand the customs of The City or even know where on the planet a place like that existed, she could relate to having to do things she didn't want to do. Maybe not to this young man's extreme, but it helped her get a better picture of her Best Friend's life.

Pantu seemed to be talking to himself, shaking his head as they walked to the store. Drum broke off from them and went in a different direction, but Pantu didn't acknowledge he noticed. As Pantu and Dill wandered around the store, the young man was still deep in thought. She walked up to him and led him to an androgynous section of the store.

Without an offer to join them, Dill walked off. Pantu looked at her with a sad smile. She assumed he thought she would mention the previous conversation with his Ma, but she just smiled back. She didn't know enough about their family dynamics to comment, nor was it the reason she wanted to speak to him.

"Way to formally meet your acquaintance," Pantu sadly stated.

"You know…my son asked me for advice about you. Well, he didn't ask directly, he hardly does. It can be quite annoying sometimes, but anyways, Queen arranged for an outing today so I could see the type of Being you are," she said, looking at Pantu's shocked reaction.

"Oh, I heard you could control your emotions unless my son was around?" she asked, not expecting or wanting an answer, but to also express to Pantu, she knew more about him than the young man assumed.

She looked at the shirts and pulled one out, lifting it up to Pantu, she measured by eye. "Hmmm, this color suits your eyes quite nicely," she said, handing the shirt to Pantu to hold as she searched for more clothes.

"Why would he do something like that?" Pantu asked.

"Well, all my son's life he has been called special by most Beings, even his own Father. But there are Beings who spread rumors he was a threat, so at the tender age of six, he started showing everyone he was an asset. He made himself indispensable to the Being Community," she told Pantu, nonchalantly.

She held up another shirt, shook her head, and put it back. "This has pissed a large group of Beings off more. It seems, the closer he gets to his family inheritance, the more these Beings are restless."

She turned her head to look directly at Pantu. "I have to decide whether you are a threat, or an asset. And you have shown me you can be both," she ended, looking at Pantu with a double meaning in her smile.

Pantu's look to her was one of fear.

"A parent's job is to provide for their children, give them better than you had as a child, raise them up in a way which is acceptable to society, but that's by human standards.

"What's acceptable to us may seem weird, different or downright insane to others not accustomed to our way of life. So, no, we will not judge the life you and your family lived to survive. We all have our own struggles, but we come together to help each other when needed."

She picked out another shirt and handed it to Pantu, without measuring. She moved over to the pants section and Pantu followed her, looking lost.

"That's what my son tried to show you last night. Do you think he didn't want to kill the little bastard himself?" she asked, watching Pantu's reactions to her words, who said nothing, but the answer was written on his face.

"He let you see a side of your parents you have refused to open your eyes to." She let it sink in as she measured pants against Pantu and added them to his growing pile of clothes.

"Do you think it was easy getting you out of a country closed off to the rest of the world for over a millennial? Escaping from a place nobody even knows exists on this planet? The constant running and hiding will tax anyone's Mind, spirit, and Energy. I'm impressed your parents did it for so many years." By now she was openly and happily shopping for Pantu, giving him all the clothes she picked out, to hold.

"We left The States after a serious incident to our family and hid out here until Drum decided on his Path for life. So, we can understand. But my son has always been a respectful young man to his parents.

"He truly believes if a person who has good parents can't respect them, they will never respect the person they are in a relationship with." She paused and looked at Pantu. "Even if the relationship is as friends."

She turned to fully face him. "My son has lived by his values his entire life. He's never done anything without reason. It's obvious to me he cares about you, but I have never allowed anyone into my family member's lives who will change them for the worse.

Regardless of the cost," she stated, and she knew by the look on Pantu's face, he more than heard her, he understood.

Become an asset or leave Drum alone. By the look on Pantu's face, she wasn't the first to tell him this. And Pantu's actions would directly affect his Ma's friendship. Getting a read on the young man standing in front of her was as difficult as Drum said it would be.

She appreciated the looks on Pantu's face, but he was still able to keep his true thoughts to himself. She knew he understood her, but how he would use this knowledge was still unknown to her. She smiled as the young man whose personality was showing he wasn't used to any of this, did something she assumed he'd never asked of his parents.

"I have no knowledge of what to do," Pantu admitted. "I feel like I have lost myself living here. I am unsure if the Other I was in The City is the Being I want to be here. I have lived so many lives in The City; it is confusing to me. Is the Other I was in The City so horrible? Does this mean I am not me?" Pantu honestly asked her.

"Here would be a suitable place to freely find yourself. Your likes or what you dislike. See if your values, your morals from The City, can be the foundation you need to build on. Take your time and figure out who you want to be, what you can do and how you will use your Abilities," she stated plainly.

For or against Drum was what she left unsaid.

"There are Beings here who can help you. I'm sure being in advanced classes and as intelligent as my son knows you are, you can figure this out?" she ended, as Drum walked up with a smile.

"Mom," Drum said, as he handed her a small bag.

PANTU: WHATEVER MAKES YOU SMILE
WEEK FOUR: SATURDAY

He wouldn't look at Drum as he was still thinking. His arms dropped as Drum took the clothes and walked away to check out.

If I could figure out all my Talents, I could use them to save my G-Pas. Maybe then there would be no need to stay behind, and they will leave my family alone. I would be able to protect them. I want to be able to protect those I care about, those I love. His thoughts made him smile.

I have always had to be perfect, but here, I have made mistake after mistake that would have had me killed back home. What am I saying? That no longer has to be my home. I will never be a pet again. Drum and I are just friends but until I understand myself, should I avoid being alone with him? Dreaming with him?

But his body and Light didn't agree with his brain, neither did his heart. He was so deep in thought he moved instinctively to follow everyone else. It was as if he was suddenly looking at himself, inside himself. The space was dark but around him and the other him, there was a faint, glowing, golden light.

"AH! You have become quite comfortable here. Did you forget what the one called Dill expressed to you?" the other Him asked.

He thought about the conversation he and Dill had not long ago. *"He's the only one powerful or smart enough to help someone as Talented as you."*

He took in this other Him, dressed in the final Perfect Pet attire he obtained. His body was about twenty pounds lighter and slender like a cat.

Damn I looked good, he thought, and the other Him smiled as his thoughts were broadcast around them, only to be enveloped by the darkness.

"You look good for her. This is how she always wanted you to look. How do you feel now?" The one he now named Pet Pantu asked.

"I feel...full," he said.

He always needed to be on a diet or use pills in The City, as he was celebrated for having the perfect male body. He never worked out, he despised it, so his body was slender but with soft curves and cold, flawless skin which made everyone want to touch him. The only time he was excited about someone touching him was with Drum.

"You know who you need to ask for help from first," Pet Pantu stated. "Until then, just do the things which will make you smile," Pet Pantu ended, before disappearing off into the darkness.

"Pantu!" Drum's voice sounded out, bringing him back to focus on the fact Drum saved him from walking right into a weird looking car.

He turned and looked at Drum to give a bright smile. "Thank you!" he said. His focus went back to the weird car. "Why is there a weird little car in the middle of the walkway?" he asked Drum, walking around it while inspecting it closely. Everyone else continued walking and talking, leaving him and Drum alone.

"It's a photo booth, designed to look like a car," Drum said.

He pulled back the curtain on one side to inspect the inside of the booth. After walking through, he opened the curtain on the other side, where Drum was standing and asked, "How does it work? It does not seem drivable?"

Drum pulled out his phone. "Would you like a hands-on instruction?"

"Yes please!" he answered happily, clapping his hands and bouncing on his feet.

"Close the other curtain and have a seat," Drum instructed while holding his phone up to the payment machine. Before closing the curtain between them, Drum explained.

"Press this button when you are ready. Look here for the camera. There will be a countdown, and you will take four photos within four seconds of each other. You can pose however you want." Drum finished and the curtain closed.

He sat there for a moment wondering how this little car was a camera before he pressed the button. The cameras in The City were old, like really old and nothing like the ones he came across while traveling here.

So, he was obviously at a loss when the camera started flashing quick lights into his eyes. The photos he took in The City were sensual poses meant to increase his points, but now there were four photos of a very confused Pantu.

Drum opened the curtain, holding a small strip of paper and his laughter in and handed the paper to him to inspect while sitting down beside him.

"Nice!" Drum said, still trying not to laugh.

"I had no idea how to pose." He pouted, crossing his arms and legs to turn his whole body away from Drum, but the sound of light laughter made his eyes roll at his Light flowing along to the softness of Drum's voice.

He stood and closed the curtain. "Let me try again?" he asked, determined to take better photos.

Drum placed his phone up to the machine until they heard the beep. He pressed the button, and Drum went to move out of the machine, but he grabbed his arm and pulled him back.

Sitting back down, Drum smiled at him as he smiled at the camera. He heard the first click and when Drum went to turn back towards the camera, he turned to Drum with a doe-eyed look and stared into his eyes, making him smile brightly as he heard another click.

Drum's eyes wouldn't leave his face even though he turned back to the camera to smile. Before the final click, Drum went to stand and he held on to Drum's arm, pulling him back down for the final click. Drum went and collected the strip, with him following behind. After looking at the photos, Drum ripped the last one off and put it in his right pocket while handing the rest to him.

Saying nothing while looking at the photos, he smiled. "I like this one better," he told Drum.

"So, may I have the first strip?" Drum asked.

He pulled the strip out of his pocket, ripped off the first one, handed it to Drum with a smile and received one back.

"Let's do one more," Drum suggested.

They went back in and after, split the last one, joking about their funny faces.

"Do you feel uncomfortable with me buying you things?" Drum asked him, out of nowhere.

He lowered his voice and looked down before he answered, "It is not that." He turned his head, avoiding Drum's eyes. "Lots of people brought me things as a pet when I lived in The City. Whatever they thought would be pleasurable for me to wear," he told Drum.

"Oh!" Drum said with understanding in his voice.

He moved closer and grabbed the front of Drum's shirt. He still wouldn't look up at Drum as he decided being around this young male made him smile, so he was going to take the advice of pet Him.

He finally turned his eyes up to meet Drum's. "My favorite color is ochre," he told Drum, who smiled and nodded.

"There's an art store. Would you like to go?" Drum asked him, and his eyes lit up.

"Yes! I need new paint, new brushes, new..." he went off in thought, listing everything he would need to paint the portrait while turning to walk.

Drum led him to the store, and he immediately went off finding everything in his head list. He spent time and care picking out his brushes and talking with the employee about the assorted brands of paint. Drum quietly followed behind with a smile on his face.

"All of this can be delivered by tonight, correct?" Drum asked the employee.

"Yes! We can also custom make canvases and have them delivered the same day!" the employee informed them.

He clapped his hands with glee and started making a list of different canvas sizes and shapes to be custom made. After the employee went to the back of the store to place his order, he cautiously looked around before moving closer to Drum.

"Dill said I should be mindful not to let others see I can touch you," he said, not looking directly at Drum while lightly playing a game of touch with Drum's right arm.

"Oh. Well, it's a good thing everyone working today is a Bee," Drum told him.

He paused and looked at Drum. "Wait, really?" he asked. He quickly counted all the Beings they saw today and realized there were no other shoppers in the mall and no cars but theirs in the parking lot. "Are we the only ones who are shopping today?" he asked.

"Yep! You heard Win, V.I.B Day," Drum responded with a smile.

The employee came back, and he quickly moved away from Drum.

"Oh, it's okay," the employee said and quickly showed him a Bee badge before tucking it away.

As he nodded in acceptance, Drum quickly and quietly moved to the back of the store to pay.

In the time it took Drum to come back, he figured out Drum was asking him to trust Queen. After the conversation with Mrs. K, he was sure they planned this day for him.

He was thinking it was planned after Drum first came to his house and saw his room. Drum was openly asking him to stay and when the young male came back, he wrapped his arms around Drum's neck.

He felt wanted and not in the way the people in The City wanted him, but like they actually wanted to get to know him. It felt as if they liked talking with and being around him. There were never any Ill Intentions or underline feelings, and it made his body more relaxed than he was used to.

They caught up with everybody else in a purse and bag store. He looked around while walking towards Dill. His eyes caught a messenger bag like the sling one Drum carried to school. It was midnight blue and gold, and he was stuck staring, so he didn't feel Drum behind him, looking over his shoulder.

"It's the latest one, unreleased to the public until next year," Drum told him.

"Ah, it is nice," he responded, before continuing to walk towards Dill.

"Do you want it?" Drum asked.

He nodded but continued to walk, not looking back. He made it to Dill, who was admiring and contemplating getting a bag.

"Come check this out!" He jumped as Drum said this over his shoulder.

He looked at Drum, with fake annoyance. After blowing out his breath, he followed Drum to the other side of the store but when his eyes caught the custom oversized midnight blue and gold canvas carrier, he did his best to hold in his squeal.

This bag was something he never knew he wanted. It was large enough to carry the custom canvases he'd just ordered and had pocket linings for his materials. As he was inspecting the bag, he was so engrossed, he didn't notice the smiles on everyone's faces as they watched him.

This canvas tote bag would be perfect, and the colors and fabric are exquisite, he thought, as his happiness swelled. *The only thing left is to find the perfect place to paint.*

Dill came over after finally deciding to get the backpack to give a nod of agreement and appreciation. "You definitely have to get that one. It fits you exactly!" Dill said to his delight.

"I have already asked—" He started to talk himself out of getting the bag.

"For nothing like this!" Dill interrupted, but he looked unsure.

The employee came up to them and asking if they needed help, started showing him the different designer canvas totes, but he clung to the one in his hand, politely listening to the young male.

Drum walked up to him, placing a hand on his back, Drum kindly said, "We will take this one and this as well." Drum motioned to the bag in his grasp and lifted up the matching messenger bag.

He could only lean back into Drum's hand to look up at Drum, trying not to express the vast amounts of happiness flowing through his body on his face. They visited every store anyone found interesting or wanted something from.

He joked and teased everyone as they returned the laughs. Drum was by his side as they continued shopping, careful not to be imposing when touching him so it was more of a game of "touch Pantu without anyone noticing" and it made him laugh.

Drum was also keeping everybody from imposing their taste on him. Drum only watched as he picked the clothes he liked, with some of those choices being flat out disapproved of by Queen.

When he placed his hands together and bowed, Vowing to never wear them around Queen, everyone laughed and Queen compromised, allowing him one Pantu outfit a week. He also asked if Queen could alter his outfits to fit his personality more, which made Queen start thinking about designs.

"You will have to show me how the clothes fit you want altered, so we can do a runway at my house!" Queen told him.

PANTU: A NEW PLACE TO PAINT
WEEK FOUR: SATURDAY

It was late afternoon when everyone was ready to leave. He looked around at everybody. Besides him and Drum no one else held bags in their hands. Drum was still holding on to the small white bag, and he never once let go of his skincare bag.

It looked as if they didn't buy much as everybody's purchases were already in the vehicle. Making it back to the parking lot, Drum and Queen stood towards the back of the van, speaking quietly.

He watched them until Mrs. K came to his side.

"I see my son took my advice," she said with a smile, before getting in the van.

What? When did she have time to tell Drum anything? Right after our conversation Drum hardly left my side and he spoke with his Ma only when we were altogether. He was at a loss but when Drum appeared next to him with a smile, he automatically relaxed and smiled in return.

Drum dropped Queen and Sport off at Queen's home as Sport's foster parents and little sister were staying there, while in town. Since both of his foster parents worked and lived in the country's capital, his Ma and he learned Sport owned his own apartment since middle school.

And Sport was at Queen's house more than his own, so he had a room there and his foster parents stayed in the guest wing with their daughter. Win was dropped off after Dill and when Drum finally pulled up to his house, he sighed, happy to be home.

He was tired and wanted a nap. He sent a text to Doctor Robin asking for an earlier time on Sunday. He was going to nap first before putting everything he got from the mall away. Walking into his room, threw him off as there were bags everywhere.

Drum must have moved everyone's bags into their homes without touching them. How did he know whose bag was whose? How powerful is he to do something on a scale this large? Did I really get this much stuff? We did visit a lot of stores, he thought to himself.

He decided to sleep in the attic but when he opened the door, he smiled. All the custom items from the art store were already delivered. He went about organizing everything until the evening. His Ma called him down for dinner and for the first time in years, he went downstairs to eat with his parents.

His Pa looked up as he sat down, but he avoided eye contact. His Ma was humming and smiling as she set the food on the table. They all thanked the Universe for the meal and began eating. They didn't talk at all, just enjoyed being at the same table, at the same time, eating.

"I am to sleep in the attic tonight," he said, as he was getting up to leave.

"Okay PanPan," his Ma said. "Your Pa has been helping me clean the kitchen, so if you want a snack, let me know!" she stated, happy it seemed like her family was finally starting to reconnect.

He nodded in his Pa's direction before putting his dishes in the sink and returning to the attic. He set up the space in the most comfortable way possible, but it was still stuffy and dark.

Work with what you have, he thought.

He sat down and took a deep breath as he recalled what it felt like when Drum used Light to make a Dome. Holding the Dome around the attic space, he started to paint. When he finished, he released his Light and looked at the cat clock hanging by the attic door, which wasn't under his Dome.

The ugly black and white cat's bulging eyes only moved side to side every minute, while the tail would only swing every hour, making the cat meow. He rolled his eyes at both the cat and the fact he only shaved his time down to half.

Let me try again with a longer time limit, he thought, as he set his Dome again and started painting.

"What are you doing?" Drum's voice sounded from behind him, making him jump and break his Dome.

He knocked over and spilled everything, wondering how Drum just appeared inside his Time Dome without any resistance, casually standing to the left of him, leaning against the wall. He turned back to see all the expensive paint Drum just brought him everywhere and was heartbroken.

He closed his eyes, silently cursing himself. He was NOT going to ask Drum to buy this for him again, so he would have to wait until he could ask his parents to buy them, one at a time.

That is how expensive this paint is. With my allowance, I would have to save for a couple of years just to buy one small container and Drum brought all extra-large containers in one go.

"Pantu?" Drum called his name.

He took a deep breath, ready for Drum to be unhappy he wasted the paint just purchased for him. But when he opened his eyes, everything was back as if he never knocked it over. He looked around, not understanding the incredible Talents Beings possessed. "I was painting."

"I can see that," Drum told him, calmly.

"I was trying to see if I could cut my painting time down. I thought if I could control the flow of time inside a Dome then it would have no effect on the time outside," he explained, staring at his unfinished painting.

"Dope idea!" Drum said with enough happiness in his voice, he turned to look at the male, who still hadn't moved.

"I can only cut time down by half," he said.

Drum finally moved off the wall but kept his hands in his pockets. When Drum walked towards him, his chest became tight and his Light was a rushing river in his veins, anticipating Drum's warmth.

"Probably because your Barrier is leaking?" Drum informed him.

"HUH!?" he unnecessarily shouted. His Mind was busy flipping through every instance of Drum's hands on his body while his brain was preoccupied with showing him every moment where he was smiling. He didn't know his Light could have a sound as the rushing waves in his veins made the loudest noise, crashing into all the places his body wanted to be touched.

"The Energy used to control time is stronger than the Barrier you set. Your Barrier has holes in it. It leaked out and affected the time in your house and around it," Drum stated, coming to stand directly in front of him.

He was sure Drum could hear his heart race as Drum's face came so close to his, their noses touched. He couldn't say anything as he bathed in the warmest honey-colored eyes he'd ever cared to look in to. His chest was tight, and every breath was forced in and out by sheer willpower to live, if only to continue to stare into Drum's eyes forever.

"I'm going to set a Barrier," Drum said. "Focus on controlling time."

He nodded and turned back to paint. After he felt Drum's Dome around the attic, he released his Light to slow the flow of time and started to paint. While holding the focus on time, he also recalled the lessons GMack taught him. It didn't seem like it took him long to finish painting and when his Light finally dissipated on its own, Drum released the Dome around the room.

"It only took fifteen minutes!" he shouted happily after a quick glance at the clock. "That painting should have taken a full regular hour, but I was able to get it completed in fifteen regular minutes!" He stood and hugged Drum.

"One hour inside the Barrier was fifteen minutes outside of it?" Drum asked. "That's way dope Pantu!" Drum hugged him back. "Did you feel how much Energy you used for the Ability?" Drum asked, and he nodded.

"Good, now double the amount to make your Barrier," Drum instructed.

He closed his eyes and remembered how much Light it took to control time, doubled it, and set a Dome. He dropped the Dome, allowing his Light to dissipate. He set it again and repeated this until it felt natural.

"The more your time decreases, the stronger your Barrier needs to be," Drum told him. As Drum kissed his neck, both his concentration and Dome broke since his Light was now more interested in the warm spot left by Drum's lips on his body.

"I. CAN. NOT. FOCUS!" he said, through clenched teeth.

"Distractions will cause your Abilities to falter or break," Drum said, as he tried to set another Dome, but it quickly crumbled when the tip of a warm tongue licked his neck.

The soft laughter in his ear distracted other parts of his body. From the first moment he heard Drum's voice, he was hard, but now he was fighting the urge to release more than his Dome.

Drum walked away, looking around the room. "It's dark and stuffy in here. Would you mind?" Drum asked him, gesturing around the room.

He shrugged, wondering what Drum could do that he hadn't tried yet to brighten up the tiny space. He could only sit in awe as Drum created a visible royal-blue Dome larger than the room.

"What color would you like the floor?" Drum asked.

"Midnight blue," he replied. "And smooth, please," he added.

"No deep yellow ochre?" Drum teased and received a pouting face as a reply.

"I did not want to be a bother," he said, looking away.

Drum laughed and waved his hand. Midnight blue and gold liquid spread from one side of the Dome to the other. His mouth dropped open as a beautiful mix of midnight blue and gold swirled around as if it was a flowing galaxy settling into a cosmos. Once the liquid filled the room and beyond, it hardened, becoming smooth and shiny.

"Epoxy finish?" he asked, admiring the floor as he left his chair to bend over and touch it. Rubbing his hands across a floor he could only ever imagine having for his own, his heart swelled, and he heard a crack. *"I have always wanted a floor like this. It is beyond beautiful!"* he whispered.

"What color for the walls?" Drum asked.

He looked up at Drum and watched as the male tried to hide his smile, but he could feel the vast amount of warm happiness coming from him. The look of wonder and joy on his face made it worse for Drum, who turned to hide the large bulge in his pants.

He giggled. "I like bay windows, large ones with an area to sit. Really open and ahh…more of a yellowish-brown ochre?" he ended, with more of a hopeful question than a statement.

Drum looked at him with a raised eyebrow. "OOH!" Drum replied.

Drum's deep voice and simple response made his body red as he realized he was on the floor, bowing to Drum with his butt in the air as he asked for what he wanted. He never bowed to anyone before, not even as a pet. His G-Ma and Indria's positions made sure of that.

Not even his owner could get him to bow, even when training him. He was shown to be amendable, but he was the only pet who could look, not only at his owner, but any other person directly in the eye and not be punished.

He was fairly sure his whole body was blushing as well. He sat up on his legs and refused to look at Drum's smiling face. He closed his eyes and took a breath. The space suddenly felt roomier and brighter, and he opened his eyes to see Drum gave him exactly what he wanted.

The room was now the size of the Dome Drum first set which doubled the size of the area. The bay windows went from floor to ceiling except the last one on each side, those came with sitting areas. The colors for the lining around the bay windows and the two sitting areas were the blend of colors he'd asked for. The ceiling was glass and gave a clear view to the darken sky, littered with tiny silver diamonds.

As he looked around the room, he started to tear up as even the cat clock was now midnight-blue and gold. It was as if the drawing he did when he was little came to life right in front of him, although more refined and way more expensive than he could have imagined as a child. He felt as if he was in the painting.

"*Impossible!*" he whispered so softly, he thought he was only thinking it.

DRUMxPANTU: AN UNANSWERED QUESTION
WEEK FOUR: SATURDAY

Drum squatted down and taking the handsomely beautiful face in his hand, he tilted Pantu's head to look directly into his eyes.

"Do you like it?" he asked softly, holding his favorite icy, brown eyes captive.

"It is perfectly me. I love it!" Pantu whispered, wanting to be in his arms, which he obliged.

He pulled the young man towards him as he went to sit down. When Pantu fell into his arms, he laughed at the 'oop' that came from a surprised Pantu.

"You have unique Abilities," he told Pantu.

"Hmm!" was all he got back.

Pantu was sitting between his legs, head against his chest, while his body relaxed to the sound of his steady heartbeat. He was both Pantu's pillow and blanket causing a smile to cross his face. He could hear how calm Pantu's heartbeat was.

He couldn't help but smile wider at a relaxed Pantu in his arms. It reminded him of the very first time he met Pantu. He took a deep breath and suppressed the memory.

"Pantu, will you be my boyfriend?" he suddenly asked.

Pantu jumped up and stared at him. The look of confused shock on Pantu's face from hearing his question, the one question everyone was waiting on him to ask, made Pantu freeze in his arms. He watched Pantu unsuccessfully try to answer. Pantu could only say the word 'boyfriend' on repeat. He laughed at Pantu's reaction, who jumped back to his senses.

"You were joking, right?" Pantu asked, scared. "It was a joke, just a joke!" Pantu reassured himself aloud.

As Pantu looked up at him to explain, he spoke first.

"Three times," he said, with a smile.

Pantu's face went from sad to confused. "Three times what?" Pantu asked.

"You have to ask me three times before I'll ask you again," he half explained.

Pantu took a deep breath and blew it out harder than he needed to. "Ask what, three times!" Pantu stated, annoyed.

He pulled Pantu close to him and whispered in his ear. *"Ask me to be your boyfriend."*

Pantu was taken aback. "That will never happen. I have never begged," Pantu said, with a disgusted look on his face and crossed arms.

"Then I guess we should set a deadline?" he proposed.

Pantu turned to look at him suspiciously.

"If by the new year, the end of this month, you haven't asked me three times to be your boyfriend, then I will leave you alone. Permanently," he offered.

"So, why not leave me alone now…since it will never happen?" Pantu asked, full of indignant pride.

"Oh! So, you won't give me a chance, huh?" he teased as he held his arms out to Pantu, who, without hesitation moved back into them and snuggled against his chest.

Feeling Drum's arms wrapped around Pantu felt too good to be true.

I will wait for you. For some reason, those words came back to his Mind from out of the darkness of his, what he thought was empty, Think Space. His eyes teared up, and his lips quivered as he knew he could never give the answer he wanted to give.

There is just too much, he thought as he put his face into Drum's chest to hide his tears. *Maybe this is wrong. If we keep going like this, he might mean it one day. I do not think Drum is gay, maybe it is the weird Talent my G-Pas taught me. They never taught me how to turn it off.*

Maybe that is it. It is just a Talent I have. I should explain this to Drum. But what if he no longer wants to touch me if he thinks I am influencing him to like me? It would be for the better, knowing what I must do.

"AH!" He jumped back up and looked at Drum, he explained, "My G-Pas taught me how to use my Talent of Influence to seduce people. Maybe this is what is happening.

"It is my Talent, but I have no idea how to turn it off since I always needed to have it on in The City and they never informed me of how," he said, looking at Drum apologetically.

Drum leaned to the side and reaching out, his face turned red with warmth as Drum moved his hair out from in front of his eyes. Drum's hand moved gently down the side of his face, caressing his cheek.

"Plenty of Beings have the Ability of Seduction," Drum said, looking at him with a slight smile. "And they're still unable to arouse me," Drum added.

His face was now flushed red as he looked around, everywhere but Drum's eyes, and slightly bounced on his legs. He was sure his whole body was red as his only thought was whether Drum would ever bite his butt again. *Do not think about it. Wait? Why am I thinking about it? Never mind.* He shook his head.

"What is it, Pantu?" Drum asked, interested.

"Just thinking…about how I may have gotten a cloud pregnant," he said softly, turning redder from realizing how it sounded out loud.

The laughter he heard was pure and as he looked at Drum, his stomach felt weird, and his heartbeat seemed unstable. He leaned forward to look Drum in his eyes, getting so close their noses touched again.

"By the new year, huh?" he asked, with a smirk. "Anything less than what you did for Kat will not be accepted," he informed Drum.

"Even though you know the truth?" Drum questioned, smiling knowingly.

"It still makes me no less unhappy of your actions for another." He pouted before kissing Drum's neck.

Drum pulled him to lie down. "How are you coming along with the book I gave you?" Drum asked, stroking his back.

"I understand why you refused to type up my papers," he told Drum, unable to stop his body from wiggling until Drum paused.

He found a comfortable position on Drum's chest and intertwined their legs. Drum silently laughed at his invasion, and waited until he stopped moving, to continue stroking his back.

"I should be finished rewriting them by Tuesday," he added, trying to control his body's reaction to being caressed, but he felt only the Universe could command his Light to stop acting so hectic with every touch from Drum.

His body shivered with every stroke, making Drum's smile wider. When his Light expressed his thoughts of being a little unhappy his clothes were still on, Drum obliged.

PANTU: THE SWEETEST SCENT
WEEK FOUR: SUNDAY

He didn't realize he fell asleep on Drum until an annoying alarm went off early in the morning. He groaned and rolled over giving both the phone, and Drum his back.

He awoke a bit later when he realized he was cold. He sat up, rubbing his eyes and stretching his upper body, he looked around at his new, naturally bright, art room and was excited.

Looking down, he didn't remember having an amazingly soft, super comfortable, twin sized mattress with his favorite anime on the sheets, blankets and pillow covers. He smiled so wide and so hard; he could only put his head in his hands.

Not going to make this easy, he thought, as he rolled off the mattress and onto the smooth midnight blue and golden floor.

He loved his studio and was wondering how he could permanently live in it. He decided to go to his room and get ready for his session with Doctor Robin. Opening the door, he looked around.

It felt different. His new clothes were hung up and his shoes put away. Everything he'd gotten yesterday was either away or set up around his room. It looked like someone lived here. His anime posters were neatly framed and hung up.

I should get a frame for the pictures we took.

He made a mental note to find a nice frame in Hollis but changed his Mind and texted Dill instead to make him a custom frame. He texted he would call later before coming over, but Dill called him immediately after he sent the message.

"Dude, were you planning on going shopping without me?" Dill's unhappy voice sounded out.

"I was just going to look for some photo frames, but I know I will not find anything I like," he whined. "I will call you when I am out of the shower." He hung up.

Placing his phone on charge, he laid it down. He liked how the air could charge their electronics if set. He hopped in the shower, which was filled with everything out of the skincare store. It was the longest shower he'd ever experienced.

He felt clean and brand new. He couldn't fathom how he didn't smell worse than Mansnake before his shower. He looked over at his bathtub and made a mental note to look for bath items.

As he went to his closet, he looked through his clothes and realized Mrs. K didn't choose a style for him, instead she picked diverse types and styles of clothes in his size. But thinking about her also made him think about the small white bag Drum carried the rest of their time shopping.

He held on to it like I held on to my bag. He tried to clear his head, *maybe it was for his Pa.*

He picked out a pair of nice shorts and a short-sleeved button-down shirt he left unbuttoned and untucked over a clean, soft baby tee shirt. He packed his new sling bag with a small sketch pad, colored pencils, and the small black box. He placed his phone and wallet in his pockets before putting on his socks and carrying his shoes downstairs, he ran into his Ma in the kitchen.

"Morning Ma!" he said, brightly smiling at her.

She returned the smile with a small laugh.

"I wanted to catch the bus to Hollis," he stated to his Ma, who slowly turned to stare at him.

"Ah, that would be..." she paused, unsure of how to continue.

"Shall I stay inside the rest of my life hiding from them. We went shopping yesterday and I still have to go to school," he told her. "I will text you when I have made it to Doctor Robin's office. I will also have her call you to verify I am there," he stated, watching her carefully.

His Ma agreed while trying to hold back tears.

Dill walked in, and after inviting him to eat breakfast, his Ma explained his day trip with Dill to his Pa. They left without eating anything his Ma made and walked down to the bus stop in front of the library. It was the only bus that connected Sunset to the other cities.

After finding their place in the back of a mostly empty bus, he asked, "Did I smell bad before?"

Dill gave him a weird look. "Umm. No. Pantu, you didn't," Dill replied, with an unsure smile.

"Really? Are you sure I did not smell like Mansnake?" he asked again, not wanting to believe Dill. He started sniffing his arms.

"Why are you asking Pantu? You never smelled bad to me," Dill explained, waiting for an answer.

"Hmm. That is weird?" he said, thinking. "I am sure I scrubbed layers of dirt off me this morning?" he asked himself, while examining his arms. "So, I must have smelled at least a little funky, right?" he asked.

"You smell way sweeter than you did before, but you have never smelled bad, or as you put it, funky," Dill answered.

He noticed Dill didn't really look at him while explaining his scent.

"Of course, I know better. I will end up dead at too young of an age," Dill added.

"Doctor Robin would torture you first!" he said, as they laughed, but his laughter came up short as he looked up. "Maybe the dirt helped to dilute the scent?" he asked Dill, as he clutched his best friend's arm for comfort.

He was looking around at the mostly empty bus but the looks he was getting back from the passengers made him uncomfortable. His Light was sounding alarm bells inside his body, and he could barely breathe from the heavy number of Ill Intentions in the air coming from those on the bus. The most and worst Intent came from the bus driver's lust, which was apparent in the looks the driver was giving him in the rearview mirror.

"Dill!" he said, now unsure about what to do.

Dill looked up and around at the other Beings on the bus and shook his head, while warning them with his eyes and hands. The other passengers didn't seem to notice Dill as their full attention was on him, and he was now trying to hide behind Dill.

His Light was now causing pain inside his body as he was unsure if Dill could fight them all off. He wasn't confident in his Dome Ability, and he never saw Dill make one before. He was trying to think as the passengers started to move closer to them. Casually sliding into other seats, they were inching closer, and he gripped Dill's arm tighter.

The bus driver suddenly braked, throwing everybody forward. Dill held him upright as the other Beings all tumbled back to the front of the bus.

DRUM: AN ADVENTUROUS DUMPLING
WEEK FOUR: SUNDAY

He didn't want to leave when his alarm went off. Even though he wanted to stay wrapped around Pantu, he still had responsibilities. As he sat on the bleachers outside of a huge warehouse, he was involved in his own thoughts.

He'd already broken his routine for the past thirteen years and spent his first weekend in Sunset. He was breaking the unspoken rule of him never visiting anyone else's home, much less spend the night.

Sport came to sit not far from him and relaxed. His best friend was the second to finish the training test and was waiting while the rest of the Beings crossed the finish line.

He and Sport were talking while watching the Beings who ran out of Energy struggle on the new, more difficult course. These Beings weren't used to being unable to replenish their Energies and were fumbling.

"Do you think they know?" Sport asked, keeping his eyes on the forest entrance of the training course.

He knew his best friend was holding himself back, but only because he asked Sport to. "Yea," he responded, knowing he was the reason for the heavy discomfort Sport was feeling these last few weeks.

"Well…why haven't they said anything. Not even a hint!?" Sport asked, his Energy visibly upset.

"Maybe they don't want you to get mixed up in what they're going through. You heard the life they lived. You really think they would endanger you now after everything they obviously did to keep you alive?" he asked his best friend, who could only turn to look at him.

He knew Sport well and could read the iris Energy flowing through his best friend. "Being patient and understanding is how you will get what you want from Beings like them. But if they leave, I won't stop you from following."

Sport's Energy was speeding through his body at the words and reluctantly nodded his head. He never stopped watching the Beings trying to finish the training and shook his head, wondering how they would face the remaining obstacles. He didn't need to be close to them, and they wouldn't know he was watching. Both he and Sport's Enhanced Vision were considered top tier.

After everyone finished, they all went back to their respected towns.

His shower felt good as he scrubbed himself. He finished, wrapping a towel around his waist, and went to apply his facial products in the mirror. He looked at his chest and all the scars that covered it and his arms. Pantu's body was unflawed. There wasn't a single scar on Pantu's body. He was certain because he checked.

Pantu's body was soft and supple, wherein, his body was toned and slender. The thought of him nibbling on Pantu made him smile and his member happy. He got dressed, wondering what he was going to do today. He never spent a full weekend at home, so he called Queen to see what he was doing.

As they were talking about hanging out at Bread Bites, a popular eatery/game room where High School and Higher Ed students hung out, he caught a whiff of Pantu's sweetened scent.

It was stronger than any Seduction Scent he ever smelled, and he knew what came along with a scent this sweet. He searched for Pantu's Energy and found him still at home.

If he stays close to home, he should be okay.

He went downstairs to eat breakfast. After, he and the twins went outside in the backyard to play football, or soccer in The States. As they were passing the ball, Pup's stuffed bunny, Clickers, was the goalie. Half the size of his owner, Clickers sat in front of the goal, calmly watching, allowing every ball to hit the net.

"It's not fun if Clickers don't at least try and block the ball," he said, scowling at Clickers.

Pup and Kitten laughed at him.

"He's a stuffed bunny, Big Brother Drum," Pup said, between his laughter.

"Yea, Big Brother Drum. Do you expect him to move without Pup's Energy?" Kitten added, shaking her head at him as she kicked the ball.

Pup used his Energy and moved Clickers to try and block the ball but was seconds late as Kitten's kick scored a goal.

"See!" Kitten said, gesturing to the goal and the now limp stuffed bunny laying on the ground.

"Yea! We would have better luck with Mr. Floppy Ears as goalie," Pup stated, laughing.

He only glanced at the chunky, plush bunny sitting in a patio chair and watching them. Mr. Floppy Ears' nose jerked up in the air, and he hopped off the chair to go about his business.

"So, if it's just a stuffed animal, why not put him in the washing machine? Why bathe him with Mr. Floppy Ears?" he asked, still eyeing the stuffed limp animal.

"Because he could lose an eye or get ripped," Pup explained.

"If you say so," he said, turning away when his phone went off. Pressing the Bluetooth in his ear, he spoke with Queen again.

"Drum! What's this scent driving the wildlife insane? They keep going on about someone whose scent is upsetting the natural balance of nature. I can't think straight!" Queen complained.

He took a second and checked where Pantu was. *If the wildlife could smell him, did he go outside the Barrier?* He found Pantu and Dill on the bus headed out of town and answered Queen.

"It's Pantu's Seduction Scent. It's gotten stronger," he informed Queen. "Pantu is on the bus with Dill. I think they're going to the bus terminal," he added.

"Pantu has an appointment with Doctor Robin today, but why would they be on the bus? Don't you think this scent is too strong to be around the humans still left in Hollis?" Queen asked him, adding, "If the wildlife here can't deal with a scent this strong, then Beings and definitely humans, won't be able to." As soon as Queen finished his thought, he felt panic from Pantu.

"Queen!" he said, as he opened a white Portal in front of Queen at his home for him, Win and Sport.

He opened one for himself and saying bye to his siblings, he walked through. They came out in the middle of the street and the bus screeched to an abrupt stop. His royal-blue Heat covered the bus, making the passengers and the driver sweat from the amount of hot pressure being pressed upon them.

He walked to the doors of the bus and yanked them open, entering the vehicle to suppress the Beings with more intense, but white Heat. They were struggling to breathe, and their skin was bright red from contact with his massive Heat Wave. He took a quick look around as he walked to the back to where Dill and Pantu were sitting.

"Drum!" Pantu shouted. "Your heat is hurting Dill!" Pantu cried out.

"Did anyone hurt you?" he asked, ignoring Dill's inability to breathe.

"NO! Dill would not let them. He never left my side, and he protected me!" Pantu pleaded with him.

He took a deep breath and slowly eased up on the Heat Wave. His best friends were unaffected and were helping the other passengers and the driver off the bus.

Pantu looked at him, upset. "How come they were not affected but Dill was?" Pantu asked him.

He didn't answer as he looked at Dill, who left to help move the rest of the passengers.

"How did you know where I was?" Pantu asked another question of him.

"Your scent has become quite strong Pantu," he stated softly. He looked at Pantu, who looked away from him.

"Did I smell bad before?" Pantu asked but didn't wait for him to answer. *"I scrubbed so much dirt off me, I think I must have smelled at least a little. As much as I stated about Mansnake not showering, and here I am, covered in dirt,"* Pantu whispered, close to tears.

"Not dirt, dead skin," he told Pantu, who looked up at him.

"Where you came from didn't have a lot of starlight, did it?" he inquired, to Pantu shaking his head no.

"There weren't any products there like the ones here," he stated, as Pantu agreed.

"Not exfoliating, saved your life," he told Pantu. "If you didn't have the layer of protection to dilute your Seduction Scent, you would've been dead by now," he said, watching Pantu's shocked reaction.

He sat down next to Pantu, with a seat in between them. Everyone was getting back on the bus, looking around as if they were lost. His best friends and Dill came back on the bus to settle in around him and Pantu.

This time when anyone other than them on the bus looked at Pantu, his calm stare quickly deterred them from trying to approach.

PANTU: A PRANK GONE WRONG
WEEK FOUR: SUNDAY

As more passengers entered the bus at the terminal, he thought it was a bad idea to head to Doctor Robin's office this way. If the bus became too crowded, someone could get hurt by bumping into Drum unintentionally. He quickly got up and weaving through the passengers, he left the bus through the back exit right before the driver closed the doors and pulled off.

As the bus drove away, he watched Drum smile at him through the window. Dill missed his chance to get off with him and was currently freaking out, running to the front to ask the driver to pull over.

The driver must have refused after the earlier incident.

He laughed at the disappearing bus. But his laughter was cut short by the mixture of Beings and humans who were starting to gather around him. His breaths came quickly from his tightening chest as he was trying to remember how to set a Dome. His Light was distracted, trying just as hard as he was to quickly set a Dome, but neither he nor his Light could concentrate due to his nerves yelling at them both.

I will never exfoliate again, he thought, as he tried to set a Dome while hyperventilating with tears falling out of his eyes.

Someone surrounding him went to reach out to touch him and his breathing stopped. He closed his eyes, waiting for contact. Instead, he felt heat and opened his eyes to see everyone on their knees, struggling to breathe.

Dill cut a path through, and Drum followed, pushing those on the ground away from him with his heat alone. Dill reached him first and checked him the same way his Ma always did to confirm he was unhurt. Dill ducked behind him and pushed him toward a quiet Drum, who stood, relaxed, with his hands in his pockets, looking at him.

Everyone else was still on the ground, some passed out and those who weren't, *are Beings, able to take more of Drum's Light than humans,* he thought.

"Drum. I think you are killing them," he said, quietly, not looking at Drum's face.

"It's what you wanted, right?" Drum asked, coming closer to him.

He looked around the terminal. Everyone else other than The Four, Dill, Drum and himself were on the ground.

Drum came close, towering over him. *"Duuuuumplinnnng?"* Drum sung softly. "Am I ugly?" Drum asked him, making him look up at Drum's face.

"It seems you don't believe me," Drum stated, looking at him, unconcerned about the people on the ground around them.

"Please Drum!" he softly begged. He didn't want Drum to kill these people because of him. It felt like he was using Drum, the same way Coin used him. *"I shall stay by your side..."* he whispered.

He didn't want to be that type of person. Not person, Being. He didn't want to be the type of Being who used others for his own benefit or thrill. Drum harshly released the heat, making those who didn't pass out cough and choke. Queen was spreading some dust in the air and Win was using the wind to spread it to everyone.

PANTU: WHO I WANT TO BE
WEEK FOUR: SUNDAY

Drum opened a royal-blue Portal for him without once breaking eye contact, and he walked through to Doctor Robin's office. The Portal closed behind him, and he looked at his Doctor's calm face.

"Good morning Pantu!" Doctor Robin said, brightly.

He couldn't take it. He dropped to his knees and started crying. Doctor Robin stood up from her desk and walked around to kneel next to him.

"It seems we have a lot to talk about," Doctor Robin said gently, as he nodded, still crying as he held onto her arms.

When he finally stopped crying, he moved to the couch. His eyes were closed, and his head bowed as he waited for Doctor Robin to settle in her chair after informing his parents he was at her office.

"This is quite the step in finding your emotions Pantu," Doctor Robin said. "Where should we start?" she asked, giving the floor to him.

"I lost my Think Space," he started. "I have nowhere to place my thoughts. No way to figure out who or what I am. In The City, I am an Other. We did not call ourselves Beings."

Doctor Robin smiled. "So, you've found the truth behind Sunset. You seem to be taking the news well, seeing as how you came through a Portal to get here."

He looked up at her. "Do you think..." he paused, not knowing how to word it, he just went for it. "Do you think I have to be the same Others I was in The City? What if the Being I want to be, is not the Others I was there. I do not hate the Others I was, but do I need to change to fit in here? Does it mean I am not myself, or am I pretending? Did I pretend to be an Other or am I pretending now?"

The questions flew out of his mouth, and he went into detail about the Others he was while living in The City. He described some of the things he endured and what he did. Six hours passed while they talked, but when he released his Dome, only an hour and a half passed.

"I see you have become adept at using Abilities," Doctor Robin commented. "Be careful when using those, you don't want to draw too much attention to yourself until you are able to understand your Abilities better. If too many Beings know, someone is bound to let it slip to the wrong ones," she warned him. "Your Abilities are unique. Many Beings would kill for your Energy."

He nodded and smiled as Doctor Robin sat with him to make a list of all the emotions he was feeling, so he could put a name to them. If there were any feelings he couldn't name, he was to text her, and she would help him figure out which emotion he was experiencing.

Doctor Robin also instructed him to write down his comparisons of what he found morally acceptable in The City versus the societal norms. He was to list his values and have all of it ready to discuss at their next session.

PANTU: GREEN WITH JEALOUSY
WEEK FOUR: SUNDAY

Doctor Robin made a call to his Ma to speak with his parents about their session over video chat. He left the office and after speaking to her assistant, made his way down the stairs. Dill was waiting for him in the lobby, and he ran over to his best friend.

He offered, "Let us go to the shopping plaza?"

Dill looked at him with what he could now name as confusion. "Sure, why not!?" Dill responded, accepting death for him.

They both laughed and walked out of the building to Win and Queen waving at them from across the street. They just left an ice cream store and were eating their treats while walking towards Dill and him. He looked around for Drum, and saw him leaning against the building, looking at his phone.

"You do not want ice cream?" he asked Drum, who didn't look up, but still answered.

"No. My human side is lactose intolerant," Drum stated.

He took a deep breath and blew it out hard. "It is fine. Dill and I will go by ourselves then." He pouted, realizing this meant he was upset Drum hadn't looked at him once.

"Okay!" Drum said with an uncaring shrug and turned to walk off.

"REALLY!?" he shouted at Drum.

"Hmm?" Drum said, nodding and still walking away.

He rolled his eyes at Drum's back and looked to Dill for help. "Which way is the plaza?"

His attitude was apparent on his face and in his stance, so Dill suppressed a smile and pointed in the direction Drum was currently taking.

You have to be fucking kidding me! His look to Dill matched his thoughts.

He resigned himself as he hurried to catch up to Drum. As Drum was walking west, he moved to Drum's right side, keeping space between them. He was busy looking around as he walked and didn't realize Drum stopped. Turning to see where Drum was, he ran back, stopping just in front of him.

"Are you THAT distracted?" he questioned, visibly upset Drum still hadn't looked at him once since leaving his Doctor's office.

Drum motioned with his head to his left side. He looked over but didn't see anything and he looked back up at Drum, waiting. Drum smiled slightly and reached his arm out to him. Without touching him, Drum moved him to the left, then continued walking, all without looking at him once.

He was confused as he didn't understand why he needed to walk to the left of Drum. He went to catch back up with Drum, this time walking on Drum's left. Drum finally closed his phone and put it in his left pocket.

He was looking at Drum apprehensively and he now knew he was proud of his Mind and brain working quickly and in tandem to help him name his emotions. Memorizing the dictionary greatly helped. "Was your phone that interesting?" he asked, trying to control the jealousy in his voice.

He knew from Dill how popular Drum was online, and he figured being the son of the richest, nope, Dill said wealthiest, man on the planet, helped. *Not to mention he is the best-looking person I have ever seen in my life. He would definitely rank number one. Hell, I would actually have to fight to stay in the top three,* he thought sadly.

Even though he is drop dead handsome, he would need more than looks to rank, and he has it. Without being able to touch him, he would still Entice the clothes off anyone with just a look. I am sure Tracey came just from Drum looking at him. He rolled his eyes, unhappy at the thought.

He took a deep breath, trying to shake the jealousy off. *Ah, I am now quite sure the drugs in a mental hospital are the best. I have never gotten jealous...ever! Especially over a male. I refuse to ask him to be MY BOYFRIEND, no matter what he does. How would he even top what he did for Kat?*

He rolled his eyes again, as they came up to a crosswalk. Drum's arm reached out to stop him from walking across the street. He stopped short of Drum's arm, and the smirk Drum gave annoyed him even more. He looked up and saw the DO NOT WALK sign flashing.

"Pantu?" Drum called him.

He looked away, refusing to look at Drum. He was trying to hold his emotions close to himself, like Drum did yesterday to keep him from feeling pain he knew was way more intense than what Drum did share. He couldn't have Drum knowing he was jealous. He just couldn't, not after he received the one question which would cause his parents and the whole town to, for some reason, explode.

"Do you still mean what you said yesterday? Or do your words change daily, depending on how *mad* you are at me?" Drum teased him.

"They have not changed! And I am NOT *mad*," he retorted, indignant of the meaning behind Drum's question. Yes, he was mad but in their sense of the word, not his.

"Then, does that mean you will still hold true to what you said earlier?"

He blew out a breath again. He was fighting himself and his anger at Drum was just his way of not being wrong for the way his Mind, brain and Light disconnected from him. "You should get your eyes checked," he said to Drum. "Or else you would see me keeping my word right now."

He crossed his arms and looked behind them. Dill, Queen, and Win were giving them space, and he wondered why. He also wondered why Sport wasn't here.

"He has a game tonight. Are you going?" Drum asked, starting to walk across the street.

He watched Drum for a moment before following. *Can he read Minds? Is it a Talent he has?* He was lost in the fact Drum just seemed to know what he was thinking, and he completely missed answering the question.

The plaza was an outdoor market, set up every Sunday by people selling handmade items and promoting their businesses online. He wanted to go since he'd first seen it after a session with his Doctor, but he didn't want to get in the habit of having keepsakes he would have to leave behind, again. After yesterday, his room looked like someone lived there, not to mention, his studio was now amazing, all thanks to Drum.

"What happened to the people at the terminal?" he asked, curious.

"The same thing that will happen to these people if someone touches you," Drum responded, not directly answering his question.

He looked at Drum shocked. If Drum left without making sure they received medical treatment, he was positive some of them would be dead.

"Drum!" he said, worried Drum would be arrested.

Drum stopped and looked at him with a smile that sent a fluttering feeling all the way down to the pit of his stomach. He was quite sure his Light was turning into butterflies inside him. He stepped closer to Drum.

"Drum?" was all he asked, but no reply was given.

He moved to stand in front of Drum, now breathing right on Drum's chest, but every inhaled breath smelled of a place he should remember because it held the same scent as the field meadow. Looking up, he said Drum's name again.

His muscles gave out when Drum leaned down and kissed him on the nose. He quickly found his senses and jumped back in surprise, frantically looking around to see if anyone saw. No one seemed to notice them, and he wondered why.

"Stay close!" was all Drum said, as they entered the plaza.

It was then he felt Drum's Light dissipate and realized the reason Dill, Queen and Win kept their distance was because Drum placed a Dome over the two of them. He was so distracted with jealousy; he didn't feel Drum's Light being used. He wanted to kick himself for missing such a detail, but instead, he blamed Drum for being such a distraction to him.

He managed to stay close to Drum while shopping and although Beings, and humans, were drawn to his scent, they couldn't get close to him as Drum's heat kept everyone at bay.

In The City, people kept their distance since he was deathly afraid of crowds. After multiple attempts on his life, the governess' daughter stated any unauthorized person who came close to him would be put to death. There was a ten feet distance placed on him to keep her favorite pet alive.

Drum, on the other hand, protected him because he hated being touched. *And probably because he does not want others touching me.* But the thought made him smile. He didn't want to be "touched" by anyone other than Drum. He didn't like it when someone invaded his space without his consent.

Drum protects my space because it is what I want. I am still scared someone will touch me or attack me. I am unsure of my comfort level and Drum protects me while giving me space to figure myself out.

The thoughts in his head produced a smile on his face as he happily shopped with Dill and three of The Four. He didn't find the frames he wanted, and he expected that, so Drum bought cured wood for Dill to turn into picture frames for him.

Queen and Win also helped him find bath items for his skin type, so he could soak. He and Dill picked out candles, while Drum was more interested in the hand-carved, mini statues. Drum seemed to be in deep conversation with the owner of the stall, and he wondered why Drum left without buying anything for himself.

He also noticed people trying to record them but would become disappointed when they looked at their phones. They would start typing as fast as they could, watching everything they did and what they brought. Any stall they purchased something from would immediately be swamped and sold out of everything before they made it to the next stall.

PANTU: LOST IN THOUGHT
WEEK FOUR: SUNDAY

He felt Ill Intent from some of the Beings and humans around him while he was shopping, so he gladly used the reason to turn on his True Vision. He decided to leave it on for a while to see how long he could hold his Vision before his Light said enough.

Looking around Hollis was different than Sunset. From the quick glimpses he was able to see, everyone in Sunset held Light inside their bodies and everything was made from Light. Here in Hollis, there were barely any Beings with Light and anything human-made looked to be deteriorating.

He noticed there were a lot less humans in Hollis than when he first arrived. Most stores had "Under New Management" signs posted; "Final: Everything Must Go" posters; or "Going Out of Business" banners.

"What is happening to Hollis?" he asked, as they were walking back towards the bus terminal.

"Humans are leaving. The city has become toxic to them," Drum informed him.

"How would a city become toxic to humans?" he wondered, aloud. Maybe he could use the same method to rid The City of humans and live there in peace with his family and the Others they protected.

"I placed a Barrier around Hollis before you arrived. It will remain Hollis but will be under the authority of Sunset Town, same as the other surrounding cities. Humans can stay under the thinnest of my Barriers, but their electronics will still abide by the Private Citizen Act.

"Now, the Barrier has been upgraded to Purifying and Replenishing, so it will make humans sick if they don't leave in enough time. Most non-Energy humans can survive about two weeks, give or take a day, with the Level at which the Barrier has been increased. The purer the land, the less time they have.

"Those humans who have an ancestorial Being somewhere in their family line, could possibly last a month, give or take a week, before all their organs fail," Drum told him, nonchalantly.

He looked at Drum and quickly averted his eyes to glance around at the remaining people in the city. Most were Beings, but there were some humans left who seemed to be on their way out. "Would it not expose us to humans to have their electronics unable to record certain people? How would you explain mass humans getting sick?"

"No Private Citizen lives in Hollis yet. And the humans have been told the land no longer belongs to them and has become toxic. They had ample time to leave before the Barrier upgraded.

"Most humans thought they could hold out for more than their business or house was worth, so now they're leaving with what they can carry before they lose their life," Drum said, not caring for the health of greedy humans. "You can tell, can't you? Who is a Being and who is human?" Drum asked, looking at him, while walking.

"Yes?" he answered, surprised Drum did all of this just so he could visit Doctor Robin once a week. "Dill told me it is not a normal Talent for Beings."

Drum shook his head. "Not the way you can," Drum informed him.

Looking around again, while making sure to avoid Drum's face, he could see the distinct differences between Beings and humans. There were balls of colorful Light inside Beings while the humans still left, carried grey chunks of jagged looking rocks. He watched the swirling Light which traveled and flowed throughout some of the Beings' bodies, while others' Light swirled around their ball.

"We call the balls of light, Cores. The grey chunks you see in the remaining humans, we call them Rock-Cores. Most Rock-Cores are just Beings outside my Barriers, who have used all their Energy without being able to replenish or humans who have a Being ancestor. Normal humans without a Being ancestor, can't tolerate Energy, unless..." Drum shrugged, leaving the rest of the thought unsaid.

"Those humans with a Being ancestor whose line have been human-ed out, have no Orb at all but some are still able to feel Light being used," he added, watching Drum's reaction.

Drum nodded. "There are other ways as well." Drum sighed before moving on. "The Light inside the Core is what makes us Beings. It's also what helps our bodies handle the swirling Light you see called Energy. The more Energy a Being has, the more they can constantly use their Abilities," Drum stated.

"There are veins we use to help channel our Light. They run from the Core throughout our bodies. They are really close to blood veins and vessels and unable to be detected by human machines. The swirling Light would be additional stored Light," he stated.

Drum stopped, stared at him, and smiled, just slightly, and he knew when any part of his body turned any color of red from this feeling, he was blushing.

He turned away from Drum. He didn't mention what Drum's Orb looked like. "Your body is over-filled with Light. It is constantly moving all over your body and pours off you in waves. Almost as if it is too much for your body to handle," he said. "What do I look like?" he quickly asked, bouncing nervously.

"May I?" Drum asked, gesturing to his body.

He understood Drum was asking permission to look inside his body, and he blushed again, knowing his True Vision was still on, making it quite difficult to look into the purest face he'd ever seen. Drum wore no mask and with a face so bright and clean, he knew Drum was who he showed.

While it was interesting, what intrigued him was feeling like there was more to this young male standing beside him. From Drum's Orb; to his Light's colors; Drum's personality; his intelligence; the Talents Drum did show him; right down to Drum's scents, he wanted to figure out everything about this young male.

"Like you could use some more Energy," Drum teased, and he was brought back to the conversation.

He deflated at the news. "So, I would be considered weak," he stated, disappointed he would never be powerful enough or worthy. *I at least thought maybe my past and the things I did, would or could be offset by being powerful enough to where it mattered not.* His complete sadness was broken by Drum grabbing his face and tilting it up to meet his eyes.

"Your Energy was severely diluted in The City. It was probably your body's way of protecting you."

As Drum said this, he looked like there was more to be added to Drum's comment, but he declined, so Drum proceeded.

"Now that you're here, you should be able to gather more Energy naturally, but since your body isn't used to holding a lot of Energy, your intake seems to be slow. When was the last time you went to the park?" Drum asked him.

"Ah, a while, not since the time we went together...I think." He was unsure of when the last time he sat in the park was. He was unable to think with Drum being so close to him.

"We will go tomorrow after tutoring," Drum said.

Drum gently tilted his face up higher. He went on his toes as Drum brushed his lips across his cheek, stopping right before their lips touched. He knew no one could see them at all.

Drum released his Dome for them to shop but left his heat as a warning not to come close. Drum respected the fact he wouldn't touch him where others could see, so Drum's compromise was to place a Dome whenever they wanted to get close.

He was sure others would guess what was happening behind the Dome, but since most knew touching Drum would result in severe burns, they could only wonder. He only touched Drum openly at the mall yesterday and once at school. It happened so fast, and he didn't burn, their schoolmates believed he was saved by Queen and Win.

On the day Drum invited him to his party, everyone saw him bump into Drum's sling backpack and since there was no skin-to-skin contact, their schoolmates really believed he was escaping death multiple times.

"Don't worry Dumpling, we'll figure this out," Drum consoled him, while whispering in his ear and caressing his neck.

He trusted every word out of Drum's mouth, as Drum never Lied to him. He didn't know what these feelings were, but he didn't want to fight them. His trouble came from accepting them. He continued to find alternate reasons and excuses as to why he felt this way about Drum.

He knew his Ma's family belief when it came to gay males and his Pa's feelings on it ever since Yolk. He thought about how his Pa would react to him stating he liked a male more than a best friend and it made him pause.

There could be a way for him to hide his feelings from his parents until he figured out what the hell to do. He was caught between wanting to stay happily wrapped up in Drum's arms forever and going back to save his G-Pas.

Ah shit! He thought as he stepped back out of Drum's arms.

He didn't look up as he knew Drum was looking at him with a questioning look. His thoughts flowed as he turned to continue walking down the sidewalk.

This is what everyone was trying to stress. I must go back to get my G-Pas. I cannot leave them there after everything they have done to protect me in that place. It is not fair I am here, a place they believed with all their hearts was real and they are still trapped there, in that hellhole.

If I leave, would Drum really follow me back there? What if he got collared? No, that would never happen since they would be unable to touch him. But what if he was killed? How could I ask him to do something like that?

But I am asking him to help me learn about my Talents. And he tutors and spoils me. We have gotten close and if I leave, what will happen to him? Am I using Drum? I do not want to use him; but he is the only one able to help me.

What if I am not good enough to be next to him? What if my Talents are not strong enough? I do not know if I can go back intact. I have been broken by freedom. Do I just accept my fate to be a pet for the rest of my short life and walk away from everything here?

He didn't realize but they were back in front of his home. Drum made a Portal, and he absentmindedly walked through. Plopping down on the ground, it was softer than he thought concrete should be, but he didn't bother to look under him. He knew he couldn't go into his home, just yet. He still needed to figure this out but every question he asked himself was carried off into the darkness. He never received an answer, so it was as if his thoughts were lost to the Universe.

Maybe I can question my way to find a solution? If I keep asking myself questions without restricting or trying to rationalize my feelings, could I possibly come up with an answer?

Is it using Drum if I learn Talents from him but still go back? If I am using those Talents to make sure I can make it back to Drum, would it still be using him? If my heart hurts when I ask myself this, does it mean I am using him and feeling bad about it?

Am I the type of Being who wants to use innocent people as a means to my own end? If I feel sick to my stomach when I ask this does it mean I do not like it, or I cannot stomach the thought of being a conniving little bastard?

It seems if I ask myself questions, I can use how I feel as an answer!

How would I feel if I stopped learning Talents from Drum if I am not going to tell him why I am wanting to learn them? Is the peace I felt the answer?

Why does it feel like Drum openly tells me about Talents and is willingly teaching me? What is this feeling of impending doom?

Does Drum know what I am planning to do once I have learned my Talents? There is no way he could know!

His head shot up to look at Drum, who was sitting on the brick ledge in front of his home. Drum sat with his leg crossed in a figure four, his hands in his pocket, his eyes closed, as his skin soaked up the rays of the starlight. As he looked at the handsomely beautiful male, he felt a crack.

"You know?" he asked Drum.

Drum didn't bother to open his eyes as he answered, "I guessed as much."

There was no malice or mistrust in Drum's voice, and it made his heart hurt more. He sat there staring at Drum, unsure of the emotion shown on his face. He noticed, without looking, where everybody else was. Dill, Queen, and Win were all lounged behind him, cooing and petting the rabbit who followed him that day. He could feel the rabbit, Mr. Floppy Ears as Dill called him, eyes on him, but he didn't bother since there was no Ill Intent. Only Drum sat on the opposite side of his gate. Queen, of course, was interested in the conversation.

He questioned aloud. "Why would you...?" He trailed off.

Drum opened his eyes and turned them towards him. "It wouldn't be fair to you for me to handicap you for my own personal reasons," Drum said, not giving away to what they were alluding.

He didn't know what to say as his alarm on his phone went off.

Drum stood up and made Portals for everyone.

"We should get ready for Sport's game," Drum said.

"I'm staying here with Pantu," Dill said, and Drum closed Dill's Portal.

Dill nodded in thanks and entered his Portal. He stood as Drum was saying bye to Queen and Win as they left through their own Portals to go home. He didn't know if he could look Drum in the eye. The emotions he was feeling were overwhelming and he was so busy trying to name them all, he didn't know how to react to them.

PANTU: A SOLID FOUNDATION
WEEK FOUR: SUNDAY

Drum, however, gathered him into a hug, with a kiss on his neck. Drum stepped back from him and held his arms out to the rabbit.

"Hey Mr. Floppy Ears, let's go home," Drum told the rabbit, who took a leap off the ledge into Drum's arms.

"This rabbit is yours?" he asked, tilting his head in confusion.

"He's not a rabbit, he's a bunny," Drum said. "He's the cutest bunny ever...aren't you, Mr. Floppy Ears?" Drum asked while snuggling his face in the rabbit's fur.

He stood staring at Drum interacting with the rabbit. "He is way too old to be a bunny," he calmly informed Drum.

Both Mr. Floppy Ears and Drum looked at him. Drum covered Mr. Floppy Ears' ears before speaking.

"He's sensitive about his age," Drum countered. "Also, if you don't want a chunk of your body missing, I suggest not alluding to him being anything more than a bunny."

He could only stand there and stare at Drum and Mr. Floppy Ears as they left through a royal-blue Portal. He walked as if he was a zombie through the white Portal Drum made and it closed behind him. He dumped himself on the beautiful floor of his art studio as Dill was walking around, oohing and ahhing over every inch.

"I do not feel like I can learn from him anymore," he said sadly to Dill. "I should just go now and wish for the best," he added, as he closed his eyes.

"What are you saying Pantu? Why can't you learn from him? If he can teach you what you need to know so we can save your G-Pas, how is it a dreadful thing?" Dill asked him the same questions he'd already asked himself.

"It is the same as using him as a means to an end if I refrain from telling him everything. It is not the kind of Being I want to be. It makes me sick to my stomach. So, unless I can tell him my plans, I should not learn anything else from him," he said, quietly realizing his true feelings.

"It feels the same way when someone else would use me for their own benefit. I felt dirty because I saw so many people become used up completely, until they were skin and bones, only to be tossed out. Literally, they would be dirty, funky, and unkempt and then be beaten out of The Center all the way to The Slums."

He hung his head. "I could never impose such a feeling on anyone I care about because I would never want them to feel the way I felt. I would never impose such a feeling on Drum," he ended, placing his head into his knees.

Dill came close and sat in front of him, tapping him three times on his head with a finger.

"Who is there?" he sadly asked.

"Your best friend!" Dill replied, with a smile in his voice.

"My best friend who?" he asked, his voice still laced with sadness.

He was unsure of how Dill would feel about charging into his hometown as his best friend understood the level of security surrounding The City. To his knowledge, no one ever left there and lived. Getting out was already a feat in itself, but to have lived as long as he and his parents have outside of The City was unheard of.

He heard of people trying to leave but they were always caught. If they did manage to make it out, the Cloaked did their job well and if they needed to, would bring back dead bodies to be stripped. Those too poor to make it out and those rich enough to not want to leave caught everyone else up in the middle.

He was sure Dill wanted to make it back to his girlfriend, so could he, right now, honestly, want Dill to go with him? If he didn't learn his Talents, he would only stupidly endanger Dill. That, he knew he didn't want.

He heard Dill's quiet voice. *"Your best friend, who is proud of the solid foundation you're building."*

His head lifted and he looked at Dill. The question on his face was answered when Dill placed his hand on his head and spoke.

"You have always been the type of Being who thinks about others before yourself. Yes, you are spoiled, but you can't fight the kind heart you have. You could have had a lot of people killed while living there, but you chose to have them sent away instead," Dill explained to him.

"A lot of good it did me. Tracey hated me for it. A lot of people hate me because I outsmarted them," he said, remembering how many people lost everything trying to bring him down.

"But they're alive to experience those feelings. Well, not Tracey, not anymore," Dill said, smiling at him. "You could've used me. You could've used Queen and Drum, but you chose to make friendships with us instead."

Dill could see the joy in his eyes every time he spoke about his G-Pas and knew how much he loved them. Dill could also see how much it hurt him to know they were left behind in a place like that.

But he still refused to bring anyone else into his problems. Dill knew he felt like a burden and understood how living in a town like this could make him feel like a semi-truck bearing down on a toddler's remote-controlled, motorized, riding car, dragging all his problems behind him. After much annoyance, Dill inserted himself into his life and instead of using Dill, they became best friends.

Dill continued, "No one has ever gotten as close as you have with The Four. Instead of just using them to help you with Mansnake, you took the time to open to them. You went to them and told them about you, asking for their understanding and their help. You told them things you never told your parents.

"But you were willing to accept their decision, no matter which way it leaned. If they didn't understand, you were okay with it and would keep trying to figure it out on your own while keeping your head down," Dill explained to him, knowing he never looked at himself this way.

He tried to be that type of Being, thinking he would only be here for a fleeting time. But Dill was the only one who saw the first day, he didn't have it in him. No matter what he needed to do in The City to survive, Dill only praised his G-Pas' Talent of establishing a good solid foundation when it came to his morals and his values, he just couldn't see it because of the mentality needed to live there.

Dill could still see the sadness written on his face, so he kept going. "You care enough to not Lie to me. You care enough to be open with me. You trusted me enough to use the black box without testing it first. You care enough to try and find a balance with our friendship. You care enough to not make me choose between my girlfriend and you," Dill listed off as he was looking at his best friend with teary eyes.

"You already have a solid foundation forged in The City by your G-Pas. You're kind and caring. You may omit some things, but I know it takes time to open up about your life there and I think they understand that as well. It's why they don't push, but I also know you haven't Lied. You haven't used anyone. You overcompensate instead," Dill told him.

Dill lifted his head to meet his eyes and holding his hands, Dill said, "You. You are different than Mansnake. He willingly sells his body wherein you were stolen and sold against your will. He uses and abuses both Beings and humans. But you. You make friends. Your family saved Others. You saved Others. He tries to Lie, cheat and murder his way into Drum's heart, while you...well you..." Dill's face turned away, trying to hide his thoughts.

He laughed from deep within him. He should have known Dill would understand him and how he was feeling. He felt like shit. He really liked Kat and The Four as friends and he was so grateful to the Universe for bringing him Dill that his laughter came with tears.

"I do not deserve to be this happy Dill!" he cried out.

Dill held his hands tighter. "Well for someone who has never killed anyone, the Universe would disagree with you. So, pardon me, best friend, if I selfishly agree with it, just this one time?" Dill said, with a smile.

He hugged his best friend. Doctor Robin and Dill were made for each other.

"And you have never killed anyone either," he said, smiling back at Dill.

Dill just looked at him. "I think if you don't feel comfortable learning from Drum unless you are completely honest, then that's what you should do. But he will notice and say something. Are you prepared to tell him?" Dill asked, measuring his level of comfort.

"He already knows. I am unsure how long he has known but he has never treated me differently or stopped being around me," he said.

Dill rolled his eyes and sighed. "Of course. Drum is more intelligent than all of us combined, so I'm not surprised. Are you ready to explain your feelings to him?" Dill asked, and he knew from the way his Light jerked inside his body, he was scared.

"Not those feelings, your feelings about learning your Abilities, goofy," Dill said, laughing at his face of mixed emotions.

He blushed a deep red and nodded. "I have never experienced the freedom to make my own choices. If it means Drum will not like who I am becoming, then I am still not sure how I would feel." He thought aloud. "I also do not think I want to change myself to fit someone else's mold of who they think I should be or how they think I should behave."

Dill nodded as he wiped away nonexistent tears. "My little PanPan, coming into his own."

"Nice. I really felt that!" he said, laughing.

His best friend always knew how to make him feel better. He was so elated he had an actual best friend; he was praying to the Universe Dill was just as happy as he was. He felt Dill deserved all the good in the world just for being a friend to someone like him.

"That," Dill told him with a smile. "That feeling right there already makes you a better Being than anyone else I have met!" Dill told him, grinning ear to ear.

PANTU: NOT WITHOUT YOUR SPOILER, YOU WILL NOT
WEEK FOUR: SUNDAY

His gratefulness spread through the room smelling of cinnamon and honey.

Dill took a deep breath. "If this is what Drum smells like to you, don't tell anyone."

He shook his head. "He does not smell of that anymore," he said. "I will tell Drum about—"

But he was interrupted by Drum appearing in his studio.

"Tell me what?" Drum's soothing voice sounded out.

He yelped and tried to jump into Dill's lap. When he found his sanity, he saw Drum, relaxed, sitting on the bay window nook, with a raised eyebrow, a smirk, and hands in his pockets. He placed himself back on the floor and gave Dill a shared look.

Dill just shook his head. *"I'm really surprised I have lived THIS long around you,"* Dill mumbled to him, but a snort let them know Drum heard as well.

He knew Drum was aware any time he was aroused, and that sitting on Dill's lap while in that state wouldn't be beneficial to Dill's health, even if Drum was the reason for his arousal.

Dill stood up to leave, and he gave a panicked look before reaching for his best friend but stopped his hand. Until he and Drum figured this out, maybe clinging to another male so openly and in front of Drum wouldn't be a promising idea.

"I'm going to say hi to Ma Sky and Pa Moon." Dill walked out of the attic, giving them space to talk.

He looked down at the floor as he rubbed his hand over it. "Thank you, Drum," he said. "For the studio. Thank you."

Drum said nothing, just reached out an arm to him, and he curled up next to Drum. His chin was resting on Drum's shoulder, and his arms were around Drum's waist.

"How did Pa Moon get his name?" Drum asked.

"GLou named him," he said, smiling at the pleasant memory of the story.

"GLou? I thought GMack was his Pa?" Drum asked, egging a conversation.

He spoke a lot about his G-Pas in their shared dreams. He told Drum a lot about himself and yet Drum's feelings and scent never wavered whenever he was around the Real Drum, whose scent was all over the RMD and so strong, he felt safe and talked his heart out, while playing with the cattail he named Natum.

"My G-Pas have been best friends since birth, as they say. So, when they each had their first kid, the other named them. GLou's favorite pastime was to camp during the double full moons.

"GLou said it was the most beautiful scene he had ever seen, so it is the name he gave my Pa. My Ma's name was supposed to be Star but one day GMack saw a moon out in full on a rare, bright day.

"He realized even when we could not see the moons, they were always there. So, he changed her name, since the Moons was always in the Sky," he explained.

Drum smiled at the story. "That's sweet. No wonder you were excited about having a best friend of your own." Drum leaned back, making his head fall to rest on Drum's chest.

"So..." Drum started, giving the conversation over to him.

He knew Drum wouldn't repeat himself and he knew what Drum wanted to know. He sat up, unfolding his legs, giving his back to Drum, he looked down while playing with his nails.

"I have to go back," he stated.

Drum looked at him questioningly. "You want to go back?"

"No. I do not want to, I must," he started. "It is not fair Drum. My G-Pas believed a place like this existed their whole lives. I stopped believing when I became a pet, but here I am, living the life they should have. They should be here to see this, experience this, live here. They deserve it, for never giving up, not like I did," he told Drum.

"So, you want to go back and rescue your G-Pas," Drum said. "How were you going to do that before learning your Abilities?"

Taking a deep breath, he told Drum. "I have some Talents I can use. If that did not work, I was going to offer myself up in exchange for my G-Pas' freedom and for them leaving my parents alone. I am who they want, so if they had me, maybe my family could live in peace." He couldn't look at Drum, his heart was hurting with the thought he would never see Drum again.

"You would leave me for a chance to give your parents and G-Pas a better life?" Drum asked, smiling at him.

"It is not like that. I did not plan on even staying this long. I did not plan to make real friendships. Then, I met Dill. I wanted to at least graduate, so my parents retained a nice memory of me before I went back, but then I thought this would be a nice, safe place for my parents to live out the rest of their lives. I wanted my G-Pas to live here as well." He got out.

It was so much, he just kept going. "I have changed and discarded so many plans, but I did so happily. I kept trying to find a better way to get back to them. I wanted to go before they found me, but for some reason..." he paused, not sure whether he should say it or not.

Drum finished his thought. "You couldn't knowingly go and endanger Dill. You didn't want to get anyone else involved for fear they would be collared."

He nodded, appreciating the fact Drum understood the Being he was trying to be. Drum's voice was matter of fact and it was soothing to him.

"I thought if I could learn some more Talents, then I would have a glimmer of hope to protect my family. I would be able to save my G-Pas. That I would be able to come back to protect them and my parents while we all lived here," he said.

"So why not do that?" Drum asked.

"Because how fair would it have been to you? There is never a hundred percent chance I would make it back. Would I learn my Talents and then disappear? Dill refuses to let me do this alone and I am so scared he will get collared. But he believes we can pull this off," he said, with a small, sad, laugh.

"By your birthday," Drum responded as Dill walked back into the attic.

He finally turned and looked at Drum. "Huh?"

"I will figure out your Energy and teach you everything I can, without overwhelming you, by your birthday," Drum started to his amazement.

"After that, I will go with you and Dill to rescue your G-Pas," Drum ended.

"Wait! Why would you..." he started. "I do not want you to..." he trailed off, stopped by the look on Drum's face.

"You would go without me? You really think I would let you and DILL go by yourselves?" Drum asked, looking at him indignantly. "What will you do if they start shooting at you?" Drum asked him.

"Put up a Dome," he responded.

Drum nodded at his response and looking him straight in the eyes, asked, "And if they told you to drop the Barrier while they held a gun to your G-Pas' heads or a knife to their throats?" Drum asked, watching the realization crawl over his face. Drum knew he would immediately drop the Dome or be unable to control it under stress.

"Fighting is more than hitting, kicking, shooting bullets, or swinging a sword. It is also psychological," Drum told him. "You two will focus on getting your G-Pas out and I will handle the fighting," Drum ended, completing their plan, without their approval.

"If you think I won't hold to my Promise, you fail to understand," Drum said. "*I Promised to protect you. That means your body, Mind, brain, heart, and Core, Pantu,*" Drum softly said and pulled him in for a hug.

DILL: A CHANCE TO TRY AGAIN
WEEK FOUR: SUNDAY

He, however, was trying not to be noticed as he came back into the studio. Before, he was around Drum in a group of Beings and he was normally with Pantu around Drum's best friends, so he was adept with blending into the background to not be noticed by Drum.

He was never around Drum so personally before, other than the one time they spoke privately, so he was trying to blend into the background when Drum looked at him.

The look of slight confusion on Drum's face trying to place his own from somewhere made him uncomfortable, and he squirmed under Drum's gaze, trying to hide.

Drum stood and with his hands in his pockets, walked towards him. "Don't I know you?" Drum asked, calmly standing a safe distance in front of him.

"He is Dill, my best friend!" Pantu said happily, sitting on the bay nook.

"Hmm. Something has been off about you. There's a weird tugging in my Mind every time I'm around you. Like I should know who you are, but I never seemed to quite put my finger on it," Drum said. "I know you, don't I?" Drum asked.

He was trying to hide his face, but he felt compelled to look into Drum's eyes. He felt Drum's Heat and started to sweat. He nodded, answering Drum's question.

"You were the ringleader, Sage, right?" Drum asked, with a slight, half smile which didn't feel inviting at all. "You're correct, it *is* a surprise you've lived this long. I thought I made it clear not to let me remember you or I would do worse to you than I did to him. Did you think I forgot what you did to me?" Drum asked.

He felt Drum push Energy out to cover his body. As Drum's Heat flashed over him, the pressure of Energy and lack of oxygen made him drop to his knees as the Heat started to blister his body.

Pantu rushed to stand in front of Drum. "NO DRUM! PLEASE! STOP!" Pantu pleaded with Drum, lightly beating Drum's chest.

"Pantu!" Drum said.

He heard the anger laced in Drum's tone and felt Drum's eyes boring a hole through him. He didn't know which was worse, the Energy pressure from Drum's Heat or Drum's stare.

"Please Drum. He is my best friend, please do not take him from me," Pantu started.

"What would you have me do?" Drum asked.

He heard the switch in tone in Drum's voice, which was now speaking softly to Pantu. He also felt Drum's eyes leave him and he could finally force a small breath. He could also hear the crack in Drum's voice, as if Drum was holding back tears but he didn't dare look up.

He could hear Pantu swallow, and he knew what Pantu was about to ask, would make it seem as if Pantu cared more about his feelings than Drum's. He couldn't find the words to stop Pantu as he struggled to take another small breath.

"Can you please try and give him a chance?" Pantu asked.

Instead of responding, all he heard was Drum's footsteps moving closer to him.

Pantu grabbed Drum. "To show you he has changed. That he is no longer the same Being. Please Drum. He was annoyingly kind to me and if it was not for Dill..." Pantu became quiet.

If it weren't for him, Pantu would have avoided Drum until he disappeared. Pantu would have never approached them or spoken with any of them. Pantu would have been like a ghost, waiting here until it was his time to pass on.

"I will," Drum stated. "If you can give Coin a second chance, then I will give Dill one."

"Pantu...you...can't..." he tried to get out. He knew where Drum was leading, and he only wanted to save his best friend. Closing his eyes to try for a deeper breath, he understood his best friend was still unaware of a lot of things about himself. Drum must have also realized, which is why Drum made such a compromise.

"It is fine. He is probably dead by now without me to convince GLou or GMack to save him." Pantu waved it off, and he knew Pantu was showing a lack of understanding his trauma.

"Okay. I agree!" Pantu said.

"Promise?" Drum asked.

To which the prompt reply out of Pantu's mouth shocked him.

"Promise," Pantu gasped out.

But Drum did more than blister his body, Drum showed him why he was on his knees. He didn't pay too much attention to the Promises Drum gave Pantu, or the fact Pantu could touch Drum, but he was pretty fucking sure Pantu said earlier that Drum no longer smelled like cinnamon and honey but now held a different scent. Drum held Pantu's double scent, like Doctor Robin held his.

The quickness in which Pantu agreed to Drum's request of a Promise was as fast as the words came out of his mouth with his girlfriend. Drum was flat out telling him, Pantu and

Drum were Fated. He could only close his eyes and say a quiet prayer to the Universe to keep his girlfriend, his Dad and best friend safe after he was burned away to nothing.

"Okay, then I will give Dill a chance. One. To prove he's changed," Drum said, looking at him with a look which said Drum wasn't happy about Pantu's stance on his behalf.

Drum took his hand out of his pocket and snapped his fingers. The Heat dissipated and he gasped for clean, cool air to fill his lungs. Pantu came to him, upset with the heat blisters on his body, again. Pantu looked at Drum, who turned away from them, as Pantu held him, but he held no strength of his own yet not to collapse into a puddle on the floor.

Drum asked without looking at them, "Aren't you going to ask me to Promise?"

"No. If I force, are you really giving him a chance?" Pantu asked back.

Pantu knew Drum was trying to make him Promise. Drum wanted the obligation of a Promise without doing the work of trying to get to know him. It was why Drum egged Pantu on, hoping for a Promise.

But of course, Pantu picked right up on it, he thought with the tiniest hint of a smile.

"Is Dill spending the night?"

Pantu made sure he could breathe properly before answering Drum. "Yes."

Drum snapped his fingers again. He finally managed, with Pantu's help, to weakly stand, but still refused to look directly at Drum. Pantu and him both noticed another twin bed not far from Pantu's. There was plenty of space between them and the new bed was covered with the logo of a kiddie show about being kind to others.

"Really Drum?" Pantu asked.

"OH!" Drum said, his eyes wide with wonder, as he turned to look at Pantu. "You would let him sleep in MY spot...on OUR bed?" Drum asked Pantu, with a dangerous smile.

Pantu didn't say a word as he quickly spoke up.

"I was going to sleep on the beanbag. Thank you very kindly for the bed," he said, not looking at Drum.

Drum turned away from them again. Pantu knew what he did as a kid and as soon as Drum realized Pantu knew, Drum almost killed him, but Pantu begged for his life, pissing Drum off even more.

"And here I thought you never begged before. That makes twice you have begged for the lives of others," Drum said, standing with pocketed hands and closed eyes.

"I have done a lot of new things, here, in this town" Pantu said, directly to Drum, as he moved to stand behind Drum. "Things I never thought I would do, I have done...here,"

Pantu told Drum. "So, thank you Drum," Pantu brightly said and gently pushed Drum towards the sitting nook.

Pantu kept pushing until Drum was standing in front of the sitting area. Turning Drum around, to face him, Pantu gently pushed Drum to sit down.

"Drum, Dill knows this will be the only chance he will have. If he ever bares his teeth against you, he knows what will happen to him," Pantu said, looking Drum directly in the eyes but being loud enough to ensure he heard. His best friend was helping him, saving his life.

Drum pulled Pantu closer. "And if I hurt him?" Drum asked.

Pantu responded, "You already have, and yet, here I am, standing in front of you. If he has no loyalty for my life, then I should return his feelings." Pantu leaned in to kiss Drum's neck.

He understood.

DRUM: AN INNER CONVERSATION
WEEK FOUR: SUNDAY

His smile, as he knew Dill understood, widened. Pantu would choose him over Dill.

As close as Pantu and Dill are, he would still choose to stand at my side.

As he thought this, coupled with the fact Pantu was kissing and licking his neck, he returned the feelings and the actions. The feelings he was giving off were stronger than what he thought it would be and Pantu whimpered. He threw a Barrier around them and controlled the time inside it, knowing Pantu was too unfocused and didn't yet know how to anchor Abilities.

There was something about the way whenever he held out his arms, Pantu would, without hesitating, come right into them, as if it was magnetic. He understood the Seduction Ability well, as he himself possessed it. He was able to make his Ability powerful, to the point he could suppress others who tried to use their Ability on him.

Pantu's Ability was severely diluted, and because of the lack of direction, it had little effect on him. But he realized how much he craved the small amount Pantu did give him and how much he didn't want to suppress Pantu.

He could only imagine the fight of willpower to take place once Pantu's Abilities were fully realized. The thought made him shiver and release again to which Pantu responded, arching his back and moaning, coming again.

Pantu fell into his shoulder, handing control over to him. He grabbed Pantu's butt in his hands, moaning at the fact Pantu's little bubble butt fit perfectly in his large hands.

As he gripped each naked cheek, he started moving Pantu to continue rubbing the veins in the back of their members against each other. Pantu's arms were now around his neck as he set the rhythm.

As he pulled Pantu closer, he felt Pantu press against his body, securing themselves with no need to use their hands. Even though they both came and released several times already, they were both still very much aroused and he wouldn't stop until His Pantu was completely satisfied. There was no way he would be leaving his aroused Pantu to spend the night alone with Dill, separate beds be damned.

But there was a problem. He knew he had this problem but the fact he was unwilling to fix it made it worse. Whenever he and Pantu were engaged this way, his abnormal Ability to multitask crumbled. Outside of his thoughts and physical actions being Pantu-centered, he couldn't focus on anything else. This left him open and vulnerable.

If it wasn't for the fact his Barriers were unbreakable, given even a little thought to them, he was begrudgingly agreeing with Dill. Even though he didn't like Dill, he wasn't stupid enough to disregard Dill's sound advice to Pantu about not touching him. If Pantu were to touch him in public, he knew his entire world would fill with Pantu, and he wouldn't be able to focus on anything else.

Pantu immediately threw their lives in array since arriving. Pantu throwing his life in array was the most dangerous thing a Being could do. There was no balance when it came to Pantu, and he knew this. It was outrageous and deadly how close Pantu was to him without choosing a side, as well as Dill's unknown influence.

He'd given himself a deadline more than Pantu. He would figure out a way to be able to touch Pantu in public without a Barrier and without endangering their lives by the New Year. He needed to, or else they probably wouldn't live past that. But it didn't mean he wasn't above enjoying every bit Pantu gave him until then.

As these thoughts filled his head, he fell into himself. He saw Himself inside his Core standing and calling to his Form while holding on to its tail.

"Not now, you have to be patient," Himself said to his Form.

He was shocked. He could, of course, see his Core and his abnormal flowing Energy but he was never inside of it before. He didn't know it was a possibility, but Pantu was showing him new things every day. He was unsure if Pantu knew what he was doing, and it made him more protective of Pantu.

As he watched and listened to the interaction between Himself and his Form, he smiled. His Form, which was a royal-blue Dragon, was considered the most beautiful, and would be seen as a water or air type, if you just base it on the colors humans used to describe things. But his Form was a Sky Fire Dragon, with the Ability to communicate with all the elements of nature.

His label as the most powerful Being was properly earned. He could do so much more than the simple Abilities he used in front of most Beings and the less those other Beings knew about him, the more confident he knew they felt.

Believing they held a chance to kill him was a nonexistent thought before, but now he knew he opened a door to invite them in. Pantu's motives and beliefs were unknown to them, but he threw his caution to the wind and pursued Pantu anyway.

As his Form settled down and returned to wrap itself around Inner Drum's body, his Form shrunk to perfectly fit and rest its head on Inner Drum's shoulder. Consoling his Form by scratching underneath its chin; Inner Drum spoke.

"You have to learn how to control yourself around him or it could be quite dangerous for us," Inner Drum told the Dragon, who nodded in understanding.

"I know it won't happen overnight, but we will work on it from here and outer Drum will work on it from there," Inner Drum said to his Form, who looked at Inner Him, skeptically.

"You are highly attracted to his Form, aren't you?" Inner Drum asked.

To which his Dragon Form raised his head, looking confused.

He looked at them, just as confused as his Form, who was looking at Pantu and started to reach for him again.

"Hey now! Calm it down. If you are going to do all that, then you might as well just tell me what his Form is," Inner Drum said to the Dragon, who paused to tilt his head to the side, eyeing Inner Drum up and down, before turning his head away to blow out a cloud of smoke.

He understood this as his Form saying, *figure it out yourself.*

He laughed a bit before realizing his Form turned to look at him. He was confused since he didn't think they would notice him. His Form left Inner Drum and glided toward him, wrapping around him. The coolness his Dragon's body held was contradicting the royal-blue flames which made up his Form.

"It helps Pantu is touching you right now," Inner Drum said.

He looked at Inner Drum.

"Besides, the cooler the Flame, the hotter it burns," Inner Drum said, with a smile.

His Form now rested his front paws on his shoulders and was playfully rubbing the underside of his head through his soft, curly hair. He moved to walk closer to Inner Drum, while reaching up with one hand to pat his Form's head, his other hand still in his pocket.

"What are you doing here?" he asked Inner Drum.

"I'm helping to control our Energy and our Form. I keep them from getting further out of hand," Inner Drum responded.

He stopped. "Who are you?" he asked Inner Drum.

"I am you and also not you," Inner Drum answered, with a smile. "You should know not to use our Form around Pantu. Not yet," Inner Drum said. "I will keep him back until it's time, so even if you try, I won't let you change in front of Pantu."

He stopped patting his Form and tilting his head to the side, he looked at his Inner Self. His Form seemed to agree with how he felt as it lifted its head to look at Inner Drum the same way.

Inner Drum held his hands up. "It's not a challenge" he said, as he went on to explain. "Our Core is severely damaged. So, your assumption of if you change, you may not be able to change back, is correct. You might also lose all sense of self."

His Form huffed out clouds of smoke from his nostrils at the explanation.

"And Pantu's Form?" he asked.

"It's only a guess but our Form seemed to suggest maybe Pantu's Form is a miracle? Knowing where it is before you can get your mental and physical reactions to Pantu under control, would only endanger us and it would be worse for him," Inner Drum started. "It seems Pantu's Form would be as upsetting to the Being community as ours was and was hidden away. Actually, I feel like it would be worse."

He nodded in agreement. "He can't replenish his Energy very well, so it would be best for him not to worry about his Form until he's able to naturally replenish. If I know what he is, I may push him too soon."

His Form though, seemed to not agree with this and huffing and puffing, moved to unwrap from around him. Both Drums laughed at the Dragon hovering above them, not wanting to touch either.

"I guess Pantu was right, I am a bit stubborn," he said to Inner Drum.

His Form nodded in agreement and Inner Drum, looking only at him, responded, "It seems like we get that from Arbie."

He looked confused. "Arbie?" he asked.

Inner Drum gestured to his Form. "His name is Arbie. It's a play on the initials of our Energy color Royal Blue. R-B spelled how you would say it, A-R-B-I-E," Inner Drum said to the prideful look of the Dragon, who wrapped itself around Inner Drum.

"Since we spend a lot of time together, it only felt right to call him by name. I didn't want to say Royal Blue every time or call him Dragon," Inner Drum said, as he scratched under Arbie's chin, much to Arbie's pleasure.

He walked up and scratched Arbie on his head. "I know you really want to connect with Pantu, but if we rush before he is ready, we might destroy him," he truthfully told Arbie, which both Drums could see, Arbie accepted.

"Patience Arbie. The Universe always finds a way," Inner Drum said, to console his Form as well.

Inner Drum looked at him as Arbie sighed contently and accepted, he was outnumbered and not willing to destroy the Being he cared about.

He looked behind them. The whole back area was covered and filled with clouds. He couldn't tell how spacious or small the space was. He felt a presence and asked, "What's back there?"

"Clouds," Inner Drum said to him, with a smile. "You might want to give Pantu a bit of our Energy before you leave," Inner Drum said, as he dissipated.

PANTUxDRUM: THE BUILDUP OF POWER
WEEK FOUR: SUNDAY

Pantu, however, was in a state of ecstasy. Even though he initiated this, he couldn't control his body after leaking and coming so much, so he gave up control to Drum. As Drum took over, he moaned.

Is this what the women in The City felt whenever I pleased them? This lingering question made him jealous with each stroke. He was seen as the best in his generation when it came to pleasing women.

He was the only pet who didn't need to spend a full night with a woman to leave her completely satisfied. Women would bid outrageous amounts just to spend less than an hour alone with him.

He was never remotely interested in any of the women he was with. He never found them attractive or was physically motivated to do anything to them. If it weren't for his G-Pas' training, he would have been lower than Coin in the rankings.

He could thoroughly physically, mentally, and emotionally please a woman without him feeling a thing for them. Not even a tingle. Although he felt like a robot, his body was able to listen and do what he needed it to do. It was enough to shoot him to number one and keep him there.

It also made him jealous of the women living in The City. He would watch, without emotion, the way the women's bodies responded to him, and he wanted to know what that felt like.

He wanted to be born a Woman so his life would be easier and so he could feel what made their bodies contort in such funny, weird ways. But he was born a male, tasked with living a life of hell and torment. Born to only give pleasure, never to receive it.

But right now, his body was receiving pleasure wrapped around Drum. His Mind no longer tried to control his body as they both moved in tandem to his feelings.

And now, there was this annoying buildup inside he wanted gone. It kept drawing his attention every time he came, and it was causing him to moan in frustration. It was an itch somewhere in his body he couldn't scratch.

But when Drum's mouth found it wrapped around his nipple, an "Aaahhh!" came out of his mouth.

When Drum's tongue flicked his nipple, the deepest, longest moan escaped his mouth as he figured out what the annoying feeling really was.

It was Drum's hands gripping his bottom, the feeling of Drum's body under his own, the sensation of him rubbing against Drum, the feeling of him touching, kissing, and licking on Drum, and having every bit of it returned to him. And although he wasn't in a position to rationalize it, the feelings he carried for everything Drum said and done for him were in there as well.

As Drum's lips wrapped around his nipple and sucked, the stacked feelings combined and exploded inside his body. The explosion went from the tip of his toes, up to the tip of his fingers and didn't stop until it reached the follicles of his hair. Every inch of him was doused with so much Light, he disconnected from his body.

"AAAAAAAAAAAHHHHHHHHHHHHhhhhhhhhh!" He pushed from wherever it was in his body, but couldn't convey everything he was feeling, there were no words. His body also knew there was no way to properly respond to what was happening to it as for the first time with Drum, he realized his Light came out of his penis.

As Pantu's body wiggled, trembled, shivered, and shook on top of Drum, he couldn't find the right words to describe what was happening to Pantu or himself. All he knew was he was trying to hang on to Pantu for dear life as they both felt the explosion seconds after each other. He was using muscle memory to continue to move Pantu until every drop was released and they were satisfied.

He was drunk off the euphoric feeling as every inch of his body shook and trembled. Pantu held him tightly, as they were trying to both calm themselves, and each other.

His final grip on Pantu's bottom ended with them both gasping for air as their members flopped over, content, and drunk happy. They held on to each other as they tried to regulate and slow down their heartbeats.

Multiple Beings understood the amount of power Pantu unknowingly possessed. It was more than the fact Pantu could do things they thought dead to Beings; it was based on the knowledge Pantu held his heart.

And now, he knew Pantu held his Form under lock and key. He completely belonged to the young man on top of him. He would do anything for Pantu, which made Pantu a dangerous Being to upset. Whether or not Pantu knew this and depending on his actions going forward, it would shape the Being world or break it.

DILL: JUST KEEP DIGGING
WEEK FOUR: SUNDAY

He also figured this out or else he wouldn't have warned Pantu, going so far as to continue to befriend the one Being who held sway over Drum. As Pantu straddled Drum, he turned away and stared out the window.

He couldn't see the Barrier, and he felt like staring would be rude while sending his Mind into shock. They were inside one of Pantu's Time Barriers, but when Pantu and Drum started, Pantu's focus dropped, so Drum created a Time Barrier around just the two of them.

He was still covered in blisters, but he knew Pantu would heal him, just like on the bus and in the bathroom. Although Drum never mentioned it, he was sure Drum noticed.

He thought, as he searched out the window, *everyone seems to think it's Pantu who scrapes by death every day, how wrong they are.*

He knew his actions as a child would be impossible for Drum to forgive, but he prayed to the Universe for just one chance to make it right. After deciding to follow Drum, he threw himself into his education.

He would read books on how to be a better person and try to implement them in his life. He wanted to show he could change for the better. He decided he would help however he could, to make sure Drum sat on the throne, even from the shadows.

The years following Drum's arrival to their town, he became obsessed with finding ways to clear Drum's Path. He never decided what would be best for Drum, but instead he watched, learning as much as he could about Drum's personality. He even knew about Drum's hidden side; the side Drum wouldn't show in Sunset.

When Pantu came to town, he was thrown for a loop. He hadn't made or wanted to make friends outside of Jax, Turn and Put, who were also trying to be better Beings, closing themselves off as they felt they had no right to engage with others. They felt they would taint their schoolmates and wanted desperately to avoid that.

But Pantu was different. It wasn't because he was new and ignorant about the things they did as children; it was because he felt remorse from Pantu.

Out of all the other emotions Pantu held walking into their classroom and introducing himself, it was the remorse which drew him to Pantu. It was as if he and Pantu were both reaching for the same goal and could reach it together.

His eyes focused in on a Being watching Pantu's house with binoculars from an apartment building a few miles away. He knew the Being wouldn't be able to see through Drum's Barrier, so he was unbothered.

The first year just doesn't know when to stop digging, does he? The deadly thing about Pantu is, he will quietly let you dig, looking for his approval to stop, while never giving it.

You have triggered Pantu, who will now watch you dig your own hole and whenever you look at him for his approval to stop, Pantu will smile at you, and you will continue to dig.

No matter how deep, Pantu will never tell you to stop, but just quietly smile at you. You would think the smile was one of encouragement, but it will be at the level of ignorance your need for his approval is.

He knew Pantu's plan for the first year did not end well for the little snake.

It was him that day, following them in the park. I never found out who the snake was following Win and Kat on their date, but now I know who was behind the attack on Kat.

He thought back to the day he happened to see Win and Kat at one of his family's theme parks. He went with his stepparent to earn some expensive materials from his Dad he needed for his latest invention.

After seeing them quietly walking around the giant theme park, he saw a snake following them and decided to capture the snake to give it to them to keep their secret. Instead, he lost the snake and never found out its identity.

Pantu has to know about Win and Kat by now, he thought. *Win is driving him to school and Kat had lunch with him, but he hasn't said a word to me about them. This is how you're different Pantu, better.*

He knew Mansnake wouldn't want the information of Win and Kat dating to reach their schoolmates before he found a chance to secure Drum's affections. If everyone knew Win was dating, Drum would be swamped with requests and unable to move around without a crowd surrounding him. It would overshadow the small little snake as he wouldn't be able to control the riot it would lead to.

Now, it was only out of respect for Kat and what she went through, that for the last two years no one really approached Drum. He was sure all the Beings who did try and give Drum a Gift were threatened by Mansnake, *but no one is willing to speak up against him. He must have dirt on every Being who gets close.*

Pantu, on the other hand, chooses to make friends. The dirt Mansnake has on Pantu, over time would be proven useless. Pantu's dirt was worse than what Mansnake had on him, and he could have spread the video, but he chose, with a smile, to let Mansnake keep digging.

You have given Pantu too much time and gotten close to him in the wrong way. He refuses to have a repeat of Yolk, so now he will silently watch you dig. He sighed happily. *It's like I'm there with you Pantu, watching him dig.*

He could also see Queen was thrilled with life since Pantu arrived. *He knew who I was. Even if he had doubts, which I find hard to believe, I outright told him that night. He hugged and consoled me instead. That's what a naturally good-natured Being looks like.*

But Drum seemed to have just figured it out today. Did Queen not tell him? It was like Drum didn't know who I was when he asked me if Pantu knew about consent. I was confused, since Drum never asked about another Being before, but I couldn't Lie to him. There was a moment when he looked at me confused but let it pass.

I told him Pantu didn't know consent existed and that was the end of our conversation. But Queen knew who I was. Why did he let me stay around Pantu? Why didn't he tell Drum? He couldn't finish his thoughts as Pantu and Drum finished.

He slowly turned around while looking at the floor, tracing the beautiful pattern mixture of midnight blue and gold with his eyes. He glanced up to see Drum with his arm lazily thrown around Pantu's shoulders, his leg crossed in a figure four, smiling at Pantu.

He looks so happy, he thought, glancing at his best friend.

Pantu was sitting under the cover of Drum's crossed leg, leaning against Drum. He didn't say anything as Pantu offered for Drum to join movie night with them.

"Sport has a game tonight, and I have never missed any," Drum said, declining to stay while looking at him. "Besides, it's the semi-finals. When we win this, we will be the first school in the championship line-up," Drum ended, looking away from him.

"I want to go!" Pantu shouted, excited. "I have never been to a sports game before. Public executions by stadium fights were the closest thing to action entertainment we had," Pantu said, eyes bright.

Drum laughed and he smiled, still trying not to become the center of attention.

"One chance," was all Drum said.

He nodded and started to bow.

"Don't!" Drum's voice stopped him.

Taking deep breaths and nodding his head in excitement, he silently shouted his thanks to the Universe for this chance.

Thank you, Universe! Thank you, Pantu, he thought, as he calmed himself down.

DILLxPANTU: AN AWKWARD START TO A SECOND CHANCE
WEEK FOUR: SUNDAY

Drum stood to stretch then bent to tap Pantu on the chest. Drum held a finger there for a moment before standing straight up to leave.

"Don't use it all in one place," Drum said and raised an eyebrow to smile at the innocent look which covered Pantu's face.

Dill didn't look at Drum but when Pantu blushed, he saw Pantu's whole body lit up red. He smiled at his best friend's cute reaction.

Drum turned to look at him. "See you at the game. Not sure how you could go in your condition but…" Drum shrugged.

Pantu popped up. "He can wear pants and a long sleeve shirt with gloves. If we add a hooded jacket, face mask, some sunglasses, and a cap, no one will know!" Pantu clapped at the idea. "Ah, long socks with high boots as well."

Drum smiled then laughed at him. Drum let go of whatever he was about to say before walking into a Portal. Pantu patiently waited until they both felt Drum's Portal close. Pantu gave it a few seconds before coming over to him.

"Take off your shirt," Pantu instructed him. "I need to see every place I need to heal."

He painfully tried to take off his shirt but couldn't lift it over his head. Pantu helped him and walked around his body, looking at his torso.

"The last time I missed some, but you neglected to tell me, so you spent all that time in pain. Unnecessary!" Pantu scolded.

He sadly smiled as he knew Pantu was working on his Healing Ability without informing Drum.

"Your pants as well. I think he got your whole body again," Pantu said to him.

He unbuttoned his pants and went to bend down to take them off, but what radiated down his thighs and up his spine, paralyzed him with pain. Pantu huffed and went to assist him.

The scene Drum saw, stepping back into Pantu's attic, made everybody freeze. Drum saw Pantu, kneeling in front of him, while pulling his pants down. His shirt was gone and all that was left completely on his body was his boxers. Drum just stared at them.

Pantu was trying to find the words to explain at the same time Drum went to say something, but it came out as an exhaled breath. He closed his eyes in quiet acceptance of his death while Drum turned to leave and Pantu found some words.

"Drum! It is not what it looks like!" Pantu rushed out, standing to walk to Drum, but paused. "I was just..." Pantu started but left it alone.

"I forgot what it was I came back for?" Drum said, before disappearing.

Pantu dropped in acceptance Drum read the room wrong and turned to look at him.

"I will remember to say nice things at your Repast," Pantu sadly said.

He nodded. "That's all I can ask for at this point," he agreed.

Pantu moved to continue taking off his pants.

"Uh Pantu? Maybe we shouldn't. Your clothes idea sounds great!" he expressed, not wanting to be caught in the same position twice.

"I want to make sure you can have an open casket," Pantu joked, getting him out of his pants.

Drum's heat blistered every part of Dill's body, but Pantu wasn't about to ask Dill to take his boxers off.

I will learn how to heal covered body parts starting with a smaller area first and then work my way up so I can heal without undressing anyone. It will be safer for all parties involved, he thought. He went to work healing Dill's body.

"You know Drum figured out something about Coin you haven't yet," Dill informed him while being healed.

"What could he have possibly figured out with what little information I gave him?" he asked, still focused on healing Dill.

"Think about it rationally, Pantu. Why else would he make you Promise to give Coin a second chance?" Dill asked, making him think about all their conversations around Drum.

"How did Yolk know who Coin was, if you nor your parents told him?" Dill's question made him stand up and he paused to think about it.

"You think Coin had something to do with me getting collared? He did nothing to stop it from happening, but I assumed it was because he was a pet as well and would die if he spoke against the governess' daughter?" he asked, looking weirdly at Dill.

"I think so. I also think Drum figured out more about Coin. There was this look in his eyes. As if he was surprised you would agree to the condition. I think he knows you haven't figured it out yet," Dill sadly said.

When he was finished, he asked Dill if there were still any blisters under his covered area. Dill had to sit, stand, and bend over every way before he would believe there wasn't any.

"You cannot withhold the truth just because you think it is too much for me. I need to know if I am doing it properly or not," he said, scolding Dill again.

Dill dressed as he dropped the Time Dome he set moments after Drum first left. They spent several hours inside his Time Dome but only thirty minutes passed since they came into his studio through Drum's Portal.

Dill looked at him. "Uh Pantu?"

"Yes, Sir Dill?" he answered, using Dill's moniker in jest.

"Does Drum just pop over whenever he feels like it?" Dill worded it to mean there was no Portal when Drum first arrived.

"I said I would give him a chance. How fair would it be if I restricted him but gave you full access to my home?" he answered. "You have a key and no need to knock." He understood Dill was expressing the inconceivable Talent Drum possessed to show up inside a Time Dome with no Portal and a Mind able to keep up with the flow of the Dome.

Dill just shrugged. He could clearly see Dill wasn't wrong, but he also didn't feel the need to acknowledge Drum's lack of a Portal.

Holy Universe! Drum is a hell of a lot more powerful than I could have imagined, he thought, as he followed Dill downstairs. *But I am not the only one unable to control myself when we are together. This is more danger than I accounted for.*

PANTUxQUEEN: RUMOR ALERT
WEEK FOUR: SUNDAY

Pantu and Dill's parents were both going to the game. As he dressed, he sent a text to Dill with a reminder to bring an overnight bag. He paused, wondering what to do about his scent being as strong as it is now. He thought he should probably stay close to Drum, without drawing too much attention to himself.

As if it is the easiest thing on the planet to do, he thought, shaking his head. *Maybe going to the game is not a clever idea.* Drum didn't seem against it, and Dill always went along with whatever he wanted to do; death be damned.

Standing half dressed, he wondered what he should do when the doorbell rang. It was the crew. Drum, Dill, Queen and Win were walking into his home followed by their parents and Sport's foster parents and little sister.

That was the quickest response the Universe has ever sent me, he thought, silently thanking the Universe as well.

He went to finish getting dressed when Drum walked into his room, followed by Dill, Queen, and Win. Queen went to plop down on his bed, but Dill stopped Queen as Win went for the mini fridge Drum purchased for his room. Dill and Queen leaned against his dresser while Drum sat in his computer desk chair, and he was so happy to have pants on.

"Your skin is flawlessly gorgeous, Pantu. Do you have ANY scars at all?" Queen asked, but he knew this wasn't the question Queen really wanted an answer to.

Dill looked over at Drum, waiting for an answer, but Drum seemed unconcerned with Dill's gaze.

"I have never held a scar," he said. "No matter what happened to me, I was never left with a physical reminder," he added. He put on his shirt and found some socks.

The uneasy air was shattered as Win's happy squeal at finding a snack in his fridge filled the room. He grabbed his wallet and keys to quickly turn away but was stopped by Drum, who grabbed his arm and pulled him in for a hug.

The others left the room with Win closing the door behind them. Without asking questions, or trying to smooth over his past, Drum just held him in a hug.

The tears came from nowhere and everywhere all at once. The memories of his training by "her" deeply haunted him. The memories of the things the women would do to him for their pleasure made him sick to his stomach and his skin crawl, but Drum didn't say a word.

Drum's silent hug was filled with understanding and acceptance of his past. That this wouldn't be near enough to drive Drum away. His arms finally moved to wrap themselves around Drum, hugging back before he went to clean his face. Drum went downstairs first, and he followed shortly after.

They all rode together in a van larger than the one they rode in before and this one came with a driver. There were two levels, and the younger Beings all relaxed up top while their parents talked and drank on the level below. He was in good spirits as they talked and laughed all the way to the school.

The game was in Hollis, and the bad blood between the schools still ran deep. Soon as everyone left the van, Queen adorned them with their school colors, along with face paint and foam tubes.

Queen wrote all over everybody's exposed limbs and when he came to Dill, Queen didn't hesitate to cover Dill. He quickly cut his eyes to Drum, who said nothing, just looked at what Queen was doing to Dill before looking away, uninterested.

Drum's Ma applied his school spirit, and Drum's Pa painted his face to look like a school spirit bunny. He snickered at Drum, who took all the quiet laughs in stride. As they walked up to the ticket booth, he and Drum hung behind, while Drum's Pa paid for everyone's tickets.

He leaned towards Drum. "You are not going to take it off?" he asked, curious.

Drum leaned towards him and whispered back, *"Why would I, when it makes you smile?"*

He giggled. "You are adorable!" he said.

Drum shrugged and looked nonchalantly at the sky. "Yea, well?" Drum said.

He giggled quietly. "Pretty conceited, are you not?" he reprimanded.

"If I'm conceited for my nonchalant attitude about being adorable, what would I call someone who is conceited about being handsomely beautiful?" Drum teasingly asked, leaning over to look at him.

He stood and looking Drum directly in the eyes, he answered, "Why, call them Dumpling, of course!" he said assuredly, to which Drum's sweet laughter filled the air.

They entered the bleachers and when he saw the closed off area with 'The Santiago Family and Friends' banner, he rolled his eyes.

"Would you rather sit amongst the crowd, smelling the way you do or would you rather I sit with everyone else?" Drum asked him.

He understood neither option was good as he was climbing the steps until he came to the third bench from the top. He slid past Dill and the two of them enjoyed the whole row to themselves as Queen and Win sat in the row behind them. They left plenty of space to which Drum filled from the top row.

Their parents sat several rows in front of him and Dill, still chatting and laughing, while also enjoying their drinks. His parents looked happy and he annoyingly, but happily, rolled his eyes closed.

He and Dill started talking about the animals and people the condemned in The City fought as punishment. He didn't notice the Beings on the other side of the enclosed area were moving closer as his back was to them. He heard his name being called and he turned to find a beautiful girl hanging off the physical barrier.

"HI!" she said brightly. "You're Pantu right?" she asked him.

He nodded, waiting for her to continue.

She waved for him to come closer. "I have to ask you something," she said, sending out a scent to her Charisma to make him move in her direction.

But he didn't move as he asked, "What is your question?"

She waved him over to her again, but he wouldn't budge.

She leaned further in. "What do you like to do?" she asked, being bold enough to unknowingly risk death to get close to him.

"I like to watch action movies with my best friend," he responded.

"OH! I like action movies as well. We should go see one together," she replied.

"I only see the movies Dill recommends," he told her, knowing where this was leading. He turned to face the field.

"OH. I SEE!" she said, drawing attention to their conversation. "Is that why you stood up #AnonBfirstdate last night?" she asked, accusing him. "Because your best friend didn't recommend the movie?"

He turned to fully face her as he spoke. "I could not have stood anyone up if I never agreed to the date," he simply stated, to the young girl's surprise.

"I thought she asked you out?" she asked, now fully interested in his side of the story.

"She tried to impose her will on me and then walked away without a response. I would hardly call that asking someone. I have neither her number nor any social media, so if she showed up for an unconfirmed, imposed date, well, it is on her," he responded.

The girl's face now held a shocked look at the amount of first-hand information he was giving. "You know she is going on a videocast to give details of you standing her up," she informed him, but he could care less.

"I hope her Lie holds weight, for heavy is the neck of a good liar," he stated, before turning away from her to finish his conversation with Dill.

By now the section next to them was trying to figure out a way to post this to social media with Queen sitting right behind Anon Being's best friend.

Pantu turned to throw them a bone. "I wonder? If you were to write something akin to a rumor alert, if Queen would be opposed to anyone confirming known rumors with verified proof." Pantu spoke without looking at any of them.

As if on cue, they all turned to look at him.

He looked thoughtful for a moment. "I think it would help to curb the word-of-mouth rumors which spread so rampantly throughout our amazing campus," he ended, agreeing to Pantu's idea.

Phones lit up as everyone wanted to be the first to post the new trend of #rumoralert. Pantu smiled at him, and he winked back.

His head, though, was organizing his plans as he contemplated the issues at hand. Crossing his long, graceful, gorgeous legs, he rested his head into his palm holding his arm up by placing his elbow onto his leg. Gently swaying back and forth, his thoughts flowed.

Life has quieted down since Pantu had the first year suspended. I wonder why he didn't file a report and have him expelled? He knew before Pantu sat down in the sacred chair he didn't have the first year expelled, but Pantu wouldn't let the information out, nor the information about the bully complaint being dropped.

It's as if he left the first year an opening. Does he want to see what the first year will come up with, so he can crush it or is that the best he could do? Is he afraid of what the first year has on him so he's being careful in the way he moves? That won't work against the first year, it will only embolden him.

The first year made it quite easy to turn our conversation in favor of Pantu with all the Lies he told. It was as if he didn't even try and thought he could use set facts to empower his claims. He dug himself right into a hole. Maybe that's what Pantu intended.

He has a thing about Lying, same as Drum, and he waited until the first year couldn't stand the fact Drum personally invited him to his party to throw the first year's mental state in array.

He's watching as the first year digs his own hole and he is letting him. By the first year thinking whatever information he has on Pantu is enough for Pantu to not fully attack him, he will keep at him until he feels like he has Pantu where he wants him.

His gut feelings were never wrong, and he smiled to himself. *My Universe, he is nowhere finished with the first year. He will strip the first year and take the one Being the first year has been obsessed with for years, right in front of him.*

The first year won't see it coming, it will be harder for him to believe because his belief is we are trying to recruit Pantu to be a part of The Four, which will probably now be called The Six as Pantu has dragged Dill along with him.

But the first year won't be fooled for long, so Pantu will have to find a way to keep the snake under control without the first year knowing what's happening to him. He closed his eyes and smiled. *Life is getting interesting.*

PANTU: CRAZY CONVERSATIONS
WEEK FOUR: SUNDAY

He and Dill went back to conversing when he noticed Jax, Turn and Put walked past their area. He nudged Dill to go talk with them, but Dill seemed like he wasn't ready to have whatever conversation with them right now.

"Go. Go. Go. Go," he said, and with every go, he pushed until Dill was standing up.

"JAX!" he called out, getting their attention. "Hey Turn! Put!" he said, waving a foam log at them.

Dill slowly walked down the stairs and towards their friends. He excitedly bounced down the stairs after Dill, only to trip over himself. Someone caught him by the arm and when he turned to thank the Being who saved him, he froze in shock.

He closed his eyes for a moment and opened them to look around, everywhere but Mr. Caleb's face. "Thank you...very kindly!" he managed to get out as Mr. Caleb already released him.

Mr. Caleb nodded at him and turned to finish his own conversations.

He carefully walked down the last few steps to join Dill and their friends at the bottom.

"Nice trip Pantu," Dill said, snickering.

"See you next fall!" he said, happily back to Dill.

Jax looked at them and asked, "Why would you guys still want to talk to us when you get to sit with *them*?"

He hit Jax with the foam log. "Jealousy is not suitable on you!" he said with a pout, making Jax blush so fast and so red, Jax turned away to face the field.

Turn and Put still hadn't said anything but stared at him like they wanted to eat him. They were frozen, unsure of what to do, so he stepped behind Dill and shyly glanced over Dill's shoulder. It only made things worse for Turn and Put, who were now trying to close the distance between them, without being obvious.

He hit Dill on the back of the head with the foam log. "I am hungry. I shall find some food. You should talk with them."

He turned to look for his Ma, but he sighed as he found her. She was red-faced and laughing happily, being naturally loud and outgoing. He sucked his teeth, but he felt Drum behind him.

Drum came down the stairs in his relaxed pose, leaving some distance between them, as he asked, "Are you hungry?"

He nodded but Drum wasn't looking at him. Drum was looking at Turn and Put, who backed up into Jax, making Jax turn and realize Drum was standing there, staring at them. Their nerves were shattered as they tried to avoid eye contact with the male they bullied as kids.

"Pantu," was all Drum said before walking out of the bleacher area.

He followed along, happily humming at the prospect of getting food.

They returned with him still holding on to his foams and Drum carrying a large order of loaded fries. There were three distinct types of cheeses, turkey bits, green onions, hot green peppers, sweet yellow peppers, salsa, avocado slices, tart black grapes, sour cream and with limes on the side.

Everyone laughed as they understood why Drum was carrying the food up the stairs. Drum acknowledged their amusement with a smile but didn't feed into it.

As he sat down in front of Win with his food, Win was staring. Not at him, but at his food and Win was starting to get upset.

He placed the foams down and moved up between Queen and Win. He turned to Win. "Would you like to share?" he asked a confused Win.

He picked up some fries and held them out for Win to eat, showing he was genuinely willing to share. Win's face lit up as he ate the food out of his hand and started eating with him, moving closer to get more of the toppings in his mouth. He was enjoying the look on Win's face as they ate.

While searching for Dill and their friends' conversation to eavesdrop on, he happened to overhear a conversation between Dean Hu and her husband.

"If he's made 'Dean of the Year' again, it will make seven years in a row!" Dean Hu said depressingly to her Husband.

"This year will be your year, Darling!" her Husband told her, trying to console her. "I know bigger and better things will happen for you."

"You've said the same thing every year since I became Dean. The school is now an "A" school—" she started.

"A+!" her Husband interjected, making her smile.

"An "A+" school. We will win every championship for sports this year, with every Senior on track to graduate on time and most have already been accepted into employment. Our school is clean and beautiful. NO student has ever been expelled since I became Dean!" She sighed. "The staff is happy, students are happy, as are their parents. What else must I do to make Dean of the Year?"

Her Husband told her with conviction in his voice. "You don't need to buy 'Dean of the Year' like he does. Your accomplishments will be all the proof you need. Be patient My Darling. This year *will* be your year. I have prayed every day and I'm sure the Universe will answer my prayers this year."

Dill came back to throw himself on the bleacher seat as he left Dean Hu and her husband's conversation. He and Win were almost finished with their food.

"How did it go?" he asked, joining Dill on their bench, leaving Win to finish the fries.

"Not good Pantu," Dill said sadly. "There's a rumor going around that you and I are dating, and I called my..." Dill stopped, realizing too much was said. Dill turned away from the unhappy look on his face.

"You called your girlfriend to see if she heard a rumor about you dating someone else? Have your Mind and brain completely disconnected?" he asked Dill, upset at the mistake made, not so much at Dill.

He grabbed Dill's head and with a quick blink, turned on his True Vision to gather Dill's head was fine before turning it off again. Even drunk, he could tell his Pa noticed and was unhappy with him using the Talent. He wondered how long his Pa would hold in his violation before getting him in trouble with his Ma.

"Do you know how much I have put in to make the two of you work? How much information have I given you to help woo your girlfriend and you think *that* was the right call to make?" He shook his head. "I am sorely disappointed in you," he ended, turning away from Dill.

He pressed his lips together to keep from smiling as Dill's head dropped.

By now Queen was interested in this information and leaned forward. "You. YOU have a girlfriend?" Queen asked. "Before Drum?"

Dill tried to shrink away from verifying the information.

"Probably not anymore," he told Queen.

Dill turned to him with pleading eyes. "Can you please help me. Again?" Dill asked.

Queen leaned forward and asked, "How exactly is Pantu, who has never been in a relationship, supposed to help you with yours?"

He turned around with the same indignant look as Dill and they both stared at Queen, who was taken aback.

"Queen. How do you think I became and stayed number one?" he asked, as he gracefully moved up to sit next to Queen, holding Queen's eyes the whole time.

Almost as if he were a feline, he slid closer to Queen. "I have left plenty of women's bodies in a state of pure ecstasy with beds soaked to capacity." He purred as his fingertips slid lightly down the side of Queen's face to the tip of his chin. "But seeing as you possess a penis, none of this will work on you," he said, and moved back to sit next to Dill.

Queen's shocked face made him suppress a smile. If it wasn't for Drum's heat on Queen's back, Queen would've succumbed to his Charisma. Queen quickly glanced at Drum and mouthed thank you before turning back to his and Dill's conversation. Queen looked at the book he Produced[46] and read the title aloud. Queen's face showed hints of suppressed laughter.

"Lessons for Sir Dill on How to Get and Keep His One and Only Girlfriend or I Will Slap Him in the Face. Written by Our Highness and Thee Great and Most Handsomely Beautiful, Pantu." Queen read before laughing.

"Does the title really need to be so long?" Win asked for Queen since Queen couldn't catch his breath.

He looked at Win and solemnly stated, "Every word needed to be expressed." He returned his attention to Dill, who was trying to get the book from him while his attention was elsewhere.

Dill failed and when he turned back, his best friend went into Cute Baby Bird Dill mode, innocently asking, "Pantu, may I please read the book? The longer I wait, the angrier she will be."

But he showed no signs of giving in. "If one should partake in the knowledge of this book, what must one do, Old Hagsaeng[47]?" he asked, knowing he was only weeks younger than Dill.

"One must follow every word, to the letter, Young Seonsaengnim[48]!" Dill responded, with folded hands.

"And if one does not?" he asked, straightening his back as much as possible to look down on Dill.

"One will be punished with the Dulock song on repeat, every night for a week," Dill said, leaning down in defeat.

He stretched out the book to Dill, who eagerly took it and flipped it open.

Dill read a page and looked up at him. "This isn't the book!" Dill exclaimed.

He showed a face faking surprise. "I know that much Sir Dill!" he said, waiting patiently for Dill's quiet acceptance.

"I will do it during half-time," Dill conceded and compromised at the same time.

---

[46] *Produce- When a Being uses their Energy to pull something already made from somewhere else. See Glossary: Universal Abilities; #16.*
[47] *Hagsaeng- Romanized Korean word meaning student.*
[48] *Seonsaengnim- Romanized Korean word meaning teacher.*

"Whatever is half-time?" he asked, curious.

"It's when they give the players a chance to catch their breath halfway through the game," Win said, a sad look on his face as he looked at the empty basket where there were once fries.

"Do you know how many people would have survived in the stadium games if there was a half-time?" he wondered aloud. "Okay. Half-time it is!" He agreed and waved his hand.

Dill flipped the book back open, finding the chapter he was looking for and started reading. Queen tried to peek but was confused by the weird squiggly lines on the page.

"Pantu? How can anybody read this?" Queen asked, hoping for the punchline to the joke.

"AH! Only Dill is authorized to read the book, so only he and the person who wrote it can understand it," he told Queen.

Dill finished and handed the book back to him. Dill left the bleachers, phone dialing, in hand.

"Ahhh. Young love. So, endearing to watch blossom, so deliciously drama filled to watch crash and burn," he said, while smiling and leaning back.

"That sounds like you want Dill and his girlfriend to fail," Win said, looking at him.

"Not by any means. GLou used to say that to me when they made me people watch. He would bet on couples' relationships to make it fun for me," he said, smiling with the memories.

"Was he any good at it?" Win asked.

He laughed. "Not. At. All. His failure was at ninety-five percent," he told them. "He would bet me and GMack and lost so much of his stuff, we pitied him; helping him win his clothes back by nudging some of his predictions."

He now had all of them laughing with him.

"He walked around for two days in public with absolutely no clothes on," he told them, while laughing along with them.

Dill was now headed back with a smile on his face and was calmer than when he left. The teams were hitting the field and his Ma turned to Mrs. K.

"So, we have to hope our team will be victorious and kill the other team, correct?" his Ma asked, trying to understand the game.

Every other adult, beside his Pa and Mr. Caleb, turned to look at his Ma in disbelief.

"Not at all, they're just trying to get the ball into the other team's goal," Mrs. K explained, pointing things out to his Ma.

"Ah, so does a team person get sacrificed if they allow a goal?" his Ma asked, wondering when the mayhem would really begin.

"Nope. They just lose and get to try again next year," Mrs. K explained.

By now Mrs. K had to know his Ma was raised and lived differently from her. It didn't stop Mrs. K from being his Ma's friend. Mrs. K seemed to genuinely like his Ma and it made him smile. His Ma was pure hearted in what she said and did.

"AH! They get brought back to life and get to try again!" his Ma exclaimed. "That's wonderful! There are other Beings here who can use the Revival Talent Pantu, and I can use. Although, Pantu uses his differently than the way I use mines to traumatize people!" His Ma's giddy laugh echoed throughout Drum's Dome.

He saw Drum erect a visible white Dome right after his Ma said, "...other Beings...", to keep the rest of the conversation out of eavesdropping ears.

Mrs. K only focused on his Ma while the other adults were now looking between him and his Ma. He looked ready to explode at the information his Ma was giving out, but his Ma's back was to him, and she was intoxicated, meaning she couldn't see or sense anything from him, so she continued.

"Yea, we Vowed not to talk about how Pantu uses his Revival Talent, so none of us can tell how it works," his Ma said, red-faced and quite drunk off Mrs. K's homemade mimosas. "Pantu doesn't like my Revival Talent, so he doesn't allow me to talk about it or use it." She hiccupped. "So, it's the family secret," his Ma said, unaware of the looks she was getting.

Mrs. K held his Ma's arm to steady her best friend. "Sky, no one here or anywhere else that we know of, has a Revival Ability," Mrs. K gently told her. "You and Pantu would be the first. So, let's talk about this when you both are ready," Mrs. K said, closing the conversation.

Without glancing at him, Mrs. K said it pointedly, so he understood Mrs. K would be mindful of his Ma's conversations.

DRUM: MORE THAN AN ASSET
WEEK FOUR: SUNDAY

He released his Barrier after his Mom's words, but his Dad didn't turn to look at him. His Dad knew not to react since his Mom would intercede. He had some time before he would create a tear in his Dad's trust in him.

He decided to have this conversation when they returned home. He knew he would have to explain being able to control time inside a Barrier as the teams were still entering the field. It was like they hadn't missed a thing.

He could see his Dad's Energy reacting to the different Beings who were around. Although his Dad's Energy wasn't pleased with two of the parental Beings in their section, his Dad's Energy was the brightest when interacting with three Beings: his Mom, Mr. Moon and now, Mrs. Sky.

While watching the Energy reactions of the Beings sitting in front of him, he was thinking how great of an ally Pantu and his family would make. He didn't feel a need to use them, but he knew with Abilities like theirs, they would be sought after.

His parents genuinely thought of Pantu's parents as actual best friends. He overheard the conversation about Pantu's parents becoming their best friends, as they currently didn't have anyone who would just be their friends without getting caught up in social media or the politics of it all.

He could see Mrs. Sky wasn't looking for popularity or trying to impose on his Mom's role as the "Light of Sunset". He also knew Mr. Moon genuinely loved his job and going to work every weekday. Per his Dad, Mr. Moon was also the type to leave work, at work.

They were simple and reminded his parents of a time before politics became their life. He decided right then and there he would support his parents' friendships with Mr. Moon and Mrs. Sky, both who were worth more to him than their Abilities.

He saw how happy his parents had become, being able to talk to someone their age about whatever, joke and relax, with it not being posted on social media or repeated. Pong was concerned but he told his older brother he wouldn't stand in the way of his parents' happiness, nor will he be the one to quiet their laughter.

He felt he was in agreement as his Dad. He knew it was almost time for his inheritance. He had his Mom confirm it with the shopping trip but asked to hold off until he secured Pantu's affections. Pantu needed to show he wasn't a threat, and his parents would give Pantu until the New Year.

The first half of the game ended with Sport having two assists and one goal of his own.

"He could have scored those goals on his own, why pass the damn ball?" Pantu asked.

His Dad turned to look at Pantu. "He's the Captain but more than that, he's a team player. He knows there are players on the team who want to go pro, so he gives them the opportunity to display their skills by not overshadowing them and helping them shine," his Dad explained.

Pantu looked at his Dad, thinking. "So, he enjoys playing the game but wants none of the fame. Although he is Captain, he gives his interviews away to his teammates."

"He also doesn't want the other team, that we are sure we will be up against in the finals, to know just how good they are, so they won't demolish this team. They will get about two or three more points, making sure they don't go over the lowest number of goals in one game recorded by the other team. They won't score more than six goals, keeping the number at around half of the projected team's best game," his Dad informed Pantu.

When he noticed his Dad's Energy towards Pantu was calmer than before, he raised an eyebrow and leaned forward, jealous of Pantu's happy facial expressions directed towards his Dad.

"He's lulling the other projected team into a false sense of security. They will let the other team score at least two points in the second half. Sport will use that as well." He looked at Pantu processing the information and watching Pantu's facial expressions as his Mind worked was enticing to him.

"So, they have not scored more than three or four goals the whole season, they also have not allowed the other teams to score as well, all while keeping their perfect winning streak. Now, they look like a team under stress and barely holding on, all while hiding their true Talent until the time is right," Pantu assessed.

"You checked their records?" he asked, surprised.

Pantu nodded. "I read the newspaper articles in the library after the mishap on my first day."

He smiled. He wanted to get Pantu to ask him at least once before he approached his Dad. If Pantu stubbornly refused, no matter what he did, he was unsure of Pantu's future. There was no way his parents would allow someone able to touch him, open his Barrier, absorb his Energy, and come close to the Sphere to freely roam the planet.

Pantu was the one he wanted standing beside him. He knew the whole just being friends wouldn't be enough anymore. They couldn't go back to that, he couldn't.

"What do you think the final championship score will be?" he asked with a smile, pleased with the way his Dumpling's Mind worked.

"Ah. That is easy, eighty-four to zero," Pantu said. "And would be based on the time limit of the first half of the game and the Talent of each team player. They will completely demolish the other team and break their spirits. Did the other team do something to upset Sport?" Pantu asked, sure Sport's plan had cause behind it.

"Last year, they posted on social media Drum paid for them to win our country's championship and our talentless team could never win against them. So, we now have an unhealthy rivalry against a whole other country. This game is to see which Higher Ed school will represent us against the Western Westlands," his Dad told Pantu.

When Pantu turned to look at him with a silent question, he glanced over at Dill who stood up with an evil laugh.

"Run, run, RUN as fast as you can. You can't catch me, I'M THE LEMONBREAD MAN!" Dill said, over exaggerating every part.

"YOU ARE A MONSTER!" Pantu cried out.

Their parents turned to look at what was happening, as no one put up a Barrier for this. Queen and Win were on the sidelines, speaking with Sport during half time and they all turned to look at the commotion.

As Dill and Pantu went back and forth between their lines, he increased the range of their voices when Pantu looked at him earlier. They were now entertaining the whole field as even the other team and their fans were listening.

Dill said his final line, "She's married to...THE CUPCAKE MAN!?"

DRUM: LET IT FLOW
WEEK FOUR: SUNDAY

Drum pressed the button on his phone for the DUN, DUN, DUNNNNN sound to close it out. It was almost impossible to keep his wits about him during this whole mini show since he was, as Pantu put it, vital to the show.

Earlier, when he and Pantu were waiting for the food to be prepared, Pantu asked for his assistance.

Pantu said, "I know Dill is going to do something stupid."

Pantu then told him that he was going to help Dill embarrass himself. Pantu told him Dill's personality was hidden, and he was self-conscious and closed off after the bullying but needed to open up if he was going to take the chance given to show who he really was.

He understood since he and Dill showed what they both thought people perceived of them, but Pantu saw under that, and was confident they both would live up to the expectations Pantu held for them while showing change. But Dill couldn't if he weren't sure of himself and Pantu asked for his help to show how much his childhood bully changed.

"If you are unwilling to give people a chance to show they can change, then does it mean you still believe I am the same person I was in The City?" Pantu asked him, genuinely wanting to know.

He was sure Pantu's meaning behind the words affected more than just Pantu and Dill, it was also meant for him. Even though he was kind, no one ever openly slighted him since the incident. Since he lived as if the bullies didn't exist to him, no one knew for certain if he was forgiving.

While the town was mostly peaceful, he saw the underline fear Beings held about him, that he would kill them with no remorse if they crossed him. He wanted to get rid of the fear and replace it with increased respect.

He agreed with the plan but how was he to know just how outrageously funny it would be? He held it in until the final dun played out and then he let it out. Pantu and Dill were surrounded by their parents, laughing and congratulating them on their performance, well not the lady named Lyra.

Even Sport came up to pat Dill on the back and joked they should perform for the championship half-time show. Pantu looked at him and mouthed the words, *thank you*, to which he could only smile in return.

As he gazed into Pantu's icy brown eyes, his smile deepened. He asked, "Hungry?", knowing the answer. Pantu nodded and held his hands apart, signaling how much food to bring back.

He left again to get Pantu's order, Queen opting to walk with him.

"Quite the Being you have found, yet again, Young Master!" Queen teased.

"I didn't find him. Someone else led me to him," he replied.

"You think Phoenix led you to him?" Queen gasped, knowing no one could hear them.

"He knows the full story of Phoenix and Wolf. He said his G-Pas told him the story when he was little," he stated, while looking at Queen's Energies reaction.

"OMU! Has he started telling you the story yet? Can you remember every detail so I can write it down? Word for word Drum, no paraphrasing or shorthand like you like to do," Queen said, and he watched Queen's Energies switch between excitement and worry.

He laughed. "He offered to tell me, but I haven't asked since then. I wanted you to hear the story first-hand as well, so I'm waiting until you and him have a better connection before I bring it up again."

He picked up the tray of extra-large orders of loaded fries and beef hot dogs from the booth, and they turned to walk back to the stands. He could see the twinkle in Queen's Energies, meaning his best friend was ready to hug him. Queen's Energies showed appreciation that he thought of Queen's equal obsession with Phoenix and didn't jump on the story without him.

"As much as I would like to think Pantu and I are good, there is still so much about his personality I can't read. It's as if the slightest provocation could send him to the other side, and THAT would be the worst possible outcome for us all," Queen said, thinking aloud as they walked back.

Pantu would be a huge asset to either side, but in separate ways. He and Queen knew the other side would strip Pantu of his Energy and Core before killing him. And they both knew what would also happen to Pantu before he was killed.

He smiled as his best friend was thinking of ways, he and Pantu could connect but Queen's Energies showed he was mentally tired and confused. Any plan Queen thought of either wasn't good enough with the information he knew or ended with a high chance of failure.

After Queen decided not to plan for it, to just see if it would happen naturally, a sigh came out of Queen's mouth. It was the first time Queen didn't plan, and Queen's Energies seemed worried. Queen glanced at him, and he quickly glanced at Queen's Energies showing his thoughts.

"That's probably for the best. If Pantu feels you are forcing it, he will shut down on you," he encouraged.

Queen nodded. "Pantu is able to sense things like that."

He and Queen made it back to the stands as the second half was starting. He placed the food down in an open spot on the bleachers in front of him and took a hot dog to eat. Pantu wanted him to get enough food for all of them and the rest of the group started to eat, while enjoying Sport's strategy play out.

The game ended exactly as his Dad said. The Hollis Higher Ed team got their hope back with two goals and Sunset looked as if they were fighting for their lives. Towards the end of the game, Sunset looked as if they just managed to score three more goals to win the semi-finals. Sport ended with two goals and four assists.

As everyone was leaving, he heard Pantu.

"Hey, there were cameras there recording the game. I was not recorded, was I? My parents?" Pantu whispered to Dill, who shook his head no.

"Pantu, you're a Private Citizen. That means no one will be able to take a photo or record you while under Drum's Barrier. There's a full-working Barrier over Hollis. Same rules apply here as well," Dill informed Pantu.

"AH!" Pantu said, pleasantly surprised. "So, it looks like you did half-time by yourself!" Pantu added, laughing.

Dill thought for a moment before he shrugged his shoulders and joined Pantu's laughter.

He watched with a small smile on his face as Pantu groaned. He figured Pantu was bothered by having to shower again to get all the body paint off before going to sleep. Pantu also noticed their parents seemed to not smell his scent as everyone else did.

"Our parents are much more used to Seductive Scents and how to block them than younger Beings," he told Pantu, as if reading his Mind. "Besides, Queen placed some special herbs in your body paint to dilute your scent."

Pantu looked at him suspiciously. "Can you read Minds?" Pantu asked.

He just shrugged and smiled before heading with his parents to leave in the vehicle they all came in. Since everyone except his family Portaled to Pantu's home, they would be Portaling home from the game.

Queen and Win were waiting to leave with Sport and now Dill was saying goodnight to his parents since he was staying with Pantu and going to school from there.

DRUM: INHERITANCE
WEEK FOUR: SUNDAY

He was finally showered and changed. He put on his slippers and Portaled outside. He knew his parents would be by his Mom's koi pond. She started the pond when she moved back.

His Mom dug out the pond and planted the Water Lotus seeds, adding water until the lotus flowers were grown and the pond was full. She placed fertilized koi eggs and raised them. The pond was his Mom's favorite place to go to on their property.

He came out of his Portal and sat in an empty, outdoor, lounge chair. He lay back, closed his eyes, and propped his feet up on the table. He laced his hands together and waited.

He felt the glance his parents gave him while relaxing in their cuddle chair. His Dad was drinking water with his feet resting on the table as well. His Mom was leaning on his Dad's chest with her feet up on the chair, drinking tea. Both their eyes on the calm pond alight with colorful lotus flowers.

He opened his eyes. "Dad, we should talk about..."

But his Dad raised a hand, and he paused, waiting for his Dad to say something. His Mom smiled and he sat up, thinking his Dad was about to speak, but his Dad just took a swig of water.

"Ahhhh, refreshing!" his Dad said, and his Mom laughed.

He was confused. He knew his parents were drinking alcohol tonight, but the liquor and alcohol was a Low-Level of Purity, so his parents weren't inebriated. They stocked the van with lower Purity-proof drinks for the other parents unable to handle their Level.

"Dad?" he asked.

"I mean...don't you have other Beings you can talk to about this?" his Dad asked.

"I don't want you to think..."

"I do think Suppade. I think what you doing is right. I'm not about to fuck it up. Keep doing what you doing, son. Yo Momma and I will support you," his Dad told him.

He smiled at his parents. He knew when his Dad used his relaxed speech, he was Daddy. It was the agreement they came to when he was six.

He ran away when they first moved here. He didn't like the tiny house they first moved into while their palace home was being built. It was only for a few days since Beings could use their Energy to build most anything, but he didn't want to be here.

It was far away from NanaPoo and Abuelo, his family, his school, his language, and his culture. He took off, deciding he would run from his title. He wanted to follow after his Mom. He knew Pong was the oldest and he thought his brother would hate him for being next in line to rule.

Because he refused to be physically trained, he also felt guilty for what happened to his Mom and younger siblings. After his parents searched the whole forest around their home, they asked for help. Pong was the one to find him.

He'd Portaled into the middle of what is now known as The Fabled Dragon's Triangle in the Optic Ocean, where ships and planes have been known to go silent or disappear. With all the crazy stories from those who made it out being treated as conspiracy theories, everyone went around it or avoided it altogether.

After living happily for two whole weeks, Pong showed up. Not physically, but Pong projected his Energy to bypass his Barrier. Once Pong convinced him to physically allow a visit, he made Pong Promise not to tell their parents where he was. Pong showed up and they came to an agreement about their futures. Pong also brokered peace between him and their Dad.

They would split their Dad's responsibilities. He would take over as the Emperor of Beings while Pong would handle the business end. Pong didn't want to be the next ruler, he wanted to follow their Dad into business, and Pong hated doing missions, he sucked at them. Pong agreed to fund his Dreams, and he agreed to take over missions.

Pong was also able to get their Dad to agree not to announce the twins' birth. Anyone in their family they told, made a Promise not to talk about the twins, or he would kill them. If anyone found out who wasn't someone, he okayed, he killed. Even at six, he was strict about keeping his siblings safe.

He also felt his Dad was business minded and would raise them like stock options. When he came back, his Dad said he could come to him about anything, or for any help.

To distinguish between business and family, his Dad used Drum's many names and his relaxed speech. It made it easy for them to understand each other. They were talking Being business, but his Dad was using his relaxed speech.

"You, Pong and Major got this!" His Dad's voice brought him back from his thoughts.

"But I will need you to find out about this Revival Talent Sky mentioned before the wrong Beings figure it out," his Dad instructed him.

He looked at his parents, knowing they would never bring it up with their best friends. His parents didn't want it to seem as if they were only interested in their best friends because of their Abilities and he smiled and nodded.

Universe, help me find a way before it's too late, he thought. He sighed, content to wait until the Universe was able to show him.

"I wanna retire...all the way 'round," his Dad said, making a circle with his hand.

He smiled brighter as his Mom laughed, happy with the conversation. His Dad figured out his Path was, at the moment, clear, so whatever decisions he was making were along the clear Path. He knew his Path could change, and it wasn't just his decisions which would change the direction of his cobblestone Path. Knowing what his family would do in order to keep his Path cleared was what worried him.

Closing his eyes, he took a deep breath and exhaled. He counted all the Beings whose decisions would now affect his Path. He invited them all into only a small part of his life, thinking if he kept them away from his life outside Sunset, they would be safe, but he was wrong. He came to depend on so many Beings, he decided to offer his trust, and they gave their trust back.

What a lot of Beings and humans didn't realize was he was the second wealthiest person on the planet. He held his own businesses around the planet and heavily invested in other countries' development, netting his control over a multitude of governments. Win handled all of that for him.

Queen knew Win handled his personal finances, but Queen didn't know the extent to which Win gained control of other countries to expand his number of Barrier Towns. He was able to hide behind his Dad's imposing figure, so most believed he was a spoiled wealthy kid, living off his family's money.

Queen also didn't know just how much of a bodyguard Sport was for him. If Queen knew Sport was the number one sniper on the number one team in The Royal Military, Queen would truly faint. He and Sport allowed Queen to continue to believe they had nothing to do with the missions Queen knew his Dad did to save Beings and sometimes without meaning to, humans. Queen never asked if he did missions and he never told Queen he did.

But Queen also didn't tell Sport or Win about the vast amount of information Queen possessed. In order to keep their enemies distracted, Queen became his rumored information hub. The ones who wanted him dead could only salivate at the rumors of Queen's personal library, filled with all the information, and experiments he and Queen have tried.

He knew their decisions would have an effect on his Path, but his family held contingency plans for his best friends, which didn't bother him. If his best friends couldn't be loyal, then they didn't deserve his trust.

It was Pantu who would cause his Path to completely crumble. He was wondering, if, at this very moment, Pantu sided with his enemies, would it break him? It scared him, realizing one day it may very well happen. He could be preemptive, kill his feelings for Pantu and let his parents lock Pantu away in a place he would never be able to leave.

Then, there would be no one on this planet who would be able to break him or counter his Energy. But the words written on his Fated Leaf came back to him. *An uncaged butterfly without Form shines brightest when reaching for the stars, either aided or crushed by The Burning Boy's hands.*

It was his decision. Will he crush the butterfly or help the butterfly reach the stars? Would he even follow the advice on his Leaf was the real question? Just because he and Pantu were Fated, it didn't mean they would end up together or even be happy with one another. They still had a choice, to choose each other or go their separate ways.

"There's something I know they can't answer," he said, opening his eyes to smile at his Dad.

"Oh?" his Dad said, his Energy intrigued.

"I'm wondering if you've ever had Energy come from your member?" he asked.

His Mom sat up. "Drum are you having sex?" she asked. Her Energy was nervous for his answer while his Dad laughed.

"Nah. He ain't done nothing like that," his Dad said, but he could only look away from his parents, knowing what he and Pantu already experienced together.

His Mom turned to look at his Dad. "Then how does he know?" They both looked at him.

"It happened during outercourse with Pantu. He would come, but my Energy came out," he explained, still not looking at his parents' Energies.

"And you've never come?" his Mom asked.

He shook his head.

"Pantu ever released?" his Dad asked.

He nodded. "At first he would only come, but he released earlier today and once before in a cloud. But that's it. I have released every time. Is it because I don't have any balls?"

His Mom's Energy went into theory mode. "It could be. Your body is more Energy and less human than everyone else. This is unfamiliar territory. But before you, releasing your

Energy means you've met your Fated. You're connected on a deeper level than just Scents and sex.

"Your Energy is the purest inside your body. When you pull your Energy out to use it, it becomes contaminated with everything in the air. Giving your Energy directly to your Fated, makes it easier to meld. It's a perfect mix of both Energies. But a balance must be held," his Mom explained.

"So, you gotta be careful. This ain't general knowledge cause most Beings go they whole lives never releasing they Energy from their genitals. It's also a way to keep producing Beings less than Full-Core to farm," his Dad told him.

"No worries. I'm willing to wait until Pantu loves me, every part of me, completely."

"Never take more than you're willing to give," his Mom reminded him.

He loved his parents. He left them alone as he Portaled back to his room. The feeling of needing to do something extreme to open Pantu's eyes to the hidden side of his life, made him sit and think.

Pantu needed to know about T-PEC. He needed a way to get Pantu to decide, sooner rather than later. He was ready to enact his plans but put the brakes on when he saved Pantu the last time and brought him here. He didn't want to move forward without Pantu by his side, but he also knew he couldn't move forward with Pantu being such a wild card.

He already put together how to get his inheritance. His NanaPoo received hers late in life while his Dad became Emperor at seventeen. Age meant nothing, so he figured finding your Fated was what triggered the passage of power. He was close.

PANTUxDRUM: UNMENTIONED FEELINGS
WEEK FOUR: SUNDAY

Pantu felt clean and the feeling made his body even more relaxed. Making his weekly phone call, he gave excuses drowned in compliments as to why the call was so late and "she" ate it up.

Feeling like his family would still be okay, he talked her into an orgasm before hanging up. His relaxed voice turned her on even more, making the call shorter than normal.

He planned to talk to Dill but passed out before Dill even finished his shower and was completely knocked out by the time Dill came back to the studio.

Even though Dill could freely go in and out of his room, Dill never spent the night in there. They always camped out in his attic or in Dill's living room when sleeping over. Dill never questioned it, and he never offered a reason.

He was strictly raised only your pets, and your Intended were allowed to sleep in your room and anyone else was seen as violating the law, punishable by death. Since he possessed neither in this town, he saw no reason for anyone other than him to sleep in his room.

He was in the field meadow, waiting, as he wasn't sure Drum would show up. He didn't want to call Drum's name repeatedly either, so he played with Natum until he felt Drum at his back.

He didn't turn around but the smile on his face was apparent. He and Natum continued to play while Drum sat down behind him. He felt warmth as Drum's arms wrapped around his waist, and when Drum pulled him back, he rested his head on Drum's chest.

"You're giving Natum more attention than me. I don't like it," Drum said.

Pantu relaxed and responded, "Well, he was here, and you were not."

He kissed the top of Pantu's head and closing his eyes, he leaned his head against Pantu's.

"Drum, what happened to you when you were six?" Pantu asked.

He didn't open his eyes. "I'm sure Dill told you, even if it was watered down, you know what I did," he replied.

"He gave me an un-watered down and his detailed version of what you did. But I want to know what happened to you?" Pantu asked again.

Taking a deep breath, he started. "When I first came here, I was different. It was a different feeling than back home. I was scared, and I felt alone. The first day I started school, there were quiet whispers and finger pointing, but no one outright said anything.

"There were whispers about my age, level of intelligence, whether they could actually touch me, and my inheritance. There were whispers about my family as well. When I refuse to acknowledge the whispers, it made my schoolmates bolder.

"It didn't take long. By the third day they were throwing things at me and openly calling me names. They would have something negative to say about every part of me, my hair, my height, body structure, my facial features, my clothes, and my accent.

"I refused to acknowledge them, and it made the bullying worse. My books, lockers and clothes were destroyed. They would write terrible things in my native tongue all over my desk about me. I still refused to respond.

"Queen, who was known as Dot then, would stand up for me. Even though I ignored him as well, he never stopped trying to block the objects thrown at me or back down when they were insulting me. He also never approached me as was the rule in the school.

"After we came back from a break, I found out I scored the highest in my class. The principal wanted to test me against the other Levels, and based on my scores, I ended up being the top student in the school. This of course pissed so many more students off.

"How could a foreigner, who can't even speak the language properly be the best student in our school? That's all I heard as the students didn't try and hide their actions from the teachers anymore. The teachers and staff all turned a blind eye to the bullying and Queen's complaints.

"Even though I had some problems with pronunciation, I could understand and write the language perfectly. Being picked on about my accent made me stop talking while I was at school.

"I wouldn't even answer any teacher's question and was sent to the principal's office a lot for insubordination. The things my parents were doing to improve this poor, underdeveloped town didn't matter at all to my schoolmates.

"So, around this time of year, an E-Level Five student approached me. He was quite a bit bigger than me, as I was considered a runt, so he tried to goad me into hitting him first. The problem with that was, I used these opportunities of bullying to hone my Abilities.

"I started making my Barrier stronger by thinning or thickening it out. I could hear conversations from far away, I could tell where a Being was from their Energy, and I also found out I could block my senses.

"My sense of touch was turned off so I could practice Spatial Awareness and erect a Barrier as fast as I could. I turned off my sense of smell, as they would leave nasty, smelly things at my desk and in my lockers. I could also tune everyone out, which is what I did that day.

"We were on the playground when a crowd gathered around me. I ignored everyone and when recess was almost over, I stood to leave. I felt him before he touched me, but I stood there.

"I could have moved, but I was tired. Tired of being bullied, tired of having to shut myself away, tired of being everyone's target practice. So, I let him touch me, knowing full well what would happen to his hand and his body.

"What I didn't account for was all the pent-up rage and anger I held onto. It was more than the bullying from the kids. They started saying rumors they heard from The States about my family.

"When the boy hit me, I snapped. I remember the sound of bones breaking and being crushed. But that was all. I remember the sounds, but I don't remember the actions. When I came to my senses, I was in the principal's office with my parents."

He stopped and looked down at Pantu sadly. "Pantu, what I did to that boy..." He cut himself off. "When my parents took me to the hospital to see the boy and his family, I thought they were exaggerating about the amount of damage I did to him. But they weren't." He hung his head, closing his eyes at the memory of the boy in the hospital bed.

"Pantu...his right arm was gone up to his elbow. I completely bashed his face in. He could no longer see, hear, talk and he couldn't breathe on his own. His stomach was destroyed by the Heat and weight of my knee holding him down. I cracked the boy's spine, and he will never walk again. Never eat on his own again.

"My parents brought in a Being who did their best. The process was painful for the boy, and my parents made me watch. For two days, I watched as the Being tried to heal the boy as best as they could. I could see the amount of pain he was in even though I could barely hear him scream." He stopped.

Pantu asked, "What happened to you?"

He looked at Pantu, smiling weakly. "My parents needed me to understand the amount of destruction I could cause at six years old, but to also understand I could use those Abilities in a unique way.

"I...I decided..." he blew out a breath before continuing, "I decided to use my Abilities to help other Beings in trouble. To try and make their lives better.

"But I was still pissed at the one who thought up new insults to hurl at me every day. The leader and the three who followed him found heavier and sharper objects to throw at me. They incited the whole school against me, and I had done nothing to them.

"I knew I couldn't go back to school and confront them. If I did, we would have to leave again and at six years old, to me, we had gone as far as we could possibly go. This was the end of the world to me. So, I locked his Energy signature inside a box in my Mind.

"I felt it when I went back. My schoolmates and the staff feared me, but not Queen. On my first day back, he sat with me at lunch. He talked to me as if I was a normal Being, not one who just destroyed a young boy's body and future.

"Once Queen and I became friends, he relayed my message, never let me remember who you are, or I will do worse to you than I did to him. And I didn't remember him, and he never approached or bullied me again.

"And over time, the longer I went without harming my schoolmates, their fear of me lessened, but it never disappeared. The guilt I still feel, eats away at me," he said, finally getting it all off his chest.

He never expressed to anyone his side of what happened that year. Even though he tried to lock it away, the fear still left in his classmates and the town's eyes, would remind him every time. Pantu leaned up, closer to him.

Pantu held his face with cooling hands and smiled. "What if I could help?" Pantu asked.

He looked into the different shades of brown, counting each distinctive tint as they melted together when the light he loved shone behind Pantu's irises. "Pantu, you're still learning Universal Abilities. Don't overload yourself and use up all your Energy," he chided.

Pantu's smile turned into a pout. He never knew he would like Pantu's pouty face so much. He was trying to hide the fact he was aroused. Pantu squished his face together and giggled.

"Silly Spoiler!" Pantu said and moved slowly, akin to a cat. Pantu's actions ended only after straddling him.

He was taken aback and looked up at Pantu, who was now bolder about touching him in their Shared Space. He grinned and allowed the invasion to his personal space and his body.

Pantu leaned against his ear to whisper, *"You already know I can, why try and stop me?"*

The shiver which went through him as he felt the rush of cool air enter his body from Pantu's mouth made him lose his balance and fall back, hitting the ground with an "oomph". He slid his hands under Pantu's shirt and pulled him down to kiss Pantu's forehead.

Pantu's head nested on his shoulder. "You should just give me what I want," Pantu said, before kissing his neck.

"Always," he stated.

"I want to be able to help you. The things you do, I need to be able to stand on my own," Pantu said. "I do not understand everything about living in a town like this, but I learn quickly, so can you trust me?" Pantu questioned.

He looked at Pantu. "Dumpling, do you know what you're asking of me?" he questioned back.

Pantu's head lifted to look at him. "Is trusting me so difficult?" Pantu pouted.

"No Dumpling, it's not that," he said. He put his hand to rest under his head and closed his eyes before speaking again. "I trust you Dumpling," he ended, as he fell asleep.

Pantu snuggled on him and fell asleep as well.

PANTU: A WRONG TURN
WEEK FIVE: MONDAY

He thought school would be a lot easier and he could rest for the next week until Mansnake came back, but he quickly found out, he could not. There was more free time, and he was trying to find things to do. Their classmates now knew he was aware of Beings and with the school's investigation being closed, this freed them up to use their Talents again.

He was in awe at the fact the whole campus during day courses acted as if they were humans and didn't show their Talents. The week he was supposed to start on campus, there were incidents of students using their Talents against each other. There was a ban on using Talents while on campus, and Portals were set up on the outskirts until the investigations were closed.

He did learn any student caught using their Talents before the ban was lifted, would be expelled, and expulsion from this school automatically meant no Higher Ed transfers or after graduation opportunities in the Being communities. He assumed the punishment probably also included a one-on-one conversation with Drum.

Even though Queen, nor Drum, didn't tell him who he could and shouldn't hang out with, he picked up on the sentiment quickly. He knew Queen wouldn't allow anyone to bully him and touching him would result in Drum's attention to the unlucky Being.

Just because no one can touch you does not mean I have to live that way as well, he thought to himself, *besides, you used your Talents on campus, but I guess you were never caught or reported.*

But he smiled and rolled his eyes at the thought of Drum protecting his personal space. Even though others could touch him, it didn't mean he wanted them to. He was over-touched in The City, and he hated it whenever anyone entered his personal space uninvited.

Thinking of Queen, he knew he couldn't easily crack the young male. *I wonder if Queen knows his Grace is a natural Talent enhanced by the Level of Compatibility he has with his Light?*

He understood Drum and Queen were the ones to start the invite requests, while Sport and Win just went along with it. So, he only played a bit with Sport and Win.

His real targets were Drum and Queen. Yes, he liked them both well enough, *well, I really like Drum, more than I should,* but he was never one to allow others to do whatever they wanted to him and walk away. It would mean death in The City.

The one thing he was not, was an entry rug. And since the invites weren't even Malicious, he decided not to break their Minds, just put a crack in their view of him.

Dill also refrained from telling him there was a whole club dedicated to relieving The Four of their statuses. It was disguised as Torven's Planetary Empowerment Club (T-PEC) and when he received a card in the book requests inviting him, he went.

Knocking before turning the knob, he walked into the room. The warm welcome he received was laced with bad intentions and he immediately sensed he made a mistake. These students harbored Ill Intent towards The Four and their scents towards him were wavering.

It will be based on whatever answers I give them, he started to quickly think. *Even if I give them what they want, they would never actually like me or want to be friends. They would never accept my past; they do not feel inviting at all.*

His smile lit up the room and made a few relax around him. *Weak,* he thought, quickly blinking to turn on his True Vision.

A dark-haired young woman with ugly dusky pink Light spoke. "Hello. You're Pantu, correct? Also known as #AnonB online?" she asked.

He felt a small amount of anger in his Light at the multitude of different Light shades inside her and the number of black scars on the left side of her face and neck, but he only nodded, and she continued.

"My name is April. I'm the vice-president and a founding member of this school club. It's nice to meet you. Take a seat." April motioned to a chair right next to her. The other members gathered around, and she asked him to introduce himself.

"Hello. MY name is PANTU. I recently moved...HERE to finish the...last YEAR of Higher Education." He started nervously. "My parents and I traveled...a lot the last...few years before THEY...decided to settle HERE. I lived with humans the first...fifteen or so years of my life...so I never knew places like this...actually existed."

April nodded her head. "That sounds exciting, where did you move from?" she asked, with a smile he knew to be fake, since it was the smile most people in The City used with him. The scent April was giving off matched the disgusting look of her True Face.

He forced himself to look at April's ugly True Face. "I am from the north."

"Where up north, are you from? Like what country?" April asked again, more pointedly and he held back a gag as the black scars on April, slithered over her face, making her left eye look like an empty hole.

"Were you all born in the Eastlands?" he asked to her surprise.

"No! We come from all over Torven," April told him, and he could hear the disgust in her voice. "Hence, the Planetary in our name."

"Ah, then I should fit right in!" he responded, with a small smile and April lost the indignant look on her face to smile back at him. And with that one small smile he crushed April's smelly Seduction Scent.

April turned to the young, blond-haired male sitting across from her and lost her smile as the male stared hard at her.

"Pantu, we're only trying to see if you would be a good fit for our club," the young male said, leaning forward with his eyes still on April, who was looking away to gather herself.

"Should I not also see if the club is a good fit for me? I only know April's name, yet you all know mines. Am I to be in a club with people whose names I do not know?" he asked, looking around at the younger members' uneasy reactions to see they had no black scars on their faces and only their Light inside their bodies.

He recognized this look. It was the same look pets gave before they knew they were about to be killed. He met those pets two weeks after he was collared. His owner introduced him to the lowest ranking pets and showed him what happens to pets unable to make a living for their owners or pets who were disobedient.

"We are Beings, not people. And my name is Will. I'm a Liberal Arts Senior graduating this year and headed to another country for a job soon after," Will told him. "April and I are both Seniors like you, the rest..." Will tossed his head towards the rest of the group "...are LA sophomores, juniors and first years," Will ended.

He was just as disgusted with Will's True Face as he was with April's. Will's whole face was covered with black scars which flowed down Will's neck and went just past Will's shoulders. Will's Light was so muddled with other Beings' Lights; he was sure Will forgot the original color of his own Light.

He looked at the other Beings in the room and none of them bothered to introduce themselves or look him in the eyes, so he turned to look at April.

"What does your club do?" he asked, curious.

April took a glance at Will, who explained, "We find other like-minded Beings to join together in our fight for planetary empowerment." Will stood and retrieved a pamphlet off the desk by the door.

"Seems you don't know, but there are other towns like Sunset, all over Torven. Our goal is equality with Humans. Humans and Beings living and joining together to make the whole of Torven better, not just our own towns and communities."

Will walked back to his seat and handed him the pamphlet. "We have the resources to help Humans, so why not try and build a better planet, a healthier Torven, together with them?"

Will leaned closer to him. "But there are *Beings* who believe in keeping us separated from Humans. We live under these barriers with the false belief that if we leave, we won't be able to survive long.

"You and your parents are proof we can. They believe we're not smart or strong enough to protect ourselves against mere Humans, so they enforce their rules on us.

"But Humans will notice now that they have taken over so much land. Lately, Sunset has expanded to cover the whole southern east tip of the continent.

"More cities have been taken over by these Beings, while kicking Humans out. Generations of Humans who have settled on this continent, forced to leave.

"We should act now before other Humans realize what was done. We need to come together as a community and seek peace, not war. It will be the death of us all if we don't." Will sat back and took in his face at the information pitch.

"But are there not a lot of us?" he asked. "Why would humans start a war with us?"

"There are way more Humans on Torven than Beings. It's close to nine hundred billion Humans and only about five hundred million of us. We are greatly outnumbered. That's why we should take the first step and offer peace," April interjected.

"Beings and humans, living in harmony," he said aloud.

April leaned closer to him. *"You've lived with Humans. You should know what we're saying is true!"* she said gently.

"Joining our club just means you want Humans and Beings to live together in harmony. They want us to believe the barrier is what's keeping us alive, but really, it's their way of controlling us, herding us like sheep," Will said, looking at his face, hoping to invoke a reaction.

"You have lived fifteen years amongst Humans with no barrier and survived," Will ended, looking at April, and she gave him a signal to continue.

"To reach that end, we share information to help each other as we have clubs all over Torven." Will smirked. "We noticed The Four is trying to recruit you, is there a reason why they're so interested in you?" Will asked.

He nodded. "Queen says I am a gem because I can make him speechless or make him laugh," he said, seemingly proud of his Talent to invoke a reaction out of Queen.

April rolled her eyes. "So, he wants you for comic relief? What an ass!"

He looked disturbed by April's assessment, and his eyes found the floor. "He has always treated me nicely. A bit playful, but always nice," he said in defense of Queen.

Will shook his head. "Who do you think started the whole invite bullshit? I heard you sat in "The Chair" and no one told you until after. It's like he wants you for his jester and if you want to keep your friend intact, you should have him stay away from The Four. If he is seen as a threat, Queen will dispose of him," Will said, with disgust.

He looked up, questioningly. "Huh?"

The look on his face gave April the opening she was looking for, and she placed a hand on his back. "Oh, dear. You still don't know? Queen and Dill were the only Beings trying to be friends with Drum when he first moved here.

"Queen wasn't happy Drum and Dill became friends since Queen is quite possessive of Drum's friendship. So, one day, Queen pushes Drum to go crazy and he almost killed one of Dill's friends, who just wanted to ask him a simple question. So, Queen became Drum's best friend instead.

"When Dill gave his statement against Drum, Queen promised to one day do worse to him than Drum did to the other guy. We found out the truth behind it from one of Dill's close friends," she Lied as she rubbed his back with a smirk at his shocked reaction.

Not shocked from believing April's story but shocked she so openly Lied to him.

"After Drum returned to school, Queen started recruiting Beings and from there, the information system known as Bees came about. Queen has been using Drum to strike fear in everyone because he wants a spot next to Drum..." She trailed off and looked at Will.

"Because he's using Drum's claim as the most powerful Being on Torven as a means to suppress Beings all over the world. Segregating us from Humans.

"Drum has always been a bully in school, but now he is being used to expand worldwide, backed by his father's money. Dill probably didn't tell you because he's still afraid Queen will have Drum put him in the hospital as well. Or even kill him," Will Lied.

By now, April was holding his hands in her own as she spoke. "It's more than that," she started as she quickly looked at Will. "Queen wants the spot next to Drum...because he's in love with him. All these years, Queen has been Seducing Drum and will use Drum in order to make you submit. To keep you locked inside this barrier until he grows bored with you. If you want, we can help you. Help you protect your friend, Dill. Help protect you. We have the resources."

He was really and truly shocked as he couldn't believe what was being said. *They have no idea Drum is privately tutoring me, if they did, they would not be trying to recruit me.*

Mansnake's dumb ass neglected to tell anyone? He missed a golden opportunity to have a bull's-eye on my back. If he said something earlier, they would be trying to kill me instead. It is most likely the same reason he never talked about Kat and Win, he thought to himself.

He'd noticed the excessive amounts of touching April was doing but didn't pull away. He was prepared, deciding when he would allow her to touch him, since he caught on from the looks between April and Will that it was her goal.

April's scent failed, so she was going to seduce him by touch. As his face was trying to decide whether to speak up about not liking being touched, April and Will thought this was an opening for them.

"So, you have been here awhile. Have you found out what abilities you can do?" April asked, softly.

"Ahhhh...a Barrier?" he absentmindedly responded.

"Can we see?" Will asked.

He remembered how Sport set up his Dome and added his own hand movements to release a small one of his own but when Will touched it, it crumbled.

"Oh. So, barriers aren't your thing?" April said.

"I am still working on it!" He pouted. He set a small restriction on his Dome to crumble and release an almost unnoticeable scent if anyone other than him touched it. He was happy Drum told him about his own Domes. Now he knew they could be made with restrictions.

"Anything else?" Will asked, breathing in the scent he was subtly releasing.

But he was still pouting about Will breaking through his Dome. "Can you make a Barrier?" he asked Will.

Will made a Dome and when he touched it, it shattered into tiny, bright, red sparkles. April's surprise was quickly replaced by her making a Dome and watching him shatter it into tiny, deep pink sparkles as well. Although no one else seemed to see it, or maybe they thought it was natural, the murky color of both Will and April's Energies could clearly be seen with his True Vision.

"Making barriers may not be your thing but breaking them seems to be!" April said, happy and impressed. "The way you break barriers is so beautiful and unique."

April was looking at him with an unfulfilled longing. He read April's quick look at Will and understood April thought maybe he could break Drum's Dome and that's why he was being kept close.

"Have anything else you can do?" April asked.

He made a small circle with his Light, making sure to keep his Light color from being seen and stuck his finger through, pulling it back covered in ice cream. He happily sucked the ice cream off his finger, making everyone in the room blush and look away.

"I am able to make small Portals to places I have seen," he said, proudly.

Will shrugged. "It doesn't seem like you have a lot of energy. Your portal and barrier are both small." Will seemed uninterested and looked at April who shrugged as well.

"I guess. If there is nothing else...?" April turned back to him and touched his leg as she left the question open.

He looked embarrassed but offered up the information. "I am working on not tripping when moving fast," he meekly said, invoking a response from the room. April realized how Will was looking at him and kicked Will.

"Ow!" came Will's surprised response. "Well, let's clear a space and see," he added.

Will nodded to the other members in the group, who hadn't said a word. They made room for him to go from the hallway facing windows to the outside facing windows.

He stood and took a deep breath before moving fast to the window. He stopped short of bumping into it, turning with a smile and both thumbs up to April. But on his way back he went a little off course and ended up tripping and falling over the chair to land on his back.

"Owww!" he moaned, as he held his left arm.

No one offered a hand or even moved to assist him. He made his way up off the floor and limped to his chair.

"I think I should go," he said, as he stretched his body until he heard a locking sound. He checked his left arm, and a large bruise was visible when he opened his cuff and rolled it back. "I am headed to the nurse's office to see if there is any cream for this. Damn it. This better not leave discoloration!" he said, mostly to himself.

"It's just a small bruise," Will said. "If we want equality, we have to share information and eventually, we have to fight for it."

He looked at Will and turned his head slightly. "I have a flawless body. There is not a single scar nor hint of discoloration on it, and it will stay that way!" he stated.

Will looked him up and down, licking his bottom lip with a smile. April kicked Will again and Will nodded as he grabbed his bag and headed out the front classroom door.

PANTUxDRUM: A PLAYFUL SIDE
WEEK FIVE: MONDAY

Pantu stopped outside the door to look at his bruise again and sucked his teeth. *"Were they testing me to see if I could smell their Lies? It stinks to low hell in there. Tsk, I deserve it,"* he said quietly to himself, as he rolled his sleeve down.

"Deserve what?" He heard from down the hall.

He turned to his right, and his eyes found Drum. Relaxed, with his hands in his pockets, Drum stood by the doors at the other end of the hallway.

He turned and ran to the doors closest to him leading outside but stopped short when he opened them and saw Drum standing outside the doors, relaxed. He yelped in surprise and quickly closed the door to run back down the hall to the other end.

The students still left inside the room, looked at him running and came to the windows to see what was going on. Before he made it to the doors, Drum appeared in front of them, making him stop short to turn and run the opposite way.

When he ran by again, someone from the room opened the door to look out but the door was quickly slammed shut by a heat wave. Not a second later, Drum appeared in front of him again, only for him to bump right into Drum's chest. Holding his hands in front of him, he slowly backed up as Drum came into the frame of the classroom window.

He used his Talent of Observation to see April, who was on her phone, end the conversation. *"Drum's here"* she whispered, before hanging up.

He watched without looking as April slid her phone as discreetly as she could, into her pocket. He could feel April's lust as she watched Drum slowly approach him.

Drum's casual way of walking with his hands in his pockets and a slight smile on his face, would make anyone mad. He could read the underline hate April held at how attractive Drum was and when the younger members moved to the back of the room, he felt her redirect her anger at them.

After hearing Drum ask him, "You're quite playful, aren't you?", he side-stepped Drum's advance to bolt out the doors.

"Quite playful indeed!" Drum said to no one.

He was standing at a window facing outside, watching Pantu run across the field and towards the back gate. Pantu tried using his Ability to Ground-step but ended up overshooting the distance and crashing into the gate.

He softly laughed. "Stubborn," he commented, before turning to walk through the same doors as Pantu, not bothering to spare those in the classroom a glance.

He could hear the younger students in the classroom breathe a sigh of relief when April's phone went off again. It was the one who was behind the club, the president.

He followed Pantu into the wooded area behind their school.

"Pantu is going to get lost," he said to himself.

He sniffed the air and followed the Scent to see a confused Pantu, turning in circles, trying to figure out which way to go.

"If I wait for nightfall, I can use the stars to guide me out," Pantu reasoned with himself.

"And would you use the Cannabis Major or Feline Minor constellation?" he asked, leaning against a nearby tree, relaxed.

Pantu screamed and fell to the ground.

He watched as Pantu took a moment to catch his breath and slow down his heart, before looking up at him. "It is only a bruise from me tripping over myself," Pantu explained. "I was trying to use the Ground-step Talent." Pantu looked down, knowing what he was going to say.

"Your Energy isn't balanced, and it's throwing you off. If you continue to use them when you're not ready, it will become a hard habit to break," he chided Pantu.

"I know...I know," Pantu relented. *"I am just scared,"* Pantu whispered.

"Scared of...?" he asked.

"You, Drum!" Pantu said, looking up at him.

He stood up off the tree and turned to walk away.

"I am not scared you will hurt me; I am scared you will hurt others because of me," Pantu stated.

He stopped and turned to look at Pantu. "Will you tell them?" he asked.

Pantu looked unsure of his implications.

"Not to invade your personal space?" he clarified.

Pantu looked down and shook his head.

"So, you're okay with anyone touching you, whenever *they* want to?" he stated, while looking at Pantu, who shook his head again.

"Then what should I do Pantu, whenever I feel you are scared, frightened, terrified or in pain?" he asked, to which Pantu looked up at him. "Every time you feel those emotions, I know. Am I not supposed to come to you?" he added and Pantu's shocked look softened him.

"What? So, am I not supposed to feel any variant of fear or pain?" Pantu asked, and he could see Pantu was trying to figure out how to hide himself away.

"*Dumpling, don't.* I'll protect your personal space as long as you need me too. Besides, I always warn them first. It's their choice what happens after, so don't blame yourself for others' decisions," he told Pantu, who relaxed at his words.

As he came to stand in front of Pantu, he reached out his right hand. Pantu immediately grabbed him, and he gently pulled Pantu up. He was wondering what the stuff in Pantu's left hand was for when Pantu bumped into his chest, making them lock eyes. Then, using his free hand, Pantu smeared mud and leaves all over the back of his pants. He turned his closed eyes to the sky as Pantu rubbed mud over his butt.

"There. Now we both have dirty butts!" Pantu giggled.

He brought his head back down to look directly into Pantu's eyes.

"So very playful," was all he said, with a slight smile.

Pantu's sweet laughter sounded out, making his own smile wider.

 "You like it!" Pantu teased.

He turned his face away and closed his eyes again, while taking a deep breath. Turning to look at Pantu, he responded, "I do like it...a lot."

Pantu just stared into his eyes. There were no Lies or ill intent from his words. They were pure and he meant them. He held Pantu's gaze until Pantu realized they were still holding hands. Pantu looked nervously at their clasped hands before looking around to see if anyone could see them.

No one could since he put up a Time Barrier. After seeing the Barrier around them, Pantu seemed to drift into thoughts. He didn't want to interrupt but Pantu obviously didn't hear it.

"Dumpling."

Pantu's eyes snapped up to look at him.

"Your phone," he told Pantu, who finally heard his phone ringing.

Pantu stepped back, taking the one clean hand from him to answer the phone.

"It is my Ma," Pantu said, before answering. "Hello? Okay...sounds good...be out in a moment." Pantu looked up at him. "We are going to a bakery before going home, would you like anything?" Pantu sweetly asked, looking at him with a face to match.

"I want whatever you were going to eat while waiting for the stars to come out," he joked and grinned as Pantu's exposed body parts all turned bright red.

But instead of being embarrassed, Pantu just laughed and looked around at his pants to see if they were clean, which they were. Pantu turned back to grin hard at him. With a kiss on Pantu's forehead, he opened a visible royal-blue Portal for Pantu to leave.

DRUMxAPRIL: AN ALMOST PERFECT MEMBER
WEEK FIVE: MONDAY

Once Drum's Portal closed behind Pantu, his Time Barrier fell, and he knocked. Opening the door, he stepped into the classroom Pantu left two minutes before. Under his Barrier in the woods, no time was lost, and he was able to get back to the room before the T-PEC members left.

He picked up a pamphlet with his free hand and slowly walked, close to the inner windows, with his right hand in his pocket. He paused to read the inside, looking rather amused at the concept. April, who was still on the phone when he entered, was now hiding her phone behind her.

He spoke first. "This reminds me, I've yet to join a club this year. This seems interesting. It says meetings are scheduled as needed. A club that only meets when necessary. I like it. Gives me plenty of free time but still looks good on my employment application."

He looked up at Will and April standing two rows over from him and a quick glance behind them to see the other members. "Where can I sign up?" he asked with a smile, making Will swallow hard and April shiver at his voice.

"Umm...the club is full. We aren't accepting new members...at the moment," Will informed him while moving to stand in front of April and he chuckled.

"Is it because you just got a new member? I saw someone leave in a hurry. Did you scare the Being off?" he asked, looking around the room.

"We don't have any more space," April said, from behind Will's back.

"Oh!" he responded. "It does seem like this room is filled to capacity with members or is it just the seven of you all?" he asked, as he continued his slow walk to the back door.

"Our numbers should be of no concern to you!" Will stated.

"It's not for me." He laughed. "But for Queen!" he said. He halted and pulled out a gold badge from his right pocket.

The members all gasped at seeing a mythical object produced and freely shown. Queen's gold badges were talked about, but no one had ever seen one.

The badges were communication devices set in pure gold. It was thin and surprisingly lightweight to carry. One side had a hollowed-out B which lit up with his royal-blue Energy, and his initials SXCS were embossed around the letter.

At the very bottom was a number, marking the order of importance. The lower the number, the more information you could access, with Queen rumored to be number zero.

He showed them that side first, and they all gasped again when they realized he was number one. He flipped the badge to show a screen littered with information and April's muddy dusky pink Energy started to tingle.

He knew the rumors. A regular Bee badge supposedly gave access to some of Queen's information based on your number. Those with gold badges could access higher levels of Queen's uploaded information.

He already knew T-PEC tried unsuccessfully to infiltrate Queen's Bees, even trying to place others around Queen, but they came up empty. He smiled, knowing they stole a yellow and green badge and tried to break into the system, but found out Energy is almost impossible to hack. He knew no one on T-PEC's side possessed the Ability since his Barriers would be the first thing T-PEC would attack.

The amount of loyalty the Bees held for Queen was unfathomable and it was hard to tell who was or wasn't a Bee, making T-PEC all a bit paranoid, and The Four laugh.

April pinched Will.

We had it right. Even Drum is under Queen's command. It's him we need to get to first, she said, in code on Will's back.

Will signed back in agreement. *Who would have thought Pantu would give us this without saying much,* Will coded back.

He looked at Will with a face questioning Will's action, but Will took it as him waiting for an answer to his question.

"Why should you care about a closed club?" Will asked, avoiding giving any information, or so he thought.

He looked at the pamphlet again. "It says "like-minded" individuals. Am I not of the same mindset as you all? Saving Beings?" he asked, goading them.

Will's Energy held disgust and was flowing fast at his implications, but Will could only return the small smile he gave with calmer flowing Energy and a wide smile back.

April stepped from behind Will. "We have the same number of members as Queen has gold badges or is the information about our size unknown to Queen?" she smugly asked back.

He turned his badge, so the screen faced him and typed on it. "Oh! Never mind, it says here that there are four thousand, eight hundred and sixty-seven members of Torven's Planetary Empowerment Club or T-PEC in Sunset, Makis Ridge and Hollis!

"With one thousand, two hundred and fifty-five members currently enrolled at SHE. Current leaders and the next generation of Beings live here. Most are slated to hold high positions in the future!"

He looked at them and gave a full smile. "Seems like I fit the bill for all three descriptions, wouldn't you say?" He laughed at the shock Will and April's Energies gave them, making them clench their fists.

"I guess we should change it to one thousand, two hundred and fifty-six at SHE, huh?" he asked, with an eyebrow raised.

"Pantu didn't officially join us. Pantu tripped over that chair and left," April said, turning to point at the still overturned chair, which he looked at as well and nodded, accepting her answer.

"There are ten gold badges. Of course, you know Queen and I both have one, so there are eight more out there," he said, as he turned to walk out the back door. "Here's two hints, one badge was stolen and after it happened, you will never be able to steal a badge from the remaining nine." He tapped the pamphlet on the last desk when Will spoke up.

"There's no need to leave with the pamphlet."

He stopped and looked back, not caring to make eye contact with anyone. "It says free on it, and you seem to have plenty left for a closed club. But, if you really want it back, come take it from me."

He lounged lazily while standing. No one made a move to stop him.

"By the way April, it seems you *just* learned to respect others' personal space. Congratulations!" He looked directly at April. "Inform your president I hope to hear more than just his breathing next time," he ended, going to walk out the door.

"YOU CAN'T BULLY US!" Will shouted at him.

"I'm only a bully because you fear me, not because I've ever done anything wrong to you personally," he said. He slid the pamphlet into his right pocket and walked out of the room.

April's phone rang and she hurriedly picked it up. "Understood!" she said, before hanging up. "You three go and follow Drum. Inform me when he's made it to wherever," she told the younger members. "You two clean this room up. I don't need the Cleaning Club complaining about unauthorized use." She went to disconnect the hidden cameras.

"I think..." Will started, but her finger to her mouth made him close his.

They started collecting their cameras from around the room when she received a message stating Drum was in The Queen's Hive.

"Other than the fact of keeping us separate from Humans, Drum really would be a perfect fit for our club," she said to Will, giving him the okay to talk.

"I think he's lying about the badges," Will finally said.

She stopped what she was doing and looked at Will like he was stupid. "You really weren't following the conversation, were you? He willingly gave us information about Queen's badges because he wanted to know if Pantu joined our club or not. Drum has never been a liar, no matter how we twist his words for our benefit. Neither of us smelled a Lie from him at all.

"We had info he wanted, and he had info we didn't know we needed. That's the only reason he showed us the golden badge. We now know it's not a myth and that's valuable information.

"Since there are more than we thought, we might be able to figure who else has one or who stole a badge." She continued to pack. "Besides, now we know for a fact they're interested in Pantu, so we will place someone."

Will stopped and looked at her. "Why would he care so much about Pantu joining our club? We have recruited plenty of other Beings in the school, but he never questioned us until now?!" Will asked, confused.

She shook her head. "We might be right about Pantu being able to break his barrier." She shrugged.

Will paused to think. "It was more than that. It was as if he was only concerned about how Pantu was hurt." He shook his head and continued to pack. "He was willing to give valuable information, just for a simple answer about Pantu."

She paused, re-thinking the conversation and what Will stated. "You think he likes Pantu?"

Will nodded. "You felt it. Pantu has some ability when it comes to Seduction. Maybe Drum fell for it?"

DRUM: THE REAL TARGET
WEEK FIVE: MONDAY

"You have a lot of free time for a private tutor," Queen teased as he walked through the door to The King's Lounge. They both laughed as he set a white Barrier.

"Who else would've thought of something so dope?" he responded as Queen's Energies agreed.

"I don't get it?" Win stated and popped another grape in his mouth.

"Pantu invented another use for Barriers and taught Drum," Queen explained, and Win nodded, not caring what the new use was.

He walked into the kitchen where Queen was putting together some snacks while Win was already eating them and dropped the pamphlet on the table.

"Seems he hightailed it out of there and gave exactly how much you said he would. He even stood up for you," he informed Queen. His best friend looked at him, and he could tell Queen was surprised by the way Queen's Energies flowed inside him.

"April can read and control others by touch, on top of having the Ability to control others with her Seduction Cloud and you are telling me Pantu gave her nothing, even then? And had the balls to stand up for me, knowing one wrong word would have a bull's-eye on his back?" Queen stated more than asked.

He chuckled. "I may have given Pantu a bit of my Energy. He used it to dilute his scent and also block April's Ability," he nonchalantly said.

Queen shook his head and finished setting the table. "Don't say it like it's normal Drum. We both know it's another Ability Pantu shouldn't be able to do." Queen paused and thought aloud. "He's able to naturally absorb your Energy and use it however he wants. He would be a gold mine for the other side, but they wouldn't care enough to figure any of this out."

Win nodded in agreement. "April's base Ability has been amplified, and she added other Abilities as well. That means she really is one of the higher levels." Win walked to the table and sat down. "If anything, she would want Pantu's Abilities as her own, seeing how she never got over you, Yooouuunnnggg Maaassssttteeeerrr!" Win teased him and he knew his face showed obvious disgust at the thought.

"I'll die first," he responded.

Queen looked at him. "Are you sure you don't want to blindly run into a wall a couple of times first?" Queen teased, to which they all laughed.

"That's the cleanest burn I've ever heard!" He laughed again. "I led them right to you. Their focus is again on the badges, this time the golden ones," he said, sitting down with plenty of space between him and his best friends.

"Good, maybe they can lead us to the one who stole it," Queen commented.

"That stupid fucking first year," Win said out of nowhere, and both he and Queen stared at Win.

He could see his best friend's white Energy rushing through Win's body and he knew Win was pissed.

"We keep thinking he's harmless, but we didn't even know he had a Form until Pantu told us! I've checked and that fucker is registered as disabled. There's also something you both don't know," Win said, and stopped eating.

He looked surprised and could tell Queen's Energies matched his face. Win pausing from eating, meant it was serious.

"Drum, I know you Promised Pantu to let him handle it, so I will follow your decision because of what he did for Kat." Win took a breath. "Kat let me touch her again. We held hands, hugged, even kissed.

"She said Pantu healed her completely, even her Mind felt brand new. So, if Pantu wants to be the one to take that snake down, I'm going to help him in any way I can," Win informed them.

"That first year was behind the attack on Kat?" Queen asked, and the entanglement of Queen's tri-colored Energies was shooting spikes through Queen's body.

Win just nodded, calm about the situation.

"How can you be so calm about this?" Queen asked, his Energies dancing furiously inside him.

"Panya." He called to get his best friend's attention and waited until Queen finally calmed down enough to look at him.

"Do you understand why Win is calm about this? Yes, it was a frightening experience for all of us. Mostly for Win and it was definitely traumatic for Kat. She hasn't been able to talk about it since it happened.

"But she shared with Pantu, and he healed her. Win is right, we need to figure out everything about Manpa before we make a move," he said.

"YOU KNEW!?" Win shouted.

He shrugged. "She told me Pantu healed her, but she didn't share who was behind the attack. She wanted to talk to you about it first," he informed them.

"That's a rare side Ability to water. Do you think it has something to do with Pantu's Revival Ability? Do you think his base is water?" Queen asked him.

He popped a piece of pinesnap in his mouth and shook his head. "Pantu's base Ability IS healing. He doesn't use water to heal like those known with the Ability, he uses his own Energy," he told a now shocked Queen, and happily surprised Win.

"Whatever Revival Ability he has is probably an advanced healing technique," he told them, leaving out the most essential information.

Pantu may be powerful enough to heal the Cores of Beings, he thought to himself. It was one of the reasons why he was personally invested in helping Pantu restore his Energy and figure out his Abilities. "He hasn't told me about this Ability," he said, informing them to not say anything and they nodded in agreement.

Win perked up. "Then how do you know?"

He looked at the plate of food. "He showed me, yesterday...he healed Dill, thrice. Once on the bus, then the shopping bathroom break and later in his studio. Although I caught them in a compromising situation, Pantu never gave up he could heal."

Now, Queen was interested. "Com-pro-mis-ing?" Queen teased.

He laughed and explained what happened and how the locked box inside his Mind broke and he recognized Dill as Sage.

"I laughed when I realized his name wasn't much different from his old one, but he seems solid and he never got caught up in T-PEC, so I didn't see a reason to say anything," Queen told him, and he nodded.

"No reason to break the box before it was ready," he agreed.

Queen took over the conversation. "Okay putting Pantu's Abilities and Dill's redemption to the side, Let's focus on Win's situation. He wants to help Pantu without breaking Drum's Promise, so here is all the information I have on the first year..." Queen started, and the tip of a key was produced out of his right hand.

Queen pulled the key out of his body and unlocked the air in front of them. They disappeared. To anyone else, it would seem like a normal, empty room. They wouldn't be able to see the three Beings, still sitting at the table, having a conversation.

PANTU: REMORSE DAY
WEEK FIVE: MONDAY

He heard knocking at exactly five o'clock ss (star-set) and he opened his door seconds later.

"You could just Portal in," he said, acting annoyed.

"I've only received permission to Portal into your studio. Seems a bit weird to come downstairs in your home," Drum teased.

"Well, you have permission to Portal anywhere in my home, except my parents' bedroom, of course," he said.

"Hmm," was all Drum said, and smiled at him.

Drum disappeared and he panicked, looking around. He slammed his front door and ran back into his home, only to find Drum setting up at the table.

"You did not use a Portal." He pouted. "You can do a lot more than you have told or showed me."

"Ditto!" Drum responded, sitting down to start going over the remainder of his past due work.

"So, if I tell you everything I can about myself, will you tell me everything about you?" he asked.

"There are things about yourself you can't say and likewise," Drum informed him.

"So, I guess we will never know." He shrugged.

"We will, one day. Depends on whether you want to openly show me," Drum told him, while still checking his work.

He gave a huge sigh and dropped himself into his chair. "Why is everything on me?" he complained. He was upset Drum was able to catch on so quickly. Drum was right, no he couldn't tell them, but he made no Vows about showing his Talents.

Drum was still busy checking his work. "Has my Scent ever wavered with you?" Drum asked, which surprised him.

"Ah, No. It has not," he answered to which Drum nodded.

"Has my scent wavered?" he asked.

"Yes. All the time," Drum told him. "There's only one sheet which needs to be reviewed. The rest are completed, and you can turn them in tomorrow. Start on your homework so I can check it before I leave, and I will go over your essays," Drum instructed him.

He looked at the paper Drum set in front of him and started on it. "Why have you not set a Dome?" he asked.

Drum shrugged and kept reading one of his essays.

He was confused and upset with himself. He knew he was still trying to understand what he was feeling. There were new feelings he had yet to even call by name as he himself did not know.

He also knew he rationalized, pushed, or ignored things as well. He cursed his Attention to Detail Talent. He wanted to learn Abilities. All the cool things he saw everyone doing, he wanted to do as well.

He took a deep breath. *Ignoring the issue again, are we not?*

He set a Time Dome and went to finish his work. As he was working on his homework, he watched Drum make his laptop and a small printer appear to start typing up his essays.

The speed at which Drum typed one essay was astounding. He watched as Drum printed it out but was confused as to why there were so many pages.

"My essay was not that long?" he questioned aloud.

"It's not just one essay, I typed all of them," Drum told him.

He looked at Drum weirdly shocked. "You typed all eight essays, from memory? After only reading them once?" he asked.

"Hmm," was all he got back.

He was confused. Drum hadn't "touched" him all day and he was beginning to wonder if it was because of his scent wavering.

Maybe he no longer wants to touch me. Is it because I have yet to decide anything? It has been over a month since I moved here, maybe I am taking too long. I wonder if he would have had to wait this long for anyone else?

"Pantu," Drum interrupted his thoughts.

"It's wavering," was all Drum said, packing his essays into nice folders, separated by class.

He slumped in his chair. "Are you going to stop tutoring me?" he asked, sadly. *If Drum does not want to be around me, what...?* He didn't finish the thought as he climbed onto Drum's lap.

The look covering Drum's face as Drum froze, trying to figure out what was happening, made him even more aroused. Before he could settle himself, Drum spoke.

"No." Drum's simple answer stunned and confused him.

He awkwardly returned to his chair, feeling embarrassed. He never had the displeasure of being turned down before and he was absolutely sure he didn't appreciate the way the feeling made his Light flow inside his body.

"I said I would tutor you and I will. Once your assignments have been turned in…" Drum started but didn't bother to finish.

"You will stop tutoring me?" he asked Drum.

Drum sighed. "Once your assignments are turned in, yes, I will stop tutoring you. But I will continue to help you learn as much as I can teach you about Abilities up until your birthday and help you rescue your G-Pas. After that, you can do whatever."

Drum's nonchalant attitude obviously disturbed his Light flow. No one was ever so dismissive of him before, and he didn't like it.

"By the way, the gym will be finished tomorrow, and they'll be holding a ceremony the next day. You and Dill should be there, since you both contributed the most to the remodel," Drum told him. "I will also have fourth period again after that, so you will have the Manga Room to yourself starting from then."

He didn't understand the look he gave Drum since his emotions were everywhere.

"I will also be leaving for work this weekend," Drum added.

He was overwhelmed with all the information Drum was pouring out. No more time alone in the Manga Room, no weekends together, and soon, no more private tutoring.

*Is he interested in someone else, and putting distance between us? Is he upset about me asking for a second chance for Dill? There is no way T-PEC was right about him, Queen, or Dill. I do not understand him. He does not seem at all bothered by the fact…*he started to drift deeper into sadness.

"Are you ready to go to the field?" Drum asked him, moving the conversation along.

He reluctantly nodded and before he could blink, they were in the field meadow. Shaking off the shock of scenes instantly changing before his eyes, he realized the real field meadow on Drum's family property was replicated exactly the same inside his dream. He looked around and walked towards where Natum would be.

He leaned down and noticed the cattail seemed to have the same reaction to him as Natum in his dreams. He was puzzled, as he petted the cattail and wondered if this was in fact Natum.

Drum moved to the middle of the field meadow to stand with closed eyes and pocketed hands. He looked at Drum and wondered how he was going to get through the day without Drum being around. He wanted to be closer to Drum's warmth and was surprised when he was standing right next to Drum. He looked around, trying to figure out if he himself did it or if Drum pulled him.

"You," Drum told him. "The Energy you lost using the Time Barrier is being replaced, but it doesn't seem like you're taking in any extra," Drum said. "Queen!" Drum called out. "Can you come to Pantu's home and make some tea? Contact her to make sure we can proceed without incident," Drum spoke aloud.

He looked around for Queen, but paused with a confused look, directed at Drum.

"Are you going to the RMD tonight?" Drum asked him, ignoring his silent question.

He shook his head. He didn't want to share a dream with someone who was so easily dismissive of him.

"You should come. It might help," Drum told him, before turning away to close his eyes back to the sky.

He took in the young male standing in front of him. Drum's skin glowed under the rays of starlight. Drum's face and neck seemed to soak in the light and glow from within.

It has only been his face and neck, he thought. *He keeps the rest of his body covered.* "Why is the Neutral Light here a pale violet color?" he asked instead.

Drum's eyes opened to stare at him for a moment before speaking. "An ancient artifact's Energy, which has been diluted over the years, is constantly being funneled through everything here."

"You keep saying by my birthday. It is what you all call the day you drew your first breath on this planet?" he asked.

Drum nodded. "What did you call it in The City?"

"Remorse Day," he told Drum. He saw Drum's eyes form a question and continued.

"Gifts are purchased for the Woman who suffered through the pain of giving you life. If she is unavailable, then your G-Ma would receive the gift for surviving the pain of giving life to your Ma.

"We celebrate the strength of Women and curse ourselves for causing pain to a Woman by being born. Throwing a party to celebrate one's day of life is akin to slapping your Ma in the face." He sighed.

"Is it punishable by death?" Drum teased, but he nodded.

"Being born a Woman in The City was a blessing. I cursed myself for not being born a girl. I used to wonder all the time how different my life would have been, had I been born one. I would have never been a pet. I would have grown up in The Slums, unbothered.

"Maybe my parents would have gone back and lived in The Center if I was born a girl. I would have claim to both my families' businesses and would have held more power than the governess herself. Maybe her demon spawn and I would have been best friends?" He shrugged and sighed again.

Drum only looked at him, and he felt his sadness grow since he couldn't feel Drum's emotions.

"Hmm," Drum said. "We should go. Queen should be close to your home by now," Drum stated without mentioning anything else.

PANTU: A NEW FRIEND
WEEK FIVE: MONDAY

Yeah, he is over me. I have worn off on him. Of course, it would not have lasted long, he is way more powerful than me. Maybe he just wanted to experiment. It was fun while it lasted. I can now be an unknown student, just trying to graduate. I will keep my head down and everybody will forget I exist.

Pantu's thoughts as they went back to his house were his resolve to make it through the remainder of the year. *Mansnake will leave me alone once Drum stop helping me, I guess.* He shrugged at his thoughts as his doorbell rang. He looked up at Drum then the door, before moving to open it.

Standing on his doorstep was Queen and Doctor Robin.

"PAAAANNNNNNTTTTTUUUUUU!!" Queen exclaimed, going in for a hug.

He smiled, genuinely happy to see Queen and hugged back. He was giving his Doctor a curious look.

"I'm here to help make sure everything goes smoothly, as your Doctor and your friend." Doctor Robin smiled at him.

He nodded. He could really use some company to take his Mind off Drum. He welcomed them in. Queen headed straight to his kitchen and made himself at home, looking around for everything he needed.

Doctor Robin sat down across from his seat at the table. "Drum." She acknowledged, with a slight bow.

"Robin," Drum responded back. "Thank you for taking the time," Drum politely added.

Doctor Robin smiled and nodded at him as he sat next to Drum. He made sure to keep plenty of space between them and after checking he wouldn't accidentally hit Drum; he focused on Doctor Robin.

"So, Drum is tutoring you?" Doctor Robin asked, looking between the two of them. "In your home. Alone?" she added, making her line of questioning clear.

He nodded.

"Seems like you made another friend. I was really hoping for a painting," Doctor Robin teased.

He smiled weakly. "Yes. Friends, Doctor Robin," was his reply.

"Then we are all here as friends. Drop the Doctor and just call me Robin," Robin said, with a smile.

He only nodded again. He was thinking how Drum told him Mansnake wouldn't leave him alone, but he knew Mansnake would never win a game only Mansnake was playing.

Mansnake would never get as close to Drum as he had. After knowing Drum only a few weeks, he knew if Drum wasn't interested in Mansnake before him, Drum most certainly wouldn't be interested after him.

"How are you and Dill getting along?" Robin asked.

"We are fine. Currently, we are working on a bow," he said, his voice slipping deeper into sadness.

"I thought you two were working on a spaceship. What happened to that idea?" Robin questioned, and Queen turned to look at him.

"The numbers look messy to me. Dill suggested I take a break to do something fun and then maybe the answer will come to me," he replied, ignoring Queen's look.

"So, you haven't started painting again? I know you said your attic is set up for you to paint. Have you started again?"

He looked away. "It is more of a studio now."

Robin looked surprised. "Do you mind if I take a look?"

He nodded his head and quickly rose from his chair to lead her out of the uncomfortable room. He led Robin up to the attic.

When she stepped in, Robin gasped. "OH! This is gorgeous!" she exclaimed, walking around the room to get a better feel. "So, you and your Pa are speaking now?" Robin asked, touching the walls.

He shook his head.

"Your Ma did this?" Robin asked.

He shook his head again. "Drum did," he stated, not saying anything more.

Robin looked at him, and he knew she was reading him. "Well..." Robin took a pause, "it's good to see you have made a new friend, maybe even a best friend," Robin commented, her eyes back to admiring the room.

"I guess," he said, moving to sit in one of the bay nooks.

Robin moved to sit beside him. "Do you not want to be friends with Drum?" Robin asked.

He shrugged. "I am unsure if he wants to even be friends anymore," he replied.

Robin looked out the window. "I do that too." She giggled.

He looked at Robin weirdly.

"I make up reasons, excuses and scenarios in my head and then apply them to Dill, all without asking him how he feels first. It happens when you are exploring new emotions that scare you. You try and find a way to protect yourself from being hurt," Robin related, smiling to which he weakly smiled back.

"I have never been in a relationship with anyone before. The best friend I thought I had in The City was just using me. The demon spawn was obsessed with me. Only my G-Pas cared about me there. I feel like I am asking too much from everybody, with nothing to give in return," he lamented.

"I'm amazed that's how you feel," Robin commented.

He looked at Robin, expectedly.

"You were raised around humans who never think about what others do for them. They think about how they can get more and more to enrich their own lives, even at the downfall of everyone around them." Robin looked at him. "You, on the other hand, don't."

He looked down. "I lived several lives in The City. It makes me unsure of who I am outside of there."

Robin smiled at him. "Then be all of them," she said.

He looked at Robin, and his sharp inhale of breath made her laugh.

"I saw people in the mental hospital with multiple personalities. They were the only patients on more medicine than me." He looked scared.

"Well, they were human, you aren't. Besides, nothing you've told me about the way you lived in The City would lead me to believe you don't already have a good Being moral foundation. In any life you've lived," Robin said, and a smile brightened his face.

"Have you ever had any bad interactions with humans?" he asked. He knew it was personal, but he liked Robin, and she honestly praised his G-Pas, which always softened him.

Robin nodded.

ROBIN: ONCE BEFORE
FLASHBACK: AGE FOURTEEN TO SIXTEEN

"When I was fourteen and a First Year, I fell in love with a junior in my High School. Of course, I was too young for a boyfriend, but I thought we were friends at first, so I waited."

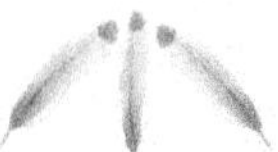

Fourteen-year-old Robin first saw him while walking down the hallway of her new High School. She thought he was incredibly handsome. He reminded her of a young Eric, without all the silver. She was fine with it since she didn't want it to be so obvious she had a *major* crush on Eric.

She forced herself to calmly walk by. She didn't feel anything from him, meaning he was human. She sighed. Her parents told her to stay out of relationships with humans but never why she should.

We live amongst humans but can't date them? I've seen plenty of Being/human marriages. They can even have kids, so what's the big OH NO when it comes to our family and humans? It's because we're royalty, isn't it? I never asked to be born into this family. I should be able to date who I want.

Her conversations with her parents always went the same way. Even NanaPoo wouldn't side with her. She sighed again as she came to her locker. It was the first day of the school year and she was more focused on boys than her advanced classes.

"Matters not. I won't have time to date anyways," she lamented to herself.

"No way I have a locker next to the hottest girl in school, and she has no time to date," a voice right next to her said.

She jumped and slowly turned to see the young Eric lookalike opening the locker on her left. She turned back without a word and opened her locker. She started taking her books out and putting them in her backpack.

"Advanced honors!?" the young Eric lookalike said, impressed. "Makes me being the quarterback seem less impressive." He laughed.

She heard the difference in their vocal tones. Where Eric's tone was deep, this guy's tone was mellow and light. She closed her locker and went to walk away but the Eric lookalike hurried around her to lean on the locker to her right.

"You really won't have time to date?" he asked, smiling at her.

"My parents won't allow me to date and even if they did, between advanced honors classes and after school college courses, there won't be any time to date," she said, moving into the halls to walk to class.

He walked beside her, smiling at her the whole time. "So, are you not allowed to have friends?" he asked, his eyes slyly looking at her while he held his friendly smile.

She shrugged.

"Then let's be friends," he said, blocking her from entering her class. "You can come watch me practice after school."

"After. School. College. Classes." she said.

"Any classes on Saturday?" he asked, and she shook her head.

"Then come to my games on Saturday and cheer for me. As a friend," he said. "I'll throw a touchdown for you," he offered. "As a friend," he added.

She nodded and he moved out of her way.

"By the way, my name is Ian," he said to her back.

"Robin," she said, without looking back.

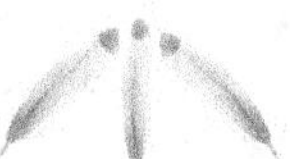

"And we were friends. We would talk between classes, and I went to every game for a year. On my Granddad's side of the family, we're Islanders, and speak Spanish. We also celebrate the human holidays and hold the human traditions. When I was fifteen and a Sophomore in High School, my family threw a Quinceañera for my birthday."

"IAN!" She was waiting by her locker for him.

He smiled at her as he walked up. "You look excited. What's up?"

"I'm having a Quinceañera for my birthday. I wanted to know if you would go?" she asked. "As my date?" she added.

Ian looked at her surprised. "Thought you couldn't date because of your parents and the whole thing about being busy?" he asked, opening his locker.

"My parents said I could invite a date. It would make a great impression on my parents if you could come. You could meet my family," she said, smiling brightly at him.

Ian nodded, not looking at her. "Yea. I'll go as your date," he said.

"Okay," she said. "The color theme is burgundy and gold," she informed him.

He nodded and smiled back at her. "Cool! I'll look for suits that match."

"Are you sure you can make it?"

"Yea. I promise I'll be there," he answered.

"As it started getting closer to the date, he complained his parents refused to buy the suit he wanted to wear, so he couldn't show up as the birthday girl's date in jeans and a tee shirt. I asked him how much the suit was and gave him the money for it.

"But he didn't show. I ended up having a friend of one of my cousins be my date about two minutes before it started. I was so sad; I didn't enjoy my own Quinceañera. The next day at school, he told me his parents wouldn't let him be out that late on a school night with a test the next day.

"I believed him. Even though I knew it was a Lie, I wanted to believe him. I really liked him. So, I ignored it and continued to go to his games. He pretty much stopped talking to me in school and his locker was moved closer to the gym since he was now a starting player.

"He was in his final year and was scouted by the college I was already attending. I thought we would be able to see more of each other, so I shook off the feelings I was having as my nerves getting the best of me.

"He would find me before I left for my college classes to complain about something, always money related and I would think I was being a good friend by "helping" his financial woes.

"Before my sixteenth birthday, my parents said I could date. I was in my third year of High School and Ian was a first-year college student. I was immediately looking for Ian on campus. I thought I could bridge a connection between Beings and humans. At least it's how I justified wanting to date a human."

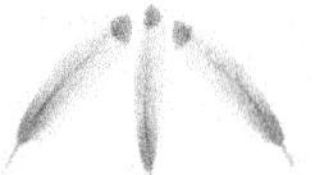

She knew he would be in the gym, working out. She paid for a day and walked in, looking around for him. She found him surrounded as the players were betting on who could lift the most.

She saw him lying on the bench, struggling to lift the heavy weights. She used her Energy to slowly help him lift the weight. One of the team members turned to look at her but she didn't acknowledge his stare.

He must be a Being. How come I've never noticed him on campus? She waited until Ian put the bar back and sat up, being congratulated by his teammates.

The Being shook his head at her and walked away. Ian didn't notice her, so she waited until one of his teammates bumped into her. They all looked at her and the smiles which came across their faces made her uneasy. Ian quickly stood and pulled her off to the other side of the room. His teammates still looking her way while making obscene gestures about her body.

"What the fuck are you doing in here?" he whispered hurriedly to her. "You need to leave, now!" he said, grabbing her arm to lead her off.

She yanked her arm back from him. "Ian, stop!" she said. "I came to tell you my parents said I could date. Since we go to the same college, we can see more of each other," she said, slightly pleading.

"I'm not in high school anymore, I'm *in* college now Robin. I can't be seen dating a third-year high schooler. My teammates would never let me live it down," he told her.

She looked shocked. She took a deep breath to hold her tears in and turned away to leave. Ian grabbed her arm.

"We can still be friends Robin. Just...let me grab my stuff and we'll talk elsewhere. Whatever you do, don't talk to any of these guys, they're assholes," he warned her.

She nodded and went outside the gym to sit on a bench. *Why should I wait for him to explain we should just be friends? He's made it clear he won't date a High Schooler. I should leave.* She went to stand but sat back down as the Being on the team was towering over her.

"Didn't yo parents tell you not to date humans?" he asked, his southern accent coming out.

She glared at him.

He laughed. "You been told but wanna do it anyway." He shook his head. "That boy gone hurt your heart in a way only humans can. You should've gone to a Higher Ed school," the Being lectured.

"And we both know you're only here because you look better playing against humans than against Beings," she shot back.

He smiled at her and walked away as Ian walked up. He grabbed her arm, pulling her off to a space between the buildings where they couldn't be seen.

"I thought I told you not to talk to them!" he said to her. He pushed her up against the wall and roughly kissed her.

She pushed him away. "What are you doing?" she asked, pissed off at him. "You just said you can't date a High Schooler, then you attack me?"

"I said that in front of them. Do you know what they do to newbies girlfriends?" He explained, "We can date but they can't know you're my girlfriend, not until I'm a starting player. I don't care if you're still in high school, but I don't want them to hurt you," he said, slowly pushing her back against the wall to make out.

"We started secretly dating. Ian's birthday was about a month before mine and he was going on about his perfect birthday gift. It was this wildly expensive car.

"I couldn't go to his birthday party, since he said it would be full of his teammates. I made plenty of money doing my part-time job and my savings account was healthy, so I bought the car as a surprise for him.

"I gave the car to him the day before his party along with my first sexual experience. He told me that night his parents were letting him, and his friends go on a guy's trip, so he also needed money. He was frustrated he couldn't make money playing until he was a starter. I funded his whole trip.

"After he came back, he was different. Our schedules always seem to just miss each other unless he wanted something. Money, food, expensive items, sex. Whenever he would call or text me, I would drop everything and run to him. He never had time to take me on a date though?

"My 'Sweet Sixteen' party was coming up, and I was over the moon. I was sure Ian would come this time; I mean he was my *boyfriend*. I thought I was so in love. He Promised he would be there. He Promised to be my date and meet my family.

"But once again, he stood me up. This time, all I did during my party was cry. My cousins were pissed he didn't bother to show up. No call or text. He'd missed my Quinceañera and now my Sweet Sixteen. So, they went to his house."

Eric knocked on Ian's parents' door. The surprise on their faces as they took in Eric, Jay, and X, standing on their doorstep, caused them to lose their thoughts.

"Hello," Eric politely and deeply said. "We looking for Ian."

"We were supposed to party tonight but when he didn't show, we got worried. He's alright?" Jay asked.

"Yes!" Ian's mom said. She was staring at them, knowing who they were. She knew this family lived in their city, but she never thought she would meet them.

"He's out on a date with his girlfriend," Ian's dad spoke up. He knew Eric from Realtor magazines and Jay from Business magazines. The young boy behind them was unknown to them.

"Maybe he was coming to the party after his date. I told you he was fine, but you just had to check," X said.

"Sorry for being concerned," Jay said.

"Wow! Our son has some...good friends!" Ian's dad said, smiling. "He went to that new Frentaly restaurant downtown," he added, still smiling at them.

After thanking Ian's parents, they went back to the car which she was waiting in. They told her what his parents said, and she started crying. Her tears stained her beautiful, silk, ivory-colored, princess dress with diamonds and lace.

Her cousins drove downtown, parking the car across the street from the restaurant, where Ian and his date could be clearly seen. X got out of the car, stood by the door for a moment before getting back in with a small device in his hand. X pulled a blue screen from the small device so they could hear and see what was happening at the table.

She looked at her cousin. "When did you?" she asked, still surprised by the awesome things her cousins could do.

X shrugged and focused back on the device. She could see and listen clearly to Ian's conversation.

"She's such a stupid little bitch," Ian's girlfriend said. "Did she really think buying you a car would get you to dump me!? I'm the co-captain of the cheerleading squad. Football players and cheerleaders go together like tart and green apple," she said, and Ian laughed.

"Did she really think you would go to a high schooler's *Sweet Sixteen* as her date? How fucking stupid is she?" Ian's girlfriend asked.

"She thinks by waving her family's money in front of my face, I'm just going to do whatever she wants. I got into this school with my own talent. A full scholarship," Ian bragged.

"I went to every game. I helped him. His stats increased because I used my Energy...to help him," she whispered.

Her cousins looked at her.

"So, you spent your hard-earned money and your Energy on this fucker?" Jay asked in disbelief.

She could only cry silently.

"You should tell her to give you more money so we can take another romantic vacation. Our trip to the Monarch Islands for your birthday was amazing!" She reached across the table to hold Ian's hand. "All the expensive jewelry she bought me almost makes me want to pretend to be her best friend." She laughed but Ian didn't.

"She's smart as fuck. I have to stay away from her as much as possible, or she will figure out I'm using her for her family's money and influence. If she didn't show up in the gym that day, I would still be riding pine." Ian looked at his girlfriend. "Stay away from her!" he warned.

His girlfriend pouted. "It's almost like you're trying to protect her. You haven't cheated on me with her, have you?" she asked.

Ian shook his head. "I wouldn't dare touch a high schooler, and I would never cheat on you. Wait until I get scouted for the Pros. Even if I ride the pine my first year, I can still get paid. Once I leave school, you can become her best friend to keep the money flowing," Ian said.

"Cut it off!" she screamed. "Cut that shit off now X!" She was now crying her eyes out. She was choking on her cries caught in her throat. "I will kill both those fucking assholes!" She went to get out of the car, but X stopped her.

"Not in front of everybody. Let's wait. You will have your revenge." X looked at her.

She trusted him, so she relaxed herself and closed her eyes to wait. She didn't open them when Eric drove off after them. She didn't care where they were going, her cousin told her she would get her payback, so she waited.

When the car stopped, her cousins all exited the car, leaning against it, waiting for her. She took a deep breath, stepping out of the car to walk over to the car she purchased for Ian. She looked through the window.

"Not enough of my money left over for a hotel room, so you parked at Quiet Cliff? Your girlfriend does eat like a fucking pig," she said, surprising them.

"Oh shit!" A half-dressed Ian scrambled to get out of the car.

"Ian! What the fuck? The little bitch is stalking you now?" Ian's girlfriend asked.

"Robin. Listen. Baby, listen. She means nothing to me," Ian tried desperately to explain. "Oh…oh…remember what I told you about team girlfriends? She's a team girlfriend. I had to do it. My teammates…they forced me," Ian pleaded.

By now his girlfriend was out of the car. "Ian? What are you fucking saying!? I'm your girlfriend. We've been dating since freshman year of high school!" She went to grab Ian.

He jerked away from her. "She's lying Robin. You're my girlfriend. You know you are. I've only been with you. This is the first time I'm being hazed by my teammates. I didn't know what else to do, so I just…I was trying to do it. I'm so happy you stopped me," Ian pleaded with her.

By now her cousins made their way over to the car. They were looking around inside the car, admiring the make and model along with the features. Ian turned to look at them and when he realized who they were, his face showed shock.

His girlfriend's face was stuck with her mouth open. Her eyes went from Eric, to X, to Jay, repeatedly. She couldn't decide which guy she wanted since her brain was stuck, same as her face.

"Set it on fire," she said to her cousins.

Ian screamed as flames erupted from his car. He looked around for anything he could use to put out the fire. Her cousins laughed as a half-naked Ian ran around in circles trying to save his car.

Ian's girlfriend was still stuck on stupid right up to the moment her fist connected with his girlfriend's face. The girl flew back into the burning car, cracking her head on the door. She slid down and slumped over.

Ian looked surprised as no one moved to save the girl from the burning car. The hot metal started to melt the back of the girl, but she didn't feel the flames start to engulf her body. There were no screams as Ian realized the girl was already dead. She killed the girl with one punch.

"What you wanna do with him?" Eric asked, nodding towards Ian.

She didn't look at Ian, who started begging for his life. He was on his knees, crawling towards her, crying.

"Don't kill him," she said, her eyes still on the girl's burning body.

Ian looked up at her. "Robin baby. Thank you. You know I love you. I'm so sorry I had her in our car. I will never do it again. Baby, I love you so much." He clung to her legs.

"I want him to live the rest of his life with the knowledge of what he did to me." She kneeled to look him in his face. "You will remember how you treated me for the last three years every time it rains."

She stood up. "Break his throwing arm," she said with no emotion. "And a leg for good measure," she told her cousins. They nodded and moved towards him.

Ian started screaming. "No Robin! I need my arm. It's going to take us to the Pros. We can live a good life. Please!" he begged, but her cousins Eric and Jay already had him by his legs, pulling him off her.

"Which leg?" Jay asked.

"The left one," she stated, and Jay nodded.

"If you do this, I will sue your whole family. I will post this all over the internet and tell everyone you killed Erica!" Ian screamed. "You will all go to prison for the rest of your lives! I will own everything you have!"

X walked up to Erica's still burning body and touched it. What was left, dusted away to nothing and Ian's eyes went wide. Ian watched as X touched the burning car and X closed his eyes. The whole car slowly dusted off as well. X's eyes opened to look at her.

"Robin, text Ian and tell him, since he missed your Quinceañera and your Sweet Sixteen, you're blocking him. Say because you know he's cheating on you with Erica, he's a horrible boyfriend and you're breaking up with him."

Ian was so focused on X; he heard the crack before he felt the pain. Ian screamed as Jay broke his left leg in several places. When Eric held his arm up, he could only cry from the amount of pain his leg was feeling until Eric broke his arm. He screamed again. By the time Eric finished breaking his arm in several places, Ian had already passed out.

ROBIN: LEAVING AN OPEN DOOR
WEEK FIVE: MONDAY

She took a deep breath. "When he woke up, he was so delirious, no one believed anything he said. He was charged with Erica's disappearance but killed himself and his parents when he was out on bail.

"Turns out, they were in a scheme with Erica's parents to milk rich and wealthy kids out of money using their own kids. Ian's parents did it during their school days and taught their kids how too as well.

"Several families were in on it. He outed them all in his murder suicide note and blamed them for ruining his future. Prominent families were noted as targets."

She looked down. "I cut myself off from relationships after that. I felt I couldn't trust any man who wasn't family, and I really couldn't trust myself. It took a serious slap back to reality the more I learned about psychology.

"But Pantu, that's part of growing, learning life lessons and figuring out how to better yourself. This includes interacting with others and finding balance. You are already doing that with Dill, so why stop?" she asked.

"Drum is not Dill," Pantu said, as he looked out the window. "Just when I think we are okay, my scent wavers with him and it makes me scared he will..." Pantu drifted off.

"Did your scent waver with Dill?" she asked.

"Yes. But he said it was steady now," Pantu responded.

"Do you know what you did to make it stable?" she questioned.

"It is not the same," Pantu told her. "In The City, liking a male is punishable by death. I realized I was clinging to Dill and needed to give him room to breathe. I was suffocating him with my friendship," Pantu ended.

"But with Drum...?" she continued for Pantu.

"But with Drum, I am unsure of what I feel. I have never felt these feelings before, and I am confused. Do I want him to be just a friend? Is he already more than a friend? Or was?" Pantu questioned himself, more than her. "He asked me to be his boyfriend, but I could not answer. Since then, he has been distant," Pantu added.

"Do you know how I learned to trust again?" she asked.

Pantu thought for a moment but shook his head.

"I learned it's completely up to me how much I let a person into my life," she told Pantu. "If you want someone in your life, then keep a door cracked for them. Never leave a door wide open. See if they want to enter, this way you can control the flow of your own room. If you feel uncomfortable, slam that shit!" she said, clapping her hands together and making Pantu laugh.

"One way to do that is to start a conversation to see how the other Being feels," she told Pantu.

"And if they are uninterested?" Pantu asked, and she could see on Pantu's face, he was unsure if he would agree with her answer.

"Then it's their decision not to walk through and your decision whether to close the door or not. And we respect others' decisions about their own life because we would like the same respect back, right?" she asked. She looked at Pantu as she said this, wanting to see if he would become like Manpa, completely obsessed and pass the point of reason.

Pantu nodded, reluctant acceptance on his face of the fact he may have to let go of Drum. She watched as the look on Pantu's face changed and knew he wasn't thinking about Drum anymore.

"Thinking about Manpa?" She knowingly smiled.

"He is my blueprint for the kind of Being I do not want to be. But how can you be okay with me doing this?" Pantu asked her, astounded.

"Do you know how many students I and my colleagues have to see because of him? I want to take him down myself, but as their Doctor, there is nothing I can say or do." She huffed, with a pleading look in her eyes.

"So, I will help you. Besides…" she waved off, "we aren't fully human. Our way of life is different. I have to be a Doctor following human standards, but when it comes to Beings, we see things differently." She shrugged.

"I don't have to worry what humans think anymore since they are all leaving Hollis, but there are Beings who want me to lose my human license, so I still have to move carefully, to help others…for now," she hinted. "It doesn't bother you that I killed someone?" she asked.

Pantu shook his head. "Your face is pure and beautiful. If you really did kill the girl and she was innocent, your face would look…blemished."

She smiled at him. She felt comfortable telling Pantu this when she hadn't told Dill everything. She felt she could now. If he could be best friends with Pantu and not judge Pantu's past, maybe Dill would understand her.

"I'm so scared if I tell Dill I killed someone, he wouldn't want to be with me anymore. He would think I'm evil," she lamented. "It doesn't help, I always have to talk myself into not sitting around thinking Dill is cheating on me," she added.

Pantu giggled. "Dill is so afraid of hurting you, he has no time to cheat. His Pa's wife disgusts him, and he never wants to be anything like her. You have nothing to worry about when it comes to Dill. He is devoted to you," Pantu assured her.

She hugged him tightly. "Thank you Pantu. Thank you for understanding me. Thank you for not dumping Dill as a friend when we started dating. And I know you push him to spend more time with me, so thank you! We should join the others downstairs," she said, as she stood up.

PANTU: THE SUNSET CREW
WEEK FIVE: MONDAY

He nodded and went with her back downstairs. Before he made it off the attic stairs, he heard Dill's voice.

"I brought flowers to give to my girlfriend, but Ma Sky said I should rearrange them to suit my girlfriend's taste," Dill happily said.

"You love saying that word, don't you?" Win teased.

He smelled something delicious, and hurried downstairs. He rounded the kitchen corner to find Sport cooking. Dill turned to say hello, but he was peeking around Sport to see what smelled like heaven.

"What is that?" he asked, pointing to a pan.

"Dinner," Sport, said with a laugh. "Your Ma is hosting a book club for Mrs. K at the store, so she will be late coming home. I thought I would make dinner for you and your Pa, so you both don't starve to death," Sport teased.

He smiled in appreciation of Sport's kindness but then looked at Sport suspiciously. *Does he know?*

"Pannnttttuuuu," Queen softly called him over to the table.

He gave up trying to figure out what Sport was doing and went happily to Queen.

"Sit down and drink," Queen instructed him.

He sat down and looked at the cup of tea. "The last time I drank some tea; I lost two or three days." He pouted.

Queen looked at him with anticipation.

"My GMack made some tea for me and when I woke up, we had traveled so far from The City, I must have lost some days," he said, looking at Queen innocently.

Queen's face turned red as he laughed. "I'm not drugging you in that sense Pantu. This tea is to help with your Energy intake." Queen looked at Robin as she walked in. "Robin?"

Dill turned in response to hearing the name to come face to face with Robin.

"It will also finish flushing out the remaining human drugs in your system. I came to make sure the dosage is correct and there are no adverse side effects," Robin said to him, but never took her eyes off Dill, who hurried to hide the flowers behind his back.

"PANTU! You didn't tell me your Doctor was going to be here," Dill loudly and clumsily whispered, but he was drinking his tea, unbothered.

"Oh. So, I'm just Pantu's Doctor, huh?" Robin asked, moving closer to Dill, who stiffened. "What's behind your back?" Robin asked, trying to catch a glimpse.

"Um, my hand?" Dill responded to Win's amused laugh and Queen's restraint of a smile.

"What's in your hand behind your back?" Robin asked, moving closer to reach behind Dill and grab the flowers.

Dill let go of the flowers and Robin gasped at the arrangement of wildflowers she pulled from behind Dill's back.

"These are beautiful! Are they for someone special?" Robin asked, curious.

"Umm. Umm. You can have them...if you want," Dill nervously said, as Robin sniffed the flowers while looking up at Dill with a shy smile.

"I wouldn't want to take a Gift meant for someone else," Robin teased, and Dill became flustered.

"Um. I was...there was...over in the..." Dill fumbled over his words as he tried to explain. Instead, Dill chose to grab and drag him into the laundry room, teacup be damned.

"DUDE! Why? Why didn't you tell me she was going to be here!?" Dill freaked out.

He said nothing as he continued to blow on and drink what was left of his tea.

"What if they find out Robin and I are dating? What do I do?" Dill asked, while still freaking out.

Dill's back was to the door, so he told him. "Well, if they were ignorant about it before, you totally just told them."

While he was content to drink his tea, Dill slowly turned to see Robin, with a huge smile on her face, standing in front of Queen, Win and Sport, who were all looking rather impressed.

Dill slowly turned to look back at his calm best friend. "Hey Bestie!" Dill said, faking his smile. "BE-FORE!" Dill said, and he burst out laughing.

"Sucks sour tits, does it not?" he said, as he continued to laugh and make his way out of the room.

Queen, Win and Sport laughed and followed, leaving Dill and Robin to talk alone. They made it back to the kitchen and dining room area where Sport went back to cooking and the rest sat down around the table.

Drum had yet to leave his seat or contribute much to the conversation, too distracted with whatever was on his laptop. He glanced at him, but Drum was too engaged with whatever was on his screen.

He rolled his eyes. *Just friends*, he thought. *Get over yourself Pantu!*

"How do you feel after drinking the tea? Feeling drugged?" Queen teased.

He cracked a smile. "Nope. I feel good," he said.

Dill and Robin came back into the room, holding hands and smiling at each other.

"Um. I know it's a lot to ask, but could you all not say anything about Robin and me? We're just now getting..." Dill started.

"You didn't say anything about Kat and me, so my lips are sealed," Win interrupted with a smile.

Dill looked just as surprised as Queen and even Sport turned around, shocked.

"Dill knew about you two?" Sport asked.

Win nodded. "He knew since before the incident. We went on a date to one of his family's theme parks during a slow day, and he was there," Win informed them.

Queen looked at Dill, who refused to meet anyone's eyes.

"I'm sorry!" Dill whispered to Win.

"Huh?" Win asked.

"I'm sorry. It's my fault. I tried but I failed, and I didn't know..." Dill started, as the tears fell.

Win got up and walked closer to Dill. "Failed what Dill?" Win asked, confused.

"You should have some tea. It is really calming." He offered his cup to Dill, who snatched it and gulped it down.

Everybody waited until Dill, with the help of Robin's hands on his arm, started.

"That day, I saw you and Kat at the park. There was a snake around you. At first, I thought it was a park snake but when you got up and left, the snake purposefully followed you. So, I followed it to make sure I wasn't going crazy."

Dill took a breath. "I tried to capture it, but the slippery bastard got away. I never knew who it was, and I checked every registered snake's whereabouts that day and they were all accounted for," Dill said. "I never knew it was him until..." Dill looked at him, but he was uninterested in joining the conversation.

Win turned to look at him as well. "Until Pantu told us." Win turned back to look at Dill. "Dill that's not your—"

Dill cut Win off. "If I only knew how to make a Barrier, I would have—" Dill was cut off by Win hugging him.

"Thank you!" Win told Dill. "Thank you for even trying and never using the information against us," Win expressed to Dill.

Dill nodded and hugged Win back.

"Pantu, did you know?" Queen asked.

He shrugged. "But I know he has a way around Domes," he added.

Everyone turned to look at him, but he was feeling good and relaxed. He was dancing to a song in his head.

This information made Drum look up from his laptop. "He's been back?" Drum asked.

He nodded. "I only know because there is a pair of pants missing from my closet. I noticed last night, which means he was here while we were in Hollis."

Queen looked disturbed. "How could he break Drum's Barrier?"

Drum looked thoughtful. "Not break, evade. The Barrier I set is untouched with no cracks or breaks. He might have gone under, or he has found a way to dampen his Energy," Drum thought aloud. "That means he can do a lot of the Universal Abilities, his base Ability Level is strong, and any side Abilities from that. He may even be able to use multiple Abilities," Drum informed them, and went back to his laptop, again distracted.

"He only took your pants, by the way," he told Drum, resisting the urge to laugh.

"Why would Drum's pants be in your closet?" Sport asked, with wide eyes.

Queen and Dill both exited the conversation, finding other things to do with their eyes, hands, and face.

"By the way Queen, he has moved into an apartment in Sunset," he informed Queen. "Drum figured Mansnake's focus was my bedroom window. Dill found out which apartment after Drum mentioned it," he said, with a frown while ignoring Sport's question. He knew the previous residents didn't disappear just to break their lease.

There was a knock on the door, and he looked confused as to who else would be coming to his house. He went to open the door, and he excitedly greeted Kat,

"I forgot to mention I invited Kat as well. HELP!" He heard Win meekly say.

Win was nervously looking for a place to hide as he and Kat walked in, and Win's whole body froze. Win slowly turned just his head, his face was one of a deer caught in headlights. "Oh, Pantu, um..." Win started.

He waved Win off. "Kat is welcomed into my home whenever," he said, smiling as he and Kat side-hugged each other.

Kat looked at Win smiling and slightly bowed her head to acknowledge him. Kat went to say hello to everyone else, but Win interrupted her.

"They all know. Oh, and check this out," Win said, while pointing to Robin and Dill still holding hands.

Kat's mouth dropped open, and she looked happy. She ran into Win's arms, and they kissed to everyone who wasn't Drum, Queen, and his surprise. Drum made more chairs appear for everyone to sit down around the table.

What surprised him was Drum made chairs which were the same as the ones already at the table, as if Drum knew where these chairs were and pulled them here with Light. But he felt something different about the way in which Drum used Light for this Talent. Drum's phone rang and he went to answer it while moving out of the room.

"I wonder what he's planning?" Queen asked, motioning for him to check out Drum's laptop, but he shook his head at Queen with his eyes wide. He was scared, if Drum was online, his punishment from his parents would be worse than his punishment for using his True Vision without just cause.

He watched as Win waved a hand to use the air and turned the laptop towards himself, then a surprised look crossed Win's face. "This is an awesome plan. I can't wait to see it in action!" Win said, as he and Kat were looking at the screen.

Drum came back in. "Dill, a moment," he said, and turned to walk away again.

Dill got up and followed Drum to the outside patio area.

"Let me see," Queen said, and Win closed the laptop, sliding it over to Queen.

After opening it and inputting Drum's password, Queen looked happy about whatever he saw. When Drum and Dill returned, Queen closed Drum's laptop and slid it back. Drum opened it and was again immersed in it.

"Well, I think we should find a way to deal with Mansnake together, that way we aren't divided when it comes to our plans," Queen offered.

"The Sunset Crew is all here. Now would be a suitable time to work together. It appears we haven't given him enough credit for being rather crafty and fucking despicable," Sport said, sitting.

Robin and Dill were sitting at the head of the table, while Queen was to Robin's right, followed by Sport. Kat and Win were at the opposite end, with Drum and him across from Sport and Queen.

Kat turned to Sport. "The food smells delicious," she commented shyly.

He wanted to remember the shade of red Sport's face turned, and he smiled as Sport refused to look at Kat.

"It's dinner for Pantu and his Pa, since neither of them can cook," Sport replied, but put distance between him and Kat, leaning more towards Queen.

Kat looked hurt. "Oh. Okay!" she said softly, as she looked at Win, who smiled and threw his arm around her.

He cursed his Attention to Detail. "Yes, but they are all staying for dinner, so if you leave Kat, I will be offended," he told her, with a serious look on his face. Everyone else at the table looked at him with surprise since he never invited any of them to stay. Even Drum's eyebrow was raised at him.

Kat smiled wide at him. "I wouldn't want to offend," she said back.

After a look at Robin, a nod came from Drum and Queen made another cup of tea appear in front of him.

"Drink up," Queen said, glad the tea was working. "I will come by every day for five more days to make your tea. Robin doesn't want to flush the human drugs too quickly because it may send your body into shock." Queen added, "I hope you don't mind the intrusion."

He smiled as his Light flowed happily inside his body, knowing that although Robin and Queen were doing this for him, it was Drum, keeping his word to help with his Light. He wanted to hide his smile at the thought, so he shook his head and sipped on the tea. "You are welcomed."

DRUM: A TEMPER OUT OF CONTROL
WEEK FIVE: MONDAY

"Let's start," he said and finally closed his laptop to look up. "Pantu, Barrier," he stated, and Pantu complied. He set white Energy inside the Barrier to control time. "Stronger," he told Pantu, who took a moment to feel how much Energy he used before increasing the strength of the Barrier to double the amount of Energy he was using. After checking for holes or leaks, he nodded.

"There's a reason all of you are here. Robin can give a profile on Mansnake," he started to explain but when he saw the smile grace Pantu's cute, pink lips at him using the moniker Pantu started, he couldn't help but add a smile to his face and his words.

"Kat is here because all of Mansnake's victims either know each other or know of each other. Kat can be our voice for them and to them. Queen can control the truthful narrative online while gathering any additional information needed.

"Win can keep track of Mansnake's finances to see if we can follow a trail, maybe even cut off his source of income. Dill can build whatever you all need," he laid out for everyone. His eyes found his best friend's iris Energy. "Sport," was all he said and received a head bow from Sport.

"Sport what?" Pantu asked, curious about Sport's role.

"Sport can do what he does best..." he paused and looked at Sport's Energy with a smile, "cook." He saw Sport's Energy give a red tint and he knew his best friend was blushing at his compliment and his smile.

"And what can you do?" Pantu asked.

He turned to fully look into Pantu's eyes, moving his knee to connect with Pantu's. Of course, no one could see under the table but Pantu's wide eyes at their touch, made his heart rate speed up. "I can inform you that you and Dill don't have to do this by yourselves. It's your decision whether you and Dill will accept our help."

Pantu thought for a moment before looking at Dill, who seemed apprehensive at accepting their help. Everyone else at the table was silently watching Pantu and Dill write on a slip of paper and slide it back and forth. Dill read whatever Pantu wrote and sighed, nodding.

"Okay we will accept help to deal with Mansnake, although Dill thinks I should tell you all, we in the Kim bloodline are cold-blooded. I will not let death be the end all, be all for this little son of a bitch." Pantu looked around as they all nodded in agreement.

Win's personal laptop came out, and Win went to type, getting lost in the screen. Queen pulled out his gold badge with the number zero on it and went to work while Kat pulled out her phone and started typing on it. Sport went to check on the food and Robin's files were out.

"He will have two weeks to plan something, no matter how incomplete or faulty it may seem to us, we shouldn't be caught off guard," he started. "He is now more of a threat than just a pain in the…" He stopped, and everybody except Pantu nodded.

"Pain in the what?" Pantu asked, confused.

"Pain in the ass," Sport said from the kitchen.

"Drum doesn't cuss," Robin added.

Pantu looked at him as if he was a talking zombie. "You have never cussed before? No use of colorful words?" Pantu asked, to which he shook his head.

"But it will change," he said, with a smile.

"Why?" Pantu asked.

"Life changes us all," was all he said about the matter, so Pantu dropped it.

"If we collectively put everything, we know about him together, what new information could we derive from it?" He threw the question out there.

"He has an office," Pantu said. "Maybe we can find it and see what he has been up to."

He could see Queen's Energies was disgusted by the comment. "Why do you think he has an office, Pantu?" Queen asked, knowing what Pantu was implying.

Dill raised a hand. "He wants the power you hold with the amount of information you have. Otherwise, why go up against you in front of everyone? He was trying to make himself look good, but he wanted to trip you up, hoping Drum would notice him," Dill said.

Robin looked up from her files. "He's willing to do anything to get the spot next to Drum, but it seems like Pantu has been able to split his attention, so he's been making mistakes," Robin added. "Normally after one round with Mansnake, other Beings bow out, scared of the information he has on them."

They all looked at Pantu, drinking his tea.

"What information does he have on you Pantu?" Kat asked, gently.

Pantu laughed. "He heard a conversation in which the things I said could be seen as a threat to my parents. There is a saying in The City, "Bad parents do not deserve to live, and a filial child knows when to end it", but it matters not.

"He missed his window of opportunity with me. The longer he waits to tell anybody the more it will just be a baseless rumor. He has no hard proof, other than he said, he said. And we see how well his words hold up in front of the general public." Pantu and Dill both leaned in together to chuckle.

"He really thought he could control you with that!? He failed to realize without hard proof, now no one will believe anything he says about you," Dill loudly whispered. "It's a good thing he didn't think to record you," Dill joked and everyone laughed.

"I have shown him his words are useless, but he will try to find out more," Pantu loudly whispered back. "He tried to attack my social standing, hoping to leave me isolated, so he could manipulate me, but it backfired, thanks to Queen." Pantu smiled at Queen. "And Drum...I guess," Pantu added and quickly cut those shining brown eyes away from him.

He only sighed while taking and releasing a deep breath. He turned to look at everyone. "Instead of approaching Pantu in public after what happened the first time, he sent others.

"The girl who approached Pantu during movie night and the one who approached him at the game, seems to be a part of the network he's building. We need to tear it down.

"Because Pantu refused to back down, it forced Mansnake to physically approach us. I laughed when he still approached me after Queen shut him down about the invite Lie. Why? Why still approach me and ask me to tutor him?" he questioned.

Queen placed his badge on the table. "His social standing is hit, so his network of information should be interrupted or at least, he can't add to it. It must be slowly eating away at his mental and emotional states," Queen offered.

Robin sat forward. "It is. He sees his window slowly closing. He may have thought he had until your inheritance to win you over but now Pantu and Drum have become the "IT" fanfic couple, he feels pressed for time.

"He doesn't want it to seem like you're open to dating or interested in anyone. It would cause chaos he can't control. It's why he never said anything about Win and Kat, going so far as to extort her into being quiet about their relationship," Robin explained.

"You haven't been around by yourself, have you?" Kat asked Pantu.

"Once I walked to the library and back home. Then I went to a cafe across the street from Robin's office by myself, both on a Sunday. I walk to my classes by myself, but it does not seem like I have gone anywhere else alone," Pantu thought aloud.

"AH!" Pantu exclaimed. "I stood out in front of the school by myself to wait for Dill on Anime Night. I also left the campus the same night, but I did not get far. And I went to a club meeting with T-PEC. Seven altogether!"

He caught the look Robin and Dill shared before looking at the table. They ignored the glances between them and Pantu.

"I was only asking because I was caught by myself. I don't want it to happen to you," Kat said and looked away.

"The only way to interrupt his ability to gather info, is to have his victims come forward. He's been using them to get information," Sport chipped in.

"No one is going to come forward with the information he has on them," Kat said.

For the first time, Sport looked at Kat. "You finally did," Sport stated.

Kat's ocean blue Energy was tinted red as she looked at Pantu. "I felt Pantu could understand my feelings," Kat said. "But the longer Mansnake stays away from school, the more his victims will flock to Pantu. Everyone knows we talked, and I just made a post in the BTC private community on Opinionated. They're putting it together online that #AnonB has won every time Mansnake tried to attack."

"What's BTC?" Sport asked.

"Behind the Camera," Kat said and looked down at her folded, twisting hands. Win looked away from his laptop to console Kat.

"The evidence of your blackmail is recorded, but not by Mansnake, by someone else. The job of people who have been recorded is to record others to keep your own secret quiet. It's how he adds to his information system. BTC is the Beings who were behind the recordings." Kat's tears dropped onto Win's hands.

He and everyone around the table realized Kat was admitting to recording someone else's extortion. No one could say anything, but he watched the Energy reactions of everyone at the table. No one's Energy held anything other than understanding and resolve to break the hold this first year held over innocent Beings.

"We have to find the information he has on them and destroy it," Win firmly stated.

Kat shook her head. "That won't be enough, Bubbly. Sure, they will "believe" you, but if you let them destroy it themselves..." Kat shyly suggested.

Queen smiled and nodded. "I like that plan."

"What about the physical part?" Dill asked. "Did that change?"

"Yes!" Pantu nodded. "Changed it today as a matter of fact!" Pantu smiled but he felt uneasy at the way the smile sat on Pantu's face.

"Details please!" Robin said, and Queen looked at her.

"You're helping us? Does that go against some code or something?" Queen asked, the bright yellow, light brown and deep green Energy inside his best friend being pleasantly surprised.

"Only if he was my patient and since he has never been, this is me as a concerned friend, helping. Besides, I have never given any information which would go against my oath," Robin informed Queen.

Pantu took a deep breath. "So…ahhh…I was thinking. Since we have no way to know what Mansnake will do, why not have someone else figure it out for us?"

He smiled as everyone else looked at Pantu, trying to understand what Pantu meant.

"Send him to T-PEC," he said, with a laugh. "If he really does have multiple Abilities and can use Universal ones, that side would covet him. He would also be an easier target."

"Slight problem," Queen spoke up. "We don't know how much correct information he has on us, and we think he has a gold badge."

Kat piped in, "It might still work. They are quite clumsy and will withhold information from each other to Level Up."

"What do you mean?" Win asked.

"When everybody thought Drum and I would be a couple, they placed someone in my friend group. I guess no one I was already hanging around wanted to join but when she kept asking how to become a Bee, that was the first white flag for me.

"She kept asking why we didn't hang with "The Four" since Drum and I was supposed to like each other. The second white flag and my friend group became smaller," Kat offered up.

"Do you think they would be clumsy enough to lead us to his office?" Queen asked, and Kat nodded.

"There's at least one on campus" he said. "I thought it was weird he kept trying to get back on campus after hours, but the Barrier is set to reject his Energy until after his suspension is over.

"That's why I think he can dampen his Energy, maybe even erase it. Him returning to Pantu's house after I set a Barrier is evidence," he stated, as he folded his hands together to think. That smile was bothering the hell out of him.

"We can find his office ourselves then," Win said.

Robin shook her head. "Yeah, you can look for his office. But remember, no matter what, he will be pushed into T-PEC when he realizes Drum wants nothing to do with him. His obsession of lust will turn into rage at not being able to get what he wants, so why not send him there earlier?

"It would be better if it seemed like he went there on his own or T-PEC forces him themselves," Robin advised. "We will have to give T-PEC something more than a Being with Universal Abilities."

Dill was thinking and not paying attention to the conversation. *"Do you think they're trying to put someone around us?"* Dill whispered to Pantu, who shook his head.

"The physical is more than that, right Pantu?" Sport continued the conversation.

He knew he could count on Sport, who was watching as Pantu looked for an opening to move on to the next subject. It was Pantu's smile, which was still unsettling to him, and he was glad his best friend asked it instead of him.

Pantu looked at Sport and looked away. *Fuck!* was written all over Pantu's face.

"What's the second part of the physical?" Dill asked, looking directly at Pantu.

The look on Pantu's face made the Heat inside his body Flare up. Pantu felt his Heat along with his annoyance and avoided his line of sight. He pulled back, asking his Energy not to make Pantu uncomfortable because he couldn't handle his own emotions. He was calming himself down, trying to get his Energy and his emotions stable.

"It is a combination of his mental and emotional state cracking," Pantu answered, walking around the question.

Dill jumped up. "PANTU, ARE YOU FUCKING CRAZY? DO YOU WANT TO ATTEND ALL OF OUR REPASTS ON THE SAME DAMN DAY!" Dill shouted to everyone else's confusion, but not his.

"What will happen if he hurts you Pantu?" he quietly asked.

Pantu rolled his eyes and gave an exasperated sigh. "It is not as if I will not heal from it. I have been through worse than a physical fight. Chill," Pantu said, with clear disgust in his voice.

He got up and left the table, knowing his Heat was increasing in intensity and no one would be able to handle the Level of Heat, except the one who followed and one more sitting at the table. He was unsure of two Beings when it came to handling his Energy, so to keep confusion down, he treated everyone outside his family the same.

"You act as if you care. Why should it bother you whether I get a scar?" Pantu gritted out, the look of anger on Pantu's face apparent.

A wave of Heat blasted out from his body, breaking the Barrier and he took back-to-back deep breaths to lower his Energy temperature. "Maybe it shouldn't bother me then, Pantu. Do whatever you want, but I won't sit around and watch when I Promised to protect you," he told Pantu, trying to control the level in his voice.

He never yelled at anyone since he moved to this town, but Pantu knew how to get under his skin. He knew he messed up, telling everyone in Pantu's house he made a Promise to Pantu, but how else could he respond to the handsomely beautiful man standing in front of him with a look of defiant anger written all over the gorgeous face he loved gazing at.

"IT IS ONLY BECAUSE OF A STUPID PROMISE! IF IT WAS ANYTHING ELSE, YOUR EYES WOULD NOT BLINK. YOU WOULD CARE LESS THAN YOU DO NOW!" Pantu yelled at him.

"So, NOW my Promise is STUPID!?" he asked, appalled. "When it's an inconvenience for you, it's stupid, but when there are people from The City here, I guess that's the only time it means anything to you," he lashed back, but was unable to keep the disgust out of his voice.

Pantu took a deep breath and stared hard at him, forcing the breath out. "Will you touch me even less if I am not flawless? I do not need you to protect me when you act as if you are the only one allowed to have scars."

He stared back hard at Pantu, wondering if Pantu hurt his soft and supple chest with releasing such a hard breath. "Pantu!" The threat in his voice was clear. "Do not ever compare my scars to you willingly offering yourself up to a slimy snake. And for what? So that you can goad your superiority over him? All so you can say what we already know? Would you harm yourself on purpose just to win against him? Just so you can shout from the mountaintop you defeated a worthless runt?" he asked, his anger showing.

He wasn't about to let Pantu plans involve him being physically hurt. He wanted to take the snake down just as much as everyone sitting at the table, but not at the cost of Pantu's safety.

"It would only be your decision what I do with my body if I were to wear your collar. Am I?" Pantu shot back at him before stomping upstairs, tripping over a step he kicked in frustration, hurting himself more. "DAMN IT ALL TO THE SLUMS!" Pantu shouted as he slammed his bedroom door closed.

He stood, stunned by Pantu's question. Out of the corners of his eyes, he noticed Dill moved to go to Pantu, but Robin's hand on his arm and a shake of her head made Dill sit back down. Dill's Energy was obviously pissed at the way he talked to Pantu and Robin leaned over to whisper to Dill.

"Let them work this out between them," Robin gently told Dill, who breathed out and agreed with a nod.

Everybody else's Energies were shocked at what just happened between him and Pantu. They never heard him argue with or yell at anyone before. He hadn't moved, but stood there and with his eyes closed, tried to control his anger.

When Pantu's phone, which was left on the table, rang, he heard Dill pick it up.

"Ma Sky, it's me Dill," Dill answered. "He's in his room now. What? The bedroom window is opened?" Dill's Energy was frenzied, and he went to go to Pantu again, but Robin stopped him, took the phone out of Dill's hands, and started talking with Mrs. Sky, while pulling Dill to sit back down.

PANTU: TELL ME
WEEK FIVE: MONDAY

Sitting on the ledge of his bedroom bay window, he was enjoying the cooling breeze tickling his face. He honestly didn't know why it wasn't snowing in this part of the continent yet, but he admitted to himself the weather was still nice.

When he felt the hottest rush of heat, hotter than any campfire he'd ever experienced, his body instinctively turned towards the source and he slipped, falling out of his window.

Drum was there to catch him by the arm, yanking him back through the window and into Drum's sturdy arms, His screams of terror turned into screams to be put down. He kicked and tried to wiggle out of Drum's strong arms.

"PUT ME DOWN RIGHT NOW DRUM!" he cried out.

Drum moved over to his bed and tossed him on it, closing the window and the blinds without even looking or motioning. Drum stood there and watched as he struggled to regain his equilibrium and focus.

When his Mind finally settled down around his brain, he sat up, but Drum was immediately above him, pushing him back down and roughly shoving his shirt up to start kissing on his neck while one hand pinched the soft, brown, hardened mound on his chest. Drum was holding himself with one hand as the other moved from his chest to find what he was blindly searching for in his boxers.

"Tell me to stop Pantu..." Drum breathed into his neck as all he could do was loudly moan. None of his body parts wanted his mouth to say those words and worked together to keep him incoherent of language as his body soaked up every bit of pleasure it was receiving.

"...Not to...touch you. Tell me...not to protect you," Drum breathed out between the kisses as Drum's hand found him already leaking.

Wrapping one hand around his penis, the other slid under his neck as Drum was back to kissing and sucking on him.

He was weakly trying to move under Drum, until the warm hand landed on his penis. The melody from the soft flow of his Light relaxed him and all he could do was grab onto Drum's shoulders to hold on for dear life. The buildup was instantaneous but when Drum gently bit his neck, his back arched, and his Light exploded.

It went everywhere, all over him and Drum. His moans and Drum's hand didn't stop until every bit was out, and his penis flopped over, content. His arched body finally relaxed and all that could be heard was their heavy breathing. Drum laid down, an arm still under him.

"Dumpling," Drum called to him.

He rolled over and snuggled into Drum's chest as he felt Drum's arm wrap around him.

"You're asking me to stand by and allow someone to hurt you when I Promised to protect you. I made that Promise because I wanted to," Drum told him.

"I always heal, so it will be temporary," he tried to counter.

"If you want to feel pain, I can always smack your butt, make it as red as your blushing face," Drum joked to his embarrassment.

"It hurts to see you in pain. And there are things in our community we can't always account for, like a snake that's able to avoid Barrier detections or control Energy snakes. Dumpling..." Drum looked in his eyes, their foreheads and noses touching.

"No one sitting down there is willing to look the other way while you get hurt. If you really want to go through with this, I will get the knife myself and let you plunge it into my Core, before I allow that snake to be the reason I no longer get to hold you," Drum told him, making it clear what would happen if he decided to continue.

"Your Core?" he asked, touching Drum's chest.

"It's already cracked, and at this point, it would break apart," Drum explained.

He looked through Drum's chest and saw his Orb. He didn't know why Drum's Orb was a fusion of chaotic colors which seemed to settle on royal-blue, but it was already severely cracked and damaged.

"I do not want you to get hurt because of me Drum." He looked back into Drum's eyes. "We can find another way to break him down mentally. Maybe my Ma can help with the mental and it will disrupt his emotional as well," he thought aloud.

Drum questioned him with a look.

"My Ma might help if I explain to her," he told Drum.

Drum nodded in agreement and left the conversation alone. Drum went to get up, but he placed his hand on Drum's chest.

Is there a reason you no longer want to touch me?" he asked, quietly.

"I was trying to set up some things. I didn't mean to ignore you, but I'm also trying to figure out how to touch you in public without losing my Awareness," Drum informed him.

"Huh?" he asked. "Your Awareness?"

Drum nodded. "It's an Ability I have, but I seem to lose all common sense whenever we touch and it's dangerous for both of us," Drum stated, looking up at the ceiling.

"Then let me help you!" He jumped up, into Drum's face. "Once you figure out my Light, we can practice Awareness together so we can keep each other safe!" he said, happily.

He felt Drum's smile was genuine. "That right there is why I want you to be completely mine," Drum said, and kissed his nose. "Let's go back" Drum added.

They came downstairs and sat at the table. He refused to look at anyone since he didn't know if they heard what happened upstairs, but when everyone tried not to look at him and smile, he figured they had.

"Are you okay?" Dill asked with distrustful eyes directed at Drum.

"I shall delete the second part of the physical plan," he told them.

He watched as everyone relaxed, happily agreeing with him, and he snuck an annoyed glance at Drum. He looked in his cup and was disappointed there was no tea left. Sport brought him a glass of chocolate milk, and his elation spread. It was his favorite drink since he left The City.

"Thank you, Sport," he joyfully said, bouncing in his chair a little.

"Hey Pantu?" Win started. "How did your Ma know your window was open?"

"Because of what happened like some months ago," he told them, knowing they would want more details.

He reached out his hand for his phone and Robin returned it.

"My phone is completely locked. I can only call or text the four people my parents approved of. My Ma, Robin, my Pa, and Dill. There is no net, social media, games, or apps. I cannot even change the settings on the phone.

"My parents must make changes, and it is GPS enabled, so I always must have it on me. My bank card is as well. My bedroom windows and door have sensors on them which alert my parents whenever I open or close them."

"Were you trying to escape out the window?" Sport asked, trying not to laugh.

He shook his head. "No, I was not. I was sitting on my ledge, looking out the window, and enjoying the breeze. DRUM scared the shit out of me, and I fell out the window." His embarrassing look made the group snicker. He slid his phone to Win.

"There's nothing on here, not even pictures!" Win said, shocked, after opening the phone and looking through it,

He nodded. "Well, it would be my own fault. I was careless before and was unknowingly in the background of someone else's photo, which was uploaded to the net. It is how she found me. Came to personally take me back. She and some Cloaked kidnapped me right out of my bedroom, while my parents were asleep in the next room over," he explained.

"Are you okay with all those restrictions?" Kat asked, looking over Win's shoulder at his phone.

He sighed sadly. "I cannot measure who was more frightened after that, me, or my parents. It was not until we came here that I had my own room again. It took a lot to be able to sleep on my own, but even now, I hardly sleep in my bedroom, I mostly sleep in my studio," he informed them.

The fear of what happened this past weekend rose in him and when Drum moved his chair closer to touch his leg, he looked surprised. Robin and Kat both had the same look as him but theirs quickly turned into giggles as the Ladies looked at each other.

"I'm really amazed you don't know all this about Pantu?" Queen said to Robin.

"I only know what Pantu is willing to share," Robin replied.

Queen looked at Dill, who shook his head no.

"It would destroy the trust Robin, and I built with Pantu," Dill said to Queen while Robin nodded.

"If he wants you to know, he'll tell you himself when he's ready," Dill stated.

Queen looked impressed with both Robin and Dill. "Wow. That's a strong relationship!" Queen commented, praising them, to which they both looked at each other and blushed.

"We have more things to talk about," Robin said, smiling at Dill.

"Yea, but is it as interesting as Pantu's life?" Win genuinely asked and laughter sounded out from everybody around the table.

SKY: TRUE FEELINGS AND FACES
WEEK FIVE: MONDAY

Laughter was cut short by the front door being kicked open and her rushing in straight to Pantu. Grabbing her child's head in her hands, she hugged his face to her body and kissed the top of his head.

"My precious PanPan. Ah, I was so worried, I rushed here to make sure you're okay," she said, as she continued to kiss the top of Pantu's head and he reluctantly allowed her.

"Your Pa is on the way as well," she informed him, and Pantu stiffened for a moment but took a breath to calm himself.

"What smells so damn delicious! PanPan, did you order food?" she asked, forgetting her concern for her child and following the smell.

Sport was in the kitchen, smiling at the compliment. "I made dinner since you have book club after the store closes. I didn't want Pantu and Mr. Moon to starve, and so you didn't have to worry about it," Sport explained, as she was taking deep breaths of the food.

"AH!" She turned to Sport, touching his arm. "That's so sweet of you!" she exclaimed, smiling brightly at Sport, who blushed and nodded awkwardly.

Pantu was up and pulling her away from Sport, while eyeing him.

"I am on to you," Pantu told Sport, defiantly.

Sport laughed as she gave confusing looks to them both.

"I can be by to make dinner every night, so you can manage the store. I can also bring your dinner to you when I go to book club," Sport offered.

Pantu stepped in front of her. "I am her oldest claimed child. Even without the name Kim as my own, I am a proud descendant of the family line!" Pantu said, puffing out his chest while trying to stand tall.

Sport was quite taller than them both and although Pantu looked up at Sport, he lowered his eyelids to still look down on Sport. When she lightly tapped Pantu upside the back of his head, knowing Pantu just used his True Vision again, Pantu deflated.

"I can take my Ma's dinner to her," Pantu meekly said, once his Mind settled while Sport was trying to hide a smile.

"PanPan, be nice!" She playfully peeked around Pantu to look at the food again, but her words held a double meaning and Pantu nodded.

"Mrs. Sky, I hope I'm not intruding…" Sport started but was interrupted.

"Call me Ma Sky, or Ma will work!" she said, brightly to Sport. "Ah, your foster parents live out of town, correct?" she asked, but didn't give Sport a chance to answer.

"If you want, there's an extra room next to Pantu's. You can live here. I mean, if you're going to make dinner every night, it would just be easier!" she said, as Pantu slowly turned around to look at her.

"Did you speak with Pa before you just started moving Beings in? You have this tendency to jump in head…" Pantu started in a faint voice.

The way she eyed Pantu shut him up, but Pantu was still waiting on her answer.

"I guess we have enough extra bedrooms for all the Beings you've welcomed into our home, just today alone!" she responded and Pantu slowly turned back around to face Sport.

"This only works if you call me Big Brother," Pantu said, with a clever smile at Sport.

"OH! Thank you, Big Brother!" Sport responded to Pantu's delight.

Pantu clapped his hands and smiled. "I have always wanted to be a big brother!" he said, gleefully.

"Ah! This feels right, having another child at home!" She was gleeful as well. She figured it would be easier to show Sport first, then tell him once they cleared things up with Sport's foster parents. "Wait, you're a member of the book club?" she asked, astounded.

Sport nodded. "I was the first to sign up. I'm on the bookstore's V.I.B. email list, so I got the announcement first," Sport informed her.

"Have you read the book for tonight?" she asked, now gravitating towards Sport.

Pantu threw his hands up in the air and went back to his seat.

"Yes. And I love the concept that you must read the passage of the book which explains your theory, belief, or comment. This way we can tell if you actually read the book…"

Sport started but they both finished the thought, "Or if you're talking out your ass!"

She squealed in delight and hugged Sport.

Pantu watched them and sucked his teeth. *"Tsk.* He will fit right in." Pantu looked at Queen. "Is he not living in your home?" Pantu asked.

Queen rolled his eyes. "Yea, but he thinks…" Queen started.

"Feels," Sport corrected Queen.

Queen looked away from Pantu, leaning his head into his left hand to respond. "Ugh. He FEELS my HOME is too BIG for him."

She watched the natural movements of the young man named Queen and raised an eyebrow. Queen was more graceful than any Woman she'd ever met, and she knew Queen would make a killing in The City as an etiquette trainer.

Sport looked at Queen in disbelief. "I live on the other side of your home Queen. I have to call or text you to communicate," Sport explained.

Queen ignored Sport and looked at Pantu. "Sport prefers cozy over spacious," Queen explained.

"Okay...we will go with your home is spacious," Sport agreed. "May I move in tonight, after book club, Ma?" Sport asked her.

She clapped her hands together. "That sounds perfect. Welcome home!" she exclaimed.

Sport looked at Pantu.

"What?" Pantu shrugged. "Fine, I will help you unpack and by that, I mean, I can direct you. I shall not lift anything. Feels too much like exercising," Pantu told Sport, to everyone's amusement.

She looked at her son. "PanPan, you're being awfully agreeable about this?" she questioned. She moved closer to Pantu to look him in the face, but he avoided her eyes and looked around, away from her.

"I need your help," Pantu said, still not looking at her.

"We," Drum corrected.

"WE need your help," Pantu corrected, smiling at Drum.

"AH! Does it have something to do with the strawberries on your neck?" she asked Pantu, teasing as her eyes settled on Drum, who refused to meet her eyes but slyly smiled.

Pantu's hands went to his neck, surprised. "What!? NO!" Pantu said, embarrassed and looked down at the table to avoid all the giggles and laughs from those probably too polite to mention it earlier.

She just stared at Drum, who still refused to look in her direction. She turned around and walked a bit away from the table. She put her head in her hands as she took deep breaths to keep from crying.

He is slowly letting go of all the bullshit ingrained in him. He's made so many friends. The absurd rules that kept him from being free are slowly being replaced. The less he fears death, the more he opens himself up.

She could feel her thoughts of her son were misinterpreted by some at the table and Sport. She turned back around and Pantu looked at her for a moment before casually finishing his milk.

"Why do you call hickeys strawberries?" Kat asked.

"Because of the mark they would leave. They reminded people of strawberries which are forbidden," Pantu told Kat.

Queen's eyes never left her, and the young man continued to watch her reaction.

Win asked, "Is it punishable by death?"

Pantu looked at Win. "Is there anything that is not?" Pantu asked, laughing.

Everyone was uncomfortably waiting on her, so their laughter was quiet and short.

Taking a final deep breath, she brightly asked, "How can I help, PanPan?"

Queen looked unsure of her reaction, and she looked back at Queen, determined.

"You know I'm gay, right?" Queen asked her.

"What? No, I didn't know that," she said, unconcerned.

"How do you feel about men being in love with men?" Queen asked, cautiously. "I know a man in your family was publicly put to death for being gay, so it was highly frown upon," Queen added.

She waved off Queen's comment. "Ah please. He was killed for other reasons. Yes, he was in love with a man, but he offered himself up to save the life of the man he loved and his child," she explained to them. "That kind of devotion doesn't care about your gender. Love is love, regardless," she said, with a happy smile on her face.

"Besides, his lover and kid were able to escape The City because of him, so I say, his death was worth his feelings!" she ended, looking at Pantu. "The way it is told by the women in The City is meant to keep the men in line," she informed Pantu, directly.

"One day, I would love to hear that story," Queen said, smiling brightly.

Pantu's confused face processed the information as Queen looked lovingly at her.

"So, my help?" she asked.

Pantu quickly pushed his thoughts to the side and looked at her.

"I...We...need you to use your Talents on someone," Pantu told her.

It was her turn to look surprised. "Pantu. Are you okay with me using them?" she asked, perplexed Pantu was openly asking her to use the Talents he once threw the biggest fit about, until she was banned from using them around him.

The look Pantu gave made her smile and nod. She was watching in real time, all the riddles she hated hearing from Pa Mack coming true, so she decided to listen to her and her Husband's parents, since they seemed to know the future.

Dill stood up and offered his seat. "Ma Sky, have a seat," Dill said, as he moved to stand in the kitchen with Sport, who was finishing dinner and paying attention to the conversation as well.

"There is a Lame male..." Pantu started, but she held up her hand.

"Understood," she cut Pantu off. "I need to see him," she said.

"Absolutely not. You will not have any personal contact with him, understand!?" Pantu demanded. "And you met him before in the Dean's front office. The first year who threatened me. You heard the recordings," Pantu told her, a look of hope on his face she could do it from memory.

"Pantu, why are you playing around with this fucking reusable cum bucket? It's not like you to play with your steppingstones?" she questioned Pantu, watching his face.

Everyone but Dill and Pantu's eyes went wide at her comment and snickering along with repressed laughter filled the room.

"The laws are different here. Until I can get a handle on the law of the land and Being law, I will refrain from going all out," Pantu explained, just as upset as she was this was taking up so much of his time.

She nodded. "But I can't do anything if I can't see him!" She pouted, shyly glancing up at Pantu.

Her demeanor was showing where Pantu received his playful, bashful, but outspoken nature from. They looked at her with smiles on their faces.

"How about a photo? Will that work?" Queen asked, highly interested in her Talents.

She thought for a minute. "I've never tried it based off a photo before. Let's see if it will work?" she conceded.

Queen pulled up a photo of the first year and showed it to her. The look on her face as she looked at Queen's phone confounded everyone except Pantu. She was disgusted, confused, shocked, surprised, and unsure all over again as she remembered the little boy in the office.

Pantu nudged her and she looked at him before he signed with his hands. She nodded, tilting her head towards the rest of the group but Pantu shook his head.

"Ah. That's right. You can't tell them, so they don't know," she said. "Are you okay with me telling them?" she cautiously asked and Pantu nodded, anxious to get the information out.

She pointed to the photo. "This isn't his real face," she told everyone.

The looks of shock and disbelief went all around the group, even Sport moved to look over her shoulder.

"Say what now?" Drum asked, respectfully.

"This isn't his real face or his skin. It belongs to someone else. I don't know if he personally killed them, but he stripped their body and is now wearing them," she told them, to Pantu's slumped relief.

"Finally! I have wanted to tell you all from the beginning but..." Pantu paused and looked at Drum.

"You made a Promise. We understand," Drum told Pantu with a smile.

Pantu nodded. "At first, I thought even if I could tell you, you all would call me crazy. There seem to be things we can do that you have not seen before, and I was unsure if you would believe me. So, I tried telling you about his stench. There are times he smells like a rotting body."

"That's what I smelled in the Manga Room that day?!" Drum asked, surprise in his eyes.

Sport commented, "He's a snake and they shed their skin. He found a way to shed others' skin instead of his own." The look of disgust on Sport's face echoed his feelings in his words.

Drum and everyone else were at a loss at the added information. Pantu signed to her again and she nodded.

"Pantu said I can tell you. Whether they are Being or humans, we each have a different Talent for seeing the True Faces of others," she explained to them.

"True Faces?" Queen asked.

"Yes. *Most* every human and some *Beings* in The Center and throughout The City changed their faces using parts from other people's bodies. Our ancestors, over time, gained a Talent. We're able to see they wear a mask and if you are proficient, you can see under, to their True Face," she explained.

Queen was now overloaded with valuable information. "I need a moment," Queen said, standing up.

"If you leave now, you'll miss it," Drum said, smiling at Queen's fight against his curiosity, which won out, and Queen sat back down.

Win was staring at a screen while Kat was trying to put all this together. Robin was having an internal conversation with herself, expressed by her hand movements. Dill either accepted the current information quickly or knew before she said anything and was waiting on everybody else to catch up.

Pantu was looking at Drum out the corners of his eyes, watching for a reaction as Drum turned to smile at him. Pantu blushed and quickly turned his attention back to her.

"On someone like this, Pantu and I can't see past a certain point, for varied reasons. But if I can't see his True Face, I can't use my Talents," she told them. "*We need your Pa's help,*" she added softly, making Pantu bristle.

MOONxSKY: SHARING SOME FAMILY SECRETS
WEEK FIVE: MONDAY

As if he heard his Wife mention him, Moon walked through the broken front door. He placed his work bag down after changing into house slippers to come into the dining room. He stopped short and looking at the ground, exited the room and came back in through the kitchen opening.

"Did you cook dinner Skylove?" he asked, walking up to the stove to look in every pot and pan to see what was being made.

Everybody felt the change of atmosphere in the room as he tried to avoid Pantu but still be in the same space. Pantu's anger was apparent as his son flat out refused to acknowledge him.

"Umm. I did Mr. Moon," Sport said, walking up to him.

He looked at Sport with admiration. "It smells delicious!" he praised.

"It's almost ready, so dinner will be served soon," Sport proudly informed him.

"Thank you!" he said, with a playful smile and he saw Pantu's eyes roll, so he lowered his head to look back at the floor.

Robin stood and moved to sit next to Drum. "Mr. Moon, you can have my seat. At your table. In your home," she said, realizing the joke.

Everybody but him laughed uneasily as they respected Pantu's feelings but seemed confused by his actions.

He nodded to Robin without looking up. *"Thank you for coming to help Doctor Robin. Is he okay?"* he quietly asked, as he stood behind his Wife. Without looking at Pantu or speaking to him, he nervously allowed his Wife to direct him to sit.

"I'm just here as a friend, not his Doctor," Robin said, with a smile.

Everybody's heads moved to look between him and Pantu.

He turned to his Wife. *"Love, what happened?"* he asked, concerned but keeping his voice calm and low, so he didn't upset Pantu and have his Wife break something on their child's body.

"Ah. I have no idea. He was fine when I came home, so his wellbeing was overshadowed by the intoxicating smell filling up the house," Skylove happily said. "By the way, our son will be moving in tonight. Welcome Sport," Skylove added, unconcerned with his reaction.

He turned to look at Sport, who was serving drinks with Dill's assistance. "Call me Pa," was all he said to Sport, who smiled in acceptance.

"Pa," Sport said, trying out the name.

He looked back at his Wife and softly spoke to her. "*You're hiding something from me. You have been blocked off.*"

Skylove pouted and looked at Pantu. "He won't..." But Pantu's quick look of annoyance shut her up.

He lowered his eyes and turned his body away from the table.

"*PanPan. We need his Talent. Besides, you wanted to tell them, but we can't, so let's show them instead,*" Skylove said softly to Pantu, reaching to touch Pantu's arm.

Dill stopped and shared a look with Pantu, who nodded and sluggishly got up and went upstairs. Skylove turned to him, touching his arm and smiling brightly, she kissed him on the cheek, making him blush. Robin watched the whole interaction and left to follow Pantu upstairs.

He declined to join the conversation, and he averted his eyes away from Drum, who seemed to be able to read him. His Wife waited until Robin and Pantu returned to the table and sat down.

Pantu gave in to the conversation and reduced the tension in the air, so he refrained from saying anything until his Wife nodded at Pantu and turned to inform him of the situation. After explaining, along with Robin and Queen's help, what they were trying to do and why, he understood and agreed.

His Wife left out the part about the one they were calling Mansnake's True Face and decided playfully to let him see for himself. He took Queen's phone and looked at it while his Wife excitedly talked into his ear.

"Look there's social media where you can put stuff on a fictional page and talk to Beings all over the planet they can like with a heartie thing or share your posties with their friends and from all over the planet people can follow you to see everything you put on there isn't it cool?" his Wife asked, not taking a break in between her words.

"*Hm,*" he agreed. "Skylove. *It is very cool. Shall we un-restrict him as well?*" he asked to his Wife's quick disgust.

"Oh no. I don't want to. Something like this would be aggravating as hell. It's why my publisher has someone else to manage my faceless author profile," his Wife said. "I just thought the execution of the system is magnificent. The numbers are beautiful." His Wife watched as Queen pulled the picture back up on the phone in his hand.

"It's a great concept though. Beings able to connect with other Beings across the planet without fear of humans!" his Wife unknowingly praised Drum.

"You're right Love, it's an amazing con...cept?" His voice faltered as he stared at the photo, stunned. He slowly turned to look at his Wife. "What the hell did he do to his face?" he asked, so appalled by what he saw he forgot to keep his voice down, making Pantu wince.

"We don't know. We can't see his True Face, only that this one isn't it," Sky said.

"Is he okay with this? He isn't going to...leave it...is he?" Moon asked, scared.

"Yes and of course not! He asked for help and is okay with us using our Talents," she stated.

Moon didn't look at Pantu but nodded. *"I still have to go to work tomorrow..."* Moon said, and Pantu gave the loudest sigh in the middle of his sentence.

Moon took a deep breath and looked at the photo again. *"He should close his eyes for this one,"* Moon said. *"Anyone who is a bit squeamish should as well."*

Win and Kat immediately closed their eyes and held on to each other, while peaking at Moon. Everyone else leaned forward to see what was about to happen. Dill and Sport came to watch as well.

Moon set up Queen's phone on the table and looked at the picture on it. Stretching his neck and shoulders, Moon massaged his face. She and Pantu followed suit and prepared for Moon to use his Talent. She relaxed her eyes and placed her hand on both Moon and Pantu's heads. Pantu closed his eyes with his book open and pencil in hand.

Everyone watched as Moon's face started to distort and move. His bones cracked as his face twisted and Pantu started to draw. Moon's hair also changed to match the first year's True Face. When Moon was finished, the gruesome face everyone saw compounded with what Moon just did, left everyone but Robin, Drum and Sport speechless.

The right half of Moon's face was burned off and scarred over. The left side was sagging so much, it looked like it was barely holding on while melting off to match the right. The sunken, black eyes held no life in them and the first year was missing most of his nose.

The thin, dry, chapped lips sloped downwards in a frown like a clown unhappy with his makeup. The first year's forehead was littered with popped, healed pus bumps and boils. The crispy, short, blond hair was cut close to the first year's head with scabbed, burned patches.

Win's eyes were wide with disgusted shock, but Kat's eyes snapped shut when she saw Moon's face start to move. Most looked away to hold down their vomit. Pantu finished his sketch, and she dropped her hands. Moon's face was still shaped like the first year and he glanced at Pantu, who didn't look at his Pa but held his hand up and sent his Light, reshaping his Pa's face back.

"Aww...my sweet little PanPan. I knew you wouldn't leave your Pa like that," she cooed at Pantu, who smiled a little.

Drum's mouth was slightly open in surprise. Pantu smiled apprehensively at Drum and handed over the picture. Drum looked at it and passed it to Robin, who took a disgusted look and passed it to Win, who skipped Kat, her eyes still fully closed and passed it to Queen, who looked at the photo with Sport and Dill standing over him.

She reached out her hand for the photo and stood up after receiving it.

"Do you need help, Love?" Moon asked her, with concern in his voice.

She nodded and both Moon and Pantu stood up to place a hand on each of her shoulders.

"There's a lot, so just don't freak out, okay?" she asked everyone. "PanPan, close your eyes, sweetie. Close yourself off," she instructed Pantu, and he followed her directions.

She stared at the photo. "All those whose life you have slain, heed my call, your apparitions I now claim," she recited.

The Beings at the table watched as apparitions of people started to appear, one after the other. She repeated the phrase while the ghostly, watery forms filled up the house and spilled over into the yard.

"Drum can you expand the Dome please? There are too many," Pantu asked, his eyes still closed.

Drum stretched his Barrier to include the empty house next door, and the apparitions filled the yard as well. Once she was finished, Pantu dropped his hand and while his eyes were still closed, wandered with his hands outstretched back towards his seat.

Drum grabbed Pantu's hand and led her son to his chair. Pantu put his head down on the table and wrapped his arms around to block out what he knew was coming. The apparitions started to drift towards Pantu, moaning and crying.

"Give life."

"Not time."

"Alive me."

"Kill him."

"Snake bad."

"Pity me."

The apparitions went to touch Pantu, and he stiffened up. There was a severe heat wave that blasted through the first floor of her home, and the apparitions stopped their advance on Pantu to turn towards Drum.

"The home next door is empty, freely reside there, but don't touch the Barrier around it or you will disappear forever. For this Favor, you will protect this home and those in it. Don't enter this home again unless invited," Drum told the apparitions.

The apparitions turned and her home emptied out. Pantu lifted his head and looked at Drum, eyes full of wonder. She stared at Drum with a surprised smile.

No one had ever been able to control her apparitions before and Pantu always suffered through reliving their death whenever she used her Talent around him.

Queen looked at Drum with a full smile. "Wow!" was all Queen could say before staring wide-eyed off into space.

Kat looked horrified. "He's killed so many!" Kat cried, as she buried her face in Win's body.

Win looked upset and Sport and Dill looked determined, while Robin was carefully thinking, working out a psychological assessment of the first year to help.

"I hope I didn't scare you all. I only use my Talent against those who would mean my family and friends harm," she meekly said, hoping Pantu's friends wouldn't be afraid, and her son would lose the only real friends he made because of her.

"Those are some AMAZING Abilities you all have. Is this what you meant by Revival Talent?" Queen asked, standing to reach for her hand. Queen flipped her hand over and a cup of tea appeared. "Here drink this, it will help instantly renew your Energy," Queen told her, and made one appear for her Husband as well.

"Thank you!" she and Moon said in unison.

Queen walked through the living room and out the side door to the patio. Drum stood and followed Queen.

"Do you think I frightened them. Are they afraid of me?" she asked aloud, her voice and body shaking so bad, she was spilling some of her tea. "I'm so sorry PanPan. Your friends..." She started to cry.

Pantu stood and touched her hand. "Ma, Queen is just overexcited. He loves seeing new Talents. We just overloaded his system. Fresh air is all he needs," Pantu consoled her. "Now drink your tea before I do. It is so good," Pantu added, eyeing her cup.

She and Moon downed their tea as Dill and Sport started setting food on the table.

"We will finish the conversation later tonight, after book club," Drum informed everyone as he came back in, followed by an elated Queen.

DRUMxPANTU: A QUICK RMD
WEEK FIVE: MONDAY

After a rather fun dinner, with little discomfort between Pantu and his Pa, the group started to disperse. Mrs. Sky, Mr. Moon, and Sport went to the book club; Queen ran off elsewhere to do something; Dill, Robin, Win and Kat all decided to get dessert.

Drum placed his credit card on the table for Win. "Based on what we know so far, I added restrictions to the Personal Barriers I set up for you two and added one for Dill and Robin," he told Win, who excitedly grasped his card and thanked him.

Everyone agreed to meet back at Pantu's home later to finalize their plans. It was just him and Pantu left alone again, and he smiled as Pantu's shyness kicked in.

Pantu went outside and laying down in the grass, stared up into the stars. He joined Pantu after making sure the ghosts in the house next door understood his instructions and what they were brought back for.

Laying down next to Pantu with his hands behind his head, he smiled at the stars. "There're so many," he commented.

Pantu asked, without looking at him. "Do you think this planet is the only one with life on it?"

He replied, "There's multiple universes with numerous galaxies out there, it's conceited of me to think only we exist."

Pantu looked at him and smiled. "My G-Pas told me our ancestors didn't originate here. Both us and humans came from different planets, from other galaxies, from different universes. I have always wondered if there are still Entities on our home planet," Pantu said, watching for his response.

"Humans came from a planet called Earth, located somewhere in what was called the Milky Way galaxy. They called their home universe The Cosmos before they destroyed it," he said.

After seeing multiple interactions between Pantu and his Pa while assuming Yolk's graduation was behind Pantu's disposition towards the man, he knew the rift between them wouldn't and couldn't be easily fixed. He could see Pantu still stubbornly refused to see his own Pa's True Face and purposefully ignored all the signs that his Pa wasn't the man Pantu thought he was.

He decided to just state it. "You know, in order to understand what really happened in The City, this is a needed step," he told Pantu, unexpectedly.

"I have nothing to say to him. After what he did..." Pantu stopped to keep from crying.

"I don't know why he did it, but it seems like you only know half of the little I know," he said.

"Doctor Robin said almost the same words. But whatever reason he will give is not enough," Pantu told him. "How can I possibly forgive him?" Pantu asked.

"In this situation, forgiving a person isn't for them," he said, as he turned to look Pantu in the eyes. "It's for you. Your peace of Mind. Even if they never know you have forgiven them," he said, smiling at Pantu. "If you want, I'll be there with you," he offered.

Pantu turned slightly and with a sad, grateful smile, nodded. "Do you mind if Dill is there as well?" Pantu asked.

He shook his head. "Not at all Dumpling."

Pantu's smile grew bigger, and moved closer, enjoying the warmth which came from him.

He knew Drum was trying to get him and his Pa to have a better relationship. He retained what Mrs. K told him and as much as he wanted to let go, there was something or someone inside of him who clung tightly to the feeling.

Although Drum may be upset with him when it came to his Pa, he didn't' know if Drum would call him crazy for thinking there were other planets with life on them or that Beings came here from another planet, but he was happy to know Drum agreed with him.

"Are Entities the name Beings in The City, called themselves?" Drum asked.

He was ecstatic Drum changed the topic again, but a little upset at himself for allowing Drum to control the conversation. "No. We called ourselves Others. Where did the classification of Beings come from?" he asked, teasing Drum about his words to Tracey.

Drum smiled and slight chuckle made his Light feel more like a graph of brain waves, pointy and uneven, instead of soft, ocean waves.

"Well, when humans came here, they called themselves human beings. Once we mixed in with them, we called ourselves Beings as we weren't quite human, and we were no longer like our ancestors," Drum told him.

"Wow. You are well informed. Humans also classified themselves Homo-sapiens and they once considered Anothers either gods or demons," he told Drum. He turned to lay on his stomach so he could look at Drum while talking. "Are you not interested in me telling you the story of Phoenix?" he asked.

Drum smiled. "I am. I haven't asked because you aren't ready to tell it."

He looked confused.

"I'm not the only one who needs to hear the story and until you can trust others, I will refrain from asking to hear it," Drum added.

"Why is it so important I trust them?" he asked, curious.

"I would like for you to be able to fully trust everyone who sat around the table and ate with you," Drum implied. "Actually, more than them, but for now, let's start small."

He thought about it. "There are times when I can feel your friends' sincerity, and I can talk to them. You seemed unbothered with me being around them, living with them or showing some of my Talents, so I can try it," he agreed.

Drum caressed his face. "Do you trust me?" Drum asked.

He nodded. "Yes!" he responded immediately.

"Completely?" Drum asked.

He smiled and nodded again. "Yes!" he said, with no reserve.

Drum pulled his face close, and the intense look Drum gave him ignited desires in them both. Drum's eyes trailed down to stare at his lips while pulling his face closer, and his breathing quickened. Drum leaned in but stopped short of their lips touching, before kissing his nose instead.

He could feel his disappointment show on his face. "Have you never kissed anyone before?" he asked, feeling dejected and unwanted.

"I have only ever kissed my family. Never on the lips though," Drum explained.

"AH!" he said, surprised but the feeling quickly turned into understanding. "Do you not want to kiss me?" he asked.

"I want to," Drum stated.

"Then why not? Is it because my scent wavers?" he inquired and received a nod.

He sat up and wrapped his arms around his legs while Drum did something on his phone. Drum pulled him back down and he laid on Drum's chest, wondering how he could stop his scent from wavering with Drum. If he didn't or couldn't, he would never figure out the young male whose heartbeat was rhythmically easing his worries.

"Dumpling. Sleep!" Drum commanded.

He woke up in their Dream Space. *I know I was not sleepy yet*, he thought. He remembered Drum telling him to sleep and he looked around. Drum came up from behind him and grabbed his hand.

"Come with me," Drum said, before pulling him to follow.

He took in everything as they went through the forest and arrived at another open field. It wasn't as big as the one they just left but Drum set a royal-blue Dome over it. Drum took his hand and held it up against the Dome. Instead of falling open, the Dome's color changed to a golden ochre, and he gasped.

"I have set restrictions where only your Energy now controls the Barrier," Drum said, looking at him with a slight smile.

"Why? What?" He was lost.

"You need a Think Space, right? Your other one imploded, so I thought maybe you could use one which wasn't so far away and still completely your own," Drum mentioned. "I will respect your privacy, and this will be a space only for you, which is why I relinquished control of the Barrier," Drum added, smiling at the overjoyed look on his face.

"Can I go in?" he asked, excitedly bouncing on his toes while trying not to squeal with delight and clap his hands.

Drum laughed at his excited bounce. "It's your space to use whenever you want, however you want. I will go keep Natum company."

Drum handed his phone over. "When the alarm goes off, we have to wake up," Drum informed him, before walking off to talk with Natum.

PANTU: THINKING INSIDE A DOME
WEEK FIVE: MONDAY

Pantu entered his new Think Space and looked around. The solid, royal-blue backdrop to the golden stars was a stark difference from the black, watery one in his old Think Space. This one felt clean, private, and safe.

He walked in circles, looking up and around at the beautiful imagery and felt he was truly walking amongst the stars in space. Someone grabbed his shoulders and stopped him. He didn't freak out as Pet Pantu seductively leaned over his shoulder.

"This is a really gorgeous Think Space your male has set up for us," Pet Pantu cooed in his ear.

"He is not my male," he responded, shooing Pet Pantu off.

Pet Pantu hopped around him. "So, does it mean I can have a taste of the deliciously tall, sexy male who always seems to be around. Have you seen his...?" Pet Pantu pointed to his genitals and giggled. "I am excited to see what he can do with it!" Pet Pantu laughed.

"Petu, if you touch him, I will erase you from existence," he threatened.

"Petu? Who the hell is that? Is that *my* name?" Pet Pantu asked, surprised.

"Hmm," he agreed, as he decided to decorate this place with all the items he cherished. "I can bring physical things into this space to keep here," he thought aloud. "They would be safer here, than out there," he agreed with himself.

Petu looked at him. "You think the hot "Not Your Male" will keep his word not to come in here? We should have made him Vow," Petu goaded.

He ignored Petu as he set up podiums made of deep yellow wood. He placed an image of Drum's shirt on one and an image of the photos they took on their shopping day. He started adding images of items to be replaced with the originals later. He made space to place his paintings and set up easels for displaying them.

"So, you are uninterested in him yet no one else can taste him. You are way more spoiled than I ever was," Petu told him, sulking.

"This space seems to go on forever!" He expressed amazement while ignoring Petu.

"Yes, duh! "Not Your Male" created it. It will become as big as you want. You control the space; it listens to you," Petu informed him.

His smile was so big, and he was so happy, even Petu smiled in response. He took some of the thoughts, questions, concerns, and knowledge out of his Mind and tossed them up into the open-air space. He rearranged them so he could read them clearly. He smiled, completely in love with his new space.

He turned to Petu. "Do you like your name, Petu?" he asked while smiling.

Petu shrugged but smiled as well.

"I can call you Oryn, if you like?" he teased, but the sour look on Petu's face made him laugh.

"That name belongs to neither of us," Petu responded, rolling his eyes.

"Okay Petu. You can stay, but if you ever touch "Not Your Male", I will toss you out, into nothing. You will be erased from me," he told Petu, with the kindest smile, making Petu freeze.

"Good. You understand!" he said, as he turned around to look at the space again.

"Do you think he will not come in here regardless of your permission? Do you really think Ma does not listen in on our calls with Dill?" Petu asked, trying to provoke him.

"Ma knows if our trust is broken, it cannot be easily repaired. We should already know this about ourselves. We know "Not Your Male" is respectful of others privacy, so no, he will not come inside unless I give permission," he stated. "I trust him, completely. I will leave the Dome open so he can come in anytime he wants. If he comes in without my permission, you can have at him," he ended.

"Then why do we need our own space to think? Why not think out there? With him?" Petu urged.

"Because of Personalities like you. It is easier to contain you in a safe space then let you run free all over Drum and my shared dream." He turned to look at Petu, who perked up at the mention of more Personalities.

"They will come around soon. Make sure they know. If they do not, I will hold you personally responsible, since you are the one whom I adore and trust the most." His response dripped in honey and danger.

Petu nodded. "I like this space, the blue feels way better than the black," he agreed. "By the way, can you make this opaque from the inside out, the view outside must be amazing!" Petu asked, sneakily.

He nodded as he knew Petu wanted to see glimpses of Drum and honestly, who could blame him. He made it so the view was no further than the edge of the trees, leaving him and Drum privacy in the field meadow. He looked around one more time and turned to leave.

"Keep our space safe Petu," he said, and waved as he walked out of the Dome.

He was now in the middle of a forest with no idea how to get back to the field meadow. He noticed a tree seemed to wave at him and he waved back. Another tree further down, seemed to lean forward and he followed the trees' movements until he came to the field meadow.

He turned around and bowed to the forest. "Thank you!" he graciously told them.

The trees responded by dancing and swaying in a windless breeze. Drum, who was sitting, was indeed talking with Natum and he hurried over to them. He jumped on Drum's back and wrapped his arms around Drum's neck, kissing all over the side of Drum's face, making him laugh, while holding on to his arms.

"Was Natum being bad?" he asked, looking at Natum reach for him. He held out his hand and petted the cattail.

"Not at all. I taught him something new, watch," Drum remarked. "Put your leaves in the air and wave them side to side," Drum instructed Natum, who followed Drum's movements, raising his leaves and swaying.

"To the left one time." Both Drum and Natum leaned to their own left.

"To the right this time." And both leaned to their own right.

"Now crazy sway!" And both Natum and Drum shook their heads and arms left and right in a crazy manner.

He laughed at the adorableness of it all and fell on the ground, holding his stomach. "You stole my Natum!" he exclaimed through the laughter.

Drum laughed and denied it. "No, I didn't. We're friends. Right Natum?" Drum asked, but Natum stood still and to their surprise, bowed to Drum.

"Oh! That's different!" Drum said, now looking at Natum with a thoughtful expression.

Even he was shocked. "How much can he understand?" he asked.

The alarm on Drum's phone went off and they both said, "Wake up."

They were back in his backyard, laying down together when their eyes opened. He sat up and stretched but shivered mid-way when Drum's finger lightly followed the arch in his back up to his neck.

Drum sat up. "Do you like your new Think Space?"

He nodded, happily. "It is just as beautiful as my studio. Thank you, Drum. I thought it imploded because I had no need of it anymore, but now I have one again, it feels right."

Drum smiled. "So, can we get rid of the old one?" Drum cautiously asked.

He looked at Drum and wondered aloud, "I have no reason to decline. It is only taking up space." He shrugged and wondered how to get rid of what was once his Think Space.

Drum touched the side of his head and gently pulled away. The watery, black, Think Space was pulled into a square shaped Dome Drum created and held there. The black liquid didn't shock him, but the confused look on his face was from how Drum figured it out.

He looked down at his body and felt it start to fill with Light. It was pouring in at an alarming rate, and he started to freak out. Drum's hand on his back calmed his breathing and he stopped fighting, accepting the Light.

When it settled, Drum smiled. "That's better!" Drum complimented, rubbing his back.

He turned and looked at Drum. "Is it a lot?" he asked, excitedly.

Drum smiled. "It's getting there. You have to drink the tea from Queen and only eat what Sport gives you for the next five days." Drum reached up and moved his hair while caressing his face.

"That doesn't include tonight. Don't be stubborn and sneak anything else. If you're hungry, tell Sport. And other than the tea, only drink water or whatever Sport and Queen gives you for now," Drum directed.

He pouted at the instructions but agreed, knowing Drum was indeed keeping his word to figure out and increase his Light.

"Do you know what this is?" he asked, pointing to the moving liquid inside the Dome.

"Not sure, but it was surviving by eating away at your Energy." Drum looked at it weirdly. "I have to go somewhere real quick. This needs to be placed somewhere safe, until I can figure out what it is," Drum said, looking at him.

He avoided eye contact. "You should check anyone I and my parents have been around," he said, giving what information he could. "Just in case," he added.

Drum lifted his head to look him in his eyes. "I understand Dumpling. Thank you!" Drum smiled.

He was ecstatic Drum just seemed to know what he was talking about. There was so much, and he immediately wanted to tell Drum everything rather than show him. But the Vows he made never affected him before since he didn't care to share anything about himself. Now he was feeling the effects of wanting to be honest but having to settle for being patient and waiting for the right time.

His G-Pas told him if he rushed, he would die, and he almost did with Yolk. He knew Yolk was going to make a false confession but was killed before he had a chance. He went to Yolk's home to talk him out of it and to try and offer to help him become number two, but he was too late, or right on time, depending on how you look at it.

The night ended with them coming up with a detailed plan. After he insisted, they left room for the plan to change if necessary. They set up their phones to alert them to any change, with Robin and Dill being the point of contact between him and everyone else.

The first part of their plan would be completed by the end of the month, as Drum wanted more time to train him on how to use his Light and to make sure he didn't fall behind with his schoolwork or exams.

Everyone left and went home but before he went to bed, he knocked on Sport's door to say good night and hugged Sport. He slept in his room that night, as he felt safer with Drum's Dome and Sport around.

PANTU: A PROTECTIVE FRIEND
WEEK FIVE: TUESDAY

Both he and Sport now rode with Win to school. Sport read in the back seat, while he and Win sang Bianca B songs loudly and danced in the front seat.

"Sport, it seems like you do not like Bianca B?" he asked.

Sport shrugged. "I have nothing good to say about her," Sport answered, while still reading.

"Does Queen know you feel this way?" he teased, and Win laughed.

Sport glanced at Win before going back to his book. When they arrived at school, they noticed news vans with reporters blocking the main entrance to the campus. Win drove the long way around to the Senior-Level building and parked.

"What is going on?" he asked, as Dill ran up to him.

"Mr. Caleb is here to see the progress for the gym remodel. They're finishing it up and holding the opening ceremony at the end of day classes," Dill informed him.

"Ah!" was all he said.

Drum and Queen were waiting for them on the steps of the building. Drum was casually sitting on the handrail, smiling at him.

He smiled back as they walked up to them. "I thought the opening was supposed to be tomorrow?" he asked, confused.

Drum shrugged. "My Dad changed the date because he won't be available tomorrow."

He noticed April and Will looking at him and shaking their heads, while whispering.

He left the group and openly approached them. "Hi," he said, meekly.

He showed his arm to Will. By the look of surprise on both Will and April's faces, he baited them as they realized the bruise was completely gone. April went to reach for his arm but stopped after a quick glance at Drum.

"That was an ugly bruise you got yesterday. How did it disappear so fast?" Will asked him.

He looked at his arm. "Some cream for the pain but my body has always healed quicker than anyone else. I guess it is an "Ability" I have," he said smiling at them.

April's eyebrow lifted at the latest information and his willingness to give it.

He stepped closer to them. *"We should talk elsewhere,"* he whispered to them, quickly cutting his eyes at The Four and Dill watching the interaction.

Will and April smiled and motioned for him to follow them. Without looking back, he went with them.

When they entered an empty storage room, April started. "So, you have a healing ability?" she asked, as Will set a Dome.

He shrugged. "My body just always seems to heal itself, so I guess."

Will nodded, obliviously happy with this information. "You know, Queen could probably give you information on healing abilities. His office is packed with information," Will eluded.

He looked confused. "You want me to ask Queen for information on Abilities?"

Will answered, "See if Queen will show you where the information is himself."

April nodded. "I hope they aren't mean to you just because we're friends now," she sweetly said. "If you ever feel unsafe, you can come to us," she added, having false concern about his wellbeing.

He smiled at April. "I really do not like the feeling of being stuck behind a Barrier my whole life and being told what to do and where I can go. I want the freedom to go wherever I want and if someone gets in the way of that, then..." He left the thought unfinished.

"You can always just break Drum's barrier!" April laughed, but he looked thoughtful.

"Should I test it out?" he commented, with a sneaky look on his face.

Will smiled. "Well, whatever you do find out, send it to this," Will said, handing him a tiny, thin, round, black device.

"This is?" he asked, checking the device.

"Something important. If they catch you with it, they might..." April started.

"Just don't let them see you have it and from now on, we can't communicate in public as much. They have to think you turned us down. We will have someone stay around, to protect you," Will told him.

"I doubt Dill will be happy with that. When he figures it out, he will be upset I have been Lying to him," he warned them.

"All the more reason to get him to join us. Dill is...a good friend to have," Will stated.

"If you do a good job getting information or improving your abilities, the President of the club just might *promote* you!" April informed him.

He felt something when she said it, and he didn't think being promoted was a good thing, but he happily nodded. He opened his bag and taking his sketchbook out, he hid the small device in the back cardboard. Will and April both approved of the hiding spot.

"I will let you know what I can, if your Promise to protect Dill is still valid?" he asked.

"Yes, it is. See if maybe you can slowly convince him that he really should be on our side, seeing how Queen is only keeping him around in order to control you," April said.

"Well, would you be interested to know Drum and Queen have turned their attention to someone else?" he asked, with a curious look on his face.

Will raised an eyebrow. "They're quietly recruiting other Beings for their Bee system?" he inquired. "If we know for sure this Being is a Bee, we can follow them and figure out the Beings under Queen's thumb." Will smiled, thinking of the reward for cracking Queen's system.

"Not sure about that, but they think a student here with what you all call Universal Abilities, managed to get something called a...gold badge? They have yet to find it on campus, so they are trying to see if the student has a place off campus," he gave them.

April looked at Will, both of them shocked.

There is no way we would get the information this quickly, April signed to Will.

Will shook his head. "Pantu did they tell you this?"

"I listened in on a conversation that was had," he offered, confused as to how April and Will knew the sign language of The City.

"Where was this conversation?" April asked.

"My house," he told them.

Now, both Will and April went into shock. He knew Drum never went to anybody's home. Not even Queen's. Everyone figured it was easier for Drum not to be in close confines with Beings, so no accidental touching. He also knew Will and April could smell Lies, so he knew he had to be careful how much information he put out.

"Pantu, are you gay?" Will asked.

"We do not have gay people where I come from. It is punishable by death," he informed Will.

Will rolled his eyes. "Okay," Will tossed out.

His demeanor changed. His overconfident attitude of knowing he was far too handsome was felt in his pose. The sensation of being able to thoroughly satisfy a woman filled the small room. The look on his face matched his pose and April was tightening her thighs to keep it all in.

"April?" He whispered his full question in her name, and she started walking to him, entranced.

His smile to her as Will grabbed her by the back of her shirt and pulled her back, released her from her trance. She embarrassingly looked everywhere but their faces.

He turned to Will, dropping his demeanor and smiled at Will as he proved his point. Will was staring at the smile he was receiving. Will's penis jumped and leaked, staining Will's pants and he looked away, embarrassed as well.

"Those you call Gay are killed but those you call Lesbians are celebrated," he stated to both Will and April's shocked confusion. His soft smile to them both was only because he now knew they learned the sign language from someone, not from living or visiting The City. They were quite sloppy with it, assuming no one would know what they were signing.

"So, this student?" April said, bringing the conversation back.

"If they are interested in me, then I think you should look into those around me," he said.

"You mean like Dill?" April asked.

He shrugged. "I do not know if Dill would still be standing if he has an unauthorized gold badge, but Drum and Queen have yet to make a move, because this Being can get around Drum's Barriers."

"Could it be the Alex guy? #NoComp?" Will shocked face wasn't buying it.

"Why would you think of him?" April asked.

"Well, Pantu said someone around him, not someone close to him. I don't think Drum or Queen would hesitate if they had easy access to the Being," Will explained.

April went into thought mode as well. "Alex does hate the shit out of Pantu and rumor has it, he's obsessed with Drum."

"We should add his name to the list," Will said and April nodded.

"Is this enough to be promoted?" he sweetly asked.

"What?" April waved it off, preoccupied with the amount of information they were receiving.

"We'll pass this information to our head president and see what he says," Will told him, still trying to sort through everything he was telling them and the Abilities he was showing.

"Well, is this enough for your Promise Dill will remain unharmed?" he gently prodded.

"Yea, we won't touch Dill," April agreed.

"Promise?" he sweetly asked.

"Promise!" Will and April said at the same time, dismissing him to think about the massive amount of information they just heard.

He smiled as he watched April and Will, lost in thought. He knew what a Promise lock felt like, and the level of distraction needed to not notice. He'd filled the room with his scent to make them drop their guard. Knowing someone was able to get around Drum's Domes with a possible gold badge would be enough to get him what he wanted. Protection for Dill.

"I am taking my leave now," he said, mostly to himself.

"Yea," April waved him off.

He nodded and opened the door to leave, breaking Will's Dome in the process. Will and April's daze was released as he left the room. He was followed by a lost April and Will. The Four plus Dill was still waiting on the steps, and he stopped. He looked back at April and Will, scared and Will came up to him.

"If you change your mind and want to join our club, come find me," Will said, loud enough for everyone to hear.

Will flashed a dazzling smile and his cheeks flushed. He saw Will's penis stiffened at the sight of his smooth, plump cheeks turning bright red. Whatever Will was imagining made him blush in return. April elbowed Will as hard as she could in the ribs and Will's focus broke. Will waved and April pulled Will off in another direction, while shooting daggers at Pantu.

Dill ran up to him. "Why would you be hanging with them?" Dill asked, knowing there was a small crowd.

"I am not. Not anymore. I decided not to join since I need an after-school club which will offer more volunteer hours, but I still wanted to be friends." He pouted.

Dill eyed his bag, and he gave the slight signal he had it. Queen was right, they would place a listening device on him since he is the only one close enough to The Four willing to talk to them.

It worked in his favor that he used to live with humans. T-PEC would want to use him and his parents as an example, but they wanted as much information as they could get first, before using him as their poster boy.

"You can't be friends with everybody Pantu. This isn't like when you lived with humans, not everybody here means you good," Dill tried to explain.

He waved Dill off. "Have you ever lived with humans before?" he asked, pointedly.

Dill looked offended. "Humans lived here when I was little, but I don't remember much about them," Dill responded.

"Then, would you understand?" he said more than asked. He saw their schoolmates watching and listening to the conversation.

Put and Turn came up to them.

"What's good?" Turn asked.

He whined. "Dill is being mean to me!" he said, grabbing Turn's arm. "He is unhappy I lived with humans, and he has been living here his whole life. It seems to be my fault!" he complained, as he pulled Turn off to walk to homeroom.

Dill sighed loudly and moved to follow him and Turn to class. The students were confused as to why it seemed like he held the same ideas as T-PEC and whether he was going to join The Four or not.

PANTUxPUT: CAUGHT BETWEEN A ROCK AND A HARD PLACE
WEEK FIVE: TUESDAY

Lunch came around and Pantu was content eating with his friends. Sport packed him a lunch, since he couldn't eat anything else. The Four weren't in the lunchroom and it only sparked more conversation. He noticed Put kept looking at him like he wanted to talk alone.

"Put, you are free fourth period, right?" he asked, and Put nodded.

"Can you come to the Manga Room and help me out? The requests have become numerous," he sweetly asked.

Put just looked at him for a minute before agreeing with a sweet but nervous smile.

They finished eating and went their separate ways, with him and Put headed towards the library. After they entered the Manga Room, he made sure to put his stuff in Drum's chair. He went and gathered the books with Put's help.

They joked and laughed about their favorite foods, which only made him hungry again. They sat down at the table, and he gave Put the books to separate while he started on the nametags.

Put started, "Pantu, Alex has something on you, doesn't he?"

He wasn't expecting this question, but he answered honestly, "He thinks he does."

Put looked away. "Aren't you scared he is going to show everyone?"

He shook his head. "He only heard some things. He has nothing concrete on me," he informed Put, who looked depressed.

"Put, are you okay?" he asked, concerned.

Put looked at him. "I need help Pantu. I'm caught and I'm scared. Please help me!"

He put what he was doing to the side and gave his full attention.

Put nervously started. "I joined T-PEC with my parents a few years after an incident that left me scared for my life. I was young and scared of Drum and they offered to protect me. It seemed like a clever idea to have powerful adults on my side.

"They asked me to get the others to join as well, but I never asked them. I kept telling T-PEC, they turned me down. The longer I stayed in the club the more I saw and heard, and it scared me more than Drum.

"They want to do more than take the Barriers down, they want to rule over us while pretending to be friends with humans. Without Drum's Barriers, once our Energy depletes, it makes it easier for humans to overpower us. It also makes it easy to sell us to humans. They know all of this. They want to kill him Pantu, and they will do anything to find a way.

"When they wanted me to Level Up, I was excited because I thought I would become powerful enough to protect myself and not need them anymore. My parents were so proud of my accomplishments, but I hadn't done anything to warrant Leveling up.

"But when I saw what Leveling up was, I turned it down. They stripped a Being of their Energy. They dug the Core out, gathered all the Energy inside it, grounded it down and gave it to April so she could ingest it. She gained the Being's Energy and Abilities.

"I left the group, not officially, because I saw too much, but I was always busy. Never available. My parents never received an offer to Level Up. They weren't good enough except when it came to paying their dues. They died before my Senior year in High School. But during my Senior year, I..." He stopped and looked at Pantu.

"Please don't judge me," he pleaded and when Pantu nodded, he continued. "I was hooking up with a Professor from Makis Ridge Higher Ed," he said, not looking at Pantu. "At first, I didn't know she was a Professor, I thought she was a Higher Ed student. She was so kind and understanding about what I was going through, I fell in love with her.

"It wasn't until Alex found out I got her pregnant, she told me the truth after being blackmailed by him. She could lose her livelihood if the school found out. So, Alex has been extorting me for information on the club, trying to find out all the members and who the head president really is.

"I never got that close, so I don't know, but I have no new information, and Alex has been restless since you started here. If it wasn't for you becoming my friend, they would have stripped me last month. I saw the list, Pantu...my name was on the list to be stripped, to be "PROMOTED!" he cried out.

"You saved my life and my fiancé's career. Alex and T-PEC both want information on you, so if I tell them things about you, I won't be stripped, and Alex will keep his mouth shut.

"I'm how they know whenever you're around The Four. I give them information about you and T-PEC won't out me to my friends as a member and Alex keeps what he knows quiet. He's super pissed you sat in "the chair." He finished.

He was trying to honestly get everything off his chest. He decided to tell Pantu about Alex, since Pantu was the only one to ever stand up against Alex and win. He knew he needed to tell Pantu what T-PEC was really about, before Pantu became too close with them. He knew what he did as a child was horrible and what he was currently doing to his friend wasn't much better.

But if Drum was hanging out with Dill, maybe he had a chance to protect his own child and the woman he loved. He was willing to have his friends hate him for being a part of T-PEC and even if Pantu hated him for telling his business to the one Being who hated Pantu's existence, he still needed to try and save his family.

He was willing to bow to Drum to accomplish that. He was willing to die if his son and fiancé could be safely moved. He knew from T-PEC there were impenetrable Barriers held by Drum across the planet, where rumors of Beings who are high on T-PEC's list to acquire lived.

He was on the edge, ready to jump if Pantu hadn't come to town and sat with them during lunch. Everybody wanted to know about Pantu, anything about his friend. The intranet had yet to find out any information on Pantu, who was really a ghost, in their town and online.

He finally looked up at Pantu, tears filled his eyes. "I'm willing to do anything to keep my fiancé and my child safe. They didn't ask for this. It's my fault we're in this mess. Pantu, I'm so sorry for giving Alex and T-PEC information on you. I will stop. I will find someplace where we can hide, from both T-PEC and Alex."

"Do not bother," Pantu said.

"I'm so sorry Pantu!" he said, trying not to cry, but his voice was laced with remorse.

"I only mean for you to keep telling the snake everything he wants to know about me until we can figure this out. I want him to know how close I am to Drum. I want to upset him more. I will be the distraction we need to trap the little fucker," Pantu said.

He looked at Pantu, scared. "Pantu! Be careful with Alex. He's slippery and has gotten away with harming and extorting a lot of Beings here. He won't hesitate to kill you over Drum," he warned.

"We should go camping this weekend," Pantu absentmindedly said. "To bond," Pantu added, smiling.

He was confused. *Why would he want to?* But his thoughts were cut off by Pantu's response.

"This only works if you trust me. This will only last if you trust Drum," Pantu gently said.

He nodded. "Drum would be willing to help?" He almost cried asking.

"I know what happened when you were younger, but people can change. You have changed." Pantu shrugged. "Besides, there are innocent lives involved, even if he will not, I will," Pantu confidently said.

Their serious conversation ended with Pantu offering one of his Favor cards to him. He told Pantu the difference between the gold and black Favor cards and the yellow, green, and brown ones.

Pantu didn't even know about the other Favor cards, so Pantu was surprised only the black and gold cards offered up Drum's assistance. He took a deep breath and offered up information Pantu didn't know he would get so soon.

PANTUxDRUM: SETTING A TRAP
WEEK FIVE: TUESDAY

That evening, everyone was at Pantu's, and now, Sport's home again. Dill took the listening bug out of the small communication device before they went to lunch and crushed it, uninterested in figuring out how it worked.

"Sit down for this!" he told Dill, who complied.

He told them what Put told him earlier in the Manga Room and Dill's face of disbelief and sadness was to be expected. Robin held Dill as he tried to come to terms with Put's confession.

"You were correct Kat; they're figuring it out and starting to come to Pantu," Robin stated, looking kindly at Kat.

"We have to find the evidence he has on them, or it will all be for nothing," Win piped in.

"Hmm," Drum said, as he pulled out his phone and opened it. "Sup son?" Drum joked into his phone, garnering weird looks from everyone except Robin. "Can ya talk? Ya busy? What's poppin' the next couple of days? No?

"You should come see me for a while. Don't you miss my handsome smiling face? Bring your brother along for a vacation. Yea, relay any info we have to him. Okay. What? Why would I have to…okay, fine." Drum agreed before hanging up his phone.

Everybody looked at Drum waiting.

"Oh, I have people from The States coming through for a few days. Don't worry, they'll stay to themselves," Drum told them as he snapped a photo of Queen and started texting.

"Why can't we meet your people?" Queen asked, a slightly curious look on his face.

"They're a different breed," Drum replied.

"Are you a different breed when around them?" he asked.

Drum nodded. "Yup!" Drum said in English.

He and Queen looked at each other.

"Now I really want to meet them." Queen's eyes sparkled.

"Me too!" he said, his excitement leaking the cinnamon and honey scent.

"I wonder how different he really is?"

"Maybe we should impose?"

The conversation between him and Queen had everyone else looking between the two of them and Drum.

Drum showed no signs of feeding into their conversation but ended it. "One day," was all he said, and they quieted down.

He thought he could keep his life in The States separate from his life here, but Pantu quickly ended that plan by existing. He knew he would have to join them all together if this was going to work.

They would all have to be on the same page of the same book, reading at the same pace. He realized, with a slight smile, everyone around him and Pantu would be essential to their survival. He had plans for all his friends, so he needed to make sure they could get along.

It should be somewhere fun, he thought as his smile grew bigger. He knew when he would introduce them all and as he finished his thoughts, everybody was still looking at him, waiting patiently.

Pantu spoke up first. "I gave him one of my Favor cards," Pantu said, looking for his reaction.

Dill also looked at him nervously.

He accepted it with a shrug. "If you feel he showed you his True Face and didn't Lie to you, then there's no reason for me to disagree," he stated, glancing at Dill.

He felt Queen's Energies smile at his acceptance. Queen knew what Pantu was trying to do when it came to him and his childhood bullies. Queen approved and didn't butt in since Pantu was doing what Queen couldn't yet wanted to do; show everyone he *was* kind and forgiving.

Queen knew it would lessen the fear Beings held for him, and Queen already planned how to show their friendship online once they cleared the air. It would also clear up the narrative T-PEC was pushing, that Queen was controlling him to subdue Beings.

"I suggested we go on an overnight camping trip this weekend to bond." Pantu looked at him. "I know you will be gone, so I will inform Queen, and he can fill you in whenever you get back."

His eyes bore a hole through Pantu, who focused anywhere but his hard stare. Pantu was trying not to laugh and started drinking his tea instead as everyone else was doing a poor job of keeping their laughter in.

"AN-E-WAYS!" he emphasized. "Mansnake comes back next week. We now know the location of his school office, thanks to Put, but we'll need someone to go to his parents' house the day he gets back. I'll also have someone discreetly follow him, see if there's anywhere else he goes on an irregular basis. He could, if he's smart, have information stored elsewhere," he instructed.

"Who should the "someone" be?" Kat asked, her ocean blue Energy slightly scared she would have to go.

"Not anyone from here. I'll have my people from The States handle it. I'm not sure if he knows the scent of everyone here and we don't need to leave any trace of us behind in any of his places. He'll be on alert if he thinks we're on to him," he explained, easing Kat's fears.

"They will pass over any information they find, specifically any evidence he has on other Beings. Break his communications off so he has no choice but to run to them," he ended, confident in the silent part of his plan.

"I have Will and April interested. They said they will pass the information to the president," Pantu informed everyone.

"This could lead to us finally pulling the S.O.B out of the shadows," Sport commented.

"I'm so sure he's a night student!" Queen expressed.

He sighed. He didn't want to delve too deep, but he could no longer withhold the information. "He *is* a night student. His nickname is Shy, and surprise, surprise, he wants to personally kill me," he revealed.

The whole room was quiet as they stared at him, waiting for him to continue.

"His little brother was my best friend when I lived in The States. His name was what Mansnake is calling himself now. He disappeared one night. Shy is sure I killed him. So, he wants a life for a life," he explained. He would let his best friends handle T-PEC in school. The less he and Shy interacted, the better.

PANTU: AN EPIPHANY
WEEK FIVE: TUESDAY

He was annoyed with himself that he wanted Drum's attention. One could almost say he demanded it. Now, he would have even less of it. He turned in his make-up work and gave his essays to the Grammar Professors to correct before he would rewrite them and turn them in.

So, tomorrow, no Manga Room and no more tutoring. He guessed he would be seeing less of everyone except Dill, maybe less of him as well, since Robin and him were moving along perfectly.

Without thinking about his actions, he left the table and moved to sit in his backyard to gather any thoughts he could. With his arms wrapped around his knees, he quietly sat, until he looked up to pray to the Universe.

"AHHHHH!" He jumped as Drum's relaxed and quiet pose scared the shit out of him.

Drum just looked at him for a moment, with a slight smile, before turning to look up at the sky. "You aren't alone Pantu," Drum told him.

He looked at Drum with a pout. "You can read Minds, can you not?" he asked.

Drum just smiled. "Other than a few Beings in there, your scent wavers with everyone else. They aren't sure if you really want to be friends or not," Drum informed him.

He jumped up, brushing the grass off his butt. "I really do like everyone in there!" he exclaimed; visibly upset he couldn't seem to do anything right. "I do not want my scent to waver with them," he cried, anxiously racking his brain to figure out how.

Drum's right arm wrapped around his waist, pulling him in close.

"Maybe your scent wavers because you know. Your Energy is different now than when you lived in The City, isn't it?" Drum asked.

"There are things I cannot say, maybe that is the reason? I feel I cannot be completely honest because of Vows already made?" he questioned.

Drum shrugged. "Whenever there's something you can't tell us, you won't be breaking a Vow if we figure it out, would you?" Drum lightly inquired.

He thought about it. He couldn't come right out and tell them, but his Ma was able to tell them some of it and after they knew, he felt more at ease.

He nodded. "But it would have to be along the lines of the conversation, I will not be able to bring it up or explain. My G-Pas are very thorough." He smiled weakly.

"I figured as much. In fact, I figured out quite a bit from what you don't say." Drum laughed.

"Because you can read Minds, right?" he questioned. He was going to find out if Drum could or not, even if he had to ask a thousand times.

"Your determination to find out is way more than your determination to be my boyfriend," Drum joked. "I guess I just can't measure up to cool Abilities," Drum said, playfully, kissing him on the nose.

He rolled his eyes. *Failed again,* he thought, smiling to himself.

"You still planning on leaving?" Drum asked, looking up to the sky.

He looked up at Drum and then up to also search the sky. "I have no idea where to go," he answered. "But I know living and dying on this rock is not my Dream. I do not want to be here anymore.

"I am so over this planet and the humans on it. I want to leave and never look back," he said, as he laid his forehead on Drum's chest. "But the numbers are messy, and I have hit a wall," he added, sad his plan to leave may never come to fruition.

"Surely you don't plan on leaving us behind?" Queen surprised him as everyone walked outside.

He smiled at the group, and it quickly hit him like a speeding bus. He smacked his forehead and groaned. "How stupid am I?" he stated. "I accounted for the Beings but without an adjustment for the additional weight, which is why the balance was off."

Drum gently removed his hand from his head. "Epiphanies are not stupid," Drum told him. "What else?" Drum asked, with a knowing smile.

He couldn't help but smile back. "What if we could take every Being who wanted to leave, with us?" he asked to the murmurs of the group.

They all looked at each other since they knew Drum's Dream was to leave this planet and they were all on board, and here was a Being with the same ideas as them.

Win stepped up and asked, "Accounting for all known Beings, the ship would be too large to hide from humans," he commented, working the numbers out in his head.

"And there's the problem of feeding that many Beings when we don't know how far we're going and how long it would take," Queen thought aloud. "And with Win and Pantu on board..." Queen drifted off as everyone giggled and snickered at the truth.

"What if there was a way to put Beings in stasis? Like how there are Beings with the Ability to force others to sleep," Robin asked.

"Good idea, but still too many Beings to properly transport," Win said thinking.

"What if we put them in stasis and then shrink them?" Queen whispered.

"Do we have a way to bring them back unharmed?" Robin asked, surprised.

"Yes," Queen whispered.

He smiled. "We need to work on a container which can transport Beings safely, work on enlarging and shrinking both Beings and the container. Once I know the size and weight of the containers with and without Beings in them, I can work on new specs for a ship. We can revamp the ramp and shuttle from there." He laid out a plan.

"Or..." Drum started. "I really don't have any plans to leave the land I Purified behind for humans to suck the life out of."

A light went off in his head. "What if no one needed to be asleep? What if we could shrink the Purified lands with Beings on it and place it in a room that will..." He started thinking.

"Be behind a Barrier to hold it in place while we traveled," Dill finished for him. "That way Beings will still be able to live their everyday life while not taking up the majority of space on the ship."

"Those needed to run the ship could Portal travel between. That way they could still be with their families!" Queen said, delighted with the idea.

"We would need to figure out the weight of the land with all the surrounding water I'm going to Purify," Drum stated. "How long will it take to build a spaceship?"

"Properly and with our Abilities, anywhere between two to four years," Dill answered. "That's after we have specs," Dill added.

Drum nodded. "This gives me yet another brilliant idea!" Drum said, smiling. "OH! And I could do that as well." Drum was lost in thought as he added to future plans.

He and Queen stared at Drum's face, wondering what new plans Drum was coming up with.

PANTU: A BEAUTIFUL APPARITION
WEEK FIVE: TUESDAY

Pantu was feeling more at ease since he was now out of his slump. He had a best friend, there was a Dome around his home, Sport lived with him, Drum was in his arms, and he had more friends than he could have ever imagined having.

As long as he stayed caught up with classwork and homework, he felt more confident in handling other issues. Being able to make a Time Dome was icing on an already fattening cupcake. He smiled as he thought this, but a shudder quickly diminished the feeling. One of the apparitions was calling to him.

"Golden Healing Boy!" A light Woman's voice called to him, over and over.

He tried to ignore it, but the voice soon started to sing it, getting louder each time. He thought he was the only one to hear it, but when Drum opened the Domes between the houses and she came in, everyone looked at Drum, stunned. He hid behind Drum's back as the apparition floated closer to him.

"DRUM!" he called out, trying to shrink himself behind Drum's back.

Drum held up his hand, and the apparition stopped, playfully swaying back and forth. She giggled in her hands, but no one except him and Drum seemed to be able to hear her.

"I have something to tell you!" she sung.

He peeked at her before peeking up at Drum, who nodded.

"What do you have to tell me?" he asked.

She swung around in a circle, enjoying the warm Light Drum was giving off. "His Energy is quite a lot. I can barely contain myself!" she mentioned to him, who looked at Drum, upset about sharing the warmth he claimed as his own.

However, Drum's eyes never left the young Woman, even as he responded. "Why thank you. I take pride in my Energy." Drum's reply left the young Woman in shock.

"He can hear me as well!?" She gasped.

"What is your name?" he asked, changing the subject.

"Delia," she replied.

"Hi, Delia. I am Pantu. This is Drum. Over there, it is Robin, Kat, Dill, Queen, Win, and Sport," he introduced everyone.

Delia kept her eyes on Queen, which made Queen's eyebrows furrow in thought.

"Once you put it together, the Flaming Bird will come to find you," she sung, still looking at Queen.

"HUH?" he asked, confused.

He repeated what she said aloud to everyone, who looked at Queen as well. Shrugging his shoulders and looking more lost and confused than everyone else, Queen said nothing.

She pointed to him. "You have to put it together. It will be a beacon, and the Flaming Bird will find you," she sung again, never taking her eyes off Queen.

He repeated what she said.

"So, why is she looking at Queen like that?" Win asked, scared she might have fallen for Queen after death.

"I didn't expect the Queen to be so beautiful!" she sung out, hiding her soft smile behind her hands.

He smiled and blushed at Queen, whose head shook in frustration, waiting for him to translate. When he said what Delia thought to him, Queen himself blushed as everyone started commenting on Queen's Ability to make even dead people fall in love with him.

"So, what do you need to put together?" Kat asked him, who shrugged.

"The quad Energy. Energy which has been separated into four other bodies and must be joined back together if you want to leave," she told him.

His thoughts were sidetracked as a thought popped into his head. "Flaming Bird...Flaming Bird...Flaming Bird?" He kept saying over and over, as if he was trying to remember something else related.

"Phoenix. She means Phoenix, right?" Queen asked, shutting down the compliments and teasing.

But he couldn't hear Queen. There is something there...*where is it*? He was deep in thought as he whispered, *"Flaming Bird...Flaming Bird...burn...burning...something is burning...what is it which is burning...the boy... the boy is burning...The Burning Boy."*

He didn't notice Drum was now looking at him intensely and Queen stood still and stared at him as well. He was still trying to figure out what Burning Boy meant to him and how he knew the phrase. When Queen gracefully collapsed to the ground, he snapped out of his thoughts.

Queen held his head in his hands. "We're all dead. I'm going to die young and beautiful!" Queen cried out, genuine tears streaming down his face.

Dill kneeled beside Queen, rubbing his back. "Yeah, the realization is quite traumatic." Dill consoled Queen, who looked up at Dill.

"How? How did you find out? How do you do it? Everyday? How could you willingly put yourself so close to death?" Queen asked Dill.

"Hmmm. I guess you could say, I foolishly wanted a best friend more than I fear death," Dill told Queen. "Someone who didn't feel obligated to me or would use me. Someone who understood me and would rather I be myself than what others perceived of me," Dill explained. "*We both know how rare it is, and we both would risk death,*" Dill gently said to Queen, who nodded through the tears.

"I should call my Mom. Tell her goodbye and give her a to-do list, just in case." Queen sniffled.

By now everybody else, except Drum and the two Beings on the ground, were completely confused by Queen's breakdown.

"Why are we all going to die?" Robin asked, confused. "Drum, did you bring me here just to kill me? You gave me your word! You gave my parents your word!" she asked, now shocked.

Dill looked up, uncertain of what Robin just said. "Wait, Drum brought you HERE?" Dill asked, pointing to the ground.

Robin looked like she just let a huge secret leak. She refused to answer or meet anyone's eyes, so they all collectively looked at Drum, who shrugged and also avoided eye contact.

"You two knew each other in The States?!" Everyone who was left asked a variation of the question, as Queen already walked off, talking to his Mom.

Robin played with her hands.

Drum took a deep breath. "We're related. Her Momma is my Daddy's little sister. She's my cousin," Drum told them, looking at Dill as he said this.

The "I am so dead" look Dill gave as he understood he was fully entangled in the life of the male who he used to bully.

Dill is best friends with me and now in a relationship with Drum's family member. He suppressed a giggle as Dill's tears dropped, and Dill let out a groan he knew was felt in Dill's soul.

Is the Universe playing a trick on him? He questioned, his thoughts overflowing. *Apparently, there is something to the connection Drum and I have, and Dill is my best friend. Not to mention his girlfriend knew her connection and who Dill was when they started dating.*

He and Dill seem to have the same thoughts as the revelation made Dill look up at Robin, who smiled, and of course, Dill melted.

Totally worth it, he thought as Dill smiled back.

A sly smile came over Dill as he decided to let it slip. "Well, when they change Scents, you just know," Dill said, glancing at him.

He wasn't paying attention anymore since he was looking around for Delia, who seemed to have wandered off and into his home.

Drum looked at Dill, and Dill shut up but Robin, Win and Kat all understood. As the small group's epiphany hit, they collectively groaned and fell to their knees, some crying. They now understood the amount of power he really held.

They looked up at a relaxed Drum, with his hands in his pockets, to see he was still standing behind Drum's back, his arms tightly wrapped around Drum's right arm.

He was looking at them weirdly and wondered where the white mats under their knees came from and *why the hell are they all on the ground crying?* He looked at Sport for some clarification but all he received was a lost look and a shrug.

Sport walked up to Dill. *"Hey, what's going on?"* Sport whispered, glancing around at everyone else on the ground.

Dill grabbed Sport's hand and pulled him down to kneel on the mat left by Queen.

Linking their fingers and holding on to Sport's hand for dear life, Dill stated, "Sport, my guy, stay innocent. At least until after the championship game. No reason to unnecessarily stress you out."

Kat's hand went to her mouth as she gasped. "We have to make it until then. Sport has to completely shit on the other team!" Kat said, with a smile.

Sport looked away. *"It's a team effort,"* Sport mumbled, trying his hardest not to be seen blushing.

Kat missed Sport's look and sat back dejected.

Win went to console her, placing his arm around her. "It's okay. If he couldn't figure this out, he really is just an innocent," Win joked, trying to lighten the mood.

Sport turned and just stared at Win. "Innocent?" Sport repeated, the pause before he continued, was deafening. "Yea let's go with innocent," he finished, turning back to talk to Dill.

Win looked shocked. "Were you about to say something offensive?" Win asked Sport, indignantly.

"Hmm!" Sport said. "I put a filter," Sport added, now fully turned to look at Dill.

"You would filter your conversation with ME!?" Win shouted, dismayed.

Sport ignored Win and spoke to Dill. "Well, I guess as long as we can live until after the game, that's good enough for me." He agreed with Dill's plan.

Drum watched without a word, but he was still distracted looking for Delia, trying to make sure she didn't come close to him, while still trying to follow the conversation.

"Drum?" he asked. "Why are they all saying they are going to die?"

Drum looked at him and smiled at the mix of innocence and fear on his face. "Most of them just had an epiphany," Drum answered, trying not to laugh.

"Well, will everybody be alive for us to leave?" he asked, looking at Drum like it was all his fault.

Drum looked appalled. "They're being overdramatic. GLou would have had his hands full with this group," Drum stated, as he rolled his eyes up to the sky and shook his head. Drum decided to pay Dill back. "You are getting pretty good at this," Drum commented, nodding his head towards Dill.

His eyes snapped towards Dill angrily. "Yes, he is, is he not?" he agreed, the threat clear in his voice.

Drum looked at Dill with a sneaky smile and a raised eyebrow.

Dill's quick thought came right out. "I was taught well by my Shifu, as his Shifu taught him. Your praise of me is only a reflection of my Shifu's wise teachings." Dill made a bow to him, who softened at Dill praising both him and GLou.

The respect shown on Drum's face was quickly masked by his inability to hold his laughter in. Drum nodded to their hands and Dill quickly caught on.

"Oh, we should probably let go now," Dill said, as he raised their clasped hands together.

"Why were we holding hands?" Sport asked, confused.

"For comfort," Dill said, nonchalantly.

"Whose comfort?" Sport asked, warily.

Dill unlinked their hands in a huff. "Does it matter? We both feel better, that's the main point," Dill said, as he stood up, looking away from Sport's sarcastic face and the laughter of everyone else.

Delia came back, and Queen ended his conversation with his Mom. Queen moved over to the patio seating area to converse with his Mom without missing out on the conversation still to be had by his friends. He came back as Delia made her way to the group.

She turned to face Queen, moving her arms and her body in front of him. Queen looked at her weirdly and then at him, who shrugged and shook his head. When Queen received the same response from Drum, he turned his attention back to Delia. She was moving her body to speak to him.

As Queen watched, he understood. "Okay, book...read. No read...Pantu...give...me. No read...book...give...Pantu...seven...morning...nights...continual...six...together...six," Queen stated as he understood the actions. "Give Pantu the unreadable book in six weeks?" Queen asked her.

Her joy and elation at Queen's quick understanding made her dance and twirl around the yard. But he was mindful of where she was, and he moved around Drum to avoid her movements.

"Who gave her a message like that?" Sport asked, his eyes watching Delia and his brows furrowed in confusion.

Delia stopped dancing and put a finger to her mouth.

"If there aren't any other Beings who can do what Ma does, then that means the message was given before she died?" Sport added, sadness written on his face.

"Wait, so she knew she would die?" Win asked, stunned.

"Why wouldn't she avoid death, if she knew?" Kat asked, scared.

When Delia quickly moved to stand in front of Drum, he instantly went completely behind Drum's back. Although closing his eyes and holding on to Drum's shirt for dear life while trying to shrink himself at the same time didn't work, Delia made no moves to touch him.

Delia held her hands out in front of her, palms down and Drum copied her. She looked at both of his hands, pointing first to his vow ring and secondly at three more fingers. She pointed at her throat and after a quick tilt of his head and a raised eyebrow, Drum snapped his fingers next to her throat.

"Ahhh...ummm...hmmm," Delia sung, clearing her throat. "OH! I haven't heard my own voice in so long. He said it was too beautiful to let me die with, so he took it!" She talked while singing.

Everyone's different emotions about what they now knew to be Delia's voice coming from Mansnake, made Delia shyly glow.

"You did something to push the time forward...by a lot," she said, softly to Drum. "That's the reason Ma Sky used her Talent years before she was supposed to," she told them.

He peeked from around Drum to join the conversation. "What could Drum have possibly done?" he asked.

"He changed something?" she said, looking at Drum.

Drum was deep in thought as if he was searching in his past, trying to figure out exactly what he did.

"Did you know you were going to die?" Sport asked her. "Just to send a message?"

Delia looked away. "My death is a set point in time. If it didn't happen, then so many things would fall apart. It's holding off as much as it can, but this is the final attempt. They came to me and asked me to relay this message, and I was honored to do so," she said, as she lightly twirled from side to side.

He perked up. "They?" he asked to Delia's giggle.

She nodded and placed her finger to her mouth again. Everybody understood this to mean GMack and GLou had something to do with this.

"I CAN NOT wait to meet them!" Queen said, excitedly.

His soft smile at Queen made him blush and quickly look away.

"Meet who?" Delia asked.

"GMack and GLou," Queen stated.

"Oh? Who are they?" Delia asked, making the group more confused.

He tugged on Drum's shirt, looking up at Drum questioningly. Drum nodded and he stepped from behind Drum. He moved to stand in front of Delia, holding out his hands, palms up.

Delia hid her smile behind her hands. "Are you sure?" she asked.

He nodded. "Your death may have been set, but I am not in agreement with the reasoning," he stated.

"They said you would do this. She said you have a pure heart," Delia's light turned a light green as she blushed at him.

He smiled in return. "They seem to know me well."

She placed her hands on his, and the look on everyone, except Drum, faces were of complete astonishment. They watched as he closed his eyes, and her body started to Form from her hands until she was a fully complete person. She was human when she died, so it was easier for him to Form her body. It helped with the hand Drum placed on his back to give him white Light.

But Beings bodies didn't work the same way a simple human body did. He found it difficult to recreate a working Being body as he wasn't aware of why human bodies could carry Orbs and Light. After a shout of surprise, Delia passed out in Queen's arms.

PANTU: WHAT A TIME TO BE NAKED
WEEK FIVE: TUESDAY

They moved Delia to the couch.

"Is there a reason she can't lay in you or Sport's room?" Queen asked.

"Only your Intended is welcome to sleep in your bed. It is a family value my G-Pas instilled in me," he explained.

Sport nodded in agreement, knowing the rule would apply to him as well.

"If you are a woman, your pet could sleep in your bed, but I never did. My G-Pas never allowed it," he stated, looking down at Delia.

His Energy, or what his G-Pas call his Light, was now easier to use and more powerful than when he was in The City. It would have taken him several hours to bring her back, but he did it in minutes. Drum never Vowed to help him, only gave his word, and kept it without the obligation of a Vow.

He was wondering if Drum would figure it out since he was really interested in what had changed. He knew his G-Pas had their hand in shaping his future, but he was lost to who Delia mentioned. He was just as confused about Delia's use of she, *maybe she meant GAmani?*

Was it GMa and GMack? Without GLou? It didn't make sense to him. His G-Pas held a lot of Talents, and he knew their Light was stronger when they were together, which was why they are pretty inseparable. He knew everyone was still processing what he did, and Drum was piecing together what he changed, so other common conversation was needed.

"Now that I think about it, GLou and GMack should have plenty of accusations against them. They are so close, accusing them of a romantic relationship would not have seemed off," he thought out loud, mostly to fill the empty air.

"They aren't, are they?" Queen asked.

He shook his head. "It never seemed like it. They would always tell me they are two sides of the same coin," he said. He pulled out his gold coin. Flipping it in the air, it landed on Positive Thoughts.

"That was GMack's coin. He always found a way to find a positive outlook on life. His paintings were the most expensive and sought after for the feelings they invoked in people. He taught me how to paint," he explained.

He flipped the coin to show Good Vibes Only on the other side.

"That was GLou's coin. He hates those who would ruin a fun time, since there were very little of those for us. It is also the name of his playhouse. He personally tossed out any hecklers." He smiled as he remembered the play GLou dragged him into.

"There's a story behind that smile, isn't it?" Win asked, whose eyes lit up in anticipation.

He laughed. "Remember how I told you GLou is shit when it comes to betting on relationships?" he asked, to the nods of everyone, except Kat and Robin.

He briefly explained. "GLou would bet me and GMack on the lengths of relationships and whether they would last. He lost so much he ended up losing his clothes, ALL of them, to us.

"He walked around The City for two days with no clothes on. We thought he would stay home, but he said in order to win his clothes back, he needed to bet. When people asked him why he was walking around naked, he told them he was working on an all-nude play...starring his grandson," he said as he tried not to laugh.

Everyone else thoughts were making them try to laugh silently but they weren't doing a decent job.

"Did...did you...do it?" Kat asked, between her giggles.

"It was pretty freeing!" he commented, now laughing with them.

"What was the play about?" Sport asked, as he caught his breath.

"It was about Dragons and humans. The humans killed almost all the Dragons in a one-sided war. A Wizard, who was banished because he chose not to fight, believed Dragons and humans could live together, so he turned the last Dragon into a baby and raised him as a human," he explained. "GLou was the Wizard, and I was the last Dragon. I even had an Intended, but because of demon spawn, it was only a rock," he said, laughing harder.

Laughter filled his home as he told the story.

"I made it as comfortable as possible to fuck. It was heartbreaking when it was destroyed at the hands of humans," he said, with sadness.

"Please...I can't...It's too...much..." Robin was saying between breaths.

Even Drum, who wasn't holding back his laughter, had tears falling. The fact everyone was imagining this with a naked Pantu, was making it harder not to laugh.

"Completely naked?" Robin asked, finally catching her breath.

He nodded. "There were several small dance numbers and a huge one at the end," he added, making everyone fall out laughing again.

"I need to see this play!" Queen cried through his laughter.

He shook his head. "GLou's personal plays are infamous. He held one play a year with both him and I in it and only for three days. If you missed it, word of mouth was the only way to find out anything about the play.

"But this play lasted a week and was sold out four months before rehearsals even started." He looked sheepishly at them. "That is the length of time it took him to convince me to do the play."

He slid down to the floor of his living room and quickly noticed a mat appeared under him. "GLou did three days in The Center, with one day in The Inner Ring, one day in the Outer Ring and two days in The Slums.

"It only made me more popular. My name was, from then on, known all around The City. I was the poster boy for my GMa and Indria's businesses and other companies as well. It was a freeing experience, and I also spent less time alone with the demon spawn.

"GMack negotiated my contracts, and they attended to me on every project. Demon spawn went along with it since it was increasing my points. My G-Pas were able to negotiate two days off a week from being a pet so I could fulfill my contracts. First pet in history to ever have a day off!" he said, proudly.

"GMack and GLou are quite powerful, aren't they?" Win asked.

He smiled. "All three of them. GMa, GMack and GLou. It is worse when they are together. No one can refuse them. They get whatever they want, when they want it."

Everyone looked impressed. As much as he talked about his G-Pas, they all felt a connection with them as well.

"*Ohmm!*" Delia moaned as she placed her hand on her forehead. She jumped up, realizing she could feel her forehead again.

"She is human with Being ancestry," he told them, so they knew there was a time limit to get her from under the Dome.

Robin stepped forward, wrapping her arm around the young Woman. *"Delia, do you know where your parents live?"* she asked, gently.

Delia nodded. "If they haven't moved."

Robin wrapped Delia up in a hug as Delia started to cry.

"Can I go home? You would take me home?" Delia asked, sobbing at the thought.

"I will contact your parents and arrange for your flight home. You will stay with me, and I will personally see you to your parents' arms," Robin told her. She turned to look at Dill apologetically, who accepted her commitment to Delia with a smile of understanding.

Delia looked at Drum. "Have you figured it out?" she asked, curious.

Drum nodded but didn't offer any more information.

"Good. I don't know what you did, but I could tell it wasn't the time told to me. If you know, you can plan ahead," Delia encouraged Drum.

Drum agreed and looking at Sport, he quickly nodded, and Sport stood up and left through a white Portal. Drum stood and moved to the eating room table. He sat at the head, and everyone slowly gathered around. Sport came back with human food and started cooking for Delia.

Drum asked Queen for calming tea and Queen obliged for everyone. Sport placed human tea in front of Delia, and she sweetly thanked him, garnering a smile and blush from Sport. Kat noticed and rolled her eyes.

Drum started. "Delia's message was meant as encouragement," he explained.

Everybody looked at Drum and Delia smiled.

"Why would we need encouragement? We're on a roll?" Queen asked.

Drum shook his head, looking down. *"I was thinking…about giving it all up,"* Drum stated quietly, to Queen's dismay.

The anger which filled the room scared everyone, and it all came from Queen.

"Say that again Suppade. I didn't quite hear," Queen said, his voice laced with threats.

"Panya, how long have we…" Drum started.

"And I will spend the rest of my life following you and only you," Queen interrupted.

"It's not fair, Panya…" Drum started again.

"Life isn't fair, but it damn sure has been interesting and eventually fun," Queen said, peeved.

Drum said nothing else as he looked down at his folded hands.

Queen took a deep breath and expelled it before drinking his calming tea. "I understand. We have been doing this since we were kids. It's a long time to keep the hope. But look at us, Suppade. We made it this far. If you want to keep going, then we will. If you want to stop, then we will.

"If you want to travel, party and bullshit, then do that, have fun, relax and take a load off. If you just want to lounge around, doing nothing but watching T.V and eating, then do it. After everything you have done for us, you deserve to be happy," Queen told Drum.

He could tell by the look on Queen's face, Queen understood what Drum was trying to tell him, even if the rest of them were lost. The sad look on Drum's face told Queen what Drum was thinking, and Queen looked away. He could see the unspoken words between best friends, even if he couldn't understand them.

He stood, looking around the table at everyone's faces. "If you want to give up, then fine," he said. "But I refuse to live on this planet for the rest of my life. I have no clue everything you all have done to get to this point, but nothing will stop me from leaving this planet, even if I must do the rest alone. Even if it takes the majority of my life, I will leave this fucking planet!" He turned to slowly look at Drum. "Even if I have to drag you, kicking and screaming," he threatened.

Drum's happy, surprised look was to mask the smile he was trying to hold in. Drum failed, looking down at the table and smiling uncontrollably.

Queen looked between Drum and him. "Well, I guess we're leaving then," Queen commented. "Although...I wouldn't mind seeing the kicking and screaming part," Queen added, laughing into his hand.

He nodded and looked around at the rest of the table. "Are we leaving willingly, or do I need to hog-tie a few of you?" he asked.

Everyone laughed at the thought, breaking the tension in the air.

"Good. Now let's clean up our plans. We have a lot to do together and separately. I would like to be off the planet before I turn thirty, give or take one to two years," Drum stated.

Delia giggled and held her hands a good space apart before bringing them closer together.

"The time has decreased?" he asked, excitedly bouncing on his feet, his elation spreading.

Drum smiled at him. *"Let's get to work,"* Drum said, gently.

PANTU: NOT HIS NICHE
WEEK FIVE: WEDNESDAY & THURSDAY

The group didn't know just how right Kat was when she said the longer Manpa stayed away from school, the more his victims would flock to him. They were putting it together, but he was sure Kat and Put were helping as well. The Manga Room turned into his private office for dealing with victims of both T-PEC and Manpa.

He could tell which ones wanted information and tried to use Lies and deception to get it out of him. He gently sent them on their way, confused and without any viable information. Some students gave him information via the book requests.

He had time to deal with this as Drum's class resumed and he himself was busy dealing with schoolmates and actual book requests, which only wanted his custom tag.

He didn't do a tag for everyone, only those he wanted to, others' names were plainly written on their order. He knew there would be backlash, and he didn't care, he would draw what he wanted, when he wanted.

There was also extra time to figure out he didn't like this. Having an office, dealing with Being's problems head on. He felt weird, like he was stepping on Queen's toes. This wasn't what he wanted to do, nor did he enjoy it. By the end of day classes Thursday, he posted the room was for book requests only.

He also knew T-PEC wouldn't ask him about the device's listening function being destroyed, as it never worked right from the moment it was given to him. The device going completely silent before lunch wouldn't seem out of the ordinary.

On campus, he kept his distance from both groups; as he didn't want anyone to see him touch Drum and he didn't want to seem overly friendly with T-PEC, mostly April and Will.

SHYxALEX: FALLING INTO A TRAP
WEEK FIVE: THURSDAY

Shy was leaning against a desk in a makeshift office, looking through some notes on certain Beings when the owner of the room Portaled in. He looked up with a smile at the surprised look on the owner's face at the intrusion.

"Finally," he said, standing to greet the owner. "I was wondering if you would come here today."

"Who are you?" Alex asked.

"My name is Shy," he answered, walking around some kneeling Beings in front of the desk. "I'm a night student and the President of the T-PEC club here on campus. I heard you've been looking for me?"

Alex's eyes grew wide. No one knew who he was, since he stayed in the shadows, only coming out when there was a "special" Being he wanted to meet. No one Alex was extorting in T-PEC knew he was the President and with this knowledge, none of the kneeling Beings would be allowed to spread the information. The closest Alex could get was April as the outspoken vice-president.

He quickly hid his smile when, after glancing at April's smiling face, Alex's face showed dread. Instead, Alex glanced around his office and saw they carelessly went through all his stuff and didn't bother to put any of it back.

Whatever Alex was thinking was answered when his eyes found the Beings kneeling behind him. These were the T-PEC Beings Alex thought he was extorting for information about the club, so Alex must have realized they would keep an eye on him as well. Alex's eyes found him before finding the floor, waiting to see what they would do.

"Seems you know a lot about our club but never wanted to join," Will stated.

Alex glared at Will, unwilling to say anything. He thought maybe Alex was traumatized by the conversation with Queen and even being suspended because of this Being named Pantu. He laughed.

"No reason to be afraid of me. I'm not going to hurt you Alex," he said, and Alex's head jerked towards him.

He knew Alex wanted the name to catch on, and he would be willing to call this cute Being by his dead little brother's name. He preferred it. It made it easier for him, sexually. Alex seemed surprised to hear the name come so easily from his mouth and it made Alex take a deep breath.

"I was never invited to join T-PEC. Guess I'm just not Special enough," Alex finally said.

"Drum and Queen seem to think you're special. They have their eyes on you," he said.

"Only because of Pantu."

"I think it's more than that, Alex. You are special, aren't you?" he asked. "I only want special Beings standing around me, since I'm so close to the next Emperor Marcus," he said, smiling at Alex.

"Drum is slated to be the next ruler," Alex stated and he noticed Alex's head was the only part of the Being to move. Alex kept the rest of his body completely still.

"Is that why you're so obsessed with him? Because he was chosen by some old ass artifact?" he asked. "Should we really be pinning our hopes and dreams on a busted sphere or a Being who will make sure we can live amongst Humans with no fear?"

When Alex didn't respond, only looked down at the floor, he continued, "Marcus is already in talks with different leaders of other countries, making laws to protect Beings. But those laws won't go into effect as long as these stupid barriers are up.

"Humans think we are withholding resources from them, and they wouldn't be wrong," he said, gauging Alex's reaction to his words. "This is what our club is about, making Torven an equal place for everyone to live freely."

"That's a nice thought," Alex replied.

"So, you agree?" he asked.

"I think there is far too few of us to fight against humans. We would be at their mercy," Alex responded.

"Well, that's what the laws would be for," he said. "Our protection."

"So, we would have to depend on the humans to protect us? To abide by their own laws?" Alex asked.

He laughed. "You're quick on the uptake. But unfortunately, I can't tell you much of Marcus' plan pass the laws, since you aren't a High-ranking Member of the club. But I will tell you as long as Drum refuses to share, it will only make things worse for us."

Alex nodded but rolled his eyes as well. Select Humans and Beings all over Torven knew Marcus openly claimed the rights to the throne as the leader of T-PEC. Beings knew Marcus wanted Humans and Beings to live together in harmony across Torven. This wasn't any new information, so Alex could care less about what he was saying.

"How about I give you some sensitive information and you answer a question, just one, that I have," he offered.

"And if your information is garbage or already known?" Alex asked.

"Then we keep going until I give you information that isn't," he said, piquing Alex's interest.

"Humans know about purification and they want it. They want Torven itself to be purified, the water, land, and food. They want to be more like us. And we could do it, if Drum would stop being so fucking stingy," he started.

Alex's head shook and he took it to mean Alex already met Humans who knew Beings existed and this information.

"Hmm," he said, watching Alex closely. "Marcus has a way to make a Being more powerful."

Alex shrugged.

"Okay," he said, moving closer to Alex. "Drum has fallen in love with Pantu."

Alex froze, forgetting to breathe. He knew. He knew Drum held feelings for Pantu, but he was in denial. As long as no one else outright said it, he could deny it to himself. But Shy knew. Everyone in the room knew. He could tell by Will and April's faces, it was true. When he remembered to breathe, his breaths were angrily pushed in and out of his body.

"I know," he said, gritting his teeth. "I have seen him in front of Pantu's home. He put a Barrier around Pantu's fucking house! Why would he do it if he didn't? I know they spend time alone in the Manga Room and Drum is personally tutoring Pantu. He even invited Pantu to his fucking birthday party over my invite. I FUCKING KNOW THAT!"

"They also know you stole a gold badge," Shy stated and he looked at Shy, surprised.

"So, you didn't know!" Shy said smiling. "Now for my question. Where is it?"

He looked away, defeated. Shy was damn good at using information and his feelings for Drum to get what he wanted. While he was thinking he would get information on Marcus, Shy gave public knowledge, making him drop his guard and led him right where Shy wanted him to go, to the gold badge. How Drum knew he was given one was now the mystery he needed to solve.

His eyes quickly glanced towards the fake wall as he turned away from it to wrap himself in his arms. A look of surprise crossed his face when Shy's arms wrapped around him, and his breathing became erratic.

"Just because Drum is too stupid to see how special you are, doesn't mean I am," Shy said as April and Will opened the false wall to reveal the room behind it.

"We have a plan. Drum will die. The barriers will fall. Marcus will be the next Emperor, and we will live peacefully on Torven. I want you by my side Alex," Shy whispered to him.

He chose not to say anything as he felt Shy's kisses on his neck. His eyes fluttered as his Mind understood he was trapped. Shy's sights were set on him and although he wished to high heaven it was Drum kissing on him, he didn't move or stop Shy. He knew rejecting Shy would be detrimental to his health.

Shy and Marcus are cousins; he is the highest-level T-PEC I could ever get close to. Any information I find out, Drum could use, he thought.

"We can't touch it!" April yelled from the other room.

Shy stopped kissing on him and looked at him with a raised eyebrow.

"It's under a Barrier made of several different Beings' Energies to keep what I assume is a GPS tracker blocked," he answered.

"That's smart as hell seeing as how they don't know where you're keeping it," Shy said, smiling at him before going back to kissing on his neck.

PANTU: A MEMORY REVISITED
WEEK FIVE: FRIDAY

The two days flew by, and he realized in the Manga Room it was Friday. Drum would be leaving for the weekend.

Not to worry, you have a camping trip tomorrow night. You can keep yourself busy outside of Drum, he thought but the ache was still there.

He was mentally trying to console himself and think of different things he could do after school. He'd turned in all his first week's makeup work and was completely caught up, so it meant no more tutoring from Drum.

Drum could have stretched it out to two and a half weeks. He just had to get it done in two, he thought, as he slowly found all the requested books.

Dill would be with Robin today, and he wasn't sure what the rest of The Four normally did after school. He felt alone. He was deep in his thoughts when a knock at the door snapped him out of it.

How many more Beings does Manpa have his foot on, he thought, opening the door. Standing in front of him was a tall, beautiful Woman.

He looked at her. She was wearing the AH student campus uniform. She wore heels, making her as tall as Drum and her makeup was as flawless as Queen's. Her eyelashes were long and luscious around her dark orange irises. Her burnt orange, tightly coiled hair only made her mahogany brown skin shine.

"Hello Pantu, I'm Sharon. I was asked to give you this," she said, as she held out a small envelope.

"Ah, all requests are to be placed at the counter, and I will get to them as I can," he said, motioning towards the front desk while his eyes never left her face. He did notice her perfectly manicured nails with orange nail color and butterfly designs. He also noticed her breasts were either really tiny or nonexistent.

Sharon looked at him weirdly, almost as if she were uncomfortable. She showed him the front and back of the envelope. His nickname from Drum was beautifully written and the back held a Dragon wax seal. Sharon extended the envelope again and he nodded, accepting it.

She sucked her teeth and went to walk away when he explained, "Where I come from, natural beauty is hard to find," he said to her. "You are an incredibly beautiful person," he added, wanting to remember her face to paint.

Sharon blushed and holding her breath, she nodded and bowed slightly to him before quickly leaving the doorway. He entered the room and sat down at the table. It was a note. Drum sent him a note, and his smile couldn't be contained.

He still thinks about me, he thought, as he carefully opened the envelope.

The note was brief. *"Dear Dumpling, I won't be in class today so I can't see your handsomely beautiful face before I leave..."*

His heart dropped. "We will not even get to see each other before he leaves. He never tutored me on Fridays, so no reason to be surprised."

He went back to reading. *"...so, I'm hoping you will practice the Abilities we have worked on and be ready for me to see if you have completed your self-study."*

He rolled his eyes and sucked his teeth at that part.

"Even though I know you rolled your eyes and sucked your teeth..."

He looked around as if Drum could see him now, but *he already wrote this! HE IS IN MY HEAD!!* He thought as he looked down to finish the note.

"...you can always ask Sport for help with Barriers, Win for help with your Ground-step and Queen for help with Portals. I will come to see you Sunday night to test your Abilities. And to hold you in my arms again. -X."

He read the last line, repeatedly before realizing there was more written further down on the paper.

"P.S. How many times did you read the last line? Are you going to miss me as well?"

His shy smile and blushing red face made him happy he wasn't in front of anyone else. He couldn't contain his excitement.

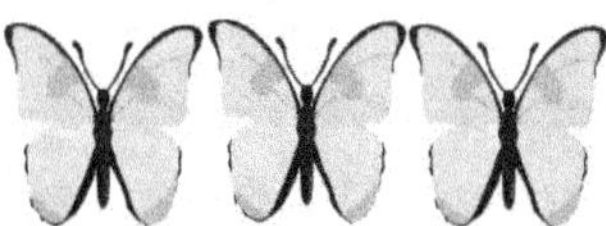

His feelings of happiness gave him a thought as he laid in his own bed that night. He relived the memory of Yolk so why couldn't he relive good memories as well. He decided to go back to one of his days off, his Remorse Day and spy on his G-Pas.

It wasn't complete happiness but there were more good times in that one day than he'd had in the years leading up to it. He snuggled under his blanket and went into his and Drum's shared space. After saying hi and talking with Natum for a bit, he relaxed and thought about the day, every detail vividly seen in his Mind, he pushed out to surround him.

He was back in his memory, in The City, no less. He knew where his G-Pas always went for drinks. He looked up to a bright, clear sky and smiled. It was one of the few days a year this dreadful place received starlight.

He placed a Dome around himself and hurried to the private room his G-Pas owned in a teahouse. Going unnoticed throughout The City felt nice. He smiled, wishing his life could have been like this, an unnoticed individual just living quietly and unbothered.

He made it to the room and quietly sneaked in with the server. He sat in the corner. His G-Pas didn't seem to notice him, and he smiled. They ordered and chatted for a bit about Pantu's upcoming promotional responsibilities and being the first pet with days off, before the server came back with the food and drinks.

After making sure they wouldn't be bothered for a bit, once the server left, both their heads turned and looked directly at him, quietly sitting in the corner. He jumped out of his skin, and he wasn't quite sure if he tried to hide in the wall or crawl up it.

"Come now, we ordered food for you," GMack said, with a smile.

"I am unsure if the wall is okay with you touching it so sensually like that?" GLou joked.

He realized and slowly put his hands down. He looked at his G-Pas with tears in his eyes. "You can see me?" he asked, through the crying.

"Aww, come here, Little PanPan," GMack said, holding his arm out, and while still crying, he went into GMack's arms and hugged him tightly. GLou came around and hugged them as well.

While this was happening, elsewhere in The City, the other him was about to meet someone who wandered in.

DRUM: A SURPRISE GONE WRONG, OR RIGHT? WHO CAN TELL ANYMORE?
WEEK FIVE: FRIDAY

He set an alarm on his phone, quickly made a Portal to his bedroom, and lay down to sleep. He wasn't supposed to be home; he was currently working in the open part of The Desertlands with some of his Record Label's artists.

It was daytime there and he planned his schedule to be free during this time. He wanted to surprise Pantu in their RMD. He arrived as Pantu was talking to Natum but before he could leave the forest, the scene changed.

He was now in what he assumed was The City again. The air outside the small café where he was standing was suffocating. He focused on taking small breaths until he was able to comfortably breathe. He looked up to see starlight and the confusion of the air muddled his Mind as someone walked right past him.

The person stopped and turned to look up at him. "Have you not been claimed and trained yet? Untrained servants are not allowed outside without supervision," said the person who looked to be a police officer from the far past.

He didn't say anything but looked around as a small crowd started to gather. He knew he was out of place as his clothes were more modern, and he was taller than everyone here.

"YOU WOULD DARE TO LOOK YOUR BETTERS IN THEIR FACE!?" the police officer shouted, raising a baton high in the air to strike him.

The police officer's hand stopped as a short, young boy stood in front of him. He couldn't see the boy's face, but a familiar feeling settled inside him.

"Forgive him Officer Goya. He is new and unregistered. He will be professionally trained."

The sweet voice made him relax as he realized who was in front of him.

The boy turned and looked up at him. "Head down, eyes averted. A simple trip to get you new clothes and to pick up my Remorse Day gift and you cannot even stay close!" the young boy kindly scolded.

The crowd's murmuring about how this boy was going to punish his new servant had money passing hands.

"It is your Remorse Day, Young Lord Oryn?" the police officer asked, as he took a knee and bowed to this Oryn guy, who looked just like his Pantu. "Sorry to bother you, please forgive me for ruining High Lady Hana Lianhua's sacred day," he said, and Oryn nodded.

The police officer straightened up and said, "I know he will be a well-trained servant under your tutelage, My Young Lord." Then the police officer dispersed the crowd.

Oryn turned towards him. "Walk about three steps behind me and never lift your head, even if you have to drop to your knees," Oryn told him before walking off.

He was surprised and confounded but did as he was told. He noticed how the people looked and whispered about them as they walked. He knew he heard someone say his skin would be a treasure to have and he wanted to strike the person in the face but released his anger with a hard breath.

"It is more of a compliment than you know," Oryn told him as they walked.

His hands were in his pockets as he followed Oryn into a small dark shop.

"Greetings Master Gold. I have come to claim my Remorse gift," Oryn said politely to the shop owner.

The old man grunted and went into the back of his store. Oryn said nothing to him, and he kept quiet, not knowing the rules here. He glanced around the dark and dreary store to see it sold some of everything.

It reminded him of a pawn shop in the less expensive parts of his States hometown. Anything a person could sell was in here. It wasn't a set store, and it seemed like the old man had his hand in some of everything.

Master Gold came back with a box which was placed in front of Oryn and tossed some clothes at him. He looked at Master Gold, who barely gave him more than a glance, before pointing to the back room. He changed as quickly as he could.

My Abilities don't seem to work in this city. They worked the last time, why not now? he asked himself. As he was changing, he heard the conversation between Master Gold and Oryn.

"Where did you pick him up at?"

"Off the street. He was in a bit of trouble."

"You always had a soft spot for strays. Your Senora Madre's home is full of them."

"Yes, it is better than killing a person, because they are new and ignorant."

"I guess. Most newbies have a challenging time accepting their new reality here and try to escape, leading to trouble for their boss. Are you sure this one will not try and run off? He seems a bit high-strung."

"I do not know. My GMa's home is probably the best place to train wondering newbies, since GMack and GLou handle it."

"Well, it is true none of the servants there have ever tried to run away or have been publicly punished. Must be that sweet scent of yours which keeps them there."

He walked out on the comment, unhappy with what it implied. Keeping his eyes down he went to stand behind Oryn in his new but incredibly old clothes. Master Gold tapped his nails on the counter, and he was confused.

"Give him the clothes you were wearing in exchange for the clothes he has given you," Oryn told him, and he reluctantly placed his suit on the counter.

He'd really wanted His Pantu to see him in this custom-made suit of expensive, soft, midnight-blue Vicuna with yellow-ochre stitching.

"You looked really nice in the suit, but it stands out too much here," Oryn said, trying not to laugh at the simple clothes he was now wearing.

He kept on the long-sleeved shirt he was wearing with his suit and when neither Oryn nor Master Gold said anything about it, he figured it was okay and sighed in relief.

Master Gold informed him, "Be careful what you do and say here in public, since the littlest thing could cost your life and endanger Young Lord Oryn as well, seeing as how he vouched for you."

He nodded and Oryn thanked the shop owner again before leaving.

DRUM: THE BANES OF ORYN'S EXISTENCE
WEEK FIVE: FRIDAY

He carefully followed Oryn and as they walked, he was taking in the layout of the place. Even though the starlight was out, the buildings looked sad and depressed as if they cowered in darkness their entire existence.

The people here seemed to not enjoy starlit days as flimsy, old umbrellas and large, ugly hats with colorful feathers seemed to be in fashion. He didn't feel out of place as almost everyone on the street covered everything but their faces. He and Oryn was the only ones with their hands uncovered.

His eyes were down but he was trying to sense anything he could, since he couldn't feel his Energy flowing in him, so he switched to his physical abilities, relying on years of missions and brutal training by Major instead.

He counted the steps he took from Officer Goya to Master Gold's and visualized the width of each of those steps. He remembered the names and heights of the buildings from where he first appeared.

He then repeated the width of each step he took from Master Gold's. He visualized the stone walkway, mapping out each turn they took while quick glances at each building they passed, allowed him to determine the height of his surroundings.

They were in the business and shopping area. He felt like he was back in a time when technology was first created several thousand years ago. Everything was so old and outdated, he wasn't sure if any of it would work outside The City, even in human air.

He was back to a time when wide, metal skirt ball gowns and old-school three-piece suits were the norm for those with money, but the simple linen shirt and pants marked him as poor. The white, thick socks made the hard loafer shoes tight and snug.

He realized from the way everyone else was dressed, he was the only one in linen. They stood out and he knew His Pantu said he was the number one most celebrated person in The City, the number one pet. His Pantu would still receive these looks, even without him here. He also noticed there weren't a lot of people on the streets.

"Most of the year, it is cloudy and dreary. So, when there is starlight, most people stay indoors for the day as their skin would not be able to handle the direct light," Oryn quietly explained as they were walking.

Once they were out of the shopping area, he saw more activity. He noticed metal boxed cars, shiny and new, parked in large parking lots. There were more linen-clothed people on the street carrying boxes and bags to the shiny old cars. The linen people never went past a huge gold line painted on the wide road, nor did any cars. The men carried everything to the gold line and the linen people collected from there.

He could tell the lawns and flowers were fake. The only real greenery was the vines and wall shrubs growing on the buildings, gates, and houses. They moved quietly on the sidewalk as a few cars traveled on the road. He knew Young Lord Oryn was right, there were way more people inside for the day.

"I am unsure if luck is on your side today. We are close to my home," Oryn informed him as they turned a corner to walk right into a small group of people.

These people were different from the Oryn standing in front of him. There were two linen servants, like him, one holding an umbrella over a person and another lightly fanning the person with a huge Burlesque fan made of puffy, colorful feathers. However, Oryn was with him, holding his own gift while he could only walk behind Oryn, helpless.

This person was barely dressed, and he could see the man's pale, milky skin. He was sure if he ever decided to become a medical doctor, the first thing he would do would be to prescribe this person several years of exposed starlight. The man standing in front of them wore what looked like an expensive, jeweled thong. Other than the jewelry which draped the man's wrists, ankles, throat, ears, and shoes, he was naked.

Oryn donned a three-piece suit, and even if he only saw clothes of this design in history books, Oryn made the suit look edible while the pet looked sick. He also noticed; Oryn didn't have a collar on.

"Well, well, well. If *it is* a Pet on his day off, who would know?" the man said to Oryn.

He froze at the voice. It was Tracey. He couldn't see Tracey's face, but he knew the horrible voice of the person who sounded like a smoker of three or four packs of cigarettes a day.

"But Master Tracey, no Pet has ever had a day off!?" one of Tracey's servants said, faking astonishment.

"And no Pet has ever spent the day collarless. Seems like this Pet is and has always been special," Tracey said, which made Oryn bristle at the word.

"What? You do not like being special?" Tracey asked, moving closer to Oryn.

He could tell Tracey was trying to seduce Oryn with his voice and movements. Oryn said nothing nor did he look at Tracey, Oryn looked through him, as if Tracey wasn't there.

"Then give me everything which makes you special and I will put it to good use," Tracey whispered, in his gruff voice.

He quickly realized a crowd formed. How so many people surrounded them without him sensing them, scared him. He could protect Oryn if he needed but it would be without the use of his Abilities.

I will have to use my training instead, he thought, preparing himself.

Oryn said one word, "Bow," and all the servants, even those in the crowd, dropped to their knees. Out of the corners of his eyes, he also saw women quickly nod their heads and the men in suits, bow at the waist. Oryn went to walk past Tracey, showing no emotion.

He heard what should have been whispers, but it was just rather loud, frank conversations in public. They were tactless comments in his eyes, but it seemed to be the norm here to just say whatever you want, if you weren't a servant, or a low-ranking pet.

When the sounds reached his ears, his lowered eyes darted to see several men touching themselves while moaning in public. He was even more shocked by the fact there were linen men under the dresses of women, pleasuring them while other linen men pleasured other parts of the women.

Some women were bent over, being pleased by the men in suits' members while being orally pleased by linen men to the confrontation. Oryn was already more than three steps ahead of him and he went to catch up, but Tracey stepped in front of him.

"Well, what do we have here? What a delectable treat. Is he going to be used to help you during your Final Training?" Tracey asked, as Oryn froze but didn't turn around.

"Come!" was all Oryn said to him, and he sidestepped Tracey but was blocked again by Tracey's servants.

"If you have no intention of wanting to use him for Training, let me have him," Tracey said, while sliding against him.

Can all the people here touch me? The surprise and confusion in his thoughts was written on his face, but Tracey mistaken it as fear.

"There is no reason to be afraid, I can be gentle...when I want to be," Tracey gruffly whispered in his ear.

He felt the force of Tracey roughly being pulled off him.

"Do not *ever...touch* what is not yours." The coldness of Oryn's voice sent a shiver through everyone there. As Oryn slammed Tracey into the nearest wall, he heard the moaning increase. Since his natural sense of smell was as top-tier as an EOR[49], he could tell several people came.

---

[49] *Expert Olfactory = Rare. See Universal Abilities #10*

Tracey slumped down. "You know my Owner will not let you get away with this. Attacking me over a servant will land you in the cells for a few painful lessons on hierarchy," Tracey gloated.

Oryn pulled his whole body down to look Tracey in the eyes before slapping him. Tracey's look of surprise was met with another slap. Every time Tracey looked Oryn in his eyes, he was slapped. After five slaps, which increased force and blood with each hit, Tracey would no longer look Oryn in his face.

"It seems to me like you are only just beginning to understand the hierarchy. My title of Young Lord is a Level you will never reach. MY servants are above EVEN you. They are not for your eyes to enjoy or your hands to touch without my expressed permission.

"Your whore of an owner will do WHAT to me? You say it as if my owner is someone your owner does not fear. You say it as if your owner does not FEAR ME." Oryn's voice control was astounding as he invoked fear into Tracey's eyes and those servants around him.

"Just because someone in The Center paid coins to fuck you does not mean you will ever live here, you fucking simple dick. Know your place," Oryn stated to a now dazed and scared Tracey.

Officer Goya was also in the crowd and Oryn motioned to him. "Make sure they spend a few days in the cells. It would be good if he learned his lessons somewhere where he will not disturb my eardrums with his horrid screaming," Oryn said as he rose to leave.

With those words Tracey found himself. "WHAT!? You cannot order my punishment; you are just a Pet! You have no right!" Tracey spat out in anger.

"As the pet of the future Governess of The City and a Young Lord, he does have the right," a grating voice sounded out.

Everyone in the crowd quickly found their knees on the ground, but he and Oryn.

"Ah, your servant does not know whose presence he is in?" the voice sounded out.

"No, young goddess. He is new and untrained. I am taking him back to my Senor Padres," Oryn said, standing to look the woman in the eyes. "Please forgive him. He will be professionally trained the next time he has the pleasure of being in your glowing presence."

He was at a loss for words, which was probably for the best.

The woman melted at the compliment and placing her hands on Oryn's chest, she cooed at him, "Aaaah, Oryn. I miss you so much. To appease me, let us publicly kill them!" she excitedly offered, pointing at Tracey and his servants, who cowered, mumbling for their lives.

Oryn removed her hands from his chest and took a few steps back. "It is my day off. If killing them makes your day then do it, but it would only be an insult for me to celebrate on my Day of Remorse," Oryn coldly said to her. "You are not supposed to be around me during my days off. It defeats the purpose," Oryn added.

The look which Oryn gave the young woman made him jealous and her shiver in parts he was sure he himself wanted to gut. He continued to say nothing, and it was as if Oryn understood he would never bow to this woman standing in front of him, so Oryn deflected the conversation elsewhere, but only after not taking the blame for having an untrained servant in public.

"Was there a new shipment I was unaware of?" she asked as her attention went back to him.

He kept his eyes down as far as he could, knowing his eye colors would send these simple-eyed people into a frenzy. Most people possessed normal single-colored eyes, but his mixture of eye color was seen around the world as beautiful since less than point zero, zero, one percent of the Beings and humans on this planet possessed two-toned eyes.

It was a rarity and if these people were this interested in his skin, only seeing his face, neck and hands, his eyes would cause them to faint. He understood all this when Oryn told him to drop to his knees if he had to. The small woman went to move towards him, but Oryn's voice stopped her.

"Should I inform Senor Padre Dal our contract has not been upheld, therefore payment is not required?" Oryn asked her, making her blanch underneath the powdery makeup.

She went to hug Oryn, but his hand stopped her again.

"It will always be your choice, no payment or an additional day off?" Oryn coldly said to the woman.

She looked sadly at Oryn, who didn't budge.

"Orrrryyyyyyynnnn. I so spoil you. I have given you quite a lot," she said with a flip of her hair. "You are lucky to have an Owner like me. No other Woman would treat you the way I do." She praised and hugged herself, trying her hardest to look sweet and innocent, but Oryn's face showed no emotion.

"And how your luck changed when I became your pet means nothing to you?" Oryn asked, with a sad voice.

She melted, trying to move closer to Oryn.

"I have let the first violation of our contract bypass us, yet, if you insist on touching me again on my day off, both choices cease to exist and together, become the only option," Oryn informed her.

She paused her advance and after a quick thought, slowly and trying to use sensual movements, she advanced towards Oryn. "Then I guess my only option...is to hug you!" she said and wrapped her arms around Oryn's neck.

He was disgusted by what he was hearing. People already went back to pleasuring themselves in public, some even having sex again as they watched.

Oryn took a deep breath and let it out before wrapping his arms around her waist and hugging her back.

"See! You do miss me!" she said excitedly. "Your penis is as hard as a rock right now!" she said, as she touched Oryn there and all he experienced in the moment was a deep red color fill his Mind and eyes.

"Hmm?" Oryn said as he pushed her back. "I will inform Senor Padre Dal no payment needs to be sent and of the extra day I now have off," Oryn said as he turned to leave. "Come!" Oryn added, and he pushed his Fury down while he walked past the woman, closing his eyes, since she was shorter than him.

"AH MY! He is already Trained to never look his Betters in their eyes. I have hope Senor Padre Tsuyoi will Train him and then you will send him by my room," she said with a giggle, which sounded more like a cackle to him.

"I will make the suggestion to Senor Padre Tsuyoi," Oryn stated, and walked away.

He was so enticed by what happened and the smoothness of it all, he started thinking about His Pantu.

"Control your emotions!" Oryn harshly whispered to him.

He snapped back and pictured the powdery-face woman in his Mind and was instantly soft. He felt Oryn hide a smile while walking in front of him.

"Do not forget about your End of Second-Level Agreements when you come back my darling Oryn. After that, your Final Training will begin," she shouted after them, but Oryn made no move to show he even heard her, he only kept walking, gift in hand, towards his home.

ORYNxDRUM: CALL ME BY MY NAME
WEEK FIVE: FRIDAY

Oryn was refusing to stop or talk before he made it to his house but short of the slow pace he was walking, so he did not draw any more attention to them, it seemed like it was taking forever. When they finally reached the gates of a medieval estate, he hurried inside.

They quickly walked over to the right side of the extremely large, overgrown mansion which looked connected, but anyone could see the thick wall between. He reached the door, quickly opened it, and pulled the male inside.

He peeked out the door windows while he turned the lock and when he was sure no one saw them enter, he slid down to the floor, sighing as if the weight of Torven was lifted from his shoulders.

"Sorry for the trouble, but I thank you for the effort to protect me," the male said, standing in the middle of the foyer, head still down.

He blew out a very loud breath. "You can quit pretending now. We both know you have never bowed your head to anyone before. Master Gold was right, high-strung," he said, as he started to pick himself up from the floor.

The male extended a hand, and he immediately grabbed it and pulled himself up to bump into the male's chest.

"Ahhh," he said, as his eyes searched for somewhere else to look other than this male. *They were willing to strip him of his looks and skin quicker than anyone else who wandered into this hellhole, yet I can see nothing.*

It was an unpleasant thought to have as he took his shoes off to move around the male.

"Servants do not wear shoes inside, only out," he said, as he laid out a pair of slippers for the male to wear.

He felt the male smile while changing shoes.

"Master Gold will have your suit cleaned and ready by tonight, so I suggest you trade it in for some money and then hide out in The Slums," he informed the male. "Too many people have seen you and will be wanting personal time with you or they would want to..." He trailed off leaving the comment unfinished.

He decided to continue, "Even though you are too old to be a pet, you are still a male and if any woman wants to fuck you, as you saw, they can make you in public.

"As long as a male is not a pet or of a higher status, he is free property for any woman. Whether she is married or not means nothing," he said, giving the male an overview of life here. "If you are a man, then you would be off limits as well," he added, quickly glancing at the male's right hand.

"Oh?" the male responded, looking around as they walked into a living room area.

His home was all one spacious room with a curtained off loft above what should be the kitchen. Walking straight in from the foyer on the right was a half bathroom with a flushable toilet and a sink with plumbing.

There were tables along the large windows which housed different animal figurines made from all kinds of materials. Several types of wood and metals made the collection of figurines, mostly of cats and butterflies quite intriguing.

Further past the windows and tables was a stairway to the loft. It was enclosed with two thin, brownish-yellow, silk dividers. To the left, there was the sitting area. There were two loveseat couches facing one long couch with a tea table in the middle. Facing the couches was a single, comfy, oversized chair.

Past the sitting area was a bookshelf filled with books and more tables which were unusual sizes and heights. Some held distinct size animal figurines while others held real plants on them.

The male came into the sitting area to notice a huge painting above his fireplace. It was the centerpiece of his whole home, and the male stood staring at the portrait of him in a barely there midnight-blue cat outfit.

He was sitting with his butt between his covered cat paws, slightly apart. His body was facing away, but his face was turned so everyone could see the blue cat nose complete with whiskers.

The cat ears he wore had one ear down, while he used one of his cat paws to hold him up and the other to cover his mouth. He was shirtless but the tight shorts he wore came down mid-thigh and the connected tail was up and curved. His face innocent.

The male seemed stuck and could only stare at the painting.

"GMack painted it for me," he said, giggling at the male's inability to look away.

"It's...ummm...it's nice!" the male said, finding his voice and sanity again.

"Just nice?" he asked, slowly lowering his eyelashes to blink.

The male's head snapped around to look at him, and he returned what felt like a smile.

"Why doesn't your kitchen have a stove or an oven. Just a fireplace?" the male asked.

"It is against the law for men and males to cook, so I only have a fridge with snacks and a fireplace to make tea. I receive all my prepared food from the main house," he stated, looking at the male with a soft smile.

The male nodded and avoided glancing at him. As the male walked around the room, looking at everything closely, he followed. Every figurine the male picked up and placed back down, he straightened before moving to continue following the male. While he was busy fixing several figurines the male displaced, the male moved slowly up the steps leading to his bedroom.

"Hey! What's up here?" the male asked, walking up a few more steps.

He grabbed the male's arm, trying to pull him back down. The male paused, looking at his efforts with a feeling which screamed 'runt', and he knew what the male wasn't saying, making him pout.

"You cannot go up there! My bedroom is there and only my Intended is allowed in!" he explained as he tried to pull the male back down the stairs.

But the male didn't budge.

"Besides, my G-Pas said I have yet to experience my growth spurt!" He pouted again, making the male move to follow him back downstairs.

As he reached the last step, he tripped, almost falling face first if the male hadn't caught his arm and held him in place until he was beside him. Pulling him straight up into his chest, he felt the male gaze into his eyes or try to.

Oryn eyes looked everywhere but Drum's face. He backed up and placed his hands in his pockets and started lazily looking around again. Oryn didn't follow him this time, but Oryn's eyes never left him.

"You said it's your Remorse Day. How old are you?" he asked.

"It has been sixteen years since I drew my first breath," Oryn informed him.

Oryn's statue didn't help his age either. He knew he looked older, assuming it had something to do with his height, but even short, Oryn seemed mature and knowledgeable.

Seems is the word though, he thought as he took in the sixteen-year-old.

It was unfair to him this boy grew up before his time. In fact, it was his breaking point when children weren't allowed to be children and just enjoy life. It was the main reason he did what he did, so he could place children who lost their parents and or who had to grow up too fast, with families who would care for and raise them as their own.

"You must be rather old, so I will not ask your age. For fear of embarrassment," Oryn said, looking at him with a smile.

His hands went up to his face. "Never...never say that in front of..." He paused, thinking he should be careful with his words. It was as if this Oryn was trying to get him to talk without asking him any questions.

"In front of your Intended," Oryn incorrectly finished.

He laughed. "I don't have one of those," he said, not looking at Oryn.

"Ah! I would think you would be married and a Pa by now, since you have a ring on your finger," Oryn commented.

"I'm only nineteen and this isn't the finger used to declare marriage where I'm from," he said.

The look of disbelief and shock was mixed with suspicion on Oryn's face, and it made him close his eyes and take a deep *I know this runt didn't* breath as Oryn giggled so hard, he tripped over the single comfy chair and landed in it.

"It is only because you are so tall and feel mean looking," Oryn said.

He sucked his teeth, letting it go as he turned to place his hands back in his pockets and look out the window.

He could feel Oryn wanted his look to be redirected and he turned to look at Oryn, whose face held a look of sweet surprise.

"Young Lord Oryn, what shall we do now?" he asked and smiled at the way Oryn was lazily propped up in the chair.

"Do not call me by a name which does not belong to me," Oryn told him, looking away from him.

He took a few steps closer. "Then, instead of Young Lord, shall I call you, "Our Highness"?" he teased, and Oryn looked at him and smiled.

"I am not a prince!" Oryn said giggling, making it his turn to look away.

Oryn looked down and whispered, *"Even though I am not wearing my collar right now, I am still a pet. Like the one you met today, Tracey. Oryn is the name she gave me when I became her pet.*

"But my family calls me Pantu. I still love my name. It reminds me of all the fun and love we held for each other, before..." Oryn, now wanting to be called Pantu explained.

"You can never say my name in public, or my punishment will be extremely painful. When I refused to answer to the name Oryn, she forced it on me. My G-Pas told me they would always call me Pantu, but to keep me from experiencing additional punishment, they only call me Pantu when we are alone," Young Pantu informed him.

The look of sadness and hopelessness made him want to tell Young Pantu things would get better, but he felt something was way too off for him to be sprouting of future events, even in a memory. So, he leaned down in the chair and hugged Young Pantu instead.

When Young Pantu hugged him back, he fell into the chair. After a moment, he leaned to stand up but was held in place by Young Pantu's hands clutching his shirt.

Looking at him. "*What is your name. I will call you by your name, even after my GMa changes it,*" Young Pantu asked, so softly he was tempted to kiss this young guy.

"Xavier," he told Young Pantu.

Young Pantu looked delighted. "It is such a beautiful name, Xavier," Young Pantu said, trying it out.

He looked away into the creases of the chair and caught his breath as his name came out of Young Pantu's mouth.

"*Pantu!*" he whispered into Young Pantu's ear and watched as it turned bright red. He lightly blew on Young Pantu's ear, making him shiver and his body turn a darker shade of red. He nibbled on the deep red earlobe and heard a small moan escape Young Pantu's mouth.

XAVIER: A GUEST FOR TEA
WEEK FIVE: FRIDAY

"What in the fuck is going on here?" He heard a voice from the doorway ask.

Young Pantu pushed and kicked him off onto the floor and scurried to stand.

He stared at the two old…or young…he couldn't tell their exact ages, men standing in the entrance. One of the men was rather buff and almost as big as Major. The man looked like he could possibly make him sweat in a non-Ability fist fight while the other was dainty, slender and looked flexible enough to pretzel his body.

They were both about Xavier's height and he understood why Young Pantu thought he was older than he was. He remembered the rule and lowered his eyes. He didn't know why these men were here and if he had to fight, he could probably take them, but where would that leave This Pantu? The rest of his thoughts were cut off by Young Pantu going to the two men and hugging them.

"GMack, GLou, you are here!" Young Pantu exclaimed, not answering the question.

He was very tempted to look at these men again, now knowing who they were, but kept his eyes down as he wasn't sure how they would react. He wasn't their beloved grandson and after the scene they walked in on, he was betting his Fate might be worse than Yolk. He invoked a reaction out of Young Pantu that would cost This Pantu his life if the wrong person were to figure this out.

My Pantu would never forgive me if I hurt his G-Pas, even if it's to save my own life. He's willing to come back to this horrid place just for a chance at their freedom, he thought as he tried to figure a way out of this unbelievably unpleasant situation.

One of Young Pantu's G-Pas walked over to him. "Who is this young male?" the slender man he thought was GLou asked.

"I have yet to see him around The Center," the other man added.

"I think he might have somehow made his way into The Center. I found him on the street about to be beaten by Officer Goya," Young Pantu explained, somewhat pleading with his voice.

"So, she has Officer Goya…" who he thought was GMack started.

"…following you on your days off?" Possible GLou finished asking.

"Yes. Every time I leave the estate, he is somewhere close," Young Pantu answered, disheartened.

"Did he see the two of you..." Possible GLou started.

"...enter your home?" Possible GMack asked.

Young Pantu shook his head. "I kept him busy by throwing Pencil Penis into a cell for private lessons!" Young Pantu answered, happily swaying his head side to side while conducting an orchestra with his hands.

"Also, there is to be no payment sent to her for the next four days, as she violated the contract," Young Pantu said, with a smile to the slender man. Young Pantu turned to look at the buff man standing next to him. "She wants you to personally train him and send him to her."

He was figuring out who was GMack and who was GLou. *Senor Padre Dal. Dal is an old Earth Korean name. Mr. Moon is of Korean descent, so Senor Padre Dal would be his Pa and the one who handles This Pantu's contracts. Senor Padre Tsuyoi. Tsuyoi is an old Earth Japanese name, so he would be Mrs. Sky's Pa and This Pantu's bodyguard.*

He made the connection his trainer was to be the buff man standing closer to the door, probably in case he tried to run. *Which means the man standing before me is GMACK!?*

He always imagined how GMack and GLou looked since His Pantu never described their physical attributes. He had it backwards. He would have never guessed GLou would be so built and sturdy, being a theater actor and for some reason, he thought GMack would be big, like a Mac semi-truck, all based on a name.

Book, cover, was all he thought as he shook his head and smiled to himself. *This family never ceases to amaze me.*

"Why is he still on the ground," GMack started to ask, still standing over him and GLou finished, "acting as if he has ever bowed to anyone before?"

Young Pantu laughed. "He is new here. In the Center. He must learn, right?" Young Pantu asked.

"He will not be a good servant to have," GLou stated, looking at him weirdly.

Young Pantu looked upset. "But you two are the best trainers around. Surely you can train him properly as well. I have never had a servant before." Young Pantu pouted while stomping his foot and crossing his arms.

Both men turned to look at Young Pantu as he slowly stood up and smiled.

"It is not about training him..." GLou started.

"...it is about keeping him away from everybody," GMack ended.

"Why? Is it because they would want to strip him?" Young Pantu sadly asked.

Both men slowly nodded, but he could see there was more behind the nod then the two men let on.

Young Pantu seemed to realize it as well. "*I told him selling his suit and hiding in The Slums would be the safest option for him,*" Young Pantu mumbled.

He realized Young Pantu misread the situation and his G-Pas' meaning.

GLou huffed. "Seems like you have been either inattentive with your own lessons..."

GMack shook his head. "...or maybe, he is overly distracted?" He tried to smooth out.

GMack sat on the loveseat to the left of him and GLou walked to the one on his right and sat down. GMack looked at Young Pantu, and he went into what is considered a kitchen for males and lit a fire. He stood up from the fire to look out into the sitting area.

"I only have chamomile tea," Young Pantu stated, not giving anyone a chance to object.

As Young Pantu was busy making platters, the two men focused their attention on him.

"Well, this is the first time..." GLou said.

"...a guest has visited Pantu in his home before," GMack ended.

He was seeing what Pantu meant when he said his G-Pas were two sides of the same coin. Almost every sentence was split into two with them finishing each other's spoken thoughts. He overlooked the meaning behind those words and sat down.

"Sooooo...where did you come from?" GMack asked.

He looked back and forth between them.

"Stay on your toes," GLou joked.

He smiled. He saw Pantu got his playfulness from more than his Ma.

"Feeling a bit restricted..." GMack seemed to ask.

"...as if you cannot breathe properly?" GLou ended.

He nodded.

"It takes generations..." GLou said.

"...upon generations," GMack added.

"...for one to be born able to breathe properly here..." GLou said.

"...in The Center. Outside of the Inner Ring..." GMack begin to explain with a shrug of his shoulders.

"...you would probably be able to adjust better," GLou added.

"Yes Sirs," he answered, understanding he would have to leave The Center in order to eventually be able to use any of his Abilities.

"How long…" GLou started again.

"…do you plan on staying?" GMack inquired.

He rose to leave. "I should go before—" He was interrupted by GMack.

"You have the ultimate pleasure of being served Pantu's chamomile tea?" GMack teased.

GLou motioned to him. "Sit down, we have not exchanged names yet," GLou stated to him, and he sat back down, looking between the two of them.

He liked how they divided his attention to opposite sides of the room and used the seconds between him looking from one to the other to communicate. They wouldn't allow him to be out of their sight.

Sitting here, in Young Pantu's home, being served tea by him, was a big deal in this place and he felt fear. For the first time in the longest, he was a literal threat. These young-looking old men knew he was a Being.

I should say Others when speaking to them. They already know I'm not from here, that's pretty obvious. I thought it was just his bedroom he'd never invited anyone into, but apparently, it's his whole home. His G-Pas have unfettered access but that's to be expected, given their relationship with Pantu.

But here is a strange man in their beloved grandson's home, *making him blush, no less. I wouldn't want me out of my own sight as well. They will want to get me away from The Center as soon as they can, away from their grandson. They told me all of this with a simple conversation. I think I might have messed up. If they kill me…*his thoughts stopped for a moment. *I need to be careful what I say.* He felt something was off.

These men only looked at him, they may have spoken, but he felt as if it were to direct the conversation a certain way. All that was still inconsistent with the fact they didn't bother to finish the conversation or ask him additional questions about himself. His thoughts were interrupted by Young Pantu coming to sit a platter on the long coffee table, while sitting down on his knees to serve the tea.

"How do you like your new tea table?" GLou asked, still looking at him.

"It is quite the modern item for any sitting area," Young Pantu said, slightly bouncing.

He knew Young Pantu was happy, but for what reason, he was unsure.

"Thank you for the tea table GLou. And GMack, your portrait of me, is more than nice, as my guest commented," Young Pantu slyly said, not bothering to look at the terror on his face.

He looked between GMack and GLou and he was about to close his eyes, when he noticed Young Pantu was pouring his cup first.

Isn't it supposed to go from the host's left and around? Why would he pour my tea first?

He looked at GLou, who was on the edge of the sofa, with his elbows on his knees, and his hands folded between his legs, staring directly at him. He looked at GMack, who was sitting back comfortably, his legs crossed, his arm around the back end of the sofa, also staring at him.

Something definitely isn't right; I have got to get out of here.

Young Pantu finished serving the tea and placing the snacks on the table, he moved to snuggle in between GLou and the sofa arm, directly to his right.

Of course, they like to throw everybody off. They're amazing! I didn't even have time to process before they redirected the conversation to throw off my thoughts. Calm down Xavier. But his attention was now on the fact he could hear Inner Drum calling out to him. He felt weird.

"They can read your Mind, be careful, they can read your Mind, be careful…" played out over and over inside him, not in his thoughts, but in his Core.

Ohhh, I thought so. I have to find a way out of here and back to my home.

He started thinking of ways to get out of The City and as his Mind flipped through millions of possible routes, he noticed GMack and GLou looked away from him, collecting their own thoughts. His only focus was on how to get out of The City, and his thoughts were overbearing to GLou and GMack.

"I heard GMack ask you earlier where you are from, but I did not hear your response?" Young Pantu asked him.

He looked at Young Pantu. "I didn't give it," he said calmly. "Where I come from doesn't matter. I need to get back there," he responded before turning to look at his tea.

Young Pantu made his tea exactly how he liked it but used fresh ingredients. The vanilla beans were cut and steeped in the tea as he could still see the tiny beans floating. The sweet smell was mixed with the scent of fresh honey and lemons.

"The ingredients are really fresh, I picked them all from my garden, just this morning!" Young Pantu proudly said.

The gasp unintentionally left his mouth. "YOU? You garden?" he said, before trying hard not to laugh in Young Pantu's face. "You just don't seem the type," he said, as a small laugh escaped.

Young Pantu stared at him indignantly. "Being able to afford greenery and the upkeep in this environment, is a sign of wealth here. Being able to grow a garden is a Talent few have here," Young Pantu coolly stated, his eyes steady.

He glanced outside and back at Young Pantu. "Seems difficult with so much starlight," he commented, with a smirk.

Young Pantu took a deep breath and rolled his eyes. "How ignorant," Young Pantu stated.

Young Pantu looked back towards his face and the calm demeanor he held and glanced down at his teacup.

He understood, no one would drink before the guest. They already established he wasn't ever going to be a servant with him sitting in Young Pantu's home, with slippers on, he smiled and laughed out loud.

I was set up from the beginning. He leaned forward, placing his elbows on his knees and his forehead into the raised, laced fingers. *I chose to wear the slippers offered; I fell right into it*. He groaned; *how could a surprise go so wrong. I want to see HIM, just one last time before I…* but his thoughts were cut off by a huff from Young Pantu.

He raised his head to look at Young Pantu's face of jealousy, and he tried to hide his smile. He took a deep breath and reached for his cup. "Hmm…there is tea, honey, lemon and vanilla in this cup, all fresh, right?" he asked, as he took a sip while looking at Young Pantu, who gave him a *"you are a weirdo for asking"* look back. He slowly moved his eyes to glance at GMack, who laughed.

"It seems we will be spending the next four days training," GLou said, looking at Young Pantu, who sighed in disappointment.

"You have yet to learn how to read the room under certain circumstances," GMack added.

He understood Young Pantu couldn't read Minds, so his G-Pas were teaching him how to "read the room" but really, Young Pantu should be reading emotions and intent.

Why does it seem like he isn't able to sense my intent? he thought.

"Because it has never been hostile towards him," GMack said inside of his Mind, making him freeze slightly before taking another sip.

He continued raising the cup to his lips as the shock settled. He took another sip. "I thought all the food here would be bland and tasteless. Why is this tea so delicious?" he asked, mostly to change his thoughts.

"I grew everything myself!" Young Pantu said, proudly. "This tea is limited and very expensive to purchase."

His surprised look as he turned towards Young Pantu was laced with a smile. "You run a business!?" he asked, shocked and amused.

Young Pantu shook his head. "My G-Pas handle all of that, I just grow the ingredients," Young Pantu nonchalantly said.

"That makes more sense," he said, still smiling.

Young Pantu's expression changed quickly to one of indignant pride. "Excuse you?" he asked, as his G-Pas were hiding their smiles.

He finished his tea and Young Pantu was busy making him some more.

"We assume, you would want to leave..." GMack started.

"...but it would be impossible for you to physically leave," GLou finished.

His face and thoughts showed no intention of giving up. He stared at GLou, unsure if he knew what saying *that* word in front of him meant.

"Wait...you want to leave?" Young Pantu asked, slightly panicked.

"I have to get back," he softly said, looking at Young Pantu.

The look in Young Pantu's eyes hurt him to his heart, but he couldn't stay here.

"Is there someone you have to get back to?" Young Pantu asked, scared.

He nodded.

"I thought you did not have an Intended?" Young Pantu coldly asked.

"I don't. But there is someone who I deeply care for back home," he gently said.

XAVIER: A REMORSE DAY TO REMEMBER
WEEK FIVE: FRIDAY

Young Pantu was visibly upset, casting his eyes down and refusing to look at anyone. Whatever Young Pantu was thinking was clearly written all over his face.

"Pantu," GMack's calm voice pulled Young Pantu back from his thoughts and anger. Turning to face him, GMack asked, "What is your name?"

He didn't look at GMack but at GLou. "Xavier," he answered, and both the young-looking, old men laughed.

He figured it out. The voice inside his head almost sounded like the voice GLou used to speak for GMack. He was highly trained so he could hear the slightest vocal change and the shock of hearing GMack's real voice inside his head helped him to understand.

This tea was helping him regain his Abilities and he was slowly feeling his Energy return, but his training never faltered. He also understood GMack was the biggest threat to him in the room. GLou was using a ventriloquist method to speak for GMack.

There was one of three reasons, the first was GMack was mute and could only speak into someone's Mind. The second was GMack and GLou were being playful, and the third was if GMack were to speak, who could deny him? He felt the first reason was by choice and to keep the choice hidden, GLou spoke for him.

This only added to the playfulness these two had to make people think they were being childish all while covering up GMack's "Talent" to the humans. He wondered how far apart the "Talent" would work and received an answer to his unspoken question.

"It does not matter…" GLou started.

"…how far apart we are…" GMack pretended to say.

"…it works all over The City," GLou ended, both of them smiling at him.

Young Pantu still hadn't caught on to what he knew, and it was making him smile.

"You must really be upset he called you ignorant earlier…" GLou started.

"…that you just had to make him the butt of an unspoken joke," GMack thought inside his head.

Well, everybody's head as Young Pantu looked shocked his G-Pas would openly expose their Talents in front of him.

"He figured it out a while ago…" GMack thought out.

"...he was just waiting for the right time to show us," GLou finished out loud.

"Definitely had nothing to do..." GMack thought.

"...with you calling him out," GLou said.

The three of them laughed at the look on Young Pantu's face as he realized he read the whole situation wrong. Young Pantu looked between both his G-Pas and started to pout.

"He is not like us, Pantu and you know this is fact," GLou said.

"He has to go back..." GMack leaned forward, "...there is no way of knowing, what will happen if he does not." GMack's voice sounded inside everyone's Mind.

"We have a way. One and only one way. To get you out." GMack told only him and GLou.

"Save it for when you really need it. It wouldn't be of any use to me," he said, thinking, *"I need to find him. He must be here, if I am."*

"Gone," GMack thought only to GLou and him.

The look of shock on his face at being left behind caused annoyance to flash across Young Pantu's face.

A thought passed his Mind; *how can I still be here but HE is not?*

"Was anyone else informed you would be here?" GLou asked, with a knowing smile.

They already met him here. They know more than I could have ever told them, just from seeing him. They even offered the one way out of The City to me, knowing it would trap Pantu here forever.

Playful. Now how to get out of this situation without giving away anything else. His thoughts were interrupted by Young Pantu roughly dropping his cup back onto the saucer.

He turned to look at Young Pantu, and a smile slowly crossed his face. "I was planning a surprise for someone and ended up here instead," he said, his eyes never leaving Young Pantu's face.

"If you want, we can take you to a place which would help you regain your Talents," GLou offered. "It would take a few days to get there..." he started.

"...but time works differently here," GMack informed him.

Young Pantu knew they were purposefully leaving him out of certain parts of the conversation and pouted.

"Thank you, very kindly Sirs, but I think I figured out a way..." he stated, smiling.

Young Pantu forgot he was pouting, to blush and look away. "You said you were planning a surprise for someone, is it for your Intended?" Young Pantu asked, not looking at him while wiggling his body to stop blushing.

"Do you wish an Intended on me that badly?" he asked, still smiling at Young Pantu's reaction.

"Wearing a ring on any finger here means you have an Intended or you are already married," Young Pantu said with a shrug. "Who would you be planning a surprise for, if not your Intended or your wife?"

He heard the jealousy in Young Pantu's voice, and he fought not to laugh while reaching for his tea, but the cup was pushed away.

Young Pantu's arms crossed and huffed at him as if to say, "*you will get nothing more from me if you like someone else*" with his whole body.

His wide-eyed shock only reinforced his decision. Did Young Pantu's G-Pas offer him several days with the young man, yes...yes, they did. But he turned them down, not knowing the ramifications of his actions.

"Where I come from, there is only one finger a ring can be on to show you are Intended or married. Since I have no ring on said finger, I have neither," he answered. "*The surprise was for the person I care for*," he gently stated and quickly glanced at GMack and GLou.

"Do you not know if this person cares for you? Why do so much for someone who may not be willing to return your feelings?" Young Pantu bluntly asked.

"I do it so I can see this person smile," he said, smiling gently at Young Pantu, who blushed again. "It makes me happy, knowing I can make them smile. I want to make their Dream a reality and I'm willing to spend the rest of my life doing just that," he explained.

Young Pantu looked up at him in surprise. "You want to marry this person?" Young Pantu asked, upset.

He said nothing more. He said what he needed to Young Pantu's G-Pas. He knew they understood since they knew he came here with His Pantu and was unknowingly left behind.

He knew they understood he wasn't from here and neither was the Pantu they met earlier. GMack and GLou knew a lot more than they let on, but he could see it, he could understand what they were implying.

He moved around the room, first opening the fridge and glancing inside. He snickered at the lack of sweets, but there was an abundance of veggies and fruits. As he leaned up and closed the door, Young Pantu fell into his trap once he followed.

"What is so amusing about the items in my fridge?" Young Pantu asked with a haughty attitude.

He said nothing but walked around to touch and slightly move each figurine on the tables leading up to the bookshelf. GMack and GLou said nothing as they let him make his own choice.

He pulled at one of the shelves on the bookcase while Young Pantu was busy straightening the figurines and mumbling to himself, detaching it from the wall to swing open. Young Pantu looked up surprised as he looked behind the shelf and pulled out a small painting of a tall, dark blue flame, holding hands with a small boy about five or six.

He showed Young Pantu and asked, "What's this? WHO is this? YOUR Imaginary Friend?" he joked, with a silly smile.

"It is you, silly. The Burning Boy," Young Pantu answered, and he paused before looking at the painting again.

Is this how he's seeing me right now? How could he not be afraid of a big ball of fire kissing on his neck? He thought to himself, but as he gazed at the painting, it was of a small Pantu. Meaning, Pantu met him several times before but only saw him as a burning blue flame who speaks. *Wait, how could everyone else see me as a normal person but Pantu doesn't?*

"I cannot see your True Self, something is blocking me from seeing who you are," Young Pantu answered. "It is what crossed your Mind, no?" Young Pantu asked, putting the last of the figurines back in place and turned to take the painting out of his hand to put it back.

But he opened the shelf wider and went to press the small gold button inside.

Young Pantu yelped and grabbed his wrist before he could press it. "Why would you press a button, when you know not what it does?" Young Pantu asked him, shocked and the playful smile he gave made Young Pantu melt.

"Because it's pushable!" he responded with a shrug, reaching again to press the button, only to smile at Young Pantu's whimpers for him to stop.

He had no idea he would be attracted to City Pantu, and this surprised him. He didn't think he would ever meet This Pantu, and he had to know. "You don't find it strange a big ball of blue fire has been coming to see you since you were a kid?" he asked, as he took the painting from Young Pantu and placed it back.

Young Pantu shook his head. "It was worse when you had no form. You gave me scary dreams, but you told me to think of you as something I find comforting. I asked you what your favorite color is, and you told me, just blue.

"You were always so warm, like a campfire, so it is how you became a ball of blue fire and not a faceless, scary, tall male," Young Pantu told him, looking at him sadly. "But it would mean nothing for you to remember, since your Mind is filled with someone else...*even as I stand before you.*"

The soft whisper at the end hurt him to his heart and he turned away from Young Pantu to walk around, his eyes looking up to land on the big portrait. He stopped and just stared at it again, keeping his Mind completely blank.

"You can always commission one to be painted," GLou said, making GMack laugh as GLou snickered at his inability to look away.

"You should fix the shelf," he stated, finally pulling his eyes away. "Anyone with a trained eye can tell it's false," he added.

"Well, we will take it into consideration, in case Pantu invites anyone else into his home," GLou joked as GMack was now crying tears while laughing.

He couldn't help but love these two men sitting on the sofas. He saw everything which made them special to His Pantu and while he might have said it in order to keep His Pantu from doing a suicide mission, now, he really wanted to come get them. He smiled as he felt these feelings instead of thinking them. He decided to keep to his plan to leave.

"GMack painted it as a gift for my Remorse Day," Young Pantu said, proudly.

"This Remorse Day?" he asked nervously but relaxed when Young Pantu nodded his head.

"And you received a tea table. So, gifts are given on Remorse Day?" he asked, cautiously.

"Normally, only your Ma receives a gift, but my G-Pas have always snuck and given me a gift on my Remorse Day. It is also something we do not share with anyone else," Young Pantu said, informing him that he was being told a lot of things no one else knew.

YOUNG PANTU: REMORSE GIFTS, FREELY GIVEN
WEEK FIVE: FRIDAY

"If I knew, I would have brought a Gift," Xavier stated, walking to the tables in front of the window.

Xavier started moving figurines slightly until he switched them into different spots, twisting them around to distract and annoy him further. As he arranged the figurines back, Xavier went up the stairs and threw back the cover to his bedroom.

"Wow, I like this idea of covering open spaces!" Xavier commented, walking into his room.

He was immediately behind Xavier, trying to pull the male back out. "Only my Intended may enter my room!" he cried out. "GMack, GLou, help!" he yelled at them.

Xavier walked up to the bookshelf in his room, pulling him along as he was hanging from Xavier's arm. He turned to look at both his G-Pas standing in the doorway of his room. They looked around and closed the curtain, before he heard them walking back downstairs, whispering amongst themselves.

He dropped his hands from around Xavier's arm and stared at the young male in front of him. "How could you come in?" he asked, his face showing no emotion.

"I walked in, just like you did," Xavier replied, flipping through a book. "Why do these books have words in them, but the ones downstairs don't?" Xavier asked, looking back at him.

"How did you get through the Dome around my room?" he bluntly asked.

"What Dome?" Xavier asked, looking around to notice the opening in the Dome at the doorway.

"You would walk through my Dome while holding another in your heart?!" he stated, his anger apparent in his voice and his action of snatching the book out of Xavier's hand and tossing it across the floor.

As Xavier whispered his name, he felt himself falling onto his bed, his wrists being held above his head by only one of Xavier's hands. When he caught his breath, he was livid! He was never handled by a man or male in such a way!

He glared at Xavier, even knowing the Blue Flame's name didn't help to put a face to him. But he could feel what the flame was feeling, and it was directed at him.

As he whimpered and wiggled under the flame, he felt his legs being pushed open and the flame settle in between. He moaned as he felt his skin heat up.

"I am highly upset. Would you handle me in such a way? You brought no Gift for my Remorse Day, and you have found another to call your own," he started, barely raising his voice. "Why come to see me if you do not want to be here? Why hurt me so?" he asked, close to tears.

Xavier paused from inhaling his scent by way of his neck and asked, "Have I always brought a Gift for your Remorse Day?"

"You started the tradition when I was but a baby, and my G-Pas thought it a good idea," he answered, and Xavier nodded.

"You said one day, you would come here and know nothing," he whispered. *"But I did not know, it was due to another being in your heart,"* he sadly ended, whispering to Xavier.

"Paaaaannnnnnttttttuuuu" Xavier whispered in his ear, making his body try and run from the sheer force of emotions laced into Xavier's tone.

The weight from Xavier's body on top of his, made him unable to do more than squirm and whimper, much less, get away. "If you do not want me, then stop coming here. Leave me alone. Find someone else to tease and annoy, GeGe."

Xavier's grip on him tightened before asking him about the name and was told, "Because today was the first day you ever told me your name. It upsets me everyone else can see you, but I cannot. At first, only I could see you as a shadow man, but once I told my G-Pas about you, they told me they could see you as well.

"My parents never believed you were real, so they never saw you. But today, everybody could see you, what you really look like. But you have always been faceless and mostly formless to me. Do you hide yourself from me because you do not like me?" he asked.

"I don't know why only you see me this way. But one day, I will find a way to show you. I will show you everything," Xavier gave his word.

"Give me my Remorse Day Gift," he demanded, still stuck under the blue flame and unable to move his arms.

Xavier laughed. "I have no physical Gift. What would you like instead?"

"A Vow." The words weighed heavily in the room.

"I can't Vow anything that will contradict Vows already made," Xavier informed him.

"You would restrict me?" he asked, looking at Xavier with such innocence that Xavier looked away.

"It would kill me," Xavier answered, turning back to look at him.

He looked away. "It is as if you know not of our Vow to give me a Gift every year. So, I will request it as my Gift for this year," he said, not directly asking Xavier to Vow.

"I will find a way to bring you a Gift, every year, on your Remorse Day," Xavier answered.

"Okay, then thank you kindly for my Gift," he said, trying to end the conversation and stand.

Xavier held him down and he could feel the flame smiling. "Anything else, Our Highness would want on his Remorse Day?" Xavier teased him by moving his hand underneath his shirt to touch his cool, smooth, soft skin, making them both shiver.

His voice was quiet as he answered, "*If it belongs only to you, and no one else, I would like your ring?*" His eyes held hope as he looked at the blue flame, he knew his whole life.

He started off as a faceless male and scared baby Pantu once. But the faceless male didn't show back up until he was two, and that's when he told his parents and G-Pas.

When he was three, the faceless male returned, with a gift. That was the year his G-Pas started secretly giving him gifts for his Remorse Day.

When he was four, he was asleep when the faceless male appeared in his room at night, leaving a gift. He woke up to the quiet in the air and saw the faceless male beside his bed, with a wrapped gift on the floor, next to his head.

It was also when he realized, he always received a gift from the faceless male even when he thought he had not. He was never hurt by him, in fact, the faceless male felt warm and inviting.

He hugged the faceless male and whispered, "*Thank you, but you do not have a face, and it is quite scary,*" in the male's ear.

The faceless male smiled but he could only feel it, not see it.

"Then imagine me as something not so scary," the faceless male thought inside his head.

He couldn't see anything which would help him remember the male's face and he pouted. "*What is your favorite color?*" he whispered.

"*Blue.*" The answer was said in his head.

"Just blue?" he thought, and the faceless male shrugged.

He smiled and imagined a tall blue flame, the darker colors starting from the middle of his chest and was a shade lighter spreading out.

"Burning Boy," he thought inside his head, looking at the beautiful blue flame in front of him.

Burning Boy nodded and Pantu felt him smile. Burning Boy laid him back down and covered him up, patting him on the head until he drifted back off. Every year after that, no matter where he was, Burning Boy would come to find him and give him a gift.

Burning Boy would also come and leave books, with GLou teaching him how to read well above his age and giving GMack painting supplies for him. Of course, his G-Pas hid all of the gifts in their secret place they would visit some nights.

Xavier relaxed at the look on his face. "One day, I will."

The statement left dead air between them as he looked at Xavier, surprised.

"But what about the person already in your heart. Will they not be upset?" he asked, his surprise turned into a shy glance at Xavier.

"They will understand and come to terms with my decision," Xavier answered, his voice devoid of any doubt.

He nodded and giggled, happy to hold on to hope that one day he would have the one item Xavier kept on his person, *I can hold on until then*, he thought.

"There's one more thing, isn't there?" Xavier questioned.

He could feel the inquiry was genuine.

"I have lived so long here, unable to leave. But you can come and go as you please," he looked up at Xavier, "I do not want to spend the rest of my life here."

Xavier froze and stared at him.

"I would like for you to take me from here," he said to Xavier.

"One day I will take you far from here. Give me time," Xavier answered.

He smiled. "I believe you. You have come every Remorse Day, so I shall be patient but just know, by the new year, she wants to subject me to final training. I am unwilling to boost her status any further by having male trainers."

While Xavier may not have known exactly what final training was, he knew he didn't want to experience it. Xavier nodded and the simple gesture was enough to get him through whatever came his way, until Xavier could get him out of here. He could wait.

Xavier stared into his eyes, and he saw a light flicker behind where he thought Xavier's eyes would be before Xavier's lips found his and he was wrapped in a warmth he'd never experienced before with such a cold body. When Xavier released his wrists, he wrapped his arms around Xavier's neck and responded by sinking deeper into the kiss, allowing Xavier's feelings to envelop him.

PANTUxDRUM: A MEMORY REWRITTEN
WEEK FIVE: FRIDAY

Pantu was already sitting back in the field meadow, dancing and singing with Natum. He was happy after his trip to see his G-Pas. The last Remorse Day he vividly remembered was Yolk and the thought made him shiver. He only wanted to go back to memories which weren't traumatizing, and his sixteenth Remorse Day was uneventful. At least, it always seemed to be.

Wait, did I kiss Burning Boy? No, his name is Xavier. When did I know his name? My sixteenth Remorse Day, the Burning Boy Xavier, we kissed?

As he tried to remember, he saw the memory replay in his head. Burning Boy, caught on the streets of The Center, everybody but him being able to see Burning Boy, being the first and only guest in his home, walking through the Dome set by his G-Pas, giving his word to give him his ring, to take him from The City, kissing him.

Is that really how it went? He fell back into his younger self, or more like he was pulled as he heard a call to him.

"…"

He was on his bed, Burning Boy on top of him, staring into his eyes. He still couldn't see Xavier's face, but he felt a familiar warmth, smelled a familiar scent. When Xavier kissed him, he felt Xavier's feelings pouring into him.

"Return."

The word sounded in his Mind, and he was back in the field meadow, the starlight bright and blinding. He quickly tried to get used to the light as he looked around him. He was alone in the field meadow. The Burning Boy didn't return with him?

Did Xavier realize I was not THAT Pantu and forced me out? I do not remember anything much after that. He sat confused in the field meadow.

If Burning Boy and he kissed, what could he possibly say to Drum? He never remembered this before and here was a vivid memory of him passionately kissing another person. A male at that.

He told Dill and The Four he'd personally never liked anyone before, but was the Burning Boy even human? He was the only one who saw him as a blue flame and everyone else saw him as human, so he was a real person, right?

He sat in stupor, trying to figure out this new memory and why he was short a figurine, while Natum gently lay on his shoulder.

DRUM

Drum was back in the woods, outside of the field, where he was when Pantu first went into the memory, and he touched his pocket.

He was in his room again and he went to sit up in his bed to look down at his clothes. He was in the same clothes he wore in The City, which meant his own clothes were now sitting somewhere in Master Gold's shop in The Center.

He pulled the cat figurine out of his pocket, wondering when Young Pantu would realize it was missing. It was the cat Young Pantu's painting portrait was based on. He moved to sit on the side of his bed to look at his bedside table.

There was a yellow ochre, wooden, photo frame with two photos, one of Pantu's nametag and one of his. He also placed the photos they took at the mall around the frame inserted in smaller, midnight-blue, wooden frames. He placed the figurine next to his frame and stood up from his bed to stretch.

Less than an hour passed since he came back to surprise Pantu, his lunch break. He didn't have time to think it over as cleanly as he needed to, but once he concluded that even though Pantu never talked about his first crush, he did tell them he was never interested in anyone.

He knew there would be some confusion. But seeing as it happened before he went back and changed the future, he was sure Win wouldn't care, and Sport would accept what he was told as truth. Even if there was no explanation for it, if he said it was true, Sport believed him, unconditionally.

Queen would need to be told beforehand. Mostly so he could figure this out with a partial party and a little bit because he knew his best friend would be overly excited to hear it firsthand and get to help him understand it. He smiled to himself, it was really so he could see Queen explode, with him giving his best friend a personal gift.

Queen was a Dreamer. The best gift for him was turning his Dreams into reality. One of Queen's Dreams was to meet a Being with Abilities crazier than his and he was about to tell Queen Pantu could travel back in time through his memories.

He wouldn't miss it for the world. His smile grew as his clothes changed into a custom, tailor-made, dark blue suit, with black cufflinks with the initial DxS in gold. He opened a Portal into his office and went back to work.

PANTUxDELIVERY MALE: A FAIR EXCHANGE
WEEK FIVE: SATURDAY

Pantu was packed and ready for the night. He couldn't believe his parents would allow him to go off with friends and spend the night at a campsite. His parents were really relaxed about his restrictions when it came to a lot of what he wanted to do here.

Social media and the intranet were still off limits, as was his camera and any apps, but he could move around with a lot more freedom than he'd previously had in the last four plus years.

Some of the restrictions before were because of mental institutions and the rest were his own inability to want to make friends, so his parents' restrictions never bothered him until they came here.

But his parents were quick to allow him freedom, even though his Ma threatened castration before returning him to The City if he didn't physically attend Higher Education when they arrived here. He knew when he graduated, he would be considered a legal adult and entitled to all his trust fund money.

It was how his G-Pas set his funds up, no education, no money. In The City, Higher Education was Training for the position of Minister. He was already slated to be Minister from an early age, so he thought his G-Pas wanted to ensure the title would be his.

With the amount of funds in his personal account, being the first pet to ever achieve the title of "Perfect Pet", being educated to become Minister, and what he thought was a good size penis, he was on every single woman's wish list in The City. He was also in the 'I wish' dreams of married women. He would raise any woman he married to the level of the governess herself.

Both his GMa and Indria's money and power made sure of that, even if they only received it by marrying his G-Pas. GMack and GLou were the only children born to their parents, on the same day, at the same time. Because they were males, they could hold no power, so whomever they married would acquire the power which came with marrying his G-Pas. He was no different, even as Minister, he would be a puppet for the governess to control The City.

A handsomely beautiful doll puppet, he thought, with a soft smile.

He was sure the memory of his sixteenth Remorse Day must have been him dreaming of how he wished it could have gone. He didn't understand why The Burning Boy seemed so familiar to him and why he would react that way towards another male in The City, but he chose to write it off as a dream, as he didn't remember what one felt like.

A quick glance around his room to make sure he had everything he thought he would need sent him into the bathroom for a final look as well. He walked back into his room and looked around. It reminded him of his room from The City. It was larger than his old bedroom but the amount of his own items in the room made it feel way more comfortable. Instead of pictures of flowers and his garden, he had framed anime posters.

"Maybe I should garden here, there is a lot more starlight, so it would be...easier..." He paused as he remembered the joke Xavier made about his garden. His hand went up to his chest, and he clenched it.

Why? Why does it hurt to think about him? The Burning Boy, Xavier. He looked over at his night table and smiled, the photos from his shopping trip with Drum were in a custom-made frame. *I must figure out who this Burning Boy is and why he is in my memories.*

He went downstairs and found Sport in the kitchen. "Hey Little Brother, what are you doing?" he asked peeking around the massive six-foot six and a half Sport. He realized he was a runt of the group at only six-foot two, and he rolled his eyes at the thought.

"I am prepping food to be cooked later on," Sport informed him.

"Oh, it's quite sad I won't be here to enjoy it," he said, happy to be going camping.

Sport turned and looked at him weirdly. "Why are you speaking like that?" Sport asked him.

"I am trying to speak as you all do," he said, turning away from Sport to sit down at the table. "Would you happen to know anyone named Xavier?"

Thinking for a minute, Sport responded, "Not to my knowledge. Looking for someone?"

He nodded his head, unwilling to say more. It didn't feel right, and he resolved to figure it out on his own, *which will be next to impossible without asking around town.*

He didn't want Drum to hear of him inquiring or looking for another male while Drum was actively trying to be his boyfriend. *"Could you not say anything to anyone. I would like to figure this out on my own?"* he asked, quietly.

Sport nodded. "Not a problem, Big Brother. Besides, if Drum knew, he would probably make sure you would never *accidentally* run into whomever you are inquiring about." Sport said this laughing, and he giggled as well, but they both knew it was true.

"Thank you!" he kindly said, happy.

"I am surprised you did not ask me for a Vow!" Sport teased.

He looked at Sport and laughed. Truly laughed. Sport was speaking like someone from The City, and it only helped to put him more at ease. He doubted he would have been more comfortable with anyone else living in his home other than Sport. Yes, he got along decently with everyone, but he doubted he would have been able to live under the same roof with Dill without ruining their friendship.

"You are my Little Brother, I trust you," he said, with a smile.

Sport beamed at the admission and turned to happily finish his work while humming.

The knock at the door made him leap up in excitement. "Dill!" he exclaimed as he ran to the door and threw it open.

It wasn't Dill. Instead, there was a delivery male.

"Delivery for a (smack, smack) My...Dumpling (smack, smack)," the male said, looking down at his clipboard.

The male was talking to him while chewing gum and he stood there, annoyed, and completely uninterested. His dead face look to the male was followed by him preceding to slam the door in the male's face. Sport caught the door, and he turned to walk off but Sport caught him as well.

"Yes, Dumpling lives here. I'll sign for it," Sport said.

He crossed his arms and shot daggers at the delivery male, still loudly chewing gum.

"Alright, (smack) sign here (smack)," the male said, between chews.

Sport signed the papers, and the male went to his truck to open the back.

He turned to Sport and grabbed him by the apron. "Why must he smack so loudly!?" he asked, upset at the lack of respect. "To speak while something is in your mouth is uncouth." He could not, for the life of him, understand some of the customs outside of The City, and while he dismissed or plainly accepted most of them, he still had his annoyances.

"Maybe there is a reason, if you care to ask," Sport told him. "Instead of trying to find a way to manifest your mental torture of the male," Sport added, with a raised eyebrow and a look of respectful surprise.

"*At least you know I would not kill him,*" he mumbled, looking ashamed and proud, one right after the other.

The delivery male came back carrying a tall, wide shelf, encased in glass. When he sat the glass case in front of the young Beings at the door, he started talking. "Where did you (smack) order this from? My girlfriend (smack) is in the (smack) gardening club (smack) here in town (smack) and she would love something like this (smack)."

One of the young Beings looked at him, annoyed. "Why do you smack so loudly when speaking to a person?" the young Being asked, politely, but he could tell the young Being's nerves were grated.

"Oh. My girlfriend (smack) is pregnant (smack), and I used to (smack) smoke. It's a habit (smack) of chewing gum (smack) I picked up (smack) while quitting. We're both (smack) Full-Core Beings, (smack) so we are hoping (smack) for a healthy (smack) baby," he informed the young Being.

"It is an annoying habit to pick up. Is your girlfriend not driven insane yet?" the young Being asked, obviously peeved about his explanation.

"It's fine," he said and turned, spitting the gum out in the young Beings' yard.

The young Being's eyes closed, and the Being's face turned to the sky to take a deep breath. He froze, realizing he just upgraded from annoying this young Being, to insulting. The young Being walked down a few steps and stood in front of him. As the strong, young man moved the display into the house with ease, the young Being in front of him, held him by the shoulders.

"*You really should not let it be known I touched you,*" the young Being quietly told him.

"What...why...I..." he stumbled. "Why would anyone care that you touched me?" he asked, confused, thinking it was a playful joke.

The young Being however only looked directly in his face. "Do you notice anyone living in either house next to me?" the young Being asked, and he looked at both homes before shaking his head.

"No one lives across from me or behind me. There is a Barrier over my home. Why is that?" the young Being coldly asked, and he felt a chill run over his skin to settle in his bones.

His face was slowly sinking into terror, and he shrugged, unwilling to guess.

"Do you know my brother who just signed for the package?" the young Being questioned.

By now, he was scared and would try to look the young Being in the eyes but couldn't, so he nodded and quietly answered the question. *"His name is Sport and he's famous as an exceptional Higher Ed sports player."*

The young Being leaned closer. "He is also my personal bodyguard. If you tell others you were touched by me, *they* will find out and want to experiment on you, since *they* cannot get to me. Maybe even on your girlfriend and your unborn child. Anything *they* can use, *they* will," the young Being stated, in a cold, deadly manner.

It was coming together in his head. It was known Sport had a younger foster sister, but the Being standing in front of him was too old to be Sport's little sister. He was thinking maybe the little sister was experimented on and was now under the private protection of The Royal Family. It was probably why there was no actual name for the delivery. He nodded, now completely scared he knew something he shouldn't.

The young lady glanced down at the ground where he spit his gum, before looking back at him.

He nodded, frightened, and bent down to search the ground for the gum as Sport returned to stand at the door, arms crossed, just watching. He found the gum, holding it up for the young Beings to see, before turning to run down the stairs.

"There is a can right outside the gate, next to the curb," the scary young lady called after him.

He didn't acknowledge he heard the young lady until he made it to the can, opening the lid to drop the chewed gum in it. He also emptied his pockets of all the gum he stuffed in there. He went to his truck, quickly tossing every pack into the garbage can, before bowing slightly to the young Beings. Then he hauled ass out of there.

PANTU: A HELPING MIND
WEEK FIVE: SATURDAY

He sucked his teeth and went back inside with Sport. He slammed the door behind him and locked it.

"Was it really necessary to scare the male to death while you healed him?" Sport asked him, standing in front of the glass case.

He answered as he went to join Sport. "He went from rude, to downright insulting," he explained. "*He is lucky it is all I did,*" he mumbled under his breath. "Do you think he understands?" he asked Sport, worried the male might say something and must face Drum, because he chose to heal him.

"I think…he is too afraid of you to come back here. Once he thinks clearly, to him, it will be like he was scared out of it, not that you healed him. If we receive any more deliveries, it will not be from him," Sport reassured him.

He came to stand in front of the display, and he stared at the top shelf, unable to say anything. As Sport commented on the shelf, he stood, frozen.

"This is really nice. Each small individual shelf holds a different herb or tea. The construction of this is abstract, so well thought out and put together. Each small shelf connects in some way. The colors are your favorite, right?" Sport asked, snapping him out of his thoughts.

"Yes. I never knew I liked midnight-blue so much until I saw it as a backdrop for yellow ochre," he said, in a trance-like voice.

The back and inside of the shelves were midnight-blue, as was the writing of each herb or tea name. The front outlines of the shelves were yellow ochre. The display was beautifully constructed, but he couldn't take his eyes off the top shelf.

"Hey! Some of these are the teas and herbs Queen has been using for your recovery!" Sport pointed out.

"AH!" he said, justifying his thoughts of why this particular plant was sitting at the top of the shelf.

"Do you want to leave it here or place it elsewhere?" Sport asked, waiting for instructions.

"Place it in my room, please. I will start a garden. Once I have fertilized the ground enough, I will plant these there," he said, absentmindedly.

Sport nodded and carried the display upstairs.

He followed, numb as his thoughts flew around in his head, *I should take a nap. I can move some things into my think space and pull some questions out of my head to keep it from crowding up.*

He stared at the display Sport placed next to his window to receive starlight. After Sport walked out, politely closing the door, he reached behind his bed, in a small slit, he pulled Drum's shirt and notes from his mattress.

He hid these after the first intrusion and left them there even after the Dome. He laid down on his bed and went to sleep. He woke up in the field meadow and quickly greeted Natum. He explained his trip was short, and he would come back to spend time with him.

Natum seemed to accept his quick hello, and he proceeded to his Think Space. After walking in, he headed straight for the podium with the mental image of Drum's notes and placed them there.

"Finally! I thought you forgot about me!" Petu pouted and hung off his shoulders.

"I will not stay long. I am going camping with some friends," he explained, moving from under Petu's arms to the next podium. Folding the shirt, he placed it name side up.

Petu read off the shirt. "Drum, Suppade XC Santiago. Why would you place a shirt of another here? Is this the name of the male who is not yours?" Petu asked.

He turned and looked at Petu. "Do you remember The Burning Boy?" he questioned.

Petu was quiet for a moment before looking around. "This place is so empty. We must sit on the floor, there is no food, nothing to read or entertain ourselves with..." Petu said, slyly looking at him.

He looked around at the other Personalities he'd found, keeping their distance from him. Placing his fingers to his head, he created replicas of all the things needed to give them a tiny area to feel like home. A few Personalities quickly moved into the area he expanded for them.

"Why yes! I remember Burning Boy. He would come every year and leave a gift for our Remorse Day. When we were sixteen, he kissed us," Petu told him.

He was shocked. "So, it was more than just a dream!?" he exclaimed and Petu nodded.

"Wait, I do not remember him bringing me gifts?" he questioned.

Petu nodded again, looking at him with a question. "He did. It is what started GMack and GLou to give us gifts. We will start to remember things which seem like a dream, but they are not. It really happened," Petu told him.

He groaned and slid down to the floor, placing his head into his hands.

Petu squatted down in front of him. "What is wrong?" Petu's concern was clear in his voice, knowing their existence depended on his mood and mental state, so Petu was more concerned about his own well-being than him.

But like Petu, he was more concerned with his own problems as well. "If Burning Boy is real, then it means I actually liked a male while living in The City. I told everyone I have never liked anyone before but now I am having memories which seem like mine, but they are different from how I remember living them.

"If HE finds out, I am unsure of what he will do." He panicked. He either had to find Burning Boy Xavier before Drum found out what he was doing, leave Drum to search for this person, or forget about him, completely.

He took several deep breaths before standing back up to throw out his thoughts and questions into space. "See if you can make some sense of this for me and the next time I come, I will try to bring sweets," he sweetly requested of Petu, who was now excited about the prospect of sweets.

"Will Sport be the one to make them?" Petu asked, his eyes gleaming with happiness.

"I will ask it of him," he responded.

Petu clapped his hands together and squealed. "We will do everything we can, to figure out, what we can."

"I should go. It appears you have a handle on the Personalities here. I will look for others," he stated. He handed a list of names to Petu, who nodded.

He held Petu and gave some of his Light to him. "It will help but use it sparingly. Also, stay within the Dome," he instructed to Petu's smile and nod.

PANTU: NOT ON THE SAME PAGE
WEEK FIVE: SATURDAY

He woke up to conversation downstairs and realized Dill was here. He jumped up, excited he was finally leaving for the campsite. He grabbed his heavy duffle bag and immediately dropped it.

Holy shit, this is heavier than I thought. He grabbed his backpack instead and went to open his door so he could push the bag down the stairs.

Dill was standing on the other side. "Need help?" Dill joked.

"It is heavy as hell. I really believe I packed too much!" he whined.

Dill laughed. "As spoiled as you are, I could only imagine what you would need while in the wild." Dill moved into the room to pick up the bag, but his interest was quickly redirected to the new stand in his room. "Where did that come from?" Dill asked, moving closer to look.

"Drum!" he said, smiling uncontrollably.

Dill's appreciation was apparent, and it made him even happier.

"We should go downstairs. I am so ready to leave!" he mentioned as he moved out of the room.

Dill picked up the heavy bag with ease and followed him.

He was standing on the last step at the bottom of the stairs, staring straight ahead of him. Dill, who wasn't paying attention, bumped into him, making him take a tumble off the step and into Drum's arms.

He caught me? Of course, he caught me.

He was confused why Drum was here when he should be elsewhere, working. Dill dropped the bag next to Drum and went to go in the kitchen with Sport but was grabbed when he took himself out of Drum's arms to drag Dill into his Pa's home office.

"Why is Drum here? He should be at work?" he asked Dill, scared his plan would be ended before he could even start it.

Dill looked at him weirdly. "Hmm. Let me think. The person I like, *a lot*, by the way, is spending the night in the woods with four of my childhood bullies. Two of those bullies' allegiances is unknown and one is with T-PEC.

"You also have a scent that could Seduce the stars out of the sky. Do you think I wouldn't freak out if Robin did something like this?" Dill asked, but the silly look on Dill's face answered him.

Blowing out a loud sigh, he spoke, "Is Robin coming as well? It is like I cannot do anything I want to do without him being around. Is he...?" He didn't get a chance to finish as Drum came to the open door.

"No worries, I won't be there. You can enjoy your trip without me getting in the way," Drum stated, giving him a pained look before turning around to leave.

He rolled his eyes, but the look on his face didn't match. He couldn't feel Drum's heat and knowing Drum was keeping him from experiencing the possible pain Drum was probably experiencing now, saddened him.

Dill turned to him in surprise. "With the weather being so nice, every weekend has been camping season for more than just us students. All the campsites were completely booked for the rest of the month. I asked Drum if we could get in with a last-minute reservation, and he arranged it," Dill explained but he only looked at Dill, waiting for more information.

Dill continued, "Drum's family owns the best campsites. I had to ask him to reserve a spot for us, so our reservations are under his name. He has to go with us to get us through the gate."

He felt conflicted. "Why not just Portal in?" he wondered. "Why is there a check-in gate?" He didn't understand why, with such abundant Neutral Light, they still did things which were so human and mundane.

Dill frankly explained, "No one can Portal in or out. No one. There's a Barrier with only one entrance, and the exit is right next to it. You have to walk from the entrance to the campsite and back. Even though the camping ground is huge, it's to keep the campgrounds from becoming overcrowded.

"It also helps to give space and privacy to those camping. It keeps crime down. If everyone checks in and no one can Portal in or out, if someone is missing..." Dill's look to him was interrupted by a text.

"I called and turned the campsite over to your name," Dill read out loud. "Shit! I wonder how much it cost him to do last minute!" Dill's shock registered in his voice.

Dill looked at him, pleading, "Pantu, I asked Drum to come on the trip with us. Put has your Favor card and wants to call it in. Queen was already coming because he has to make your tea fresh and Sport, because he has to make your meals.

"So, I invited Win, since you both have a shared thing with food. Pantu, everybody was supposed to be there, and I really didn't think you would mind Drum, of ALL Beings, being there." Dill finished, still pleading with him as he slid down to sit on the floor and covered his face.

He couldn't respond to Dill and felt so bad, tears started to form behind his hands. Dill threw his hands up to turn and walked out of the office. He and Dill were not on the same page.

They were nothing like GMack and GLou or Drum and Queen. Dill planned it this way for his sake. He didn't realize how much he missed Drum until he saw him. He fucked everything up. It seems as if he couldn't do anything right.

Everybody unknowingly added the pressure of Drum liking him and he didn't know how to be in a relationship or to be a boyfriend. But everybody assumed he was an expert, and he felt treated as such when he knew he was not.

Having an owner wasn't the same as having a girlfriend or being in a relationship but no one seemed to understand him. Did they forget he was raised to never like a male, that he couldn't be gay? Or did they assume he would be okay since he wasn't in The City anymore?

Everyone acts as if only Drum is innocent and ignorant of relationships, he thought as the image of The Burning Boy came back to him. *Maybe if I just forget about him then it will not matter.* But he knew his memories of Burning Boy would be coming back, and he probably wouldn't be able to control them.

I can figure this out without anyone getting killed. Now to try and forget that kiss. As he thought this, his hands went up to his lips as he remembered how Burning Boy's lips felt against his. The softness mixed with the pressure of being unable to express everything they wanted to say with just a kiss, made his heart ache.

He felt alone. Even with everyone around him, he felt isolated. He felt unable to express or explain himself to even Dill right now. He just wanted to shut himself off from the world until it was his time to pass into the next life.

He stood and went to the kitchen. He noticed his bag was missing from the front area, but he only stopped when he reached the kitchen with Dill and Sport trying to figure out how to, as he understood it, correct his mistake.

"Drum can go, I will stay here," he plainly stated before turning and running up the stairs to his studio.

He proceeded to slam the door and started destroying everything in there. His chairs, canvases, paint, his brushes, anything he could get his hands on, he broke. Sport came rushing through the door with Dill close behind him.

After blocking him from doing any further damage to the studio, he turned and ran to his room, looking to destroy everything there. He locked his door and let his anger, frustration, and sadness out on everything in his room. Nothing but his bathroom was spared.

What could he do? He picked through the wreckage and found a photo of him and Drum from their shopping trip, and he cried as he stared at it. He pulled his phone out of his pocket and for the first time, he called his Ma.

PANTU: FOLLOW YOUR HEART
WEEK FIVE: SATURDAY

It was only the second ring, and he was ready to hang up when he heard his Ma pick up.

"PanPan! You called me!" his Ma exclaimed, her excitement wafting through the phone.

He said nothing and the silence was telling to his Ma.

"PanPan, what is it? I'm on my way. Don't do anything, just wait until I get there. PanPan! PanPan!" his Ma tried to call out to him, but he wouldn't answer.

His Ma started talking to calm him down. "Whatever it is, you and I can work through it. Nothing is too big for us to handle, right PanPan? We have been in really bad situations, and we have always made it through. Please PanPan, wait for me. I'm almost home. Two seconds, no, one second, PanPan."

Still on the phone, his Ma knocked. "PanPan, it's Ma. Open the door *Little PanPan*," she gently said.

He unlocked and opened his door to show everyone his room. His Ma looked unsurprised and walked in, closing the door behind her. His Ma held him in her arms. She didn't say anything, just held him for a while, rubbing his back.

He wanted to think he experienced another episode, but he was told these were normal emotions he hadn't experienced in years. In The City, he needed to be "perfect", so having emotions was bad for him.

Given who his family was and the legacy which came along with their names, where Coin failed miserably, he had no choice but to succeed. He couldn't make friends there, and since everyone wanted his spot more than they cared about his feelings, he cut his feelings off. But his Ma knew he'd done more than that.

Even after leaving, the medicines he was taking made him even more withdrawn than when he was in The City. He would at least speak to his Ma, no matter how rude, but after starting the medicines, he was so out of it, most times, he didn't realize they existed. Other times, he was moody and agitated. The only time he would focus was when his parents placed schoolwork in front of him.

The last couple of months, before coming here, Doctor Robin was one of the ones helping them to make it here, both physically and mentally. Doctor Robin was always available, and she started decreasing his dosage until he was finally coherent.

His Ma pulled him away from her to look at him. *"It's okay Pantu. It's okay to be sad. It's okay to be upset. These are feelings everyone feels. Do not be afraid Little PanPan,"* his Ma said, gently.

He broke like a dam, and his Ma hugged him again. She didn't ask as she knew he would only tell her if he wanted to. In The City, he spoke only when he felt the need to, never used unnecessary words and if he didn't feel like explaining, he wouldn't. It was why this town was different. He hadn't spoken this much since he was a child, living in The Slums.

His Ma took in the situation. *"If you really want him there, ask him to come,"* she quietly stated. *"Follow what you feel inside."*

He only nodded. The tears finally stopped, and his resolve was set. His Ma followed him back down to the concerned faces of Dill and Sport. He smiled weakly but refused to look anyone in the eyes.

Sport nodded. "I'm ready to go, whenever you are," Sport stated.

He looked around the kitchen. All the food Sport prepped and prepared was gone and he looked confused.

"It takes a lot of Energy to move that much stuff, so Dill and I loaded it into the jeep. Win and Queen are loading their stuff now and everyone else will meet us at the gate," Sport explained.

He agreed with a small smile. "I left something in my room, be right back." He quickly grabbed the makeshift Portal bag and returned, hugging his Ma tightly before leaving out the front door. At the car, their Ma hugged Sport just as tight.

"It's just one night" Sport joked. "You and Pa should go out and enjoy yourselves," Sport added, smiling brightly at her.

His Ma agreed with a smile and waved them all into her jeep they were using, since she was banned from driving. He knew she'd run all the way from the bookstore to their home, and the thought hurt his heart.

With Win as the driver, Queen in the passenger seat, Dill and he were in the second row, Sport had the whole third row to himself to spread out.

"I feel honored you trust my driving skills, but seatbelts are for the other crazy ass drivers on the road," Win chided Sport, who snapped his fingers, and his seatbelt moved itself to click.

Queen rolled down his window. "Bye Ma Sky! Tell Pa Moon, we miss him already!" Queen shouted as they pulled out of the driveway and took off.

His Ma laughed and waved them off.

The whole ride, he was quiet and deep in thought as Sport read, Dill tinkered but would occasionally join in with Queen and Win, singing songs off Queen's playlist. He only looked out the window as they passed through several rural towns headed northeast, away from the ocean and deeper inland.

He noticed just how big Drum's Dome was over these places as the air smelled the same all the way to the campgrounds. A few hours later, they pulled up to a gate marked private entrance. Jax, Turn and Put were waiting for them.

After everyone left the vehicle, Put nervously looked around. "Is Drum not coming?" Put asked, his voice laced with fear and worry.

He could only look away with guilt in his eyes as he searched for his duffel bag.

Queen spoke up instead, "Drum said to call him on video chat and you two will hash out the details then." As Queen spoke, he soothed the fear in Put's eyes, but Put's face was still full of worry.

He continued to say nothing as they checked in and started to walk three miles to the campsite. Everybody stopped and looked at him.

"Umm?" Win said, speaking for everyone else. "Are you going to be okay walking three miles…over this kind of terrain?"

He looked up in surprise and then giggled and nodded. "My G-Pas and I went camping plenty of times before. I will be okay with three miles." He continued to walk, retreating inside himself to think and plan.

The night went smoothly once they made it to the campsite. It was the most beautiful site he'd ever seen. The deep greens made the small lake they were camped next to glow and sparkle, a beautiful shade of cobalt blue.

He took a deep breath, and the scent and scene calmed him. They set up camp and Put went off to video chat with Drum. Put came back relieved and finished helping to set everything up.

They ate, talked, laughed, and had a wonderful time. He didn't have to force himself to join in the fun. They went swimming in the lake until late, before returning to camp to tell scary stories in front of the fire.

His tale of the haunted little girl seemed more like a real story to those who knew what his Ma could do. He said it was a story his Ma told him during nightly thunderstorms, which made it scarier.

"Why has it never rained in Sunset?" he asked everyone.

No one wanted to answer him as they all mumbled something different and refused to look his way.

He accepted it with a nod. "I am turning in for the night. How are the tents set up?" he asked, this time hoping for a clear answer.

"Oh, you can have the tent there at the front and the rest of us are single or doubled up," Queen explained.

He didn't make a fuss as he looked exhausted. He went inside his tent and zipped it up after saying goodnight to everyone.

QUEEN: CAMPSITE MAYHEM
WEEK FIVE: SUNDAY

He stretched and yawned. Taking a deep breath, he smiled. He hadn't slept this well in a while. He crawled over to the zipper on the tent he was sharing with Sport and Win. He looked back at them and smiled again.

Sport was the meat to their bread. He wasn't one for camping, but he did have fun last night. The scary stories and food were compliment to the company he was in. The guys who bullied Drum and ignored him as kids, grew up to be decent young men.

He saw their zipper was a little bit open and as he unzipped the tent, he also noticed how bright it was outside. *We must have been really tired to sleep in so late*, he thought to himself, before moving to crawl out the tent.

His hand landed in some yellow powder, and he looked down. His confusion increased as he examined the powder. "SPORT! WIN! WAKE UP!" he shouted.

He moved quickly out of the tent to take a look around. There was yellow powder in front of the three tents they used last night but none in front of Pantu's or the empty one.

Sport was at Pantu's tent and ripped it open, unable to fathom why he didn't see his brother. "PANTU IS GONE!" Sport cried out.

"Sport let's stay calm," he gently said. "Let's see if Pantu went to use the bathroom. Maybe Pantu got caught up talking to other campers?"

He was formulating a plan in his head. "Sport, Jax and Dill, break off and go check every bathroom and surrounding camp sites. Turn will go to the gate and see if Pantu was seen around there. Put, Win and I will clean up. We can't leave until the camp site is cleaned. We will all stay connected by using the Walkie App," he commanded.

Everyone nodded and started. He knew Sport needed to keep busy to stop him from freaking out. This may seem like an impromptu family Sport started living with, but he knew this felt different to Sport.

He understood his best friend never felt such a bond with his foster parents, who left him to live in Sunset by himself while they moved to the capital with their younger, biological, Full-Core child.

We have to find his big brother, he nervously thought to himself. He would never forgive himself if Sport's one glimmer at hope for a loving family was shattered. He knew Win felt the same way from just a look they shared as Sport sped off, desperately searching for his brother.

Win and Put used their Energy to quickly clean up the grounds, while he collected the yellow powder in front of their tents. Once they were packed, Dill and Jax were back, panting from overusing their Energy. Sport showed up seconds later, freaking out.

"I can't find Pantu! Ma and Pa are going to kill me!" Sport cried as he dropped to the ground.

Win was hugging Sport. "I doubt your parents would want to lose either of their children," Win consoled.

"We will find Pan—" He started to console Sport before being interrupted by the Walkie app beeping on his phone.

"There's a Being working the exit who said Pantu signed out at o'one thirty sr after verification we were all still alive," Turn's voice sounded through. "Pantu isn't on camera, but you can see an employee talking to the air before papers were signed," Turn informed them.

"We're packed. Send an employee to check while we move to the gate. That way we can leave once we get there," he instructed Turn.

"Roger that," Turn stated.

"Let's go," he said, and everyone started to move.

They made it to the gate and signed out after confirming their grounds were cleaned and everyone left was present and alive. They packed up into their cars as he spoke to the employee.

"Did Pantu say anything or ask any questions?" he inquired.

"Pantu asked how long it would take to get to the nearest diner by foot, and I told her probably half a morning? I offered her a ride, but she declined, wanting to walk instead." The employee shrugged.

He smiled and nodded. "Thank you!" he brightly said, making the employee smile back while leaning forward to smell more of his scent. He waved and walked away.

He sat in the passenger seat of the jeep and pulling up a map, they found the nearest diner and drove there. They all went in and looked around, with Sport trying to smell Pantu's scent.

"It's like Pantu has been erased," Sport lamented. "*Should we call Drum?*" Sport quietly asked.

The collective "NO!" from everyone but Dill, made Sport fight back tears.

He was talking to a server at the 40/7 diner. No current server saw Pantu, so he was getting information as she was making calls to the other server who would have been working the shift when the young Being he described would have possibly been here. He finally found something when the server received a call back from the shift manager.

"Yea, some really gorgeous Being came in, ate alone, paid the bill, and left. But the Being did ask how far it was to the diner that sells peach cobbler by foot. I told the Being a few hours if they bend at the curve instead of going straight then circling back.

"Robbie, a regular offered to give the Being a ride, since he hunts in the area. They left together," the manager informed them. "I thought it was weird the Being didn't show up on any of our cameras. I wouldn't have minded a picture," the manager added, chuckling.

"Oh, my sweet Karma! Thank you all so much!" he gushed to them, taking pictures with servers and customers while agreeing to be tagged, liking and commenting on the posts.

He went outside as everyone, but Sport and Dill were eating the food they ordered while waiting for him.

"Pantu went to another diner for peach cobbler!" he said, smiling. "Sport we will find Pantu," he confidently stated.

Sport nodded, fighting to accept the progress.

They took the curve the manager told him about and arrived at the diner within an hour. He quickly went in to speak to the staff. He came running back out, with peach cobbler for the cars.

"Pantu and Robbie stopped here. One of the bussers overheard Pantu asking Robbie about a cheese factory!" He was excited, they still had leads on Pantu. No camera proof but he didn't smell any Lies from the Beings speaking to him.

"That's outside of the Barrier," Win said, looking at his phone.

He took a deep calming breath. "Pantu is absolutely fine having lived outside a Barrier, so Pantu knows using Energy is risky with no way to replenish it," he theorized.

Sport furiously nodded. "Pantu does, Queen! It's why Pantu is hitching rides or walking, to keep from using Energy."

He looked at Sport. "Call your parents. Have them meet us at the Barrier," he commanded.

They all jumped back into the cars and sped to the Barrier.

Sport was on the phone with his parents, trying not to freak out as he stumbled across an explanation.

They pulled up to the Barrier and jumped out as Sport's Pa's SUV drove out a Portal to swerve to the side of the road.

SPORTxDRUM: A TRAIL OF PANTU
WEEK FIVE: SUNDAY

When Mr. C and Mrs. K exited the front of the car, Sport's Ma and Pa exited from the backseats. His parents ran straight to him, hugging him tightly. His Ma started checking all over his exposed limbs, asking him over and over if he was okay as his Pa patted him on the back.

After finally reassuring his Ma, he was alright, he hung his head. "Ma, Pa, my deepest apologies. I was careless and Pantu left alone," he said, fighting back tears.

His Pa hugged him. "Son, you are not responsible for the actions of another," his Pa consoled, while still rubbing his back.

His Ma, however, was gazing off. She swayed slightly and his Pa Ground-stepped, quickly catching her. Watching his parents, he couldn't help but feel responsible for what was happening. If he were just a little bit better as a son and brother, maybe Pantu wouldn't have left.

"Love?" his Pa asked, gathering his Wife's face in his hands. "Love? How are you feeling?" his Pa lightheartedly asked.

His Ma seemed to come out of a daze. "Ah! I'm fine Mo-ling?" she asked back.

His Pa nodded, smiling cautiously at his Wife. *"That's amazing Love. Fine is a top tier feeling, we love top tier feelings, yes Love?"* his Pa gently said to his slightly dazed and happy Wife.

"We will bring our child back this time, right Mo-ling? Pantu always comes back. Pantu came back for me the first time. You brought our child back the second time. We will bring Pantu back!" his Ma brightly said to her Husband, leaving his arms to walk slowly to the Barrier.

He tried not to let his tears fall. He had no idea what was wrong with his Ma and his heart was hurting as he watched Mr. C walk a bit behind his Ma as Mrs. K was getting the full picture from Queen.

"Pa? What's wrong with Ma?" he quietly asked.

"She has a lot on her Mind Sport," his Pa answered. His Pa placed a hand on his shoulder and looked at him sadly. "My apologies Son. Seems like your family is more trouble than we're worth," his Pa told him.

He shook his head, determined not to lose his connection with his family. "Then I am as well," he stated.

Mr. C looked at Queen. "What were your plans outside the Barrier?" Mr. C asked, keeping his Ma from touching the Barrier.

His Ma looked up at Mr. C. "We must bring our child back. Pantu can't be far from me. PANTU HAS TO COME BACK!"

His Ma started to freak out, and his breaths were being harshly pushed out. He was trying to understand everything that was happening, but his Ma's sorrow was hurting him, and he wanted to see her smile again.

Mr. C held his Ma as she broke down, and he pulled his phone out. "Drum," Mr. C stated, and the group collectively shivered.

"Find me," Mr. C told his son.

Drum appeared. Closing his phone, he took a look around, noticing everyone was here except Pantu. He was at each car, checking inside. He stood away from everyone and looked at them.

He turned away, quiet as he looked at his Barrier. He spoke without looking at anyone. "Turn, Jax, make sure Put gets home safe. Be packed and ready to go," he instructed.

Jax stepped forward. "We can help look. More eyes. Pantu is OUR friend," Jax demanded.

"Put. I made you a Promise. I'm trusting Jax and Turn will get you home safely until I arrive," he spoke to Put, ignoring Jax, who relaxed when he offered his trust.

He was going to trust the guys who made his life hell. He was even willing to help Put. Jax nodded and went to the car, getting in with Turn and Put to drive off.

He said nothing until they were out of sight. He stood staring at his Barrier, listening to Mrs. Sky cry. Someone walked out of the forest behind him. He didn't move as the man walked up to them.

The man looked at Mrs. Sky. "Oop. Was that yo child who left through the Barrier?" the man asked.

"Are you Mr. Robbie?" Queen asked, quickly stepping to the man.

"Oop, the one in the same. I figured someone would come looking. That child is really too goodlooking to be traveling alone and hitching rides. Not everybody is as nice as we are," Mr. Robbie shook his head as he spoke. "I hunt in these woods regularly, good meat and..." Mr. Robbie trailed off.

"Do you know for sure if the Being is going to the cheese factory?" Queen asked, pulling Mr. Robbie's Mind back.

"Oop! The child seemed really excited about it. Kept asking about different cheeses there. I dropped the child off right here before heading to my hunting spot," Mr. Robbie said. "I ain't never been to a cheese factory so I have no idea what the child was so excited about? It's just cheese, right? Who would be..." Mr. Robbie trailed off again.

"Thank you, sir," he said, producing an unlabeled bottle filled with Purified, dark blue water. He tossed it to Queen, who gave it to Mr. Robbie.

"Oop! Holy shit! I heard 'bout these. Thank you very kindly," Mr. Robbie happily said. "By the way, I hope you find your friend sooner rather than later. It ain't safe outside the Barrier. The stories coming from out there..." Mr. Robbie shook his head. "I tried to talk the child back, but the child was adamant 'bout leaving."

"Thank you for your concern," Queen sweetly said, and touched Mr. Robbie on the shoulder.

"Oop! If you hear your child got into a red pickup truck, all hope might be lost," Mr. Robbie warned before walking off back into the woods after an alert to his animal tracker went off.

"Win, you drive Queen and Dill. Only Queen needs to use his Energies. Dill, you replenish him," he calmly said as he turned around. "NO ONE ELSE IN THE CAR WASTE THEIR ENERGY!" he added, raising his voice as he stared hard at them.

The three all looked down, nodding. His Mom and Mr. Moon looked at him, their Energies shocked by his outburst.

His expression softened, wanting to explain his outburst was to hide his fear. *"I'm not willing to lose you as well,"* he whispered. "Pantu would never forgive me if something happened to you Dill," he added.

They nodded, sniffling while holding back their tears.

"Sport and I will be in the air," he said, as he tossed two bottles of Purified water he Produced to Sport. He waved his hand, and several bottles appeared in the back of Mrs. Sky's jeep.

He turned to his parents. "Dad, can you and Mom see Mr. Moon and Mrs. Sky home? We will be back as soon as we find Pantu," he asked.

"Wait!" Mrs. Sky said, getting up. "We lived outside a Barrier, we can help!" she pleaded.

He refused to look at her. "Mr. Moon, it would be best if fewer Beings expend their Energy outside the Barrier. We will find Pantu," he explained.

Mr. Moon nodded. He went to his Wife, holding her face in his hands, he looked into her eyes. *"Love, we can help. How Calm is your Mind?"* Mr. Moon asked gently.

Mrs. Sky shook her head. "Pa would never let me train with a Mind this unsteady," she rationalized. "I can't look for Pantu. They will bring our child back, right?" She cried as she fell into her Husband's arms.

His Dad was already at the car, turning it on as his Mom and Mr. Moon helped Mrs. Sky to the car. Win, Queen and Dill were in the jeep, ready to leave. Sport stood by his Barrier; wearing cargo camo pants to hold the water bottles.

DRUMxQUEEN: UNDERSTANDING THE TRAIL
WEEK FIVE: SUNDAY

Drum waited until his Dad drove through the white Portal he made, directly to Pantu's street. He stepped through his Barrier as Sport was followed by Win driving slowly. He stopped and Win drove up.

He turned and looked at Queen's scared Energies. "Don't push yourself to exhaustion before Replenishing. I will set a Portal to the cheese factory. Sport and I will catch up after checking the roads."

Queen nodded, taking rapid deep breaths. Once Queen's breathing slowed, he smiled at his best friend.

"We'll find Pantu. This isn't my decision to make," he sadly said. "But Pantu will make that decision to my face."

Queen closed his eyes as Win drove through the Portal. He made a white cloud for Sport, while he created a royal-blue one for himself. They took off, checking every road which led to the cheese factory.

Once they were close enough while still being far enough away to not be seen, he and Sport jumped down from their clouds, and he lifted them up into the sky. Those in the car were waiting in front of the cheese factory when he and Sport arrived. They entered the factory and found the host.

"OH, MY GOD! She is totally gorgeous, almost turned me into a lesbian, or maybe I am after seeing her. Yea, she came here, did the tour, and tried every cheese we have. She was so polite and kind and her excitement about cheese made us laugh. Umm, I believe she was with Dim's group though," she told them, pointing to a young man walking up.

"Another tour!" Dim exclaimed. "That's two tours in one day! We're quite popular today huh?" Dim brightly said. "The cost is twenty-five SB per person, groups of four or more, pay twenty SB per person," Dim happily said.

Queen looked at him, and he pulled his wallet out, laying the money down, paying for all of it. He also placed two hundred SB on the table for the lady host.

"Can you show my best friend the surveillance cameras, while we tour?" he asked, smiling at the young woman, who was stuck staring. He could see her Energy holding a pinkish-red glow for him.

The host's breaths were coming quickly as he gazed at her, making her sink further in. Sport stepped to her side, gently pulling her from the sticky vat. She nodded, embarrassedly walking off to lead Sport to the security room, glancing back, multiple times at him.

Their tour guide led them into the building. Dim explained the start of the company and the owners. Dim talked about the functionality of the factory before leading them into the main workroom. Dim described the different cheeses and how they were made.

He noticed several of the employees' Energies were sad and depressed as they passed. Their tour guide led them into an employee's only area past the workroom.

He went in last and was immediately in the furthest corner, away from everybody. Their tour guide looked around, outside the door. Dim waited with nervous Energy, checking the door until several employees came in. They huddled in a group, looking at them.

"We are only telling you this because we know who you and Queen are, Young Master," their tour guide, Dim told them. "My name is actually Grant, and I'm quite sure you can tell we're Beings. We live and work amongst humans, so using our Energy is a huge no," Grant started off saying.

"Every other place has cameras, so we can only talk in here. Your friend came here for a tour. She did the tour with four other guys who tried to pay for her.

"After they finished the tour, the guys offered her a ride to the next city. We all live there with humans, and we know these guys. They are hugely popular and post online as The SYB Guys," Grant explained.

"The Steal Your Bitch Guys?" Queen asked, confused.

Grant nodded. "They go around finding couples and sweet-talking them into walking off with them. They don't care if it's a guy or a girl, they go after anyone. Billions of views online," Grant said, shaking his head.

"But we know them. They aren't good humans. Their parents are wealthy and control a lot of our city. There were rumors they post videos to the dark web of the things they do to people last seen with them. Anyone unlucky enough to catch their eye is always found a few days later, tortured, raped, and mutilated.

"A leaked video showed them raping someone who was later found dead. After putting the information together, the police officers wanted to arrest them, but a judge blocked them, allowing them to be free during the entire process.

"They were found not guilty of murder, with the jury of their wealthy peers saying, rape wasn't enough evidence they also killed them. Everyone in this room has lost someone to them," Grant sadly ended.

Queen's Energies showed shock as Dill's Energy had him nervously fumbling with his hands, building something. He said nothing as Win sniffed around for food the whole time.

"*What the hell?*" Queen finally whispered.

"Your friend was really nice to everyone and so excited about cheese," Grant sadly laughed. "For some reason, when we saw her, there was this cooling but peaceful feeling that settled over us."

A small young lady stepped forward, and he could see her lack of Energy was why she was so short. "I know the hotel where they are last seen with people. My Mom works there. Of course, it's owned by one of the guys' parents and zoned as private property, to keep the police from entering without permission," the young lady stated. "I really hope you can save your friend," she said as she handed Queen a piece of paper with the hotel name, address, and telephone number. There was also the young lady's Mother's name.

Queen hugged her. "Thank you. We will have a chat with The SYB Guys. See what they know," Queen said, the threat clear in his voice.

"Do they drive a red pickup truck?" he asked while trying to control his breathing, his sadness, and his fear.

The employees shook their heads.

"They drive a fancy black Suburban," someone spoke up. "They need it for all their camera equipment," the Being added.

He nodded; his fear lessened as there was hope Pantu was still okay. "*My deepest condolences. We can't bring your loved ones back, but we can get them justice,*" he softly spoke to them.

He knew he would have to kill The SYB Guys. He didn't smell any Lies from the Beings standing in the room and he could see the sadness and anger in their Energies after losing someone close to them who didn't have a chance to fully live their own lives.

"Cyber!" he called out, and a tiny, turquoise orb appeared.

"Yes, Young Master?" Cyber's voice sounded out, making everyone look at him, surprise in all their Energies.

"Gather everything you can for proof of The SYB crimes and those who helped them get away with countless murders against our people. Have Major direct teams to off those who helped, and I'll handle The SYB Guys myself," he ordered Cyber, whose orb disappeared after a 'Yes, Young Master'.

Some of them started crying while hugging each other.

"I will lead you back to the front," Grant told them.

They met Sport back at the entrance. Sport motioned to his phone, and after tipping Grant, he left out the door to watch the video.

"I will set a Portal to the hotel, Sport and I will catch up," he told them. His voice was even, so no one knew how he was feeling. "Drink some water, Queen," he added.

He created a Portal right in front of the door and after Win drove through, disappearing right in front of the door host' face, the human gasped.

After he tapped his foot on the ground to Up-jump onto a royal-blue cloud he pulled down from the sky, and Sport also Up-jumped onto the white cloud, the door host fainted. They moved back to the road on their clouds, before zipping off down the highway.

They were at the hotel, and the commotion made Queen turn to Win and Dill. "Stay by the car," he crisply directed while he walked off to find out what was happening.

"What happened here?" he asked the nearest person, who shrugged. He slowly made his way to the front of the blocked off crowd, asking what was happening.

He received partial answers the closer he got to the front. He noticed a group of Being employees standing off to the side, in front of the physical line barrier. He slowly made his way over.

"*Anita?*" he softly called out.

One of the Being women turned, shocked he knew her name and was calling her. She slowly backed up, bringing the group with her. They milled around, having light conversations, while they came closer to him.

One of the Beings nudged the barrier, letting him into their group. They milled around, this time moving closer to the building, away from the crowd and the police, who were still occasionally watching them.

"*How do you know my name?*" Anita finally asked him.

"*Your daughter works at the cheese factory. She gave us this location to find The SYB Guys. They have our friend,*" he spoke low, blending in with the staff as he changed his clothes once surrounded.

"*No, they don't,*" one of the men gruffly said.

He looked confused. "*They didn't come here?*" He almost cried.

"*They did. Five people came, four died,*" Gruff Man said, watching the police.

He looked scared. "*Who died?*" His voice was shaking as he asked.

No one said anything until Gruff Man gave a signal.

Anita quickly whispered, *"The SYB Guys came here with a beautiful young woman, more beautiful than I've ever seen. She excitedly looked at everything and was so adorably sweet! They ordered food and took her up to the penthouse suite, where we know they make their videos.*

"When the bellhop," Anita tapped the Gruff Man, *"went up to deliver the food, he found one of them with a gunshot wound to the head. When he went up, two of the guys came down, one by stairs, the other by elevator. They ran at each other screaming..."* Anita was cut off by a signal.

Anita started back up when Gruff Man signaled her. *"They were yelling about how the handsome God Panda killed their friends. That they will kill him. They attacked each other.*

"One had a sword and stabbed his friend, before hacking his head off and holding it up chanting that he killed the God Panda. Another friend came running down the stairs. He shouted, "Fuck you! You're no God, Panda!" before shooting his friend in the head." Anita stopped.

"So, one is still alive?" he questioned.

After a moment Anita answered, *"No, he went to the pool and looked in. He started shooting the water. He stopped and looked at his reflection before saying, "Oh wait, I'm the God Panda!". He shot himself in the head and his body fell into the pool,"* Anita explained. *"That's going to be a bitch to clean,"* Anita thought out loud.

"You don't seem sad about their deaths?" he asked.

They all turned to look at him.

"Fuck them and their whole family," Gruff Man said.

"They got away with killing a lot of young people around here. We're ecstatic whenever they take their channel on the road and frightened whenever they come home." Anita's eyes teared up.

He knew she lost someone close to her to these murderous assholes.

"We have tried to save so many and were forced into silence. Now they want us to talk, and we have nothing to fucking say to them. They can kiss our asses. The young woman didn't show up on camera, so the police only see four guys walking in.

"They can see the guys talking to the air. They want to know if there was someone else and why they didn't show up on video," Gruff Man said, staring holes into the police and the detectives.

"Watch the fucking video is all we have to say. Every Being employee here, mouth is closed. Milly has been whispering to the human employees to forget, and we will as well," Anita

said, tears streaming down her face. *"It was the most satisfying moment in my life. To watch them kill each other."*

"That young woman was sent from the Universe," Gruff Man said. *"I owe her an unpayable debt. She went east, towards the ocean. Find her and tell her we said, fucking thank you,"* Gruff Man said.

A white Portal appeared and he stepped through. "Did you hear all that?" he asked, wondering when Sport and Drum made it to the car.

Drum nodded and Dill tossed Queen a bottle of water. A human grey blob walked up, stopping away from them. The detective's head was focused on him.

"You aren't from around here, are you?" the human detective asked, only speaking to him.

"No, we're not," he answered, his hands in his pockets. He lazily leaned against the front of the jeep, his eyes never leaving the human.

"Where you from?" the human briskly asked, standing up tall to try and look down on him.

His half-sneer proceeded his words. "Not from here, so we will take our leave," he told the human, standing up. He was over seven inches taller than the little human and he looked down on the man, from a short distance.

"I can't just let you leave. You will come with me to the station to answer some questions," the human detective said, walking towards him.

Sport and Dill were immediately in front of the human. A barrier of bodies stopped the human detective.

"Move out the way or you will have to come down to the station as well," the human detective threatened.

"Touch him and lose your life," Sport threatened back.

Dill added, "It would be stupid of us to let you unknowingly endanger yourself without proper warning."

Queen looked at Dill with measured respect in Queen's Energies at Dill standing solid in front of him.

The appalling deep grey laced with red in the human blob, let him know the human was angry while trying to push through Sport and Dill but was yanked back by another detective.

"What the fuck are you doing?" The Other Detective asked the angry, human detective.

"I'm bringing in a suspicious person," the human said, pointing at him. The human received a back head slap from The Other Detective.

"Ain't shit about him suspicious. Or is being a possible Desertlander enough to restrain a person?" The Other Detective asked the human one, while shaking his head, The Other Detective's Energy showing disgust.

"Look at how he looks at me!" angry human detective shouted while pointing at his sneering profile.

"And why is he just standing around back here?" the human added.

"If sneering were a crime, you would have to arrest everyone who meets you. Look at the young man behind him," The Other Detective said, moving angry, human detective's head to see.

"That's Queen. The SYB Guys are dead. The internet will be on fire. He IS the Queen of Social Media, so of course, it makes sense he would want firsthand information," The Other Detective explained.

The angry, human detective looked at Queen with the realization of who his best friend was, and the human's blob showed surprise.

"One of his best friends is Sport here," The Other Detective pointed to Sport. "One of the ones you thought you could barrel through."

The angry human detective looked at Sport, holding such admiration in his blob, then embarrassment. It was clear the human definitely followed S.H.E sports teams but was so wrapped up with taking him in, the human failed to notice who was around him.

"I hope you can accept my apologies for my stupid ass partner. Just know I have never let him arrest anyone without documented proof. I hope your Father will forgive his transgression as well," The Other Detective apologized. "Give Mr. Caleb Santiago, my best regards," The Other Detective said, bowing to him. "Young Master," The Other Detective added.

The angry human detective looked at his partner with shock and fear written across every inch of blob. Everybody knew his Dad's name. Mr. Caleb Santiago was the wealthiest man on the planet. The human slowly turned to see a full sneer with a look of disdain written on his face.

Shaking, the human told everybody standing around, the human knew he fucked up. The human fucked up bad. The human started to look for a way out. "I'm under a lot of pressure to find an invisible God we don't even know a proper name for. Who the fuck is Panda?" the human detective tried to justify.

"If that's enough to impair your judgment, maybe you should find a different line of work," he told the human. His face unchanged.

"Go see if the employees will say anything more than watch the video yet," The Other Detective instructed.

"Remember," he told the human. "The employees aren't trained professionals like you. Be kind and understanding," he chided, his sneer turning into a smile and the human detective meekly nodded before shuffling off.

"I don't know what happened here, but with no information and video showing them kill each other, their parents are grasping at whatever they can to find someone to blame," The Other Detective said, scratching his head.

"Never thought I would ever meet you all and I don't know why you happen to be here, Young Master, but I will keep this out of any of his paperwork." The Other Detective went to walk off. "If you find your friend, tell her I said thank you," he added.

"Forced silence?" he asked.

The Other Detective nodded and continued to walk back to the crime scene but stopped with what he said.

"There will be more deaths. Everyone who covered up The SYB Guys crimes against our people will be held responsible. I would suggest you use the human way of forced silence on the matter," he instructed the Being.

The Other Detective nodded, then turned to bow to him. "Yes, Young Master!"

QUEENxPANTU: LEAVING SUNSET
WEEK FIVE: SUNDAY

They moved east until they were out of sight of everything happening at the hotel. Drum and Sport rode clouds next to the jeep, while Win drove the rest of them. Queen was looking up places to eat Pantu may have stopped at, so Sport and Drum could break off to check any areas off road before meeting back up with a still driving Win.

After driving over three hours, He got a beep on the walkie app from Sport.

"Someone seen Pantu here!" Sport shouted through the app.

Win continued to drive as a white Portal appeared in front of the jeep. Win drove through and slowed down, taking in the surroundings. They parked and left the jeep to join Drum and Sport at the door.

"Pantu was here, ate and left with a regular named Gina in a red pickup truck," Sport's voice cracked saying this.

"Which way did they go?" he asked.

Sport shook his head, tears falling, so he went into the restaurant.

"Hello! I am looking for my friend who came through here. The person is so tall with an incredible face, light brown eyes, and hair?" he questioned.

The host blew out a breath. "I told the other guy I don't know which way they went," she said annoyed. "If you don't want to eat here, please leave."

He smiled at the human. "Thank you for your help!" he said. "We will take a table for two," he added, looking kindly at her while sliding several bills onto the podium.

The host looked surprised and smiled. "Of course, I will sit you in the area she was in," she said, grabbing two menus.

He called Win to join him, and they walked to the table and sat down, waiting for the server. Dill came in and speaking to the host, she called a manager over her walkie talkie and Dill went off towards the back.

Their server came and she smiled brightly at them. "What can I get you today?" she asked.

Win ordered three different burgers with fries and two milkshakes. He only ordered a side salad and sweet tea. They patiently waited for their food. As the server brought back their order, they saw Dill leave. He placed several bills on the table and their server looked confused.

"It's for information," he commented, looking at the human server.

The server grabbed the money. "What do you want to know?" she asked, counting the bills.

"Our friend was in your section earlier. The host said the person left with Gina. In a red pickup truck?" he asked.

The server nodded, bending down to lower her voice. *"The rumors about Gina are crazy. Some say she's a serial killer, or that she sells people. She's a regular here, so most laugh it off, but she only picks up hitchhikers, so we can't ever tell if they make it to where they're going. It only fuels the rumors.*

"Along with the fact no one knows where she lives around here, but she comes every day and only helps lonely travelers. Your friend left happily with Gina. She was so kind. She's a great tipper and a joy to talk to.

"I was telling her I was saving up to go swimming with dolphins, and she seemed interested." The server leaned back up. "I saw them headed inland, which was odd since dolphins live in the water," she told them.

Win asked for a to go box as he had yet to eat, while Win finished his food during the short conversation. He paid cash for their meals and left a hefty tip. He and Win also took a picture with the young lady and several other guests and employees before returning to the car. Drum and Sport were already gone as they got back on the road. Dill informed them.

"Drum said he felt fear from Pantu, so he and Sport went to check. He will send a Portal for us to catch up," Dill said, and handed him and Win water.

A Portal appeared and Win drove through without stopping. Win saw a red pickup truck pulled over to the side of the road and parked behind the truck before they all jumped out.

Sport was standing in front of the truck, and he quickly appeared at the driver's window. The driver, Gina, looked shocked at his quick appearance around her truck. When he used his Energies to turn her truck off and take the keys out of the ignition, Gina looked ready to pass out.

Pantu was relieving himself in the open field. More importantly, he was using this time to think. He was fairly sure he couldn't kill anyone, so he was trying to figure out, what to do when fear rose inside him. Seconds later he heard his name being called.

He turned so quickly, he lost his balance, falling back. When a warm hand on his arm pulled him back to stand, he blocked himself from bumping into Drum's chest with his free hand.

"I am quite okay Drum," he stated through clenched teeth. He finished peeing, pulled a wet wipe out, cleaned himself before using sanitizer on his hands. He walked back to Gina's truck.

"Is something wrong?" Gina asked, her voice racked with fear.

He rolled his eyes at Gina as he gathered his stuff.

"You would really get back in the car with a seral killer?" Drum desperately asked him.

He turned to Drum and huffed out his breath. "Why the fuck would I do that, now you are here, Drum?" he asked, upset with Drum for finding him but secretly happy Drum did.

Packing his items, he informed Drum, "By the way, she is UnCloaked. She leads six teams of Cloakless, and since I failed to see any around the restaurant, it would mean they are closer to the safehouse where she is stashing the people they are killing and selling." He shocked the sanity out of Gina, who was pretending not to know who he really was.

Gina went for the glove compartment and pulled out a gun, pointing it at him. The gun melted in Gina's hand, and she screamed out as the red-hot metal traveled down her arm. He rolled his eyes at her again and slammed her door.

He went to the truck bed and tried pulling his bigger bag out but gave up and shrugged it off. Drum pulled his bag from the bed, setting it on the ground for him. He pulled the handle and went to walk off, away from Sunset. Dill was beside him, a backpack on Dill's back and the blood red satchel of his Birth Ma across Dill's body.

Dill took the large rolling bag from him and smiled. "You always try and leave without me." Dill's voice pouted but his face was bright.

He took a deep breath and let it out, deflating himself to slump over, his head against Dill. He was tired, and even though he used very little Light, he was wound tight with this latest car ride. He wasn't sure if he could make it out of this one alive.

"I want to leave Dill. You should stay. Sunset is your home." He tiredly pushed Dill back, taking his bag from Dill's hands.

Dill shrugged and turned to walk with him. "I'm not leaving you alone, Pantu. Robin will understand."

They walked a bit until he heard Sport crying. He paused but didn't look back, he just stood there, unable to move. He felt Drum behind him, and he closed his eyes. Dill took his bag and continued to walk. He held back his tears and went to take a step.

"Pantu?" Drum's soft voice asked.

"I...need to...leave," he got out, without crying. "I need to do this. Let me leave Drum," he stated, finding his voice.

"I wasn't trying to stop you Pantu. I just needed to know. I will wait for you," Drum told him, before he felt Drum's presence leave him.

He felt the waves of hurt and sadness from behind him, but his resolve wouldn't falter, even if he wanted it too. His resolve forced his foot to move and kept forcing him until he caught up with a waiting Dill. Moving him to the shoulder of the road, Dill threw an arm around him, happy.

"Shall we go swim with the dolphins?" Dill asked, grinning brightly at him as they walked and he nodded, keeping his eyes forward and his feet moving.

AFTERWORDS-N-CONNECTIONS

I really hope you enjoyed the sweet, slice of life, slow burn of A Promised Sunset, the first book in Return to Enreya series. If you have gotten to know the characters and even have some favorites, hang on to your love of them.

Stay alert for the next book in the series which will also be released soon. If you thought Pantu and Drum's story was a comfy spice, then be prepared for the wild ride their parents, Caleb, Kannika, Moon, and Sky will send you on.

See you in the next book!

M.T. JADED {Author of Return to Enreya series}

*You can also follow me on my Amazon Author Page, which will inform you of any upcoming releases

Bluesky- @mtjadedwrites.bsky.social

Threads- @mtjadedwrites

TikTok- @mtjadedwrites

Instagram- @mtjadedwrites

Facebook- M.T. Jaded

CHARACTER PROFILES

*Drum:

Full Name: Suppade Xavier Carlito Santiago

Registered As: Suppade Santiago

Preferred Name: Drum

Nicknames: X, Zay, Zay-Zay

Age: 19

Height: 6'5 1/2. Often called a Desertlander.

Birthplace: Little Atlanta, New Georgia, The States

Current Hometown: Sunset Town, Sunset Country, Eastlands

Region: Southerner

Core Level: Born & Registered- Full-Core

Ability Level: No Public Records; likely Furtive List Level

Form: Born- Dragon; Registered- Royal-blue Dragon

Occupation: Higher Education Student- Advanced Honors Junior; Young Master; Professor Teaching Assistant (PTA); Private Tutor (Pantu only); 2+ careers

*Pantu:

Full Name: Pantu Adeyemi Kubo

Registered As: Underage Private Citizen

Nickname: Public- None; Personal- My Dumpling

Age: Underage Private Information

Height: Underage Private Information

Birthplace: Underage Private Information

Current Hometown: Sunset Town, Sunset Country, Eastlands

Region: Born- Easterner; Registered- Underage Private Information

Core Level: Born- Full-Core; Registered- Underage Private Information

Ability Level: Public- Unknown; Registered- Underage Private Information

Form: Born- Unknown; Registered- Underage Private Information

Occupation: Higher Education Student- Advanced Honors Senior

<u>Information given but not in Pantu's Private Citizen's file:</u>

Known Online As: #AnonB

City Title/Pet Name: Young Lord Oryn

*Queen: previous nickname was Dot.

Full Name: Panya Tram

Registered As: Panya Queen Tram

Preferred Name: Queen

Nickname: Knowledge

Age: 21

Height: 6'4. Often called a Desertlander.

Birthplace: Born- Unverified; Registered- Adopted

Current Hometown: Sunset Town, Sunset Country, Eastlands

Region: Born- Unverified; Registered- Easterner

Core Level: Born- Half-Core; Registered- Full-Core

Ability Level: Public- Unknown; Registered- Intermediate, Potential Rare

Form: Born & Registered- Tri-Colored Nature-Winged Fae

Occupation: Higher Education Student- Advanced Honors Junior; Business Owner (3+); Social Media Influencer

*Dill: previous nickname was Sage.

Full Name: Zion Nathan Peaks

Registered As: Zion Nathan Peaks

Nickname: Dill

Age: 21

Height: 6'4. Often called a Desertlander.

Birthplace: Born- Unverified; Registered- Sunset Country

Current Hometown: Sunset Town, Sunset Country, Eastlands

Region: Born- Unverified; Registered- Westerner

Core Level: Born & Registered- Full-Core

Ability Level: Public- Unknown; Registered- Intermediate, Potential Rare

Form: Born- Unknown; Registered- Disabled

Occupation: Higher Education Student- Advanced Honors Senior; Family Business Co-Owner; Pantu's Personal Engineer; Secret Career

<u>*Win:</u>

Full Name: Tawin Joel Quintellas

Registered As: Tawin Quintellas

Nickname: Win

Age: 21

Height: 6'3. Often called a Desertlander.

Birthplace: Born- Unverified; Registered- Adopted

Current Hometown: Sunset Town, Sunset Country, Eastlands

Region: Born- Unverified; Registered- Islander

Core Level: Born & Registered- Full-Core

Ability Level: Public- Unknown; Registered- Intermediate, Potential Rare

Form: Born & Registered- Double-horned White Stag

Occupation: Higher Education Student- Advanced Honors Senior Valedictorian; Certified Personal Accountant; Social Media Influencer

<u>*Sport: it's understood to only call Sport by his registered name.</u>

Full Name: Theeraphob Song

Registered As: Sport Song

Preferred Name: Sport

Age: 21

Height: 6'6 1/2. Often called a Desertlander.

Birthplace: Born- Unknown; Registered- Foster Child

Current Hometown: Sunset Town, Sunset Country, Eastlands

Region: Born- Unverified; Registered- Easterner

Core Level: Born & Registered- Full-Core

Ability Level: Public- Unknown; Registered- Rare, Potential Furtive List Abilities

Form: Born & Registered- Double Snake-tailed Gryphon

Occupation: Higher Education Student- Advanced Honors Junior; Chef; Secret Career

*<u>Alex</u>:

Full Name: Manpa Niranaromdee

Registered As: Manpa Niranaromdee

Preferred Name: Alex

Age: 19

Height: 5'11

Birthplace: Hollis, Sunset Country, Eastlands

Current Hometown: Hollis, Sunset Country, Eastlands

Region: Born & Registered- Westerner

Core Level: Born- Half-Core; Registered- Full-Core

Ability Level: Public- Unknown; Registered- Untested

Form: Born- Black Scaled Snake; Registered- Disabled

Occupation: Higher Education Student- Liberal Arts First Year; underground economy dealer

*<u>Kat</u>:

Full Name: Katlynn Alexandria Paris Lock

Registered As: Katlynn Lock

Nickname: Kat

Age: 19

Height: 6'1 1/2. Often called a Desertlander.

Birthplace: Born & Registered- Florencia, Telmon Country, Frentaly

Current Hometown: Sunset Town, Sunset Country, Eastlands

Region: Born and Registered- Northerner

Core Level: Born & Registered- Half-Core

Ability Level: Public- Unknown; Registered- Basic

Form: Born & Registered- Ocean-blue Water Lily

Occupation: Higher Education Student- Liberal Arts Junior

<u>*Robin:</u>

Full Name: Doctor Robin Yelitza-Marie Jinguiles

Registered As: Doctor Robin Jinguiles

Preferred Name: Robin

Nickname: None

Age: 19

Height: 6'1 1/2. Often called a Desertlander.

Birthplace: Little Atlanta, New Georgia, The States

Current Hometown: Hollis, Sunset Country, Eastlands

Region: Southerner

Core Level: Born & Registered- Full-Core

Ability Level: Public- Intermediate; Registered- Basic

Form: Born & Registered- Multi-colored Adarna Bird

Occupation: Psychiatrist, Secret Career

UNIVERSAL ABILITIES AND LEVELS
GLOSSARY

FYI: Although these Abilities are called Universal, they are not universally shared amongst Beings. Only the Aura Radar Ability is Universal.

In order to claim an Ability Level, Beings must be able to complete the requirements for each Level. This list only measures those with a Half-Core of Energy or more.

Beings can use the available abbreviations when naming their Level and regardless of Core Levels, Beings who can do multiple Intermediate or Higher Levels, either keep quiet or go missing. No Being in found history has been recorded as possessing all Universal Abilities.

Drum's shown Abilities are purposefully overlooked and not recorded, but there are people who keep a Furtive List to keep track of Drum's shown Abilities while looking for Beings who can claim any Level on this list.

1.) Aura Radar- All Beings, regardless of Core Level, can naturally sense Energy. This allows Beings to recognize each other or to tell when Energy has been used. Depending on how powerful the Energy inside another Being is or how the Energy is/has been used, people can be suppressed under the intensity of feeling Energy. Some humans can sense Energy without having it inside their own bodies, but most don't understand or disregard the feeling.

[Regardless of the intensity of a Being's Energy, this is still considered a Low-Level of *Exposed Energy*, no matter the harm caused to humans, since the Energy isn't shown, only felt.]

- Close-range = Basic (CRB)

(Sense Energy within 6 feet.)

- Med-range = Intermediate (MRI)

(Sense Energy 6-12 feet away.)

- Far-range = Rare (FRR)

(Sense Energy between 12 feet and 1 mile.)

- Remote-range = Incredibly Rare (RRIR)

(Sense Energy between 1-5 miles.)

{The furthest recorded distance in found history of Aura Radar is 5 miles}

Furtive List:

- Supreme Remote = Basic Rare (SRBR)

(Sense Energy within the country where you stand, as long as the country is 5+ miles.)

- Esteemed Remote = Incredibly Rare (ERIR)

(Sense Energy across the continent where you stand, regardless of the continent's size.)

- Exalted Remote = Impossible (ERI)

(Sense Energy across the planet.)

2.) Form- A Being uses Energy to transform into or create a non-Humanoid shape. Most Beings are born with and can only hold one Form inside their bodies. There are two types of Forms, an Energy Form, and a Physical Form.

{A Being who can use partial forms isn't considered to garner Leveling. Using a partial Form, whether Energy-based or physical is a High-Level of Exposed Energy}

[The two listed below apply to both Energy and Physical Forms.]

- No Form = Disabled (NFD)

(Born without a Form or no longer has a Form.)

- Neonate Form = Partially Disabled (NFPD)

(Being has a Form but unable/can't transform.)

***Form A (Energy Form)-** A Being creates an image of a non-Humanoid Form made of Energy, but the Humanoid body can still be seen during an Energy Form creation. The Being must be within the Energy Form to maintain control. Due to the intensity needed to perform an Energy Form, it is a High-Level of Exposed Energy no matter the Form or size.

- Energy Form = Basic (EFB)

(Create a Form in 25+ seconds.)

- Energy Form = Intermediate (EFI)

(Create a Form in 15-24 seconds.)

- Energy Form = Rare (EFR)

(Create a Form in 8-14 seconds.)

{Recorded found history list 11 seconds as the quickest Form creation}

Furtive List:

- Supreme = Basic Rare (SBR)

(Create a Form in 5-7 seconds.)

- Esteemed = Incredibly Rare (EIR)

(Create a Form in 1-4 seconds.)

- Exalted = Impossible (EI)

(Create a Form under 1 second or instantaneously.)

***Form B (Physical Form)-** Because a Being may be able to physically change their bodies, it is considered a Low-Level of Exposed Energy, unless done in front of humans and/or the Form speaks to humans.

- Physical Form = Basic (PFB)

(Complete transformation in 25+ seconds.)

- Physical Form = Intermediate (PFI)

(Complete transformation in 15-24 seconds.)

- Physical Form = Rare (PFR)

(Complete transformation in 8-14 seconds.)

<u>Furtive List:</u>

- Supreme Physical Form = Basic Rare (SPFBR)

(Complete transformation in 5-7 seconds.)

- Esteemed Physical Form = Incredibly Rare (EPFIR)

(Complete transformation in 1-4 seconds.)

- Exalted Physical Form = Impossible (EPFI)

(Instant transformation.)

<u>[A Being with Dual Forms (Energy and Physical), is automatically on the Furtive List, no matter how long they need for transformation and creation.]</u>

3.) Barrier- When a Being wants to protect, their Energy is used with this singular purpose, creating a Dome around the Being or whatever/whomever the Being wants to protect. Beings can normally create only one Barrier at a time and will expend Energy to make and hold the Barrier. Barriers are based on size, strength *(against Energy or human-made weapons)* and the amount of time you can hold a Dome. As a Barrier becomes bigger, the strength of the Barrier is affected, making it harder to hold against heavier attacks for prolonged periods of time. For some Beings, this also includes distances between multiple Barriers. Normal humans are able to live under the thinnest of Barriers.

[The color of Barriers cannot normally be seen, making it a Low-Level of Exposed Energy, no matter how the Energy usage affects humans. Beings whose Energy is restricted from entering a Barrier or humans will see whatever is projected inside their heads and/or experience whatever the Barrier makes them feel.]

- Personal Barrier = Basic (PBB)

(1 Barrier for themselves, someone else or an object. To even be considered basic, the Barrier must withstand a barrage of human bullets for five minutes.)

- Zone Barrier = Intermediate (ZBI)

(Barrier covers a neighborhood (up to 300 square miles) while withstanding a barrage of Basic Energy Blasts and human bullets for 5.1-10 minutes.)

- Metropolis Barrier = Rare. (MBR)

(Barrier can cover a city (1,000-3,600 square miles) while withstanding a barrage of Intermediate Energy Blasts and human bullets for 10 minutes or strong enough to block one missile.)

{The biggest recorded Barrier in found history, not made with machines, covered a city at 3,600 square miles. At that size, the Barrier withstood a missile and a constant barrage of Intermediate Energy Blasts for 10 minutes before breaking}

Furtive List:

- Supreme Zone = Basic Rare (SZBR)

(2-3 Zone Barriers; 1/2 mile apart; each one able to withstand a constant barrage of Basic Energy Blasts and human bullets for 5-10 minutes or be able to stop one missile.)

- Esteemed Metropolis = Incredibly Rare (EMIR)

(3-5 Metropolis Barriers; 1 mile apart; each one able to withstand a barrage of Intermediate Energy Blasts and human bullets for 10+ minutes. Each Barrier must also withstand two missiles.)

{Beings in recorded found history have made 5 city Barriers, at 3,600 square miles in diameter, over 1 mile apart, able to stop human weapons and Intermediate Energy Blasts with the longest recorded time being 1 hour before the Barrier was destroyed.}

- Exalted Metropolis = Impossible (EMI)

(6+ country-sized Barriers; on 2+ continents; held for longer than 1 hour; able to withstand all Levels of Energy blasts and all known human-made weapons for as long as the Being wants. Placing restrictions on Barriers/give the Barriers more than one purpose.)

4.) Portals- A Being connects two distant spaces together in order to move from one place to another. A Portal can be any shape the Being wants. A Being can open 1 Portal at a time and only items and people with Energy can travel through. Keeping a Portal open and allowing Beings or objects to pass through, drains Energy. Beings can use Portals to reach through and take/receive items from the places connected to their Portal. Sending/receiving a Being through a Portal drains more Energy than sending/taking/receiving items. Most Beings use

Portal Keys or phone apps to open Portals, relying on the Key or cellphone to use the remaining amount of Energy needed to hold the connection, allowing Beings to pass through or send items. **<u>This list describes Beings able to self-create Portals.</u>**

[Even though using Energy to open a Portal can be felt, normally the color of Portals can't be seen. This makes Portals a Low-Level of Exposed Energy, regardless of the effects on humans. Beings can increase the intensity of their Portal, making it visible, but will expend additional Energy, possibly making the Portal unstable and making it a High-Level of Exposed Energy.]

- Personal Portal = Basic (PPB)

(Small: under 2x3 feet; send/take 4 items smaller than a personal printer through at the same time. Depending on the size of the Being, able to send one through.)

- Sharing Portal = Intermediate (SPI)

(Medium: 3x4-6x6 feet; send/take 4-10 portal-sized items through at the same time. Or send/receive 2 portal-sized Beings through, either together or one at a time.)

- Party Portal = Rare (PPR)

(Large: 7x7-9x9 feet; send 5 adult Beings through a Portal, either altogether or individually. Or the Being is able to send 10-20 portal-sized items through together.)

<u>Furtive List:</u>

- Supreme Party (War Portal) = Basic Rare (SPBR/WPBR)

(Extreme: bring tanks, aircrafts, and small warships through. Send 6-10 adult Beings, either individually or at least 6 altogether. Send 15-25 portal-sized items.)

<u>{20 extreme items or 20 adult Beings were the most recorded in found history to pass through a Portal before the Being was forced to close it. No buildings or land have been recorded as being able to pass through a Portal}</u>

- Esteemed War Portal = Incredibly Rare (EWPIR)

(2+ War Portals at the same time; send over 25 portal-sized items and 20 Beings through.)

- Exalted War Portal = Impossible (EWPI)

(2+ Esteemed Portals simultaneously; changing a Portal(s) location without closing it.)

5.) Ground-step- When Beings use their Energy to quickly move/run from one place to another across land/water without using a Portal. Beings can use their Energy to move their body, without walking a step; they can also use their Energy to run/walk faster, which is the most common use. Each instance requires the Being to expend Energy with every push. Beings can move a certain distance with each Energy push and must continue to arrive at their destination.

[This is a Low-Level of Exposed Energy.]

- Baby Steps = Basic (BSB)

(Move less than 1 mile total while constantly pushing.)

- Dart Step = Intermediate (DSI)

(Move 1-10 miles while pushing)

- Bolt Step = Rare (BSR)

(Move 10+ miles while pushing.)

{In recorded found history, the furthest a Being was able to move while pushing was 30 miles before exhausting their Energy}

Furtive List:

- Supreme Bolt (Straight Shot) = Basic Rare (SBBR/SSBR)

(Move 10+ miles in one push)

{A 13-mile Straight Shot is the highest distance recorded in found history.}

- Esteemed Bolt = Incredibly Rare (EBIR)

(A Straight Shot 13+ miles)

- Exalted Step (Instant) = Impossible (ESI/(II)- DOUBLE I)

(Teleport to any location, no matter the distance.)

{Instant is said in whispers in the Being communities and treated like myth. This is different than Ground-step but considered the highest Level of the Ability. With

Instant, a Being could be at the southernmost tip of the planet and half a second later be at the northernmost tip}

6.) Sky-jump- When a Being uses their Energy to push themselves into a higher-than-normal jump. Sky-jump has two sections, Up-jump, and Far-jump. Beings are able to project themselves straight up and/or change directions to jump far distances. **This is the Levels a Being can jump in one push.**

***Sky-jump A (Up-jump)-** Beings can use their Energy to continually Up-jump higher but will also need to use a Barrier to protect themselves from the different atmospheric pressures. This is considered a Low-Level of Exposed Energy.

- Spring Jump = Basic (SJB)

(Up-jump 50 feet into the Breathable Ozone, about 9 human sized stacked men at normal height.)

- Aloft jump = Intermediate (AJI)

(Up-jump 51+ feet into the Breathable Ozone but under the Tropicalsphere at 68.2 miles.)

- Apex Jump = Rare (AJR)

(Up-jump pass the Tropicalsphere but under the Nexusphere at 341.2 miles. Being must also be able to create a Barrier to survive.)

{The highest recorded Up-jump in found history is Apex. The highest Level most current Beings can achieve in this Ability is Intermediate.}

Furtive List:

- Supreme Apex = Basic Rare (SABR)

(Up-jump pass the Nexusphere but under Middlesphere at 583.2 miles with Barrier.)

- Esteemed Apex = Incredibly Rare (EAIR)

(Up-jump pass the Middlesphere but under the end of Hell at 6,831.2 miles with Barrier.)

- Exalted Cusp = Impossible (ECI)

(Up-jump to the end of Heaven at 2,900,000 miles before the vacuum of space is reached with Barrier or Up-jump into space. It is unknown if a Barrier can be used to survive space.)

***Sky-jump B (Far-jump)-** Beings with enough Energy can continue to Far-jump across places to reach their destination. Beings who have ample Energy to continuously use Far-jumping are also coveted. Low-Level of Exposed Energy. These Levels are for how far Beings can Far-jump in one push.

- Bunny Hop = Basic (BHB)

(Far-jump under 1 mile.)

- Frog Leap = Intermediate (FLI)

(Far-jump 1-5 miles.)

- Pole Vault = Rare (PVR)

(Far-jump 5-10 miles.)

{*10 miles are the furthest recorded single Far-jump in found history*}

<u>Furtive List:</u>

- Supreme Vault (Country View) = Basic Rare (SVBR/CVBR)

(If the country is 10-50 miles, a Being can Far-jump it.)

- Esteemed Vault (Continent Hopper) = Incredibly Rare (EVIR/CHIR)

(Far-jump continents 50+ miles.)

- Exalted Vault = Impossible (EVI)

(Far-jump across the planet.)

7.) Energy Orb- Beings who have this Ability can pull Energy out of their bodies into a circular-like form. This Ability is used as a light source, and the Orb will follow the Being who made it. Most Beings can only make one Energy Orb at a time. Based on the intensity needed to perform this Ability, it can be seen by Beings (without Enhanced Vision) and even humans. Energy usage can be felt within a certain range.

[This is considered the worst case of Exposed Energy, at any Level.]

- Bulb Orb = Basic (BOB)

(Size of a golf ball; felt within 6 feet; most commonly used as a personal light for Beings.)

- Lantern Orb = Intermediate (LOI)

(Size of a soccer ball; felt 6-12 feet away; commonly used as streetlights in Barrier Towns.)

- Star Orb = Rare (SOR)

(Orb is 2.1x3-5x5 feet; felt up to 1/2 mile away; commonly used to explore darken places.)

{*The largest Energy Orb in recorded found history is 5x5 feet, felt 1 mile away*}

Furtive List:

- Supreme Nova = Basic Rare (SNBR)

(Zone-sized Orb; felt 300+ square miles away; lights up a metropolis.)

- Esteemed Nova = Incredibly Rare (ENIR)

(2 Supreme Novas simultaneously or 1 Metropolis-sized Orb; felt 3,600+ square mile; lights up a country.)

- Exalted Nova = Impossible (ENI)

(3+ Supreme Novas simultaneously or 2+ Metropolis-sized Orbs; lights up a continent.)

8.) Energy Blast- A Being who can make an Energy Orb, may be able to expend additional Energy to push the Orb, and upon connecting, cause damage to whomever or whatever they send their Energy towards, turning the Orb into a Blast. Beings with this Ability are normally able to make 1 Blast at a time but based on the amount of Energy inside a Being's body, they can continually make Blasts. Energy Blast Levels are measured by size, distance *(how far the Blast can travel to hit its target or before dissipating)*, damage and how many the Being can make before depleting most of their Energy.

[Even if the Being can make continual Blasts one after another, these Levels are for an individual Blast. This is a High-Level of Exposed Energy.]

- Struggle Blast = Basic (SBB)

(10+ Bulb Orbs; blasted up to 50 feet and causes minor damage.)

- Quarrel Blast = Intermediate (QBI)

(5+ Lantern Orbs; blasted up to 1 mile away with considerable damage.)

- Feud Blast = Rare (FBR)

(2+ Star Orbs; blasted 1+ mile and causes major damage.)

{Recorded found history states Feud Blast as the biggest Blast. The farthest distance recorded was a target 4 miles away being completely destroyed}

Furtive List:

- Supreme Feud = Basic Rare (SFBR)

(Supreme Nova; pushed 4+ miles; major damage.)

- Esteemed Feud = Incredibly Rare (EFIR)

(2 Supreme Feuds at the same time; massive damage.)

- Exalted Feud = Impossible (EFI)

(3+ Supreme Feuds causing destruction.)

9.) Seduction Ability- When a Being uses the scent their Energy gives off to Seduce (control) others. Beings would normally use scent to tell if another Being held a personality compatible with their own, causing the Being in question to hold a scent which smells pleasing. Because the scent of Energy is sexually intoxicating to humans, Beings have learned to use their scent to Seduce both Beings and humans. Humans easily succumb to Seduction, while some Beings can use their own Energy to block the Ability. Seduction can be used with Scent *(Cloud)* and/or Touch *(Tap)*. Humans are not included since none are recorded as having willpower strong enough to block any scent.

***Seduction A (Scent Cloud)-** A Being sends out their Energy to be breathed in. Levels are based on how many Beings a Cloud can control at the same time, within a certain distance and for an extended amount of time. This is a Low-Level of Exposed Energy.

- Essence Cloud = Basic (ECB)

(Light Scent. Seduce 1-5 Beings within a 12-foot range for 5 minutes.)

- Perfume Cloud = Intermediate (PCI)

(Heavy Scent. Seduce 6-10 Beings 13 feet-1 mile away for 10 minutes.)

- Fragrant Cloud = Rare (FCR)

(Imposing Scent. Seduce 11-20 Beings within 5 miles for 20 minutes.)

{20 was the most seduced Beings in recorded found history, within a max 5-mile range for 30 minutes}

Furtive List:

(A Being's Cloud can seduce all Beings within the designated area for longer than 1 hour.)

- Supreme Horde = Basic Rare (SHBR)

(Massive scent. Seduce Being within a Zone.)

- Esteemed Horde = Incredibly Rare (EHIR)

(Enormous Scent. Seduce Beings within a Metropolis.)

- Exalted Horde = Impossible (EHI)

(Tremendous Scent. Seduce any Being within a range larger than a Metropolis.)

***Seduction B (Touch/Tap)-** A Being sends their Energy out through a Tap to subdue a person and <u>must</u> have physical contact with anyone they are trying to Seduce. If a Being's Energy is isn't powerful enough, the Tap will be suppressed. Levels are based on how many Beings can be controlled and for how long. A Low-Level of Exposed Energy.

- Bait Tap = Basic Rare (BTBR)

(Tap 1-5 Beings for 10 minutes.)

- Attraction Tap = Intermediate (ATI)

(Tap 6-11 Beings for 10+ minutes.)

- Lure Tap = Rare (LTR)

(Tap 12-17 Beings for 20 minutes.)

{In found recorded history, 20 Beings were Tapped for 30 minutes}

Furtive List:

- Supreme Enticement = Basic Rare (SEBR)

(Tap 18-30 Beings for 30+ minutes.)

- Esteemed Temptation = Incredibly Rare (ETIR)

(Tap 31-50 Beings for 30+ minutes.)

- Exalted Persuasion = Impossible (EPI)

(Tap 51+ Beings for 1+ hours.)

10.) Enhanced Smell- Concentrating Energy around their nose, allows a Being to smell beyond the scope of normal humans. To be considered for this Ability requires the completion of three steps. First, a Being is required to break down the scientific compound of simple items and properly identify each scent; secondly, the Being must also detect exactly where Energy was/being used and third, the Being must be able to do both within a certain range.

[This is a Low-Level of Exposed Energy.]

- Just-A-Sniff (JAS) = Basic (JASB)

(Distinguish 10,000-100,000 simple scents and Energy usage within 20 miles.)

{The furthest recorded Enhanced Smell Ability in found history is within 20 miles with 10,000 simple scents}

- Mature Nose = Intermediate (MNI)

(Distinguish 100,001-500,000 simple scents and Energy usage 20-50 miles away.)

- Expert Olfactory = Rare (EOR)

(Distinguish 500,001+ simple scents and Energy usage 50-100 miles away.)

Furtive List:

(In order to be considered for this list, a Being must be able to smell Energy, even if it hasn't been used and can identify people by the scent of their Energy.)

- Supreme Critic = Basic Rare (SCBR)

(Distinguish 10,000-100,000 complex scents 50-100 miles away.)

- Esteemed Specialist = Incredibly Rare (ESIR)

(Distinguish 100,001-500,000 complex scents 101-200 miles away.)

- Exalted Expert = Impossible (EEI)

(Distinguish 500,001+ complex scents 201+ miles away.)

11.) Enhanced Hearing- When a Being is able to concentrate their Energy around their eardrums, allowing them to hear conversations within a certain distance.

[This is considered a Low-Level of Exposed Energy.]

- Overhear = Basic (OB)

(Hear conversations 1-5 miles away.)

- Snoop = Intermediate (SI)

(Hear conversations 6-15 miles.)

- Unearth = Rare (UR)

(Hear conversations 16-30 miles away.)

{The furthest recorded found history distance is 27 miles}

Furtive List:

- Supreme Unearth = Basic Rare (SUBR)

(Hear conversations 31-50 miles away.)

- Esteemed Unearth = Incredibly Rare (EUIR)

(Hear conversations 51-80 miles away.)

- Exalted Aerial Receiver = Impossible (EARI)

(Hear any conversation anywhere on the planet.)

12.) Enhanced Vision- Concentrating Energy behind and into eyes to see further than normal.

[This is a Low-Level of Exposed Energy.]

- Infant Sight = Basic (ISB)

(Eyesight 10-20 miles away.)

- Panoramic View = Intermediate (PVI)

(Eyesight 21-65 miles away.)

- High Observation = Rare (HOR)

(Eyesight 67-100 miles away.)

{*The furthest Enhanced Vision in recorded found history is 92 miles*}

Furtive List:

- Supreme Eyes = Basic Rare (SEBR)

(Eyesight 100-200 miles away.)

- Esteemed Optics = Incredibly Rare (EOIR)

(Eyesight 201-300 miles away.)

- Exalted Awareness = Impossible (EAI)

(Unlimited Eyesight.)

[Any Ability listed below is only on the Furtive List]**

13.) Retriever (Grabber)- Sending Energy, a certain distance to wrap around a Being or object and pull them to you. A Retriever can still have a Portal Ability but doesn't use it to transport items or Beings. Using this Ability on a Being could cause mental disorientation. Using this Ability multiple times on the same Being, can cause mental decline. Retrieving humans will result in mental decline or death since their Energy-empty brains and bodies can't withstand or understand Energy.

[It doesn't matter if you can only retrieve items or how many, the base of this Ability is seen as Supreme Level. Low-Level of Exposed Energy if only used on Beings and not in front of or on humans.]

- Snatcher = Basic Supreme (SBS)

(Retrieve within 5 miles.)

- Fetcher = Intermediate Supreme (FIS)

(Retrieve within 5-20 miles.)

- Reclaimer = Rare Supreme (RRS)

(Retrieve within 21-60 miles.)

{Recorded found history lists 37 miles as the furthest distance a Being used this Ability}

- Esteemed Procurement = Incredibly Rare (EPIR)

(Retrieve within 61-150 miles away.)

- Exalted Liberator = Impossible (ELI)

(Retrieve 150+ miles anywhere on the planet.)

14.) Sender (Giver)- Placing Energy around a Being or object to send them a certain distance away. A Sender can still have a poral Ability but doesn't use it to transport items or Beings. Using this Ability on a Being could cause mental disorientation. Using this Ability multiple times on the same Being can cause mental decline. Sending humans will result in mental decline or death since their Energy-empty brains and bodies can't withstand or understand Energy.

[Low-Level of Exposed Energy if only used on Beings and not in front of or on humans.]

- Delivery Drop = Basic Supreme (DDBS)

(Send within 5 miles.)

- Router = Intermediate Supreme (RIS)

(Send within 5-20 miles.)

- Transporter = Rare Supreme (TRS)

(Send within 21-60 miles.)

{Recorded found history lists 42 miles as the furthest distance a Being used this Ability}

- Esteemed Distributor = Incredibly Rare (EDIR)

(Send within 61-150 miles away.)

- Exalted Transference = Impossible (ETI)

(Send 150+ miles anywhere on the planet.)

15.) Creator- (also known as **Materializing**.) The Ability to turn your Energy into any compound material to craft solid objects. It doesn't matter if a Being can only turn their Energy into one simple compound, this is considered the highest and only Level for this Ability.

16.) Produce- This is a multi-part Ability. The first part is the Ability to create an alternate space made of Energy. The second step is to place items there in storage. The third step is to use the Retriever Ability to pull those items, making them appear wherever needed.

17.) Charm- When a Being can take away the free will of others, making them fall in love or become obsessed. Once used, this Ability will stay active until the person(s) Charmed dies.